Ruth Rendell
INSPECTOR WEXFORD

This edition first published by Cresset Editions
in 1993
an imprint of the Random House Group
20 Vauxhall Bridge Road
London SW1V 2SA

First published by Hutchinson Ltd

ISBN 0 09 182131 0

Jacket photograph by Tony Nutley

Typeset in Baskerville 11.5/13.5 by
Pure Tech Corporation, Pondicherry, India
Printed and bound in Great Britain by
Mackays of Chatham PLC, Chatham, Kent

From Doon With Death

The verses at the beginning of each chapter and the
inscriptions in Minna's books all appear in *The
Oxford Book of Victorian Verse*.

CONTENTS

For Don

From Doon
With Death

You have broken my heart. There, I have written it. Not for you to read, Minna, for this letter will never be sent, never shrink and wither under your laughter, little lips prim and pleated, laughter like dulcimer music. . . .

Shall I tell you of the Muse who awaited me? I wanted you to walk beside me into her vaulted halls. There were the springs of Helicon! I would furnish you with the food of the soul, the bread that is prose and the wine that is poetry. Ah, the wine, Minna. . . . This is the rose-red blood of the troubadour!

Never shall I make that journey, Minna, for when I brought you the wine you returned to me the waters of indifference. I wrapped the bread in gold but you hid my loaves in the crock of contempt.

Truly you have broken my heart and dashed the wine-cup against the wall. . . .

CHAPTER ONE

Call once yet,
In a voice that she will know,
'Margaret, Margaret!'

Matthew Arnold, *The Forsaken Merman*

'I think you're getting things a bit out of proportion, Mr Parsons,' Burden said. He was tired and he'd been going to take his wife to the pictures. Besides, the first things he'd noticed when Parsons brought him into the room were the books in the rack by the fireplace. The titles were enough to give the most level-headed man the jitters, quite enough to make a man anxious where no ground for anxiety existed: *Palmer the Poisoner, The Trial of Madeleine Smith, Three Drowned Brides, Famous Trials, Notable British Trials.*

'Don't you think your reading has been preying on your mind?'

'I'm interested in crime,' Parsons said. 'It's a hobby of mine.'

'I can see that.' Burden wasn't going to sit down if he could avoid it. 'Look, you can't say your wife's actually missing. You've been home one and a half hours and she isn't here. That's all. She's probably gone to the pictures. As a matter of fact I'm on my way there now with my wife. I expect we'll meet her coming out.'

'Margaret wouldn't do that, Mr Burden. I know her and you don't. We've been married nearly six years and in all that time I've never come home to an empty house.'

'I'll tell you what I'll do. I'll drop in on my way back. But you can bet your bottom dollar she'll be home by then.' He started moving towards the door. 'Look, get on to the station if you like. It won't do any harm.'

'No, I won't do that. It was just with you living down the road and being an inspector. . . .'

And being off duty, Burden thought. If I was a doctor instead of a policeman I'd be able to have private patients on the side. I bet he wouldn't be so keen on my services if there was any question of a fee.

Sitting in the half-empty dark cinema he thought: Well, it is funny. Normal ordinary wives as conventional as Mrs Parsons, wives who always have a meal ready for their husbands on the dot of six, don't suddenly go off without leaving a note.

'I thought you said this was a good film,' he whispered to his wife.

'Well, the critics liked it.'

'Oh, critics,' he said.

Another man, that could be it. But Mrs Parsons? Or it could be an accident. He'd been a bit remiss not getting Parsons to phone the station straight away.

'Look, love,' he said. 'I can't stand this. You stay and see the end. I've got to get back to Parsons.'

'I wish I'd married that reporter who was so keen on me.'

'You must be joking,' Burden said. 'He'd have stayed out all night putting the paper to bed. Or the editor's secretary.'

He charged up Tabard Road, then made himself stroll when he got to the Victorian house where Parsons lived. It was all in darkness, the curtains in the big bay downstairs undrawn. The step was whitened, the brass kerb above it polished. Mrs Parsons must have been a house-proud woman. Must have been? Why not, still was?

Parsons opened the door before he had a chance to knock. He still looked tidy, neatly dressed in an oldish suit, his tie knotted tight. But his face was greenish grey. It reminded Burden of a drowned face he had once seen on a mortuary slab. They had put the glasses back on the spongy nose to help the girl who had come to identify him.

'She hasn't come back,' he said. His voice sounded as if he had a cold coming. But it was probably only fear.

'Let's have a cup of tea,' Burden said. 'Have a cup of tea and talk about it.'

'I keep thinking what could have happened to her. It's so open round here. I suppose it would be, being country.'

'It's those books you read,' Burden said. 'It's not healthy.' He looked again at the shiny paper covers. On the spine of one was a jumble of guns and knives against a blood-red background. 'Not for a layman,' he said. 'Can I use your phone?'

'It's in the front room.'

'I'll get on to the station. There might be something from the hospitals.'

The front room looked as if nobody ever sat in it. With some dismay he noted its polished shabbiness. So far he hadn't seen a stick of furniture that looked less than fifty years old. Burden went into all kinds of houses and he knew antique furniture when he saw it. But this wasn't antique and nobody could have chosen it because it was beautiful or rare. It was just old. Old enough to be cheap, Burden thought, and at the same time young enough not to be expensive. The kettle whistled and he heard Parsons fumbling with china in the kitchen. A cup crashed on the floor. It sounded as if they had kept the old concrete floor. It was enough to give anyone the creeps, he thought again, sitting in these high-ceilinged rooms, hearing unexplained inexplicable creaks from the stairs and the cupboard, reading about poison and hangings and blood.

'I've reported your wife as missing,' he said to Parsons. 'There's nothing from the hospitals.'

Parsons turned on the light in the back room and Burden followed him in. It must have a weak bulb under the parchment lampshade that hung from the centre of the ceiling.

About sixty watts, he thought. The shade forced all the light down, leaving the ceiling, with its plaster decorations of bulbous fruit, dark and in the corners blotched with deeper shadow. Parsons put the cups down on the side-board, a vast mahogany thing more like a fantastic wooden house than a piece of furniture, with its tiers and galleries and jutting beaded shelves. Burden sat down in a chair with wooden arms and seat of brown corduroy. The lino struck cold through the thick soles of his shoes.

'Have you any idea at all where your wife could have gone?'

'I've been trying to think. I've been racking my brains. I can't think of anywhere.'

'What about her friends? Her mother?'

'Her mother's dead. We haven't got any friends here. We only came here six months ago.'

Burden stirred his tea. Outside it had been close, humid. Here in this thick-walled dark place, he supposed, it must always feel like winter.

'Look,' he said, 'I don't like to say this, but somebody's bound to ask you. It might as well be me. Could she have gone out with some man? I'm sorry, but I had to ask.'

'Of course you had to ask. I know, it's all in here.' He tapped the bookcase. 'Just routine enquiries, isn't it? But you're wrong. Not Margaret. It's laughable.' He paused, not laughing. 'Margaret's a good woman. She's a lay preacher at the Wesleyan place down the road.'

No point in pursuing it, Burden thought. Others would ask him, probe into his private life whether he liked it or not, if she still hadn't got home when the last train came in and the last bus had rolled into Kingsmarkham garage.

'I suppose you've looked all over the house?' he asked. He had driven down this road twice a day for a year but he couldn't remember whether the house he was sitting in had two floors or three. His policeman's brain tried to reassemble the retinal photograph on his policeman's eye. A bay window at the bottom, two flat sash windows above it and – yes, two smaller ones above that under the slated eyelids of the roof. An ugly house, he thought, ugly and forbidding.

'I looked in the bedrooms,' Parsons said. He stopped pacing and hope coloured his cheeks. Fear whitened them again as he said: 'You think she might be up in the attics? Fainted or something?'

She would hardly still be there if she'd only fainted, Burden thought. A brain haemorrhage, yes, or some sort of accident. 'Obviously we ought to look,' he said. 'I took it for granted you'd looked.'

'I called out. We hardly ever go up there. The rooms aren't used.'

'Come on,' Burden said.

The light in the hall was even dimmer than the one in the dining-room. The little bulb shed a pallid glow on to a woven pinkish runner, on lino patterned to look like parquet in dark and lighter brown. Parsons went first and Burden followed him up the steep stairs. The house was biggish, but the materials which had been used to build it were poor and the workmanship unskilled. Four doors opened off the first landing and these were panelled but without beading and they looked flimsy. The flat rectangles of plywood in their frames reminded Burden of blind blocked-up windows on the sides of old houses.

'I've looked in the bedrooms,' Parsons said. 'Good heavens, she may be lying helpless up there!'

He pointed up the narrow uncarpeted flight and Burden noticed how he had said 'Good heavens!' and not 'God!' or 'My God!' as some men might have done.

'I've just remembered, there aren't any bulbs in the attic lights.' Parsons went into the front bedroom and unscrewed the bulb from the central lamp fitting. 'Mind how you go,' he said.

It was pitchy dark on the staircase. Burden flung open the door that faced him. By now he was certain they were going to find her sprawled on the floor and he wanted to get the discovery over as soon as possible. All the way up the stairs he'd been anticipating the look on Wexford's face when he told him she'd been there all along.

A dank coldness breathed out of the attic, a chill mingled with the smell of camphor. The room was partly furnished. Burden could just make out the shape of a bed. Parsons stumbled over to it and stood on the cotton counterpane to fit the bulb into the lamp socket. Like the ones downstairs it gave only an unsatisfactory light, which, streaming faintly through a shade punctured all over with tiny holes, patterned the ceiling and the distempered walls with yellowish dots. The window was uncurtained. A bright cold moon swam into the black square and disappeared again under the scalloped edge of a cloud.

'She's not in here,' Parsons said. His shoes had made dusty footprints on the white stuff that covered the bedstead like a shroud.

Burden lifted a corner of it and looked under the bed, the only piece of furniture in the room.

'Try the other room,' he said.

Once more Parsons went through the tedious, maddeningly slow motions of removing the light bulb. Now only the chill radiance from the window lit their way into the second attic. This was smaller and more crowded. Burden opened a cupboard and raised the lids from two trunks. He could see Parsons staring at him, thinking perhaps about what he called his hobby and about the things trunks could contain. But these were full of books, old books of the kind you sometimes see in stands outside second-hand shops.

The cupboard was empty and inside it the paper was peeling from the wall, but there were no spiders. Mrs Parsons was a house-proud woman.

'It's half past ten,' Burden said, squinting at his watch. 'The last train doesn't get in till one. She could be on that.'

Parsons said obstinately, 'She wouldn't go anywhere by train.'

They went downstairs again, pausing to restore the light bulb to the front bedroom. There was something sinister and creepy about the stair-well that could have been so easily dispelled, Burden thought, by white paint and stronger lights. As they descended he reflected momentarily on this woman and the life she lived here, going fussily about her chores, trying to bring a little smartness to the mud-coloured wood-work, the ugly ridged linoleum.

'I don't know what to do,' Parsons said.

Burden didn't want to go back into the little diningroom with the big furniture, the cold tea-dregs in their two cups. By now Jean would be back from the cinema.

'You could try phoning round her friends at the church,' he said, edging towards the front door. If Parsons only knew how many reports they got in of missing women and how few, how tiny a percentage, turned up dead in fields or chopped in trunks. . . .

'At this time of night?'

Parsons looked almost shocked, as if the habits of a lifetime, the rule that you never called on anyone after nine o'clock, mustn't be broken even in a crisis.

'Take a couple of aspirins and try to get some sleep,' Burden said. 'If anything comes up you can give me a ring. We've told the station. We can't do anything more. They'll let you know as soon as they hear.'

'What about tomorrow morning?'

If he'd been a woman, Burden thought, he'd beg me to stay. He'd cling to me and say, Don't leave me!

'I'll look in on my way to the station,' he said.

Parsons didn't shut the door until he was half-way up the street. He looked back once and saw the white bewildered face, the faint glow from the hall falling on to the brass step. Then, feeling helpless because he had brought the man no comfort, he raised his hand in a half-wave.

The streets were empty, still with the almost tangible

silence of the countryside at night. Perhaps she was at the station now, scuttling guiltily across the platform, down the wooden stairs, gathering together in her mind the threads of the alibi she had concocted. It would have to be good, Burden thought, remembering the man who waited on the knife edge that spanned hope and panic.

It was out of his way, but he went to the corner of Tabard Road and looked up the High Street. From here he could see right up to the beginning of the Stowerton Road where the last cars were leaving the forecourt of The Olive and Dove. The market place was empty, the only people to be seen a pair of lovers standing on the Kingsbrook Bridge. As he watched the Stowerton bus appeared between the Scotch pines on the horizon. It vanished again in the dip beyond the bridge. Hand in hand, the lovers ran to the stop in the centre of the market place as the bus pulled in close against the dismantled cattle stands. Nobody got off. Burden sighed and went home.

'She hasn't turned up,' he said to his wife.

'It *is* funny, you know, Mike. I should have said she was the last person to go off with some man.'

'Not much to look at?'

'I wouldn't say that exactly,' Jean said. 'She looked so – well, respectable. Flat-heeled shoes, no make-up, tidy sort of perm with hair-grips in it. You know what I mean. You must have seen her.'

'I may have done,' Burden said. 'It didn't register.'

'But I wouldn't call her plain. She's got a funny old-fashioned kind of face, the sort of face you see in family albums. You might not admire it, Mike, but you wouldn't forget her face.'

'Well, I've forgotten it,' Burden said. He dismissed Mrs Parsons to the back of his mind and they talked about the film.

CHAPTER TWO

One forenoon the she-bird crouched not on the nest,
Nor returned that afternoon, nor the next,
Nor ever appeared again.

Walt Whitman, *The Brown Bird*

Burden slept quickly, used to crises. Even here, a market town he had expected to find dull after Brighton, the C.I.D. were seldom idle.

The telephone rang at seven.

'Burden speaking.'

'This is Ronald Parsons. She hasn't come back. And, Mr Burden – she hasn't taken a coat.'

It was the end of May and it had been a squally cold month. A sharp breeze ruffled his bedroom curtains. He sat up.

'Are you sure?' he asked.

'I couldn't sleep. I started going through her clothes and I'm positive she hasn't taken a coat. She's only got three: a raincoat, her winter coat and an old one she does the gardening in.'

Burden suggested a suit.

'She's only got one costume.' Parsons' use of the old-fashioned word was in character. 'It's in her wardrobe. I think she must have been wearing a cotton frock, her new one.' He stopped and cleared his throat. 'She'd just made it,' he said.

'I'll get some things on,' Burden said. 'I'll pick you up in half an hour and we'll go to the station together.'

Parsons had shaved and dressed. His small eyes were wide with terror. The tea-cups they had used the night before had just been washed and were draining on a homemade rack of wooden dowel rods. Burden marvelled at the ingrained habit of respectability that made this man, at a crisis in his life, spruce himself and put his house in order.

He tried to stop himself staring round the little hole of a kitchen, at the stone copper in the corner, the old gas stove on legs, the table with green American cloth tacked to its top. There was no washing machine, no refrigerator. Because of the peeling paint, the creeping red rust, it looked dirty. It was only by peering closely when Parsons' eyes were not on him that Burden could see it was in fact fanatically, pathetically, clean.

'Are you fit?' he asked. Parsons locked the back door with a huge key. His hand shook against crazed mottled tiles. 'You've got the photograph all right?'

'In my pocket.'

Passing the dining-room he noticed the books again. The titles leapt at him from red and yellow and black covers. Now that the morning had come and she was still missing Burden wondered fantastically if Tabard Road was to join Hilldrop Crescent and Rillington Place in the chronicle of sinister streets.

Would there one day be an account of the disappearance of Margaret Parsons under another such book-jacket with the face of his companion staring from the frontispiece? The face of a murderer is the face of an ordinary man. How much less terrifying if the killer wore the Mark of Cain for all the world to see! But Parsons? He could have killed her, he had been well instructed. His textbooks bore witness to that. Burden thought of the gulf between theory and practice. He shook off fantasy and followed Parsons to the front door.

Kingsmarkham was awake, beginning to bustle. The shops were still closed, but the buses had been running for two hours. Occasionally the sun shone in shafts of watery brilliance, then vanished again under clouds that were white and thick or bluish with rain. The bus queue stretched almost to the bridge; down towards the station men hurried, singly or in pairs, bowler-hatted, armed with cautious umbrellas, through long custom unintimidated by the hour-long commuting to London.

Burden pulled up at the junction and waited for an orange-painted tractor to pass along the major road.

'It all goes on,' Parsons said, 'as if nothing had happened.'

'Just as well.' Burden turned left. 'Helps you keep a sense of proportion.'

The police station stood appropriately at the approach to the town, a guarding bastion or a warning. It was new, white and square like a soap carton, and, rather pointlessly, Burden thought, banded and decorated here and there in a soap carton's colours. Against the tall ancient arcs of elms, only a few yards from the last Regency house, it flaunted its whiteness, its gloss, like a piece of gaudy litter in a pastoral glade.

Its completion and his transfer to Kingsmarkham had coincided, but sometimes the sight of it still shocked him. He watched for Parsons' reaction as they crossed the threshold. Would he show fear or just the ordinary citizen's caution? In fact, he seemed simply awed.

Not for the first time the place irritated Burden. People expected pitch pine and lino, green baize and echoing passages. These were at the same time more quelling to the felon, more comforting to the innocent. Here the marble and the tiles, irregularly mottled with a design like stirred oil, the peg-board for the notices, the great black counter that swept in a parabola across half the foyer, suggested that order and a harmony of pattern must reign above all things. It was as if the personal fate of the men and women who came through the swing doors mattered less than Chief Inspector Wexford's impeccable records.

He left Parsons dazed between a rubber plant and a chair shaped like the bowl of a spoon, a spongy spoon, cough-mixture red. It was absurd, he thought, knocking on Wexford's door, to build a concrete box of tricks like this amid the quiet crowded houses of the High Street. Wexford called him to come in and he pushed open the door.

'Mr Parsons is outside, sir.'

'All right.' Wexford looked at his watch. 'I'll see him now.'

He was taller than Burden, thick-set without being fat, fifty-two years old, the very prototype of an actor playing a top-brass policeman. Born up the road in Pomfret, living most of his life in this part of Sussex, he knew most people and he knew the district well enough for the map on the the buttercup-yellow wall to be regarded merely as a decoration.

Parsons came in nervously. He had a furtive cautious look, and there was something defiant about him as if he knew his pride would be wounded and was preparing to defend it.

'Very worrying for you,' Wexford said. He spoke without emphasizing any particular word, his voice level and strong. 'Inspector Burden tells me you haven't seen your wife since yesterday morning.'

'That's right.' He took the snapshot of his wife from his pocket and put it on Wexford's desk. 'That's her, that's Margaret.' He twitched his head at Burden. 'He said you'd want to see it.'

It showed a youngish woman in cotton blouse and dirndl skirt standing stiffly, her arms at her sides, in the Parsonses' garden. She was smiling an unnaturally broad smile straight into the sun and she looked flustered, rather short of breath, as if she had been called away from some mundane household task – the washing-up perhaps – had flung off her apron, dried her hands and run down the path to her husband, waiting with his box camera.

Her eyes were screwed up, her cheeks bunchy; she might really have been saying 'Cheese!' There was nothing here of the delicate cameo Jean's words had suggested.

Wexford looked at it and said, 'Is this the best you can do?'

Parsons covered the picture with his hand as if it had been desecrated.

He looked as if he might flare into rage, but all he said was:

'We're not in the habit of having studio portraits taken.'

'No passport?'

'I can't afford foreign holidays.'

Parsons had spoken bitterly. He glanced quickly at the venetian blinds, the scanty bit of haircord carpet, Wexford's chair with its mauve tweed seat, as if these were signs of a personal affluence rather than the furnishings supplied by a detached authority.

'I'd like a description of your wife, Mr Parsons,' Wexford said. 'Won't you sit down?'

Burden called young Gates in and set him tapping with one finger at the little grey typewriter.

Parsons sat down. He began speaking slowly, shamefacedly, as if he had been asked to uncover his wife's nakedness.

'She's got fair hair,' he said. 'Fair curly hair and very light blue eyes. She's pretty.' He looked at Wexford defiantly and Burden wondered if he realized the dowdy impression the photograph had given. 'I think she's pretty. She's got a high sort of forehead.' He touched his own low narrow one. 'She's not very tall, about five feet one or two.'

Wexford went on looking at the picture.

'Thin? Well built?'

Parsons shifted in his chair.

'Well built, I suppose.' An awkward flush tinged the pale face. 'She's thirty. She was thirty a few months ago, in March.'

'What was she wearing?'

'A green and white dress. Well, white with green flowers on it, and a yellow cardigan. Oh, and sandals. She never wears stockings in the summer.'

'Handbag?'

'She never carried a handbag. She doesn't smoke or use

make-up, you see. She wouldn't have any use for a handbag. Just her purse and her key.'

'Any distinguishing marks?'

'Appendicitis scar,' Parsons said, flushing again.

Gates ripped the sheet from the typewriter and Wexford looked at it.

'Tell me about yesterday morning, Mr Parsons,' he said. 'How did your wife seem? Excited? Worried?'

Parsons slapped his hands down on to his spread knees. It was a gesture of despair; despair and exasperation.

'She was the same as usual,' he said. 'I didn't notice anything. You see, she wasn't an emotional woman.' He looked down at his shoes and said again, 'She was the same as usual.'

'What did you talk about?'

'I don't know. The weather. We didn't talk much. I have to get off to work at half past eight – I work for the Southern Water Board at Stowerton. I said it was a nice day and she said yes, but it was too bright. It was bound to rain, too good to last. And she was right. It did rain, poured down all the morning.'

'And you went to work. How? Bus, train, car?'

'I don't have a car. . . .'

He looked as if he was about to enumerate all the other things he didn't have, so Wexford said quickly:

'Bus then?'

'I always catch the eight-thirty-seven from the market place. I said good-bye to her. She didn't come to the door. But that's nothing. She never did. She was washing up.'

'Did she say what she was going to do with herself during the day?'

'The usual things, I suppose, shopping and the house. You know the sort of things women do.' He paused, then said suddenly: 'Look, she wouldn't kill herself. Don't get any ideas like that. Margaret wouldn't kill herself. She's a religious woman.'

'All right, Mr Parsons. Try to keep calm and don't worry. We'll do everything we can to find her.'

Wexford considered, dissatisfaction in the lines of his face, and Parsons seemed to interpret this characteristically. He sprang to his feet, quivering.

'I know what you're thinking,' he shouted. 'You think I've done away with her. I know how your minds work. I've read it all up.'

Burden said quickly, trying to smooth things down. 'Mr Parsons is by way of being a student of crime, sir.'

'Crime?' Wexford raised his eyebrows. 'What crime?'

'We'll have a car to take you home,' Burden said. 'I should take the day off. Get your doctor to give you something so that you can sleep.'

Parsons went out jerkily, walking like a paraplegic, and from the window Burden watched him get into the car beside Gates. The shops were opening now and the fruiterer on the opposite side of the street was putting up his sunblind in anticipation of a fine day. If this had been an ordinary Wednesday, a normal weekday, Burden thought, Margaret Parsons might now have been kneeling in the sun, polishing that gleaming step, or opening the windows and letting some air into those musty rooms. Where was she, waking in the arms of her lover or lying in some more final resting place?

'She's bolted, Mike,' Wexford said. 'That's what my old father used to call a woman who eloped. A bolter. Still, better do the usual check-up. You can do it yourself since you knew her by sight.'

Burden picked up the photograph and put it in his pocket. He went first to the station but the ticket-collector and the booking clerks were sure Mrs Parsons hadn't been through.

But the woman serving at the bookstall recognized her at once from the picture.

'That's funny,' she said. 'Mrs Parsons always comes in to pay for her papers on Tuesdays. Yesterday was Tuesday but

I'm sure I never saw her. Wait a minute, my husband was on in the afternoon.' She called, 'George, here a sec.!'

The bookstall proprietor came round from the part of the shop that fronted on to the street. He opened his order book and ran a finger down the edge of one of the pages.

'No,' he said. 'She never came. There's two-and-two outstanding.' He looked curiously at Burden, greedy for explanations. 'Peculiar, that,' he said. 'She always pays up, regular as clockwork.'

Burden went back to the High Street to begin on the shops. He marched into the big supermarket and up to the check-out counter. The woman by the till was standing idly, lulled by background music. When Burden showed her the photograph she seemed to jerk back into life.

Yes, she knew Mrs Parsons by name as well as by sight. She was a regular customer and she had been in yesterday as usual.

'About half ten it was,' she said. 'Always the same time.'

'Did she talk to you? Can you remember what she said?'

'Now you are asking something. Wait a minute, I do remember. It's coming back to me. I said it was a problem to know what to give them, and she said, yes, you didn't seem to fancy salad, not when it was raining. She said she'd got some chops, she was going to do them in a batter, and I sort of looked at her things, the things she'd got in her basket. But she said, no, she'd got the chops on Monday.'

'Can you remember what she was wearing? A green cotton frock, yellow cardigan?'

'Oh, no, definitely not. All the customers were in raincoats yesterday morning. Wait a tic, that rings a bell. She said, "Golly, it's pouring." I remember because of the way she said "Golly", like a school-kid. She said, "I'll have to get something to put on my head," so I said, "Why not get one of our rain-hoods in the reduced line?" She said didn't it seem awful to have to buy a rain-hood in May? But she took one. I know that for sure, because I had to check it separately. I'd already checked her goods.'

She left the counter and led Burden to a display of jumbled transparent scarves, pink, blue, apricot and white. .

'They wouldn't actually keep the rain out,' she said confidingly. 'Not a downpour, if you know what I mean. But they're prettier than plastic. More glamorous. She had a pink one. I remarked on it. I said it went with her pink jumper.'

'Thank you very much,' Burden said. 'You've been most helpful.'

He checked at the shops between the supermarket and Tabard Road, but no one remembered seeing Mrs Parsons. In Tabard Road itself the neighbours seemed shocked and helpless. Mrs Johnson, Margaret Parsons' next-door neighbour, had seen her go out soon after ten and return at a quarter to eleven. Then, at about twelve, she thought it was, she had been in her kitchen and had seen Mrs Parsons go out into the garden and peg two pairs of socks on to the line. Half an hour later she had heard the Parsonses' front door open and close again softly. But this meant nothing. The milkman always came late, they had complained about it, and she might simply have put her hand out into the porch to take in the bottles.

There had been a sale at the auction rooms on the corner of Tabard Road the previous afternoon. Burden cursed to himself, for this meant that cars had been double parked along the street. Anyone looking out of her downstairs windows during the afternoon would have had her view of the opposite pavement blocked by this row of cars standing nose to tail.

He tried the bus garage, even rather wildly the car-hire firms, and drew a complete blank. Filled with foreboding, he went slowly back to the police station. Suicide now seemed utterly ruled out. You didn't chatter cheerfully about the chops you intended cooking for your husband's dinner if you intended to kill yourself, and you didn't go forth to meet your lover without a coat or a handbag.

Meanwhile Wexford had been through Parsons' house from the ugly little kitchen to the two attics. In a drawer of Mrs Parsons' dressing-table he found two winceyette nightdresses, oldish and faded but neatly folded, one printed cotton nightdress and a fourth, creased and worn perhaps for two nights, under the pillow nearest the wall on the double bed. His wife hadn't any more nightgowns, Parsons said, and her dressing-gown, made of blue woolly material with darker blue braiding, was still hanging on a hook behind the bedroom door. She hadn't a summer dressing-gown and the only pair of slippers she possessed Wexford found neatly packed heel to toe in a cupboard in the dining-room.

It looked as if Parsons had been right about the purse and the key. They were nowhere to be found. In the winter the house was heated solely by two open fires and the water by an immersion heater. Wexford set Gates to examining these fireplaces and to searching the dustbin, last emptied by Kingsmarkham Borough Council on Monday, but there was no trace of ash. A sheet of newspaper had been folded to cover the grate in the dining-room, and this, lightly sprinkled with soot, bore the date April 15th.

Parsons said he had given his wife five pounds house-keeping money on the previous Friday. As far as he knew she had no savings accumulated from previous weeks. Gates, searching the kitchen dresser, found two pound notes rolled up in a cocoa tin on one of the shelves. If Mrs Parsons had received only five pounds on Friday and out of this had bought food for her husband and herself for four or five days, leaving two pounds for the rest of the week, it was apparent that the missing purse could have contained at best a few shillings.

Wexford had hoped to find a diary, an address book or a letter which might give him some help. A brass letter-rack attached to the dining-room wall beside the fireplace contained only a coal bill, a circular from a firm fitting central-heating plant (had Mrs Parsons, after all, had her dreams?), two soap coupons and an estimate from a contractor for rendering and making good a damp patch on the kitchen wall.

'Your wife didn't have any family at all, Mr Parsons?' Wexford asked.

'Only me. We kept ourselves to ourselves. Margaret didn't...doesn't make friends easily. I was brought up in a children's home and when she lost her mother Margaret went to live with an aunt. But her aunt died when we were engaged.'

'Where was that, Mr Parsons? Where you met, I mean.'

'In London. Balham. Margaret was teaching in an infants' school and I had digs in her aunt's house.'

Wexford sighed. Balham! The net was widening. Still, you didn't travel forty miles without a coat or a handbag. He decided to abandon Balham for the time being.

'I suppose no one telephoned your wife on Monday night? Did she have any letters yesterday morning?'

'Nobody phoned, nobody came and there weren't any letters.' Parsons seemed proud of his empty life, as if it was evidence of respectability. 'We sat and talked. Margaret was knitting. I think I did a crossword puzzle part of the time.' He opened the cupboard where the slippers were and from the top shelf took a piece of blue knitting on four needles. 'I wonder if it will ever be finished,' he said. His fingers tightened on the ball of wool and he pressed the needles into the palm of his hand.

'Never fear,' Wexford said, hearty with false hope, 'we'll find her.'

'If you've finished in the bedrooms I think I'll go and lie down again. The doctor's given me something to make me sleep.'

Wexford sent for all his available men and set them to search the empty houses in Kingsmarkham and its environs, the fields that lay still unspoilt between the High Street and the Kingsbrook Road and, as afternoon came, the Kingsbrook itself. They postponed dragging operations until the shops had closed and the people dispersed, but even so a crowd gathered on the bridge and stood peering over the parapet at the wading men. Wexford, who hated this particular kind of ghoulishness, this lust for dreadful sights thinly disguised under a mask of shocked sympathy, glowered at them and tried to persuade them to leave the bridge, but they drifted back in twos and threes. At last when dusk came, and the men had waded far to the north and the south of the town, he called off the search.

Meanwhile Ronald Parsons, dosed with sodium amytal, had fallen asleep on his lumpy mattress. For the first time in six months dust had begun to settle on the dressing-table, the iron mantelpiece and the linoed floor.

CHAPTER THREE

Ere her limbs frigidly
Stiffen too rigidly,
Decently, kindly,
Smooth and compose them,
And her eyes, close them,
Staring so blindly!

Thomas Hood, *The Bridge of Sighs*

On Thursday morning a baker's roundsman, new to his job, called at a farm owned by a man called Prewett on the main Kingsmarkham-to-Pomfret road. There was no one about, so he left a large white loaf and a small brown one on a window-ledge and went back to where he had parked his van, leaving the gate open behind him.

Presently a cow nudged against the gate and pushed it wide open. The rest of the herd, about a dozen of them, followed and meandered down the lane. Fortunately for Mr Prewett (for the road to which they were heading was derestricted) their attention was distracted by some clumps of sow thistles on the edge of a small wood. One by one they lumbered across the grass verge, munched at the thistles, and gradually, slowly, penetrated into the thickets. The briars were thick and the wood dim. There were no more thistles, no more wet succulent grass. Trapped and bewildered, they stood still, lowing hopefully.

It was in this wood that Prewett's cowman found them and Mrs Parsons' body at half past one.

By two Wexford and Burden had arrived in Burden's car, while Bryant and Gates brought Dr Crocker and two men

with cameras. Prewett and the cowman, Bysouth, primed with
knowledge from television serials, had touched nothing, and
Margaret Parsons lay as Bysouth had found her, a bundle of
damp cotton with a yellow cardigan pulled over her head.

Burden pushed aside the branches to make an arch and
he and Wexford came close until they were standing over her.
Mrs Parsons was lying against the trunk of a hawthorn tree
perhaps eight feet high. The boughs, growing outwards and
downwards like the spokes of an umbrella, made an almost
enclosed igloo-shaped tent.

Wexford bent down and lifted the cardigan gently. The
new dress had a neckline cut lowish at the back. On the skin,
running from throat to nape to throat, was a purple circle like
a thin ribbon. Burden gazed and the blue eyes seemed to stare
back at him. An old-fashioned face, Jean had said, a face you
wouldn't forget. But he would forget in time, as he forgot them
all. Nobody said anything. The body was photographed from
various angles and the doctor examined the neck and the
swollen face. Then he closed the eyes and Margaret Parsons
looked at them no more.

'Ah, well,' Wexford said. 'Ah, well.' He shook his head
slowly. There was, after all, nothing else to say.

After a moment he knelt down and felt among the dead
leaves. In the cavern of thin bending branches it was close
and unpleasant, but quite scentless. Wexford lifted the arms
and turned the body over, looking for a purse and a key.
Burden watched him pick something up. It was a used matchstick, half burnt away.

They came out of the hawthorn tent into comparative light
and Wexford said to Bysouth:

'How long have these cows been in here?'

'Be three hour or more, sir.'

Wexford gave Burden a significant look. The wood was
badly trampled and the few naked patches of ground were
boggy with cattle dung. A marathon wrestling match could

have taken place in that wood before breakfast, but Prewett's cows would have obliterated all traces of it by lunchtime; a wrestling match or a struggle between a killer and a terrified woman. Wexford set Bryant and Gates to searching among the maze of gnat-ridden brambles while he and Burden went back to the car with the farmer.

Mr Prewett was what is known as a gentleman farmer and his well-polished riding boots, now somewhat spattered, did no more than pay service to his calling. The leather patches on the elbows of his tobacco-coloured waisted jacket had been stitched there by a bespoke tailor.

'Who uses the lane, sir?'

'I have a Jersey herd pastured on the other side of the Pomfret road,' Prewett said. He had a county rather than a country accent. 'Bysouth takes them over in the morning and back in the afternoon by way of the lane. Then there is the occasional tractor, you know.'

'What about courting couples?'

'A stray car,' Prewett said distastefully. 'Of course this is a private road. Just as private in fact, Chief Inspector, as your own garage drive, but nobody respects privacy these days. I don't think any of the local lads and lasses come up here on foot. The fields are much more – well, salubrious, shall we say? We do get cars up here. You could stick a car under those overhanging branches and anyone could pass quite close to it at night without even seeing it was there.'

'I was wondering if you'd noticed any unfamiliar tyre marks between now and Tuesday, sir?'

'Oh, come!' Prewett waved a not very horny hand up towards the entrance to the lane and Burden saw what he meant. The lane was all tyre marks; in fact it was the tyre marks that made it into a road. 'The tractors go in and out, the cattle trample it. . . .'

'But you have a car, sir. With all this coming and going it's odd nobody saw anything unusual.'

'You must remember it's simply used for coming and going. No one hangs about here. My people have all got a job of work to do. They're good lads and they get on with it. In any case you'll have to discount my wife and myself. We've been in London from Monday until this morning and we mostly use the front entrance anyway. The lane's a short cut, Chief Inspector. It's fine for tractors but my own vehicle gets bogged down.' He stopped, then added sharply, 'When I'm in town I don't care to be taken for a horny-handed son of toil.'

Wexford examined the lane for himself and found only a morass of deeply rutted trenches zig-zagged with the tread marks of tractor tyres and deep round holes made by hoofs. He decided to postpone talking to Prewett's four men and the girl agricultural student until the time of Mrs Parsons' death had been fixed.

Burden went back to Kingsmarkham to break the news to Parsons because he knew him. Parsons opened the door numbly, moving like a sleep-walker. When Burden told him, standing stiffly in the dining-room with the dreadful books, he said nothing, but closed his eyes and swayed.

'I'll fetch Mrs Johnson,' Burden said. 'I'll get her to make you some tea.'

Parsons just nodded. He turned his back and stared out of the window. With something like horror Burden saw that the two pairs of socks were still pegged to the line.

'I'd like to be alone for a bit.'

'Just the same, I'll tell her. She can come in later.'

The widower shuffled his feet in khaki-coloured slippers.

'All right,' he said. 'And thanks. You're very good.'

Back at the station Wexford was sitting at his desk looking at the burnt matchstick. He said musingly:

'You know, Mike, it looks as if someone struck this to get a good look at her. That means after dark. Someone held it until it almost burnt his fingers.'

'Bysouth?'

Wexford shook his head.

'It was light, light enough to see – everything. No, whoever struck that match wanted to make sure he hadn't left anything incriminating behind him.' He slipped the piece of charred wood into an envelope. 'How did Parsons take it?' he asked.

'Difficult to say. It's always a shock, even if you're expecting it. He's so doped up on what the doctor's giving him he didn't seem to take it in.'

'Crocker's doing the post-mortem now. Inquest at ten on Saturday.'

'Can Crocker fix the time of death, sir?'

'Some time on Tuesday. I could have told him that. She must have been killed between half twelve and – what time did you say Parsons rang you on Tuesday night?'

'Exactly half past seven. We were going to the pictures and I was keeping an eye on the time.'

'Between half twelve and seven-thirty, then.'

'That brings me to my theory, sir.'

'Let's have it. I haven't got one.'

'Well, Parsons said he got home at six but no one saw him. The first anyone knew he was in the house was when he phoned me at half past seven. . . .'

'Okay, I'm listening. Just stick your head out of the door and get Martin to fetch us some tea.'

Burden shouted for tea and went on:

'Well, suppose Parsons killed her. As far as we know she doesn't know anyone else around here and, as you always say, the husband is the first suspect. Suppose Parsons made a date with his wife to meet him at Kingsmarkham bus garage.'

'What sort of a date?'

'He could have said they'd go and have a meal somewhere in Pomfret, or go for a walk, a picnic . . . anything.'

'What about the chops, Mike? She didn't have a date when she was talking to your supermarket woman.'

'They're on the phone. He could have telephoned her

during his lunch hour – it had begun to clear up by then – and asked her to pick up the bus at the garage at ten to six, suggested going into Pomfret for a meal. After all, maybe they make a habit of going out to eat. We've only got his word for what they did.'

Martin came in with the tea and Wexford, cup in hand, went over to the window and looked down into the High Street. The bright sun made him screw up his eyes and he pulled at the cord of the blind, half closing the slats.

'The Stowerton bus doesn't go to Pomfret,' he objected. 'Not the five-thirty-five. Kingsmarkham is the terminus.'

Burden took a sheet of paper out of his pocket.

'No, but the five-thirty-two does. Stowerton to Pomfret, via Forby and Kingsmarkham.' He concentrated on the figures he had written. 'Let me put it like this: Parsons phones his wife at lunchtime and asks her to meet the Stowerton bus that gets into Kingsmarkham at five-fifty, two minutes before the other bus, the one that goes into the garage. Now, he could have made that bus if he left a minute or two early.'

'You'll have to check that, Mike.'

'Anyway, Mrs P. catches the bus. It passes through Forby at six-one and reaches Pomfret at six-thirty. When they get to the nearest bus-stop to the wood by Prewett's farm Parsons says it's such a nice evening, let's get off and walk the rest of the way. . . .'

'It's a good mile this side of Pomfret. Still, they might be keen on country walks.'

'Parsons says he knows a short cut across the fields to Pomfret. . . .'

'Through a practically impenetrable dark wood, thistles, long wet grass?'

'I know, sir. I don't like that bit myself. But they might have seen something in the wood, a deer or a rabbit or something. Anyway, somehow or other Parsons gets her into that wood and strangles her.'

'Oh, marvellous! Mrs Parsons is going out to dinner in a fashionable country pub, but she doesn't object to plunging into the middle of a filthy wet wood after a rabbit. What's she going to do with it when she's caught it, eat it? Her old man follows her and when she's in the thickest part of the wood he says, "Stand still a minute, dear, while I get a bit of rope out of my pocket and strangle you!" God Almighty!'

'He might have killed her in the lane and dragged her body into the bushes. It's a dark lane and there's never anyone walking along the Pomfret road. He might have carried her – he's a big bloke and you wouldn't see the tracks after those cows had been all over it.'

'True.'

'The bus leaves Pomfret again at six-forty-one, gets to Forby at seven-nine, Kingsmarkham garage seven-twenty. That gives him about fifteen minutes in which to kill his wife and get back to the bus-stop on the other side of the Pomfret road. The bus gets there at about six-forty-six. He runs up Tabard Road and gets into his own house in five minutes, just in time to phone me at seven-thirty.'

Wexford sat down again in the little swivel chair with the purple cushion.

'He was taking an awful risk, Mike,' he said. 'He might easily have been seen. You'll have to check with the bus people. They can't pick up many passengers at the stop by Prewett's farm. What did he do with her purse and her key?'

'Chucked them in the bushes. There wasn't any point in hiding them, anyway. The thing is, I can't think of a motive.'

'Oh, motive,' Wexford said. 'Any husband's got a motive.'

'I haven't.' Burden was incensed. Someone knocked at the door and Bryant came in.

'I found this on the edge of the wood on the lane side, sir,' Bryant said. He was holding a small gilt cylinder in the tips of his gloved fingers.

'A lipstick,' Wexford said. He took it from Bryant, covering his fingers with a handkerchief, and upended it to expose a circular label on its base. ' "Arctic Sable," ' he read, 'and something that looks like eight-and-six written in violet ink. Anything else?'

'Nothing, sir.'

'All right, Bryant. You and Gates can get over to the Southern Water Board at Stowerton and find out exactly – and I mean precisely to the minute – what time Parsons left work on Tuesday evening.'

'This makes your theory look bloody silly, Mike,' he said when Bryant had gone. 'We'll get the fingerprint boys on it, but, I ask you, is it likely to be Mrs Parsons'? She doesn't take a handbag, she doesn't use make-up and she's as poor as a church mouse (dinner in Pomfret, my foot!), but she takes a lipstick with her in her purse or stuffed down her bosom – an eight-and-sixpenny lipstick, mark you – and when they get to the wood she sees a rabbit. She opens her purse to get out her shotgun, I presume, slings the lipstick into the ditch, runs after the rabbit, striking a match to show her the way, and, when she's in the middle of the wood, sits down and lets her old man strangle her!'

'You sent Bryant off to Stowerton.'

'He's got time on his hands.' Wexford paused, staring at the lipstick. 'By the way,' he said, 'I've checked on the Prewetts. There's no doubt they were in London. Mrs Prewett's mother's seriously ill, and according to University College Hospital they were at her bedside pretty well continuously from before lunch on Tuesday until late that night, and there on and off all day yesterday. The old girl rallied a bit last night and they left their hotel in the Tottenham Court Road after breakfast this morning. So that lets them out.'

He picked up the sheet of paper on which he had placed the Arctic Sable lipstick and held it out for Burden to see. The prints were smudged, but there was a clear one on its domed top.

'It's a new lipstick,' Wexford said. 'It's hardly been used. I want to find the owner of that lipstick, Mike. We'll go over to Prewett's again and talk to that land girl or whatever she calls herself.'

CHAPTER FOUR

Thou hast beauty bright and fair,
Manner noble, aspect free,
Eyes that are untouched by care;
What then do we ask of thee?

Bryan Waller Procter, *Hermione*

When Wexford had been told the prints on the lipstick definitely hadn't been made by Mrs Parsons they went back to
the farm and questioned each of the men and the land girl
(as Wexford called her in his old-fashioned vocabulary) separately. For all but one of them Tuesday afternoon had been
busy and, in a very different way from murder, exciting.

Prewett had left the manager, John Draycott, in charge,
and on Tuesday morning Draycott had gone to Stowerton
market accompanied by a man called Edwards. They had
taken a truck and used the front entrance to the farm. This
was a long way round, but it was favoured because the lane
to the Pomfret road was narrow and muddy and the week
before the truck had got stuck in the ruts.

Bysouth and the man in charge of Prewett's pigs had
remained alone at the farm, Miss Sweeting, the land girl,
having had the day off on Tuesday to attend a lecture at
Sewingbury Agricultural College. At half past twelve they had
eaten their dinner in the kitchen, a meal cooked for them, as
usual, by Mrs Creavey, who came up to the farm each day
from Flagford to cook and clean. After dinner at a quarter
past one the pig man, Traynor, had taken Bysouth with him
to see a sow that was about to farrow.

At three Draycott and Edwards returned and the manager

FROM DOON WITH DEATH

began immediately on his accounts. Edwards, who included gardening among his duties, went to mow the front lawn. The man hadn't been constantly under his eye, Draycott told Wexford, but for the next hour he had been aware of the sound of the electric mower. At about half past three Draycott was interrupted by Traynor, who came in to tell him he was worried about the condition of the sow. Five piglets had been delivered, but she seemed to be in difficulties and Traynor wanted the manager's consent to call the vet. Draycott had gone to the sties, looked at the sow and talked for a few seconds to Bysouth, who was sitting beside her on a stool, before telephoning for the vet himself. The vet arrived by four and from then until five-thirty the manager, Edwards and Traynor had remained together. During this hour and a half, Traynor said, Bysouth had gone to fetch the cows in and put them in the milking shed. In order to do this he had had to pass the wood twice. Wexford questioned him closely, but he insisted that he had seen nothing out of the way. He had heard no untoward sound and there had been no cars either in the lane itself or parked on the Pomfret road. According to the other three men he had been even quicker than usual, a haste they attributed to his anxiety as to the outcome of the farrowing.

It was half past six before the whole litter of pigs had been delivered. The vet had gone into the kitchen to wash his hands and they had all had a cup of tea. At seven he left by the same way as he had come, the front entrance, giving a lift to Edwards, Traynor and Bysouth, who all lived in farm workers' cottages at a hamlet called Clusterwell, some two miles outside Flagford. During the Prewetts' absence Mrs Creavey was staying at the farm overnight. The manager performed his final round at eight and went home to his house about fifty yards down the Clusterwell road.

Wexford checked with the vet and decided that, apart from mystery story miracles, no one had had time to murder

Mrs Parsons and conceal her body in the wood. Only Bysouth had used the lane that passed the wood, and unless he had abandoned his charges dangerously near a derestricted road he was beyond suspicion. To be sure, Mrs Creavey had been alone and out of sight from three-thirty until six-thirty, but she was at least sixty, fat and notoriously arthritic.

Wexford tried to fix the time Bysouth had passed down and then up the lane, but the cowman didn't wear a watch and his life seemed to be governed by the sun. He protested vehemently that his mind had been on the sow's travail and that he had seen no one on the track, in the wood or walking in the fields.

Dorothy Sweeting was the only one of them who might remotely be supposed to have owned the Arctic Sable lipstick. But there is a particularly naked raw look about the face of a woman in an unpainted state when that woman habitually uses make-up. Dorothy Sweeting's face was sunburnt and shiny; it looked as if it had never been protected from the weather by cream and powder. The men were almost derisive when Wexford asked them if they had ever seen lipstick on her mouth.

'You didn't go to the farm all day, Miss Sweeting?'

Dorothy Sweeting laughed a lot. Now she laughed heartily. It seemed that to her the questioning was just like part of a serial or a detective story come to life.

'Not *to* it,' she said, 'but I went near it. Guilty, my lord!' Wexford didn't smile, so she went on: 'I went to see my auntie in Sewingbury after the lecture and it was such a lovely afternoon I got off the bus a mile this side of Pomfret and walked the rest of the way. Old Bysouth was bringing the cows in and I did just stop and have a chat with him.'

'What time would that have been?'

'Fiveish. It was the four-ten bus from Sewingbury.'

'All right, Miss Sweeting. Your prints will be destroyed after the check has been made.'

She roared with laughter. Looking at her big broad hands, her forearms like the village blacksmith's, Burden wondered what she intended to do with her life after she had qualified for whatever branch of bucolic craft she was studying.

'Hang on to them by all means,' she said. 'I'd like to take my place in the rogues' gallery.'

They drove back to Kingsmarkham along the quiet half-empty road. There was still an hour to go before the evening rush began. The sun had dimmed and the mackerel sky thickened until it looked like curds and whey. On the hedges that bordered the road the May blossom still lingered, touched now with brown as if it had been singed by fleeting fire.

Wexford led the way into the police station and they had Miss Sweeting's prints checked with the ones on the lipstick. As Wexford had expected, they didn't match. The student's big pitted fingertips were more like a man's than a woman's.

'I want to find the owner of that lipstick, Mike,' he said again. 'I want every chemist's shop in this place gone over with a small toothcomb. And you'd better do it yourself because it's not going to be easy.'

'Does it have to have any connection with Mrs Parsons, sir? Couldn't it have been dropped by someone going up the track?'

'Look, Mike, that lipstick wasn't by the road. It was right on the edge of the wood. Apart from the fact that they don't use the lane, Sweeting and Mrs Creavey don't wear lipstick and even if they did they wouldn't be likely to have one in a peculiar shade of pinkish brown like this. You know as well as I do, when a woman only uses lipstick on high days and holidays, for some reason or other, a sense of daring probably, she always picks a bright red. This is a filthy colour, the sort of thing a rich woman might buy if she'd already got a dozen lipsticks and wanted the latest shade for a gimmick.'

Burden knew Kingsmarkham well, but he got the local trade directory to check and found that there were seven

chemists in Kingsmarkham High Street, three in side roads
and one in a village which had now been absorbed as a suburb
into Kingsmarkham itself. Bearing in mind what Wexford had
said about a rich woman, he started on the High Street.

The supermarket had a cosmetics counter, but they kept
only a limited stock of the more expensive brands. The assistant knew Mrs Parsons by name, having read that she was
missing in a newspaper. She also knew her by sight and was
agog. Burden didn't tell her the body had been found and he
didn't waste any more time on questions when he learnt that,
as far as the girl could remember, Mrs Parsons had bought
only a tin of cheap talcum powder in the past month.

'That's a new line,' said the assistant in the next shop. 'It's
only just come out. It comes in a range of fur shades, sort of
soft and subtle, but we don't stock it. We wouldn't have the
sale for it, you see.'

He walked up towards the Kingsbrook bridge past the
Georgian house that was now the Youth Employment Bureau,
past the Queen Anne house that was now a solicitor's office,
and entered a newly opened shop in a block with maisonettes
above it. It was bright and clean, with a dazzling stock of pots
and jars and bottles of scent. They kept a large stock of the
brand, he was told, but were still awaiting delivery of the fur
range.

The waters of the brook had settled and cleared. Burden
could see the flat round stones on the bottom. He leaned over
the parapet and saw a fish jump. Then he went on, weaving
his way between groups of schoolchildren, High School girls
in panamas and scarlet blazers, avoiding prams and baskets
on wheels. He had called at four shops before he found one
that stocked the fur range. But they had only sold one and
that in a colour called Mutation Mink, and they didn't put
prices on their goods. The girl in the fifth shop, a queenly
creature with hair like pineapple candy-floss, said that she was
wearing Arctic Sable herself. She lived in a flat above the shop

and she went upstairs to fetch the lipstick. It was identical to the one found in the wood except that it had no price written on its base.

'It's a difficult shade to wear,' the girl said. 'We've sold a couple in the other colours but that sort of brownish tint puts the customers off.'

Now there were no more shops on this side of the High Street, only a couple of big houses, the Methodist Church – Mrs Parsons' church – standing back from the road behind a sweep of gravel, a row of cottages, before the fields began. He crossed the street at The Olive and Dove and went into a chemist's shop between a florist's and an estate agent's. Burden had sometimes bought shaving cream in this shop and he knew the man who came out from the dispensary at the back. But he shook his head at once. They didn't stock any cosmetics of that make.

There were only two left: a little poky place with jars of hair cream and toothbrushes in the window, and an elegant emporium, double-fronted, with steps up to the door and a bow window. The vendor of hair cream had never even heard of Arctic Sable. He climbed up a short ladder and took from a shelf a cardboard box of green plastic cylinders.

'Haven't sold a lipstick inside a fortnight,' he said.

Burden opened the door of the double-fronted shop and stepped on to wine-coloured carpet. All the perfumes of Arabia seemed to be assembled on the counters and the gilded tables. Musk and ambergris and new-mown hay assaulted his nostrils. Behind a pyramid of boxes, encrusted with glitter and bound with ribbon, he could see the back of a girl's head, a girl with short blonde curls wearing a primrose sweater. He coughed, the girl turned and he saw that it was a young man.

'Isn't it a delightful shade?' the young man said. 'So young and fresh and innocent. Oh, yes, definitely one of ours. I mark everything with this.' And he picked up a purple ball-point pen from beside the cash register.

'I don't suppose you could tell me who you sold this one to?'

'But I love probing and detecting! Let's be terribly thorough and have a real investigation.'

He opened a drawer with a knob made of cut glass and took out a tray of gilt lipsticks. There were several in each compartment.

'Let me see,' he said. 'Mutation Mink, three gone. I started off with a dozen of each shade. Trinidad Tiger – good heavens, nine gone! Rather a common sort of red, that one. Here we are, Arctic Sable, four gone. Now for my thinking cap.'

Burden said encouragingly that he was being most helpful.

'We do have a regular clientele, what you might call a segment of the affluent society. I don't want to sound snobbish, but I do rather eschew the cheaper lines. I remember now. Miss Clements from the estate agent's had one. No, she had two, one for herself and one for someone's birthday present. Mrs Darrell had another. I do recall that because she took Mutation Mink and changed her mind just as she was going out of the shop. She came back and changed it and while she was making up her mind someone else came in for a pale pink lipstick. Of course, Mrs Missal! She took one look – Mrs Darrell had tried the shade out on her wrist – and she said, "That is absolutely me!" Mrs Missal has exquisite taste because, whatever you may say, Arctic Sable is really intended for red-heads like her.'

'When was this?' Burden asked. 'When did you get the fur range in?'

'Just a tick.' He checked in a delivery book. 'Last Thursday, just a week ago. I sold the two to Miss Clements soon after they came in. Friday, I should say. I wasn't here on Saturday and Monday's always slack. Washing, you know. Tuesday's early closing and I know I didn't sell any yesterday. It must have been Tuesday morning.'

'You've been a great help,' Burden said.

'Not at all. You've brought a little sparkle into my worka-day world. By the by, Mrs Missal lives in that rather lovely bijou house opposite the Olive and Dove, and Mrs Darrell has the maisonette with the pink curtains in the new block in Queen Street.'

As luck had it, Miss Clements had both lipsticks in her handbag, her own partly used, and the other one she had bought for a present still wrapped in cellophane paper. As Burden left the estate agent's he glanced at his watch. Half past five. He had just made it before they all closed. He ran Mrs Darrell to earth in the maisonette next to her own. She was having tea with a friend, but she went down the spiral staircase at the back of the block and up the next one, coming back five minutes later with an untouched lipstick, Arctic Sable, marked eight-and-six in violet ink on its base.

The Stowerton-to-Pomfret bus was coming up the hill as he turned out of Queen Street and crossed the forecourt of The Olive and Dove. He checked with his watch and saw that it was gone ten to six. Maybe it had been late leaving Stowerton, maybe it often was. Damn those stupid women and their lipsticks, he thought; Parsons must have done it.

The lovely bijou house was a Queen Anne affair, much done up with white paint, wrought iron and window-boxes. The front door was yellow, flanked with blue lilies in stone urns. Burden struck the ship's bell with a copper clapper that hung on a length of cord. But, as he had expected, no one came. The garage, a converted coach-house, was empty and the doors stood open. He went down the steps again, crossed the road and walked up to the police station, wondering as he went how Bryant had got on with the Southern Water Board.

Wexford seemed pleased about the lipstick. They waited until Bryant had got back from Stowerton before going down to The Olive and Dove for dinner.

'It looks as if this clears Parsons,' Wexford said. 'He left the Water Board at five-thirty or a little after. Certainly not before. He couldn't have caught the five-thirty-two.'

'No,' Burden said reluctantly, 'and there isn't another till six-two.'

They went into the dining-room of The Olive and Dove and Wexford asked for a window table so that they could watch Mrs Missal's house.

By the time they had finished the roast lamb and started on the gooseberry tart the garage doors were still open and no one had come into or gone out of the house. Burden remained at the table while Wexford went to pay the bill, and just as he was getting up to follow him to the door he saw a blonde girl in a cotton dress enter the High Street from the Sewingbury Road. She walked past the Methodist Church, past the row of cottages, ran up the steps of Mrs Missal's house and let herself in at the front door.

'Come on, Mike,' Wexford said.

He banged at the bell with the clapper.

'Look at that bloody thing,' he said. 'I hate things like that.'

They waited a few seconds. Then the door was opened by the blonde girl.

'Mrs Missal?'

'Mrs Missal, Mr Missal, the children, all are out,' she said. She spoke with a strong foreign accent. 'All are gone to the sea.'

'We're police officers,' Wexford said. 'When do you expect Mrs Missal back?'

'Now is seven.' She glanced behind her at a black grand-father clock. 'Half past seven, eight. I don't know. You come back again in a little while. Then she come.'

'We'll wait, if you don't mind,' Wexford said.

They stepped over the threshold on to velvety blue carpet. It was a square hall, with a staircase running up from the centre at the back and branching at the tenth stair. Through an arch on the right-hand side of this staircase Burden saw a dining-room with a polished floor partly covered by Indian rugs in pale colours. At the far end of this room open french windows gave on to a wide and apparently endless garden. The hall was cool, smelling faintly of rare and subtle flowers.

'Would you mind telling me your name, miss, and what you're doing here?' Wexford asked.

'Inge Wolff. I am nanny for Dymphna and Priscilla.'

Dymphna! Burden thought, aghast. His own children were John and Pat.

'All right, Miss Wolff. If you'll just show us where we can sit down you can go and get on with your work.'

She opened a door on the left side of the hall and Wexford and Burden found themselves in a large drawing-room whose bow windows faced the street. The carpet was green, the chairs and a huge sofa covered in green linen patterned with pink and white rhododendrons. Real rhododendrons, saucer sized heads of blossom on long stems, were massed in two white vases. Burden had the feeling that when rhododendrons went out of season Mrs Missal would fill the vases with delphiniums and change the covers accordingly.

'No shortage of lolly,' Wexford said laconically when the girl had gone. 'This is the sort of set-up I had in mind when I said she might buy Arctic Sable for a gimmick.'

'Cigarette, sir?'

'Have you gone raving mad, Burden? Maybe you'd like to take your tie off. This is Sussex, not Mexico.'

Burden restored the packet and they sat in silence for ten minutes. Then he said, 'I bet she's got that lipstick in her handbag.'

'Look, Mike, four were sold, all marked in violet ink. Right? Miss Clements has two, Mrs Darrell has one. I have the fourth.'

'There could be a chemist in Stowerton or Pomfret or Sewingbury marking lipsticks in violet ink.'

'That's right, Mike. And if Mrs Missal can show me hers you're going straight over to Stowerton first thing in the morning and start on the shops over there.'

But Burden wasn't listening. His chair was facing the window and he craned his neck.

'Car's coming in now,' he said. 'Olive-green Mercedes, nineteen-sixty-two. Registration XPQ189Q.'

'All right, Mike, I don't want to buy it.'

As the wheels crunched on the drive and someone opened one of the nearside doors, Burden ducked his head.

'Blimey,' he said. 'She is something of a dish.'

A woman in white slacks stepped out of the car and strolled to the foot of the steps. The kingfisher-blue and darker-blue patterned silk scarf that held back her red hair matched her shirt. Burden thought she was beautiful, although her face was hard, as if the tanned skin was stretched on a steel frame. He was paid not to admire but to observe. For him the most significant thing about her was that her mouth was painted not brownish pink but a clear golden-red. He turned away from the window and heard her say loudly:

'I am sick to my stomach of bleeding kids! I bet you anything you like, Pete, that lousy little Inge isn't back yet.'

A key was turned in the front-door lock and Burden heard Inge Wolff running along the hall to meet her employers. One of the children was crying.

'Policemen? How many policemen? Oh, I don't believe it, Inge. Where's their car?'

'I suppose they want me, Helen. You know I'm always leaving the Merc outside without lights.'

In the drawing-room Wexford grinned.

The door opened suddenly, bouncing back from one of the flower-vases as if it had been kicked by a petulant foot. The red-haired woman came in first. She was wearing sunglasses with rhinestone frames, and although the sun had gone and the room was dim, she didn't bother to take them off. Her

40

husband was tall and big, his face bloated and already marked with purple veins. His long shirt-tails hung over his belly like a gross maternity smock. Burden winced at its design of bottles and glasses and plates on a scarlet and white checkerboard.

He and Wexford got up.

'Mrs Missal?'

'Yes, I'm Helen Missal. What the hell do you want?'

'We're police officers, Mrs Missal, making enquiries in connection with the disappearance of Mrs Margaret Parsons.'

Missal stared. His fat lips were already wet, but still he licked them.

'Won't you sit down,' he said. 'I can't imagine why you want to talk to my wife.'

'Neither can I,' Helen Missal said. 'What is this, a police state?'

'I hope not, Mrs Missal. I believe you bought a new lipstick on Tuesday morning?'

'So what? Is it a crime?'

'If you could just show me that lipstick, madam, I shall be quite satisfied and we won't take up any more of your time. I'm sure you must be tired after a day at the seaside.'

'You can say that again.' She smiled. Burden thought she suddenly seemed at the same time more wary and more friendly. 'Have you ever sat on a spearmint ice lolly?' She giggled and pointed to a very faint bluish-green stain on the seat of her trousers. 'Thank God for Inge! I don't want to see those little bastards again tonight.'

'Helen!' Missal said.

'The lipstick, Mrs Missal.'

'Oh, yes, the lipstick. Actually I did buy one, a filthy colour called Arctic something. I lost it in the cinema last night.'

'Are you quite sure you lost it in the cinema? Did you enquire about it? Ask the manager, for instance?'

'What, for an eight-and-sixpenny lipstick? Do I look that poor? I went to the cinema —'

'By yourself, madam?'

'Of course I went by myself.' Burden sensed a certain defensiveness, but the glasses masked her eyes. 'I went to the cinema and when I got back the lipstick wasn't in my bag.'

'Is this it?' Wexford held the lipstick out on his palm, and Mrs Missal extended long fingers with nails lacquered silver like armour-plating. 'I'm afraid I shall have to ask you to come down to the station with me and have your fingerprints taken.'

'Helen, what is this?' Missal put his hand on his wife's arm. She shook it off as if the fingers had left a dirty mark. 'I don't get it, Helen. Has someone pinched your lipstick, someone connected with this woman?'

She continued to look at the lipstick in her hand. Burden wondered if she realized she had already covered it with prints.

'I suppose it is mine,' she said slowly. 'All right, I admit it must be mine. Where did you find it, in the cinema?'

'No, Mrs Missal. It was found on the edge of a wood just off the Pomfret Road.'

'What?' Missal jumped up. He stared at Wexford, then at his wife. 'Take those damn' things off!' he shouted and twitched the sunglasses from her nose. Burden saw that her eyes were green, a very light bluish green flecked with gold. For a second he saw panic there; then she dropped her lids, the only shields that remained to her, and looked down into her lap.

'You went to the pictures,' Missal said. 'You said you went to the pictures. I don't get this about a wood and the Pomfret Road. What the hell's going on?'

Helen Missal said very slowly, as if she was inventing: 'Someone must have found my lipstick in the cinema. Then they must have dropped it. That's it. It's quite simple. I can't understand what all the fuss is about.'

'It so happens,' Wexford said, 'that Mrs Parsons was found strangled in that wood at half past one today.'

She shuddered and gripped the arms of her chair. Burden

thought she was making a supreme effort not to cry out. At last she said:

'It's obvious, isn't it? Your murderer, whoever he is, pinched my lipstick and then dropped it at the . . . the scene of the crime.'

'Except,' Wexford said, 'that Mrs Parsons died on Tuesday. I won't detain you any longer, madam. Not just at present. One more thing, though, have you a car of your own?'

'Yes, yes, I have. A red Dauphine. I keep it in the other garage with the entrance in the Kingsbrook Road. Why?'

'Yes, why?' Missal said. 'Why all this? We didn't even know this Mrs Parsons. You're not suggesting my wife . . .? My God, I wish someone would explain!'

Wexford looked from one to the other. Then he got up.

'I'd just like to have a look at the tyres, sir,' he said.

As he spoke light seemed suddenly to have dawned on Missal. He blushed an even darker brick red and his face crumpled like that of a baby about to cry. There was despair there, despair and the kind of pain Burden felt he should not look upon. Then Missal seemed to pull himself together. He said in a quiet reserved voice that seemed to cover a multitude of unspoken enquiries and accusations:

'I've no objection to your looking at my wife's car but I can't imagine what connection she has with this woman.'

'Neither can I, sir,' Wexford said cheerfully. 'That's what we shall want to find out. I'm as much in the dark as you are.'

'Oh, give him the garage key, Pete,' she said. 'I tell you I don't know any more. It's not my fault if my lipstick was stolen.'

'I'd give a lot to be able to hide behind those rhododendrons and hear what he says to her,' Wexford said as they walked up the Kingsbrook Road to Helen Missal's garage.

'And what she says to him,' Burden said. 'You think it's all right leaving them for the night, sir? She's bound to have a current passport.'

Wexford said innocently: 'I thought that might worry you, Mike, so I'm going to book a room at The Olive and Dove for the night. A little job for Martin. He'll have to sit up all night. My heart bleeds for him.'

The Missals' garden was large and roughly diamond-shaped. On the north side, the side where the angle of the diamond was oblique, the garden was bounded by the Kingsbrook, and on the other a hedge of tamarisk separated it from the Kingsbrook Road. Burden unlocked the cedarwood gates to the garage and made a note of the index number of Helen Missal's car. Its rear window was almost entirely filled by a toy tiger cub.

'I want a sample taken from those tyres, Mike,' Wexford said. 'We've got a sample from the lane by Prewett's farm. It's a bit of luck for us that the soil's practically solid cow dung.'

'Blimey,' Burden said, wincing as he got to his feet. He re-locked the doors. 'This is millionaires' row, all right.' He put the dried mud into an envelope and pointed towards the houses on the other side of the road: a turreted mansion, a ranch-style bungalow with two double garages and a new house built like a chalet with balconies of dark carved wood.

'Very nice if you can get it,' Wexford said. 'Come on. I'm going to get the car and have another word with Prewett, and, incidentally, the cinema manager. If you'll just drop that key in to Inge, or whatever she calls herself, you can get off home. I shall have to have a word with young Inge tomorrow.'

'When are you going to see Mrs Missal again, sir?'

'Unless I'm very much mistaken,' Wexford said, 'she'll come to me before I can get to her.'

CHAPTER FIVE

If she answer thee with No,
Wilt thou bow and let her go?

W. J. Linton, *Faint Heart*

Sergeant Camb was talking to someone on the telephone when Wexford got to the station in the morning. He covered the mouthpiece with his hand and said to the Chief Inspector:

'A Mrs Missal for you, sir. This is the third time she's been on.'

'What does she want?'

'She says she must see you. It's very urgent.' Camb looked embarrassed. 'She wants to know if you can go to her house.'

'She does, does she? Tell her if she wants me she'll have to come here.' He opened the door of his office. 'Oh, and, Sergeant Camb, you can tell her I won't be here after nine-thirty.'

When he had opened the windows and made his desk untidy – the way he liked it – he stuck his head out of the door again and called for tea.

'Where's Martin?'

'Still at The Olive and Dove, sir.'

'God Almighty! Does he think he's on his holidays? Get on to him and tell him he can get off home.'

It was a fine morning, June coming in like a lamb, and from his desk Wexford could see the gardens of Bury Street and the window-boxes of the Midland Bank full of blown Kaiserskroon tulips. The spring flowers were passing, the summer ones not yet in bud – except for rhododendrons. Just as the first peals of the High School bell began to toll faintly in the distance Sergeant Camb brought in the tea – and Mrs Missal.

'We'll have another cup, please.'

She had done her hair up this morning and left off her glasses. The organdie blouse and the pleated skirt made her look surprisingly demure, and Wexford wondered if she had abandoned her hostile manner with the raffish shirt and trousers.

'I'm afraid I've been rather a silly girl, Chief Inspector,' she said in a confiding voice.

Wexford took a clean piece of paper out of his drawer and began writing on it busily. He couldn't think of anything cogent to put down and as she couldn't see the paper from where she was sitting he just scribbled: *Missal, Parsons; Parsons, Missal.*

'You see I didn't tell you the entire truth.'

'No?' Wexford said.

'I don't mean I actually told lies. I mean I left bits out.'

'Oh, yes?'

'Well, the thing is, I didn't actually go to the pictures by myself. I went with a friend, a man friend.' She smiled as one sophisticate to another. 'There wasn't anything in it, but you know how stuffy husbands are.'

'I should,' Wexford said. 'I am one.'

'Yes, well, when I got home I couldn't find my new lipstick and I think I must have dropped it in my friend's car. Oh, tea for me. How terribly sweet!'

There was a knock at the door and Burden came in.

'Mrs Missal was just telling me about her visit to the cinema on Wednesday night,' Wexford said. He went on writing. By now he had filled half the sheet.

'It was a good picture, wasn't it, Mrs Missal? Unfortunately I had to leave half-way through.' Burden looked for a third tea-cup. 'What happened to that secret-agent character? Did he marry the blonde or the other one?'

'Oh, the other one,' Helen Missal said easily. 'The one who played the violin. She put the message into a sort of musical code and when they got back to London she played it over to M.I.5.'

'It's wonderful what they think of,' Burden said.

'Well, I won't keep you any longer, Mrs Missal. . . .'

'No, I must fly. I've got a hair appointment.'

'If you'll just let me have the name of your friend, the one you went to the cinema with. . . .'

Helen Missal looked from Wexford to Burden and back from Burden to Wexford. Wexford screwed up the piece of paper and threw it into the wastepaper basket.

'Oh, I couldn't do that. I mean, I couldn't get him involved.'

'I should think it over, madam. Think it over while you're having your hair done.'

Burden held the door open for her and she walked out quickly without looking back.

'I've been talking to a neighbour of mine,' he said to Wexford, 'a Mrs Jones who lives at nine, Tabard Road. You know, she told us about the cars being parked in Tabard Road on Tuesday afternoon. Well, I asked her if she could remember any of the makes or the colours and she said she could remember one car, a bright red one with a tiger in the back. She didn't see the number. She was looking at them from sideways on, you see, and they were parked nose to tail.'

'How long was it there?'

'Mrs Jones didn't know. But she says she first saw it about three and it was there when the kids got home from school. Of course, she doesn't know if it was there all that time.'

'While Mrs Missal is having her hair done, Mike,' Wexford said, 'I am going to have a word with Inge. As Mrs Missal says, Thank God for Inge!'

There was a tin of polish and a couple of dusters on the dining-room floor and the Indian rugs were spread on the crazy paving outside the windows. Inge Wolff, it seemed, had duties apart from minding Dymphna and Priscilla.

'All I know I will tell you,' she said dramatically. 'What matter if I get the push? Next week, anyhow, I go home to Hanover.'

Maybe, Wexford thought, and, on the other hand, maybe not. The way things were going Inge Wolff might be needed in England for the next few months.

'On Monday Mrs Missal stay at home all the day. Just for shopping in the morning she go out. Also Tuesday she go shopping in the morning, for in the afternoon is closing of all shops.'

'What about Tuesday afternoon, Miss Wolff?'

'Ah, Tuesday afternoon she go out. First we have our dinner. One o'clock. I and Mrs Missal and the children. Ah, next week, only think, no more children! After dinner I wash up and she go up to her bedroom and lie down. When she come down she say, "Inge, I go out with the car," and she take the key and go down the garden to the garage.'

'What time would that be, Miss Wolff?'

'Three, half past two. I don't know.' She shrugged her shoulders. 'Then she come back, five, six.'

'How about Wednesday?'

'Ah, Wednesday. I have half-day off. Very good. Dymphna come home to dinner, go back to school. I go out. Mrs Missal stay home with Priscilla. And when comes the evening she go out, seven, half past seven. I don't know. In this house always are comings and goings. It is like a game.'

Wexford showed her the snapshot of Mrs Parsons.

'Have you ever seen this woman, Miss Wolff? Did she ever come here?'

'Hundreds of women like this in Kingsmarkham. All are alike except rich ones. The ones that come here, they are not like this.' She gave a derisive laugh. 'Oh, no, is funny. I laugh to see this. None come here like this.'

When Wexford got back to the station Helen Missal was sitting in the entrance hall, her red hair done in elaborate scrolls on the top of her head.

'Been thinking things over, Mrs Missal?' He showed her into his office.

'About Wednesday night . . .'

'Frankly, Mrs Missal, I'm not very interested in Wednesday night. Now, Tuesday afternoon. . . .'

'Why Tuesday afternoon?'

Wexford put the photograph on his desk where she could see it. Then he dropped the lipstick on top of it. The little gilt cylinder rolled about on the shiny snapshot and came to rest.

'Mrs Parsons was killed on Tuesday afternoon,' he said patiently, 'and we found your lipstick a few yards from her body. So, you see, I'm not very interested in Wednesday night.'

'You can't think . . . Oh, my God! Look, Chief Inspector, I was here on Tuesday afternoon. I went to the pictures.'

'You must just about keep that place going, madam. What a pity you don't live in Pomfret. They had to close the cinema there for lack of custom.'

Helen Missal drew in her breath and let it out again in a deep sigh. She twisted her feet round the metal legs of the chair.

'I suppose I'll have to tell you about it,' she said. 'I mean, I'd better tell the truth.' She spoke as if this was always a last distasteful resort instead of a moral obligation.

'Perhaps it would be best, madam.'

'Well, you see, I only said I went to the pictures on Wednesday to have an alibi. Actually, I went out with a friend.' She smiled winningly. 'Who shall be nameless.'

'For the moment,' Wexford said, un-won.

'I was going out with this friend on Wednesday night, but I couldn't really tell my husband, could I? So I said I was going to the pictures. Actually we just drove around the lanes. Well, I had to see the film, didn't I? Because my husband always . . . I mean, he'd obviously ask me about it. So I went to see the film on Tuesday afternoon.'

'In your car, Mrs Missal? You only live about a hundred yards from the cinema.'

'I suppose you've been talking to that bloody little Inge. You see, I had to take the car so that she'd think I'd gone a long way. I mean, I couldn't have gone shopping because it was early closing and I never walk anywhere. She knows that. I thought if I didn't take the car she'd guess I'd gone to the pictures and then she'd think it funny me going again on Wednesday.'

'Servants have their drawbacks,' Wexford said.

'You're not kidding. Well, that's all there is to it. I took the car and stuck it in Tabard Road . . . Oh God, that's where that woman lived, isn't it? But I couldn't leave it in the High Street because . . .' Again she tried a softening smile. 'Because of your ridiculous rules about parking.'

Wexford snapped sharply:

'Did you know this woman, madam?'

'Oh, you made me jump! Let me see. Oh, no, I don't think so. She's not the sort of person I'd be likely to know, Chief Inspector.'

'Who did you go out with on Wednesday night when you lost your lipstick, Mrs Missal?'

The smiles, the girlish confidences, hadn't worked. She flung back her chair and shouted at him:

'I'm not going to tell you. I won't tell you. You can't make me! You can't keep me here.'

'You came of your own accord, madam,' Wexford said. He swung open the door, smiling genially. 'I'll just look in this evening when your husband's at home and we'll see if we can get everything cleared up.'

The Methodist minister hadn't been much help to Burden. He hadn't seen Mrs Parsons since Sunday and he'd been surprised when she didn't come to the social evening on Tuesday. No, she had made no close friends at the church and he couldn't recall hearing anyone use her Christian name.

Burden checked the bus times at the garage and found that the five-thirty-two had left Stowerton dead on time. Moreover, the conductress on the Kingsmarkham bus, the one that left Stowerton at five-thirty-five, remembered seeing Parsons. He had asked for change for a ten-shilling note and they were nearly in Kingsmarkham before she got enough silver to change it.

'Fun and games with Mrs Bloody Missal,' Wexford said when Burden walked in. 'She's one of those women who tell lies by the light of nature, a natural crook.'

'Where's the motive, sir?'

'Don't ask me. Maybe she was carrying on with Parsons, picked him up at his office on Tuesday afternoon and bribed the entire Southern Water Board to say he didn't leave till after five-thirty. Maybe she'd got another boy friend she goes out with on Wednesdays, one for every day of the week. Or maybe she and Parsons and Mr X, who shall be nameless (God Almighty!), were Russian agents and Mrs Parsons had defected to the West. It's all very wonderful, Mike, and it makes me spew!'

'We haven't even got the thing she was strangled with,' Burden said gloomily. 'Could a woman have done it?'

'Crocker seems to think so. If she was a strong young woman, always sitting about on her backside and feeding her face.'

'Like Mrs Missal.'

'We're going to get down there tonight, Mike, and have the whole thing out again in front of her old man. But not till tonight. I'm going to give her the rest of the day to sweat in. I've got the report from the lab and there's no cow dung on Mrs Missal's tyres. But she didn't have to use her own car. Her husband's a car dealer, got a saleroom in Stowerton.

Those people are always chopping and changing their cars. That's another thing we'll have to check up on. The inquest's tomorrow and I want to get somewhere before then.'

Burden drove his own car into Stowerton and pulled into the forecourt of Missal's saleroom. A man in overalls came out from the glass-walled office between the rows of petrol-pumps.

'Two and two shots, please,' Burden said. 'Mr Missal about?'

'He's out with a client.'

'That's a pity,' Burden said. 'I looked in on Tuesday afternoon and he wasn't here. . . .'

'Always in and out he is. In and out. I'll just give your windscreen a wipe over.'

'Maybe Mrs Missal?'

'Haven't seen her inside three months. Back in March was the last time. She come in to lend the Merc and bashed the grid in. Women drivers!'

'Had a row, did they? That sounds like Pete.'

'You're not joking. He said, never again. Not the Merc or any of the cars.

'Well, well,' Burden said. He gave the man a shilling; more would have looked suspicious. 'Marriage is a battlefield when all's said and done.'

'I'll tell him you came in.'

Burden switched on the ignition and put the car in gear.

'Don't trouble,' he said. 'I'm seeing him tonight.'

He drove towards the exit and braked sharply to avoid a yellow convertible that swung sharply in from Maryfield Road. An elderly man was at the wheel; beside him, Peter Missal.

'There he is, if you want to catch him,' the pump attendant shouted.

Burden parked his own car and pushed open the swing doors. He waited beside a Mini-car revolving smoothly on a scarlet roundabout. Outside he could see Missal talking to the driver of the convertible. Apparently the deal was off, for the other man left on foot and Missal came into the saleroom.

'What now?' he said to Burden. 'I don't like being hounded at my place of business.'

'I won't keep you,' Burden said. 'I'm just checking up on Tuesday afternoon. No doubt you were here all day. In and out, that is.'

'It's no business of yours where I was.' Missal flicked a speck of dust from the Mini's wing as it circled past. 'As a matter of fact I went into Kingsmarkham to see a client. And that's all I'm telling you. I respect personal privacy and it's a pity you don't do the same.'

'In a murder case, sir, one's private life isn't always one's own affair. Your wife doesn't seem to have grasped that either.' He went towards the door.

'My wife . . .' Missal followed him and, looking to either side of him to make sure there was no one about, hissed in an angry half-whisper: 'You can take that heap of scrap metal off my drive-in. It's causing an obstruction.'

CHAPTER SIX

Who was her father?
Who was her mother?
Had she a sister?
Had she a brother?
Or, was there a dearer one
Still, and a nearer one
Yet, than all other?

Thomas Hood, *The Bridge of Sighs*

The murder books had been taken away and the top shelf of the bookcase was empty. If Parsons was innocent, a truly bereaved husband, Burden thought, how dreadfully their covers must have screamed at him when he came into the shabby dining-room this morning. Or had he removed them because they had served their purpose?

'Chief Inspector,' Parsons said, 'I must know. Was she . . .? Had she . . .? Was she just strangled or was there anything else?' He had aged in the past days or else he was a consummate actor.

'You can set your mind at rest on that score,' Wexford said quickly. 'Your wife was certainly strangled, but I can assure you she wasn't interfered with in any other way.' He stared at the dull green curtains, the lino that was frayed at the skirting board, and said impersonally, 'There was no sexual assault.'

'Thank God!' Parsons spoke as if he thought there was still a God in some nonconformist heaven and as if he was really thanking Him. 'I couldn't bear it if there had been. I couldn't go on living. It would just about have killed Margaret.' He realized what he had said and put his head in his hands.

Wexford waited until the hands came down and the tearless eyes were once more fixed on his own.

'Mr Parsons, I can tell you that as far as we know there was no struggle. It looks as if your wife was sleeping until just before she was killed. There would have been just a momentary shock, a second's pain – and then nothing.'

Parsons mumbled, turning away his face so that they could catch only the last words, '... For though they be punished in the sight of man, yet is their hope full of immortality.'

Wexford got up and went over to the bookcase. He didn't say anything about the missing library of crime, but he took a book out of one of the lower shelves.

'I see this is a guide to the Kingsmarkham district.' He opened it and Burden glimpsed a coloured photograph of the market place. 'It isn't a new book.'

'My wife lived here – well, not here. In Flagford it was – for a couple of years after the end of the war. Her uncle was stationed with the R.A.F. at Flagford and her aunt had a cottage in the village.'

'Tell me about your wife's life.'

'She was born in Balham,' Parsons said. He winced, avoiding the Christian name. 'Her mother and father died when she was a child and she went to live with this aunt. When she was about sixteen she came to live in Flagford, but she didn't like it. Her uncle died – he wasn't killed or anything – he died of heart disease, and her aunt went back to Balham. My wife went to college in London and started teaching. Then we got married. That's all.'

'Mr. Parsons, you told me on Wednesday your wife would have taken her front-door key with her. How many keys did you have between you?'

'Just the two.' Parsons took a plain Yale key from his pocket and held it up to Wexford. 'Mine and – and Margaret's. She kept hers on a ring. The ring has a silver chain with a horseshoe charm on the end of it.' He added simply in a calm voice: 'I gave it to her when we came here. The purse is a brown one, brown plastic with a gilt clip.'

'I want to know if your wife was in the habit of going to Prewett's farm. Did you know the Prewetts or any of the farm workers? There's a girl there called Dorothy Sweeting. Did your wife ever mention her?'

But Parsons had never even heard of the farm until his wife's body had been found there. She hadn't cared much for the country or for country walks and the name Sweeting meant nothing.

'Do you know anyone called Missal?'

'Missal? No, I don't think so.'

'A tall good-looking woman with red hair. Lives in a house opposite The Olive and Dove. Her husband's a car dealer. Big bloke with a big green car.'

'We don't . . . we didn't know anyone like that.' His face twisted and he put up a hand to hide his eyes. 'They're a lot of snobs round here. We didn't belong and we should never have come.' His voice died to a whisper. 'If we'd stayed in London,' he said, 'she might still be alive.'

'Why *did* you come, Mr Parsons?'

'It's cheaper living in the country, or you think it's cheaper till you try it.'

'So your coming here didn't have anything to do with the fact that your wife once lived in Flagford?'

'Margaret didn't want to come here, but the job came up. Beggars can't be choosers. She had to work when we were in London. I thought she'd find some peace here.' He coughed and the sound tailed away into a sob. 'And she did, didn't she?'

'I believe there are some books in your attic, Mr Parsons. I'd like to have a good look through them.'

'You can have them,' Parsons said. 'I never want to see another book as long as I live. But there's nothing in them. She never looked at them.'

The dark staircases were familiar now and with familiarity

they had lost much of that sinister quality Burden had felt on his first visit. The sun showed up the new dust and in its gentle light the house seemed no longer like the scene of a crime but just a shabby relic. It was very close and Wexford opened the attic window. He blew a film of dust from the surface of the bigger trunk and opened its lid. It was crammed with books and he took the top ones out. They were novels: two by Rhoda Broughton, *Evelina* in the Everyman's Library and Mrs Craik's *John Halifax, Gentleman*. Their fly-leaves were bare and nothing fluttered from the pages when he shook them. Underneath were two bundles of school stories, among them what looked like the complete works of Angela Brazil. Wexford dumped them on the floor and lifted out a stack of expensive-looking volumes, some bound in suède, others in scented leather or watered silk.

The first one he opened was covered in pale green suède, its pages edged with gold. On the fly-leaf someone had printed carefully in ink:

> If love were what the rose is,
> And I were like the leaf,
> Our lives would grow together
> In sad or singing weather...

And underneath:

Rather sentimental, Minna, but you know what I mean. Happy, happy birthday. All my love, Doon. March 21st, 1950.

Burden looked over Wexford's shoulder.

'Who's Minna?'

'We'll have to ask Parsons,' Wexford said. 'Could be second-hand. It looks expensive. I wonder why she didn't keep it downstairs. God knows, this place needs brightening up.'

'And who's Doon?' Burden asked.

'You're supposed to be a detective. Well, detect.' He put the book on the floor and picked up the next one. This was the *Oxford Book of Victorian Verse*, still in its black and pearl-grey jacket, and Doon had printed another message inside. Wexford read it aloud in an unemotional voice.

'*I know you have set your heart on this, Minna, and I was so happy when I went to Foyle's and found it waiting for me. Joyeux Noel, Doon, Christmas, 1950.*' The next book was even more splendid, red watered silk and black leather. 'Let's have a look at number three,' Wexford said. '*The Poems of Christina Rossetti*. Very nice, gilt lettering and all. What's Doon got to say this time? *An un-birthday present, Minna dear, from Doon who wishes you happy for ever and ever. June 1950.* I wonder if Mrs P. bought the lot cheap from this Minna.'

'I suppose Minna could *be* Mrs P., a sort of nickname.'

'It had just crossed my mind,' Wexford said sarcastically. 'They're such good books, Mike, not the sort of things anyone would give to a church sale, and church sales seem to have been about Mrs Parsons' mark. Look at this lot: *Omar Khayyám*; Whitman's *Leaves of Grass*; William Morris. Unless I'm much mistaken that *Omar Khayyám* cost three or four pounds. And there's another one here, the *Verses of Walter Savage Landor*. It's an old-fashioned kind of book and the leaves haven't even been cut.' He read the message on the fly-leaf aloud:

> '*I promise to bring back with me*
> *What thou with transport will receive,*
> *The only proper gift for thee.*
> *Of which no mortal shall bereave.*

'*Rather apt, don't you think, Minna? Love from Doon. March 21st, 1951.*'

'It wasn't very apt, was it? And Minna, whoever she is, didn't receive it with transport. She didn't even cut the pages. I'm going to have another word with Parsons, Mike, and then we're going to have all this lot carted down to the station. This attic is giving me the creeps.'

But Parsons didn't know who Minna was and he looked surprised when Wexford mentioned the date, March 21st.

'I never heard anyone call her Minna,' he said distastefully, as if the name was an insult to her memory. 'My wife never spoke about a friend called Doon. I've never even seen those books properly. Margaret and I lived in the house her aunt left her till we moved here and those books have always been in the trunk. We just brought them with us with the furniture. I can't make it out about the date – Margaret's birthday was March 21st.'

'It could mean nothing, it could mean everything,' Wexford said when they were out in the car. 'Doon talks about Foyle's, and Foyle's, in case you don't know, my provincial friend, is in London in the Charing Cross Road.'

'But Mrs P. was sixteen in 1949 and she stayed two years in Flagford. She must have been living only about five miles from here when Doon gave her those books.'

'True. He could have lived here too and gone up to London for the day. I wonder why he printed the messages, Mike. Why didn't he write them? And why did Mrs P. hide the books as if she was ashamed of them?'

'They'd make a better impression on the casual caller than *The Brides in the Bath* or whatever it is,' Burden said. 'This Doon was certainly gone on her.'

Wexford took Mrs Parsons' photograph out of his pocket. Incredible that this woman had ever inspired a passion or fired a line of verse!

'Happy for ever and ever,' he said softly. 'But love isn't what the rose is. I wonder if love could be a dark and tangled wood, a cord twisted and pulled tighter on a meek neck?'

'A cord?' Burden said. 'Why not a scarf, that pink nylon thing? It's not in the house.'

'Could be. You can bet your life that scarf is with the purse and the key. Plenty of women have been strangled with a nylon stocking, Mike. Why not a nylon scarf?'

He had brought the Swinburne and the Christina Rossetti with him. It wasn't much to go on, Burden reflected, a bundle of old books and an elusive boy. Doon, he thought, Doon. If Minna was anything to go by Doon was bound to be a pseudonym too. Doon wouldn't be a boy any more but a man of thirty or thirty-five, a married man with children, perhaps, who had forgotten all about his old love. Burden wondered where Doon was now. Lost, absorbed perhaps into the great labyrinth of London, or still living a mile or two away. . . . His heart sank when he recalled the new factory estate at Stowerton, the mazy lanes of Pomfret with a solitary cottage every two hundred yards, and to the north, Sewingbury, where road after road of post-war detached houses pushed outwards like rays from the nucleus of the ancient town. Apart from these, there was Kingmarkham itself and the daughter villages, Flagford, Forby. . . .

'I don't suppose that Missal bloke could be Doon,' he said hopefully.

'If he is,' Wexford said, 'he's changed one hell of a lot.'

The river of my years has been sluggish, Minna, flowing slowly to a sea of peace, Ah, long ago how I yearned for the torrent of life!

Then yesternight, yestere'en, Minna, I saw you. Not as I have so often in my dreams, but in life. I followed you, looking for lilies where you trod. . . . I saw the gold band on your finger, the shackle of an importunate love, and I cried aloud in my heart, I, I, too have known the terrors of the night!

But withal my feast has ever been the feast of the spirit and to that other dweller in my gates my flesh has been as an unlit candle in a fast-sealed casket. The light in my soul has guttered, shrinking in the harsh wind. But though the casket be atrophied and the flame past resuscitation, yet the wick of the spirit cries, hungering for the hand that holds the taper of companionship, the torch of sweet confidence, the spark of friends reunited.

I shall see you tomorrow and we shall ride together along the silver streets of our youth. Fear not, for reason shall sit upon my bridle and gentle moderation within my reins. Will all not be well, Minna, will all not be pleasant as the warm sun on the faces of little children?

CHAPTER SEVEN

When she shall unwind
All those wiles she wound about me. . . .

Francis Thompson, *The Mistress of Vision*

A black Jaguar, not new but well tended, was parked outside
the Missals' house when Wexford and Burden turned in at the
gate at seven o'clock. The wheels only were soiled, their
hub-caps spattered with dried mud.

'I know that car,' Wexford said. 'I know it but I can't place
it. Must be getting old.'

'Friends for cocktails,' Burden said sententiously.

'I could do with a spot of gracious living myself,' Wexford
grumbled. He rang the ship's bell.

Perhaps Mrs Missal had forgotten they were coming or
Inge hadn't been primed. She looked surprised yet spitefully
pleased. Like her employer's, her hair was done up on top of
her head, but with less success. In her left hand she held a
canister of paprika.

'All are in,' she said. 'Two come for dinner. What a man!
I tell you it is a waste to have men like him buried in the
English countryside. Mrs Missal say, "Inge, you must make
lasagna." All will be Italian, paprika, pasta, pimentoes. . . . Ach,
it is just a game!'

'All right, Miss Wolff. We'd like to see Mrs Missal.'

'I show you.' She giggled, opened the drawing-room door
and announced with some serendipity, 'Here are the policemen!'

Four people were sitting in the flowered armchairs and
there were four glasses of pale dry sherry on the coffee-table.

For a moment nobody moved or said anything, but Helen Missal flushed deeply. Then she turned to the man who sat between her and her husband, parted her lips and closed them again.

So that's the character Inge was going on about in the hall, Burden thought. Quadrant! No wonder Wexford recognized the car.

'Good evening, Mr Quadrant,' Wexford said, indicating by a slight edge to his voice that he was surprised to see him in this company.

'Good evening, Chief Inspector, Inspector Burden.'

Burden had long known him as a solicitor he often saw in Kingsmarkham magistrates' court, long known and inexplicably disliked. He nodded to Quadrant and to the woman, presumably Quadrant's wife, who occupied the fourth armchair. They were somewhat alike, these two, both thin and dark with straight noses and curved red lips. Quadrant had the features of a grandee in an El Greco portrait, a grandee or a monk, but as far as Burden knew he was an Englishman. The Latin lips might have first drawn breath in a Cornish town and Quadrant be the descendant of an Armada mariner. His wife was beautifully dressed with the careless elegance of the very rich. Burden thought she made Helen Missal's blue shift look like something from a chainstore sale. Her fingers were heavily be-ringed, vulgarly so, if the stones were false, but Burden didn't think they were false.

'I'm afraid we're intruding again, sir,' Wexford said to Missal, his eyes lingering on Quadrant. 'I'd just like to have a talk with your wife, if you don't mind.'

Missal stood up, his face working with impotent rage. In his light-weight silver-grey suit he looked fatter than ever. Then Quadrant did a strange thing. He took a cigarette out of the box on the table, put it in his mouth and lit the cork tip. Fascinated, Burden watched him choke and drop the cigarette into an ashtray.

'I'm sick and tired of all this,' Missal shouted. 'We can't

even have a quiet evening with our friends without being hounded. I'm sick of it. My wife has given you her explanation and that ought to be enough.'

'This is a murder enquiry, sir,' Wexford said.

'We were just going to have dinner.' Helen Missal spoke sulkily. She smoothed her blue skirt and fidgeted with a string of ivory beads. 'I suppose we'd better go into your study, Pete. Inge'll be in and out of the dining-room. God! God damn it all, why can't you leave me in peace?' She turned to Quadrant's wife and said: 'Will you excuse me a moment, Fabia, darling? That is, if you can bear to stay and eat with the criminal classes.'

'You're sure you don't want Douglas to go with you?' Fabia Quadrant sounded amused, and Burden wondered if the Missals had warned them of the impending visit, suggested perhaps that this was to enquire into some parking offence. 'As your solicitor, I mean,' she said. But Wexford had mentioned murder and when he lit that cigarette Quadrant had been frightened.

'Don't be long,' Missal said.

They went into the study and Wexford closed the door.

'I want my lipstick back,' Helen Missal said, 'and I want my dinner.'

Unmoved, Wexford said, 'And I want to know who you went out with when you lost your lipstick, madam.'

'It was just a friend,' she said. She looked coyly up at Wexford, whining like a little girl asking permission to have a playmate to tea. 'Aren't I allowed to have any friends?'

'Mrs Missal, if you continue to refuse to tell me this man's name I shall have no alternative but to question your husband.'

Burden was becoming used to her sudden changes of mood, but still he was not quite prepared for this burst of violence.

'You nasty low-down bastard!' she said.

'I'm not much affected by that sort of abuse, madam. You see, I'm accustomed to moving in circles where such language is among the terms of reference. His name, please. This is a murder enquiry.'

'Well, if you must know it was Douglas Quadrant.'

And that, Burden thought, accounts for the choking act in the other room.

'Inspector Burden,' Wexford said, 'will you just take Mr Quadrant into the dining-room (never mind about Miss Wolff's dinner) and ask him for his version of what happened on Wednesday night? Or was it Tuesday afternoon, Mrs Missal?'

Burden went out and Wexford said with a little sigh, 'Very well, madam, now I'd like to hear about Wednesday night all over again.'

'What's that fellow going to say in front of my husband?'

'Inspector Burden is a very discreet officer. Provided I find everything satisfactory I've no doubt you can convince your husband that Mr Quadrant was consulted simply in his capacity as your solicitor.'

This was the line Burden took when he went back into the drawing-room.

'Is there some difficulty about Mrs Missal, then, Inspector?' Fabia Quadrant asked. She might have been asking some minion if he had attended to the wants of a guest. 'I expect my husband can sort it out.'

Quadrant got up lazily. Burden was surprised that he offered no resistance. They went into the dining-room and Burden pulled out two chairs from the side of the table. It was laid with place mats, tall smoky purple glasses, knives and forks in Swedish steel and napkins folded into the shape of water-lilies.

'A man must live,' Quadrant said easily when Burden asked him about his drive with Helen Missal. 'Mrs Missal is perfectly happily married. So am I. We just like to do a little dangerous living together from time to time. A drive, a drink . . . No harm done and everyone the happier for it.' He was being disarmingly frank.

Burden wondered why. It didn't seem to tie up with his manner when they had first arrived. Everyone the happier for it? Missal didn't look happy . . . and the woman with the rings? She had her money to console her. But what had all this to do with Mrs Parsons?

'We drove to the lane,' Quadrant said, 'parked the car and stood on the edge of the wood to have a cigarette. You know how smoky it gets inside a car, Inspector.' Burden was to be brought in as another man of the world. 'I'm afraid I know nothing about the lipstick. Mrs Missal is rather a happy-go-lucky girl. She tends to be careless about unconsidered trifles.' He smiled. 'Perhaps that's what I like about her.'

Had he seen him? Part of the time, yes, but he certainly hadn't had Quadrant under his eye all day.

'I suppose all this did happen on Wednesday,' Burden said, 'not Tuesday afternoon?'

'Now, come, Inspector. I was in court all day Tuesday. You saw me yourself.'

'We'd like to have a look at your car tyres, sir.' But as he said it Burden knew it was hopeless. Quadrant admitted visiting the lane on Wednesday.

In the study Wexford was getting much the same story from Helen Missal.

'We didn't go into the wood,' she said. 'We just stood under the trees. I took my handbag with me because it had got quite a bit of money in it and I think I must have dropped my lipstick when I opened the bag to get my hanky out.'

'You never went out of sight of the car?'

The net was spread and she fell in it.

'We never went out of sight of the car,' she said. 'We just stood under the trees and talked.'

'What a nervous person you must be, Mrs Missal, nervous and extremely cautious. You had Mr Quadrant with you and you were in sight of the car, but you were afraid someone might try to steal your handbag under your very eyes.'

She was frightened now and Wexford was sure she hadn't told him everything.

'Well, that's how it happened. I can't be expected to account for everything I do.'

'I'm afraid you can, madam. I suppose you've kept your cinema ticket?'

'Oh, my God! Can't you give me any peace? Of course I don't keep cinema tickets.'

'You don't show much foresight, madam. It would have been prudent to have kept it in case your husband wanted to see it. Perhaps you'll have a look for that ticket and when you've found it I'd like you to bring it down to the station. The tickets are numbered and it will be simple to determine whether yours was issued on Tuesday or Wednesday.'

Quadrant was waiting for him in the dining-room, standing by the sideboard now and reading the labels on two bottles of white wine. Burden still sat at the table.

'Ah, Chief Inspector,' Quadrant said in the tone he used for melting the hearts of lay magistrates. ' "What a tangled web we weave when first we practise to deceive"!'

'I wish you could convince Mrs Missal of the truth of that maxim, sir. Very unfortunate for you that you happened to choose that particular lane for your . . . your talk with her on Wednesday night.'

'May I assure you, Chief Inspector, that it was merely a matter of misfortune.' He continued to look at the bottles of Barsac, misted and ice-cold. 'Had I been aware of the presence of Mrs Parsons' body in the wood I should naturally have come straight to you. In my position, my peculiar position, I always take it upon myself to give every possible assistance to you good people.'

'It is a peculiar position, isn't it, sir? What I should call a stroke of malignant fate.'

In the drawing-room Missal and Mrs Quadrant were sitting in silence. They looked, Burden thought, as if they had little in common. Helen Missal and the solicitor filed in, smiling brightly, as if they had all been playing some party game. The charade had been acted, the word discovered. Now they could all have their dinner.

'Perhaps we can all have our dinner now,' Missal said.

Wexford looked at him.

'I believe you were in Kingsmarkham on Tuesday afternoon, Mr Missal? Perhaps you'll be good enough to tell me where you were exactly and if anyone saw you.'

'No, I won't,' Missal said. 'I'm damned if I do. You send your henchman —'

'Oh, Peter,' Fabia Quadrant interrupted. 'Henchman! What a word.'

Burden stood woodenly, waiting.

'You send your underling to show me up in front of my clients and my staff. You persecute my wife. I'm damned if I tell you what I do with every minute of my time!'

'Well, I had to,' Helen Missal said. She seemed pleased with herself, delighted that the focus of attention had shifted from herself to her husband.

'I'd like a sample from your car tyres,' Wexford said, and Burden wondered despairingly if they were going to have to scrape mud from the wheels of every car in Kingsmarkham.

'The Merc's in the garage,' Missal said. 'Make yourself at home. You do inside, so why not make free with the grounds? Maybe you'd like to borrow the lawn for the police sports.'

Fabia Quadrant smiled slightly and her husband pursed his lips and looked down. But Helen Missal didn't laugh. She glanced quickly at Quadrant and Burden thought she gave the ghost of a shiver. Then she lifted her glass and drained the sherry at a single gulp.

Wexford sat at his desk, doodling on a piece of paper. It was time to go home, long past time, but they still had the events of the day, the stray remarks, the evasive answers, to sift through and discuss. Burden saw that the Chief Inspector was writing, apparently aimlessly, the pair of names he had scribbled that morning when Mrs Missal had first come to him: *Missal, Parsons; Parsons, Missal.*

'But what's the connection, Mike? There must be a connection.' Wexford sighed and drew a thick black line through the names. 'You know, sometimes I wish this *was* Mexico. Then we could keep a crate of hooch in here. Tequila or some damn' thing. This everlasting tea is making me spew.'

'Quadrant and Mrs Missal . . .' Burden began slowly.

'They're having a real humdingin' affair,' Wexford interrupted, 'knocking it off in the back of his Jag.'

Burden was shocked.

'A woman like that?' he said. 'Why wouldn't they go to an hotel?'

'The best bedroom at The Olive and Dove? Be your age. He can't go near her place because of Inge and she can't go to his because of his wife.'

'Where does he live?'

'You know where Mrs Missal keeps her car? Well, up on the other side, on the corner of what our brothers in the uniformed branch call the junction with the Upper Kingsbrook Road. That place with the turrets. She couldn't go there because of darling Fabia. My guess is they went to that lane because Dougie Q. knows it well, takes all his bits of stuff there. It's quiet, it's dark and it's nasty. Just the job for him and Mrs M. When they've had their fun and games in the back of the car they go into the wood. . . .'

'Perhaps Mrs Missal saw a rabbit, sir,' Burden said innocently.

'Oh, for God's sake!' Wexford roared. 'I don't know why they went into the wood, but Mrs Missal might well fancy having a bit more under the bushes in God's sweet air. Maybe they saw the body. . . .'

'Quadrant would have come to us.'

'Not if Mrs Missal persuaded him not to, not if she said it would mean her Peter and his Fabia finding out about them.

She got to work on him and our courteous Dougie, whom
ne'er the word of No woman heard speak – I *can* read, Mike –
our courteous Dougie agrees to say nothing about it.'

Burden looked puzzled. Finally he said: 'Quadrant was
scared, sir. He was scared stiff when we came in.'

'I suppose he guessed it was going to come out. His wife
was there. That's quite natural.'

'Then wouldn't you have expected him to have been more
cagey about it all? But he wasn't. He was almost too open
about it.'

'Perhaps,' Wexford said, 'he wasn't scared we were going
to ask about it. He was scared of *what* we were going to ask.'

'Or of what Mrs Missal might say.'

'Whatever it was, we didn't ask it or she gave the right
answer. The right answer from his point of view, I mean.'

'I asked him about Tuesday. He said he was in court all
day. Says I saw him there. I did, too, off and on.'

Wexford groaned. 'Likewise,' he said. 'I saw him but I
wasn't keeping a watch on him and that makes a mighty lot
of difference. I was up in Court One. He was defending in
that drunk driving case downstairs. Let me think. They adjourned at one, went back at two.'

'We went into the Carousel for lunch. . . .'

'So did he. I saw him. But we went upstairs, Mike. He
may have done too. I don't know. He was back in court by
two and he didn't have the car. He walks when he's that near
home.'

'Missal could do with taking a leaf out of his book,' Burden
said. 'Get his weight down. He's a nasty piece of work, sir.
Henchman!' he added in disgust.

'Underling, Mike,' Wexford grinned.

'What's stopping him telling us where he was on Tuesday?'

'God knows, but those tyres were as clean as a whistle.'

'He could have left the car on the Pomfret Road.'

'True.'

'I suppose Mrs Missal could have got some idea into her head that Quadrant was carrying on with Mrs P. —'

Wexford had begun to look fretful. 'Oh, come off it,' he said. 'Dougie Q. and Mrs P.? He's been knocking it off on the side for years. It's common knowledge. But have you seen the sort of things his taste runs to? I tell you, on Saturday mornings the High Street is littered with his discards, consoling themselves for their broken maidenheads or their broken marriages by showing off their new Mini-Minors. Mrs P. just wasn't his style. Anyway, Mrs Missal wouldn't have done murder for him. He was just a different way of passing a dull evening, one degree up on the telly.'

'I thought it was only men who looked at it that way.' Burden was always startled by his chief's occasional outbursts of graphic frankness. Wexford, who was always intuitive, sometimes even lyrical, could also be coarse. 'She was risking a lot for a casual affair.'

'You want to buck your ideas up, Mike,' Wexford snapped. 'Minna's *Oxford Book of Victorian Verse* is just about your mark. I'm going to lend it to you for your bedtime reading.'

Burden took the book and flicked through the pages: Walter Savage Landor, Coventry Patmore, Caroline Elizabeth Sarah Norton.... The names seemed to come from far away, the poets long dust. What possible connection could they have with dead, draggled Minna, with the strident Missals? Love, sin, pain – these were the words that sprang from almost every verse. After Quadrant's flippancies they sounded like ridiculous anachronisms.

'A connecting link, Mike,' Wexford said. 'That's what we want, a connection.'

But there was none to be found that night. Wexford took three of the other books ('Just in case our Mr Doon underlined anything or put in any fancy little ticks') and they walked out into the evening air. Beyond the bridge Quadrant's car still waited.

CHAPTER EIGHT

One of my cousins long ago,
A little thing the mirror said. . . .

James Thomson, *In the Room*

A bird was singing outside Wexford's office window; a black-bird, Burden supposed. He had always rather liked listening to it until one day Wexford said it sang the opening bars of 'The Thunder and Lightning Polka', and after that its daily reiteration annoyed him. He wanted it to go on with the tune or else vary a note or two. Besides, this morning he had had enough of blackbirds and larks and nightingales, enough of castle-bound maidens dying young and anaemic swains serenading them with lute and tabor. He had sat up half the night reading the Oxford Book and he was by no means convinced that it had had anything to do with Mrs Parsons' death.

It was going to be a beautiful day, too beautiful for an inquest. When Burden walked in Wexford was already at his desk, turning the pages of the suède-covered Swinburne. The rest of the Doon books had been removed from the house in Tabard Road and dumped on Wexford's filing cabinet.

'Did you get anything, sir?' Burden asked.

'Not so's you'd notice,' Wexford said, 'but I did have an idea. I'll tell you about it when you've read the report from Balham. It's just come in.'

The report was typed on a couple of sheets of foolscap. Burden sat down and began to go through it:

Margaret Iris Parsons (he read) was born Margaret Iris Godfrey to Arthur Godfrey, male nurse, and his wife, Iris Drusilla Godfrey, at 213 Holderness Road, Balham, on March

21st, 1933. Margaret Godfrey attended Holderness Road Infants' School from 1938 until 1940 and Holderness Road Junior School from 1940 until 1944. Both parents killed as a result of enemy action, Balham, 1942, after which Margaret resided with her maternal aunt and legal guardian, Mrs Ethel Mary Ives, wife of Leading Aircraftman Geoffrey Ives, a member of the regular Air Force, at 42 St John's Road, Balham. At this time the household included Anne Mary Ives, daughter of the above, birth registered at Balham, February 1st, 1932.

Leading Aircraftman Ives was transferred to Flagford, Sussex, R.A.F. Station during September 1949 (date not known). Mrs Ives, Anne Ives and Margaret Godfrey left Balham at this time, Mrs Ives having let her house in St John's Road, and took up residence in Flagford.

On the death of Geoffrey Ives from coronary thrombosis (Sewingbury R.A.F. Hospital, July 1951) Mrs Ives, her daughter and Margaret Godfrey returned to Balham and lived together at 42 St John's Road. From September 1951 until July 1953 Margaret Godfrey was a student at Albert Lake Training College for Women, Stoke Newington, London.

On August 15th, 1952, Anne Ives married Private Wilbur Stobart Katz, U.S. Army, at Balham Methodist Chapel, and left the United Kingdom for the United States with Private Katz in October 1952 (date not known).

Margaret Godfrey joined staff of Holderness Road Infants' School, Balham, September 1953.

Ronald Parsons (clerk) aged twenty-seven, became a lodger at 42 St John's Road, in April 1954. Death of Mrs Ethel Ives from cancer (Guy's Hospital, London), registered at Balham by Margaret Godfrey, May 1957. Margaret Godfrey and Ronald Parsons married at Balham Methodist Chapel, August 1957, and took up residence at 42 St John's Road, the house having been left jointly to Mrs Parsons and Mrs Wilbur Katz under the will of Mrs Ives.

42 St. John's Road was purchased compulsorily by Balham Council, November 1962, whereupon Mr and Mrs Parsons removed to Kingsmarkham, Sussex, Mrs Parsons having resigned from the staff of Holderness Road School.

(Refs: Registrar of Births and Deaths, Balham; Rev. Albert Derwent, Minister, Methodist Chapel, Balham; Royal Air Force Records; United States Air Force Records; London County Council Education Dept.; Guy's Hospital; Balham Borough Council.)

'I wonder where Mrs Wilbur Katz is now?' Burden said.

'You got any cousins in America, Mike?' Wexford asked in a quiet, deceptively gentle voice.

'I believe I have.'

'So've I and so have half the people I've ever met. But nobody ever does know where they are or even if they're alive or dead.'

'You said you'd had an idea, sir?'

Wexford picked up the report and stabbed at the second paragraph with his thick forefinger.

'It came to me in the night,' he said, 'in the interval between Whitman and Rossetti – sound like a couple of gangsters, don't they? Sweet Christ, Mike I ought to have thought of it before! Parsons said his wife came here when she was sixteen and even then it didn't click. I assumed, backwoods copper that I am, that Mrs Parsons had left school by then. But, Mike, she was a teacher, she went to a training college. When she was in Flagford she must have gone to school! I reckon they came to Flagford just after she'd taken her School Cert., or whatever they call it these days, and when she got here she went right on going to school.'

'There are only two girls' schools around here,' Burden said. 'The Kingsmarkham County High and that convent place in Sewingbury. St Catherine's.

'Well, she wouldn't have gone there. She was a Methodist and, as far as we know, her aunt was too. Her daughter got married in a Methodist chapel at any rate. It's just our luck that's it's Saturday and the school's shut.

'I want you to root out the head – you can dip out on the inquest, I'll be there. The head's a Miss Fowler and she lives in York Road. See what you can dig up. They must keep records. What we want is a list of the girls who were in Margaret Godfrey's class between September 1949 and July 1951.'

'It'll be a job tracing them, sir.'

'I know that, Mike, but somehow or other we've got to have a break. This just might be it. We know all about Margaret Parsons' life in Balham, and by the look of it it was mighty dull. Only two sensational things ever happened to her as far as I can see. Love and death, Mike, love and death. The thing is they both happened here in my district. Somebody loved her here and when she came back somebody killed her. One of those girls may remember a boy friend, a possessive boy friend with a long memory.'

'I wish,' Burden said, 'I wish some decent public-spirited cop-loving citizen would walk in here and just tell us he knew Mrs P., just tell us he'd taken her out in 1950 or even seen her in a shop last week.' He brooded for a second over the Balham report. 'They were an unhealthy lot, weren't they, sir? Cancer, coronary thrombosis . . .'

Wexford said slowly: 'When Parsons was telling us a bit of his wife's history I did just wonder why he said, "Her uncle died, he wasn't killed." It's a small point, but I see it now. Her parents *were* killed, but not in the way we mean when we talk about killing.'

After he had gone across the courthouse behind the police station Burden telephoned Miss Fowler. A deep cultured voice answered, carefully enunciating the name of the exchange and the number. Burden began to explain but Miss Fowler interrupted him. Yes, Margaret had been at the High School, although she could scarcely remember her from that time.

However, she had seen her recently in Kingsmarkham and had recognized her as the murdered woman from a newspaper photograph.

'Honestly, Inspector,' she said, 'what a very shocking thing!' She spoke as if the killing had offended rather than distressed her, or, Burden thought, as if the education meted out at her school should automatically have exempted any pupil from falling victim to a murderer.

He apologized for troubling her and asked if she could let him have the list Wexford wanted.

'I'll just give our school secretary, Mrs Mortlock, a ring,' Miss Fowler said. 'I'll get her to nip along to school and have a look through the records. If you could call on me about lunchtime, Inspector?'

Burden said he was most grateful.

'Not at all. It's no trouble,' Miss Fowler said. 'Honestly.'

The inquest was over in half an hour and Dr Crocker's evidence occupied ten minutes of that time. Death, he said, was caused by strangulation by means of a ligature; a scarf possibly or a piece of cloth. Mrs Parsons' body was otherwise unbruised and there had been no sexual assault. She had been a healthy woman, slightly overweight for her height. In his evidence Wexford gave his opinion that it was impossible to say whether or not there had been a struggle as the wood had been heavily trampled by Prewett's cows. The doctor was recalled and said that he had found a few superficial scratches on the dead woman's legs. These were so slight that he would not care to say whether they had been made before or after death.

A verdict was returned of murder by person or persons unknown.

Ronald Parsons had sat quietly throughout the inquest, twisting a handkerchief in his lap. He kept his head bowed as the coroner offered some perfunctory expressions of sympathy and indicated that he heard only by a slight movement, a tiny nod. He seemed so stunned with misery that Wexford was surprised when he caught up with him as he was crossing the flagged courtyard and touched him on the sleeve.

Without preamble he said, 'A letter came for Margaret this morning.'

'What d'you mean, a letter?' Wexford stopped. He had seen some of Mrs Parsons' letters; advertisements and coal bills.

'From her cousin in the States,' Parsons said. He took a deep breath and shivered in the warm sun.

Looking at him, Wexford realized that he was no longer stupefied. Some fresh bitterness was affecting him.

'I opened it.'

He spoke with a kind of guilt. She was dead and they had plundered her possessions. Now even her letters, letters posthumously received, were to be picked over, their words dissected as meticulously as her own body had been examined and exposed.

'I don't know . . . I can't think,' he said, 'but there's something in it about someone called Doon.'

'Have you got it with you?' Wexford asked sharply.

'In my pocket.'

'We'll go into my office.'

If Parsons noticed his wife's books spread about the room he gave no sign. He sat down and handed an envelope to Wexford. On the flap, just beneath the ragged slit Parsons had made, was a handwritten address: *From Mrs Wilbur S. Katz, 1183 Sunflower Park, Slate City, Colorado, U.S.A.*

'That would be Miss Anne Ives,' Wexford said. 'Did your wife correspond with her regularly?'

Parsons looked surprised at the name.

'Not to say regularly,' he said. 'She'd write once or twice a year. I've never met Mrs Katz.'

'Did your wife write to her recently, since you came here?'

'I wouldn't know, Chief Inspector. To tell you the truth,

I didn't care for what I knew of Mrs Katz. She used to write and tell Margaret all about the things she'd got – cars, washing machines, that sort of thing . . . I don't know whether it upset Margaret. She'd been very fond of her cousin and she never said she minded hearing about all those things. But I made it plain what I thought and she stopped showing me the letters.'

'Mr Parsons, I understand Mrs Ives' house was left jointly to your wife and Mrs Katz. Surely —?'

Parsons interrupted bitterly: 'We bought our share off her, Chief Inspector. Every penny of seven hundred pounds we paid – through a bank in London. My wife had to work full-time so that we could do it, and when we'd paid the lot, just paid off the lot, the council bought the place off us for nine hundred. They had a sort of order.'

'A compulsory-purchase order,' Wexford said. 'I see.' He stuck his head round the door. 'Sergeant Camb! Tea, please, and an extra cup. I'll just read that letter, if you don't mind, Mr Parsons.'

It was written on thin blue paper and Mrs Katz had found plenty to tell her cousin. The first two pages were entirely taken up with an account of a holiday Mr and Mrs Katz and their three children had spent in Florida; Mrs Katz's new car; a barbecue her husband had bought her. Mr and Mrs Parsons were invited to come to Slate City for a holiday. Wexford began to see what Parsons had meant.

The last page was more interesting.

Gee, Meg (Mrs Katz had written), *I sure was amazed to see you and Ron had moved to Kingsmarkham. I'll bet that was Ron's idea, not yours. And you have met up with Doon again, have you? I sure would like to know who Doon is. You've got to tell me, not keep dropping hints.*

Still, I can't see why you should be scared of Doon. What of, for the Lord's sake? There was never anything in that. (You know what I mean, Meg.) I can't believe Doon is still keen. You always had a suspicious mind!!! But if meeting Doon means trips in the car and a few free meals I wouldn't be too scrupulous.

When are you and Ron going to get a car of your own? Wil says he just doesn't know how you make out . . .

There was some more in the same vein, sprinkled with exclamation marks and heavily underlined. The letter ended:

. . . Regards to Ron and remind him there's a big welcome waiting for you both in Sunflower Park whenever you feel like hitting Colorado, U.S.A. Love from Nan. Greg, Joanna and Kim send hugs to their Auntie Meg.

'This could be very important, Mr Parsons,' Wexford said. 'I'd like to hang on to it.'

Parsons got up, leaving his tea untasted.

'I wish it hadn't come,' he said. 'I wanted to remember Margaret as I knew her. I thought she was different. Now I know she was just like the rest, carrying on with another man for what she could get out of him.'

Wexford said quietly: 'I'm afraid it looks like that. Tell me, didn't you have any idea that your wife might be going out with this man, this Doon? It looks very much as if Doon knew her when she lived in Flagford and took up with her again when she came back. She must have gone to school here, Mr Parsons. Didn't you know that?'

Did Parsons look furtive, or was it just a desire to hold on to some remnants of his private life, his marriage broken both by infidelity and by death, that made him flush and fidget?

'She wasn't happy in Flagford. She didn't want to talk about it and I stopped asking her. I reckon it was because they were such a lot of snobs. I respected her reticence, Chief Inspector.'

'Did she talk to you about her boy friends?'

'That was a closed book,' Parsons said, 'a closed book for

both of us. I didn't *want* to know, you see.' He walked to the
window and peered out as if it was night instead of bright day.
'We weren't those kind of people. We weren't the kind of
people who have love affairs.' He stopped, remembering the
letter. 'I can't believe it. I can't believe that of Margaret. She
was a good woman, Chief Inspector, a good loving woman. I
can't help thinking that Katz woman was making up a lot of
things that just weren't true, making them up out of her own
head.'

'We shall know a bit more when we hear from Colorado,'
Wexford said. 'I'm hoping to get hold of the last letter your
wife wrote to Mrs Katz. There's no reason why it shouldn't
be made available to you.'

'Thank you for nothing,' Parsons said. He hesitated, touched
the green cover of Swinburne's verses and walked quickly from
the room.

It was some sort of a break, Wexford thought, some sort
of a break at last. He picked up the telephone and told the
switchboard girl he wanted to make a call to the United States.
This had been a strange woman, he reflected as he waited, a
strange secretive woman leading a double life. To her husband
and the unobservant world she had been a sensible prudent
housewife in sandals and a cotton frock, an infants' teacher
who polished the front step with Brasso and went to church
socials. But someone, someone generous and romantic and
passionate, had been tantalized and maddened by her for
twelve long years.

CHAPTER NINE

Sometimes a troop of damsels glad . . .

Tennyson, *The Lady of Shalott*

Miss Fowler's was an unacademic bookless flat. Burden, who was aware of his own failing of cataloguing people in types, had tried not to expect old-maidishness. But this was what he found. The room into which Miss Fowler showed him was full of hand-made things. The cushion covers had been carefully embroidered, the amateurish water-colours obviously executed with patience, the ceramics bold. It looked as if Miss Fowler could hardly bear to reject the gift of an old scholar, but the collection was neither restful nor pleasing.

'Poor, poor Margaret,' she said. Burden sat down and Miss Fowler perched herself in a rocking chair opposite him, her feet on a petit-point footstool. 'What a very shocking thing all this is! That poor man too. I've got the list you wanted.'

Burden glanced at the neatly typed row of names.

'Tell me about her,' he said.

Miss Fowler laughed self-consciously, then bit her lip as if she thought this was no occasion for laughter.

'Honestly, Inspector,' she said, 'I can't remember. You see, there are so many girls . . . Of course, we don't forget them all, but naturally it's the ones who achieve something, get Firsts or find really spectacular posts, those are the ones we remember. Hers wasn't a very distinguished year. There was plenty of promise, but none of it came to very much. I saw her, you know, after she came back.'

'Here? In Kingsmarkham?'

'It must have been about a month ago.' She took a packet

of Weights from the mantelpiece, offered one to Burden, and puffed bravely at her own as he held a match to it.

They never really grow up, he thought.

'I was in the High Street,' she went on. 'It was just after school and she was coming out of a shop. She said, "Good afternoon, Miss Fowler." Honestly, I hadn't the faintest idea who she was. Then she said she was Margaret Godfrey. You see, they expect you to remember them, Inspector.'

'Then how did you . . .?'

'How did I connect her with Mrs Parsons? When I saw the photograph. You know, I felt sorry we hadn't talked, but I'm always seeing old girls, but I honestly couldn't tell you who they are or their ages, come to that. They might be eighteen or thirty. You know how it is, you can't tell the ages of people younger than yourself.' She looked up at Burden and smiled. 'But you *are* young,' she said.

Again he returned to the list. The names were in alphabetical order. He read aloud slowly, waiting for Miss Fowler's reactions:

'*Lyn Annesley, Joan Bertram, Clare Clarke, Wendy Ditcham, Margaret Dolan, Margaret Godfrey, Mary Henshaw, Jillian Ingram, Anne Kelly, Helen Laird, Marjorie Miller, Hilda Pensteman, Janet Probyn, Fabia Rogers, Deirdre Sachs, Diana Stevens, Winifred Thomas, Gwen Williams, Yvonne Young.*'

Under the names Mrs Morpeth had written with an air of triumph: *Miss Clare Clarke is a member of the High School teaching staff!!!*

'I'd like to talk to Miss Clarke,' he said.

'She lives at Nectarine Cottage down the first lane on the left on the Stowerton Road,' Miss Fowler said.

Burden said slowly, 'Fabia is a very unusual name.'

Miss Fowler shrugged. She patted her stiffly waved grey hair. 'Not a particularly unusual type,' she said. 'Just one of those very promising people I was telling you about who never amounted to much. She lives here somewhere. She and her husband are quite well known in what I believe are called social circles. Helen Laird was another one. Very lovely, very self-confident. Always in trouble. Boys, you know. Honestly, so silly! I thought she'd go on the stage, but she didn't, she just got married. And then Miss Clarke, of course . . .'

Burden had the impression she had been about to include Miss Clarke among the failures, but that loyalty to her staff prevented her. He didn't pursue it. She had given him a more disturbing lead.

'What did you say happened to Helen Laird?'

'I really know nothing, Inspector. Mrs Morpeth said something about her having married a car salesman. Such a waste!' She stubbed out her cigarette into an ashtray that was daubed with poster paint and obviously home-baked. When she went on her voice sounded faintly sad. 'They leave, you know, and we forget them, and then about fifteen years later a little tot turns up in the first form and you think, I've seen that face before somewhere! Of course you have – her mother's.'

Dymphna and Priscilla, Burden thought, nearly sure. Not long now, and Dymphna's face, the same red hair perhaps, would revive in Miss Fowler's memory some long-lost chord.

'Still,' she said, as if reading his thoughts, 'there's a limit to everything and I retire in two years' time.'

He thanked her for the list and left. As soon as he got to the station Wexford showed him the Katz letter.

'It all points to Doon being the killer, sir,' Burden said, 'whoever he is. What do we do now, wait to hear from Colorado?'

'No, Mike, we'll have to press on. Clearly Mrs Katz doesn't know who Doon is and the best we can hope for is to get some of the background from her and the last letter Mrs P. sent her before she died. Doon is probably going to turn out to be a boy friend Mrs P. had when she was at school here. Let's hope she didn't have too many.'

'I've been wondering about that,' Burden said, 'because honestly – as Miss Fowler would say – those messages in Minna's books don't look like the work of a boy at all, not unless he was a very mature boy. They're too polished, too smooth. Doon could be an older man who got interested in her.'

'I thought of that,' Wexford said, 'and I've been checking up on Prewett and his men. Prewett bought that farm in 1949 when he was twenty-eight. He's an educated person and quite capable of writing those messages, but he was in London on Tuesday. There's no doubt about it, unless he was involved in a conspiracy with two doctors, an eminent heart specialist, a sister, God knows how many nurses and his own wife.

'Draycott's only been in the district two years and he was in Australia from 1947 to 1953. Bysouth can scarcely write his own name, let alone dig up suitable bits of poetry to send to a lady love, and much the same goes for Traynor. Edwards was in the Army throughout 1950 and 1951, and Dorothy Sweeting can't possibly know what was going on in Minna's love life twelve years ago. She was only seven.'

'Then it looks as if we'll have to ferret out what we can from the list,' Burden said. 'I think you'll be interested when you see some of the names, sir.'

Wexford took the list and when he came to Helen Laird and Fabia Rogers he swore fiercely. Burden had pencilled in *Missal* and *Quadrant*, following each surname with a question mark.

'Somebody's trying to be clever,' Wexford said, 'and that I won't have. Rogers. Her people are old man Rogers and his missus at Pomfret Hall. They're loaded. All made out of paint. There's no reason why she should have told us she knew Mrs P. When we talked to Dougie this Doon angle didn't seem that important. But Mrs Missal . . . Not know Mrs P. indeed, and they were in the same class!'

He had grown red with anger. Burden knew how he hated being taken for a ride.

'I was going to forget all about that cinema ticket, Mike, but now I'm not so sure. I'm going to have it all out again with Mrs Missal now.' He stabbed at the list. 'While I'm gone you can start contacting these women.'

'It would have to be a girls' school,' Burden grumbled. 'Women change their names, men don't.'

'Can't be helped,' Wexford said snappily. 'Mr Griswold's been on twice already since the inquest, breathing down my neck.'

Griswold was the Chief Constable. Burden saw what Wexford meant.

'You know him, Mike. The least hint of difficulty and he's screaming for the Yard,' Wexford said, and went out, leaving Burden with the list and the letter.

Before embarking on his womanhunt Burden read the letter again. It surprised him because it gave an insight into Mrs Parsons' character, revealing a side he had not really previously suspected. She was turning out to be a lot less pure than anyone had thought.

... *If meeting Doon means rides in the car and a few free meals I wouldn't be too scrupulous*, Mrs Katz had written. But at the same time she didn't know who Doon was. Mrs Parsons had been strangely secretive, enigmatic, hiding the identity of a boy friend from a cousin who had also been an intimate friend.

A strange woman, Burden thought, and a strange boy friend. It was a funny sort of relationship she had with this Doon, he said to himself. Mrs Katz says, *I can't see why you should be scared*, and later, on, *there was never anything in that*. What did she mean, anything in that? But Mrs P. was *scared*. What of, sexual advances? Mrs Katz says she had a suspicious mind. Fair enough, he reflected. Any virtuous woman would be scared and suspicious of a man who paid her a lot of attention. But at the same time there was never anything in it. Mrs P. mustn't be too scrupulous.

Burden groped vainly. The letter, like its recipient, was a

puzzle. As he put it down and turned to the telephone he was certain of only two facts: Doon hadn't been making advances; he wanted something else, something that frightened Mrs Parsons but which was so innocuous in the estimation of her cousin that it would be showing excessive suspicion to be scrupulous about it. He shook his head like a man who has been flummoxed by an intricate riddle, and began to dial.

He tried Bertram first because there was no Annesley in the book – and, incidentally, no Pensteman and no Sachs. But the Mr Bertram who answered said he was over eighty and a bachelor. Next he rang the number of the only Ditchams he could find, but although he listened to the steady ringing past all reason, there was no reply.

Mrs Dolan's number was engaged. He waited five minutes and tried again. This time she answered. Yes, she was Margaret Dolan's mother, but Margaret was now Mrs Heath and had gone to live in Edinburgh. In any case, Margaret had never brought anyone called Godfrey to the house. Her particular friends had been Janet Probyn and Deirdre Sachs, and Mrs Dolan remembered them as having been a little shut-in clique on their own.

Mary Henshaw's mother was dead. Burden spoke to her father. His daughter was still in Kingsmarkham. Married? Burden asked. Mr Henshaw roared with laughter while Burden waited as patiently as he could. He recovered and said his daughter was indeed married. She was Mrs Hedley and she was in the county hospital.

'I'd like to talk to her,' Burden said.

'You can't do that,' Henshaw said, hugely amused. 'Not unless you put a white coat on. She's having a baby, her fourth. I thought you were them, bringing me the glad news.'

Through Mrs Ingram he was put on to Jillian Ingram, now Mrs Bloomfield. But she knew nothing of Margaret Parsons except that at school she had been pretty and prim, fond of reading, rather shy.

'Pretty, did you say?'

'Yes, she was pretty, attractive in a sort of way. Oh, I know, I've seen the papers. Looks don't necessarily last, you know.'

Burden knew, but still he was surprised.

Anne Kelly had gone to Australia, Marjorie Miller . .

'My daughter was killed in a car crash,' said a harsh voice, full of awakened pain. 'I should have thought the police of all people would know that.'

Burden sighed. Pensteman, Probyn, Rogers, Sachs . . . all were accounted for. In the local directory alone he found twenty-six Stevenses, forty Thomases, fifty-two Williamses, twelve Youngs.

To track them all down would take best part of the afternoon and evening. Clare Clarke might be able to help him. He closed the directory and set off for Nectarine Cottage.

The french windows were open when Inge Wolff let Wexford into the hall and he heard the screams of quarrelling children. He followed her across the lawn and at first saw nobody but the two little girls: the elder a sharp miniature fascimile of her mother, bright-eyed, red-headed; the younger fat and fair with a freckle-blotched face. They were fighting for possession of a swing-boat, a red and yellow fairground thing with a rabbit for a figurehead.

Inge rushed over to them, shouting.

'Are you little girls that play so, or rough boys? Here is one policeman come to lock you up!'

But the children only clung more tightly to the ropes, and Dymphna, who was standing up, began to kick her sister in the back.

'If he's a policeman,' she asked, 'where's his uniform?'

Someone laughed and Wexford turned sharply. Helen Missal was in a hammock slung between a mulberry tree and the wall of a summerhouse and she was drinking milkless tea from a glass. At first he could see only her face and a honey-coloured arm dangling over the edge of the canvas. Then, as he came closer, he saw that she was dressed for sunbathing. She wore only a bikini, an ice-white figure of eight and a triangle against her golden skin. Wexford was embarrassed and his embarrassment fanned his anger into rage.

'Not again!' she said. 'Now I know how the fox feels. He doesn't enjoy it.'

Missal was nowhere about, but from behind a dark green barrier of macrocarpa Wexford could hear the hum of a motor mower.

'Can we go indoors, Mrs Missal?'

She hesitated for a moment. Wexford thought she was listening, perhaps to the sounds from the other side of the hedge. The noise of the mower ceased, then, as she seemed to hold her breath, started again. She swung her legs over the hammock and he saw that her left ankle was encircled by a thin gold chain.

'I suppose so,' she said. 'I don't have any choice, do I?'

She went before him through the open doors, across the cool dining-room where Quadrant had looked on the wine, and into the rhododendron room. She sat down and said:

'Well, what is it now?'

There was something outrageous and at the same time spiteful about the way she spread her nakedness against the pink and green chintz. Wexford turned away his eyes. She was in her own home and he could hardly tell her to go and put some clothes on. Instead he took the photograph from his pocket and held it out to her.

'Why did you tell me you didn't know this woman?'

Fear left her eyes and they flared with surprise.

'I didn't know her.'

'You were at school with her, Mrs Missal.'

She snatched the photograph and stared at it.

'I was not.' Her hair fell over her shoulders, bright copper like a new penny. 'At least, I don't think I was. I mean, she

was years older than me by the look of this. She may have
been in the sixth when I was in the first form. I just wouldn't
know.'

Wexford said severely: 'Mrs Parsons was thirty, the same
age as yourself. Her maiden name was Godfrey.'

'I adore "maiden name". It's such a charitable way of
putting it, isn't it? All right, Chief Inspector, I do remember
now. But she's aged, she's differnt. . . .' Suddenly she smiled,
a smile of pure delighted triumph, and Wexford marvelled that
this woman was the same age as the pathetic dead thing they
had found in the wood.

'It's very unfortunate you couldn't remember on Thursday
evening, Mrs Missal. You've put yourself in a most unpleasant
light, firstly by deliberately lying to Inspector Burden and
myself and secondly by concealment of important facts. Mr
Quadrant will tell you that I'm quite within my rights if I
charge you with being an accessary —'

Helen Missal interrupted sulkily. 'Why pick on me? Fabia
knew her too, and . . . Oh, there must be lots and lots of other
people.'

'I'm asking you,' he said. 'Tell me about her.'

'If I do,' she said, 'will you promise to go away and not
come back?'

'Just tell me the truth, madam, and I will gladly go away.
I'm a very busy man.'

She crossed her legs and smoothed her knees. Helen
Missal's knees were like a little girl's, a little girl who has never
climbed a tree or missed a bath.

'I didn't like school,' she said confidingly. 'It was so
restricting, if you know what I mean. I just begged and begged
Daddy to take me away at the end of my first term in the
sixth —'

'Margaret Godfrey, Mrs Missal.'

'Oh, yes, Margaret Godfrey. Well, she was a sort of cipher
– isn't that a lovely word? I got it out of a book. A sort of

cipher. She was one of the fringe people, not very clever or nice-looking or anything.' She glanced once more at the picture. 'Margaret Godfrey. D'you know, I can hardly believe it. I should have said she was the last girl to get herself murdered.'

'And who would be the first, Mrs Missal?'

'Well, someone like me,' she said, and giggled.

'Who were her friends, the people she went around with?'

'Let me think. There was Anne Kelly and a feeble spotty bitch called Bertram and Diana Something...'

'That would be Diana Stevens.'

'My God, you know it all, don't you?'

'I meant boy friends.'

'I wouldn't know. I was rather busy in that direction myself.' She looked at him, pouting provocatively, and Wexford wondered, with the first flicker of pity he had felt for her, if her coyness would increase as her beauty declined until in age she became grotesque.

'Anne Kelly,' he said, 'Diana Stevens, a girl called Bertram. What about Clare Clarke, what about Mrs Quadrant? Would they remember?'

She had said that she hated school, but as she began to speak her voice was softer than he had ever known it and her expression gentler. For a moment he forgot his anger, her lies, the provocative costume she wore, and listened.

'It's funny,' she said, 'but thinking of those names has sort of brought it back to me. We used to sit in a kind of garden, a wild old place. Fabia and me and a girl called Clarke – I see her around sometimes – and Jill Ingram and that Kelly girl and – and Margaret Godfrey. We were supposed to be working but we didn't much. We used to talk about... Oh, I don't know....'

'About your boy friends, Mrs Missal?' As soon as the words were out Wexford knew he had been obtuse.

'Oh, no,' she said sharply. 'You've got it wrong. Not then, not in the garden. It was a wilderness, an old pond, bushes, a seat. We used to talk about . . . well, about our dreams, what we wanted to do, what we were going to make of our lives.' She stopped and Wexford could see in a sudden flash of vision a wild green place, the girls with their books and hear with his mind's ear the laughter, the gasp of dizzy ambition. Then he almost jumped at the change in her voice. She whispered savagely, as if she had forgotten he was there: 'I wanted to act! They wouldn't let me, my father and my mother. They made me stay at home and it all went. It sort of dissolved into nothing.' She shook back her hair and smoothed with the tips of two fingers the creases that had appeared between her eyebrows. 'I met Pete,' she said, 'and we got married.' Her nose wrinkled. 'The story of my life.'

'You can't have everything,' Wexford said.

'No,' she said, 'I wasn't the only one. . . .'

She hesitated and Wexford held his breath. He had an intuitive conviction that he was about to hear something of enormous significance, something that would iron out the whole case, wrap it up and tie it ready to hand to Mr Griswold. The green eyes widened and lit up; then suddenly the incandescence died and they became almost opaque. Outside in the hall a floorboard squeaked and Wexford heard the squashy sound of a rubber sole on thick carpet. Helen Missal's face became quite white.

'Oh God!' she said. 'Please, please don't ask about the cinema ticket. Please don't!'

Wexford cursed inwardly as the door opened and Missal came in. He was sweating and there were damp patches on the underarms of his singlet. He stared at his wife and in his eyes was a strange mixture of disgust and concupiscence.

'Put something on,' he shouted. 'Go on, put some clothes on.'

She got up awkwardly and Wexford had the illusion that

her husband's words were scrawled across her body like the obscene scribble on a pin-up picture.

'I was sunbathing,' she said.

Missal wheeled round on Wexford.

'Come to see the peep-show, have you?' His face was crimson with exertion and with jealousy. 'What the copper saw.'

Wexford wanted to be angry, to match the other man's rage with his own colder kind, but he could feel only pity.

All he said was, 'Your wife has been able to help me.'

'I'll bet she has.' Missal held the door open and almost pushed her through. 'Been kind, has she? That's a speciality of hers, being kind to every Tom, Dick and Harry.' He fingered his wet shirt as if his body disgusted him. 'Go on,' he said, 'start on me now. What were you doing in Kingsmarkham on Tuesday afternoon, Mr Missal? The name of the client, Mr Missal. Your car was seen in the Kingsbrook Road, Mr Missal. Well, go on. Don't you want to know?'

Wexford got up and walked a few paces towards the door. The heavy blossoms, pink, puce and white, brushed against his legs. Missal stood staring at him like an overfed, under-exercised dog longing to let out an uninhibited howl.

'Don't you want to know? Nobody saw me. I could have been strangling that woman. Don't you want to know what I was doing? Don't you?'

Wexford didn't look at him. He had seen too many men's souls stripped to relish an unnecessary spiritual skinning.

'I know what you were doing,' he said, skipping the name, the 'sir'. 'You told me yourself, just now in this room.' He opened the door. 'If not in so many words.'

Douglas Quadrant's house was much larger and far less pleasing to the eye than the Missals'. It stood on an eminence amid shrubby grounds some fifty feet back from the road. A huge cedar softened to some extent its austere aspect, but when he was half-way up the path Wexford recalled similar houses he had seen in the north of Scotland, granite-built, vaguely gothic and set at each end with steeple-roofed towers.

There was something odd about the garden, but it was a few minutes before he realized in what its strangeness consisted. The lawns were smooth, the shrubs conventionally chosen, but about it all was a sombre air. There were no flowers. Douglas Quadrant's garden presented a Monet-like landscape of grey and brown and many-shaded green.

After Mrs Missal's blue lilies, the rhododendrons real and artificial in her drawing-room, this stately drabness should have been restful. Instead it was hideously depressing. Undoubtedly no flowers could bloom because none had been planted, but the effect was rather that the soil was barren or the air inclement.

Wexford mounted the shallow flight of broad steps under the blank eyes of windows hung with olive and burgundy and pigeon grey, and pressed the bell. Presently the door was opened by a woman of about seventy dressed amazingly in a brown frock with a beige cap and apron. She was what was once known, Wexford thought, as 'an elderly body'. Here, he was sure, there would be no frivolous Teutonic blondes.

She in her turn looked as if she would designate him as 'a person', a creature not far removed from a tradesman, who should have known better than to present himself at the front door. He asked for Mrs Quadrant and produced his card.

'Madam is having her tea,' she said, unimpressed by Wexford's bulk, his air of justice incarnate. 'I'll see if she can speak to you.'

'Just tell her Chief Inspector Wexford would like a word with her.' Affected by the atmosphere, he added, 'If you please.'

He stepped over the threshold and into the hall. It was as big as a large room and, surprisingly enough, the tapestries of hunting scenes stretched on frames and attached to the walls did nothing to diminish its size. Again there was the same absence of colour, but not quite a total absence. Worked into the coats of the huntsmen, the palfreys of their mounts, Wexford caught the gleam of dull gold, ox-blood red and a hint of heraldic murrey.

The old woman looked defiantly at him as if she was prepared to argue it out, but as Wexford closed the front door firmly behind him someone called out:

'Who is it, Nanny?'

He recognized Mrs Quadrant's voice and remembered how the night before she had smiled at Missal's crude joke.

Nanny just got to the double doors before him. She opened them in a way he had only seen done in films and, incongruously, grotesquely, there rose before his eyes a shot, ridiculous and immensely funny, from a Marx Brothers picture. The vision fled and he entered the room.

Douglas and Fabia Quadrant were sitting alone at either end of a low table covered by a lace cloth. Tea had apparently only just been brought in because the book Mrs Quadrant had been reading was lying open and face-upwards on the arm of her chair. The soft old silver of the teapot, the cream jug and the sugar bowl was so brightly polished that it reflected her long hands against the sombre colours of the room. It was forty years since Wexford had seen a brass kettle like this one boiling gently over a spirit flame.

Quadrant was eating bread and butter, just plain bread and butter but crustless and cut thin as a wafer.

'This is an unexpected pleasure,' he said, rising to his feet. This time there were no clumsy incidents with cigarettes. He restored his cup almost gracefully to the table and waved Wexford into an armchair.

'Of course, you know my wife?' He was like a cat, Wexford thought, a slim detached tom-cat who purred by day and went out on the tiles at night. And this room, the silver, the china, the long wine-coloured curtains like blood transmuted into velvet! And amidst it all Mrs Quadrant, dark-haired, elegant in black, was feeding cream to her cat. But when the lamps were lit he stole away to take his feline pleasures under the bushes in the creeping dark.

'Tea, Chief Inspector?' She poured a driblet of water into the pot.

'Not for me, thank you.' She had come a long way, Wexford thought, since those days in the wilderness garden, or perhaps, even then, her gym tunic had been of a more expensive make, her hair more expertly cut than the other girls'. She's beautiful, he thought, but she looks old, much older than Helen Missal. No children, plenty of money, nothing to do all day but feed cream to a ranging cat. Did she mind his infidelity, did she even know about it? Wexford wondered curiously if the jealousy that had reddened Missal had blanched and aged Quadrant's wife.

'And what can I do for you?' Quadrant asked. 'I half expected a visit this morning. I gather from the newspapers that you aren't making a great deal of headway.' Lining himself up on the side of the law, he added, 'An elusive killer this time, am I right?'

'Things are sorting themselves out,' Wexford said heavily. 'As a matter of fact it was your wife I wanted to speak to.'

'To me?' Fabia Quadrant touched one of her platinum ear-rings and Wexford noticed that her wrists were thin and her arms already corded like a much older woman's. 'Oh, I see. Because I knew Margaret, you mean. We were never very close, Chief Inspector. There must be dozens of people who could tell you more about her than I can.'

Possibly, Wexford thought, if I only knew where to find them.

'I didn't see her at all after her family moved away from Flagford until just a few weeks ago. We met in the High Street and had coffee. We discovered we'd gone our separate ways and – well!'

And that, Wexford said to himself, contrasting Tabard Road with the house he was in, must be the understatement of the case. For a second, building his impressions as he always did in a series of pictures, he glimpsed that meeting: Mrs Quadrant with her rings, her elaborately straight hair, and Margaret Parsons awkward in the cardigan and sandals that had seemed so comfortable until she came upon her old companion. What had they in common, what had they talked about?

'What did she talk about, Mrs Quadrant?'

'Oh, the changes in the place, people we'd known at school, that sort of thing.' The governess and the lady of the manor. Wexford sighed within himself.

'Did you ever meet anyone called Anne Ives?'

'You mean Margaret's cousin? No, I never met her. She wasn't at school with us. She was a typist or a clerk or something.'

Just another of the hoi-polloi, Wexford thought, the despised majority, the bottom seventy-five per cent.

Quadrant sat listening, swinging one elegant leg. His wife's condescension seemed to amuse him. He finished his tea, crumpled his napkin and helped himself to a cigarette. Wexford watched him take a box of matches from his pocket and strike one. Matches! That was odd. Surely if he had behaved consistently Quadrant would have used a lighter, one of these table lighters that look like a Georgian teapot, Wexford thought, his imagination working. There had been a single matchstick beside Mrs Parsons' body, a single matchstick half burnt away. . . .

'Now, Margaret Godfrey's boy friends, Mrs Quadrant. Can you remember anyone at all?'

He leant forward, trying to impress her with the urgency of his question. A tiny flash of something that might have been malice or simply recollection darted into her eyes and was gone. Quadrant exhaled deeply.

'There was a boy,' she said.

'Try to remember, Mrs Quadrant.'

'I ought to remember,' she said, and Wexford was sure she could, certain she was only stalling for effect. 'It was like a theatre, a London theatre.'

'Palladium, Globe, Haymarket?' Quadrant was enjoying himself. 'Prince of Wales?'

Fabia Quadrant giggled softly. It was an unkind titter, sympathetic towards her husband, faintly hostile to the Chief Inspector. For all his infidelity Quadrant and his wife shared something, something stronger, Wexford guessed, than ordinary marital trust.

'I know, it was Drury. Dudley Drury. He used to live in Flagford.'

'Thank you, Mrs Quadrant. It had just crossed my mind that your husband might have known her.'

'I?' As he spoke the monosyllable Quadrant's voice was almost hysterically incredulous. Then he began to rock with laughter. It was a soundless cruel mirth that seemed to send an evil wind through the room. He made no noise, but Wexford felt scorn leap out of the laughing man like a springing animal, scorn and contempt and the wrath that is one of the deadly sins. 'I, know *her*? In that sort of way? I assure you, dear Chief Inspector, that I most emphatically knew her not!'

Sickened, Wexford turned away. Mrs Quadrant was looking down into her lap. It was as if she had withdrawn into a sort of shame.

'This Drury,' Wexford said, 'do you know if she ever called him Doon?'

Was it his imagination or was it simply coincidence that at that moment Quadrant's laughter was switched off like a wrenched tap?

'Doon?' his wife said. 'Oh, no, I never heard her call anyone Doon.'

She didn't get up when Wexford rose to go, but gave him a dismissive nod and reached for the book she had been reading. Quadrant let him out briskly, closing the door before he reached the bottom of the steps as if he had been selling brushes or reading the meter. Dougie Q! If there was ever a fellow who could strangle one woman and then make love to another a dozen yards away . . . But why? Deep in thought, he walked down the Kingsbrook Road, crossed to the opposite side of the road and would have passed Helen Missal's garage unseeing but for the voice that hailed him.

'Did you see Douglas?' Her tone was wistful but she had cheered up since he had last seen her. The bikini had been changed for a printed silk dress, high-heeled shoes and a big hat.

The question was beneath Wexford's dignity.

'Mrs Quadrant was able to fill in a few gaps,' he said.

'Fabia was? You amaze me. She's very discreet. Just as well, Douglas being what he is.' For a moment her pretty face was swollen with sensuality. 'He's magnificent, isn't he? He's splendid.' Shaking herself, she drew her hand across the face and when she withdrew it Wexford saw that the lust had been wiped away. 'My Christ,' she said, once more cheerful and outrageous, 'some people don't know when they're well off!' She unlocked the garage doors, opened the boot of the red Dauphine and took out a pair of flatter shoes.

'I had the impression,' Wexford said, 'that there was something else you wanted to tell me.' He paused. 'When your husband interrupted us.'

'Perhaps there was and perhaps there wasn't. I don't think I will now.' The shoes changed, she danced up to the car and swung the door open.

'Off to the cinema?' Wexford asked.

She banged the door and switched on the ignition.

'Damn you!' Wexford heard her shout above the roar of the engine.

CHAPTER TEN

We were young, we were merry, we were very very wise,
And the door stood open at our feast. . . .

Mary Coleridge, *Unwelcome*

Nectarine Cottage lay in a damp hollow, a bramble-filled basin behind the Stowerton Road. The approach down a winding path was hazardous and Miss Clarke was taking no chances. Notices pencilled on lined paper greeted Burden at intervals as he descended. The first on the gate had commanded *Lift and push hard*; the second, some ten feet down the path, *Mind barbed wire.* Presently the brambles gave place to faint traces of cultivation. This was of a strictly utilitarian kind, rows of sad cabbages among the weeds, a splendid marrow plant protected from the thistles by a home-made cloche. Someone had pinned a sheet of paper to its roof, *Do not remove glass.* Evidently Miss Clarke had clumsy friends or was the victim of trespassers. This Burden could understand, for there was nothing to indicate habitation but the vegetables and the notices, and the cottage only came into view when he was almost upon it at the end of the path.

The door stood wide open and from within came rich gurgling giggles. For a moment he thought that, although there were no other houses in the lane, he had come to the wrong place. He rapped on the door, the giggles rose to a gale and someone called out:

'Is that you, Dodo? We'd almost given you up.'

Dodo might be a man or a woman, probably a woman. Burden gave a very masculine cough.

'Oh, gosh, it isn't,' said the voice. 'I tell you what, Di. It must be old Fanny Fowler's cop, a coughing cop.'

Burden felt uncommonly foolish. The voice seemed to come from behind a closed door at the end of the passage.

He called loudly, 'Inspector Burden, madam!'

The door was immediately flung open and a woman came out dressed like a Tyrolean peasant. Her fair hair was drawn tightly back and twisted round her head in plaits.

'Oh, gosh,' she said again. 'I didn't realize the front door was still open. I was only kidding about you being Miss Fowler's cop. She rang up and said you might come.'

'Miss Clarke?'

'Who else?' Burden thought she looked very odd, a grown woman dressed up as Humperdinck's Gretel. 'Come and pig it along with Di and me in the dungeon,' she said.

Burden followed her into the kitchen. *Mind the steps*, said another notice pinned to the door and he saw it just in time to stop himself crashing down the three steep steps to the slate-flagged floor. The kitchen was even nastier than Mrs Parsons' and much less clean. But outside the window the sun was shining and a red rose pressed against the diamond panes.

There was nothing odd about the woman Miss Clarke had called Di. It might have been Mrs Parsons' double sitting at the table eating toast, only this woman's hair was black and she wore glasses.

'Di Plunkett, Inspector Burden,' Clare Clarke said. 'Sit down, Inspector – not that stool. It's got fat on it – and have a cup of tea.'

Burden refused the tea and sat on a wooden chair that looked fairly clean.

'I've no objection if you talk while I eat,' said Miss Clarke, bursting once more into giggles. She peered at a tin of jam and said crossly to her companion: 'Confound it! South African. I know I shan't fancy it now.' She pouted and said dramatically, 'Ashes on my tongue!' But Burden noticed that she helped herself generously and spread the jam on to a doorstep of bread. With her mouth full she said to him: 'Fire away. I'm all ears.'

'All I really want to know is if you can tell me the names of any of Mrs Parsons' boy friends when she was Margaret Godfrey, when you knew her.'

Miss Clarke smacked her lips.

'You've come to the right shop,' she said. 'I've got a memory like an elephant.'

'You can say that again,' said Di Plunkett, 'and it's not only your memory.' They both laughed, Miss Clarke with great good humour.

'I remember Margaret Godfrey perfectly,' she said. 'Second-class brain, anaemic looks, personality both prim and dim. Still, *de mortuis* and all that jazz, you know. (Prang that fly, Di. There's a squeegy-weegy sprayer thing on the shelf behind your great bonce.) Not a very social type, Margaret, no community spirit. Went around with a female called Bertram, vanished now into the mists of obscurity. (Got him, Di!) Chummed up with one Fabia Rogers for a while – Fabia, forsooth! not to mention Diana Stevens of sinister memory —'

Miss or Mrs Plunkett broke in with a scream of laughter and waving the fly-killer made as if to fire a stream of liquid at Miss Clarke's head. Burden shifted his chair out of range.

Ducking and giggling, Clare Clarke went on: '. . . Now notorious in the Stowerton rural district as Mrs William Plunkett, one of this one-eyed burg's most illustrious sons!'

'You are a scream, Clare,' Mrs Plunkett gasped. 'Really, I envy those lucky members of the upper fourth. When I think of what we had to put up with —'

'What about boy friends, Miss Clarke?'

'*Cherchez l'homme*, eh? I said you'd come to the right shop. D'you remember, Di, when she went out with him the first time and we sat behind them in the pictures? Oh, gosh, I'll never forget that to my dying day.'

'Talk about sloppy,' said Mrs Plunkett. ' "Do you mind if I hold your hand, Margaret?" I thought you were going to burst a blood-vessel, Clare.'

'What was his name?' Burden was bored and at the same time angry. He thought the years had toughened him, but now the picture of the green and white bundle in the wood swam before his eyes; that and Parsons' face. He realized that of all the people they had interviewed he hadn't liked a single one. Was there no pity in any of them, no common mercy?

'What was his name?' he said again wearily.

'Dudley Drury. On my sacred oath, Dudley Drury.'

'What a name to go to bed with,' Mrs Plunkett said.

Clare Clarke whispered in her ear, but loud enough for Burden to hear: 'She never did! Not on your sweet life.'

Mrs Plunkett saw his face and looked a little ashamed. She said defensively in a belated effort to help:

'He's still around if you want to trace him. He lives down by Stowerton Station. Surely you don't think he killed Meg Godfrey?'

Clare Clarke said suddenly: 'She was quite pretty. He was very keen on her. She didn't look like that then, you know, not like that ghastly mockery in the paper. I think I've got a snap somewhere. All girls together.'

Burden had got what he wanted. Now he wanted to go. It was a bit late in the day for snaps. If they could have seen one on Thursday it might have helped but that was all.

'Thank you, Miss Clarke,' he said, 'Mrs Plunkett. Good afternoon.'

'Well, cheeri-bye. It's been nice meeting you.' She giggled. 'It's not often we see a man in here, is it, Di?'

Half-way down the overgrown path he stopped in his tracks. A woman in jodhpurs and open-necked shirt was coming up towards the cottage, whistling. It was Dorothy Sweeting.

Dodo, he thought. They'd mistaken him for someone called

Dodo and Dodo was Dorothy Sweeting. From long experience Burden knew that whatever may happen in detective fiction, coincidence is more common than conspiracy in real life.

'Good afternoon, Miss Sweeting.'

She grinned at him with cheerful innocence.

'Oh, hallo,' she said, 'fancy seeing you. I've just come from the farm. There's a blinking great crowd like a Cup Final in that wood. You ought to see them.'

Still not inured to man's inhuman curiosity, Burden sighed.

'You know that bush where they found her?' Dorothy Sweeting went on excitedly. 'Well, Jimmy Traynor's flogging twigs off it at a bob a time. I told Mr Prewett he ought to charge half a crown admittance.'

'I hope he's not thinking of taking your advice, miss,' Burden said in a repressive voice.

'There's nothing wrong in it. I knew a fellow who had a plane crash on his land and he turned a whole field into a car park he had so many sightseers.'

Burden flattened himself against the hedge to let her pass.

'Your tea will be getting cold, Miss Sweeting,' he said.

'Whatever next?' Wexford said. 'If we don't look sharp they'll have every stick in that wood uprooted and taken home for souvenirs.'

'Shall I have a couple of the lads go over there, sir?' Burden asked.

'You do that, and go and get the street directory. We'll go and see this Drury character together.'

'You aren't going to wait to hear from Colorado, then?'

'Drury's a big possibility, Mike. He could well be Doon. I can't help feeling that whatever Parsons says about his wife's chastity, when she came back here she met up with Doon again and succumbed to his charms. As to why he should have killed her – well, all I can say is, men *do* strangle women they're having affairs with, and Mrs P. may have accepted the car rides and the meals without being willing to pay for services rendered.

'The way I see it, Mike, Doon had been seeing Mrs P. and asked her out on Tuesday afternoon with a view to persuading her to become his mistress. They couldn't meet at her home because of the risks and Doon was going to pick her up on the Pomfret Road. She took the rain-hood with her because the weather had been wet and she didn't bank on being in the car all the time. Even if she didn't want Doon for her lover she wouldn't want him to see her with wet hair.'

The time factor was bothering Burden and he said so.

'If she was killed early in the afternoon, sir, why did Doon strike a match to look at her? And if she was killed later, why didn't she pay for her papers before she went out with him and why didn't she explain to Parsons that she was going to be late?'

Wexford shrugged. 'Search me,' he said. 'Dougie Q. uses matches, carries them in his pocket. So do most men. He's behaving in a very funny way, Mike. Sometimes he's co-operative, sometimes he's actively hostile. We haven't finished with him yet. Mrs Missal knows more than she's saying —'

'Then there's Missal himself,' Burden interrupted.

Wexford looked thoughtful. He rubbed his chin and said: 'I don't think there's any mystery about what he was doing on Tuesday. He's as jealous as hell of that wife of his and not without reason as we know. I'm willing to take a bet that he keeps tabs on her when he can. He probably suspects Quadrant and when she told him she was going out on Tuesday afternoon he nipped back to Kingsmarkham on the off-chance, watched her go out, satisfied himself that she didn't go to Quadrant's office and went back to Stowerton. He'd know she'd dress herself up to the nines if she was meeting Dougie. When he saw her go off in the car along the Kingsbrook Road in the same clothes she was wearing that morning he'd bank on her going shopping in Pomfret – they don't close on Tuesdays – and he'd be able to set his mind at rest. I'm certain that's what happened.'

'It sounds like him,' Burden agreed. 'It fits. Was Quadrant here twelve years ago, sir?'

'Oh, yes, lived here all his life, apart from three years at Cambridge and, anyway, he came down in 1949. Still, Mrs P. was hardly his style. I asked him if he knew her and he just laughed, but it was the way he laughed. I'm not kidding, Mike, it made my blood run cold.'

Burden looked at his chief with respect. It must have been quite a display, he thought, to chill Wexford.

'I suppose the others could have been just – well, playthings as it were, and Mrs P. a life-long love.'

'Christ!' Wexford roared. 'I should never have let you read that book. Playthings, life-long love! You make me puke. For pity's sake find out where Drury lives and we'll get over there.'

According to the directory, Drury, Dudley J. and Drury, Kathleen lived at 14 Sparta Grove, Stowerton. Burden knew it as a street of tiny pre-war semi-detached houses, not far from where Peter Missal had his garage. It was not the kind of background he had visualized for Doon. He and Wexford had a couple of rounds of sandwiches from the Carousel and got to Stowerton by seven.

Drury's house had a yellow front door with a lot of neatly tied climbing roses on the trellis round the porch. In the middle of the lawn was a small pond made from a plastic bath and on its rim stood a plaster gnome with a fishing rod. Someone had evidently been polishing the Ford Popular on the garage drive. As a vehicle for clandestine touring Mrs Katz would probably have despised it, but it was certainly shiny enough to have dazzled Margaret Parsons.

The door-knocker was a cast-iron lion's head with a ring in its mouth. Wexford banged it hard, but no one came, so he pushed open the side gate and they entered the back garden. On a vegetable plot by the rear fence a man was digging potatoes.

Wexford coughed and the man turned round. He had a red glistening face, and although it was warm, the cuffs of his long-sleeved shirt were buttoned. His sandy hair and the whiteness of his wrists confirmed Wexford's opinion that he was probably sensitive to sunburn. Not the sort of man, Burden thought, to be fond of poetry and send snippets of verse to the girl he loved, surely not the sort of man to buy expensive books and write delicate whimsical messages in their fly-leaves.

'Mr Drury?' Wexford asked quietly.

Drury looked startled, almost frightened, but this could simply be alarm at the invasion of his garden by two men much larger than himself. There was sweat on his upper lip, again probably only the result of manual toil.

'Who are you?'

It was a thin highish voice that sounded as if its development towards a greater resonance had been arrested in puberty.

'Chief Inspector Wexford, sir, and Inspector Burden. County Police.'

Drury had looked after his garden. Apart from a couple of square yards from which potatoes had been lifted, there were various freshly turned patches all over the flower-beds. He stuck the prongs of the fork into the ground and wiped his hands on his trousers.

'Is this something to do with Margaret?' he asked.

'I think we'd better go into the house, Mr Drury.'

He took them in through a pair of french windows, considerably less elegant than Mrs Missal's, and into a tiny room crowded with post-war utility furniture.

Someone had just eaten a solitary meal. The cloth was still on the table and the dirty plates had been half-heartedly stacked.

'My wife's away,' Drury said. 'She took the kids to the seaside this morning. What can I do for you?'

He sat down on a dining chair, offered another to Burden and, observant of protocol, left the only armchair to Wexford.

'Why did you ask if it was something to do with Margaret, Mr Drury?'

'I recognized her photograph in the paper. It gave me a bit of a turn. Then I went to a do at the chapel last night and they were all talking about it. It made me feel a bit queer, I can tell you, on account of me meeting Margaret through the chapel.'

That would have been Flagford Methodist Church, Burden reflected. He recalled a maroon-painted hut with a corrugated-iron roof on the north side of the village green.

Drury didn't look scared any longer, only sad. Burden was struck by his resemblance to Ronald Parsons, not only a physical likeness but a similarity of phrase and manner. As well as the undistinguished features, the thin sandy hair, this man had the same defensiveness, the same humdrum turn of speech. A muscle twitched at the corner of his mouth. Anyone less like Douglas Quadrant would have been difficult to imagine.

'Tell me about your relationship with Margaret Godfrey,' Wexford said.

Drury looked startled.

'It wasn't a relationship,' he said.

What did he think he was being accused of? Burden wondered.

'She was one of my girl friends. She was just a kid at school. I met her at chapel and took her out . . . what, a dozen times.'

'When did you first take her out, Mr Drury?'

'It's a long time ago. Twelve years, thirteen years . . . I can't remember.' He looked at his hands on which the crusts of earth were drying. 'Will you excuse me if I go and have a bit of a wash?'

He went out of the room. Through the open serving hatch

Burden saw him run the hot tap and swill his hands under it.
Wexford moved out of Drury's line of vision and towards the
bookcase. Among the Penguins and the *Reader's Digests* was a
volume covered in navy-blue suède. Wexford took it out
quickly, read the inscription and handed it to Burden.

It was the same printing, the same breathless loving style.
Above the title – *The Picture of Dorian Gray* – Burden read:

*Man cannot live on wine alone, Minna, but this is the very best bread
and butter. Farewell. Doon, July, 1951.*

CHAPTER ELEVEN

They out-talked thee, hissed thee, tore thee,
Better men fared thus before thee.

Matthew Arnold, *The Last Word*

Drury came back, smiling cautiously. He had rolled up his sleeves and his hands were pink. When he saw the book Wexford was holding the smile faded and he said aggressively:

'I think you're taking a liberty.'

'Where did you get this book, Mr Drury?'

Drury peered at the printing, looked at Wexford and blushed. The tic returned, pumping his chin.

'Oh dear,' he said, 'she gave it me. I'd forgotten I'd got it.'

Wexford had become stern. His thick lower lip stood out, giving him a prognathous look.

'Look here, she gave me that book when I was taking her out. It says July here and that's when it must have been. July, that's right.' The blush faded and he went white. He sat down heavily. 'You don't believe me, do you? My wife'll tell you. It's been there ever since we got married.'

'Why did Mrs Parsons give it to you, Mr Drury?'

'I'd been taking her out for a few weeks.' He stared at Wexford with eyes like a hare's caught in the beam of headlights. 'It was the summer of – I don't know. What does it say there? Fifty-one. We were in her aunt's house. A parcel came for Margaret and she opened it. She looked sort of mad and she just chucked it down, chucked it on the floor, you see, but I picked it up. I'd heard of it and I thought ... well, I thought it was a smutty book if you must know, and I wanted to read it. She said, "Here, you can have it, if you like." Something like that. I can't remember the details of what she said. It was a long time ago. Minna had got fed up with this Doon and I thought she was sort of ashamed of him . . .'

'Minna?'

'I started calling her Minna then because of the name in the book. What have I said? For God's sake, don't look at me like that!'

Wexford stuck the book in his pocket.

'When did you last see her?'

Drury picked at the cord that bound the seat of his chair. He began pulling out little shreds of red cotton. At last he said:

'She went away in the August. Her uncle had died . . .'

'No, no. I mean recently.'

'I saw her last week. That isn't a crime, is it, seeing somebody you used to know? I was in the car and I recognized her. She was in the High Street, in Kingsmarkham. I stopped for a minute and asked her how she was, that sort of thing . . .'

'Go on. I want all the details.'

'She said she was married and I said so was I. She said she'd come to live in Tabard Road and I said we must get together sometime with her husband and Kathleen. Kathleen's my wife. Anyway, I said I'd give her a ring, and that was all.'

'She told you her married name?'

'Of course she did. Why shouldn't she?'

'Mr Drury, you said you recognized her photograph. Didn't you recognize her name?'

'Her name, her face, what's the odds? I'm not in court. I can't watch every word I say.'

'Just tell the truth and you won't have to watch your words. Did you telephone her?'

'Of course I didn't. I was going to, but then I read she was dead.'

'Where were you on Tuesday between twelve-thirty and seven?'

'I was at work. I work in my uncle's hardware shop in Pomfret. Ask him, he'll tell you I was there all day.'

'What time does the shop close?'

'Half past five, but I always try to get away early on Tuesdays. Look, you won't believe me.'

'Try me, Mr Drury.'

'I know you won't believe me, but my wife'll tell you, my uncle'll tell you. I always go to Flagford on Tuesdays to collect my wife's vegetable order. There's a nursery there, see, on the Clusterwell Road. You have to get there by half five otherwise they're closed. Well, we were busy last Tuesday and I was late. I try to get away by five, but it was all of a quarter past. When I got to Spellman's there wasn't anybody about. I went round the back of the greenhouses and I called out, but they'd gone.'

'So you went home without the vegetables?'

'No, I didn't. Well, I did, but not straight away. I'd had a hard day and I was fed up about the place being closed, so I went into The Swan and had a drink. A girl served me. I've never seen her before. Look, does my wife have to know about that? I'm a Methodist, see? I'm a member of the chapel. I'm not supposed to drink.'

Burden drew in his breath. A murder enquiry and he was worrying about his clandestine pint!

'You drove to Flagford along the main Pomfret Road?'

'Yes, I did. I drove right past that wood where they found her.' Drury got up and fumbled in vain along the mantelpiece for cigarettes. 'But I never stopped. I drove straight to Flagford. I was in a hurry to get the order... Look, Chief Inspector, I wouldn't have done anything to Minna. She was a nice kid. I was fond of her. I wouldn't do a thing like that, kill someone!'

'Who else called her Minna apart from you?'

'Only this Doon fellow as far as I know. She never told me his real name. I got the impression she was sort of ashamed of him. Goodness knows why. He was rich and he was clever too. She said he was clever.' He drew himself up and looked at them belligerently. 'She preferred me,' he said.

He got up suddenly and stared at the chair he had mutilated. Among the dirty plates was a milk bottle, half full, with yellow curds sticking to its rim. He tipped the bottle into an empty tea-cup and drank from it, slopping a puddle into the saucer.

'I should sit down if I were you,' Wexford said.

He went into the hall and beckoned to Burden. They stood close together in the narrow passage. The carpet was frayed by the kitchen door and one of Drury's children had scribbled on the wallpaper with a blue crayon.

'Get on to The Swan, Mike,' he said. He thought he heard Drury's chair shift and, remembering the open french windows, turned swiftly. But Drury was still sitting at the table, his head buried in his hands.

The walls were thin and he could hear Burden's voice in the front room, then a faint trill as the receiver went back into its rest. Burden's feet thumped across the floor, entered the hall and stopped. There was utter silence and Wexford edged out of the door, keeping his eye on Drury through the crack.

Burden was standing by the front door. On the wall at the foot of the narrow staircase was a coat-rack, a zig-zag metal affair with gaudily coloured knobs instead of hooks. A man's sports jacket and a child's plastic mac hung on two of the knobs and on the one nearest to the stairs was a transparent pink nylon hood.

'It won't take prints,' Wexford said. 'Get back on that phone, Mike. I shall want some help. Bryant and Gates should be coming on about now.'

He unhooked the hood, covered the diminutive hall in three strides, and showed his find to Drury.

'Where did you get this, Mr Drury?'

'It must be my wife's,' Drury said. Suddenly assertive, he added pugnaciously, 'It's no business of yours!'

'Mrs Parsons bought a hood like this one on Tuesday morning.' Wexford watched him crumple once more in sick despair. 'I want your permission to search this house, Drury. Make no mistake about it, I can get a warrant, but it'll take a little longer.'

Drury looked as if he was going to cry.

'Oh, do what you like,' he said. 'Only, can I have a cigarette? I've left mine in the kitchen.'

'Inspector Burden will get them when he comes off the phone,' Wexford said.

They began to search, and within half an hour were joined by Gates and Bryant. Then Wexford told Burden to contact Drury's uncle at Pomfret, Spellman's nursery and the manager of the supermarket.

'The girl at The Swan isn't on tonight,' Burden said, 'but she lives in Flagford at 3 Cross Roads Cottages. No phone. Her name's Janet Tipping.'

'We'll get Martin over there straight away. Try and get a phone number out of Drury where we can get hold of his wife. If she's not gone far away – Brighton or Eastbourne – you can get down there tonight. When I've turned the place over I'm going to have another word with Mrs Quadrant. She admits she was "friendly" with Mrs P. and she's practically the only person who does, apart from our friend in the next room.'

Burden stretched the pink scarf taut, testing its strength.

'You really think he's Doon?' he asked incredulously.

Wexford went on opening drawers, feeling among a mêlée of coloured pencils, Snap cards, reels of cotton, scraps of paper covered with children's scribble. Mrs Drury wasn't a tidy housewife and all the cupboards and drawers were in a mess.

'I don't know,' he said. 'At the moment it looks like it, but it leaves an awful lot of loose ends. It doesn't fit in with my fancies, Mike, and since we can't afford to go by fancies...'

He looked through every book in the house – there were not more than two or three dozen – but he found no more from Doon to Minna. There was no Victorian poetry and the only novels apart from *The Picture of Dorian Gray* were paperback thrillers.

On a hook in the kitchen cabinet Bryant found a bunch of keys. One fitted the front door lock, another the strong box in Drury's bedroom, two more the dining-room and front-room doors, and a fifth the garage. The ignition keys to Drury's car were in his jacket on the coat-rack and the key to the back door was in the lock. Wexford, looking for purses, found only one, a green and white plastic thing in the shape of a cat's face. It was empty and labelled on the inside: *Susan Mary Drury*. Drury's daughter had taken her savings with her to the seaside.

The loft was approached by a hatch in the landing ceiling. Wexford told Bryant to get Drury's steps from the garage and investigate this loft. He left Gates downstairs with Drury and went out to his car. On the way he scraped some dust from the tyres of the blue Ford.

A thin drizzle was falling. It was ten o'clock and dark for a midsummer evening. If Drury had killed her at half past five, he thought, it would still have been broad daylight, much too early to need the light of a match flame. It would have to be a match they had found. Of all the things to leave behind a matchstick was surely the least incriminating! And why hadn't she paid for her papers, what had she done with herself during the long hours between the time she left the house and the time she met Doon? But Drury was terribly frightened... Wexford too had observed the resemblance between him and Ronald Parsons. It was reasonable to suppose, he argued, that this type of personality attracted Margaret Parsons and that she had chosen her husband because he reminded her of her old lover.

He switched on his headlights, pulled the windscreen wiper button, and started back towards Kingsmarkham.

CHAPTER TWELVE

Were you and she whom I met at dinner last week,
With eyes and hair of the Ptolemy black?

Sir Edwin Arnold, *To a Pair of Egyptian Slippers*

The house looked forbidding at night. In Wexford's headlights the rough grey granite glittered and the leaves of the flowerless wistaria which clung to it showed up a livid yellowish green.

Someone was dining with the Quadrants. Wexford pulled up beside the black Daimler and went up the steps to the front door. He rang the bell several times; then the door was opened, smoothly, almost offensively slowly, by Quadrant himself.

For dining with Helen Missal he had worn a lounge suit. At home, with his wife and guests, he ascended to evening dress. But there was nothing vulgar about Quadrant, no fancy waistcoat, no flirtation with midnight blue. The dinner jacket was black and faultless, the shirt – Wexford liked to hit on an apt quotation himself when he could – 'whiter than new snow on a raven's back'.

He said nothing but seemed to stare right through Wexford at the shadowy garden beyond. There was an insolent majesty about him which the tapestries that framed his figure did nothing to dispel. Then Wexford told himself sharply that this man was, after all, only a provincial solicitor.

'I'd like another word with your wife, Mr Quadrant.'

'At this hour?'

Wexford looked at his watch and at the same time Quadrant lifted his own cuff – links of silver and onyx glinted in the muted lights – raised his eyebrow at the square platinum dial on his wrist and said:

'It's extremely inconvenient.' He made no move to let Wexford enter. 'My wife isn't a particularly strong woman and we do happen to have my parents-in-law dining with us ... '

Old man Rogers and his missus, Pomfret Hall, Wexford thought vulgarly. He stood stolidly, not smiling.

'Oh, very well,' Quadrant said, 'but keep it brief, will you?'

There was a faint movement in the hall behind him. A brown dress, a wisp of coffee-coloured stuff, appeared for an instant against the embroidered trees on the hangings, then Mrs Quadrant's nanny scuttled away.

'You'd better go into the library.' Quadrant showed him into a room furnished with blue leather chairs. 'I won't offer you a drink since you're on duty.' The words were a little offensive. Then Quadrant gave his quick cat-like smile. 'Excuse me,' he said, 'while I fetch my wife.' He turned with the slow graceful movement of a dance measure, paused briefly and closed the door behind him, shutting Wexford in.

So he wasn't going to let him bust in on any family party, Wexford thought. The man was nervous, hiding some nebulous fear in the manner of men of his kind, under a massive self-control.

As he waited he looked about him at the books. There were hundreds here, tier upon tier of them on every wall. Plenty of Victorian poetry and plenty of Victorian novels, but just as much verse from the seventeenth and eighteenth centuries. Wexford shrugged. Kingsmarkham was surrounded by such houses as this one, a bastion of affluence, houses with libraries, libraries with books ...

Fabia Quadrant came in almost soundlessly. Her long dress was black and he remembered that black was not a colour but just a total absorption of light. Her face was gay, a little hectic, and she greeted him cheerfully.

'Hallo again, Chief Inspector.'

'I won't keep you long, Mrs Quadrant.'

'Won't you sit down?'

'Thank you. Just for a moment.' He watched her sit down and fold her hands in her lap. The diamond on her left hand burned in the dark nest between her knees. 'I want you to tell me everything you can remember about Dudley Drury,' he said.

'Well, it was my last term at school,' she said. 'Margaret told me she'd got a boy friend – her first, perhaps. I don't know. It's only twelve years ago, Chief Inspector, but we weren't like the adolescents of today. It wasn't remarkable to be without a boy friend at eighteen. Do you understand?' She spoke clearly and slowly, as if she were instructing a child. Something about her manner angered Wexford and he wondered if she had ever had to hurry in her life, ever had to snatch a meal standing up or run to catch a train. 'It was a little unusual, perhaps, but not odd, not remarkable. Margaret didn't introduce me to her friend but I remember his name because it was like Drury Lane and I had never heard it before as a surname.'

Wexford tried to crush his impatience.

'What did she tell you about him, Mrs Quadrant?'

'Very little.' She paused and looked at him as if she was anxious not to betray a man in danger. 'There was only one thing. She said he was jealous, jealous to the point of fanaticism.'

'I see.'

'He didn't care for her to have any other friends. I had the impression that he was very emotional and possessive.'

Traits you would hardly understand, Wexford thought, or would you? He remembered Quadrant's inconstancies and wondered again. Her voice, uncharacteristically sharp and censorious, interrupted his reverie.

'He was very upset that she was moving back to London. She said he was in a terrible state, his life wouldn't be worth living without her. You can imagine the sort of thing.'

'But he'd only known her a few weeks.'

'I'm simply telling you what she said, Chief Inspector.' She smiled as if she was an immense distance from Drury and

Margaret Godfrey, light years, an infinity of space. 'She didn't seem to care. Margaret wasn't a sensitive person.'

Soft footsteps sounded in the hall and behind Wexford the door opened.

'Oh, there you are,' Fabia Quadrant said. 'Chief Inspector Wexford and I have been talking about young love. It all seems to me rather like the expense of spirit in a waste of shame.'

But that wasn't young love, Wexford thought, trying to place the quotation. It was much more like what he had seen on Helen Missal's face that afternoon.

'Just one small point, Mrs Quadrant,' he said. 'Mrs Parsons seems to have been interested in Victorian poetry during the two years she lived in Flagford. I've wondered if there was any special significance behind that.'

'Nothing sinister, if that's what you mean,' she said. 'Nineteenth-century verse was part of the Advanced English syllabus for Higher School Certificate when we took it in 1951. I believe they call it "A" Levels now.'

Then Quadrant did a strange thing. Crossing the library between Wexford and his wife, he took a book out of the shelves. He put his hand on it without hesitation. Wexford had the impression he could have picked it out blindfold or in the dark.

'Oh, Douglas,' Mrs Quadrant said, 'he doesn't want to see that.'

'Look.'

Wexford looked and read from an ornate label that had been pasted inside the cover:

Presented to Fabia Rogers for distinguished results in Higher School Certificate, 1951.

In his job it didn't do to be at a loss for words, but now he could find no phrase to foster the pride on Quadrant's dark face, or mitigate the embarrassment on his wife's.

'I'll be going now,' he said at last.

Quadrant put the book back abruptly and took his wife's arm. She rested her fingers firmly on his jacket sleeve. Suddenly they seemed very close, but, for all that, it was a strangely sexless communion. Brother and sister, Wexford thought, a Ptolemy and a Cleopatra.

'Good night, Mrs Quadrant. You've been most co-operative. I apologize for troubling you . . .' He looked again at his watch. 'At this hour,' he said, savouring Quadrant's enmity.

'No trouble, Chief Inspector.' She laughed deprecatingly, confidently, as if she was really a happy wife with a devoted husband.

Together they showed him out. Quadrant was urbane, once more courteous, but the hand beneath the sleeve where his wife's fingers lay was clenched and the knuckles showed like white flints under the brown skin.

A bicycle was propped against the police-station wall, a bicycle with a basket, practical-looking lights and a bulging tool bag. Wexford walked into the foyer and almost collided with a fat fair woman wearing a leather windcheater over a dirndl skirt.

'I beg your pardon.'

'That's all right,' she said. 'No bones broken. I suppose you wouldn't be him, this Chief Inspector bod?'

Behind the desk the sergeant grinned slightly, changed the grin to a cough, and covered his mouth with his hand.

'I am Chief Inspector Wexford. Can I help you?'

She fished something out of her shoulder bag.

'Actually,' she said, 'I'm supposed to be helping you. One of your blokes came to my cottage. . . .'

'Miss Clarke,' Wexford said. 'Won't you come into my office?'

His hopes had suddenly risen unaccountably. It made a change for someone to come to him. Then they fell again when he saw what she had in her hand. It was only another photograph.

'I found it,' she said, 'among a lot of other junk. If you're sort of scouring the joint for people who knew Margaret it might help.'

The picture was an enlarged snapshot. It showed a dozen girls disposed in two rows and it was obviously not an official photograph.

'Di took it,' Miss Clarke said. 'Di Stevens that was. Best part of the sixth form are there.' She looked at him and made a face as if she was afraid that by bringing it she had done something silly. 'You can keep it if it's any use.'

Wexford put it in his pocket, intending to look at it later, although he doubted whether it would be needed now. As he was showing Miss Clarke out he met Sergeant Martin coming back from his interview with the manager of the supermarket. No records had been kept of the number of pink hoods sold during the week, only the total sale of hoods in all colours. The stock had come in on Monday and Saturday night twenty-six hoods had been sold. The manager thought that about twenty-five per cent of the stock had been pink and on a very rough estimate he guessed that about six pink ones had been sold.

Wexford sent Martin over to Flagford in search of Janet Tipping. Then he rang Drury's number. Burden answered. They hadn't found anything in the house. Mrs Drury was staying with her sister in Hastings, but the sister had no telephone.

'Martin'll have to get down there,' Wexford said. 'I can't spare you. What did Spellman say?'

'They closed at five-thirty sharp on Tuesday. Drury collected his wife's vegetable order on Wednesday.'

'What's he buying vegetables for, anyway? He grows them in the garden.'

'The order was for tomatoes, a cucumber and a marrow, sir.'

'That's fruit, not vegetables. Talking of gardening, I'm going to get some lights over to you and they can start digging. I reckon that purse and that key could be interred with Drury's potatoes.'

Dudley Drury was in a pitiful state when Wexford got back to Sparta Grove. He was pacing up and down but he looked weak at the knees.

'He's been sick, sir,' Gates said.

'Hard cheese,' Wexford said. 'What d'you think I am, a health visitor?'

The search of the house had been completed and the place looked a lot tidier than it had before they began. When the lighting equipment arrived Bryant and Gates started digging over the potato patch. White-faced, Drury watched from the dining-room windows as the clods of earth were lifted and turned. This man, Wexford thought, had once said life would be unlivable without Margaret Parsons. Had he really meant it would be unendurable, if another possessed her?

'I'd like you to come down to the station now, Drury.'

'Are you going to arrest me?'

'I'd just like to ask you a few more questions,' Wexford said. 'Just a few more questions.'

Meanwhile Burden had driven over to Pomfret, awakened the ironmonger and checked his nephew's alibi.

'Dud always gets off early on Tuesdays,' he grumbled. 'Gets earlier and earlier every week, it does. More like five than a quarter past.'

'So you'd say he left around five last Tuesday?'

'I wouldn't like to say five. Ten past, a quarter past. I was busy in the shop. Dud came in and said, "I'm off now, Uncle." I'd no call to go checking up on him, had I?'

'It might have been ten past or a quarter past?'

'It might have been twenty past for all I know.'

It was still raining softly. The main road was black and stickily gleaming. Whatever Miss Sweeting may have seen in the afternoon, the lane and the wood were deserted now. The top branches of the trees moved in the wind. Burden slowed down, thinking how strange it was that an uninteresting corner of the countryside should suddenly have become, because of the use to which someone had put it, a sinister and dreadful hiding place, the focal point of curious eyes and the goal, perhaps for years to come, of half the visitors to the neighbourhood. From henceforth Flagford Castle would take second place to Prewett's wood in the guide book of the ghoulish.

He met Martin on the forecourt of the police station. Janet Tipping couldn't be found. As usual on Saturday night she had gone out with her boy friend, and her mother had told Martin with a show of aggressive indifference that it was nothing for her to return as late as one or two o'clock. The cottage was dirty and the mother a slattern. She didn't know where her daughter was and, on being asked to hazard a guess, said that Janet and her friend had probably gone for a spin to the coast on his motor-bike.

Burden knocked on Wexford's door and the Chief Inspector shouted to him to come in.

Drury and Wexford sat facing each other.

'Let's go over Tuesday evening again,' Wexford was saying. Burden moved silently into one of the steel and tweed chairs. The clock on the wall, between the filing cabinet where Doon's books still lay and the map of Kingsmarkham, said that it wanted ten minutes to midnight.

'I left the shop at a quarter past five and I drove straight to Flagford. When I got to Spellman's they were closed so I went down the side and looked round the greenhouses. I called out a couple of times but they'd all gone. Look, I've told you all this.'

Wexford said quietly, 'All right, Drury. Let's say I've got a bad memory.'

Drury's voice had become very high and strained. He took out his handkerchief and wiped his forehead.

'I had a look round to see if the order was anywhere about, but it wasn't.' He cleared his throat. 'I was a bit fed-up on account of my wife wanting the vegetables for tea. I drove slowly through the village because I thought I might see Mr Spellman and get him to let me have the order, but I didn't see him.'

'Did you see anybody you know, anybody you used to know when you lived in Flagford?'

'There were some kids,' Drury said. 'I don't know who they were. Look, I've told you the rest. I went into The Swan and this girl served me. . . .'

'What did you have to drink?'

'A half of bitter.' He blushed. At the lie, Burden wondered, or at the breach of faith? 'The place was empty. I coughed and after a bit this girl came out from behind the back. I ordered the bitter and paid for it. She's bound to remember.'

'Don't worry, we'll ask her.'

'She didn't stay in the bar. I was all alone. When I'd finished my drink I went back to Spellman's to see if there was anyone about. I didn't see anyone and I went home.'

Drury jumped up and gripped the edge of the desk. Wexford's papers quivered and the telephone receiver rattled in its rest.

'Look,' he shouted, 'I've told you. I wouldn't have laid a finger on Margaret.'

'Sit down,' Wexford said and Drury crouched back, his face twitching. 'You were very jealous of her, weren't you?' His tone had become conversational, understanding. 'You didn't want her to have any friends but you.'

'That's not true.' He tried to shout but his voice was out of control. 'She was just a girl friend. I don't know what you mean, jealous. Of course I didn't want her going about with other boys when she was with me.'

'Were you her lover, Drury?'

'No, I was not.' He flushed again at the affront. 'You've got no business to ask me things like that. I was only eighteen.'

'You gave her a lot of presents, didn't you, a lot of books?'

'Doon gave her those books, not me. She'd finished with Doon when she came out with me. I never gave her anything. I couldn't afford it.'

'Where's Foyle's, Drury?'

'It's in London. It's a bookshop.'

'Did you ever buy any books there and give them to Margaret Godfrey?'

'I tell you I never gave her any books.'

'What about *The Picture of Dorian Gray?* You didn't give her that one. Why did you keep it? Because you thought it would shock her?'

Drury said dully, 'I've given you a specimen of my printing.'

'Printing changes a lot in twelve years. Tell me about the book.'

'I have told you. We were in her aunt's cottage and the book came in a parcel. She opened it and when she saw who'd sent it she said I could have it.'

At last they left him to sit in silence with the sergeant. Together they went outside.

'I've sent Drury's printing over to that handwriting bloke in St Mary's Road,' Wexford said. 'But printing, Mike, and twelve years ago! It looks as if whoever printed those inscriptions did so because his handwriting was poor or difficult to read. Drury's writing is very round and clear. I got the feeling he doesn't write much and his writing's never matured.'

'He's the only person we've talked to who called Mrs P. Minna,' Burden said, 'and who knew about Doon. He had one of those hood things in his house and while it could be one of the other five it could be Mrs P.'s. If he left his uncle's at five-ten or five-fifteen even he could have been at Prewett's by twenty past and by then Bysouth had had those cows in for nearly half an hour.'

The telephones had been silent for a long time now, an

unusually long time for the busy police station. What had happened to the call they had been awaiting since lunchtime? Wexford seemed to read his thoughts almost uncannily.

'We ought to hear from Colorado any minute,' he said. 'Calculating roughly that they're about seven hours behind us in time, suppose Mrs Katz was out for the day, she'd be getting home just about now. It's half past twelve here and that makes it between five and six in the West of the United States. Mrs Katz has got little kids. I reckon she and her family have been out for the day and they haven't been able to get hold of her. But she ought to be coming home about now and I hope they won't be too long.'

Burden jumped as the bell pealed. He lifted the receiver and gave it to Wexford. As soon as he spoke Burden could tell it was just another bit of negative evidence.

'Yes,' Wexford said. 'Yes, thank you very much. I see. Can't be helped. . . . Yes, good night.'

He turned back to Burden. 'That was Egham, the handwriting fellow. He says Drury could have printed those inscriptions. There's no question of the printing being disguised, but he says it was very mature for a boy of eighteen and if it's Drury's he would have expected a much greater development than Drury's present specimen shows.

'Moreover, there's another point in his favour. I took a sample from the treads of his tyres and although they haven't finished with it, the lab boys are pretty certain that car hadn't been parked in a muddy lane since it was new. The stuff I got was mostly sand and dust. Let's have some tea, Mike.'

Burden cocked his thumb at the door.

'A cup for him, sir?'

'My God, yes,' Wexford said. 'How many times do I have to tell you? This isn't Mexico.'

CHAPTER THIRTEEN

And I am sometimes proud and sometimes meek,
And sometimes I remember days of old . . .

Christina Rossetti, *Aloof*

Margaret Godfrey was one of five girls on the stone seat and she sat in the middle of the row. Those who stood behind rested their hands on the shoulders of the seated. Wexford counted twelve faces. The snapshot Diana Stevens had taken was very sharp and clear and the likenesses, even after so long, were good. He re-created in his mind the face he had seen on the damp ground, then stared with awakened curiosity at the face in the sun.

The others were all smiling, all but Margaret Godfrey, and her face was in repose. The white forehead was very high, the eyes wide and expressionless; her lips were folded, the corners tilted very slightly upwards, and she was looking at the camera very much as the Gioconda had looked at Leonardo. Secrecy vied with something else in those serene features. This girl, Wexford thought, looked as if she had undergone an experience most of her fellows could never have fathomed, and it had marked her not with suffering or shame but simply with smug tranquillity.

The gym tunic was an incongruity. She could have worn a high-necked dress with puffy sleeves. Her hair, soft then, not crimped and waved as it had been later, skimmed her cheekbones and lay across her temples in two shining arcs.

Wexford glanced across to the silent Drury, now sitting some five yards from him. Then, screening it once more with his hands, he looked long at the photograph. When

Burden came in he was still gazing and his tea had grown cold.

It was almost three o'clock.

'Miss Tipping is here,' Burden said.

Wexford came out of the sunny garden, covered the snapshot with a file and said:

'Let's have her in, then.'

Janet Tipping was a plump healthy-looking girl with a cone of lacquered hair above a stupid suspicious face. When she saw Drury her expression, vacuous and uncomprehending, was unaltered.

'Well, I can't say,' she said. 'I mean, it was a long time ago.'

Not twelve years, Burden thought, only four days.

'I could have served him. I mean, I serve hundreds of fellows with bitter....' Drury stared at her, round-eyed, as if he was trying to drive recognition into her dim, tired consciousness. 'Look here,' she said, 'I don't want to get anybody hung.'

She came closer, peering, in the manner of one attracted by a monstrosity in a museum. Then she retreated, shaking her head.

'You must remember me,' Drury shouted. 'You've got to remember. I'll do anything, I'll give you anything if you'll only remember. You don't realize, this means everything to me....'

'Oh, do me a favour,' the girl said, frightened now. 'I've racked my brains and I don't remember.' She looked at Wexford and said, 'Can I go now?'

The telephone rang as Burden showed her out. He lifted the receiver and handed it to Wexford.

'Yes...yes, of course I want her brought back,' Wexford said. 'That was Martin,' he said to Burden outside. 'Mrs Drury said she bought that rain-hood on Monday afternoon.'

'That doesn't necessarily mean —' Burden began.

'No, and Drury got in after six-thirty on Tuesday. She remembers because she was waiting for the tomatoes. She wanted to put them in a salad for their tea. If he wasn't killing Mrs P., Mike, that was a hell of a long drink he had. For an innocent man he's practically crazy with terror.'

Again Burden said, 'That doesn't necessarily mean —'

'I know, I know. Mrs Parsons liked them green and goosey, didn't she?'

'I suppose there wasn't anything in the garden, was there, sir?'

'Five nails, about a hundredweight of broken bricks and a Dinky Toy Rolls-Royce,' Wexford said. 'He ought to thank us. It won't need digging in the autumn.' He paused and added, 'If he's still here in the autumn.'

They went back into the office. Drury was sitting utterly immobile, his face lard-coloured like a peeled nut.

'That was a mighty long drink, Drury,' Wexford said. 'You didn't get home till after six-thirty.'

Drury mumbled, his lips scarcely moving: 'I wanted the order. I hung about. There's a lot of traffic about at six. I'm not used to drink and I didn't dare to drive for a bit. I wanted to find Mr Spellman.'

Half a pint, Burden thought, and he didn't dare to drive? 'When did you first resume your relationship with Mrs Parsons?'

'I tell you there wasn't a relationship. I never saw her for twelve years. Then I was driving through the High Street and I stopped and spoke to her. . . .'

'You were jealous of Mr Parsons, weren't you?'

'I never met Parsons.'

'You would have been jealous of anyone Mrs Parsons had married. You didn't have to see him. I suggest you'd been meeting Mrs Parsons, taking her out in your car. She got tired of it and threatened to tell your wife.'

'Ask my wife, ask her. She'll tell you I've never been unfaithful to her. I'm happily married.'

'Your wife's on her way here, Drury. We'll ask her.

Drury had jumped each time the telephone rang. Now as it sounded again after a long lull, a great shudder passed through him and he gave a little moan. Wexford, for hours on tenterhooks, only nodded to Burden.

'I'll take it outside,' he said.

Bryant's shorthand covered the sheet of paper in swift spidery hieroglyphics. Wexford had spoken to the Colorado police chief, but now as he stood behind Bryant he could hear nothing of that thick drawl through the headphones, only watch the words fall on to paper in a tangled code.

By four it had been transcribed. His face still phlegmatic, but to Burden vital with latent excitement, Wexford read the letter again. The dead words, now coldly typed on official paper, seemed still to have the force of life, a busy bustling life led by a woman in a country backwater. Here in the depths of the night, among the office furniture and the green steel filing cabinets, Mrs Parsons was for a moment – one of the few moments in the whole case – resurrected and become a real person. There was no drama in her words and only the whisper of a small tragedy, but because of her fate the letter was a dreadful document, the only existing recorded fragment of her inner life.

Dear Nan (Wexford read),

I can picture your surprise when you read my new address. Yes, we have come back here and are living a stone's throw from school and only a few miles from the dear old cottage. We had to sell auntie's house and lost quite a bit on it, so when Ron got the chance of a job out here we thought this might be the answer. It is supposed to be cheaper living in the country, but we have not noticed it yet, I can tell you.

In spite of what you all thought, I quite liked living in Flagford. It was only you-know-what that turned me off it. Believe me, Nan, I was really scared *over that Doon business, so you can imagine I wasn't too pleased to run slap bang up against Doon again a couple of weeks*

*after we moved in. Although I'm a lot older I still feel frightened and
a bit revolted. I said it was better to let things rest but Doon will not
have this. I must say it is quite pleasant to get a few rides in a nice
comfortable car and get taken out for meals in hotels.*

*Believe me, Nan, it is as it has always been, just friendship. When
Doon and I were younger I really don't think we knew it could be
anything else. At least, I didn't. Of course the very thought disgusts me.
Doon only wants companionship but it is a bit creepy.*

*So you are going to get another new car. I wish we could afford one
but at present it is beyond our wildest dreams. I was sorry to hear about
Kim having chicken pox so soon after measles. I suppose having a family
has its drawbacks and its worries as well as its advantages. It does not
look as if Ron and I will have the anxiety or the happiness now as I
have not even had a false alarm for two years.*

*Still, I always say if you have a really happy marriage as we have,
you should not need children to keep it together. Perhaps this is just sour
grapes. Anyway, we are happy, and Ron seems much more relaxed now
we are away from town. I never will understand, Nan, why people like
Doon can't be content with what they have and not keep crying for the
moon.*

*Well, I must close now. This is quite a big house really and not
exactly filled with mod. cons.! Remember me to Wil and your offspring.
Regards from Ron.*

Love from Meg

A happy marriage? Could a marriage be happy, rocking
uneasily on a sea of deceit and subterfuge? Burden put the
letter down, then picked it up and read it again. Wexford told
him of his conversation with the police chief and his face
cleared a little.

'We'll never prove it,' Burden said.

'One thing, you can go and tell Drury Gates'll take him
home now. If he wants to sue us I daresay Dougie Q. will be
nothing loth to lend a hand. Only don't tell him that and
don't let me see him. He's upsetting my liver.'

It was beginning to grow light. The sky was grey and misty and the streets were drying. Wexford, stiff and cramped with sitting, decided to leave his car and walk home.

He liked the dawn without usually being sufficiently strong-minded to seek it unless he must. It helped him to think. No one was about. The market place seemed much larger than it did by day and a shallow puddle lay in the gutter where the buses pulled in. On the bridge he met a dog, going purpose-fully about its mysterious business, trotting quickly, head high, as if making for some definite goal. Wexford stopped for a second and looked down into the water. The big grey figure stared back at him until the wind disturbed the surface and broke up the reflection.

Past Mrs Missal's house, past the cottages. . . . He was nearly home. On the Methodist church notice-board he could just make out the red-painted letters in the increasing light: 'God needs you for his friend.' Wexford came closer and read the words on another notice pinned beneath it. 'Mr R. Parsons invites all church members and friends to a service in memory of his wife, Margaret, who died so tragically this week, to be held here on Sunday at ten a.m.'

So today, for the first time since she had died, the house in Tabard Road would be empty. . . . No, Wexford thought, Parsons was at the inquest. But, then . . . His thoughts returned to certain events of the afternoon, to laughter shut off in full spate, to a book, a fierce transposition of emotion, to a woman dressed for an assignation.

'We'll never prove it,' Burden had said.

But they could go to Tabard Road in the morning, and they could try.

My demands were modest, Minna. I wanted so little, but a few hours out of the scores of hours that make a week, infinitesimal eddies in the great ocean of eternity.

I wanted to talk, Minna, to spread at your feet the pains

and sorrows, the anguish of a decade of despair. Time, I thought, time that planes out the rough edge of cruelty, that dulls the cutting blade of contempt, that trims the frayed fringe of criticism, time will have softened her eye and made tender her ear.

It was a quiet wood we went to, a lane where we had walked long ago, but you had forgotten the flowers we had gathered, the waxen diadem of the Traveller's Joy.

I talked softly, thinking you were pondering. All the while I thought you listening and at last I paused, hungry for your gentle praise, your love at last. Yes, Minna, love. Is that so bad, so evil, if it treads in the pure garments of companionship?

I gazed, I touched your hair. Your eyes were closed for you found dull sleep more salutary than my words and I knew it was too late. Too late for love, too late for friendship, too late for anything but death. . . .

CHAPTER FOURTEEN

Such closets to search, such alcoves to importune.

Robert Browning, *Love in a Life.*

Parsons was dressed in a dark suit. His black tie, not new and worn perhaps on previous mourning occasions, showed the shiny marks of a too-hot, inexpertly handled iron. Sewn to his left sleeve was a diamond-shaped patch of black cotton.

'We'd like to go over the house again,' Burden said, 'if you wouldn't mind leaving me the key.'

'I don't care what you do,' Parsons said. 'The minister's asked me to Sunday dinner. I shan't be back till this afternoon.' He began to clear his breakfast things from the table, putting the teapot, the marmalade jar away carefully in the places the dead woman had appointed for them. Burden watched him pick up the Sunday paper, unopened and unread, and tip his toast crusts on it before depositing it in a bucket beneath the sink. I'm selling this place as soon as I can,' he said.

'My wife thought of going along to the service,' Burden said.

Parsons kept his back turned to him. He poured water from a kettle over the single cup, the saucer, the plate.

'I'm glad,' he said. 'I thought people might like to come, people who won't be able to get along to the funeral tomorrow.' The sink was stained with brown now; crumbs and tea-leaves clung along a greasy tide-mark. 'I suppose you haven't got a lead yet? On the killer, I mean.' It was grotesque. Then Burden remembered what this man had read while his wife knitted.

'Not yet.'

He dried the crockery, then his hands, on the tea towel.

'It doesn't matter,' he said wearily. 'It won't bring her back.'

It was going to be a hot day, the first really hot day of the summer. In the High Street the heat was already making water mirages, lakes that sparkled and then vanished as Burden approached; in the road where actual water had lain the night before phantom water gleamed on the tar. Cars were beginning the nose-to-tail pilgrimage to the coast and at the junction Gates was directing the traffic, his arms flailing in blue shirt sleeves. Burden felt the weight of his own jacket.

Wexford was waiting for him in his office. In spite of the open windows the air was still.

'The air conditioning works better when they're shut,' Burden suggested.

Wexford walked up and down, sniffing the sunlight.

'It feels better this way,' he said. 'We'll wait till eleven. Then we'll go.'

They found the car Wexford had expected to see, parked discreetly in a lane off the Kingsbrook Road near where it joined the top end of Tabard Road.

'Thank God,' Wexford said almost piously. 'So far so good.

Parsons had given them the back-door key and they let themselves silently into the kitchen. Burden had thought this house would always be cold, but now, in the heat of the day, it felt stuffy and smelt of stale food and frowsty unwashed linen.

The silence was absolute. Wexford went into the hall, Burden following. They trod carefully lest the old boards should betray them. Parsons' jacket and raincoat hung on the hallstand, and on the little square table among a pile of circulars, a dirty handkerchief and a heap of slit envelopes, something gleamed. Burden came closer and stared, knowing better than to touch it. He pushed the other things aside and

135

together they looked at a key with a horseshoe charm on the end of a silver chain.

'In here,' Wexford whispered, mouthing the words and making no sound.

Mrs Parsons' drawing-room was hot and dusty, but nothing was out of place. Wexford's searchers had replaced everything as they had found it, even to the vase of plastic roses that screened the grate. The sun, streaming through closed windows, showed a myriad dance of dust particles in its shafts. Otherwise all was still.

Wexford and Burden stood behind the door, waiting. It seemed like an age before anything happened at all. Then, when it did, Burden could hardly believe his eyes.

The bay window revealed a segment of deserted street, bright grey in the strong light and sharply cut by the short shadows of trees in the gardens opposite. There was no colour apart from this grey and sunlit green. Then, from the right-hand side, as if into a film shot, a woman appeared walking quickly. She was as gaudy as a kingfisher, a technicolor queen in orange and jade. Her hair, a shade darker than her shirt, swung across her face like heavy drapery. She pushed open the gate, her nails ten garnets on the peeling wood, and scuttled out of sight towards the back door. Helen Missal had come at last to her schoolfellow's house.

Wexford laid his finger unnecessarily to his lips. He gazed upwards at the ornate ceiling. From high above them came a faint footfall. Someone else had heard the high heels of their visitor.

Through the crack between the door and its frame, a quarter-inch-wide slit, Burden could see a knife-edge section of staircase. Up till now it had been empty, a vertical line of wallpaper above wooden banister. He felt the sweat start in his armpits. A stair squeaked and at the same moment a hinge gave a soft moan as the back door swung open.

Burden kept his eyes on the bright, sword-like line. He

tensed, scarcely daring to breathe, as the wallpaper and the wood were for a second obscured by a flash of black hair, dark cheek, white shirt shadowed with blue. Then, no more. He was not even certain where the two met, but it was not far from where he stood, and he felt rather than heard their meeting, so heavy and so desperate had the silence become.

Four people alone in the heat. Burden found himself praying that he could keep as still and at the same time as alert as Wexford. At last the heels tapped again. They had moved into the dining-room.

It was the man who spoke first and Burden had to strain to hear what he said. His voice was low and held under taut control.

'You should never have come here,' Douglas Quadrant said.

'I had to see you.' She spoke with loud urgency. 'You said you'd meet me yesterday, but you never came. You could have come, Douglas.'

'I couldn't get away. I was going to, but Wexford came.' His voice died away and the rest of the sentence went unheard.

'Afterwards you could. I know, I met him.'

In the drawing-room Wexford made a small movement of satisfaction as another loose end was tied.

'I thought . . .' They heard her give a nervous laugh, 'I thought I'd said too much. I almost did . . .'

'You shouldn't have said anything.'

'I didn't. I stopped myself. Douglas, you're hurting me!'

His reply was something savage, something they couldn't hear.

Helen Missal was taking no pains to keep her voice down and Burden wondered why one of them should show so much caution, the other hardly any.

'Why have you come here? What are you looking for?'

'You knew I would come. When you telephoned me last night and told me Parsons would be out, you knew it. . . .

They heard her moving about the room and Burden imagined the little straight nose curling in disgust, the fingers outstretched to the shabby cushions, drawing lines in the dust on the galleried sideboard. Her laughter, disdainful and quite humourless, was a surprise.

'Have you ever seen such a horrible house? Fancy, she lived here, she actually lived here. Little Meg Godfrey....'

It was then that his control snapped and, caution forgotten, he shouted aloud.

'I hated her! My God, Helen, how I hated her! I never saw her, not till this week, but it was she who made my life what it was.' The ornaments on the tiered shelves rattled and Burden guessed that Quadrant was leaning against the sideboard, near enough for him to touch him but for the intervening wall. 'I didn't want her to die, but I'm glad she's dead!'

'Darling!' They heard nothing, but Burden knew as if he could see her that she was clinging to Quadrant now, her arms around his neck. 'Let's go away now. Please. There's nothing here for you.'

He had shaken her off violently. The little cry she gave told them that, and the slithering sound of a chair skidding across lino.

'I'm going back upstairs,' Quadrant said, 'and you must go. Now, Helen. You're as conspicuous in that get-up as ...' They heard him pause, picking a metaphor, '... as a parrot in a dovecote.'

She seemed to stagger out, crippled both by her heels and his rejection. Burden, catching momentary sight of flame and blue through the door crack, made a tiny movement, but Wexford's fingers closed on his arm. Above them in the silent house someone was impatient with waiting. The books crashing to the floor two storeys up sounded like thunder when the storm is directly overhead.

Douglas Quadrant heard it too. He leapt for the stairs, but Wexford reached them first, and they confronted each other in the hall. Helen Missal screamed and flung her arm across her mouth.

'Oh God!' she cried, 'Why wouldn't you come when I told you?'

'No one is going anywhere, Mrs Missal,' Wexford said, 'except upstairs.' He picked up the key in his handkerchief.

Quadrant was immobile now, arm raised, for all the world, Burden thought, like a fencer in his white shirt, a hunter hunted and snared. His face was blank. He stared at Wexford for a moment and closed his eyes.

At last he said, 'Shall we go, then?'

They ascended slowly, Wexford leading, Burden at the rear. It was a ridiculous procession, Burden thought. Taking their time, hands to the banister, they were like a troop of house hunters with an order to view or relatives bidden upstairs to visit the bedridden.

At the first turn Wexford said:

'I think we will all go into the room where Minna kept her books, the books that Doon gave her. The case began here in this house and perhaps there will be some kind of poetic justice in ending it here. But the poetry books have gone, Mr Quadrant. As Mrs Missal said, there is nothing here for you.'

He said no more, but the sounds from above had grown louder. Then, as Wexford put his hand to the door of the little room where he and Burden had read the poetry aloud, a faint sigh came from the other side.

The attic floor was littered with books, some open and slammed face-downwards, others on their spines, their pages spread in fans and their covers ripped. One had come to rest against a wall as if it had been flung there and had fallen open at an illustration of a pigtailed girl with a hockey stick. Quadrant's wife knelt among the chaos, clutching a fistful of crumpled coloured paper.

When the door opened and she saw Wexford she seemed

to make an immense effort to behave as if this were her home, as if she was hunting in her own attic and the four who entered were unexpected guests. For a second Burden had the fantastic notion that she would attempt to shake hands. But no words came and her hands seemed paralysed. She began to back away from them and towards the window, gradually raising her arms and pressing her be-ringed fingers against her cheeks. As she moved her heels caught one of the scattered books, a girls' annual, and she stumbled, half falling across the larger of the two trunks. A star-shaped mark showed on her cheek-bone where a ring had dug into the flesh.

She lay where she had fallen until Quadrant stepped forward and lifted her against him. Then she moaned softly and turned her face, hiding it in his shoulder.

In the doorway Helen Missal stamped and said, 'I want to go home!'

'Will you close the door, Inspector Burden?' Wexford went to the tiny window and unlatched it as calmly as if he was in his own office. 'I think we'll have some air,' he said.

It was a tiny shoe-box of a room and khaki-coloured like the interior of a shoe-box. There was no breeze but the casement swung open to let in a more wholesome heat.

'I'm afraid there isn't much room,' Wexford said like an apologetic host. 'Inspector Burden and I will stand and you, Mrs Missal, can sit on the other trunk.'

To Burden's astonishment she obeyed him. He saw that she was keeping her eyes on the Chief Inspector's face like a subject under hypnosis. She had grown very white and suddenly looked much more than her actual age. The red hair might have been a wig bedizening a middle-aged woman.

Quadrant had been silent, nursing his wife as if she were a fractious child. Now he said with something of his former scorn:

'Sûreté methods, Chief Inspector? How very melodramatic.'

Wexford ignored him. He stood by the window, his face outlined against clear blue.

'I'm going to tell you a love story,' he said, 'the story of Doon and Minna.' Nobody moved but Quadrant. He reached for his jacket on the trunk where Helen Missal sat, took a gold case from the pocket and lit a cigarette with a match. 'When Margaret Godfrey first came here,' Wexford began, 'she was sixteen. She'd been brought up by old-fashioned people and as a result she appeared prim and shockable. Far from being the London girl come to startle the provinces, she was a suburban orphan thrown on the sophisticated county. Isn't that so, Mrs Missal?'

'You can put it that way if you like.'

'In order to hide her gaucheness she put on a curious manner, a manner compounded of secretiveness, remoteness, primness. To a lover these can make up a fascinating mixture. They fascinated Doon.

'Doon was rich and clever and good-looking. I don't doubt that for a time Minna – that's the name Doon gave her and I shall refer to her by it – Minna was bowled over. Doon could give her things she could never have afforded to buy and so for a time Doon could buy her love or rather her companionship; for this was a love of the mind and nothing physical entered into it.'

Quadrant smoked fiercely. He inhaled deeply and the cigarette end glowed.

'I have said Doon was clever,' Wexford went on. 'Perhaps I should add that brilliance of intellect doesn't always go with self-sufficiency. So it was with Doon. Success, the flowering of ambition, actual achievement depended in this case on close contact with the chosen one – Minna. But Minna was only waiting, biding her time. Because, you see...' He looked at the three people slowly and severally. '...You *know* that Doon, in spite of the wealth, the intellect, the good looks, had one insurmountable disadvantage, a disadvantage greater than any deformity, particularly to a woman of Minna's background, that no amount of time or changed circumstances could alter.'

Helen Missal nodded sharply, her eyes alight with memory. Leaning against her husband, Fabia Quadrant was crying softly.

'So when Dudley Drury came along she dropped Doon without a backward glance. All the expensive books Doon had given her she hid in a trunk and she never looked at them again. Drury was dull and ordinary – callow is the word, isn't it, Mrs Quadrant? Not passionate or possessive. Those are the adjectives I would apply to Doon. But Drury was without Doon's disadvantage, so Drury won.'

'She preferred me!' Burden remembered Drury's exultant cry in the middle of his interrogation.

Wexford continued:

'When Minna withdrew her love, or willingness to be loved, if you like, Doon's life was broken. To other people it had seemed just an adolescent crush, but it was real all right. At that moment, July 1951, a neurosis was set up which, though quiescent for years, flared again when she returned. With it came hope. They were no longer teenagers but mature. At last Minna might listen and befriend. But she didn't and so she had to die.'

Wexford stepped forward, coming closer to the seated man.

'So we come to you, Mr Quadrant.'

'If it wasn't for the fact that you're upsetting my wife,' Quadrant said, 'I should say that this is a splendid way of livening up a dull Sunday morning.' His voice was light and supercilious, but he flung his cigarette from him across the room and out of the open window past Burden's ear. 'Please go on.'

'When we discovered that Minna was missing – you knew we had. Your office is by the bridge and you must have seen us dragging the brook – you realized that the mud from that lane could be found in your car tyres. In order to cover yourself, for in your "peculiar position" (I quote) you knew our methods, and you had to take your car back to the lane on some legitimate pretext. It would hardly have been safe to go there during the day, but that evening you were meeting Mrs Missal —'

Helen Missal jumped up and cried, 'No, it isn't true!'

'Sit down,' Wexford said. 'Do you imagine she doesn't know about it? D'you think she didn't know about you and all the others?' He turned back to Quadrant. 'You're an arrogant man, Mr Quadrant,' he said, 'and you didn't in the least mind our knowing about your affair with Mrs Missal. If we ever connected you with the crime at all and examined your car, you could bluster a little but your reason for going to the lane was so obviously clandestine that any lies or evasions would be put down to that.

'But when you came to the wood you had to look and see, you had to make sure. I don't know what excuse you made for going into the wood . . .'

'He said he saw a Peeping Tom,' Helen Missal said bitterly.

'. . . but you did go in and because it was dark by then you struck a match to look more closely at the body. You were fascinated as well you might be and you held the match until it burnt down and Mrs Missal called out to you.

'Then you drove home. You had done what you came to do and with any luck nobody would ever connect you with Mrs Parsons. But later when I mentioned the name Doon to you – it was yesterday afternoon, wasn't it? – you remembered the books. Perhaps there were letters too – it was all so long ago. As soon as you knew Parsons would be out of the house you used the dead woman's missing key to get in, and so we found you searching for what Doon might have left behind.'

'It's all very plausible,' Quadrant said. He smoothed his wife's dishevelled hair and drew his arm more tightly around her. 'Of course, there isn't the remotest chance of your getting a conviction on that evidence, but we'll try it if you like.' He

spoke as if they were about to embark on some small strata-
gem, the means of getting home when the car has broken
down or a way of getting tactfully out of a party invitation.

'No, Mr Quadrant,' Wexford said, 'we won't waste our
time on it. You can go if you wish, but I'd prefer you to stay.
You see, Doon *loved* Minna, and although there might have
been hatred too, there would never have been contempt.
Yesterday afternoon when I asked you if you had ever known
her you laughed. That laughter was one of the few sincere
responses I got out of you and I knew then that although Doon
might have killed Minna, passion would never have turned
into ridicule.

'Moreover, at four o'clock this morning I learnt something
else. I read a letter and I knew then that you couldn't be
Doon and Drury couldn't be Doon. I learnt exactly what was
the nature of Doon's disadvantage.'

Burden knew what was coming but still he held his breath.

'Doon is a woman,' Wexford said.

CHAPTER FIFTEEN

Love not, love not! The thing you love may change,
The rosy lip may cease to smile on you;
The kindly beaming eye grow cold and strange;
The heart still warmly beat, yet not be true.

Caroline Norton, Love Not

He would have let them arrest him, would have gone with them, Burden thought, like a lamb. Now, assured of his immunity, his aplomb had gone and panic, the last emotion Burden would have associated with Quadrant, showed in his eyes.

His wife pulled herself away from him and sat up. During Wexford's long speeches she had been sobbing and her lips and eyelids were swollen. Her tears, perhaps because crying is a weakness of the young, made her look like a girl. She was wearing a yellow dress made of some expensive creaseless fabric that fell straight and smooth like a tunic. So far she had said nothing. Now she looked elated, breathless with unspoken words.

'When I knew that Doon was a woman,' Wexford said, 'almost everything fell into place. It explained so much of Mrs Parsons' secrecy, why she deceived her husband and yet could feel she wasn't deceiving him; why Drury thought she was ashamed of Doon; why in self-disgust she hid the books. . . .'

And why Mrs Katz, knowing Doon's sex but not her name, was so curious, Burden thought. It explained the letter that had puzzled them the day before. *I don't know why you should be scared. There was never anything in that.* . . . The cousin, the confidante, had known all along. For her it was no secret but a fact of which she had so long been aware that she had thought it unnecessary to tell the Colorado police chief until he had probed. Then it had come out as an artless postscript to the interview.

'Say, what is this?' he had said to Wexford. 'You figured it was a guy?'

Helen Missal had moved back into the shade. The trunk she sat on was against the wall and the sun made a brighter splash on her bright blue skirt, leaving her face in shadow. Her hands twitched in her lap and the window was reflected ten times in her mirror-like nails.

'Your behaviour was peculiar, Mrs Missal,' Wexford said. 'Firstly you lied to me in saying you didn't know Mrs Parsons. Perhaps you really didn't recognize her from the photograph. But with people like you it's so difficult to tell. You cry Wolf! so often that in the end we can only find out what actually happened from the conversation of others or by things you let slip accidentally.'

She gave him a savage glance.

'For God's sake give me one of those cigarettes, Douglas,' she said.

'I'd made up my mind that you were of no significance in this case,' Wexford went on, 'until something happened on Friday night. I came into your drawing-room and told your husband I wanted to speak to his wife. You were only annoyed but Mr Quadrant was terrified. He did something very awkward then and I could see that he was nervous. I assumed when you told me that you'd been out with him that he didn't want us to find out about it. But not a bit of it. He was almost embarrassingly forthcoming.

'So I thought and I thought and at last I realized that I'd been looking at that little scene from upside down. I remembered the exact words I'd used and who I'd been looking at . . . but we'll leave that now and pass on.

'Your old headmistress remembered you, Mrs Missal.

Everyone thought you'd go on the stage, she said. And you said the same thing. "I wanted to act!" you said. You weren't lying then. That was in 1951, the year Minna left Doon for Drury. I was working on the assumption that Doon was ambitious and her separation from Minna frustrated that ambition. If I was looking for a spoiled life I didn't have to go any further.

'In late adolescence Doon had been changed from a clever, passionate, hopeful girl into someone bitter and disillusioned. You fitted into that pattern. Your gaiety was really very brittle. Oh, yes, you had your affairs, but wasn't that consistent too? Wasn't that a way of consoling yourself for something real and true you couldn't have?'

She interrupted him then and shouted defiantly:

'So what?' She stood up and kicked one of the books so that it skimmed across the floor and struck the wall at Wexford's feet. 'You must be mad if you think I'm Doon. I wouldn't have a disgusting . . . a revolting thing like that for another woman!' Flinging back her shoulders, projecting her sex at them, she denied perversion as if it would show in some deformity of her body. 'I hate that sort of thing. It makes me feel sick! I hated it at school. I saw it all along, all the time . . .'

Wexford picked up the book she had kicked and took another from his pocket. The bloom on the pale green suède looked like dust.

'This was love,' he said quietly. Helen Missal breathed deeply. 'It wasn't disgusting or revolting. To Doon it was beautiful. Minna had only to listen and be gentle, only to be kind.' He looked out of the window as if engrossed by a flock of birds flying in leaf-shaped formation. 'Minna was only asked to go out with Doon, have lunch with her, drive around the lanes where they'd walked when they were young, listen when Doon talked about the dreams which never came to anything. Listen,' he said. 'It was like this.' His finger was in the book, in its centre. He let it fall open at the marked page and began to read:

> 'If love were what the rose is;
> And I were like the leaf,
> Our lives would grow together
> In sad or singing weather. . . .'

Fabia Quadrant moved and spoke. Her voice seemed to come from far away, adding to the stanza out of old memory:

> 'Blown fields or flowerful closes,
> Green pleasure or grey grief. . . .'

They were the first words she had uttered. Her husband seized her wrist, clamping his fingers to the thin bones. If he had only dared, Burden thought, he would have covered her mouth.

> 'If love were what the rose is,' she said,
> 'And I were like the leaf.'

She stopped on a high note, a child waiting for the applause that should have come twelve years before and now would never come. Wexford had listened, fanning himself rhythmically with the book. He took the dream from her gently and said:

'But Minna didn't listen. She was bored.' To the woman who had capped his verse he said earnestly. 'She wasn't Minna any more, you see. She was a housewife, an ex-teacher who would have liked to talk about cooking and knitting patterns with someone of her own kind.

'I'm sure you remember,' he said conversationally, 'how close it got on Tuesday afternoon. It must have been very warm in the car. Doon and Minna had had their lunch, a much bigger lunch than Minna would have had here. . . . She was bored and she fell asleep.' His voice rose but not in anger. 'I don't say she deserved to die then, but she asked for death!'

Fabia Quadrant shook off her husband's hand and came towards Wexford. She moved with dignity to the only one who had ever understood. Her husband had protected her, Burden thought, her friends had recoiled, the one she loved had only been bored. Neither laughing nor flinching, a country police-man had understood.

'She did deserve to die! She did!' She took hold of the lapels of Wexford's coat and stroked the stuff. 'I loved her so. May I tell you about it because you understand? You see, I had only my letters.' Her face was pensive now, her voice soft and unsteady. 'No books to write.' She shook her head slowly, a child rejecting a hard lesson. 'No poems. But Douglas let me write my letters, didn't you, Douglas? He was so frightened . . . .' Emotion came bubbling up, flooding across her face till her cheeks burned, and the heat from the window bathed her.

'There was nothing to be frightened of!' The words were notes in a crescendo, the last a scream. 'If only they'd let me love her . . . love her, love her . . .' She took her hands away and tore them through the crest of hair. 'Love her, love her. . . .'

'Oh God!' Quadrant said, crouching on the trunk. 'Oh God!'

'Love her, love her . . . green pleasure or grey grief . . .' She fell against Wexford and gasped into his shoulder. He put his arm around her hard, forgetting the rules, and closed the window.

Still holding her, he said to Burden: 'You can take Mrs Missal away now. See she gets home all right.'

Helen Missal drooped, a battered flower. She kept her eyes down and Burden edged her through the door, out on to the landing and down the hot dark stair. Now was not the time, but he knew Wexford must soon begin:

CHAPTER SIXTEEN

The truth is great and shall prevail.

Coventry Patmore, *Magna est Veritas*

Doon had written precisely a hundred and thirty-four letters to Minna. Not one had ever been sent or even left the Quadrants' library where, in the drawer of a writing-desk, Wexford found them that Sunday afternoon. They were wrapped in a pink scarf and beside them was a brown purse with a gilt clip. He had stood on this very spot the night before, all unknowing, his hand within inches of the scarf, the purse and these wild letters.

Scanning them quickly, Burden understood now why Doon had printed the inscriptions in Minna's books. The handwriting daunted him. It was spidery and difficult to decipher.

'Better take them away, I suppose,' he said. 'Are we going to have to read them all, sir?'

Wexford had looked more closely, sifting the significant from the more obviously insane.

'Only the first one and the last two, I fancy,' he said. 'Poor Quadrant. What a hell of a life! We'll take all this lot down to the office, Mike. I've got an uneasy feeling Nanny's listening outside the door.'

Outside, the heat and the bright light had robbed the house of character. It was like a steel engraving. Who would buy it, knowing what it had sheltered? It could become a school, Burden supposed, or an hotel or an old people's home. The aged might not care, chatting, reminiscing, watching television in the room where Fabia Quadrant had written to the woman she killed.

They crossed the lawn to their car.

' "Green pleasure and grey grief",' Wexford said. 'That just about sums this place up.'

He got into the passenger seat and they drove away.

At the police station they were all talking about it, loitering in the foyer. It was an excitement that had come just at the right moment, just when they were growing tired of remarking on the heat-wave. A murderer and a woman at that. . . . In Brighton it was one thing, Burden thought, but here! For Sergeant Camb it was making Sunday duty bearable; for green young Gates, who had almost decided to resign, it had tipped the scales in favour of his staying.

As Wexford came in, setting the doors swinging and creating a breeze out of the sultry air, they dispersed. It was as if each had suddenly been summoned to urgent business.

'Feeling the heat?' Wexford snapped. He banged into his office.

The windows had all been left open but not a paper on the desk had stirred.

'Blinds, Mike. Pull down the blinds!' Wexford threw his jacket on to a chair. 'Who in hell left the windows open? It upsets the air conditioning.'

Burden shrugged and pulled down the yellow slats. He could see that the gossip he hated had shaken Wexford into impatient rage. Tomorrow the whole town would seethe with speculation, with wisdom after the event. Somehow in the morning they were going to have to get her into the special court . . . But it was his day off. He brightened as he thought that he would take Jean to the sea.

Wexford had sat down and put the letters, thick as the manuscript of a long novel or an autobiography, Doon's autobiography, on the desk. It was shady in the office now, thin strips of light seeping through the blinds.

'D'you think he knew about it when he married her?' Burden asked. He began to sort through the letters, picking here and there on a legible phrase. He read in a kind of embarrassed wonder, ' "Truly you have broken my heart and dashed the wine cup against the wall...." '

Cooler now in temperature and temper, Wexford swivelled round in his purple chair.

'God knows,' he said. 'I reckon he always thought he was God's gift to women and marrying him would make her forget all about Minna.' He stabbed at one of the letters with his forefinger. 'I doubt whether the marriage was ever consummated.' Burden looked a little sick, but Wexford went on. ' "Even to that other dweller in my gates my flesh has been as an unlit candle...." ' He looked at Burden. 'Et cetera, et cetera. All right, Mike, it is a bit repulsive.' If it had been less hot he would have brought his fist down on the desk. Fiercely he added, 'They're going to gobble it up at the Assizes.'

'It must have been terrible for Quadrant,' Burden said. 'Hence Mrs Missal and Co.'

'I was wrong about her. Mrs Missal, I mean. She was really gone on Quadrant, mad for him. When she realized who Mrs P. was and remembered what had happened at school, she thought Quadrant had killed her. Then, of course, she connected it with his behaviour in the wood. Can't you see her, Mike? . . .' Wexford was intent yet far away. 'Can't you imagine her thinking fast when I told her who Mrs P. was? She'd have remembered how Quadrant insisted on going to that lane, how he left her in the car and when he was gone a long time she followed him, saw the match flame under the bushes, called to him perhaps. I bet he was as white as a sheet when he got back to her.

'Then I talked to her yesterday and I caught her unawares. For a split second she was going to tell me about Fabia, about all her ambitions going to pot. She would have told me, too, only Missal came in. She telephoned Quadrant, then, in the five minutes it took me to get to his house and she went out to meet him. I asked her if she was going to the cinema! He didn't turn up. Coping with Fabia, probably. She phoned him again in the evening and told him she knew Fabia was Doon, knew she had had a schoolgirl crush on Mrs P. Then he must have said he wanted to get into Parsons' house and get hold of the books, just in case we'd overlooked them. Remember, he'd never seen them – he didn't know what was in them. Mrs Missal had seen the church notice-board. It's just by her house. She told Quadrant Parsons would be out. . . .'

'And Fabia had a key to Parsons' house,' Burden said. 'The key Mrs P. left in the car before she was killed.'

'Quadrant had to protect Fabia,' Wexford said. 'He couldn't be a husband but he could be a guardian. He had to make sure no one found out what things were really like for him and her. She was mad, Mike, really crazy, and his whole livelihood would have gone up in smoke if it was known. Besides, she had the money. It's only cat's meat what he makes out of his practice compared with what she's got.

'But it's no wonder he was always sneaking off in the evenings. Apart from the fact that he's obviously highly sexed, anything was preferable to listening to interminable stories about Minna. It must have been almost intolerable.'

He stopped for a moment, recalling his two visits to the house. How long had they been married? Nine years, ten? First the hints and the apologies; then the storms of passion, the memories that refused to be crushed, the bitter resentment of a chance infatuation that had warped a life.

With terrible finesse, worse than any clumsiness, Quadrant must have tried to break the spell. Wexford wrenched his thoughts away from those attempts, feeling again the convulsions of the woman in the attic, her heart beating against his chest.

Burden, whose knowledge of the Quadrants was less personal, sensed his chief's withdrawal. He said practically:

'Then Minna came back as Mrs P. Fabia met her and they went driving together in Quadrant's car. He didn't have it on Tuesday, but she did. When she got home on Tuesday night

Fabia told him she'd killed Mrs P. What he'd always been afraid of, that her mental state would lead to violence, had actually happened. His first thought must have been to keep her out of it. She told him where the body was and he thought of the car tyres.'

'Exactly,' Wexford said, caught up once more in circumstantial detail. 'Everything I said to him in Parsons' attic was true. He went to get fresh mud in the tyres and to look at the body. Not out of curiosity or sadism – although he must have felt sadistic towards Mrs P. and curious, by God! – but simply to satisfy himself that she *was* there. For all we know Fabia wasn't always lucid. Then Mrs Missal dropped her lipstick. She's what Quadrant calls a happy-go-lucky girl and that was just carelessness.

'He hoped we wouldn't get around to questioning Fabia, not for some time, at any rate. When I walked into Mrs Missal's drawing-room on Friday night —'

'You spoke to Missal,' Burden interrupted, 'but you were looking at Quadrant because we were both surprised to see him there. You said, "I'd like a word with your wife," and Quadrant thought you were speaking to him.'

'I was suspicious of him until yesterday afternoon,' Wexford said. 'Then when I asked him if he'd known Mrs P. and he laughed I knew he wasn't Doon. I said his laughter made me go cold and no wonder. There was a lot in that laugh, Mike. He'd seen Mrs P. dead and he'd seen her photograph in the paper. He must have felt pretty bitter when he thought of what it was that had driven his wife out of her mind and wrecked his marriage.'

'He said he'd never seen her alive,' Burden said. 'I wonder why not? I wonder why he didn't try to see her.'

Wexford reflected. He folded the scarf and put it away with the purse and the key. In the drawer his fingers touched something smooth and shiny.

'Perhaps he didn't dare,' he said. 'Perhaps he was afraid

of what he might do. . . .' He took the photograph out, but Burden was preoccupied, looking at another, the one Parsons had given them.

'They say love is blind,' Burden said. 'What did Fabia ever see in her?'

'She wasn't always like that,' Wexford said. 'Can't you imagine that a rich, clever, beautiful girl like Fabia was, might have found just the foil she was looking for in that . . .' He changed the pictures over, subtracting twelve years. 'Your pal, Miss Clarke, brought me this,' he said. 'It gave me a few ideas before we ever heard from Colorado.'

Margaret Godfrey was one of five girls on the stone seat and she sat in the middle of the row. Those who stood behind rested their hands on the shoulders of the seated. Burden counted twelve faces. The others were all smiling but her face was in repose. The white forehead was very high, the eyes wide and expressionless. Her lips were folded, the corners tilted very slightly upwards, and she was looking at the camera very much as the Gioconda had looked at Leonardo . . .

Burden picked out Helen Missal, her hair in outmoded sausage curls; Clare Clarke with plaits. All except Fabia Quadrant were staring at the camera. She stood behind the girl she had loved, looking down at a palm turned uppermost, at a hand dropping, pulled away from her own. She too was smiling but her brows had drawn together and the hand that had held and caressed hung barren against her friend's sleeve. Burden gazed, aware that chance had furnished them with a record of the first cloud on the face of love.

'Just one more thing,' he said. 'When you saw Mrs Quadrant yesterday you said she was reading. I wondered if . . . I wondered what the book was.'

Wexford grinned, breaking the mood. 'Science fiction,' he said. 'People are inconsistent.'

Then they pulled their chairs closer to the desk, spread the letters before them and began to read.

Some Lie
and
Some Die

*To my son, Simon Rendell, who goes to festivals,
and my cousin, Michael Richards, who wrote the song,
this book is dedicated with love and gratitude.*

CHAPTER ONE

'But why here? Why do they have to come here? There must be thousands of places all over this country where they could go without doing anyone any harm. The Highlands for instance. I don't see why they have to come here.'

Detective Inspector Michael Burden had made these remarks, or remarks very much like them, every day for the past month. But this time his voice held a note which had not been there before, a note of bitter bewilderment. The prospect had been bad enough. The reality was now unreeling itself some thirty feet below him in Kingsmarkham High Street and he opened the window to get a better – or a more devastating look.

'There must be thousands of them, all coming up from Station Road. And this is only a small percentage when you consider how many more will be using other means of transport. It's an invasion. God, there's a dirty-looking great big one coming now. You know what it reminds of? That poem my Pat was doing at school. Something about a pied piper. If "pied" means what I think it does, that customer's pied all right. You should see his coat.'

The only other occupant of the room had so far made no reply to this tirade. He was a big, heavy man, the inspector's senior by two decades, being at that time of life when people hesitated to describe him as middle-aged and considered 'elderly' as the more apt epithet. His face had never been handsome. Age and a very nearly total loss of hair had not improved its pouchy outlines, but an expression that was not so much easy-going as tolerant of everything but intolerance, redeemed it and made it almost attractive. He was sitting at his rosewood desk, trying to compose a directive on crime prevention, and now, giving an impatient shake of his head, he threw down his pen.

'Anyone not in the know,' said Chief Inspector Wexford, 'would think you were talking about rats.' He pushed back his chair and got up. 'A plague of rats,' he said. 'Why can't you expand your mind a bit? They're only a bunch of kids come to enjoy themselves.'

'You'll tell a different tale when we get car burning and shop-lifting and decent citizens beaten up and – and Hell's Angels.'

'Maybe. Wait till the time comes. Here, let me have a look.'

Burden shifted grudgingly from his point of vantage and allowed Wexford a few inches of window. It was early afternoon of a perfect summer's day, June the tenth. The High Street was busy as it always was on a Friday, cars pulling into and out of parking places, women pushing prams. Striped shop awnings were down to protect shoppers from an almost Mediterranean sun, and outside the Dragon workmen sat on benches drinking beer. But it was not these people who had attracted Burden's attention. They watched the influx as avidly as he and in some cases with as much hostility.

They were pouring across the road towards the bus stop by the Baptist church, a stream of boys and girls with packs on their backs and transistors swinging from their hands. Cars, which had pulled up at the zebra crossing to let them pass, hooted in protest, but they were as ineffectual as the waves of the Red Sea against the Children of Israel. On they came not thousands perhaps, but a couple of hundred, laughing and jostling each other, singing. One of them, a boy in a tee-shirt printed with the face of Che Guevara, poked out his tongue at an angry motorist and raised two fingers.

Mostly they wore jeans. Not long since they had been at school – some still were – and they had protested hotly at the enforced wearing of uniforms. And yet now they had their own, voluntarily assumed, the uniform of denims and shirts, long hair and, in some cases, bare feet. But there were those among them making a total bid for freedom from conventional clothes, the girl in red bikini top and dirty ankle-length satin skirt, her companion sweating but happy in black leather. Towering above the rest walked the boy Burden had particularly singled out. He was a magnificent tall Negro whose hair was a burnished black bush and who had covered his bronze body from neck to ankles in a black and white pony-skin coat.

'And that's only the beginning, sir,' said Burden when he thought Wexford had had time enough to take it all in.

'They'll be coming all night and all tomorrow. Why are you looking like that? As if you'd – well, lost something?'

'I have. My youth. I'd like to be one of them. I'd like to be swinging along out there, off to the pop festival. Wouldn't *you*?'

'No, frankly, I wouldn't. I'm sure I never would have. Those young people are going to cause a lot of trouble, make a hell of a noise and ruin the weekend for all those unfortunate citizens who live on the Sundays estate. Heaven help them, that's all I can say.' Like most people who make that remark, Burden had a lot more to say and said it, 'My parents brought me up to be considerate of the feelings of others and I'm very glad they did. A trip to the local hop on a Saturday night, maybe, and a few drinks, but to take over God knows how many acres of parkland just to indulge my tastes at the expense of others! I wouldn't have wanted it. I'd have thought I hadn't achieved enough to deserve it.'

Wexford made the noise the Victorians wrote as 'Pshaw!' 'Just because you're so bloody virtuous it doesn't mean there aren't going to be any more cakes and ale. I suppose you'll stop that boy of yours going up there?'

'I've told him he can go to Sundays tomorrow evening for two hours just to hear this Zeno Vedast, but he's got to be in by eleven. I'm not having him camp there. He's only just

fifteen. Zeno Vedast! That's not the name his godfathers and
godmothers gave him at his baptism, you can bet your life.
Jim Bloggs, more like. He comes from round here, they say.
Thank God he didn't stay. I don't understand this craze for
pop music. Why can't John play classical records?'

'Like his dad, eh? Sit at home getting a kick out of Mahler?
Oh, come off it, Mike.'

Burden said sulkily, 'Well, I admit pop music's not my
style. None of this is.'

'Your scene, Mike, your scene. Let's get the jargon right.
We're pigs and fuzz as it is. We don't have to be square as
well. Anyway, I'm sick of being an onlooker. Shall we get up
there?'

'What, now? We'll have to be there tomorrow when the
fighting and the burning starts.'

'I'm going now. You do as you like. Just one thing, Mike.
Remember the words of another Puritan — "Bethink ye, bethink ye, in the bowels of Christ, that ye may be mistaken."'

Where the Regency mansion now stands a house called Sun-
days has stood since the Norman Conquest. Why Sundays?
No one knows. Probably the name has nothing to do with the
Sabbath Day; probably — and this is the general belief — it
derives from the name of the man who built the first house,
Sir Geffroy Beauvoir de Saint Dieu.

Once the Sundays lands extended from Kingsmarkham to
Forby and beyond, but gradually fields and woodlands were
sold off, and now the house has only a small garden and a
park of a few acres. In the eyes of the preservationists Sundays
is irretrievably spoilt. Its tall cedars remain and its avenue of
hornbeams, the overgrown quarry is still untouched, but the
Italian garden is gone, Martin Silk, the present owner, grows
mushrooms in the orangery, and the view is ruined by the
newly built Sundays estate.

The Forby road skirts the park and bisects the estate. It is along here that the Forby bus runs four times a day, halting at the Sundays request stop which is outside the park gates. Wexford and Burden pulled in to a lay-by and watched the first of the young pilgrims tumble out of the two-thirty bus and hump their baggage over to the gates. These were open and on the lodge steps stood Martin Silk with half a dozen helpers ready to examine tickets. Wexford got out of the car and read the poster which was pasted over one of the gates: *The Sundays Scene, June 11th and 12th, Zeno Vadast, Betti Ho, The Verb To Be, Greatheart, The Acid, Emmanuel Ellerman.* As the busload went through and passed into the hornbeam avenue, he went up to Silk.

'Everything O.K., Mr Silk?'

Silk was a small man in late middle age with shoulder-length grey hair and the figure – at any rate, until you looked closely or saw him walk – of a boy of twenty. He was rich, eccentric, one of those people who cannot bear to relinquish their youth. 'Of course it's O.K.,' Silk said abruptly. He had no time for his own contemporaries. 'Everything will be fine if we're left alone.'

He stepped aside, turning on a big smile, to take tickets from half a dozen boys whose slogan-painted Dormobile, pink, orange and purple, had come to a stop by the lodge.

'Welcome, friends, to Sundays. Pitch your tents where you like. First come, first served. You can park the truck up by the house.'

Burden, who had joined them, watched the Dormobile career rather wildly up the avenue, music braying from its open windows.

'I hope you know what you're doing,' he said dourly. 'Beats me why you want to do it.'

'I want to do it, Inspector, because I love young people. I love their music. They've been hounded out of the Isle of Wight. No one wants them. I do. This festival is going to cost thousands and a good deal of it will come out of my pocket.

I've had to sell another bit of land to raise money and people can say what they like about that.'

Burden said hotly, 'The preservationists will have plenty to say, Mr Silk. The older residents don't want all this new building. Planning permission can be rescinded, you know.'

Seeing Silk's face grow red with anger, Wexford intervened.

'We all hope the festival's going to be a success. I know I do. I'm told Betti Ho's arriving in her own helicopter tomorrow afternoon. Is that a fact? When Silk, somewhat appeased, nodded, he went on: 'We want to keep the Hell's Angels out and try to keep trouble down to a minimum. Above all, we don't want violence, bikes set on fire and so on, the kind of thing they had at Weeley. I want to address the crowd before the concert starts, so maybe you'll allow me the use of your platform tomorrow evening. Shall we say six?'

'I don't mind as long as you don't antagonise people.' Silk greeted a group of girls, beaming on them, complimenting them on their ankle-length, vaguely Victorian gowns, approving the guitars which they wore slung from their shoulders. They giggled. At him, rather than with him, Wexford thought privately, but the encounter had the effect of putting Silk in a better temper. When the girls had wandered off into the park he said quite graciously to the policeman, 'D'you want to have a look round?'

'If you please,' said Wexford.

The encampment was to be sited on the left-hand side of the avenue where, under the limes and the cedars, a small herd of Friesians usually grazed. The cattle had been removed to pasture behind the house and the first of the tents were already up. In the midst of the park a stage had been erected, faced by arc-lamps. Wexford, who generally deplored armoured fences, was glad that Sundays park was enclosed by a spiked wall to keep what Burden called 'undesirable elements' out.

At only one point was the wall broken and this was at the side of the quarry, a deep semicircular fissure in the chalk at the Forby end. The two policemen walked up to the house, stood on the terrace and surveyed the scene.

A mobile shop selling soft drinks, crisps and chocolate had already been parked in the avenue, and a queue of hungry youth had formed alongside it. The stronger-minded were staking claims to desirable sites and banging in tent pegs. Through the gates came a thin but steady stream of new arrivals, on foot, in cars and on motor-cycles. Wexford jerked his head in the direction of the quarry and walked down the steps.

The lucky ones – those who had taken a day off work or missed a college lecture – had got there in the morning and established their camp. A boy in a Moroccan burnous was frying sausages over a calor-gas burner while his friends sat cross-legged beside him, entertaining him vocally and on a guitar. The Kingsbrook flows through Sundays park, dipping under the Forby Road and meandering between willows and alders close to the wall. It had already become a bathing place. Several campers were splashing about in the water, the girls in bras and panties, the boys in the black scants that serve as underpants or swimming trunks. Crossing the little wooden bridge, Burden looked the other way. He kept his eyes so determinedly averted that he almost fell over a couple who lay embraced in the long grass. Wexford laughed.

' "And thou," ' he said, ' "what needest with thy tribe's black tents who hast the red pavilion of my heart?" ' There's going to be a lot of that going on, Mike, so you'd best get used to it. Letts'll have to put a couple of men on that quarry if we don't want gate-crashers.'

'I don't know,' said Burden. 'You couldn't get a motorbike in that way.' He added viciously: 'Personally, I couldn't care less who gets in free to Silk's bloody festival as long as they don't make trouble.'

On the Sundays side the chalk slope fell away unwalled; on the other it was rather feebly protected by broken chestnut paling and barbed wire. Beyond the paling, beyond a narrow strip of grass, the gardens of three houses in The Pathway were visible. Each had a tall new fence with its own gate. Wexford looked down into the quarry. It was about twenty feet deep, its sides overgrown with brambles and honeysuckle and wild roses. The roses were in full bloom, thousands of flat shell-pink blossoms showing against the dark shrubby growth and the golden blaze of gorse. Here and there rose the slim silver trunks of birches. In the quarry depths was a little natural lawn of turf scattered with harebells. One of the flowers seemed to spiral up into the air, and then Wexford saw it was not a flower but a butterfly, a Chalkhill Blue, harebell-coloured, azure-winged.

'Pity they had to build those houses. It rather spoils things, doesn't it?'

Burden nodded. 'These days,' he said, 'I sometimes think you have to go about with your eyes half-closed or a permanent crick in your neck.'

'It'll still be lovely at night, though, especially if there's a moon. I'm looking forward to hearing Betti Ho. She sings those anti-pollution ballads, and if there's anything we do agree on, Mike, it's stopping pollution. You'll like Miss Ho. I must admit I want to hear this Vedast bloke do his stuff, too.'

'I get enough of him at home,' said Burden gloomily. 'John has his sickly love stuff churning out night and day.'

They turned back and walked along under the willows. A boy in the river splashed Wexford, wetting his trouser legs, and Burden shouted angrily at him, but Wexford only laughed.

CHAPTER TWO

'On the whole, they're behaving themselves very well.'

This remark was delivered by Inspector Burden on a note of incredulous astonishment as he and Wexford stood (in the words of Keats) on a little rounded hill, surveying from this eminence the *jeunesse dorée* beneath. It was Saturday night, late evening rather, the sky an inverted bowl of soft violet-blue in which the moon hung like a pearl, surrounded by bright galaxies. The light from these stars was as intense as it could be, but still insufficient, and the platform on which their own stars performed was dazzlingly illuminated, the clusters of arc-lamps like so many man-made moons.

The tents were empty, for their occupants sat or lay on the grass, blue now and pearling with dew, and the bright, bizarre clothes of this audience were muted by the moonlight, natural and artificial, to sombre tints of sapphire and smoke. And their hair was silvered, not by time but by night and the natural light of night-time. The calor-gas stoves had been extinguished, but some people had lit fires and from these arose slender spires, threads of blue melting into the deeper blue of the upper air. The whole encampment was blue-coloured, azure, jade where the parkland met the sky, tinted here and there like the plumage of a kingfisher, and the recumbent bodies of the *aficionados* were numberless dark blue shadows.

'How many, d'you reckon?' Wexford asked.

'Seventy or eighty thousand. They're not making much noise.'

> 'The moan of doves in immemorial elms
> And murmuring of innumerable bees,'

169

quoted Wexford.

'Yes, maybe I shouldn't have thought of them as rats. They're more like bees, a swarm of bees.'

The soft buzz of conversation had broken out after Betti Ho had left the stage. Wexford couldn't sort out a single word from it, but from the concentrated intense atmosphere, the sense of total accord and quietly impassioned indignation, he knew they were speaking of the songs they had just heard and were agreeing with their sentiments.

The little Chinese girl, as pretty and delicate and clean as a flower, had sung of tides of filth, of poison, of encroaching doom. It had been strange to hear such things from such lips, strange in the clear purity of this night, and yet he knew, as they all knew, that the tides were there and the poison, the ugliness of waste and the squalor of indifference. She had been called back to sing once more their favourite, the ballad of the disappearing butterflies, and she had sung it through the blue plumes of their woodsmoke while the Kingsbrook chattered a soft accompaniment.

During the songs Burden had been seen to nod in vehement endorsement, but now he was darting quick glances here and there among the prone, murmuring crowd. At last he spotted his son with a group of other schoolboys, and he relaxed. But it was Wexford who noted the small additions John and his friends had made to their dress, the little tent they had put up, so that they would appear to conform with the crowd and not be stamped as mere local tyros, day boys and not experienced boarders.

Burden swatted at a gnat which had alighted on his wrist and at the same time caught sight of his watch.

'Vedast ought to be on soon,' he said. 'As soon as he's finished I'm going to collar John and send him straight home.'

'Spoilsport.'

The inspector was about to make a retort to this when the buzzing of the crowd suddenly increased in volume, rising to a roar of excited approval. People got up, stood, or moved nearer to the stage, the atmosphere seemed to grow tense.

'Here he comes,' said Wexford.

Zeno Vedast was announced by the disc jockey who was compèring the festival as one who needed no introductions, and when he advanced out of the shadows on to the platform the noise from the audience became one concentrated yell of joy. Rather different, Wexford thought wryly, from the chorus of 'Off, off, off . . .!' which had been their response to his own well-thought-out speech. He had been proud of that speech, tolerant and accommodating as it was, just a few words to assure them there would be no interference with their liberty, provided they behaved with restraint.

The police didn't want to spoil the festival, he had said, inserting a light joke; all they wanted was for the fans to be happy, to co-operate and not to annoy each other or the residents of Kingsmarkham. But it hadn't gone down at all well. He was a policeman and that was enough. 'Off, off, off,' they had shouted and 'Out, fuzz, out.' He hadn't been at all nervous but he had wondered what next. There hadn't been any next. Happily, law-abidingly, they were doing their own thing, listening to their own music in the blue and opalescent night.

Now they were roaring for Vedast and at him. The sound of their voices, their rhythmically clapping hands, their drumming feet, assailed him in a tide and seemed to wash over him as might a wave of floodwater. And he stood still in the white ambience, receiving the tide of tribute, his head bent, his bright hair hanging half over his face like a hood of silver cloth.

Then, suddenly, he flung back his head and held up one hand. The roar died, the clamour softened to a patter, dwindled into silence. Out of the silence a girl's voice called, 'Zeno, we love you!' He smiled. Someone came up to the stage and handed him a bulbous stringed instrument. He struck a single, low, pulsating note from it, a note which had an esoteric meaning for the crowd, for a gentle sigh arose from it, a murmur of satisfaction. They knew what he was going to sing first, that single note had told them and, after a rustle of contentment, a ripple of happiness that seemed to travel through all eighty thousand of them, they settled down to listen to what that note had betokened.

'It's called "Let-me-believe",' whispered Burden. 'John's got it on an L.P.' He added rather gloomily: 'We know it better than the National Anthem in our house.'

'I don't know it,' said Wexford.

Vedast struck the single note again and began immediately to sing. The song was about love; about, as far as Wexford could gather, a girl going to her lover's or her husband's house and not loving him enough or something and things going wrong. A not unfamiliar theme. Vedast sang in a clear low voice, face deadpan, but they didn't let him get beyond the first line. They roared and drummed again; again he stood silent with head bent; again he lifted his head and struck the note. This time they let him complete it, interrupting only with a buzzing murmur of appreciation when his voice rose an octave for the second verse.

'Remember me and my life-without-life,
Come once more to be my wife,
Come today before I grieve,
Enter the web of let-me-believe . . .'

The melody was that of a folk-song, catchy, tuneful, melancholy, as befitted the lyric and the tender beauty of the night. And the voice suited it utterly, an untrained, clear tenor. Vedast seemed to have perfect pitch. His face was bony with a big nose and wide mobile mouth, the skin pallid in the moonlight, the eyes very pale in colour, perhaps a light hazel or a glaucous green. The long, almost skeletal, fingers drew not an accompaniment proper, not a tune, from the strings, but a series of isolated vibrant notes that seemed to twang into Wexford's brain and make his head swim.

'So come by, come nigh,
come try and tell why
some sigh, some cry,
some lie and some die.'

When he had finished he waited for the tide to roar over him again, and it came, pounding from and through the crowd, a river of acclaim. He stood limply, bathing in the applause, until three musicians joined him on the stage and the first chords from their instruments cut into the tumult. Vedast sang another ballad, this time about children at a fair, and then another love-song. Although he hadn't gyrated or thrown himself about, his chest, bare and bead-hung, glistened with sweat. At the end of the third song he again stood almost limply, sensitively, as if his whole heart and soul were exposed to the audience, the clapping, the roaring, flagellating him. Why then, Wexford wondered, did he feel that, for all the man's intensity, his simplicity, his earnestness, the impression he gave was not one of sincerity? Perhaps it was just that he was getting old and cynical, inclined to suspect all entertainers of having one eye on the publicity and the other on the money.

But he hadn't thought that of Betti Ho. He had preferred her childlike bawling and her righteous anger. Still, he must be wrong. To judge from the noise the crowd was making as their idol left that stage, he was alone in his opinion, apart, of course, from Burden, who had been determined from the start to like nothing and who was already off in search of John.

'God, when I think of my own youth,' said Wexford as they strolled towards an open space where a van had arrived selling hot dogs. 'When I think of the prevalent attitude that it was somehow *wrong* to be young. We couldn't wait to be older so that we could compete with the old superior ruling people. They used to say, "You wouldn't understand at your age, you're too young." Now it's the young people who know everything, who make the fashions of speech and manners and clothes, and the old ones who are too old to understand.'

'Hum,' said Burden.

'We're two nations again now. Not so much the rich and the poor as the young and the old. Want a hot dog?'

'May as well.' Burden joined the queue, coldly disregarding the hostile glances he got, and bought two hot dogs from a boy in a striped apron. 'Thanks very much.'

'Thank *you*, dad,' said the boy.

Wexford laughed gleefully. 'You poor old dodderer,' he said. 'I hope your ancient teeth are up to eating this thing. How d'you like being contemporary?' He pushed through the queue towards a stand selling soft drinks. 'Excuse me!'

'Mind who you're shoving, grandad,' said a girl.

Now it was Burden's turn to laugh. 'Contemporary? We're three nations, young, old and middle and always will be. Shall we go and look at the quarry?'

There was to be no more live music for an hour. People had got down to cooking or buying their evening meals in earnest now. A strong smell of frying rose and little wisps of smoke. Already boys and girls could be seen dressed in red and yellow tee-shirts, stamped with the words 'Sundays Scene' on chest and sleeves. The arc-lamps' range wasn't great enough to reach the river, but as the night deepened, the moon had grown very bright. No one was bathing in the clear shallow water, but bathers had left evidence behind them, trunks and bras and jeans spread over the parapet of the bridge to dry.

They walked round the rim of the quarry, brambles catching at their ankles, the tiny, newly formed berries of the wayfarer's tree occasionally tapping their faces, berries which felt like ice-cold glass beads.

The place seemed to be entirely empty, but on the estate side the barbed wire had been cut and broken down. The twisted metal gleamed bright silver in the moonlight. Neither Wexford nor Burden could remember if the wire had been like that yesterday. It didn't seem important. They strolled along, not speaking, enjoying the loveliness of the night, the scent of meadowsweet, the gentle, keening music coming from far away.

Suddenly a gate opened in the fence of the last house in The Pathway and a man came out. He was a tall man with a hard, handsome face and he looked cross.

'Are you by any chance running this' – he sought for an appropriate word – 'this rave-up?'

'I beg your pardon?' said Wexford.

The man said rudely. 'You look too superannuated to be audience.'

'We're police officers. Is anything wrong?'

'*Wrong*? Yes, plenty's wrong. My name's Peveril. I live there.' He pointed back at the house whose garden gate he had come from. 'There's been an unholy racket going on for twenty-four hours now and the pace has hotted up revoltingly in the past three. I've been attempting to work, but that's quite impossible. What are you going to do about it?'

'Nothing, Mr Peveril, provided no one breaks the law.' Wexford put his head on one side. 'I can't hear anything at present, apart from a distant hum.'

'Then you must be going deaf. The trees muffle the noise down here. I don't know what use you think you're being here. You ought to hear it from my studio.'

'You were warned in plenty of time, sir. It'll all be over tomorrow. We did advise people who live near Sundays and who felt apprehensive about the festival to notify us of their intention and go away for the weekend.'

'Yes, and have their homes broken into by teenage layabouts. Experience ought to have taught me not to expect decency

from you people. You're not even in the thick of it.' Peveril
went back into his garden and banged the gate.

'We ought to have asked him if he'd seen any interlopers,'
said Burden, grinning.

'Everyone's an interloper to him.'

Wexford sniffed the air appreciatively. He lived in country
air, he was used to it. For years he had never troubled to
savour it, but he did now, not being sure how much longer it
would last. The night was bringing its humidity, little mists
lying low on the turf, wisps of whiteness drifting over the
quarry walls. A hare started from a tangle of dog roses, stared
at them briefly and fled across the wide silver meadow, gawky
legs flying.

'Listen,' Wexford whispered. 'The nightingale . . .'

But Burden wasn't listening. He had stopped to glance into
the brake from which the hare had come, had looked further
down, done a double take, and turned, his face red.

'Look at that! It really is a bit much. Apart from being –
well, disgusting, it happens to be against the law. This, after
all, is a public place.'

The couple hadn't been visible from the Sundays side.
They lay in a small declivity on the floor of the quarry where
the lawn dipped to form a grassy basin about the size of a
double bed. Burden had spoken in his normal voice, some
twenty feet above their heads, but the sound hadn't disturbed
the boy and girl, and Wexford recalled how Kinsey had said
that in these circumstances a gun could be fired in the vicinity
and the report pass unheard.

They were making love. They were both naked, eighteen
or nineteen years old, and of an absolute physical perfection.
Across the boy's long arched back the fern-like leaves of the
mountain ash which sheltered them scattered a lightly moving
pattern of feathery black shadows. They made no sound at all.
They were entirely engrossed in each other. And yet they
seemed at the same time to be one with their surroundings,

as if this setting had been made for them by some kindly god who had prepared it and waited yearningly for the lovers to come and make it complete.

The boy's hair was long, curly and golden, the girl's black and spread, her face cut crystal in the moonlight. Wexford watched them. He could not take his eyes away. There was nothing of voyeurism in the fascination they had for him and he felt no erotic stimulus. A cold atavistic chill invaded him, a kind of primeval awe. Bathed by the moonlight, enfolded by the violet night, they were Adam and Eve, Venus and Adonis, a man and woman alone at the beginning of the world. Silver flesh entwined, encanopied by an ever-moving, shivering embroidery of leaf shadows, they were so beautiful and their beauty so agonising, that Wexford felt enter into him that true panic, the pressure of procreating, urgent nature, that is the presence of the god.

He shivered. He whispered to Burden, as if parodying the other's words. 'Come away. This is a private place.'

They wouldn't have heard him if he had shouted, any more than they heard the sudden throb which thundered from the stage and then the thumping, yelling, screaming tumult as The Verb To Be broke into song.

CHAPTER THREE

There had been no trouble. A party of Hell's Angels had come to Sundays gates and been turned away. The walls were not high enough to keep them out but they kept out their bikes. A tent had caught fire. There was no question of arson. Someone had lit a fire too close to the canvas and Silk had housed the dispossessed owners in one of his spare bedrooms.

The singing went on most of the night, the keening swell, the thunderous roars of it, audible as far as away as Forby, and calls from outraged residents – Peveril among them – came steadily into Kingsmarkham police station. By dawn all was silent and most people asleep. The fires had been stamped out and the arc-lamps switched off as the sun came up to shine on Sundays through a golden haze.

The day promised to be less hot, but it was still very warm, warm enough for the campers to bathe in the Kingsbrook and queue up afterwards for ice-cream. By noon the vendors of food and drink and souvenirs had parked their vans all the way up the avenue. The canned music and the music made by little amateur groups ceased and Emmanuel Ellerman opened the second day of the concert with his hit song, 'High Tide'. The mist which had lain close to the ground at dawn had risen to lie as a blanket of cloud through which the sun gleamed palely. It was sultry and the atmosphere made people breathless.

Burden's son John had been allowed to return and hear Zeno Vedast sing for the last time. He kept out of his father's way, embarrassed in this society to have a policeman for a parent. Burden sniffed the air suspiciously as he and Wexford walked about the encampment.

'That smell is pot.'

'We've got enough to think about here without indulging in drug swoops,' said Wexford. 'The Chief Constable says to turn a blind eye unless we see anyone actually high and whooping about or jumping over the quarry because he's full of acid. I wish I could appreciate the noise those musicians are making but it's no good, I can't. I'm too bloody old. They've finished. I wonder who's next?'

'They all sound the same to me.' Burden kept looking for his son, fearing perhaps that he was being corrupted into taking drugs, making love or growing his hair. 'And they all look the same.'

'Do stop fretting about that boy of yours. That's not him you're looking at, anyway. I saw him go off to the hamburger stall just now. Hear that noise? That'll be Betti Ho's helicopter come to fetch her away.'

The bright yellow helicopter, like a gigantic insect in a horror film, hovered and spun and finally plopped into the field behind the house. The two policemen watched it come down and then joined the stream of people passing through the gate into the field. The Chinese singer wore a yellow dress – to match her aircraft? – and her black hair in a pigtail.

'What money she must get,' said Burden. 'I won't say *earn*.'

'She makes people think. She does a lot of good. I'd rather she had it than some of these politicians. There's your John, come to see the take-off. Now, don't go to him. Leave him alone. He's enjoying himself.'

'I wasn't going to. I'm not so daft I don't realise he doesn't want to know me here. There's Vedast. God, it's like the end of a state visit.'

Wexford didn't think it was much like that. A thousand or so of the fans had massed round the helicopter while Betti Ho stood in the midst of a circle of others, talking to Vedast who wore black jeans and whose chest was still bare. There was another girl with them and Vedast had his arm round her waist. Wexford moved closer to get a better look at her, for of all the striking, bizarre and strangely dressed people he had seen since Friday, she was the most fantastic.

She was nearly as tall as Vedast and good-looking in the flashy, highly coloured fashion of a beauty queen. It seemed to Wexford impossible that anyone could naturally possess so much hair, a frothy, bouffant mane of ice-blonde hair that bubbled all over her head and flowed nearly to her waist. Her figure was perfect. He told himself that it would need to be not to look ridiculous in skin-tight vest and hot pants of knitted string, principal-boy boots, thigh-high in gilt leather. From where he stood, twenty yards from her, he could see her eyelashes and see too that she wore tiny rainbow brilliants studded on to her eyelids.

'I wonder who that is?' he said to Burden.

'She's called Nell Tate,' said Burden surprisingly. 'Married to Vedast's road manager.'

'Looks as if she ought to be married to Vedast. How do *you* know, anyway?'

'How d'you think, sir? John told me. Sometimes I wish pop was an O Level subject, I can tell you.'

Wexford laughed. He could hardly take his eyes off the girl, and this was not because she attracted him or even because he admired her looks – he didn't. What intrigued him was contemplating for a moment the life her appearance advertised, a life and way of life utterly remote, he imagined, from anything he had ever known or, come to that, anything the majority of these fans had ever known. It was said that Vedast was a local boy made good. Where did she come from? What strange ladder had she climbed to find herself here and now the cynosure of so many eyes, embraced in public by the darling of the 'scene'?

Vedast withdrew his arm and kissed Betti Ho on both cheeks. It was the continental statesman's salute that has become the 'in' thing for a certain élite. Betti turned to Nell Tate and they too kissed. Then the Chinese girl climbed into her helicopter and the doors were closed.

'Things'll break up soon,' said Burden. 'What time is it?'

'Half four. The air's very heavy. Going to be a storm.'

'I wouldn't like to be in that thing in a storm.'

The aircraft buzzed and whirred and rose. Betti Ho leaned out and waved a yellow silk arm. The fans began to drift back towards Sundays park, drawn by the sound of amplified guitars. The Greatheart, a three-man group, had taken the stage. Burden, listening to them, began to show his first signs of approval since the beginning of the concert. The Greatheart made a speciality of singing parodies of wartime hits, but Burden didn't yet know they were parodies and a half-sentimental, half-suspicious smile twitched his lips.

Martin Silk was sitting on a camp-stool by the ashes of a dead fire talking to the boy in the magpie coat. It was too warm and humid to wear a jacket, let alone a fur coat, but the boy hadn't taken it off, as far as Wexford had noticed, since his arrival. Perhaps his dark bronze skin was accustomed to more tropical skies.

'Not a spot of trouble, you see,' said Silk, looking up.

'I wouldn't quite say that. There was that fire. Someone's reported a stolen bike and the bloke selling tee-shirts has had a hell of a lot pinched.'

'It's quite O.K. to nick things from *entrepreneurs*,' said the magpie boy in a mild, soft voice.

'In your philosophy, maybe. If and when it ever becomes the law of the land I'll go along with you.'

'It will, man, it will. Come the revolution.'

Wexford hadn't actually heard anyone speak seriously of the promised revolution as a foreseeable thing since he was himself a teenager in the early thirties. Apparently they were still on the same old kick. 'But then,' he said, 'there won't be any *entrepreneurs*, will there?'

The magpie boy made no reply but merely smiled very kindly. 'Louis,' said Silk proudly, 'is reading philosophy at the

181

University of the South. He has a remarkable political theory of his own. He is quite prepared to go to prison for his beliefs.'

'Well, he won't for his beliefs,' said Wexford. 'Not, that is, unless he breaches the peace with them.'

'Louis is the eldest son of a paramount chief. One day Louis Mbowele will be a name to be reckoned with in the emerging African states.'

'I shouldn't be at all surprised,' said Wexford sincerely. In his mind's eye he could see future headlines, blood, disaster, tyranny, and all well meant. 'Philosophy doctorate, political theory, British prison – he'll soon have all the qualifications. Good luck. Remember me when thou comest into thy kingdom.'

'Peace be with you,' said the African gravely.

Burden was standing with Superintendent Letts of the uniformed branch.

'Nearly all over, Reg,' said Letts.

'Yes. I don't want to be mean, but I'd like it soon to be over. All done and trouble-free.'

'Before the storm comes too. It'll be hell getting this lot off the park in a downpour.'

Above the roof of Sundays house the sky had deepened to indigo. And the house itself was bathed in livid light, that wan, spectral light that gleams under cloud canopies before a storm. The hornbeams in the avenue, stolid, conical trees, were too stocky to sway much in the rising breeze, but the low broom-like branches of the cedars had begun to sweep and sigh against the turf and, up by the house, the conifers shivered.

It was a hot wind, though, and when Zeno Vedast walked on to the stage he was still half-naked. He sang the 'Let-me-believe' ballad again to a silent crowd made tense by the stifling, thick air.

Wexford, who had once more wandered a little apart so that he was close by the scaffolding of the stage, found himself standing beside Nell Tate. Vedast was singing unaccompanied this time and she held his mandoline or ocarina or whatever it was. There was nothing exceptional in the fact that her eyes were fixed on the singer. So were seventy or eighty thousand other pairs of eyes. But whereas the rest showed enthusiasm, admiration, critical appreciation, hers were hungrily intense. Her gleaming mulberry-coloured lips were parted and she held her head slightly back in a yearning, swan-like curve. A little bored by the song, Wexford amused himself in watching her and then, suddenly, she turned and looked him full in the face.

He was shocked. Her expression was tragic, despairing, as if she had been and was for ever to be bitterly deprived of what she most wanted. Misery showed through the plastered biscuit make-up, the rosy blusher, the green and blue eyelid paint, and showed in spite of the absurd twinkling brilliants stuck about her eyes. He wondered why. She was older than he had thought at first but still only about twenty-eight. Was she in love with Vedast and unable to have him? That seemed improbable, for when Vedast had finished his first song he stepped over to the edge of the stage, squatted down and, in taking the stringed thing from Nell's hand, kissed her impulsively, but slowly and passionately, on the mouth. Vedast began singing again and now Wexford saw that she was looking calmer, the glittering lids closed briefly over her eyes.

'Is that the lot?' he asked, going back to Burden. 'I mean, is the concert over?'

Burden slipped unprotestingly into his role as pop expert, though a less likely or less enthusiastic authority could hardly have been found. 'Two more songs from The Greatheart,' he said, 'and then we can all go home. Some are going already. They only waited to hear the Naked Ape.'

'Fighting words, Mike, sacrilege. I thought he was rather good. There goes that pink and orange van. It's got graffiti all over it – did you see? – and someone's written on one of the doors. "This truck also available in paperback".'

The tents were coming down. Gas burners and kettles and tins of instant coffee were being thrust into kit bags, and a barefoot girl wandered vaguely about looking among the heaps of litter for the shoes she had discarded twenty-four hours before. The future leader of an emerging African state had abandoned polemics for the more prosaic pursuit of rolling up his sleeping bag. Martin Silk strolled among them, smiling with regal benignity at his young guests and rather malicious triumph at Wexford.

'You can't help feeling sorry for those Greatheart people, singing their guts out to an audience who couldn't care less. They must know they only stayed for Vedast.'

Wexford's words went unheard. 'There they are,' said Burden, 'that girl and her boy friend, the ones we saw last night. Coming straight from the quarry. Well, their little honeymoon's over. And they've had a row by the look of them or been bitten by something. It's always said there are adders on Sundays land.'

'You'd like that, wouldn't you?' Wexford snapped. 'That'd be a suitable retribution for doing what comes naturally in the Garden of Eden.' The girl and the boy showed no sign of having quarrelled, nor did either of them seem disabled. They were holding hands and running like Olympic sprinters. In a dirty and tattered version of the tee-shirt-jeans uniform, their long hair wind-blown, they had lost their primeval beauty of the night before. The magic and the wonder was all gone. They were just an ordinary young couple running, breathless and – frightened. Wexford took a step in their direction, suddenly concerned.

They stopped dead in front of him. The girl's face was white her breath laboured and choked. 'You're police, aren't you?' the boy said before Wexford could speak. 'Could you come, please? Come and see what . . .'

'In the quarry,' the girl said throatily. 'Oh, *please*. It was such a shock. There's a girl lying in the quarry and she's – she's dead. Ever so dead. Her face is – blood – horrible . . . Oh *God!*' She threw herself into the boy's arms and sobbed.

CHAPTER FOUR

She was screaming hysterically.

'You tell me,' Wexford said to the boy.

'We went to the quarry about ten minutes ago.' He talked jerkily, stammering. 'I – we – I'm with a party and Rosie's with a party and – and we shan't see each other again for a month. We wanted to be private but it's still daylight and we looked for somewhere we wouldn't be seen. Oh, Rosie, don't. Stop crying. Can't you *do something*?'

A crowd had gathered around them. Wexford spoke to a capable-looking girl. 'Take her into one of the tents and make some tea. Make it hot and strong. One of you others, find Mr Silk and see if he's got any brandy. Come along now. She'll tell you all about it. She'll want to.'

Rosie let forth a shriek. The other girl, justifying Wexford's faith in her, slapped one of the wet white cheeks. Rosie gagged and stared.

'That's better,' said Wexford. 'Into the tent with you. You'll be all right when you've had a hot drink.' He went back to the boy. 'What's your name?'

'Daniel. Daniel Somers.'

'You found a girl's body in the quarry?' Suddenly The Greatheart burst into song. 'God, I wish we could have a bit of hush. Where did you find it?'

'Under some bushes – well, sort of trees – on the side where the wire is.' Daniel shuddered, opening his eyes wide. 'There were – flies,' he said. 'Her face was all over blood and it was sort of dried and there were flies – *crawling*.'

'Come and show me.'

'Do I have to?'

'It won't take long.' Wexford said gently. 'You don't have to look at her again, only show us where she is.'

By now a fear that something had gone badly wrong had flurried the encampment on the side where they were standing, rumour 'stuffing the ears of men with false reports'. People came out of tents to stare, others raised themselves on one elbow from the ground, briefly deaf to The Greatheart. A low buzz of conversation broke out as boys and girls asked each other if this was the beginning of a drug swoop.

Daniel Somers, his face as white, his eyes as aghast as his girl friend's, seemed anxious now to get the whole thing over. He scrambled down the chalk slope and the policemen followed him in less gainly fashion. As yet there was nothing to see, nothing alarming. Under the louring grey sky, thick, purplish, not a blue rift showing, the quarry grass seemed a brighter, more livid green. Light, obliquely and strangely filtered under cloud rims, gave a vivid glow to the white faces of the wild roses and the silver undersides of birch leaves, lifting and shivering in the wind. On the little lawn the harebells shook like real bells ringing without sound.

Daniel hesitated a few feet from where a young birch grew out of a dense, man-high tangle of honeysuckle and dogwood. He shivered, himself near to hysteria.

'In there.' He pointed. 'I didn't touch her.'

Wexford nodded.

'You get back to Rosie now.'

The bushes had no thorns and were easily lifted. They surrounded the root of the tree like the fabric of a tent belling about its pole. Under them, half-curled around the root, lay the girl's body. It was somewhat in the position of a foetus, knees bent, arms folded so that the hands met under the chin.

Even Wexford's strong stomach lurched when he saw the face or what had been a face. It was a broken mass, encrusted with black blood and blacker flies which swarmed and buzzed sluggishly as the leafy covering was disturbed. Blood was in the hair too, streaking the yellow fibrous mass, matting it in places into hard knots. And blood was probably on the dark red dress, but its material, the colour of coagulated blood, had absorbed and negatived it.

The Greatheart were still performing.

'A girl's been murdered,' Wexford said to Silk. 'You must get this lot off the stage. Let me have a microphone.'

The crowd murmured angrily as the musicians broke off in the middle of a song and retreated. The murmur grew more menacing when Wexford appeared in their place. He held up one hand. It had no effect.

'Quiet please. I must have quiet.'

'Off, off, off!' they shouted.

All right. They could have it straight and see if that silenced them. 'A girl has been murdered,' he said, pitching his voice loud. 'Her body is in the quarry.' The voices died and he got the silence he wanted. 'Thank you. We don't yet know who she is. No one is to leave Sundays until I give permission. Understood?' They said nothing. He felt a deep pity for them, their festival spoiled, their eager young faces now cold and shocked. 'If anyone has missed a member of their party, a blonde girl in a red dress, will he or she please inform me?'

Silk behaved rather as if Wexford himself had killed the girl and put her in his quarry. 'Everything was going so well,' he moaned. 'Why did this have to happen? You'll see, it'll be another lever in the hands of the fuddy-duddies who want to suppress all free activity and gag young people. You see if I'm not right.' He gazed distractedly skywards at the grey massy clouds which had rolled out of the west.

Wexford turned from him to speak to a boy who touched his arm and said, 'There was a girl in our party who's disappeared. No one's seen her since this morning. We thought she'd gone home. She wasn't enjoying herself much.'

'How was she dressed?'

The boy considered and said, 'Jeans, I think, and a green top.'

'Fair hair? Mauve tights and shoes?'

'God, no. She's dark and she wasn't wearing anything like that.'

'It isn't she,' said Wexford.

The rain was coming. He had a brief nightmarish vision of rain descending in torrents on the encampment, turning the trodden grass into seas of mud, beating on the fragile tents. And all the while, throughout the night certainly, he and every policeman he could get hold of would have to interrogate wet, unhappy and perhaps panicky teenagers.

The photographers had come. He saw their car bumping over the hard turf and stop at the wooden bridge. Once she had been photographed, he could move her and perhaps begin the business of identification. He felt a dash of cold water on his hand as the first drops of rain fell.

'I've been wondering if we could get them all into the house,' said Silk.

Eighty thousand people into one house? On the other hand, it was a big house . . .

'Not possible. Don't think of it.'

Behind him a girl cleared her throat to attract his attention. Two girls stood there, one of them holding a black velvet coat.

'Yes?' he said quickly.

'We haven't seen our friend since last night. She left her coat in the tent and just went off. We can't find her or her boy friend, and I thought – we thought . . .'

'That she might be the girl we found? Describe her, please.'

'She's eighteen. Very dark hair, very pretty. She's wearing black jeans. Oh, it isn't her, is it? She's called Rosie and her boyfriend . . .'

'Is Daniel.' While the girl stared at him, round-eyed, marvelling at this omniscience, he said, 'Rosie's all right.' He pointed. 'She's over there, in that tent.'

'Thanks. God, we were really scared.'

How much more of this was there to be, he wondered,

before he had to say yes, yes, it sounds like her? Then he saw
Dr Crocker, lean, trim and energetic, stalking towards him.
The police doctor wore a white raincoat and carried an
umbrella as well as his bag.

'I've been away for the weekend, Reg, taking your people's
advice. I thought I was going to keep clear of all this. What's
it about?'

'Didn't they tell you?'

'No, only that I was wanted.'

'There's a dead girl in the quarry.'

'Is there, by God? One of *them*?' Crocker pointed vaguely
into the crowd.

'I don't know. Come and see.'

The rain was falling lightly, intermittently, the way rain
does after a drought and before a deluge, as if each drop was
being squeezed painfully out. Three police cars had succeeded
in negotiating the rough ground and were parked at the quarry
edge. In the quarry itself the photographers had completed
their work, the undergrowth had been cut away and a tar-
paulin canopy erected to screen the body from view. In spite
of this, a crowd of boys and girls squatted or lolled all round
the quarry, speculating among themselves, their eyes wide.

'Get back to your tents, the lot of you,' Wexford said.
'You'll get wet and you won't see anything.' Slowly, they began
to move. 'Come on now. Ghoulishness is for ignorant old
people. Your generation is supposed to be above this sort of
thing.'

That did it. One or two of them grinned sheepishly. By
the time Wexford and the doctor had scrambled down on to
the little lawn – the harebells trodden to a mush – the
sightseers had dispersed. Crocker knelt by the body and examined it.

'She's been dead at least five days.'

Wexford felt himself relax with relief.

'She was dead before the festival started,' said Crocker,

'and she wasn't a teenager. I'd say at least twenty-seven, maybe thirty.'

Under the canopy the flies were thick and noisy. Wexford rolled the body on to its side, revealing a large handbag of mauve patent leather which lay beneath it. Handbag, shoes and tights matched each other and clashed with the dark red dress. He opened the bag, spilling the contents on to a sheet of plastic. An envelope addressed to Miss Dawn Stonor, 23 Philimede Gardens, London, SW5, fell out. There was a letter inside it addressed from Lower Road, Kingsmarkham: *Dear Dawn, I will be glad to see you Monday but I suppose it will be one of your flying visits and you won't condesend to stop the night. Granma has had one of her bad turns but is all right again now. I got the mauve slacks and blouse from the cleaners that you left there and you can take it away with you. They charged 65p. which I will be glad of. See you Monday. Love, Mum.*

He noted the illiteracies, the badly formed writing. Something else in the letter struck in his mind, but he could think about that later. The main thing was that she had been easily and rapidly identified. 'Have the body removed,' he said to Sergeant Martin, 'and then I want the quarry searched.'

There was blood on his hand, fresh blood. How could that have come from a body five days dead? He looked again and saw that it hadn't. The blood was his own, flowing from a small wound near the base of his thumb.

'Broken glass everywhere,' he said wonderingly.

'Have you only just noticed?' Crocker gave a harsh, humourless laugh. 'You needn't bother to search for a weapon.'

They had come gaily and noisily, erupting from cars and trains and buses, arriving on a summer's day to hear music and bringing their own music with them. They left downcast, in silence, trudging through the rain. Most of them had had no more than a dozen hours of sleep throughout the weekend. Their faces were shocked and dirty and pale.

No one ran. There was no horseplay. They dismantled their wet tents, shouldered their baggage, leaving behind them greyish-white mountain ranges of rubbish. Moving towards the gates in long ragged files, they looked like refugees leaving a place of disaster. Daniel walked with Rosie, one arm embracing her, the other shouldering a rolled tent which bumped against his khaki pack. Louis Mbowele passed through the gates without looking up from the book he was reading. They chewed sweets, passed wine bottles from hand to hand in silence, indifferent in their saddened freemasonry as to who paid or who drank. Huddled together, they lit cigarettes, sheltering match flames from the downpour.

Lightning split the sky over Stowerton and the thunder rolled, grumbling in the west. From fast-travelling clouds, blue and black and roaring grey, the rain cascaded, sweeping people and their belongings into the avenue like so much debris buffeted by the tide. The cedars lifted their black arms, sleeved in spiky foliage, and slapped them, rattling up and down on what had been turf. It was turf no longer. Thousand upon thousand of strong young feet had shaved the grass to stubble, to final scorched aridity. The rain fell on to acres of brown desert.

Someone had abandoned a torn tent, a red canvas tent that bounded in the wind like a huge drowning butterfly until it became waterlogged and collapsed against the footings of the stage. The river began to fill, carrying with it as it plunged under the Forby Road a bobbing flotsam of paper, cans, transistor batteries and lost shoes.

CHAPTER FIVE

With the rain came a kind of false night, a streaming, early twilight. It drove everyone indoors, everyone, that is, but the departing young people who trudged through the downpour into Kingsmarkham. Soaked and shivering, the long processions came on towards the buses, towards the station. Some stayed behind on the Forby Road, hoping to hitch, doggedly resigned when cars passed without stopping, when motorists, put off by their draggled clothes and their long wet hair, rejected them.

They invaded the centre of the town, queueing for any bus that might come, forming dispirited lines that stretched the length of the High Street. A conglomeration of youth filled the centre, but the outskirts, the back streets, were deserted. In Lower Road where all the doors and windows were shut, every curtain drawn, rain drumming on rows of pavement-parked cars, it might have been the depths of winter. Only the roses in the front gardens of these squat red-brick council houses, the drooping foliage on cherry trees, showed that there should have been sunshine, that it was a June evening.

Number fifteen was a house just like its neighbours, a similar Dorothy Perkins trailing over the front door, its acid pink flowers clashing with ochreish red brick, similar white net curtains, draped crosswise like the bodice of a negligé, across its windows. A scaffolding of television aerials sprouted from its single chimney and juddered in the gale.

Wexford went slowly up the path. The rain was falling so heavily that he had to put up his umbrella even for this short distance from the car to the front door. He hated having to question the bereaved, hated himself for intruding on their grief and for feeling, if not showing, impatience when memories

192

overcame them and tears silenced them. He knew now that Dawn Stonor had had no father. It was a woman in the barren country of deep middle age, alone and perhaps utterly broken, he had to interview. He tapped softly on the door.

Detective Polly Davies let him in.

'How is she, Polly?'

'She's O.K., sir. There wasn't much love lost between mother and daughter, as far as I can see. Dawn hadn't lived at home for ten years.'

Dreadful to feel relief at a lack of love . . . 'I'll talk to her now.'

Mrs Stonor had been driven to the mortuary and home again in a police car. Still wearing her coat, her red straw hat on the arm of her chair, she sat in the living room, drinking tea. She was a big, florid-faced woman of fifty-five with bad varicose veins, her swollen feet crushed into court shoes.

'Do you feel up to giving me some information, Mrs Stonor? I'm afraid this has been a bad shock for you.'

'What d'you want to know?' She spoke abruptly in a shrill, harsh voice. 'I can't tell you why she was in that quarry. Made a proper mess of her, didn't he?'

Wexford wasn't shocked. He knew that in most people there is something sado-masochistic, and even the newly-bereaved have an apparently ghoulish need to dwell with pleasurable horror on the injuries inflicted on dead relatives. Whether or not they express these feelings depends on their degree of cultivated repression rather than on grief.

'Who was "he", Mrs Stonor?'

She shrugged. 'Some man. There was always some man.'

'What did she do for a living?'

'Waitress in a club. Place called the Townsman up in London, up West somewhere. I never went there.' Mrs Stonor gave him a lowering, aggressive look. 'It's for men. The girls get themselves up in daft costumes like bathing suits with skirts, showing off all they've got. "Disgusting!" I said to her. "Don't you tell me about it, I don't want to know.' Her dad would have turned in his grave if he'd known what she did.'

'She came here on Monday?'

'That's right.' She took off her coat. He saw that she was heavily built, rigidly corseted. Her face was set in grim, peevish lines, and it was hard to tell whether it was more grim and peevish than usual. 'You wouldn't find a decent girl going to that quarry with a man,' she said. 'Had he done anything to her?'

The question was grotesque between people who had seen for themselves, but he knew what she meant. 'There was no sexual assault and intercourse hadn't taken place.'

She flushed darkly. He thought she was going to protest at his fairly blunt way of speaking but instead she rushed into an account of what he wanted to know. 'She came down by train, the one that gets in at half past eleven. I'd got her dinner for her, a bit of steak. She liked that.' The harsh voice wavered a little. 'She liked her bit of steak, did Dawn. Then we chatted a bit. We hadn't really got nothing in common any more.'

'Can you tell me what you talked about?'

'Nothing about *men*, if that's what you mean. She was fed-up on account of some little kid in the train had wiped his sticky fingers down her dress. It was a new dress, one of them minis, and it showed all her legs. I said she'd have to change it and she did.'

'She put on the dark red dress she was found in?'

'No, she never. That wasn't hers. I don't know where that come from. There was a mauve thing she had here as I'd fetched from the cleaners for her – they call them trousers suits – and she put that on. She was wearing mauve shoes so it looked all right. Well, like I said, we chatted a bit and she went up to see her gran – that's my mother as lives with me – and then Dawn went off to catch the four-fifteen train. Left here just before four.'

Wexford looked thoughtful. 'You thought she was going straight back to London?'

'Of course I did. She said so. She said, I've got to be in the club by seven. She took the blue dress with her in a bag and she said she'd have to run not to miss her train.'

'Two more things, Mrs Stonor, and then I'll leave you in peace. I'd like you to describe the trouser suit, if you would.'

'Very showy, it was. More like pyjamas than something you'd wear in the street. There was slacks, sort of flared, and a kind of tunic. It was mauve nylon stuff with a bit of darker mauve round the sleeves and the bottom of the tunic. Dawn liked to dress flashy.'

'Have you a photograph of her?'

Mrs Stonor gave him a suspicious glare. 'What, got up in them clothes?'

'No. Any photograph.'

'There was a photo she sent me for Christmas. Funny idea giving your mum a photo of yourself for Christmas, I thought. You can have that if you like.'

The photograph, a studio portrait, was brought. It had never been framed and, from its pristine condition, Wexford supposed that it had never been shown with pride to Mrs Stonor's friends but kept since its arrival in a drawer. Dawn had been a heavy-featured, rather coarse-looking girl, who wore thick make-up. The blonde hair was piled into puffs and ringlets, a massy structure reminding him of the head-dresses of eighteenth-century belles or perhaps of actresses playing such parts. She wore a blue silk evening gown, very low-cut and showing a great deal of fleshy bosom and shoulder.

Mrs Stonor eyed it irritably, peevishly, and Wexford could see that it would have been a disappointing gift for a mother of her type. Dawn had been twenty-eight. To have met with maternal favour, the picture should have shown not only a daughter but grandchildren, a wedding ring on those stiffly posed fingers, and behind the group the outline of a semi-detached house, well-kept-up and bought on a mortgage.

He felt a stirring of pity for this mother who was a mother no longer, a flash of sympathy which was dissipated at once when she said as he was leaving:

'About that trouser suit . . .'

'Yes?'

'It was more or less new. She only bought it back in the winter. I mean, I know a lady who'd give me five pounds for that.'

Wexford gave her a narrow glance. He tried not to show his distaste.

'We don't know what's become of it, Mrs Stonor. Perhaps the lady would like the shoes and the bag. You can have them in due course.'

The exodus continued. By now it was dark, a windswept, starless night, the rain falling relentlessly. Wexford drove back to the Sundays estate where, on both sides of the Forby road, police cars cruised along the streets or stood parked in lakes of trembling black water. Presently Burden found him and got into the car beside him.

'Well? Anything startling?'

'Nothing much, sir. Nobody remembers seeing a girl in a red dress down here during the week. But last Monday afternoon one woman from Sundays Grove, a Mrs Lorna Clarke, says she saw a blonde girl, answering Dawn's description, but wearing a . . .'

'Mauve trouser suit?'

'That's right! So it was her? I thought it must be from Mrs Clarke talking about mauve shoes and a mauve bag. Where did the red dress come from then?'

Wexford shook his head. 'It's beginning to look as if she died on Monday. She left her mother's house just before four that afternoon. When and where did your Mrs Clarke see her?'

'She got off the five-twenty-five bus from Kingsmarkham. Mrs Clarke saw her get off the bus and cross the road towards The Pathway. A few minutes later someone else saw her in The Pathway.'

'Which backs on to the quarry. Go on.'

'There are only five houses in The Pathway, two bungalows and three proper houses. If you remember, they didn't do any more buildings down there. People made a fuss about it and the ministry reversed the decision to grant planning permission. She was next seen by a woman who lives in the last house.'

'Not the wife of that bloke who came out making a to-do on Saturday night?'

Burden nodded. 'A Mrs Peveril, sir. They're both at home all day. He's a graphic designer, works at home. His wife says she saw a blonde girl in mauve go down the road at five-thirty and enter the public footpath that goes across the fields to Stowerton. She gave a very detailed description of the trouser suit, the shoes and the bag. But, of course, I couldn't be sure it was Dawn. I couldn't understand her being dressed in mauve. Mrs Peveril says the girl was holding a brown carrier bag.'

'Mm-hm. It certainly was Dawn. She changed out of a blue dress into the mauve thing and it was obviously the blue one she was carrying in the bag. She seems to have gone in for a lot of clothes changing, doesn't she? I wonder why. No other help from The Pathway?'

'No one else saw her. Each of the bungalows has only one occupant and they were both out at the relevant time. Miss Mowler's a retired district nurse and she was out on Monday till eight. Dunsand – he's a lecturer at the University of the South, philosophy or something – didn't get home from work till after half past six. I can't find anyone else who saw her on Monday or at any other time. My guess is she picked up some bloke and made a date to meet him between Sundays and Stowerton that evening.'

'Ye-es. I expect that's it. She left her mother at four and she must have caught the five-twelve bus. There are only two buses going to Forby in the afternoon, as you know. What did she do in that spare hour and ten minutes? We'll have to find out if anyone saw her in the High Street. There's the London angle too, but I've already got wheels moving there.'

'D'you want to see Mrs Peveril?'

'Not now, Mike. I doubt if we can make much progress tonight. I'll let them finish the house-to-house. They may get something more. She may have been seen later. I don't want to speculate at this stage.'

Burden left the car and, throwing his raincoat over his head, plunged off through the rain. Wexford turned the car, moving off in low gear through the torrents, the steady downpour, glancing once at Sundays where the last dispirited stragglers were leaving the park.

CHAPTER SIX

By the morning it had been established that Mrs Margaret Peveril of number five, The Pathway, was very probably the last person to have seen Dawn Stonor alive. On Monday, June sixth, Dawn had entered the pathfields at five-thirty and disappeared. By nine Wexford and Burden were back in The Pathway. By nine also an emergency interview room had been set up in the Baptist church hall where Sergeant Martin and a team of detectives waited to talk to anyone who might have seen Dawn on the previous Monday afternoon. The photograph had been blown up to poster size ready to jog memories, and another photograph prepared, this time of Polly Davies wearing a blonde wig and dressed in clothes resembling as nearly as possible Mrs Stonor's description of the mauve suit.

The rain had stopped during the night and the town and its environs looked washed, battered, wrung out to dry. All the summer warmth had gone with the storm, leaving a cloud-splashed sourly blue sky, a high sharp wind and mid-winter temperatures.

At Sundays Martin Silk was burning litter, the accumulated detritus of eighty thousand people's weekend. A row of fires blazed just behind the wall and the wind blew acrid white smoke in clouds over the Sundays estate, the Forby road and the barren brown plain of the park. Silk's little herd of Friesians had returned to their pasture. They stood in a huddle under the cedars, bewildered by the smoke.

The Pathway was shaped like an arm with bent elbow, its shoulder the junction with the Forby road, its wrist and hand – or perhaps its one pointing finger – a footpath which ran through hilly meadows and copses to Stowerton. Three houses and two bungalows had been built along this arm, but in its crook there were only open fields. The bungalows were identical, rather large pink plastered bungalows with red tiled roofs and detached garages. They stood 'in their gardens', as estate agents put it, meaning that there are sections of garden at the sides as well as at front and back. Some twenty feet separated one from the other, and a further twenty feet down stood a two-storey house. Similar building materials had been used for this house and the two dwellings on the upper arm, red brick, white stone, cedarwood, but they varied in size and in design. All had sparse lawns and flower-beds planted with unhappy-looking annuals.

'The Peverils came in first,' said Burden. 'Their place was finished in January. Miss Mowler and Dunsand both moved in in March. He came from Myringham, Miss Mowler from the town here and the Peverils from Brighton. The Robinsons retired here from London, moving in in April, and the Streets came here from up north last month.'

'Do they all have garden gates opening on to that bit of land between them and the quarry?' asked Wexford.

'Only the Peverils and the two bungalows. There was going to be a path made at the back, but someone got the planning authority to veto that.'

'We'll go and have a word with your Mrs Peveril.'

She was a very nervous woman, breathless with nerves. Wexford thought she was in her late thirties. Her hair-style and her clothes were fussy but not in any of the current modes. She dressed evidently in a somewhat modified version of the style of her youth, full, longish skirt, stilt heels. He sized her up immediately as belonging to a distinct and not uncommon type, the sheltered and conservative woman who, childless and exclusively dependent on her husband for all emotional needs, tends to be suspicious of other men and of the outside world. Such women will go to almost any lengths to preserve their security and their absolute domestic quietude, so Wexford was

rather surprised that Mrs Peveril had volunteered any information about a murder victim.

'All that smoke,' she said querulously, leading them into
an over-neat living room. 'Isn't it dreadful? I shan't be able
to get my washing out for hours. It was bad enough having
that ghastly racket over the weekend – I didn't get a wink of
sleep. The noise was frightful. I'm not surprised someone got
murdered.'

'The murder,' said Wexford, 'happened several days before
the festival started.'

'Did it?' Mrs Peveril looked unconvinced. 'When I heard
someone had been killed I said to my husband, they took too
many of those drugs they all take and someone went too far.
D'you mind not sitting on that cushion? I've just put a fresh
cover on it.'

Wexford moved on to a leather-seated and apparently
invulnerable chair. 'I believe you saw the girl?'

'Oh, yes, I saw her. There's no doubt about that.' She
gave a short nervous laugh. 'I don't know many people round
here except my friend on the other side of the estate, but I
knew that girl wasn't local. The people round here don't dress
like that.'

'What made you notice her?'

'If you're going to ask me a lot of questions I'd like my
husband to be present. I'll just call him. He's working but he
won't mind stopping for a bit. I might say – well, the wrong
thing if he wasn't here. I'll just call him.'

Wexford shrugged. In a manner of speaking, the 'wrong'
thing could easily be the thing he wanted her to say. But she
had asked for her husband as some people ask for their lawyers
and probably with less need. He saw no reason to refuse his
permission and he got up, smiling pleasantly, when Peveril
came in.

'You didn't see the girl yourself, Mr Peveril?'

'No, I was working.' Peveril was one of those men who

talk about work and working as if labour belongs exclusively to them, as if it is an arduous, exacting cross they must bear, while the rest of the world make carefree holiday. 'I work a ten-hour day. Have to what with the cost of running this place. The first I heard of any girl was when my wife told me last night she'd given information to the police.' He glared at Burden. 'I was working when you lot came.'

'Perhaps we shouldn't keep you from your work now?'

'Oh, please don't go, Edward, please don't. You said I was silly to say what I said last night and now . . .'

'I can do with a short break,' said Peveril lugubriously. 'I've been at it since eight, thanks to being made totally idle by a weekend of uproar. I'm worn out.'

Comforted but still jumpy, his wife rushed into the middle of things. 'It's a matter of chance I was here at all. I nearly went to the pictures – my husband had seen the film in London and told me to go – but it was such a lovely afternoon. I just looked out of the window there and I saw her. I saw the girl walking up towards the footpath.'

'Describe her to me. In as much detail as you can, please.'

'She was about my height and she had a lot of dyed blonde hair cut in the shaggy way they all go in for.' Mrs Peveril twitched at her own over-permed, frizzy dark hair with an unsteady hand. 'And she was very heavily made-up, tarty. She had on this trouser suit, bright mauve – it hurt your eyes – with a darker mauve edging to it, and mauve patent shoes with high heels. Her handbag was mauve, a great big showy handbag with a gilt buckle, and she was carrying a brown carrier bag. I watched her because I wanted to tell my husband what a sight she was – he's very particular in his tastes, being a sort of artist – and I save up little things to tell him when he's finished work.'

'But you didn't tell him, Mrs Peveril?'

'I must have forgotten.' She was suddenly flurried. 'I wonder why I didn't tell you, Edward?'

The 'sort of artist' turned down the corners of his mouth. 'I expect I was too tired to listen. If you've finished with her I'll get back to the grindstone.'

'I've almost finished. Where did she go?'

'Across the field,' said Mrs Peveril promptly. 'That is, down the footpath, you know. I stayed at the window a long time but she didn't come back.'

She came to the door with them and watched them nervously as they got back into their car. Wexford's driver, glancing up innocently, received from her such a sharp look that he went red and turned away.

'Well, Mike, I don't quite know what to make of the Peverils, but she certainly saw the girl. Her description was too accurate to admit of anything else. Our best bet is to conclude that Dawn went across that field to meet a man. Where would she have met him?'

'In the open, I suppose. If she was going to meet him in Stowerton she'd have gone to Stowerton – the buses go every ten minutes between four and seven. There's no shelter between here and Stowerton except trees and the old pumping station.'

Wexford nodded. He knew the place Burden spoke of, a shed containing disused pumping equipment and standing in thick woodland on the banks of the Kingsbrook.

'We'll have it searched,' he said. 'That's quite an idea. Meanwhile, I'd like to see how things are progressing in the High Street.'

Things had progressed considerably. When Wexford entered the hall of the Baptist church, Martin had two people waiting to see him, each with information that was to complicate rather than simplify the case.

The first of these, an assistant from the Snowdrop Laundry and Dry Cleaners in Kingsmarkham High Street, was a middle-aged cheerful woman who had known Dawn Stonor as a schoolgirl and since then had sometimes seen her on her rare visits to her mother.

'We sort of knew each other by sight really,' she said. 'She came in last Monday at about a quarter past four.'

'She was dressed in mauve?'

'That's right. A very smart trouser suit. I remember we cleaned it for her Easter time. When she came in on Monday I wasn't sure if she knew me, but I asked her how her mum was and her gran and she said all right. Well, she'd brought this blue frock in to be cleaned and she wanted to know if I could get it done express. She wanted to collect it the next morning. "We can just do it," I said, "seeing you've brought it before four-thirty." If they come in later than that, you see, they can't get their things back before the next afternoon.

' "I want to be on the ten-fifteen train tomorrow," she said, "so can I collect it at ten?" '

'She meant to collect it herself?' Wexford asked.

'Well, she said "I". She didn't say anything about her mum fetching it like she has in the past. No, she meant to get it herself. I said that'd be all right and I made out the slip for her. You can see our part of it if you like, I've got it here with me.'

Wexford thanked her and examined the slip, noting the name and the date.

'But she didn't collect it?'

'No. I had it all ready but she never came. I was going to pop up to her mum's with it this week and then I heard what had happened. Awful, isn't it? It made me go cold all over when I heard.'

Next Wexford saw the manager of the Luximart, a big new supermarket which stood between the Dragon and the Baptist church just beside the Forby bus stop. He was young, eager and helpful.

'The young lady came in here at half-past four. We don't get many customers late on a Monday on account of we don't sell meat on a Monday and the veg isn't fresh. Most people eat up the Sunday leftovers and shop on Tuesdays.

'She was almost my last customer and when she left she waited nearly half an hour for the Forby bus, the five-twelve. Stood outside here, she did. I cursed, I can tell you, because just after the bus had come and she'd got on it I was sweeping up in the shop and I found this slip from the cleaners.'

'May I see?'

'I was certain she'd dropped it. I was sure it hadn't been there before she came in and I was quite worried thinking maybe she'd have trouble collecting her cleaning. I reckoned she'd come back but she never did. Then when I saw your notices and heard the name . . .'

'You didn't know her?'

'Never saw her before,' said the manager, 'that I can recall.'

Wexford matched the two slips, the top and the carbon. *Miss Stonor*, he read, *15 Lower Road, Kingsmarkham. Blue dress, express, 46p.* 'Will you describe her, please?'

'Nice-looking blonde. Very smartly dressed in a sort of purple blouse slacks. I don't know, I can't describe girls' clothes. I reckon she had a purple bag. I remember thinking . . .' The manager looked up ruefully and bit his lip. 'I remember thinking she was a smashing piece, but it seems awful saying that now she's dead.'

'What did she buy?'

'I knew you'd ask me that. I've been trying to think. I was at the check-out and she called me over to the deep freeze and asked me what the strawberry sundaes were like. They're sort of mousse things in cartons. I said I'd recommend them and she put two in the trolley. Wait, I'm trying to see it, sort of get a picture . . .'

Wexford nodded, saying nothing. He knew that this method, a kind of free association, was the best way. Let the man close his eyes, transport himself mentally back into the shop, stand beside the girl, re-create the almost empty wire trolley . . .

'There was a can in the trolley.' He concentrated. 'I know what it was! Soup. Vichyssoise, the stuff you can have hot or cold. It's all coming back. She took a tin of chicken fillets off the shelf and tomatoes – yes, tomatoes in a pack. I think she bought bread, a cut loaf. She might have bought butter, I don't remember. I do remember she got a bottle of wine, though, because she had the cheapest line we do. Spanish beaujolais and some cigarettes. She hadn't a basket. I gave her a brown paper carrier.'

There was no one else to see. Wexford went back to the police station where he found Burden with the doctor. The wind rattled the windows and a thin rain spattered against the glass.

'She meant to spend the night here,' he said. 'She was going to call for the dress on Tuesday morning. And it was food she was carrying in that bag when Mrs Peveril saw her. Food for *two* people.'

'For her and her date,' said Burden.

'Then he wasn't a casual pick-up. A man she picked up would either not ask her to eat with him at all or else he'd invite her to some restaurant. You can't imagine a girl making a date with a stranger and that stranger saying, Bring a three-course meal with you and we'll have a picnic. She must have known him and known him well.' Wexford listed the items of food and said, 'What's the most interesting thing about that food, Mike?'

'It could have been eaten cold as it was or it could have been heated. In other words, it could have been bought especially to be eaten in the open air, or it could equally well have been heated – the soup and the chicken, that is – which means indoors, in a house.'

During this interchange the doctor, who had been sketching a duodenum on the back of Wexford's draft of the crime-prevention plans, looked up and said, 'It wasn't eaten at all. I've got a provisional medical report prepared for you – there'll be a more detailed one later from the experts, of course – but the girl's stomach was empty. She hadn't eaten anything for five or six hours. Maybe the boy friend ate the lot on his own.'

'Or else food and wine and carrier bag are hidden some-where with the mauve trouser suit.'

'Not the wine,' said Croker. He stopped drawing and his face was suddenly grim. 'The wine was used. Remember the glass you found, Reg, the glass you cut your hand on? There was glass embedded in her face and neck. Her dress was stained with wine as well as blood. I don't think I'm being unduly melodramatic when I say that her attacker went com-pletely mad. Perhaps you and Mike will be able to find out whatever it was she said or did to him. All I can say is that something she did tipped him over the edge. He beat her to death with that wine bottle. He beat her in such a frenzy that the glass broke against the bones of her face.'

It was dark inside the little shed, half-filled as it was by cumbersome, rusty machinery, and the men worked by the light of lamps they had brought with them. Outside the pumping station the river rattled noisily and the wind slapped the door monotonously against its rotted frame.

'If they came in here,' said Wexford at last, 'it was a very brief visit. No blood, no crumbs, no cigarette ends.' He touched his hair and brought away a handful of cobwebs. 'It's a filthy hole, not at all my idea of the sort of rendezvous likely to entice a girl like Dawn Stonor, who, I take it, was conscious of her appearance.' For a moment he watched the men lifting up old sacks and searching through coils of rotted rope. 'I wish to God I could understand why she put that red dress on,' he said. 'I've a feeling that if I could I'd have the key to the whole business.'

'Because she got dirty in here?' hazarded Burden.

'Doing what? Not eating, not smoking, not making love. Talking, maybe? Then where did the dress come from? She wasn't carrying it with her. Perhaps he was. I just don't think it's possible that in one day she got two garments soiled so as to be unwearable. The coincidence is too great, and it's beyond the bounds of credibility that he happened to have a dress with him ready for her to put on in case hers got dirty. And who was he?'

'We may get some help as far as that goes from the London end.'

'Let's hope so. Shall we go? All this dust is making me cough.'

What Burden termed help from the London end had come in while they were down by the river. It was not information, data, reported interviews, but help in actual human form. She was an attractive young woman, this girl who had shared a flat in Philimede Gardens, Earls Court, with Dawn Stonor. Wexford went into the interview room where they told him she was and found her drinking tea and chain-smoking, the ashtray on the table in front of her already choked with butts.

CHAPTER SEVEN

'My name's Joan Miall,' she said shaking hands in a very forthright manner. 'An inspector came this morning and asked me a lot of questions. He said you'd want to see me and I thought I'd save you the trouble by coming to see you.' She was dark with a very pretty intelligent face and deep blue eyes. She looked about twenty-four. 'I still can't believe Dawn's dead. It seems so fantastic.'

'It's good of you to come, Miss Miall. I shall have a great deal to ask you so I think we'll go upstairs to my office where we can be more comfortable.'

In the lift she didn't speak but she lit another cigarette. Wexford understood that this heavy smoking was an antidote to shock. He approved her plain knee-length skirt and scarlet shirt, the healthy fine-boned face which, scarcely touched with make-up, was framed in shining hair, long and parted in the centre. Her hands were ringless, the nails short and lacquered pale pink. The pleasant, semi-living room appointments of his office seemed to set her more at ease. She relaxed, smiled and stubbed out her cigarette. 'I smoke too much.'

'Maybe,' he said. 'You were very fond of Dawn?'

She hesitated. 'I don't know really. I shared a flat with her for four years. We saw each other every day. We worked together. It was a shock.'

'You both worked at the Townsman Club?'

'Yes, that was where we met. We'd both been through a bit of a bad time. Dawn had been living with a man who was almost pathologically jealous and I'd been sharing with my sister. My sister was terribly possessive. Dawn and I decided to take flat together and we made a pact not to fuss each other and not to worry if the other one didn't always come home. That's why I wasn't worried. Not until Saturday. Then I . . .'

'You're running on a bit, Miss Miall,' Wexford interrupted her. 'Tell me about last Monday first.'

The slight strain this called for demanded a fresh cigarette. She lit one, inhaled and leant back in her chair. 'Dawn had started a week's holiday the Saturday before, Saturday, June fourth. She couldn't make up her mind whether to go away or not. Her boy friend – he's called Paul Wickford and he keeps a garage near us – he wanted her to go touring in Devon with him, but she hadn't decided by that Monday morning.'

'You expected her back on Monday evening?'

'Yes, in a way. She went off in the morning to catch the train for Kingsmarkham and she wasn't very cheerful. She never was when she was going to see her mother, they didn't get on. Dawn got on better with her grandmother.' Joan Miall paused and seemed to consider. 'Paul came round at about six, but when she hadn't come by seven he drove me to the club and then he went back to our flat to wait for her. Well, when she wasn't there on the Tuesday or the Wednesday and I didn't see anything of Paul, I thought they'd gone off to Devon together. We never left notes for each other, you see. We had this non-interference pact.'

'She told her mother she was working that night.'

Joan smiled slightly. 'I expect she did. That would just be an excuse to get away. Four or five hours in her mother's company would be as much as she could stand.' She stubbed out her cigarette, flicked ash fastidiously from her fingers. 'On Saturday – last Saturday, I mean – Paul appeared again. He hadn't been in Devon. His mother died that very Monday night and he'd had to go up north to the funeral and to see about things. He didn't know where Dawn was any more than I did.

'Then yesterday when we were both getting really worried – Dawn was due back at work tonight – the police came and told me what had happened.'

'Miss Miall, when Dawn was found she was wearing a dark red dress.' He noted her quick glance of surprise but ignored it for the moment. 'Now we have that dress here,' he said. 'It's rather badly stained. I'm going to ask you if you will be very brave and look at that dress. I warn you that you could find it upsetting. Will you look at it?'

She nodded.

'Yes, if you think it'll help. I can't remember Dawn ever wearing red. It wasn't her colour. But I'll look at it.'

The dress was made of a dark red rayon fabric with cap sleeves, a shaped waist and self belt. Because of its colour, the stains didn't show up except as a great stiff patch on the bodice.

The girl whitened and compressed her lips. 'May I touch it?' she said faintly.

'Yes.'

Rather tremulously, she fingered the neck opening and looked at the label. 'This is only a size twelve,' she said. 'Dawn was quite a big girl. She took a fourteen.'

'But she was wearing this dress.'

'It wasn't hers and it must have been quite a tight fit on her.' Abruptly she turned away and shivered. 'Look, perhaps you don't know much about fashion, but that dress is old, seven or eight years out of date, maybe more. Dawn was very fashion-conscious,'

Wexford led her back to his office. She sat down and the colour returned to her cheeks. He waited a little, marvelling at the friend's distress, the mother's indifference, and then he said, 'Miss Miall, will you try and give me a sort of character sketch of Dawn? What sort of girl she was, whom she knew and how she reacted to other people?'

'I'll try.' said Joan Miall.

'I don't want to give you the impression,' the girl began, 'that she wasn't a nice person. She was. But there were some – well, rather peculiar things about her.' She lifted her head and looked at him earnestly, almost aggressively.

'I'm not asking for a character *reference*, you know. And what you say will be between us. I shan't broadcast it about.'

'No, of course not. But she's dead and I have sort of old-fashioned ideas about not speaking ill of the dead. I expect you'll think that a doll who serves drinks in a club hasn't any right to get all upstage, sort of disapprove of other people's behaviour?'

Wexford didn't answer. He smiled gently and shook his head.

'Anyway,' she said, 'I didn't exactly disapprove of Dawn. It was just that – well, it's not always easy living with a compulsive liar. You don't know where you are with people like that. You don't know *them* and the relationship is sort of unreal. I know someone said that even a really bad liar tells more truth than lies, but you still can't tell what are lies and what truth, can you?'

It was on the tip of Wexford's tongue to ask what an intelligent girl like Joan Miall was doing at the Townsman Club, but he checked the impulse.

'So Dawn was a liar?' he said instead, reflecting that this wasn't going to make his task easier. He looked into the frank, clear eyes of the girl opposite him, a girl he was sure would be transparently truthful. 'What did she lie about?'

'Well, it was boasting and name-dropping really. She'd had an awful childhood. Her father used to knock her about, and her mother sort of knocked her about mentally. She'd tell her she was immoral and no good in one breath and then in the next she'd say how she missed her and beg her to come home and marry and settle down. Mrs Stonor was always telling her they were – what was the phrase? – Oh, yes, "Just ordinary folk", and Dawn had no business giving herself airs. Then she'd say the work she did was no better than being a tart.

'It made her want to prove herself. Sorry if I'm talking

like an amateur psychiatrist but I'm interested in that sort of thing. I tried to find out what made Dawn tick. When we first lived together I thought she really did know a lot of famous people. One day she brought a dog home and said she was going to look after it for a fortnight while its owner was away. She said the owner was a famous actor, a household word more or less. He's always on television.

'Then, after the dog had gone back, we were both in the club one night and this actor came in. Some member brought him as his guest. Of course I recognised him. He didn't even know Dawn. It wasn't that they'd quarrelled and weren't speaking. You could tell he just didn't know her.' Joan shrugged. She put her cigarettes into her bag and closed the bag decisively. 'She used to look through the evening paper and she'd spot a photograph of some well-known guy and say she'd worked with him or had an affair with him. I never said much. It embarrased me. The biggest name she ever dropped was a singer, terribly famous. She said she'd known him for years and very often they'd go out together. She *said*. A couple of weeks ago the phone rang and she answered it. She looked at me and covered up the mouthpiece and said it was him, but when she started talking to him she never said his name, just "Yes" and "No" and "That'd be lovely". She never actually called him Zeno. You can pretend a phone-caller is anyone, can't you? Your flatmate's not likely to go and listen on the extension.'

'Zeno?' said Wexford. 'D'you mean she claimed acquaintance with Zeno Vedast?'

'That's rather the word, "claimed". He never came to the flat. I never saw her with him. No, it was just the same as with the TV actor, name-dropping to impress, I'm afraid.'

'Miss Miall, was Dawn the sort of girl who might pick up a stranger and spend the night with him?'

She hesitated and then said impulsively, 'She might have. It sounds hateful but Dawn was very fond of money. She never had any money when she was a child, just a shilling a week or something ridiculous, and she was supposed to save half of that in a piggy bank you couldn't open. And her parents can't have been that poor – they both worked. I'm telling you this to explain why she might have picked someone up if she thought there was anything in it for her. When she first came to the club she was told like we all are that dating a customer means instant dismissal. The members know that but some of them try it on. Well, Dawn accepted an invitation from a member, in spite of the rule. He said if she'd go away for the weekend with him he'd buy her a fur coat. She did go and he gave her ten pounds. She never got the coat and I think she felt awfully humiliated because she never did that again. She liked admiration too and if a man wanted to sleep with her she thought . . . Oh, well, that it means a lot more than it does. Sometimes when she wasn't working she'd be away for a night and I think she was with a man. She couldn't bring him home, you see, in case Paul came round. But, as I told you, we didn't ask each other questions.'

'This Mr Wickford was a steady boy friend?'

She nodded. 'They'd been going out together for two years. I think she'd have married Paul in the end. The trouble seemed to be that he wasn't rich enough for her or famous or anything. He's about thirty-five, divorced, very nice. He was frightfully upset when he heard what had happened to her and the doctor had to give him sedatives. I'm sure she would have married him if she could only have grown out of all those ideas about knowing famous people. She was a very nice girl really, generous, good fun, always ready to help anyone out. It was just that she couldn't help telling lies . . .'

'One last thing. Miss Miall. Dawn brought food in Kingsmarkham last Monday afternoon, a tin of soup, tinned chicken and two strawberry mousse things in cartons. Is it possible she bought it to take home for lunch for the two of you on Tuesday?'

'Definitely not.'

'Why are you so sure?'

'For one thing – please don't think I don't like this place, it's a very nice town – but no one who lives – er, lived – where Dawn did would buy food here to take home. We're surrounded by shops and big supermarkets. The other thing is, she wouldn't buy food for the two of us. I'm a bit of a faddist when it comes to food. Health-conscious. You wouldn't think so the way I smoke, would you?' She gave a slight laugh. 'I never eat food out of cans. Dawn knew that. We used to prepare our food quite separately unless one of us made a casserole or a salad. Dawn didn't care what she ate. She hated cooking and she used to say she ate to live.' Joan winced at the last word which had been used automatically, without thought. She lifted her eyes to Wexford and he saw that they shone with unshed tears. In a choking voice she said:

'She didn't live very long, did she?'

Michael Burden was a widower whose married life had been happy and who, as a result of this, tended to consider sexual relationships as ecstatically romantic or, when they were illicit, deeply sordid. But the solitary love affair he had had since his wife's death had slightly broadened his mind. He was now prepared to admit that unmarried people might love each other and consummate that love without degradation. Sometimes these newly enlightened views of his gave rise to romantic theories and it was one of these which he propounded to Wexford as they drank their coffee together on Tuesday morning.

'We've agreed,' he began, 'that her killer can't have been a casual pick-up because of the food-shopping angle. And we know the food wasn't bought for her and the Miall girl. Therefore, she knew the man and knew him well enough to arrange with him that she'd buy their meal and meet him after he'd finished work. The time of the meeting – surely between five-thirty and six? – indicates it was to be after he'd finished work. Right?'

'Imagine so, Mike.'

'Well, sir, I've been wondering if she and this bloke had one of those long close friendships extending over years.'

'What long close friendships? What are you on about?'

'You know my sister-in-law Grace?' Wexford nodded impatiently. Of course he knew Grace, the sister of Burden's dead wife who had looked after Burden's children when they had first lost their mother and who he had later hoped would be the second Mrs Burden. That had come to nothing. Grace had married someone else and now had a baby of her own. 'I mention her,' said Burden, 'because it was her experience that gave me the idea. She and Terry knew each other off and on for years before they got married. There was always a sort of bond between them, although they didn't meet much and each of them had other – well, friends. Terry even got engaged to someone else.'

'You're suggesting this was the case with Dawn?'

'She lived here till she was eighteen. Suppose she knew this bloke when they were both very young and they had an affair and then they both left Kingsmarkham to work elsewhere. Or he stayed here and she went to London. What I'm suggesting is that they kept in touch and whenever she came home or he went to London they had one of these dates, secret dates necessarily because he was married and she was more or less engaged to Wickford. Frankly, I think this covers every aspect of the case and deals with all the difficulties.'

Wexford stirred his coffee, looked longingly towards the sugar bowl and resisted the temptation to take another lump. 'It doesn't deal with that bloody red dress,' he said viciously.

'It does if they met in this chap's house. We'd have to admit the possibility of coincidence, that she stained the mauve outfit and then put on a dress belonging to this man's wife.'

'The wife being out presumably. She goes there, he lets

her in. What happens to the mauve garment? They had no drinks for her to spill, ate nothing for her to drop, made no love to – er, crush it. (I put it like that, Mike, to save your delicate sensibilities.) Maybe the violence of his welcoming embrace creased it up and she was so dainty about her appearance that she rushed upstairs and slipped into one of her rival's ancient cast-offs. He was so upset about her thinking more of her clothes than of him he upped and banged her with the bottle. Is that it?'

'It must have been something like that,' said Burden rather stiffly. Wexford was always pouring cold water on his flights of fancy and he never got used to it.

'Where was this house of assignation, then?'

'On the outskirts of Stowerton, the Forby side. She went by the fields because he was going to meet her there and take her back to his house. They arranged it that way just in case the wife changed her mind about going away.' He made a moue of distaste, sordidness temporarily conquering romance. 'Some people do go on like that, you know.'

'You seem to know, anyway. So all we have to do now is find a bloke living in a house on the north side of Stowerton who's known Dawn Stonor since they went to Sunday school together and whose wife was away Monday night. Oh, and find if the wife has missed a red dress.'

'You don't sound too enthusiastic, sir.'

'I'm not,' Wexford said frankly. 'The people you know may go on like that but the people I know don't. They act like *people*, not characters in a second feature film that's been thrown together for the sake of sensation rather than illustrating human nature. But since my mind is otherwise a blank, I reckon we'd better get asking Mrs Stonor who Dawn knew around Stowerton and who had a lifelong sentimental bond with her.'

CHAPTER EIGHT

'The folks round here,' said Mrs Stonor, 'weren't good enough for Dawn. She was a proper little snob, though what she'd got to be snobbish about I never will know.'

For all her frankly expressed unmaternal sentiments, Mrs Stonor was dressed in deepest black. She and the old woman who was with her, and who had been introduced as 'My mother, Mrs Peckham', had been sitting in semi-darkness, for the curtains were drawn. When the two policemen entered the room a light was switched on. Wexford noticed that a wall mirror had been covered by a black cloth.

'We think it possible,' he said, 'that Dawn went to meet an old friend on Monday night. I want you to try and remember the names of any old boy friends she had before she left home or any name she may have mentioned to you on her visit here.'

Instead of replying, Mrs Stonor addressed the old woman who was leaning forwardly avidly, clutching the two sticks that supported her when she walked. 'You can get off back to bed now, Mother. All this has got nothing to do with you. You've been up too long as it is.'

'I'm not tired,' said Mrs Peckham. She was very old, well over eighty. Her body was thin and tiny and her face simian, a maze of wrinkles. What sparse white hair she had was scragged on to the top of her head into a knot stuck full of pins. 'I don't want to go to bed, Phyllis. It's not often I have a bit of excitement.'

'Excitement! I like that. A nice way to talk when Dawn's had her head bashed in by a maniac. Come along now. I'll take your arm up the stairs.'

A small devil in Wexford's head spoke for him. 'Mrs

Peckham should stay. She may be able to help.' He said it more to irritate Mrs Stonor than because he thought her mother would be able to furnish them with information.

Mrs Peckham grinned with pleasure, showing a set of over-large false teeth. Reprieved, she helped herself to a sweet from the bag on the table beside her and began a ferocious crunching. Her daughter turned down the corners of her mouth and folded her hands.

'Can you think of anyone, Mrs Stonor?'

Still sulky from having her wishes baulked, Mrs Stonor said, 'Her dad never let her have boy friends. He wanted her to grow up respectable. We had a job with her as it was, always telling lies and staying out late. My husband tried every way we could think of to teach her the meaning of decency.'

'Tried his strap, mostly,' said Mrs Peckham. Protected by the presence of the policemen, she gave her daughter a triumphant and unpleasant grin. Wexford could see that she was one of those old pensioners who, dependent for all her needs on a hated child, was subservient, cringing, defiant or malicious as her fancy took her or circumstances demanded. When Mrs Stonor made no reply but only lifted her chin, her mother tried another dig. 'You and George ought never to have had no kids. Always smacking her and yelling at her. Knock one devil out and two in, that's what I say.'

Wexford cleared his throat. 'We don't seem to be getting very far. I can't believe Dawn never mentioned any man she was friendly with.'

'I never said she didn't. You'll get your stomach trouble again, Mother, if you don't leave them acid drops alone. The fact is, it was all lies with Dawn. I got so I let what she said go in one ear and out the other. I do know she had this man Wickford on account of her bringing him down here for the day last year. They didn't stop long. Dawn could see what I thought about *him*. A divorced man, running a garage! That was the best she could do for herself.'

'There was no one else?' Burden asked coldly.

'I said I *don't know*. You're not going to tell me she got herself done in by some boy she was at school with, are you? That's all the local boys she knew.'

Mrs Peckham, having incompletely unwrapped her latest sweet, was removing shreds of paper from her mouth. 'There was Harold Goodbody,' she said.

'Don't be so stupid, Mother. As if Harold'd have anything to do with a girl like Dawn. Harold climbed too high for the likes of her.'

'Who is this man?' asked Wexford.

The sweet lodged in a wizened cheek pouch, the noisy sucking abated, Mrs Peckham heaved a heavy but not unhappy sigh. 'He was a lovely boy, was Harold. Him and his mum and dad used to live round here in the next street. I wasn't here then, I had my own cottage, but I used to see Harold when I had my job serving dinners at the school. Oh, he was a lad! Always one for a joke was Harold, April Fools all the year round for him. Him and Dawnie was pals from their first day at school. Then I came here to live with Phyllis and George and Dawnie'd bring him back to tea.'

'I never knew that,' said Mrs Stonor, bristling. 'George wouldn't have had that.'

'George wasn't here, was he? And you was working at that shop. I didn't see no harm in Dawnie bringing her friend home.' Mrs Peckham turned her back on her daughter and faced Wexford. 'Harold was a real freak to look at, all bones and his hair nearly as white as mine. I'd have boiled eggs all ready for the three of us, but when Dawnie and me started cracking ours we'd find the empty shells. Harold'd brought a couple of empty shells to fool us. Ooh, he was funny! He had a joke ink blot and a rubber spider. Made us scream, that spider did. One day I caught him playing with the phone. He'd ring this number and when the woman answered it said he was the engineers. He said to her there was an emergency.

She was to pour boiling water down the receiver, leave it for ten minutes and then cut the lead with scissors. She was going to too, she believed him, but I put a a stop to that, though I was laughing fit to die. Harold was a real scream.'

'Yes, I'm sure,' said Wexford. 'How old was he when all this fun and games was going on?'

'About fifteen.'

'And he still lives round here?'

'No, of course he don't. That Mr Silk from Sundays took him up and he left home and went to London when he was seventeen and got famous, didn't he?'

Wexford blinked. 'Famous? Harold Goodbody?'

Mrs Peckham wagged her gnarled hands impatiently. 'He changed his name when he got to be a singer. What did he call himself? Now I'm getting on I seem to forget everything. John Lennon, that was it.'

'I hardly think . . .' Wexford began.

Mrs Stonor, who had remained silent and scornful, opened her mouth and snapped, 'Zeno Vedast. He calls himself Zeno Vedast.'

'Dawn was at school with Zeno Vedast?' Wexford said blankly. So it hadn't been all boasting, vain name-dropping? Or some of it hadn't? 'They were friends?'

'You don't want to listen to Mother,' said Mrs Stonor. I daresay Dawn saw a bit of him when they were at school. She never saw him in London.'

'Oh, yes, she did, Phyllis. She told me so last Monday when she was home. She'd tell me things she'd never tell you. She knew you'd pour cold water on everything she did.'

'What did she say, Mrs Peckham?'

'She came into my room when I was in bed. You remember Hal, don't you Gran? she says. We always called him Hal. Well, I went out to dinner with him on Friday night, she said.'

'And you believed her?' Mrs Stonor gave the brittle laugh

that is not a laugh at all. 'Harold Goodbody was in Manchester Friday night. I saw him myself on telly, I saw him live. She was making up tales like she always did.'

Mrs Peckham scrunched indignantly. 'She got the night wrong, that's all. Poor little Dawnie.'

'Don't you be so stupid. He's a *famous* singer. Though what's so wonderful about his voice I never shall know. Richard Tauber, now that was a man who *had* a voice.'

Burden asked, 'Do his parents still live here?'

Mrs Stonor looked for a moment as if she was going to tell him not to be so stupid. She restrained herself and said sourly, 'When he got rich he bought them a great big detached place up near London. All right for some, isn't it? I've always been decent and brought my daughter up right and what did she ever do for me? I well remember Freda Goodbody going round to her neighbours to borrow a quarter of tea on account of Goodbody spending all his wages on the dogs. Harold never had more than one pair of shoes at a time and they was cast-offs from his cousin. "My darling boy" and "my precious Hal" she used to say but she used to give him baked beans for his Sunday dinner.'

Suddenly Mrs Peckham waxed appropriately biblical. ' "Better a dish of herbs where love is", she said, "than a stalled ox and hatred therewith".' She took the last acid drop and sucked it noisily.

'There you are, sir,' said Burden when they were in the car. 'A lifelong friendship, like I said.'

'Well, not quite like you said, Mike. Zeno Vedast doesn't live in Stowerton, he has no wife, and I don't suppose he makes a habit of eating tinned food in fields with waitresses. The odd thing is that she *did* know him. It seems to bear out what Joan Miall said that, in the nature of things, even a chronic liar must tell more truth than lies. We all know the story of the boy who cried wolf. Dawn Stonor was a lion-hunter. She cried lion and this time the lion was real. But we haven't a shred of evidence to connect Vedast with her last Monday. Very likely he was still in Manchester. All I can say at the moment is that it's intriguing, it's odd.'

'Surely you think we ought to see him?'

'Of course we must see every man Dawn knew, unless he has a watertight alibi for that Monday night. We still don't know what Wickford was doing after seven.' The chief inspector tapped his driver's shoulder. 'Back to the station, please, Stephens.'

The man half-turned. He was young, rather shy, recently transferred from Brighton. He blushed when Wexford addressed him, rather as he had coloured under Mrs Peveril's stare.

'Did you want to say something to me?' Wexford asked gently.

'No, sir.'

'Back to the station, then. We can't sit here all day.'

By Wednesday Paul Wickford had been cleared of suspicion. After leaving Joan Miall at the Townsman Club in Hertford Street, he had gone into a pub in Shepherd Market where he had drunk one vodka and tonic before driving back to Earls Court. Waiting for him at his flat was his brother who brought the news of their mother's serious illness and asked Paul to drive with him immediately to Sheffield. Paul had then asked the tenant of the second floor flat to cancel his milk and papers and, if he happened to see Dawn Stonor, to tell her where he had gone. The two brothers had reached their mother's house in Sheffield soon after midnight, and by the following morning she was dead.

In spite of there being only thin evidence of Dawn's killer having lived on the outskirts of Stowerton, a house-to-house investigation had begun on Tuesday afternoon of the whole district. No one had seen Dawn; no one had seen a girl in mauve alone or with a man. Only two wives had been absent from home on the evening in question, one with her husband and one leaving him behind to mind their four children. No wife had been away for the whole night and no wife had missed a red dress. Wexford's men searched the fields for the trouser suit and the food. It was dreary work, for the rain fell heavily and there were fears that the river would flood.

Mrs Clarke and Mrs Peveril remained the only people who had seen Dawn after five-twenty, Mrs Peveril the last person – except her killer – to have seen her alive. Wexford concentrated on these women, questioning them exhaustively, and it wasn't long before he found something odd in their evidence. It had not previously occurred to him that they might know each other, and it was only when, sitting in Mrs Clarke's living room, listening to her answer the phone, that the thought occurred to him.

'I can't talk now, Margaret. I'll ring you later. I hope Edward soon feels better.'

She didn't say who had been at the other end of the line. Why should she? She sat down with a bright, insincere smile.

'So sorry. You were saying?'

Wexford said sharply, 'Were you talking to Mrs Peveril?'

'How *could* you know? I was, as a matter of fact.'

Then I imagine you are the one person she claims acquaintance with in this district?'

'Poor Margaret. She's so neurotic and she had an awful time with Edward. I suppose I am her only friend. She doesn't make friends easily.'

'Mrs Clarke, you were first questioned about Dawn Stonor last Sunday evening, I think? We questioned people on this side of the estate first.'

'Well, you ought to know that better than me.'

She looked a little offended, bored, but not at all frightened. Wexford considered carefully. Burden and Martin and Gates had begun their questions here at seven, not reaching The Pathway till nine. 'Did you phone Mrs Peveril on Sunday evening before nine?' Her glance became wary, defensive. 'I see you did. You told her you'd been questioned and, moreover, that you'd been able to help. It was only natural for you to talk to your friend about it. I expect you described the girl to her and told her which way you'd seen her go.'

'Is there anything wrong in that?'

'Discretion would have been wiser. Never mind. Describe Dawn Stonor to me again now, please.'

'But I've done it hundreds of times,' cried Mrs Clarke with exasperated exaggeration. 'I've told you over and over again.'

'Once more, for the last time.'

'I was coming along to get the bus into Kingsmarkham. I saw her get off the bus that went the other way. She crossed the road and went into The Pathway.' Mrs Clarke spoke slowly and deliberately as might a parent explaining for the dozenth time to a not very bright child the point of a simple story. 'She had fair hair, she was in her twenties, and she wore a lilac-coloured trouser suit and mauve shoes.'

'That's what you told Mrs Peveril?'

'Yes, and you and all your people. I couldn't say any more because I don't know any more.'

'You didn't, for instance, notice her large mauve bag with a gilt buckle or that there was a darker edging to the suit?'

'No, I didn't. I didn't notice that and you saying it doesn't bring it back to me or anything. I'm sorry but I've told you everything I know.'

He shook his head, not in denial of her statement, but at his own bewilderment. At first, briefly, when she put the phone down he had suddenly been certain that Mrs Peveril had never seen Dawn at all, that the news from her friend had sparked off an urge for sensationalism, giving her an opportunity to make herself important. He remembered how, although she said she had taken careful note of the girl's appearance in order to tell her husband about her, she had never told him. But now he knew she must have seen her. How else could she, and she alone, have known of the bag and the purple border to the tunic?

CHAPTER NINE

Three houses that backed on to Sundays, three garden gates opening on a narrow strip of land beyond which was the quarry . . . Each garden separated from its neighbours by high woven chestnut fencing, a strip of land overgrown with dense bushes and quite tall trees. Wexford thought how easy it would have been to carry a body out of one of those houses by night and drop it into the quarry. And yet, if Dawn had gone into one of those houses instead of across the fields, if Mrs Peveril had seen her do so and was a seeker after sensation, wouldn't these facts have made a far greater sensation?

'I thought you'd leave me alone after I'd told you the truth,' said Mrs Peveril fretfully. 'I shall be ill if you badger me. All right, Mrs Clarke did phone me. That doesn't mean I didn't see her too, does it? I saw her and I saw her walk across those fields.'

'She couldn't have gone into any of those houses, anyway, sir,' said Burden. 'Unless it was into Mrs Peveril's own house. In which case Mrs P. presumably wouldn't say she'd seen her at all. Dawn can't have gone into Dunsand's or Miss Mowler's. We've checked at Myringham, at the University, and Dunsand didn't leave there till six. He'd have been lucky to get home by six-thirty to seven. Miss Mowler was with her friend in Kingsmarkham till a quarter to eight.'

They went back to the police station and were about to enter the lift when a sharp draught of wind told Wexford that the double doors to the entrance foyer had been swept unceremoniously open. He turned and saw an extraordinary figure. The man was immensely tall – far taller than Wexford who topped six feet – with a bush of jet-black hair. He wore an ankle-length pony-skin coat and carried a canvas bag whose sopping wet contents had soaked the canvas and were dripping on to the floor. Once inside, he paused, looked about him confidently and was making for Sergeant Camb who sat drinking tea behind his counter when Wexford intercepted him.

'Mr Mbowele, I believe? We've met before.' Wexford put out his hand which was immediately gripped in a huge copper-coloured vice of bone-crushing fingers. 'What can I do for you?'

The young African was extremely handsome. He had all the glowing virile grace which led clothes designers and model agencies and photographers to take up the slogan – 'Black is beautiful'. Beaming at Wexford, his soft, dark eyes alight, he withdrew his hand, dropped the sodden bag on to the floor and undid his coat. Under it his chest was bare, hung with a chain of small green stones.

'I don't altogether dig this rain, man,' he said, shaking drops of water off his hair. 'You call this June?'

'I'm not responsible for the weather.' Wexford pointed to the bag. 'And rain wasn't responsible for that unless the floods have started.'

'I fished it out of the river,' said Louis Mbowele. 'Not here. At Myringham. That's quite a river now, your little Kingsbrook, man. I go down the river every morning and walk. I can think down there.' He stretched out his arms. It was easy to imagine him striding by the full flowing river, his mind equally in spate, his body brimming with vibrant energy. 'I was thinking,' he said, 'about Wittgenstein's principle of atomicity. . . .'

'About *what*?'

'For an essay. It's not important. I looked in the river and I saw this purple silk thing . . .'

'*Is that what's in the bag?*'

'Didn't you get that? I knew what it was, man, I'd read the papers. I waded in and fished it out and put it in this bag – it's my girl friend's bag – and brought it here.'

'You shouldn't have touched it, Mr Mbowele.'

'Louis, man, Louis. We're all friends, aren't we? I've no prejudice against the fuzz? The fuzz have their place in a well-organized state. I'm no anarchist.'

Wexford sighed. 'You'd better come upstairs and bring the bag with you.'

In the office Louis made himself immediately at home by taking off the pony-skin coat and drying his hair on its lining. He sat on a chair like one who is more accustomed to sit on the floor, one leg stuck out and the other hooked over the chair arm.

'Exactly where did you find this, Louis?'

'In the river between Mill Street and the college grounds. It'd been swept down from round here somewhere. Look, why freak out about it? If I'd left it there it'd be down by the sea somewhere now. Keep your cool, man.'

'I am not losing my cool,' said Wexford who couldn't help smiling. 'Was there anything else in the river?'

'Fish,' said Louis, grinning, 'and sticks and stones and a hell of a lot of water.'

It was pointless, anyway, to ask about the paper carrier of food. What carrier bag, what cardboard cartons, would survive ten days and fifteen miles of pounding in that swollen stream? The can and the jar would survive, of course. But only a miracle would have brought them to precisely the same spot in the river as the trouser suit when Louis Mbowele had found it. Maybe the Wittgenstein principle provided for that sort of coincidence, but Wexford decided not to pursue it. The bag and, to a lesser extent the coat, were soaking his carpet.

'Well, I'm very grateful to you. You've been most public-spirited.' Wexford risked his hand again and managed not to wince when the vice enclosed it. 'There's a bus goes to Myringham at ten past which you ought to be in time for.'

'I ought if I'm going to get to Len's tutorial.' He glanced at the window. It was pouring. 'Have you ever been to Marumi?'

'Marumi?'

'My country. Sometimes you get no rain there for three years. Man, is that country dry! You like the sun?'

'It makes a change,' said Wexford.

'You said I was to remember you when I came into my kingdom. It won't be a kingdom but I'll need fuzz and I could get along great with you if you got rid of your hangups. How does it grab you?'

'I'll be too old by that time, Louis.'

'Age,' said the philosopher, 'is just a state of mind.' He looked, Wexford thought, about twenty. 'It won't be that long, man, not long at all. Get yourself together. Think it over.'

From the window Wexford watched him cross the street, swinging the wet, empty bag. He chuckled. When Burden came into the room, he looked up from the mauve rags he was examining.

'Just been offered a job, Mike.'

'Doing what?'

'My own thing, man, my own thing. When the rain and boredom here freak me out I can go boss the fuzz in a sort of black Ruritania. Can you see me in epaulettes with a Mauser on each hip?'

'My God,' said Burden. He fingered the torn material fastidiously. 'Is that the missing suit?'

Wexford nodded. 'Down to the purple edging, as described by our accurate Mrs Peveril. Louis Mbowele found it in the river at Myringham. It had obviously been washed down there by the heavy rains.'

'From those fields?'

'From up there somewhere. She was killed up there. I'm as sure of that as I'm sure I'll never be the Maigret of Marumi.'

Wexford remembered Miss Mowler from when she had been a district nurse in Kingsmarkham. His wife had broken her ankle and Miss Mowler had called three times a week to bath her and keep an eye on the plaster cast. She greeted him like an old friend.

'Mrs Wexford not been climbing any more ladders, I hope? And how are your lovely girls? I saw Sheila on television last week. She's getting quite well known, isn't she? And amazingly good-looking.'

'You mean it's amazing with me for her dad?'

'Oh, Mr Wexford, you know I didn't mean that!' Miss Mowler blushed and looked very confused. She tried to cover her gaffe with a string of explanations, but Wexford laughed and cut her short.

'I've come to talk to you about this murder, Miss Mowler.'

'But I can't help you. I wasn't here.'

'No, but you were here later in the evening. If there was anything you noticed, any little oddity . . .'

'I really can't help you,' she said earnestly. 'I've only been here three months and I hardly even know my neighbours.'

'Tell me what you do know of them, of the Peverils especially.'

The hall in the bungalow was rather garishly decorated, black and gilt predominating. The black bitumastic flooring curved upwards at the edges to meet an astonishingly hideous wallpaper. Wexford was rather surprised that the sprays of lipstick-red flowers, each petal a pear-shaped scarlet blot, with spiralling black stems and glossy golden leaves, should be to Miss Mowler's taste. He did not tell her so as she led him into the living room, but he must have looked it, for she plunged into characteristic excuses.

'Awful, isn't it? The builder finished both these bungalows completely before he sold them. Dreadful taste. You see I've got blue birds and orange lilies on the walls in here. And Mr Dunsand's next door is exactly the same. I believe he's going to re-decorate completely in his holidays. But doing that is so expensive and arduous if you're a lone woman like I am. The trouble is it's very good-quality paper and completely washable. I don't know if the Peverils' is the same. I believe they were able to choose their own decorations, but I've never been in there.'

'Mrs Peveril is a strange woman.'

'A very neurotic one, I should think. I heard her quarrelling once in the garden with her husband. She was crying quite hysterically.'

'What were they quarrelling about, Miss Mowler?' Wexford asked.

'Well, she was accusing him of being unfaithful to her. I couldn't help overhearing.' Afraid of another digression in which a spate of excuses would be put forward, Wexford shook his head and smiled. 'Oh, well, it's different rather with a policeman, isn't it? It's not gossip. Mrs Peveril talked to me in the street. I hardly know her but that doesn't stop her saying the most – well, intimate things. I do think it's a mistake for a man to work at home, don't you?'

'Why, Miss Mowler?'

'He and his wife never get away from each other. And if the wife's possessive and jealous she'll resent it and begin suspecting things if ever he does go out without her. Mrs Peveril seems to depend on her husband for every sort of support, and of course the poor man isn't adequate. Who is? I don't think he wanted to come here. She was the moving spirit behind that . . . Oh, I didn't mean to make a pun. She's the sort of woman who's always running away if you know what I mean.'

'Does she ever go out without her husband?'

'Oh dear, women like that can never appreciate that what's sauce for the goose ought to be sauce for the gander. She certainly goes out to her dressmaking class every Monday evening and sometimes she has another evening out with Mrs Clarke.'

'I suppose you knew Dawn Stonor?'

Any allegation that she might have been acquainted with

a murder victim might have been expected to evoke fulsome excuses from a woman of Miss Mowler's temperament. Instead, she set her mouth and looked affronted. 'Very selfish, flighty sort of girl. I know the family very well. Naturally, I look in on the grandmother, Mrs Peckham, from time to time. It would have made a world of difference to that old lady's life if Dawn had bothered to go home more often. But there you are, that's the young people of today all over. While I was still working I used to tell Dawn about it but she fired right up at me, said she couldn't stand the place or her mother. There was some nonsense about having an unhappy childhood. They've all had unhappy childhoods, Mr Wexford, to account for every bit of bad behaviour.' She tossed her head. 'I haven't seen her in two or three years now and I can't say I'm sorry.'

It was such a change for Miss Mowler not to be able to say she was sorry that Wexford concluded Dawn's firing up must have riled her excessively. He thanked her and left. Dunsand's bungalow had the closed-up, discouraging look of a house that is seldom occupied by day, all the windows shut, a milk bottle with a note stuck in it on the doorstep. He caught sight of Mrs Peveril, neatly overalled, watering a window box. She saw him, pretending she hadn't, and rushed indoors, slamming the front door.

She was a biggish woman, the victim of premature middle-aged spread, several stones heavier than Miss Mowler who was twenty-five years her senior. He hadn't really noticed that before. She wouldn't be a size twelve, more a sixteen. But a woman can put on a lot of weight in seven years, and Joan Miall had said the dress was seven or eight years old . . .

He had himself driven to Lower Road and again he was aware of a fidgety unease on the part of young Stevens, his driver. These days the man seemed always on the point of saying something to him, of unburdening his soul perhaps. He would say 'Yes, sir' and 'No, sir', but there was no finality about these responses, rather a vague note of hesitation and often a preoccupied pause before the man turned away and started the car. Wexford tried asking him what was the matter but he was always answered by a respectful shake of the head, and he concluded that Stevens had some domestic trouble weighing on him that he longed to discuss but was too shy and too reticent to reveal.

Mrs Stonor was in her kitchen, ironing, her mother in a rocking chair beside her. It was a chair which squeaked each time it was moved and Mrs Peckham, who seemed in an even more maliciously cheerful frame of mind today, moved it constantly, taking delight in the noise it made – they say you cannot make a noise to annoy yourself – and munching Edinburgh rock.

'I never heard her mention no Peveril,' said Mrs Stonor, passing her iron across a pair of pink locknit knickers that could only have belonged to her mother yet were capacious enough to have contained the whole of that little, dried-up body. 'She was proud of *not* knowing anyone around here, called them provincials of some fine thing. There's ever such a nice woman as is manageress of the cleaners and she'd known Dawn all her life. Dawn had to pretend she'd never seen her before. What d'you think of that?'

Wexford had to keep his thoughts to himself. He was marvelling, not for the first time, at certain popular fallacies. That children naturally love their parents is a belief which has all but died away. The world still holds that parents love their children, love them automatically, through thick and thin, through disappointment and disillusion. He himself had until recently believed that the loss of a child is the one insupportable grief. When would people come to understand that the death of a son or daughter, removing the need of a parent to put a good face on things, to lie to neighbours, to sustain a false image, can be a relief?

'If she had fallen in love with a local man,' he said carefully, 'perhaps these prejudices of hers wouldn't have counted for much.' He knew as he spoke that he was talking a foreign language to Mrs Stonor.

She seized upon the one point that meant anything to her. 'She wasn't capable of loving anyone.'

Mrs Peckham snorted. With surprising psychological insight, she said, 'Maybe she didn't know how. Kids don't know how if they don't get none theirselves. Same thing with dogs.' She passed Wexford the bag and grinned when he took a piece. 'And monkeys,' she added. 'I read that in me *Reader's Digest.*'

'We're wondering, Mrs Stonor, if she went into a man's house.' With any other bereaved mother he would have softened his words; with this one any tact seemed superfluous sentimentality. 'We think she may have had an assignation with a local man while his wife was away.'

'I wouldn't put it past her. She hadn't got no morals. But she wouldn't go into a fellow's house – even I can see that. That's stupid. She'd got a flat of her own, hadn't she? Them girls was only too ready to make themselves scarce if the other one was up to any funny business.' It was atrociously put, but it was unanswerable. 'Dawn didn't even have the decency to hide any of that from me,' Mrs Stonor said fiercely. 'She told me she'd been with men in that way. She called it being honest and leading her own life. As if she knew the meaning of honesty! I'd have died before I'd have told such things to my mother.'

A shrieking cackle come from Mrs Peckham. 'You'd nothing to tell, Phyllis. You aren't 'uman.'

'Don't be so stupid, Mother. The sergeant don't want you poking your nose in all the time, and it's time you had your rest. You've been fancying yourself ever since that young man came to see you this morning, buttering you up like I don't know what.'

Amused at his sudden demotion two rungs down the ladder, Wexford, who had risen to go, gave the older woman a conspiratorial half-smile. 'A grandson, Mrs Peckham?'

'No, I never had no kids but Phyllis. More's the pity.' She
said it not as if she pined for a replica of Mrs Stonor but
perhaps for her antithesis. 'Mind you, he was like a grandson
in a way, was Hal.'

'Will you do as I ask, Mother, and get off to bed?'

'I'm going, Phyllis. I'm on me way.' An awareness that,
after all, she depended for her bed and board on her
daughter's good graces briefly softened Mrs Peckham's as-
perity, but not for long. She heaved herself up, clutching her
sweets. 'You've got it in for poor Hal just because he wasn't
all over you like he was me. He kissed me,' she said proudly.

'Mrs Peckham, am I right in thinking that Zeno Vedast
has been here to see you? Do you mean while the festival was
on? You didn't tell me that before.'

She propped herself on her walking aid, hunching her thin
shoulders. 'He come this morning,' she said. 'Looking out for
a house for hisself round here, one of them big places as we
used to call gentleman's houses. Ooh, he's very grand in his
ideas, is Hal. He's got a whole suite to hisself at that big hotel
in the Forest, but he wasn't too proud to come and see old
Granny Peckham and say how cut up he was about poor
Dawnie. He come in a big gold car and he kissed me and
brought me a two-pound box of Black Magic.' Her eyes
gleamed greedily at the thought of the chocolates, waiting for
her perhaps in her bedroom. She sighed contentedly. 'I'll get
off for me lay-down now.' she said.

CHAPTER TEN

The Burden children were old enough now to come home to an empty house and get their own tea, but more often they went straight from school to the house of their Aunt Grace, and in the holidays Pat Burden spent most of her time there, playing with the baby. Her brother led the marauding life of a teenage boy, wandering with a small gang of contemporaries in the fields, fishing in the Kingsbrook or playing the jukebox at the Carousel café. Burden knew very well that his son's life would have differed very little from this pattern even if there had been a mother at the bungalow in Tabard Road. He understood that a girl child needs an adult female on whom to model herself and he knew that she had that in Grace. But he worried incessantly about his children. Would John become a delinquent if he were out after nine in the evening? Would Pat carry a trauma through life because at the age of thirteen she was occasionally expected to open a tin or make tea? Did he give them too much pocket money or not enough? Ought he, for their sakes, to marry again? Innocent of any, he was loaded down with guilt.

He went to absurd lengths to ensure that neither of them had to do any work they would not have done had his wife lived. For this reason he was always taking them out to meals or rushing home with packages of expensive frozen food. Pat must never walk the half-mile from Grace's house to Tabard Road. He would have let her walk it without a thought if Jean had lived. But motherless children had to be fetched in father's car. He suffered agonies of frustration and recrimination if he was busy on a case and Pat had to wait an hour or even be abandoned to her aunt for an evening.

Wexford knew this. Whereas he would never excuse Burden

from essential work on these grounds, he regretfully gave up the practice of detaining the inspector after hours to sit with him in the Olive and Dove and thrash out some current problem. Burden was worse than useless as a participant in these discussions. His eyes were always on the clock. Every drink he had was 'one for the road', and from time to time he would start from his seat and express the worry uppermost in his mind. Had John come in yet?

But old habits die hard. Wexford preferred the atmosphere in the Olive to the adolescent-ruled, untidy living room of the bungalow. He felt guilty when Pat was prevented from doing her ballet exercises and John had to turn off the record player, but he had to talk to Burden sometimes, discuss things with him outside hours. As he came to the door that evening, he heard the pom-pom, the roar and the whine of pop music before he rang the bell.

Burden was in his shirt sleeves, a plastic apron round his waist. He took this off hurriedly when he saw who his caller was. 'Just finishing the dishes,' he said. 'I'll nip out for some beer, shall I?'

'No need. I've brought it. What did you think I'd got in the bag? More treasures from the river? Who's the vocalist, John?'

'Zeno Vedast,' said John reverently. He looked at his father. 'I suppose I'll have to turn it off now.'

'Not on my account,' said Wexford. 'I rather like his voice.'

Vedast wasn't singing any of the festival songs but an older hit which had for so long been number one in the charts that even Wexford had heard it. Once or twice he had heard himself humming the melody. It was a gentle folk song about a country wedding.

'Dad's going to buy me the Sundays album for my birthday.'

'That'll set you back a bit, Mike.'

'Six quid,' said Burden gloomily.

'I wonder if any of these songs will live? We tend to forget that some of the greatest songs were pop in their day. After *The Marriage of Figaro* was first performed in the seventeen-eighties, they say Mozart heard the errand boys whistling *Non piu andrai* in the streets of Vienna. And it's still popular.'

'Oh, yes?' said Burden politely and uncomprehendingly. 'You can turn it off now, John. Mr Wexford didn't come round here to talk about Zeno Vedast or Goodbody or whatever his name is.'

'That's just what I did come for.' Wexford went into the kitchen and picked up a tea towel. He began polishing glasses, resisting Burden's efforts to stop him. 'I've a feeling that before we go any further we ought to see Dawn's lion, the lion who roars like any sucking dove.'

'Wherever he may be at this moment.'

'That's no problem, Mike. He's here. Or, at any rate, he's at the Cheriton Forest Hotel.' Wexford drank the half-pint Burden had poured out for him and told the inspector about his talk with Mrs Peckham. 'I don't know that it means much. He may make a point of visiting old ladies rather on the lines of a parliamentary candidate nursing babies. Never neglect any opportunity of currying favour and influencing people. Or he may be an ordinary nice bloke who wanted to condole with the dead girl's grandma. It certainly doesn't mean he'd seen Dawn recently.'

John put his head round the door. 'I'm going out, Dad.'

Burden began to flap. 'Where? Why? What d'you want to go out now for?'

'Only down the Carousel.'

Wexford said smoothly, 'That's fine, John, because we're going out too. Your father won't be back till ten-thirty, so you'd better have the key. You're bound to be in before him, aren't you?'

Burden handed over the key in meek stupefaction and John took it as if it were something precious and wonderful. When the boy had gone – rapidly before there could be any changes of heart – Burden said suspiciously, 'You talked to him exactly as if he were grown-up.'

'Don't have any more beer, Mike. I want you to drive us.'

'To Cheriton Forest, I suppose?'

'Mm-hm. Vedast's dining in tonight. I checked.' Wexford looked at his watch. 'He ought to have just about finished his dinner.'

'Oh God. I don't know. Pat's at Grace's. John . . .'

'The boy's glad you're going out. It was a relief. Couldn't you see that? You won't go out for his sake. D'you want him to get so he can't go out for yours?'

'I sometimes think human relationships are impossible. Communication's impossible.'

'And you're a fool,' said Wexford, but he said it affectionately.

Cheriton Forest, a large fir plantation, lies some two miles to the south of Kingsmarkham. It is intersected by a number of sandy rides and one metalled road on which, in a big heathy clearing, is situated the Cheriton Forest Hotel.

This is a newer and far more fashionable hotel than the Olive and Dove in Kingsmarkham. The original building, put up in the thirties, is supposed to be a copy of a Tudor manor house. But there are too many beams and studs, the plaster is too white and the beams too black, the woodwork a decoration rather than an integral part of the structure. And the whole thing which might have mellowed with time has been vulgarized by a vast glass cocktail bar and by rows of motel bungalows added on in the late sixties.

When Wexford and Burden arrived at the hotel it was still broad daylight, a dull summer evening, windy and cool. The wind stirred the forest trees, ruffling them against a pale sky where grey clouds, rimmed in the west with pink, moved, gathered, lost their shapes, torn by the wind.

On a Saturday night the forecourt would by this time have been crammed with cars and the cocktail bar full of people. But this was mid-week. Through a mullioned window a few sedate diners could be seen at tables, waiters moving unhurriedly with trays. This dining-room window was closed as were all the others in the building except one on the floor above, a pair of french windows giving on to a balcony which was quite out of keeping with the design of the hotel. The wind sent these diamond-paned glass doors banging shut and bursting open again, and from time to time it caught the velvet curtains, beating them, making them toss like washing on a line.

There was plenty of room in the parking bays for the half-dozen vehicles which stood there. Only one was on the forecourt proper, a golden Rolls-Royce parked askew, the silver gable of its grid nosing into a flower-bed and crushing geranium blossoms.

Wexford stared at this car from the windows of his own which Burden was steering, with rule-abiding propriety, into a vacant bay. He had heard of the fashion of covering the bodywork of cars in a furry coating to seem like skin or coarse velvet, but he had never yet seen this done in use, except in glossy advertisements. The Rolls wore a skin of pale golden fur, the vibrant sand colour of a lion's pelt which gleamed softly and richly, and on its bonnet, just above the grid, was attached a statuette of a plunging lion that seemed to be made of solid gold.

'This beast-of-prey motif keeps cropping up,' he said. He approached the car to get a closer look and as he did so the driver's door opened and a girl got out. It was Nell Tate.

'Good evening,' he said. 'We've met before.'

'I don't think so. I don't remember.' It was the voice of a person accustomed to defending a celebrity from intrusive fans.

'At the festival.' Wexford introduced himself and Burden. 'I'd like a word with Mr Vedast.'

Nell Tate looked seriously alarmed. 'You can't see Zeno. He's resting. He's probably asleep. We're all trying to get a quiet evening. I only came down to get something out of the car.'

She looked as if she were in need of rest. Beautifully dressed in a long clinging gown of silver lace under which she obviously wore nothing at all, heavy platinum ornaments at neck and wrists, she had a look of hag-ridden exhaustion. Under the silver and purple paint, her left eye was very swollen, the white of it bloodshot between puffy, painful lids. Studying it covertly, Wexford thought that considerable courage must have been needed to stick false lashes on to that bruised membrane.

'There's no hurry,' he said smoothly. 'We'll wait. Are you in the motel?'

'Oh, no.' She had a false poise that was growing brittle. 'We've got what they call the Elizabethan suite. Can you give me some idea what it's about?'

'Dawn Stonor. Tell him we want to talk to him about Dawn Stonor.'

She didn't even go through the pretence of looking bewildered or asking who this was. 'I'll tell him. Couldn't you come back tomorrow?'

'I think we'll wait,' said Wexford. He and Burden followed her into the foyer of the hotel, a porter having sprung forward to open the door for her. Observing the way she swept past the man, her head going up and her shoulders wriggling, passing him without a word or a nod, Wexford hardened his heart. 'We'll give you a quarter of an hour and then we'll come up.'

She made for the lift. The spurned porter, not at all put out, watched her admiringly. Once in the lift, before the doors closed on her, she appeared multiplied three times by the mirrors which lined its walls. Four blonde girls in silver, four bruised eyes, glared at Wexford and then the doors closed and she was whisked upwards.

'Lovely,' said the porter feelingly.

'What are they doing here?'

'Mr Vedast's here to purchase a country property, sir.'

Anyone else, thought Wexford, would have just bought a house. He fished for a couple of coins and found only a fifty-pence piece. 'Any luck, yet?'

'Thank you very much, sir. They go out looking every day, sir, him and Mr and Mrs Tate. We've had a few fans outside but they didn't have no joy on account of Mr Vedast takes all his meals in his suite.'

'She was scared stiff when you said who we were,' said Burden when the porter had gone out of earshot.

'I know, but that may be only that she's afraid of having him disturbed. I wonder if it was he who gave her that black eye?'

'More likely her husband, poor devil. That's a *ménage à trois* if ever there was one. D'you think there are two bed-rooms or only one in that suite?'

'For a self-avowed puritan, Mike, you take a very lubricious interest in these things. Here you are, get your nose into *Nova* and you can pass me *The Field*.'

For fifteen minutes they leafed through the glossy periodicals provided in the Shakespeare Lounge. A very old couple came in and switched on the television. When they were satisfied that it was glowing with colour and braying forth cricket scores, they ignored it and began to read novels. A Dalmatian entered, wandered about and fell into a despairing heap in front of the cold electric heater.

'Right, time's up,' said Wexford. 'Now for the lion's den.'

CHAPTER ELEVEN

The suite was on the first floor. They were admitted not by Nell but by a small dark man of about thirty who introduced himself as Godfrey Tate and who favoured them with a narrow smile. There was something spare and economical about him from his longish thin black hair and dab of moustache to his tiny feet in lace-up boots. He wore tube-like black slacks, a very tight skimpy black shirt, and the air of one who rations his movements, his speech and his manners to the starkest barrenness social usage permits.

'Zeno can spare you ten minutes.'

They were in a small entrance hall filled with flowers, displays of roses, sweet peas and stephanotis, whose perfume hung cloyingly on the air. Burden knocked a rosebud out of a vase and cursed softly. The living room was large and not at all Elizabethan, being done up in the style of a provincial casino with panels of pink mirror on the walls, niches containing more flowers in gilt urns, and french windows, hung with velvet and opening on to a balcony. In here the atmosphere was not stuffy or soporific. All the doors were open, showing a bathroom whose floor was cluttered with wet towels, and the interiors of two bedrooms, one containing a huge double bed and the other two singles. All had been occupied until recently as the tumbled bedclothes showed, but as to who had occupied which and with whom it was impossible to tell. Both bedrooms, like the living room, were littered all over with discarded clothes, magazines, records, and suitcases spilling out their contents. A lusty gale blew through the open windows, shaking the flowers and making the curtains billow and thrash.

Nell Tate looked blue with cold, her arms spiky with gooseflesh. Not so her companion, who, bare-chested, sat at a table by the window eating roast duck with the enthusiasm of one who has been brought up on baked beans.

'Good evening, Mr Vedast. I'm sorry to disturb your dinner.'

Vedast didn't get up, but his hairless, polished-looking face, all bones and almost Slavonic planes, split into a wide grin. 'Hallo. Good evening. Have some coffee.' His voice had no affectations. It was still what it must have always been, the local mixture of Sussex burr and mild cockney. 'Make them send up more coffee, Nello, and take all this away.' He made a sweeping gesture with his arm, indicating the two other plates on which the food had only been picked at, the covered dishes, the basket of melba toast. 'Phone down now. Go on.' No one had touched the cream trifle. Vedast took the whole bowl and set in his lap.

'Maybe they'd rather have a drink,' said Godfrey Tate.

'You mean *you* would, Goffo. Didn't you know they're not allowed to drink on duty?' Spooning up trifle, Vedast grinned at Wexford. He had an ugly attractive face, *joli laid*, very white and oddly bare. His eyes were a light, clear brown that sometimes looked yellow. 'The trouble with Nello and Goffo,' he said, 'is that they never read. They're not informed. Get on with your phoning and drinking, dears.'

Like discontented slaves, the Tates did his bidding. Tate took an almost empty bottle of brandy from a pseudo Louis Quinze cabinet and tipped what remained of it into a glass. He stood drinking it and watching his wife darkly while she phoned down for more coffee. Vedast laughed.

'Why don't you sit down? Not too cold in here, is it?' He put out his hand to Nell and beckoned her, pursing his lips into a whistle shape. She came up to him eagerly, too eagerly. She was trembling with cold. It was all she could do to stop her teeth from chattering. 'Fresh air is good for Nello and Goffo. If I didn't look after their health they'd be like two little broiler chickens, shut up all day in hot hutches. I think we'll do our house-hunting on foot tomorrow, Nello.'

'Then you can count me out,' said Tate.

'Must we? You won't mind if Nello comes with me, will you?' Emaciated, starved-looking Vedast finished the dessert which had been intended for three people. 'Perhaps our visitors can tell us of all sorts of lovely houses going spare round here?'

'We aren't house agents, Mr Vedast,' said Burden, 'and we've come to ask you questions, not answer them.'

The coffee arrived before Vedast could reply to this. Tate took one look at it, swallowed his drink and searched in the cupboard for a fresh bottle of brandy. While his wife poured coffee, he found a bottle tucked away at the back and quite full though already opened. A liberal measure in his glass, he took a long deep draught.

Immediately he was convulsed, choking and clapping one hand over his mouth.

'Christ!' A dribble of liquid came out through his fingers. 'That's not brandy! What the hell is it?'

Vedast laughed, his head on one side. 'Meths and cold tea, Goffo. Just a little experiment to see if you could tell the difference.' Nell giggled, squeezed close against Vedast's side. 'I poured the brandy down the loo. Best place for it.'

Tate said nothing. He went into the bathroom and slammed the door.

'Poor little man! Never mind, we'll take him out to dinner tomorrow at that lovely place in Pomfret. Kiss, Nello? That's right. No hard feelings because I like playing tricks on your old man? How is your coffee, Chief Inspector?'

'Well, it *is* coffee, Mr Vedast. Apparently one runs a risk drinking in your establishment.'

'I wouldn't dare doctor your coffee. I've a great respect for the law.'

'Good,' said Wexford drily. 'I hope you've enough respect to tell me what was your relationship with Dawn Stonor.'

For a moment Vedast was silent but he didn't seem

disturbed. He was waiting while Nell poured cream into his cup and then added four lumps of sugar.

'Thank you, Nello darling. Now you run away and paint something. Your poor eye, for instance.'

'Do I have to?' said Nell like a child who has been told she must go to the dentist.

'Of course you do when Zeno says so. The quicker you go the sooner it will all be over. Run along.'

She ran along. She wasn't a child but a grown woman, shivering with cold and with a black eye. Vedast smiled indulgently. He walked to the bathroom door and paused, listening to Tate running taps and brushing his teeth. Then he came back, kicking shut the door of the drinks cabinet as he passed it, and stretched himself out full-length on the pink velvet sofa.

'You wanted to ask me about Dawnie,' he said. 'I suppose you've been talking to Mummy Stonor or even Granny Peckham?'

'They say you were at school with Dawn.'

'So I was. So were ever such a lot of other people. Why pick on me?'

'Mr Vedast,' said Wexford heavily, 'Dawn told her flat-mate that you and she had remained friends since you left school, and she told her grandmother that you took her out to dinner on the Friday before she died. We know that can't have been true since you were in Manchester that day, but we'd like to know how well you knew Dawn and when you last saw her.'

Vedast took a lump of sugar and sucked it. He seemed completely relaxed, one leg casually crossed over the other. Still in their raincoats, Wexford and Burden were not even comfortably warm, but Vedast, almost naked, showed no sign of being affected by the cold damp wind. The golden hairs on his chest lay flat under the light gold chain which hung against them.

'When we both lived here,' he said, 'she was my girl friend.'

'You mean you were lovers?'

Vedast nodded, smiling pleasantly. 'I was her first lover. We were sixteen. Rather moving, don't you think? Martin Silk discovered me and all sorts of exciting things happened to me which wouldn't interest you at all. Dawnie and I lost touch. I didn't see her again till this year.'

'Where did you see her?'

'In the Townsman Club,' said Vedast promptly. 'Nello and Goffo and I went there as guests of a friend of mine, and there was Dawnie serving drinks. My poor little Dawnie in a yellow satin corset and tights! I nearly laughed but that would have been unkind. She came and sat down at our table and we had a long chat about old times. She even remembered what I like to drink, orange juice with sugar in it.'

'Did you communicate with her after that?'

'Just once.' Vedast spoke very lightly, very easily, his fingers playing with the gold chain. 'Nello and Goffo had gone away to see Goffo's mum and I was rather lonely, all on my own and sad, you know.' He smiled, the unspoilt star, the poor little rich boy. 'Dawnie had written down her phone number for me at the club. Nello didn't like that a bit, you can imagine. I thought, why not give Dawnie a ring?'

'And did you?'

'Of course I did.' Now Vedast's smile was apologetic, a little rueful, the smile of the unspoilt star who longs for the companions of his humbler days to treat him as the simple country boy he really is at heart. 'But it's very off-putting, isn't it, when people sort of swamp you? D'you know what I mean? When they're terribly enthusiastic, sort of fawning?'

'You mean you got bored?' said Burden bluntly.

'It sounds unkind, put that way. Let's say I thought it better not to revive something which was dead and gone. Sorry, that wasn't very tactful. What I mean is I choked Dawnie off. I said it would be lovely if we could meet again sometime, but I was so busy at present.'

'When did this telephone conversation take place, Mr Vedast?'

'Three or four weeks ago. It was just a little chat, leading to nothing. Fancy Dawnie telling Granny Peckham we'd met! Nello and Goffo could tell you when it was they went away.' He fixed his cat's eyes, yellowish, narrow, on Wexford, opening them very wide suddenly, and again they had a sharp sly glint. 'And they'll tell you where I was on June sixth. I know that'll be the next thing you'll ask.'

'Where were you, Mr Vedast?'

'At my house in Duvette Gardens, South Kensington. Nello and Goffo and I were all there. We came back from Manchester during the Sunday night and just lazed about and slept all that Monday. Here's Goffo, all clean and purified. He'll tell you.'

Godfrey Tate had emerged from the bathroom, blank-faced, contained, wary, but showing no grudge against Vedast for the humiliating trick to which the singer had subjected him.

'Who's taking my name in vain?' he said with an almost pathetically unsuccessful attempt at jocularity.

'Tell the officers where I was on June sixth, Goffo.'

'With me and Nell.' He responded so promptly, so glibly, that it was evident the stating of this alibi had been rehearsed. 'We were all together in Duvette Gardens all day and all night. Nell can tell you the same. Nell!'

Wexford was sure she had been listening behind the door, for she exclaimed when her husband opened it as if she had been knocked backwards.

'Of course we were all there,' she said. She had covered herself with a long coat but she was still cold and she moved towards the window as if to close it. When Vedast, still smiling, shook his head, she sat down obediently, huddled in the coat, and at a glance from him, said, 'We didn't go out all day. We were exhausted after Manchester.' One hand went up to the sore eye, hovered and fell again into her lap.

'And now,' said the singer, 'tell the officers when you went off on your trip to see Goffo's mum.'

If Tate had had a tail, Wexford thought, he would at this point have wagged it. Rather like a performing dog who loves yet fears his master and who is utterly hypnotized by him, he sat up, raised his head eagerly.

'About a month ago, wasn't it?' prompted Vedast.

'We went on May twenty-second,' said Nell, 'and . . .'

'Came back on Wednesday, the twenty-fifth,' her husband ended for her.

Vedast looked pleased. For a moment it looked as if he would pat his dogs on their heads, but instead he smiled at Tate and blew a kiss at Tate's wife. 'You see, Chief Inspector? We lead a very quiet life. I didn't kill Dawnie out of passion, Goffo didn't kill her because I told him to — though I'm sure he would have done if I had — and Nello didn't kill her out of jealousy. So we can't help you. We've got masses of stuff from agents to look through tonight, so may we get on with our house-hunting?'

'Yes, Mr Vedast, you may, but I can't promise I shan't want to see you again.'

Vedast sprang to his feet in one supple movement. 'No, don't promise. I should love to see you again. We've had such a nice talk. We don't see many people, we have to be so careful.' Wexford's hand was cordially shaken. 'See them out, Goffo, and lock up the car.'

'I wish you good hunting, Mr Vedast,' said Wexford.

John Burden was at home and already in bed, having left a note for his father to tell him that Pat would be staying the night with her aunt. The key had been left under a flower-pot, which shocked the policeman in Burden while the father showed a fatuous pride in his son's forethought. He removed the Vedast L.P. from the turntable and closed the record player.

'One of these songs,' he said, 'is called "Whistle and I'll come to you, my love".'

'Very appropriate,' Wexford glanced at the record sleeve. 'He must have written that for the Tates' theme song.'

'My God, yes. Why do they put up with it?'

'She for love, he for money. Both for the reflected glory. He hit the nail right on the head when he said "Goffo" would have killed Dawn if he'd told him to. They'd do anything for him. "Being your slave, what should I do but tend upon the hours and times of your desire?" It's not just love and money and glory, but the power of the man's personality. It's sinister, it's most unpleasant. In a set-up of this kind that alibi goes for nothing. An alibi supported by slaves is no alibi. The Romans in their heyday were very chary about admitting slaves' evidence.'

Burden chuckled. 'I daresay you're right, Caesar. How did he know he needed an alibi for the sixth of June, anyway? We didn't tell him.'

'Mrs Stonor or Mrs Peckham may have told him. There was something about it in the papers, about our thinking that the probable date of her death. I don't really suppose he's involved at all. He likes playing with us, that's all. He likes sailing near the wind. Above all, he enjoys frightening the others.' Wexford added in the words of the Duke of Wellington: ' "By God, he frightens me!" '

CHAPTER TWELVE

The interior decorations of Leonard Dunsand's bungalow were precisely the same as those of Miss Mowler's. Identical red spotted paper covered the hall walls, identical birds and lilies pained the eye in the living room. But Miss Mowler, for all her genteel shudders at the builder's bad taste, had shown little more judgment in her own and had filled the place with garish furniture and mass-produced pictures. Dunsand's drab pieces, brown leather smoking-room chairs, late Victorian tables and, above all, shelf upon shelf of scholarly books, looked absurdly incongruous here. Little shrivelled cacti, lifeless greenish-brown pin-cushions, stood in pots on the window-sills. There was nothing in the hall but a bare mahogany table and no carpet on the floor. It was the typical home of the celibate intellectual, uncharacteristic only in that it was as clean as Mrs Peveril's and that, on a table in the living room, lay a stack of holiday brochures, their covers even more vividly coloured than the wallpaper.

Dunsand, who had just come home from work, asked them to sit down in a colourless but cultivated voice. He seemed about forty with thinning mousey hair and rubbery face whose features were too puffy for that tight mouth. Thick glasses distorted his eyes, making them appear protuberant. He wore an immaculate, extremely conventional dark suit, white shirt and dark tie. Neither obstructive nor ingratiating, he repeated what he had already told Burden, that he had reached home at about six-forty on June sixth and had noticed no unusual happenings in The Pathway during that evening.

'I prepared myself a meal,' he said, 'and then I did some housework. This place is very ugly inside but I see no reason why it should also be dirty.'

'Did you see anything of your neighbours?'

'I saw Mrs Peveril go down the road at half past seven. I understand she attends an evening class in some sort of handicraft.'

'You didn't go out yourself? It was a fine evening.'

'Was it?' said Dunsand politely. 'No, I didn't go out.'

'Are you on friendly terms with your neighbours, Mr Dunsand?'

'Oh, yes, very.'

'You go into their houses, for instance? They visit you?'

'No. I think I misunderstood you. I simply mean we nod to each other and say a word if we meet in the street.'

Wexford sighed to himself. He found Dunsand depressing and he pitied his students. Philosophy, he knew – although he knew little about it – is not all ethics, witty syllogisms, anecdotes about Pythagoras, but logic, abstruse mathematics, points and instants, epistemological premisses. Imagine this one holding forth for a couple of hours on Wittgenstein!

'So you can tell us nothing of Mr and Mrs Peveril's way of life, their habits, who calls on them and so on?'

'No, nothing.' Dunsand spoke in the same drab level voice, but Wexford fancied that for a brief moment he had caught a certain animation in the man's eye, a sign of life, a flash perhaps of pain. It was gone, the magnified eyes were still and staring. 'I think I can say, Chief Inspector, that I know nothing of any private life but my own.'

'And that is . . . ?' Wexford said hesitantly.

'What you see.' Dunsand cleared his throat. 'Beginning to rain again,' he said. 'If you don't want to ask me anything else I'll go and put my car away.'

'Do you ever go to London, Mr Peveril?'

'Of course I do in connection with my work.' Peveril put a gloomy and irritable emphasis on the last word. He had once more been fetched from his studio and his fingers were actually inky. Wexford couldn't help feeling that the ink had been put there deliberately just as the man's hair had been purposely shaken and made to stand up in awry spikes. 'I go up occasionally, once a fortnight, once a month.'

'And stay overnight?'

'I have done.'

'When did you last go?'

'Oh God, it would have been June first, I think. I didn't stay.' Peveril glanced towards the closed door which excluded his wife. 'Scenes,' he said stiffly, 'are made if I venture to spend a night away from the matrimonial nest.' Misanthropic, his whole manner showing how distasteful he found this probing, he nevertheless was unable to resist making frank disclosures. 'You'd imagine that a woman who has everything soft and easy for her, never earned a penny since she found someone to keep her, wouldn't deny the breadwinner a few hours of freedom. But there it is. If I go to London I have to phone her when I get there and leave a number for her to call me whenever she fancies, that means about three times in one evening.'

Wexford shrugged. It was not an uncommon type of marriage that Peveril had described; he was only one of many who had elected to make the dreariest and the longest journey with a jealous foe. But why talk about it? Because it would induce his interrogator to believe that such surveillance kept him from other women? Wexford almost smiled at such naivety. He knew that good-looking, dissatisfied men of Peveril's stamp, childless men long out of love with their wives, could be Houdini-like in the facility with which they escaped from domestic bonds. He left the subject.

'Your wife went to an evening class on that Monday evening,' he said. 'Would you mind telling me what your movements were?'

'I *moved* into my studio to work and I didn't *move* out of it until my wife got back at eleven.'

'There are no buses at that time of night. She didn't take your car?'

An edge of contempt to his voice, Peveril said, 'She can't drive. She walked into Kingsmarkham and some woman gave her a lift back.'

'You didn't think of driving her, then? It was a fine evening and it isn't far.'

'Damn it all!' said Peveril, his ready temper rising. 'Why the hell should I drive her to some daft hen party where they don't learn a bloody thing? It's not as if she was going to work, going to bring in some much-needed money.' He added sullenly, 'I usually do drive her, as a matter of fact.'

'Why didn't you that night?'

'The worm turned,' said Peveril. 'That's why not. Now I'd appreciate it if you'd let me get on with my work.'

It was on the red dress that Wexford concentrated that Friday. He called a semi-informal conference consisting of himself, Burden, Dr Crocker, Sergeant Martin and Detective Polly Davies. They sat in his office, their chairs in a circle, with the dress laid on his desk. Then Wexford decided that for them all to get a better view of it while they talked, the best thing would be to hang it from the ceiling. A hanger was produced by Polly, and dress and hanger suspended from the lead of Wexford's central light.

Laboratory experts had subjected it to a thorough examination. They had found that it was made of synthetic fibre and that it had been frequently worn probably by the same person, a brown-haired, fair-skinned Caucasian. There were no sweat stains in the armpits. In the fibre had been found traces of an unidentified perfume, talcum powder, anti-perspirant and carbon tetrachloride, a cleaning fluid. Other researches showed the dress to have been manufactured some eight or nine years previously at a North London factory for distribution by a small fashion house that dealt in medium-priced clothes. It might have been bought in London, Manchester, Birmingham or a host of other towns and cities in the British Isles. No Kingsmarkham store had ever stocked the garments from this fashion house, but they were, and had for a long time been, obtainable in Brighton.

The dress itself was a dark purplish red, darker than magenta and bluer than burgundy. It had a plain round neck, three-quarter-length sleeves, a fitted waist with self belt and a skirt designed just to show the wearer's knees. This indicated that it had been bought for a woman about five feet seven inches tall, a woman who was also, but not exceptionally, slim, for it was a size twelve. On Dawn Stonor it had been a tight fit and an unfashionable length for this or any other epoch.

'Comments, please,' said Wexford. 'You first, Polly. You look as if you've got something to say.'

'Well, sir, I was just thinking that she must have looked really grotty in it.' Polly was a lively, black-haired young woman who habitually dressed in the 'dolly' mode, mini-skirts, natty waistcoats and velvet baker-boy caps. Her way of painting her mouth strawberry red and blotching two red dabs on her cheeks made her look less intelligent than she was. Now she saw from Wexford's frown that her imprecise epithet had displeased him and she corrected herself hurriedly. 'I mean, it wouldn't have suited her and she'd have looked dowdy and awful. A real freak. I know that sounds unkind – of course she looked dreadful when she was found – but what I'm trying to say is that she must have looked dreadful from the moment she put it on.'

'You'd say, would you, that the dress itself is unattractive as a garment? I'm asking you particularly, Polly, because you're a woman and more likely to see these things than we are.'

'It's hard to say, sir, when something's gone out of date. I suppose with jewellery and so forth it might have looked all right on a dark person it fitted well. It wouldn't have looked good on Dawn because she had sort of reddish-blonde hair and she must have absolutely bulged out of it. I can't think she'd ever have put it on from *choice*. And another thing, sir, you said I'm more likely to notice these things than you are, but – well, just for an experiment, could you all say what you think of it as, say, a dress you'd like your wives to wear?'

'Anything you say. Doctor?'

Crocker uncrossed his elegant legs and put his head on one side. 'It's a bit difficult,' he began, 'to separate it from the unpleasant associations it has, but I'll try. It's rather *dull*. Let me say that if my wife wore it I'd feel she wasn't letting me down in any way. I wouldn't mind who saw her in it. It's got what I believe they call an "uncluttered line" and it would show off a woman's figure in a discreet kind of way. On the other hand, supposing I was the sort of man who took other women out, I don't think I'd feel any too thrilled if my girl friend turned up to a date wearing it because it wouldn't be – well, adventurous enough.'

'Mike?'

Burden had no wife, but he had come to terms with his condition. He was able to talk of wives now without inner pain or outward embarrassment. 'I agree with the doctor that it's rather distasteful to imagine anyone close to you wearing it because of the circumstances and so on associated with it. When I make myself look at it as I might look at a dress in shop window I'd say I rather like it. No doubt, I've no idea of fashion, but I'd call it smart. If I were – er, a married man I'd like to see my wife in it.'

'Sergeant?'

'It's a smart dress, sir,' said Martin eagerly. 'My wife's got a dress rather like it and that sort of shade. I bought it for her last Christmas, chose it myself, come to that. My daughter – she's twenty-two – she says she wouldn't be seen dead in it, but you know these young girls – beg your pardon, Polly. That's a nice, smart dress, sir, or was.'

'Now for me,' said Wexford. 'I like it. It looks comfortable and practical for everyday wear. One would feel pleasantly uxorious and somehow secure sitting down in the evening with a woman in that dress. And I think it would be becoming on the right person. As the doctor says, it follows the natural lines of a woman's figure. It's not daring or dramatic or embarrassing. It's conservative. There you are, Polly. What do you make of all that?'

Polly laughed. 'It tells me more about all you than the dress,' she said pertly. 'But what it does tell me is that it's a *man's* dress, sir. I mean, it's the sort of thing a man would choose because it's figure-flattering and plain and somehow as you said, secure. Dr Crocker said he wouldn't want to see his girl friend in it. Doesn't all this mean it's a *wife's* dress chosen by a *husband* partly because he subconsciously realizes it shows she's a good little married lady and any other man seeing her in it will know she's not made of girl-friend stuff?'

'Perhaps it does,' said Wexford thoughtfully. The window was open and the dress swayed and swivelled in the breeze. Find the owner, he thought, and then I have all I need to know. 'That's intelligent of you, Polly, but where does it get us? You've convinced me it was owned at one time by a married woman who bought it to please her husband. We already know Dawn didn't own it. Its owner might have sent it to a jumble sale, given it to her cleaner or taken it to the Oxfam shop.'

'We could check with the Oxfam people here, sir.'

'Yes, Sergeant, that must be done. I believe you said, Mike, that Mrs Peveril denies ownership?'

'She may be lying. When it was shown to her I thought she was going to faint. With that stain on it it isn't a particularly attractive object and there are, as we've said, the associations. But she reacted to it very strongly. On the other hand, we know she's a nervy and hysterical woman. It could be a natural reaction.'

'Have you talked to Mrs Clarke again?'

'She says her friend had some sort of mental breakdown last year and lost a lot of weight, so it hardly looks as if she was ever slim enough to wear the dress. But Mrs Clarke has only known her four years.'

'Eight years ago,' Wexford said thoughtfully, 'the Peverils might still have been on romantic terms. He might have been choosing clothes for her that were particularly to his taste. But I agree with you that the question of size makes that unlikely. Well, I won't detain you any longer. It's a massive plan I've got in mind, but I think it's the only course to take. Somehow or other we're going to have to question every woman in Kingsmarkham and Stowerton between the ages of thirty and sixty, show them the dress and get reactions. Ask each one if it's hers or, if not, whether she's ever seen anyone else wearing it.'

His announcement was received with groans by all but the doctor, who left quickly, declaring that his presence was needed at the infirmary.

CHAPTER THIRTEEN

The response to Wexford's appeal was enormous and immediate. Women queued up outside the Baptist church hall to
view the dress as they might have queued on the first day of
a significant sale. Public-spirited? Wexford thought their enthusiasm sprang more from a need to seem for a little while
important. People like to be caught up in the whirlwind of
something sensational and they like it even more if, instead of
being part of a crowd, each can for a brief moment be an
individual, noticed, attended to, taken seriously. They like to
leave their names and addresses, see themselves recorded. He
supposed they also liked to feast their eyes on the relic of a
violent act. Was it so bad if they did? Was it what the young
festival visitors would have called sick? Or was it rather
evidence of a strong human vitality, the curiosity that wants
to see everything, know everything, be in the swim, that when
refined and made scholarly, is the prerogative of the historian
and the archaeologist?

He had long ago ceased to allow hope to triumph over
experience. He didn't suppose that some woman would come
forward and say her husband had unexpectedly and inexplicably borrowed the dress from her that Monday evening. Nor
did he anticipate any dramatic scene in the hall, a wife
screaming or falling into a faint because she recognized the
dress and realized simultaneously what recognition implied.
No woman harbouring a guilty secret would come there
voluntarily. But he did hope for something. Someone would
say she had seen the garment on a friend or an acquaintance;
someone would admit to having possessed it and then to have
given it away or sold it.

No one did. All Friday afternoon they filed along the

wooden passage that smelt of hymn books and Boy Scouts, passed into the grim brown hall to sit on the Women's Fellowship chairs and stare at the posters for coffee mornings and social evenings. Then, one by one, they went behind the screens where Martin and Polly had the dress laid out on a trestle table. One by one they came out with the baulked, rather irritable, look on their faces of do-gooders whom ill-luck had robbed of the chance to be more than negatively helpful.

'I suppose,' said Burden, 'that she could have been picked up by a man in a car. A prearranged pick-up, of course. He might have come from anywhere.'

'In that case, why take a bus to Sundays and walk across the fields? Mrs Peveril says she saw her go into those fields and her description is so accurate that I think we must believe her. Dawn may have been early for her date – that was the only bus as we've said before – gone into the fields to sit down and wait, and then doubled back. But if she did that, she didn't go far back.'

'What makes you say that?'

'Four people saw her between the time she left her mother's house and the time she went into those fields, five-thirty. We've not been able to find anyone who saw her *after* five-thirty, though God knows, we've made enough appeals and questioned enough people. Therefore it's almost certain she went into some house somewhere just after five-thirty.'

Burden frowned. 'On the Sundays estate, you mean?'

'To put it more narrowly than that, in The Pathway. The body was in the quarry, Mike. It was carried or dragged to the quarry, not transported in a car. You know what a job it was to get our own cars down there. When the gates to the drive are locked no car could get in.' Wexford glanced at his watch. 'It's five-thirty and the Olive's open. Can't we leave Martin to carry on with this and adjourn for a drink? I'd rather talk all this out sitting down over a pint.'

Burden's brow creased further and he bit his lip. 'What about Pat? She'll have to get her own tea. She'll have to walk to her dancing lesson. John'll be alone.'

In a tone that is usually described as patient but which, in fact indicates an extreme degree of controlled exasperation, Wexford said, 'He is six feet tall. He is fifteen. By the time he was that age my old dad had been out at work eighteen months. Why can't he escort his sister to her dancing class? Taking it for granted, of course, that if she walks three hundred yards alone on a bright summer evening, she's bound to be set on by kidnappers.'

'I'll phone them,' said Burden with a shamefaced grin.

The saloon bar of the Olive and Dove was almost empty, a little gloomy and uninviting as deserted low-ceilinged places always are when the sun shines brightly outside. Wexford carried their drinks into the garden where wooden tables and chairs were arranged under an arbour. Vines and clematises made a leafy roof over their heads. It was the home-going hour, the time when the peace and the quiet of this spot was usually shattered by the sound of brakes and shifting gears as traffic poured over the Kingsbrook bridge.

Today all man-made noise was drowned by the chatter of the swollen river running beside the terraced garden. It was a steady low roar, constant and unchanging, but like all natural sound it was neither tedious to the ear nor a hindrance to conversation. It was soothing. It spoke of timeless forces, pure and untameable, which in a world of ugliness and violence resisted man's indifferent toiling of the earth. Listening to it, sitting in silence, Wexford thought of that ugliness, the scheme of things in which a girl could be beaten to death, thrown into a bower which had been made and used for love, thrown like garbage.

He shivered. He could never quite get used to it, the appalling things that happened, the waste, the pointlessness. But now he had to think of practical matters, of why and how this particular ugliness had taken place, and when Burden came to the table he said:

'You've talked to the occupants of the other two houses in The Pathway and I haven't. Would you say we could exclude them?'

'The Streets are a married couple with four children, all of whom were at home with their parents the whole evening. None of them saw Dawn. Mrs Street saw Miss Mowler come home at eight o'clock. Apart from that, none of them saw any of their neighbours that evening. They heard nothing and they remained in the front of the house from about six till about ten. Mrs Street's kitchen is in the front.

'The Robinsons are elderly. He's bedridden and they have a fiercely respectable old housekeeper. Mr Robinson's bedroom overlooks Sundays but not the quarry. His wife spent the evening with him in his bedroom as she always does and went to her own room at nine-thirty. She saw and heard nothing. The housekeeper saw Dunsand come home at twenty to seven and Miss Mowler at eight. She didn't see the Peverils and she herself went to bed at ten.'

Wexford nodded. 'How about Silk?'

'Up in London from June sixth to June eighth, making last-minute festival arrangements. Says he left Sundays at about seven on the evening of the sixth.'

'Can anyone corroborate that?'

'His wife and his two grown-up children are in Italy. They've been there since the end of May and they aren't back yet. Silk says they always go abroad for two months in the summer, but it looks to me as if they aren't as keen as he on the pop scene.'

'And it's his quarry,' said Wexford thoughtfully. 'If anybody had easy access to it, he did. I imagine he's often in London, too. I don't suppose he was at school with Dawn, was he?'

'Hardly, sir,' said Burden. 'He's as old as you.' He added generously: 'And looks a good deal more.'

Wexford laughed. 'I won't bother to grow my hair, then. It doesn't seem likely that Dawn would have played around with him, and if she had done she'd have gone straight up to the house, surely, not tried to sneak round by a back way. There was no wife at Sundays for her to hide from.'

'And no possible reason for her to bring a picnic.'

'No, I think we can exclude Silk on the grounds of age and general ineligibility. That leaves us with the Peverils, Dunsand and Miss Mowler. But Peveril wasn't alone in his house at five-thirty and Miss Mowler and Dunsand weren't even at home. And yet who but the occupants of one of those three houses could have put Dawn's body in the quarry without being seen?'

Burden glanced surreptitiously at his watch, shifting uneasily. 'Then we're saying she doubled back, sir, and was admitted to one of those houses. Somebody let her in. Not Dunsand or Miss Mowler. Peveril or Mrs Peveril, then? That must mean the Peverils are in it up to their necks. In that case, why does Mrs Peveril say she saw the girl at all? Why say anything?'

'Possibly because she isn't up to her neck in it at all. Because she *did* see Dawn go into those fields and didn't know of any connection between the girl she saw and her husband. Dawn caught that bus because it was the only bus she could catch. She loitered in the fields for two hours – remember how warm and sunny it was – and returned to Peveril's house *after* Mrs Peveril had left for her class. D'you want another drink?'

'Oh, no,' said Burden quickly. 'Good heavens, no.'

'Then we may as well get back to your place. I can't stand this watch-watching.'

Outside the Baptist church the queues had lengthened. Housewives departing to prepare evening meals had been replaced by working women released from shops and offices.

'Better get something special for the children's dinner,' said conscientious Burden. 'The Luximart stays open late on Fridays. You eating with us?'

'No, thanks. My wife'll have something for me at eight.'

They went into the shop where they were immediately recognized by the manager. He insisted on pointing out to them personally items precisely similar to those Dawn had bought from the six tomatoes in a plastic-covered tray to the bottle of cheap wine. The shop was full and the manager spoke loudly as if anxious to cash in on and reap the benefits of a particularly ghoulish form of advertising.

'Tomatoes as purchased by our very own murder victim,' said Wexford disgustedly.

Burden avoided them studiously and averted his eyes from the row of strawberry mousses. 'You forgot the food in your theory,' he whispered. 'Peveril would have already eaten. His wife would have given him his dinner before she went out.' Regardless of expense, he selected three packages of *bœuf bourguignon* from the frozen-food trough. 'She meant to stay overnight too. You forgot that. Or was Peveril going to hide her in his studio when his wife got home at eleven?'

'Everything all right, sir?' said the manager. 'How about a bottle of wine to go with that?'

'No, thanks.' Burden paid and they left, their progress watched by a dozen pairs of curious eyes. The sun was still bright, the wind brisk. Martin was fixing a fresh, larger, poster of Dawn's picture to the church-hall door.

'Anything yet?' asked Wexford.

'We've had five hundred women pass through here, sir, and not one of them able to give us a bit of help.'

'Keep on at it tomorrow.'

They walked the length of the High Street and turned left into Tabard Road. Burden's step always quickened at this point. Once he had made himself aware that no fire engines or ambulances thronged the street outside his bungalow he relaxed and his breathing became more even.

'Was Peveril going to keep her hidden all night?' he said. 'Or, failing that, maybe she got into Dunsand's place through the larder window. There's an idea for you. Poor old Dunsand who has to fend for himself like me, living on frozen food he buys on his way home, no doubt. Miss Mowler must have actually known her – district nurses know everybody. Perhaps Dawn hid in her garden until eight o'clock, keeping herself from boredom by trying on a dress she found hanging in the shed?'

'I'm the one who asks the derisive questions, not you, remember? All this reversing our roles throws me off balance.' Wexford raised his eyebrows at the three bicycles leaning against Burdens' gate and the moped parked at the kerb. 'Doesn't look as if your boy's moping in solitude,' he said. 'Good thing he's been prudent and shut the windows.'

The six teenagers who were gyrating energetically in Burden's living room stopped abashed when the policemen came in, and Pat, standing by the record player, pressed the 'reject' lever. Vedast's line, 'Come once more and be my wife', groaned away on a dying fall, the last word a melancholy moan.

'Having your dancing lesson at home tonight, my dear?' said Wexford, smiling.

The two Burden children began to make hasty excuses while their friends made for the door with the silent speed that looks like treachery but is in fact the loyalty of those accustomed to parental censure and who know it is better faced without an audience. Wexford didn't think they ought to have to apologize for innocently enjoying themselves and he interrupted Burden's half-hearted reproaches.

'Play it again, will you, Pat?'

Expertly she found the right track on the L.P. without having to check with the sleeve and lowered the pick-up arm delicately.

'I don't like you doing that,' said John. 'You'll scratch it.'

'I won't. I'm more careful with records than you are. So there!' The Burden children were usually at loggerheads and seldom missed an opportunity to rile each other. 'It's a horrible song, anyway. All sloppy love stuff. Folk music ought to have some point to it and Zeno Vedast's hasn't any point at all.'

'What d'you mean by "point", Pat?'

'Well, be anti-war, Mr Wexford, or for everybody loving each other not just one stupid girl. Or anti-ugliness and mess like Betti Ho. Zeno Vedast's songs are all for him, all for self.'

Wexford listened interestedly to this but Burden said sourly, 'Everybody loving each other! You can talk.' He sniffed. 'I don't hold with all this putting the world right.'

'Then you shouldn't be a policeman,' said Wexford. 'Play it, Pat.'

The song started with a little grinding scratch which made John frown and purse his lips. Then Vedast's strings twanged and the clear, unaffected voice began to sing:

'I don't miss her smile or the flowers,
I don't eclipse distance or hours . . .'

'He writes his own songs?' Wexford whispered.

'Oh, yes, always,' said John reverently. 'This one's two years old but it's his best.'

'Boring!' Pat ducked behind the player to avoid her brother's wrath.

It wasn't boring. Listening to the slight, delicate story which the verses and the chorus told, Wexford had a strong sense that the singer was relating a true experience.

Suddenly the backing grew loud and Vedast's voice bitter, keening:

'Now she's gone in the harsh light of day,
When she'll return the night would not say,
And I am left to vision the time
When once more she'll come and be mine.

So come by, come nigh,
come try and tell why
some sigh, some cry,
some lie and some di-i-ie.'

Burden broke the silence which followed. 'I'm going to get this food heated up.' He went into the kitchen but Wexford lingered.

'Does he ever write joke songs, John?'

'*Joke* songs?'

'Yes – I mean, well, they're hardly in the same class, but Haydn and Mozart sometimes wrote jokes into their music. If you're a joker in private life, joking often comes into your work as well. D'you know the Surprise Symphony?'

Pat said, 'We did it at school. There's a sort of soft gentle bit and then a big boom that makes us jump.'

Wexford nodded. 'I wondered if Vedast . . .'

'Some of them are a bit like that,' said John. 'Sudden loud bits or a funny change of key. And all his songs are supposed to be somebody's story or to have a special meaning for a friend.' He added eagerly: 'I'll play you some more, shall I?'

'Not now.' Burden came back to lay the table. Pat tried to take the knives and forks out of his hand, but the daughter who had been admonished for showing insufficient love must not be allowed to show it now by helping her father. He kept his hold on the cutlery and shook his head with rather a martyred air. 'Ready in five minutes. You'd better wash your hands and sit up at the table.'

Wexford followed him into the kitchen.

'I've learnt some interesting facts about our slave-driver. I wonder how long he's staying in this neck of the woods?'

'John says indefinitely. You don't really think he had anything to do with all this?'

Wexford shrugged. 'He intrigues me. I can't do what Scott advises and stop mine ear against the singer. His song is beginning to haunt me. I think I'll buy a single of it tomorrow.'

Burden switched off the oven. 'We might play it over and over in your office,' he said sarcastically. 'Get a couple of the W.P.C.s in and dance. Have ourselves a rave-up. There won't be anything else to do if no one's identified that dress.'

'There will be for me,' said Wexford, taking his leave. 'I'm going to London to have another talk with Joan Miall.'

CHAPTER FOURTEEN

Wexford bought a local paper to read in the train. The *Kingsmarkbam Courier* came out on a Friday and Dawn's body had been found on the previous Monday, so that news was stale even by local standards. Harry Wild, the chief reporter, had made what he could of it by giving headline publicity to Wexford's appeals in connection with the red dress, but by far the greater part of the front page was devoted to Zeno Vedast. A large photograph, taken by a not very expert *Courier* staff man, showed the singer and the Tates leaning against the bonnet of the golden Rolls. Nell was smiling serenely, one hand caressing the lion ornament. Wild had married his two lead stories by including his caption to the picture a frank confession from Vedast that he had been at school with Dawn Stonor. Reading it, Wexford felt even more convinced that Vedast could not be involved in Dawn's death, that he had nothing to hide. But why then was he staying on in Cheriton Forest, staying even though, as the caption stated, he had found and started negotiations for the house he intended to buy? Could it be that he was staying to see the case through, to await the outcome?

Joan Miall's flat was on the second floor of a tall shabby house between the Earls Court Road and Warwick Road. It wasn't a shabby flat, but smartly and even adventurously decorated, the ceilings painted in bold dark colours to reduce their height. A close observer could tell that the furniture was mostly secondhand, but the girls had re-covered the armchairs, put new pictures in old frames and filled the shelves with brightly jacketed paperbacks. There were a great many plants, fresh and green from recent watering.

She received him without pomp, without preparation. She

wore red trousers, a red spotted smock and no make-up. A big old vacuum cleaner, cast off perhaps by some more affluent relative, was plugged in just inside the front door. He had heard its whine die away when he rang the bell.

She was expecting him and she put on a kettle to make coffee. 'I miss Dawn,' she said. 'Especially round about lunchtime. We were almost always together then. I keep expecting to hear her call out from her bedroom that she's dying for a cup of coffee. Oh, "dying" – the expressions one uses! But she often said she was dying. Dying of boredom, dying for a drink.'

'I know so little about her. If I knew more, I might know how and why. You see, Miss Miall, there are two kinds of murder victim, those who are killed by a stranger for gain or for some obscure pathological reason, and those who are killed by someone who is not a stranger, someone who might be or have been a friend. It is in those cases that it's invaluable to know as much as may be known about the character and the tastes and the peculiarities of the victim.'

'Yes, I do see. Of course I do.' She paused, frowning. 'But people are little worlds, aren't they? There's so much in everyone, depths, and layers, strange countries if we're talking about worlds. I might just be showing you the wrong country.'

It took her a little while to get the coffee. She was a faddist, he remembered. He heard and smelt her grinding coffee beans – nothing pre-ground out of a packet for her – and when she came in with the tray he saw that the coffee was in an earthenware jug. But as soon as she sat down she lit a cigarette and she sighed with a kind of relief as she exhaled. It recalled to him her words about the strange countries in each person's make-up. She hadn't mentioned the inconsistencies which those who delve into character must encounter as bafflingly as the unknown.

'Did you both work every night at the Townsman?' he began.

'It's more complicated than that. We do lunches as well.

Members can lunch between twelve and three, so we either work an eleven till five shift or one from seven at night to two in the morning. If you do the night shift, you can be sure you won't have to do the lunchtime one next day, but otherwise it's rather haphazard. We get two full days off a week, not necessarily Saturday and Sunday, of course. Dawn and I often worked the same shift, but just as often we didn't. There were lots and lots of times when she was alone here seeing people and getting calls I knew nothing about.'

'You knew about the one particular call you told me of.'

'Yes,' she said, 'I've thought a lot about that since then, trying to sort it all out, and I've remembered all sorts of things I didn't tell you. But the things I've remembered aren't helpful. They really only prove it *wasn't* Zeno Vedast who phoned her.'

'I'd like to hear them just the same.'

'I forgot to tell you that his name came up long before the phone call. It must have been in March or April. Of course, we'd see him on TV or read about him in the papers and she'd say she'd known him for years, but she never actually spoke of him as a friend she *saw*. Then one morning – I think it was the end of March – she said he'd been in the club the night before. I hadn't been working that night and, frankly, I didn't believe her. I knew he wasn't a member. I asked one of the other girls and she said Zeno Vedast had been in and had sort of chatted Dawn up a bit. I still wasn't convinced and I'm not now – about the friendship. I mean. We get a lot of celebrities in the club and they do chat us up. That's what we're there for.'

'When did the phone call come, Miss Miall?'

'It was a Monday.' She frowned, concentrating. 'Dawn had had the day off, I'd been working the lunchtime shift. Let me see – it wasn't the last Monday in May. I think it must have been May twenty-third, about half past eight in the evening. We were sitting in here by ourselves, watching television. The phone rang and Dawn answered it. She said hallo and then something like, 'How super of you to phone me.' She covered up the mouthpiece and whispered to me to turn down the TV. Then she said, "It's Zeno Vedast." I was embarrassed. I thought she must be in a really neurotic state if she was prepared to fantasize that far.'

Wexford accepted a second cup of coffee. 'Miss Miall, suppose I told you that Vedast did recognize her in the club, that it was he who phoned that night, what would you say to that?'

'That I knew her and you didn't,' the girl said obstinately. 'He was in the club all right. I know that. He talked to her. A maharajah talked to me for half an hour one night but that doesn't make us lifelong friends. I'll tell you why I'm sure it wasn't Zeno Vedast who phoned. When some celebrity really took notice of Dawn – a film star paying her attention at the club, say – she'd be full of it for days. When it was just make-believe – or let-me-believe like in his song – when she saw someone she said she knew in a photograph or on the TV, she'd comment on it, sort of reminisce a bit, and then forget all about it. After that phone call she wasn't a bit elated. She just said, "I told you I knew him," and then she was quite gloomy, the way she was after she'd had a nasty letter from her mother or some man had stood her up.'

'Who did you think had phoned her then?'

'Some new man she'd met,' Joan Miall said firmly. 'Someone who was attracted to her but who wasn't rich enough or well known enough to be worth bragging about.' A shade of sadness crossed her pretty face. 'Dawn was getting a bit old for our kind of work and she didn't wear well. I know that sounds ridiculous. She was only twenty-eight. But it bothered her a lot, knowing she'd be past it in a couple of years. She'd have had to get a different job or – marry Paul. She was desperate to make everyone believe she was as attractive as ever and to her way of thinking you measure attractiveness by the number of successful men who want to take you out.'

Wexford sighed. When you are twenty-five, thirty seems old. That was all right, that was natural. But surely when you are forty, thirty ought to seem young? It sickened him that this girl and her dead friend had moved in a world where to a man of fifty a girl of twenty-eight was getting 'past it'.

'This new man,' he said, 'you've no foundation for believing in his existence? Nothing to make you think he existed but a phone call which I tell you Vedast himself made?'

'Yes, I have. She went out with him the following week.'

'Miss Miall,' Wexford said rather severely, 'you should have told me of this before. Is this one of the "unhelpful" things you've remembered?'

'One of the things that prove it wasn't Vedast, yes. But I don't know his name. I don't even know if he wasn't another of Dawn's dreams.'

There was a framed photograph on the mantelpiece, an enlarged snapshot of a dark young man and a girl on a beach somewhere. Wexford picked up the picture and scrutinized it.

'That's Paul,' said Joan Miall.

It took him a few moments to realize that the girl was Dawn. In shorts and a shirt, her hair wind-blown, she looked quite different from the painted, overdressed creature whose portrait on posters was stuck up all over Kingsmarkham like a cabaret star's publicity. At last, he thought, she had achieved a kind of fame. Though posthumously, she had got herself into the public eye. But she looked happier in the snapshot. No, happy wasn't the right word – content, rather, tranquil, and perhaps just a tiny bit bored?

There had been no ecstasy, no excitement, in being on a beach with her ordinary fiancé. Mrs Stonor had seen to that. By belittling her daughter, by comparing her unfavourably to others, by denying her love, she had so warped her personality that everyday affection meant nothing to her. Dawn understood love only when it came from and was directed to money and success, the love of a man who would make her rich and get her name in the papers. Well, some man had got her name in the papers . . .

'Go on, Miss Miall,' said Wexford, laying the photograph down.

'The day I'm going to tell you about was June first. It was a Wednesday and it was Paul's birthday.'

The date meant something to Wexford. He nodded, listening alertly.

'On the Tuesday, the day before, Dawn and I had both had our day off. She went out in the afternoon and bought the blue dress, the one she wore to go and see her mother. I remember I asked her if she'd bought it to take away on holiday with Paul. Well, she said she couldn't make up her mind whether she was going away with Paul or not but she wouldn't say why not, only that it might be boring. They hadn't quarrelled. Paul spent the evening with us and stayed the night with Dawn. They seemed very happy.'

'Let's come to June first.'

'Paul went off to work before we were up. He was going to come back for a birthday lunch Dawn was giving him and then take the afternoon off. Dawn and I were both due to work the evening shift. She went out to buy food for lunch, steak and salad – I insisted on fresh stuff – and after she came back, while she was laying the table, the phone rang. I answered it and a man's voice asked to speak to Dawn. I didn't ask who it was and he didn't say. I gave the phone to Dawn and I didn't stay to hear what she said. I went on with preparing the lunch. She came back into the kitchen and she was very flushed and excited-looking but a bit – well, narked too. I'm explaining this badly but I do remember just what she was like. She was excited and yet she was upset. I could see she didn't want to say who had rung her so I didn't ask.'

'Did you ever find out?'

'No, I didn't. But there's more to come. Paul was expected at half past one. By about a quarter to twelve everything was ready for lunch. We just had to grill the steaks when Paul came. Dawn was already dressed and made-up, but at twelve she went away and changed and when she came out of her bedroom she was wearing her new dress and she'd done her hair on top of her head and put on a lot more eye make-up. In fact, she'd overdone the whole thing and she was wearing far too much perfume. I was sitting in here reading a magazine. She came in and said, "I've got to go out for an hour or so. If Paul gets here before I'm back you can tell him some tale. Say I forgot the wine or something." Well, as I said, we didn't ask each other questions. I wasn't too thrilled about lying to Paul. The wine was already on the table so I couldn't say that. I just hoped she wouldn't be long.'

'Was she?' Wexford asked.

'She went out at sometime between twelve and half past. Paul was a bit late. He got here at twenty to two and still she wasn't back. I told him she had some last-minute shopping, but I could see he was hurt. After all, it was his birthday and they were more or less engaged.'

'When did she come back?'

'Ten past three. I remember the time exactly because when she came in I realized she must have been in a pub and they close at three. She'd had too much to drink, anyway. Her face was all puffy and her speech wasn't quite clear. Paul's a very good-tempered bloke but he was nearly doing his nut by this time.'

'Where did she say she'd been?'

'She said she'd met a girl who used to work in the club and was now a model – poor Dawn could never resist the fame and glamour bit – and they'd gone into a pub and forgotten the time talking.'

'You didn't believe her?'

'Of course I didn't. Later on, after Paul had gone Dawn

wrote to her mother to say she'd go and see her on the following Monday.'

'You didn't connect the pub visit with the letter?'

'I didn't at the time,' the girl said thoughtfully, 'but I do now. You see, it was very unlike Dawn to make up her mind about anything to do with her mother on the spur of the moment. She knew she had to go to Kingsmarkham sometimes but usually she'd start sort of arguing with herself about it weeks beforehand. You know, saying she'd have to go but she didn't want to and maybe she could let it ride for a few more weeks. Then she'd write a letter and tear it up and sort of swear about it. It'd take her weeks to get a letter actually written and posted. But it didn't this time. She sat down and dashed it off.'

Wexford said, 'Did she ever mention what happened on June first again?'

She nodded, looking unhappy. 'On the Saturday, the first day of her holiday. She said, "What would you think of a bloke who said he was dying to see you and the best date he could fix up was a few drinks in a pub at lunchtime?' She went to that mirror over there and put her face right close up to it, staring at herself and pulling the skin under her eyes. "If you were really crazy about a man," she said, "you wouldn't care, would you? You'd just want his company. You wouldn't worry if he was too scared or too mean to take you to a hotel for the night." I didn't really know whether she was referring to me or herself. I thought she might be talking about me because my boy friend is poor. Then Paul came and took her out and I gathered she meant to go away on holiday with him.'

Joan Miall sighed. She reached for a fresh cigarette but the packet was empty. The air in the room was blue with hanging smoke. Wexford thanked her and went away. In the Earls Court Road he went into a record shop and bought a single of 'Let-me-believe'.

CHAPTER FIFTEEN

The red dress was back in Wexford's office. Several thousand women had looked at it, handled it, backed away from the dark stain; not one had recognized it. It lay on the rosewood surface, on the wood whose colour matched it, an old shabby dress, folded, soiled, keeping its secret as implacably as ever.

Wexford touched it, glanced again at the label and at the whitish talc marks around the neckline. Dawn had worn it but she had never owned it. She had found it in Kingsmarkham and for some unfathomable reason had put it on, she who had been fashion-conscious and who was already dressed in garments which matched her shoes and her bag. She had found it in Kingsmarkham, but, unless deception had been practised, no Kingsmarkham or Stowerton woman had ever owned it. A woman never forgets any dress she has owned, not even if fifty years have elapsed between her discarding of it and her being confronted with it again, much less if only seven or eight years have passed.

Burden came into the office, glanced at Wexford, glared at the dress as if to say, Why bother with it? Why let it keep confusing us, holding us up? Aloud he said, 'How did you get on with the Miall girl?'

'It looks as if Dawn had another man friend. Mike, I'm wondering if it could have been Peveril. He was in London on June first, and on that day Dawn met a man for a drink. She went out to meet someone in an underhand way when she had a pretty pressing engagement at home. Now that date took place only five days before the day she died.'

'Go on,' said Burden, interested.

'Dawn was in Kingsmarkham at Easter. The Peverils were already living in The Pathway at Easter. Suppose Peveril picked her up somewhere in Kingsmarkham, had a drink with her, got her to give him her phone number?'

'Didn't he ever phone her?'

'According to Joan Miall, Dawn had a rather mysterious phone call from a man on Monday, May twenty-third. That could have been Peveril. His wife goes out on Monday evenings and that would have given him his opportunity.'

'Sounds promising.'

'Unfortunately, it isn't. We know Zeno Vedast phoned Dawn about that time. He says he did, and Dawn told Joan Miall it was he as soon as she answered the phone. Joan didn't believe her because afterwards she wasn't elated or excited. But, on his own admission, Vedast put her off with vague promises. Dawn wasn't a fool. She could tell he was bored and that rocked her so much that she couldn't even bring herself to brag about knowing him any more or weave any of her usual fantasies. Therefore, I think we must conclude that it was Vedast who phoned her that night and that Vedast had no further communication with her. He's out of it. But that doesn't mean Peveril didn't phone her. He could easily have done so on some occasion when Joan wasn't there.

'During the weekend following her pub date, the weekend preceding her death, she gave Joan to understand that she was embarking on an affair with a man too mean or too scared to take her to an hotel. That description would fit Edward Peveril, a man who owned a house from which his wife would be absent for several hours on a Monday evening; Edward Peveril who came out to us while we were at the festival and tried to distract our attention from the quarry as soon as he knew who we were; Edward Peveril who no longer cares for his wife and who, on Miss Mowler's evidence, is occasionally unfaithful to her.'

Burden pondered. 'What do you think happened that night, then?'

'Whatever happened, Mrs Peveril must know of it.'

'You don't mean connived at it, sir?'

'Not beforehand, certainly. She may have been suspicious beforehand. Don't forget that she told us it was a matter of chance that she was in the house at all at five-thirty. Her *husband* had tried to persuade her to go to a film in Kings-markham that afternoon and stay on for her evening class. Why didn't she do that? Because she was suspicious of his motives? Confident that he could persuade her, he asked Dawn to bring with her a meal for the two of them. But Mrs Peveril didn't go out. She saw Dawn at five-thirty, the actual time of the appointment, *and Dawn saw her*. Therefore, carrying her bag of food, she waited in those fields until she saw Margaret Peveril go out.

'Dawn was then admitted by Peveril. She began to prepare the food, changing into an old dress Peveril gave her so as not to spoil the mauve thing. Before the meal was ready, she asked Peveril if it would be all right for her to stay the night as he, knowing this couldn't be but using any inducements to get Dawn to come, had previously promised. When he told her that idea was off, they quarrelled, she threatening to stay and confront his wife. He killed her in a panic.'

Burden said, 'But when Mrs Peveril came home he threw himself on her mercy. She was needed to help him clean up and dispose of the body.'

'I don't know, Mike. I haven't great confidence in this theory. Why did Mrs Peveril mention having seen the girl at all if it's true? I can't get a warrant on this evidence but tomorrow I'm going to ask Peveril's permission to search. Tomorrow's Sunday and it's your day off.'

'Oh, I'll come,' said Burden.

'No. Have your Sunday with the kids. If we find anything I'll let you know at once.'

Wexford allowed his glance to fall once more on the dress, caught now in a ray of evening sunshine which touched it like a stage spotlight. He tried to imagine Margaret Peveril slender, rejuvenated, but he could only see her as she was, bigger and fleshier than Dawn, a woman whose whole build showed that she could never, since her teens, have worn that dress. He shrugged.

He didn't attempt to get a search warrant. With Martin and three constables, he went to The Pathway in the morning, a misty, cool morning such as heralds a fine day. The sunshine hung like a sheet of gold satin under a fine tulle veil.

Muttering and pleading that his work would be disturbed, Peveril agreed without much protest to his house being searched. Wexford was disappointed. He had expected the man to put up a front of aggressive opposition. They lifted the fitted carpets, scrutinized skirting boards, examined the hems of curtains. Mrs Peveril watched them, biting her nails. This ultimate desecration of her home had driven her into a kind of fugue, a total withdrawal into apathy and silence. Her husband sat in his studio, surrounded by men crawling on the floor and peering under cabinets; he doodled on his drawing board, making meaningless sketches which could not, under any circumstances, have been saleable.

Miss Mowler, returning home from church, came up to Wexford at the gate and asked if the men would like tea. Wexford refused. He noticed, not for the first time, how the churchgoing woman who might conveniently carry a prayer book in her handbag, always holds it ostentatiously in her hands, an outward and visible sign of spiritual superiority. Dunsand was mowing his lawn, emptying the cuttings into a spruce little green wheelbarrow. Wexford went back into the house. Presently he looked out of the window and, to his astonishment, saw Louis Mbowele approaching, his coat swinging open to allow the soft summer air to fan his brown, bead-hung chest. Louis went into Dunsand's garden, the mowing was abandoned and the two men entered the bungalow. Not so very astonishing, after all. Wexford remembered that

Louis was a philosophy student at Myringham where Dunsand taught philosophy.

'How are you doing?' he said to Martin.

'She wasn't killed here, sir. Unless it was in the bathroom. I reckon you could stick a pig in that bathroom and not leave a trace.'

'We may as well get out then. This is supposed to be a day of rest and I'm going home.'

'Just one thing, sir. Young Stevens asked me if you'd see him before he goes off duty. He's at the station. He mentioned it last night but what with all this it went out of my head. He's got something on his mind but he won't tell me what.'

The house was restored to order. Wexford apologized sparingly to Mrs Peveril.

'I told you she didn't come here,' she said with a cowed resentful look. 'I told you she went right away from here. She went across the fields.'

Wexford got into the car beside Martin. 'I wish she wouldn't keep saying that, you know, gratuitously, as it were.' He slammed the door. Martin listened politely as he was obliged to do, his mind on his Sunday dinner which would probably be spoilt by now, anyway. 'Why does she say it if it isn't true?' said Wexford.

'Maybe it is true, sir.'

'Then why didn't anyone else see her after five-thirty? Think of all those blokes coming home for their dinners at Sundays and in Stowerton around six. They'd have seen her. She was the kind of girl men notice.'

The mention of dinner made Sergeant Martin even more obtuse than usual. 'Maybe she sat in the fields for hours, sir, sat there till it was dark.'

'Oh God!' Wexford roared. 'If she was going to have to hang about for hours she'd have stayed at her mother's or if that was unbearable, gone to the pictures in Kingsmarkham.'

'But the last bus, sir?'

'It's less than a mile, man. She was a strong healthy girl. Wouldn't she have walked it later rather than sit about in a field?'

'Then Mrs Peveril never saw her.'

'Oh, yes, she did. She observed her closely, every detail of her appearance.'

The car drew up and the two men got out, Martin to depart for a long and well-deserved dinner, Wexford to see Stevens who was already waiting for him in his office. The shy and inarticulate young policeman stood to attention rigidly which made Wexford even crosser and also made him want to laugh. He told the man to sit down and Stevens did so, less at ease in a chair than stiffly on his feet.

Wexford didn't laugh. He said quite gently, 'We do have a welfare officer, Stevens, if the men have some domestic or private problem that's interfering with their work.'

'But it's work that's interfering with my work, sir,' Stevens stuttered.

'I don't know what you mean.'

The man swallowed. 'Sir.' He stopped. He said it again. 'Sir,' and then, rushing, the words tumbling out, 'Mrs Peveril, sir, I've wanted to tell you for days. I didn't think it was for me to put myself forward. I didn't know what to do.'

'If you know something about Mrs Peveril that I ought to know, you must tell me at once. You know that, Stevens. Now come on, pull yourself together.'

'Sir, I was transferred here from Brighton last year.' He waited for Wexford's nod of encouragement which came with brisk impatience. 'There was a bank robbery, sir, last summer. Mrs Peveril saw the raid and she – she came to the police voluntarily to give evidence. The superintendent interviewed her a lot, sir, and she had to try to identify the villains. We never caught them.'

'You recognized her? Her name? Her face?'

'Her face, sir, and then when I heard her name I remembered. She knew me too. She was very hysterical, sir, a bad witness, kept saying it was all making her ill. I've had it on my conscience all week and then I kept thinking, well, so what? She didn't hold up the bank clerk. And then it got so I thought – well, I had to tell you, sir.'

'Stevens,' sighed Wexford, 'you've got a lot to learn. Never mind, you've told me at last. Go away and have your dinner. I'll check all this with Brighton.'

He began to have an inkling of what had happened. But he must check before going back to The Pathway. There wasn't going to be any Sunday dinner for him.

The Peverils were just finishing theirs. It struck Wexford that this was the first time he had encountered Peveril not working or coming straight from his work or fidgeting to get back to it.

'What is it this time?' he said, looking up from roast beef and Yorkshire pudding.

'I'm sorry to disturb your lunch, Mr Peveril. I want to talk to your wife.'

Peveril promptly picked up his plate, tucked his napkin into the neck of his sweater and, having paused to grab the mustard pot, was making for the door to his studio.

'Don't leave me, Edward!' said his wife in the thin, high-pitched voice which, if it were louder, would be a scream. 'You never give me any support, you never have done. I shall be ill again. I can't bear being questioned. I'm frightened.'

'You're always bloody frightened. Don't hang on me.' He pushed her away. 'Can't you see I've got a plate in my hand?'

'Edward, can't you see, he's going to make me say who did it! He's going to make me pick someone out!'

'Mrs Peveril, sit down. Please sit down. I'd be glad if you wouldn't go away, sir. I don't think it's for me to interfere between husband and wife but, if I may say so, Mrs Peveril might not be quite so frightened if you'd try to give her the support she wants. Please, sir, do as I ask.'

Wexford's tone had been very stern and commanding. It was effective. Bullies crumple fast when sharply admonished, and Peveril, though he moved no closer to his wife and did not look at her, sat down, put his plate on the edge of the table and folded his arms sullenly. Mrs Peveril crept towards him and hesitated, biting her thumbnail. She gave Wexford the half-sly, half-desperate look of the hysteric who is trying to preserve intact the thickly packed layers of neurosis.

'Now will you both listen quietly to what I have to say?' He waited. Neither spoke. 'Mrs Peveril, let me tell you what I think happened. In Brighton you witnessed a bank robbery.' Her eyes opened wide. She gave a little chattering murmur. 'That was a most upsetting experience for you, but you very properly came forward to give information to the police. You were a key witness. Naturally, the police questioned you exhaustively. You fancied yourself badgered and you became frightened, ill perhaps with fright, both from the constant visits of the police and from a notion that some revenge might be taken against you for the information you had given. You moved here to get away from that. Am I right?'

Mrs Peveril said nothing. Her husband, who never missed a cue, said, 'Sure, you're right. Never mind where I had my roots, my contacts, my ideal studio. Madam wanted to run away so we ran away.'

'Please, Mr Peveril.' Wexford turned to the woman, sensing that he must be very careful, very gentle. Her stillness, the compulsive nail biting, the hard set furrows in her face, were ominous. 'You had only been here a few months when you realized, because of what you had seen, that you might soon be involved in another and perhaps more disturbing criminal case. Mrs Peveril, we know you saw Dawn Stonor on Monday, June sixth. You gave an accurate description of her, more precise than any other we have. I suggest to you – please don't be alarmed – that you either admitted her to this house or saw her enter another house. You told us you saw her cross the fields because you believed that would be the surest way to draw our attention, the attention you find so frightening, away from you and your own neighbourhood.'

It might have been all right. She took her hand from her mouth and bit her lip. She made a little preparatory murmur. It would have been all right if Peveril hadn't started to his feet and shouted at her, 'Christ, is that true? You bloody fool! I thought there was something fishy, I knew it. You told lies to the police and nearly landed me right in it. My God!'

She began to scream. 'I never saw her at all! I never saw her!' A slap on the face would have been effective. Instead, her husband began shaking her so that the screams came out in stifled strangled gasps. She crumpled and fell on the floor. Peveril took a step backwards, white-faced.

'Get Miss Mowler,' snapped Wexford.

By the time he returned with the nurse, Mrs Peveril was lying back in a chair, moaning softly. Miss Mowler gave her a bracing, toothy smile.

'We'll get you to bed, dear, and then I'll make you a nice strong cup of tea.'

Mrs Peveril cringed away from her. 'Go away. I don't want you. I want Edward.'

'All right, dear. Just as you like. Edward can get you to bed while I make the tea.'

At the use of his Christian name Peveril frowned ferociously, but he gave an arm to his wife and helped her up the stairs. Miss Mowler bustled about, removing plates of congealing food, boiling a kettle, hunting for aspirins. A little thin woman, she was quick in her movements and efficient. She talked all the time she worked, apologizing for non-existent faults. What a pity she hadn't been on the spot when 'it' happened. If only she had been in her garden, for instance. How unfortunate that, what with one thing and another, she had had to wash her hands and take off her overall before accompanying Mr Peveril to the house. Wexford said very little. He was thinking that he would be lucky to get any more out of Mrs Peveril that day.

The tea was taken up. Peveril didn't reappear. Wexford followed Miss Mowler back into her own bungalow where newspapers were spread over the hall carpet and a kind of late spring cleaning seemed to be in progress.

'I spilt a cup of cocoa down the wall. It's a blessing this paper's washable. I don't know what you must think of me, washing walls on a Sunday afternoon.'

'The better the day, the better the deed,' said Wexford politely. 'I want to have another look at the quarry, Miss Mowler. May I make my way there through your garden?'

He was permitted to do so but only after he had refused pressing offers of tea and coffee, sherry, a sandwich. Miss Mowler, having been assured that he didn't need her to accompany him down the path and open the gate for him, returned to her work. He let himself out of the garden and into the narrow no man's land that separated the estate from Sundays.

CHAPTER SIXTEEN

Heavy rains had fallen and now the sun had returned as bright and hot as ever. But it was too soon yet for new grass to show, too soon for even the beginnings of the green carpet which by autumn would once more cover the desert plain which Sundays park had become. Wexford sat down on the edge of the quarry. Here nature was winning, for the flowers and shrubs, the delicate yet lush herbage of June, had been assailed by only half a dozen trampling feet. New roses, new harebells, were opening to replace the crushed blossoms. He looked at the broken wire, the wall, the three gates, but they told him nothing more, and gradually the scented air, sunwarmed and soft, drove thoughts of the case from his mind. A butterfly, a Clouded Yellow, drifted languidly past him and alighted on a rose, its petals paler and creamier than the buttercup-coloured wings. Not so many butterflies these days as when he was a child, not so many as when even his daughters were children. Under his breath he caught himself humming a tune. At first he thought it was that song of Vedast's which stuck in his mind and irritated him. Then he realized it wasn't that one but a ballad of Betti Ho's in which she prophesied that her children would never see a butterfly except in a museum. The Clouded Yellow took to the air again, hovering, floating . . .

'You're trespassing!'

Wexford started to his feet, shaking himself out of his dream.

'You're trespassing,' said Silk again, half-serious, half-peevishly ironic. 'I don't see why I should always have the fuzz trampling over my land.'

Looking up into the irritable white face and the smiling black one, Wexford said, 'I'm not trampling. I was sitting and thinking. What are you two up to? Planning another festival?'

'No, we're going to try and get a commune going here during the university vacation. Louis and I and his girl friend and about half a dozen others. Louis wants to see how it works out with a view to operating a kibbutz system in Marumi.'

'Really?' said Wexford blankly. He didn't see how gathering together a house party in a fully-equipped and furnished mansion could be a rehearsal for kibbutzim in an equatorial state, but he didn't say so. 'Well, I think I'll trample off now.'

'So will I,' said Louis unexpectedly. He gave his radiant grin and patted Silk on the grey head which reached just to his shoulder. 'Peace be with you.'

They skirted the Peverils' fence and emerged at the head of The Pathway. Mrs Peveril's bedroom curtains were drawn. Dunsand was pulling puny little weeds out of his flowerless borders. Beside Miss Mowler's car a bucket of soapy water stood unattended. It was hot, sunny, a radiant day. The English do not relax in deck-chairs in their front gardens and, apart from the crouching figure of the philosophy lecturer, the place was deserted. Louis waved graciously to him.

'Want a lift into Kingsmarkham?'

'Thanks,' Louis said. 'That way I might get the three-thirty bus to Myringham.'

Wexford's car was a fair-sized one, but no car except perhaps Vedast's Rolls would have been roomy enough to accommodate Louis Mbowele comfortably. Laughing, he hunched himself inside the folds of his pony-skin and slid the passenger seat back to its fullest extent.

Wexford said, 'When you get to the top of wherever it is you're going, are you going to *make* them live in communes?'

'It's the only way of life, man.'

'And force them to be equal and dictate the pattern of their houses and the subjects of their study and operate a censorship and forbid other political parties?'

'For a time, for a time. It's necessary. They have to learn. When they see it all works and the new generation's grown up and we have peace and full bellies, then we can start to relax. It's necessary to make them do what they aren't just too crazy to do right now. So you have to make them for their own good.'

'Do you know a saying of James Boswell? "We have no right to make people happy against their will"?'

Louis nodded, smiling no longer.

'I know it, man, and I know the connection in which it was said. The slave trade. The traders excused themselves on the ground that my people would be happier on plantations than in jungles. This is different. This is for real. And it's only for a time.'

'Oh, Louis,' said Wexford, turning into the Forby road, 'that's what they all say.'

They drove into Kingsmarkham in silence. The heat of the day, his failure to get anywhere, enervated Wexford. There seemed nothing else to do with his afternoon but go home, eat his stale lunch, maybe sleep. Then, as they approached the place where the Myringham bus stopped, he became aware of the long silence and wondered if he had offended the young African. Louis looked as if he would have a hearty appetite, and the Olive and Dove did a good Sunday lunch. . . .

'Have you eaten?' he said.

'Sure. I cadged some bread and cheese off Len.'

'Mr Dunsand? Why did you have to cadge? Isn't he very hospitable?'

Louis grinned. Evidently, he hadn't been offended, only sleepy from the sun. 'He's a recluse,' he said. 'He finds it hard to communicate. Still, I took him out to lunch a while back in Myringham – last Wednesday fortnight it was – so I guess he owed me a meal. I asked him to join our commune but he's not together enough for that.'

'Strange. You'd think a lecturer in philosophy would . . .'

'Have found the way? Found himself?' Louis leapt out of the car and strode round to open Wexford's door. 'That's a popular misconception, man. It's living – a broad spectrum of living – that teaches you how to live, not philosophy. Philosophy teaches you how to *think*.'

The bus was late. Louis, scorning to join the queue, sat down on the steps of the Snowdrop Cleaners, and Wexford, leaving the car at the kerb, followed him.

'How do you get on with him?'

Louis considered. The dozen or so people in the queue bestowed upon him glances of intense, if repressed, curiosity. Few black-skinned men and women had penetrated to this country town, and to them his coat, his beads and the green silk scarf he wore round his head – although no more than fashionable 'gear' for black and white alike – perhaps appeared as tribal paraphernalia. He returned their looks with the gracious smile of a prince, a tawny Rasselas, and said to Wexford:

'He's all right as a teacher, he knows his subject. But he doesn't seem to like people. You see, he's afraid of them.'

'What else is there to be afraid of?' asked Wexford to whom this idea, in all its truth, had come suddenly as if out of the air. 'Except, maybe, thunderstorms, floods, what insurance companies call Acts of God. If you say you're afraid of bombs or war, it's people who make the bombs and the war.'

'You're right. But, oh, man, there are a lot of people and they are frightening. And it's worse when one of the people you're frightened of is yourself.' Louis gazed into the heart of the afternoon sun. 'Someone told me he was better when his wife lived with him. He used to go away on holidays then, the Majorca bit, the Costa Brava scramble. He doesn't do anything now but read and paint the house. and mow the lawn. But you can't picture him married to *her*, can you?' Louis got up, thrust out his hand. 'Here's the bus.'

'Picture her? I don't know her. Do you?'

Extending one huge furry arm to support her, Louis helped a fragile-looking old lady on to the bus platform. In the manner of one whose girlhood dreams have at last been realized and who has fallen into the hands of a sheikh, she blushed, giggled and almost panicked. The other passengers stared and whispered.

'Come along now,' said the driver. 'We haven't got all day.'

Louis grinned. Head and shoulders above the rest, he gave his fare, looking over a diminutive woman's hat at Wexford.

'I don't know her. Old Silk told me who she was at the festival, pointed her out while Zeno Vedast was singing. Man, you stood next to her.'

'I did?'

The bus started.

'Peace be with you,' Louis shouted.

'And with you,' said Wexford.

The golden car wasn't there. Perhaps it had been silly of him to think it would be. On such a fine afternoon they would all have gone out to see the house Vedast was buying. On the almost bare forecourt, blanched ashen pale by hard sunlight, his own car looked forlorn. The Cheriton Forest Hotel seemed asleep. But the porter who had admired Nell Tate was awake. He sat in the deserted hall, reading the *Sunday Express* and smoking a cigarette which he stubbed out quickly when Wexford appeared.

'I'm afraid not, sir,' he said in answer to the chief inspector's enquiry. 'Mr Vedast and Mrs Tate went out in Mr Vedast's car after lunch.'

'You don't know when they'll be back?'

Memories of fifty-pence pieces easily earned stirred in the porter's mind. He was obviously reluctant to deny Wexford anything. 'Mr Tate took his coffee out into the garden, sir. Would you care for me to . . . ?'

'No, I'll find him myself.'

'As you like sir,' said the man, philosophically contemplating the smaller coin his efforts had won him.

Wexford strolled round the gabled, studded, mullioned and heavily rose-hung building. There was nobody about. Birds sang sleepily in the deciduous trees which bordered the fir plantations. He reached the back and saw the elderly couple with whom he had shared the Shakespeare Lounge snoring in long chairs on the terrace. A gravel path wound between rosebeds to a small round lawn in the middle of which was an umbrella with a table and chair under it. A man sat in the chair, his back to the terrace. The porter, a tactful servant, had described Tate as taking his coffee in the garden and there was certainly a diminutive cup on the table beside him. But what Tate was taking was brandy. An eager hand had just grasped the bottle of Courvoisier and was about to tip a further measure into the already half-full glass.

'Good afternoon, Mr Tate.'

If Wexford had hoped to make Tate jump he was disappointed. The man didn't get up. He filled his glass, replaced the bottle top and said, 'Hallo. Have a drink.'

Wexford remembered that he was driving, that he had had no lunch, and he refused. 'I'd like to talk to you. D'you mind if I fetch myself a chair?'

'No,' said Tate economically.

Wexford fetched himself a deck-chair and drew it under the umbrella's shade. Tate didn't say anything. His face quite blank, he contemplated the view of the hilly forest, lying black and furry-looking, and a smooth blue sky. He wasn't in the least drunk. Alcoholics never get drunk. Wexford thought that this was probably Tate's misfortune, that he had drunk so much and drunk so chronically that, perpetually intoxicated, he could never now enjoy the felicity of what most people call intoxication. His skin was a rough greyish red, his eyeballs veined with red, their rims vermilion and moist. And yet he was a young man still, unlined, thin, not bad-looking, his hair untouched by grey.

'Mr Tate, I really wanted to talk to your wife.'

'She's gone out with Zeno to see the new house.'

As he had thought. 'So Mr Vedast found one to his liking?'

Tate agreed that this was so. He sipped his brandy. 'It's called Cheriton Hall.'

'Ah, yes. I think I know it. On the Pomfret side of the forest. Will you all live there?'

'We go where Zeno goes.'

Guessing, hoping, very much in the dark, Wexford essayed, 'Your wife won't find it awkward living so comparatively close to her ex-husband?'

The unhealthy colour in Tate's face deepened, the grey overpowering the red. He made no answer but he fixed on Wexford a truculent and rather puzzled stare.

'I'm right in thinking your wife was once married to Mr Dunsand?' Tate shrugged. The shrug implied an indifference to Wexford's opinions rather than a doubt as to their veracity. 'For the past week,' Wexford went on, 'I've been trying to discover a connection between Dawn Stonor and some resident of the Sundays estate, especially of The Pathway. Until now I've been unable to succeed.'

'Small world,' said Tate uneasily.

'Is it? I think it's an enormous world. I think it's extraordinary that Dawn should have last been seen alive in The Pathway where Mrs Tate's ex-husband lives. I think it particularly odd now that I know Dawn was once a close friend of Zeno Vedast who is now a – er, close friend of your wife's. And yet I'm to dismiss it as being due to the smallness-of the world.'

Tate shrugged again. 'Zeno and Nell and me were all in Duvette Gardens that night you're talking about.' He put Vedast's name before his wife's, Wexford noticed. 'We were all together and that guy Silk looked in about ten to talk about the festival.' Morosely, he said, 'We've never been near that place.'

'Surely you were when you were at the festival, very near? Didn't your wife point Mr Dunsand's house out to you?'

It was a trap and the slow-witted Tate fell into it. 'She said, that's Len's house, yes.'

Wexford pounced. 'So she knew it? He'd only lived there a matter of weeks but she knew it. Not by the street name and the number. She knew it by the look of it!'

'I shouldn't like to have your job, meddling in people's private affairs.'

'And I shouldn't like to have yours, Mr Tate,' said Wexford crisply. He leant across the table, forcing the other man to look at him. 'Whose wife is she, yours or that singer you fawn on? Yours or the man who divorced her? What sort of a set-up are you running here? Or do you do just what you're told, lie, pimp, connive at obstructing the police, anything he and she tell you?'

There was too little of one kind of spirit in Tate and too much of the other for him to react violently to these insults. He passed a hand across bleary eyes as if his head ached and said in a sour cowed voice, 'Christ, how you do go on! Never you mind my wife. I can deal with her.'

'By blacking her eye?'

'She told you? I bet she didn't tell you why.'

'I think it was because you found out she'd been seeing Dunsand. At the festival when she pointed out his house you put two and two together. You didn't mind about Vedast, that was different. Maybe you found she'd got a key to his house so you had it out with her and blacked her eye.'

Tate half-smiled. It was the smile of one who is accustomed to subservience to a superior intellect, a smile of grudging admiration. He took something out of his trouser pocket and laid it on the table. A key.

'I found it in her handbag. It'll be safer with you. She might get it away from me and use it again.' He got up abruptly, took his bottle and walked very carefully and steadily up the terrace steps and into the hotel.

Wexford pocketed the key. He tiptoed past the old couple, made his way through a cool and shadowy corridor to the front entrance. Then, seeing the golden car had arrived, he slipped back into the porch and waited.

Nell and Zeno Vedast got out. The swelling had gone down from the girl's eye and her painted face was almost serene. Her hair, freshly washed, was a yellow cloud but the bright light showed darker roots. Vedast, wearing jeans and a thin embroidered waistcoat, took a springy stride towards Wexford's car and stood contemplating it, smiling, his head on one side. His face wore very much the expression Wexford had seen there just before Tate drank the doctored liquor, and he heard him say:

'That parking ticket we got, shall we put it on his windscreen?'

'What's the point?' said Nell.

'Fun is the point, Nello darling. A joke. He'll twig it in two seconds but think how mad he'll be first. Go and get it, Nello. It's on the back seat.'

She opened the rear door of the Rolls. Hypnotized by him, obedient as ever, she gave him the ticket. But as he was lifting one of the wipers she broke out:

'I'm sick of jokes. Why can't we grow up, do things for real? I hate always playing games.'

'Do you really, Nello? You are a funny girl.' Vedast clipped the ticket under the wiper and laughed. He shook back his hair and his yellow eyes glowed. 'I don't believe you. I think you liked all that funny dressing up and pretending to be good and making cosy little plans.' He took her hand, kissed her cheek lightly. 'That's why we get on so well, dear, you and me with our little fantasies. Shall we go and rouse Goffo from his Sunday stupor?'

She nodded, clutching his arm. They went off towards the rose garden. When they had disappeared around the side of the hotel Wexford emerged thoughtfully. Having a strong objection to the scattering of litter, he placed the parking ticket under the paws of the golden lion and then he drove away.

CHAPTER SEVENTEEN

Some little good had come out of Mrs Peveril's hysterical breakdown. The information she was now willing to give was imparted too late to be of much use – Wexford knew it already, or most of it – but her despair had shocked her husband into anxiety for her.

He said soberly, 'You were pretty decent, very patient actually. I never realized what a bad state she'd got herself into. Will she have to appear in court?'

'I don't know, Mr Peveril. I still don't quite know what she did see. I must have a final word with her.'

'If she does have to I'll be there. She won't mind so much if I'm with her. The fact is I've been too wrapped up in my work. I let her face all that business in Brighton alone and it was too much for her. When this is over I'm going to scrape up the cash and take her away for a good holiday.'

The uxoriousness wouldn't last, Wexford knew that. Such a *volte-face* often takes place at crises in a marriage but it is only in romances that it becomes a permanency.

And Peveril revealed just how ephemeral it was when, as they went upstairs to see his wife, he muttered, 'You have to bloody wet-nurse some women all their lives, don't you? If I'm not wanted for the next half-hour I may as well catch up on a spot of work.'

Mrs Peveril, wan-looking but calm, sat up in bed wrapped in a jaded broderie anglais dressing gown.

'It was like you said,' she admitted. 'I wanted to make you all think she'd gone a long, long way from here. I wanted to be left in peace. When I first saw her I meant to tell Edward what I'd seen but I didn't because he gets cross with me if I gossip. He says he works for me all day and all I've got to do with myself is look out of the window and tell stories about the neighbours.' She sighed heavily. 'Then when Mrs Clarke phoned me on that Sunday night and said you were coming round asking, I thought I'd say she'd gone into the fields. If I'd said she'd gone next door you'd never have left me alone. I thought saying I hadn't seen her at all would be perjury.'

Wexford shook his head. It was quite useless to point out to her that what she had said was equally perjury.

'You saw her go next door to Mr Dunsand's? At what time?'

'At half past five. I did say,' said Mrs Peveril, eagerly attempting to retrieve her integrity, 'I saw her at five-thirty. I watched her. I saw her go into the porch and someone must have let her in because she never came out again.' Prevarication at an end now, Mrs Peveril was cheerfully burning her boats, gabbling out belated information. Wexford knew she was speaking the truth. 'I was very interested. You see, I couldn't think who she could be. Mr Dunsand never has any visitors except sometimes his students.'

'Never?' Wexford asked quickly.

She said ingenuously, 'Oh, no, I should have noticed. I spend a lot of time at my window when Edward's in his studio and you can see everything these light evenings, can't you? That's why I was so *intrigued* by this girl.' Fear touched her afresh and the wan look returned. 'You'll protect me, won't you? I mean, when I've been to the court and said how Mr Dunsand did it you won't let me come to any harm?'

'When you have been to the court and told the truth, Mrs Peveril,' Wexford corrected her, 'we'll see that you're quite safe.'

With a passing, thoughtful glance at Dunsand's bungalow, its windows closed against the midsummer evening, Wexford drove to Tabard Road. He found Burden and the children in the garden and for once there was no music playing. Burden was too respectable and had far too much social conscience

to allow record players or transistors out of doors. The boy
and girl sat at a wicker table, arguing and making some
pretence of doing their homework. John, who was always
pleased to see the chief inspector whom he regarded as an
ally and friend of oppressed youth, fetched him a chair and
said:

'Could you give me a bit of help, Mr Wexford? I've got
to do an essay on the French Revolution, and Dad's no use.
He's not educated.'

'Really!' spluttered Burden. 'Don't be so rude.'

His son ignored him. 'I've left my book at school and I
can't remember the new names the Convention gave to the
months. I'll have to know them and I thought . . .'

'I'll try.' Wexford hesitated. 'We're in *Messidor* now, that's
June. You're supposed to start with September. Let's see . . .
Vendemiaire, Brumaire, Frimaire; Nivose, Pluviose, Ventose; then *Germinal* like Zola's book, *Floreal* and *Prairial; Messidor, Thermidor*
and − wait . . .'

'*Fructidor!*' exclaimed John.

Wexford chuckled. 'You might care to know the contemporary and rather scathing English translation: Wheezy, Sneezy,
Freezy; Slippy, Drippy, Nippy; Showery, Flowery, Bowery;
Wheaty, Heaty, Sweety. There, you can put that in your essay
and maybe you'll get an A.' He cut short the boy's thanks and
said, 'One good turn deserves another. Now I want a bit of
help from you.'

'*Me?*'

'Mm-hm. About Zeno Vedast. Or, more precisely, about
Godfrey Tate. You must know something about him. You told
your father who his wife was.'

'I read about it,' John said, 'in the *Musical Express*. Anything
about Zeno's news, you see.' He put down his pen and flashed
a look of triumph at his father. 'What d'you want to know,
Mr Wexford?'

'Anything about Zeno. What you read.'

'Zeno ran her over in his car . . .'

'He *what* . . . ?'

'It was like this. He went to Myringham to give a concert – it was sponsored by that Mr Silk, Silk Enterprises – and there was a big crowd outside the theatre afterwards and she got in front of his car and got hurt. It said in the paper that Silk Enterprises paid for a private room in the hospital for her and sent her flowers and fruit and things. I expect Zeno thought that would be good publicity, don't you? It was about two years ago, maybe three. Dad,' said John resentfully, 'won't let me save copies of old magazines. He says it's hoarding. She was married to someone else, then. I think he was called Dunn, something like Dunn.'

'Go on.'

'When she got married again it was in the papers because Zeno was at the wedding and Mr Silk. I expect she'd rather have married Zeno.'

'I daresay she would, John, but he wouldn't have her so she took the next best thing. Catch as catch can.'

'Good heavens,' said Burden crossly, 'must you fill him up with these cynical views of life?'

Wexford winked indiscreetly at the boy and for the time being said no more. He was thinking of the bald story he had been told and, more particularly, of the gaps in it which only an older person with experience of life could fill. Nell was still young. She must have been very young when she first married Dunsand. He wondered what had led to that illassorted marriage, what had made her choose the reserved, repressed lecturer for a husband. An unhappy home life like Dawn Stonor's? The need to escape from some dreary backwater? If this were so, it must have been a case of out of the frying pan into the fire. He pictured her among the faculty wives, decades her senior, the long evenings at home with Dunsand, the leather chairs, Wittgenstein, the lawnmowing . . . Still a teenager at heart, she must have longed for younger people, for music, for excitement. And yet there was in her the stuff that makes a slave. Had she also been Dunsand's slave? Perhaps. But she had escaped – into a glamorous, eventful, luxurious life that was nonetheless slavery. About two years ago, at the time the song was written.

> 'So come by, come nigh,
>   come try and tell why
>   some sigh, some cry,
>   some lie and some die.'

He had sung it aloud and the others were staring at him. Pat giggled.

John said, 'Very groovey, Mr Wexford.'

In the same parlance Wexford said, 'I shouldn't make much bread that way, John. Apart from not being able to sing, I don't have the figure for it.' He raised his heavy body out of the chair and said rather sharply to the inspector, 'Come into the house.'

'First thing tomorrow,' Wexford said, 'I want you to swear out a warrant to search Dunsand's house.'

'What, another fruitless search?'

'Maybe it won't be fruitless.'

Burden took Pat's ballet shoes off the seat of one chair and John's tennis racket off another. 'On what evidence, for God's sake?'

'If Mrs Peveril has any value as a witness at all, Dawn Stonor went to Dunsand's house. She was last seen going to his house and she was never seen coming out of it, never seen again. I would calculate that it's a shorter distance from his back fence to the quarry than from any other back fence. She was killed in that house, Mike.'

'Will you ask Dunsand's consent first?'

'Yes, but he'll refuse. At least, I think so. I shall also ask

300

him not to go to work tomorrow. They come down this week, so he can't have anything very pressing to do.'

Burden looked bewildered. 'You were just as sure it happened in Peveril's house, sir. Are you saying she knew Dunsand, that it was Dunsand she met in that pub on June first?'

'No. I know it wasn't. Dunsand was in Myringham on June first. Louis Mbowele told me that.'

'And Dunsand can't have let her in on that Monday. He wasn't there at five-thirty. We're as certain as can be she didn't know Dunsand. Can you imagine him picking a girl up, asking her to come to his house?'

'You must remember that Dunsand isn't the only person who could have let her in. Nell Tate had a key.'

'She used to go and see her ex-husband?' Burden asked doubtfully.

'I should think not,' Wexford rejoined slowly. 'Mrs Peveril would have seen her if she had been and Mrs Peveril never saw her. Perhaps he sent her the key in the hope that she would visit him. The fact remains that she had a key and she could have been in Dunsand's house by five-thirty. Did you ever check on that Duvette Gardens alibi?'

Burden looked a little offended. He was conscientious, proud of his thoroughness. 'Of course I did. Although, there didn't seem much point when you got so interested in Peveril. I got the Met. on it.'

'And?'

'Vedast's car was stuck outside all day and all night, gathering his usual parking tickets. Nobody seems to have a clue whether they were inside the house. One of them may not have been. We just can't tell.'

Wexford nodded. 'The Tates would lie themselves black in the face to protect their master and he'd lie to protect his little ones. I think he cares a good deal more for "Goffo" than for "Nello", though, don't you? I wish I could see a motive. One might suggest that Nell was jealous of Dawn's relationship with Zeno Vedast, only there wasn't a relationship any more. Vedast might have had a date to meet Dawn somewhere in the neighbourhood and Nell found out about it and lured her into the house to kill her. D'you fancy that idea?'

'Of course I don't.'

'Tate might have fallen in love with Dawn when they met at the Townsman Club and got the key from his wife to use Dunsand's house for a love nest. Then Vedast killed her to prevent her spoiling their jolly little *tria juncta in uno*. Does that suit you better?'

'Well, I suppose anything's possible with people of their sort.'

'Sure it is. Nell arranged to meet Dawn there because she had Dunsand's loneliness on her conscience. She thought Dawn might make him a suitable second wife – no less suitable than his first, at any rate – but when Dawn had confessed that Vedast had phoned her, shown interest in her, Nell got into a rage. She would, of course, have instructed Dawn to bring with her a second-hand red dress because Dunsand likes second-hand clothes, red is his favourite colour, and he prefers dresses to be a tight fit.'

Burden said distantly, 'I don't see the point of all this, sir. Aren't you rather arguing with yourself? It's you who want to search the place, not I.'

'I expect I am, Mike,' said Wexford. 'I haven't an idea how it happened, but two things I'm certain of. We shall find traces of blood in Dunsand's house tomorrow, and Dunsand will confess to having killed Dawn Stonor from the chivalrous motive of protecting his former and still much-loved wife. It's going to be a heavy day so I think I'll be off home now.'

CHAPTER EIGHTEEN

While they ransacked the bungalow, Wexford sat with Dunsand in the sombre living room. The search warrant had been shown to him and he had read it carefully, scrupulously, in total silence. He lifted his shoulders, nodded and followed Wexford into the living room, pausing at the window to pick a dead flower off one of the dehydrated cacti. Then he sat down and began to leaf through one of the travel brochures in the manner of a patient in a doctor's waiting room. The light fell on his glasses, turning them into gleaming opaque ovals. His eyes were invisible, his thick mouth closed and set, so that his whole face was expressionless. But as he turned the pages and came to one on which some words had been pencilled in the margin, there came suddenly a tightening of those rubbery cheek muscles that was like a wince.

'Your wife had a key to this house, Mr Dunsand.'

He looked up. 'Yes. I sent it to her. But she's my wife no longer.'

'I beg your pardon. We believe she or a friend of hers was here on June sixth.'

'No,' he said. 'Oh no.'

Wexford thought he had closed his eyes, although he could not be sure. He was aware of a terrible stillness in the room, a profound silence, which the movements in the hall and overhead accentuated rather than disturbed. Dunsand was not in the least like Godfrey Tate to look at or in manner, yet they shared this strange reticence. Both Nell Tate's husbands possessed the rare quality of being able to answer a searching question with a straight yes or no. Had she chosen them for this or had she made them so? Had she chosen them at all?

The man Wexford could be sure she had chosen was chatty, verbose, an extrovert whom some would call charming.

He tried again. 'Do you ever see your former wife?'

'No.'

'Never, Mr Dunsand?'

'Not now. I shall never see her again now.'

'You're aware that she's staying at the Cheriton Forest Hotel?'

'Yes. I saw it in the paper, a picture of her with a lot of flowers. She used to fill the house with flowers.' He glanced at the moribund cacti and then he picked up his brochure again. Underneath it on the pile was a pamphlet advertising dishwashers and another for garden equipment. 'I'd rather not talk any more now, if you don't mind.' He added curiously, 'I'm not obliged to say anything, am I?'

Wexford left him and went into one of the bedrooms. Bryant, Gates and Loring were crawling about, examining the carpet.

'Are there any women's clothes in the wardrobes?'

'No, sir, and there's no blood. We've done the whole place. This is the last room. We've even been up in the loft.'

'I heard you. Contents of the refrigerator?'

'It's empty. He's been defrosting it. He's very houseproud, sir. If you're thinking of that food she bought, the dustbins have been emptied twice since June sixth.'

Aghast, suddenly weary, Wexford said, 'I *know* she was killed here!'

'The hall floor's bitumastic, sir, the kind of stuff that's poured on as liquid and then left to set. There are no joins. I suppose we could get it taken up. We could have the tiles off the bathroom walls.'

Wexford went back into the room where Dunsand was. He cleared his throat and then found he was at a loss for words. His eyes met not Dunsand's own but the thick baffling glass which shielded them. Dunsand got up and handed him two identical keys.

'One of these,' he said in a calm, neutral voice, 'is mine. The other I sent to my former wife and she returned it to me by post.' Wexford looked at the keys, the first of which was scraped and scarred from daily use, the second scarcely marked. 'Mrs Tate,' said Dunsand with awful precision, 'was never here. I should like to make a point of that.' Things were happening, Wexford thought, at least to some extent according to the pattern he had forecast. Dunsand swallowed, looked down at the floor. 'I found the girl here when I got home on June sixth. She must have got in by the window. The kitchen fanlight had been left unfastened. I encountered her as soon as I let myself in. She was giving the place what I think thieves call a "going over". We struggled and I – killed her. I hit her with a bottle of wine she had left on the hall table.'

'Mr Dunsand . . .' Wexford began almost despairingly.

'No, wait. Let me finish. She had brought some things with her, apart from the wine, some shopping in a bag and some clothes. Perhaps she thought my house was empty and she meant to camp there – "squat" is the word, isn't it? After it got dark I put her body in the quarry and the other things into the river under the bridge. Then I washed the floor and the walls.' Staring at Wexford, he said abruptly, 'Aren't you going to caution me? Shouldn't there be witnesses to take all this down?'

'This confession – you insist on making it?'

'Of course. It's true. I killed her. I knew it was only a matter of time before you arrested me.' He took off his glasses and rubbed them against his sleeve. His naked eyes were frightening. There was something terrible yet indefinable in their depths, a light that told perhaps of passion, of single-minded fanaticism under that flaccid exterior. He was used to teaching, to instructing. Now, in a teacher's voice, he proceeded to direct Wexford.

'The proper thing, I think, will be for me to go to the police station and make a statement.' He put on his glasses, wiped a beading of sweat from above his left eyebrow. 'I could go in my own car or accompany you if you think that wiser. I'm quite ready.'

'Well, you were right,' said Burden in grudging admiration.

'Only up to a point. We didn't find a trace of blood.'

'He must be a nut or a saint, taking that on himself to shield a woman like Nell Tate.' Burden began to pace the office, growing vehement. 'That statement he made, it doesn't even remotely fit the facts. For one thing, Dawn was let into the house. She didn't go round the back. And for another, why should she suppose Dunsand's house to have been empty – I mean, unoccupied? If she had, she wouldn't have camped there on her own. She had a home to go to. Can you see Dunsand beating a woman to death because he suspected her of breaking into his house? Crocker said her killer was mad with rage, in a frenzy. That phlegmatic character in a frenzy?'

'He and Tate,' said Wexford, 'are apparently both phlegmatic characters. They are still waters which not only run deep but which may have turbulent undercurrents. Strange, isn't it? Dunsand hasn't asked for a lawyer, hasn't put up the least resistance. He's behaved almost fatalistically. That woman breaks the men she doesn't want but can't scratch the surface of the man she does want.'

Burden shook his head impatiently. 'What do we do now? What next?'

'Go back to Dunsand's place, I suppose. Have another look round and experiment with those keys a bit.'

Bright noon in The Pathway, the hottest day yet of a summer that promised to be all halcyon. The sun had brought into blossom tiny pink flowers on the plants in Miss Mowler's garden. In the meadows in the crook of the armshaped road they were cutting hay, cropping flowers far more lush and vigorous than those man had planted. The crude pink of Dunsand's bungalow was blanched to a rosy pallor by the hard hot light.

Wexford went up to the front door and tried Dunsand's keys. Both worked. The third key, the one Tate had given him, looked different, and by now he was sure it wouldn't move the lock. It didn't.

'It's a much older key than the others,' said Burden. 'What's Tate playing at?'

'Let's go inside.'

The whole house had been searched, but for evidence of a crime, not for clues to a life. Wexford remembered how Dunsand had planned to redecorate the place. He held on to that, certain it must have some significance. In a week's time perhaps that ugly wallpaper, those wriggling black stems, those golden flowers, would have been removed. Dunsand would have stripped it down, replaced it. But Dunsand had confessed . . .

Reticently, disliking the job, he went into the living room where the cacti were, where Dunsand had sat, blindly studying his brochures, and opened the desk. He found no letters, only bills; no marriage certificates, no album of photographs. But in a small drawer under the roll-top he discovered Dunsand's address book, a brown leather-covered book very sparing of entries. A London phone number was recorded under the letter T, just a number followed by a dash and the name Helen. Wexford noted the code and thought it might probably be Vedast's. He looked under S and under D but found no reference to Dawn Stonor.

It was at this point that it occurred to him how she, the dead, she whose death was the cause of this enquiry, had for some days past seemed to fade from its screen. It was as if she, as a real person, a personality, had lost her importance, and that he was searching for the answer to some other puzzle in the ramifications of which her death had been almost incidental. And he saw her – vividly but briefly – as a pawn, a used creature, her life blundering across other, brighter lives, falling through folly and vanity into death.

But the vision went, leaving him no wiser, and he thrust his hands once more into the pigeon-holes of the desk. A bunch of photographs came to light at last. They were in an envelope stuffed into a slot at the side of the roll-top interior, and they were mostly snapshots of Dunsand, much younger, with people who were evidently his parents, but underneath them were two much larger shots which Wexford took to the window. The strong light showed him first a wedding photograph, Dunsand still young, Dunsand smiling down without reserve at his bride in her badly fitting wedding dress, her veil wind-blown, young bony hands clutching a tight posy of rosebuds. Unless he had been twice married, the bride must be Nell. Time and art had changed her so much in the intervening years – eight? ten? – since the picture was taken as to make her scarcely recognisable as its subject. Her hair was dark, cropped short, her face fresh and childlike. But it was she. The big yearning eyes were unchanged and the short upper lip, showing even in those days its petulant curl.

He brought out the other photograph, the last one, from under it. Nell again, Nell fractionally older, her hair still short and feathery, her skin apparently innocent of make-up. The portrait was coloured, tinted in the shades of old china, rose and sepia and ice-blue and plum red. Nell's new wedding ring gleamed brassily against the dull red stuff of her dress, and on the simple bodice, just below the round neckline, hung a pearl drop on a gold chain.

Wexford went ponderously out into the hall.

CHAPTER NINETEEN

On all-fours Burden was examining the floor and the hideous shiny wallpaper with its pattern of little gold flowers and tiny, regularly recurring crimson leaves, wallpaper which met a floor that curved up to join it without any intervening skirting board.

'Get up, Mike. It's useless. We've done all that already.'

'One must do something,' said Burden irritably. He got up and brushed his hands against each other. 'What's the matter? You've found something!'

'This.'

'It's the dress! But who's the girl?'

'Nell Tate.'

Burden stared incredulously at the portrait. Then he put it beside the wedding picture, nodded, looked up at the chief inspector. 'I like her better how she was,' he said quietly.

'So would most men, but maybe she doesn't know that.' Wexford slipped the two photographs back into the envelope. 'Mike, I've a curious feeling I'm losing touch with Dawn Stonor, that she's fading away from me and I'm coming to grips with something stranger, something almost more terrible than her actual death. There must be many murder victims,' he said slowly, 'who meet their deaths without knowing in the least why they are to die.'

'Most of them, I should think. Victims of poisoners, old shopkeepers who know the till's empty, all children.'

'She wasn't a child,' said Wexford. 'Perhaps your list isn't completely comprehensive. I don't know, Mike. I'm only dreaming, not really getting anywhere. This is a gloomy place, isn't it? The windows are huge and yet the light doesn't seem to get in. Of course, it's an illusion, it's something to do with the dulling, deadening influence of the man's personality.'

RUTH RENDELL

They moved back into the living room where the books frowned on the blue birds and the orange lilies that covered the walls.

Burden said, 'We're getting too dreamlike for me. I'd be happier if I could understand about the keys, if I could see how Dawn got in here.'

'Someone let her in. Someone asked her to come and that someone was here to let her in when she arrived at five-thirty. Not Dunsand.'

'But he cleared up the mess. He was left to dispose of the body he found when he got home.'

'I suppose so. You talk about mess, Mike. What mess? Where is it? Where are the traces of it? Is the killer the one killer we've ever come across who can commit a crime as bloody as this one and leave no blood? I don't believe it.'

'This place will have to be taken apart,' Burden said, crossing the passage and entering the bathroom. 'If it was done without leaving any apparent trace it must have been done in here.' He looked at the gleaming taps, the spotless bath and basin. The sunlight showed no film of dust on glass, no fingermarks on mirrors.

Wexford nodded. 'Yes,' he said, 'the tiles off, the pipes out. And if that yields nothing, the same with the kitchen.'

'Dunsand may crack. He may tell us what at the moment he's doing his utmost to conceal.'

'If he has anything to conceal.'

'Come on, sir. He must know more than he's told us. He must know why his wife would kill an unknown girl in his house, how it happened, the circumstances. He must know that.'

'I wonder?' said Wexford. 'Does he know any more than that his wife – the woman he still thinks of as his wife – may be in danger? I believe he knows very little, Mike, as little of the whole of it as the girl who died.'

Wexford stared up at the ceiling, scanned the smooth glossy walls. The whole place smelt soapy, too clean.

'Mind you don't trip,' said Burden. 'Your shoelace is undone. It's no good looking up there. It's no use looking at all. If she was killed here, someone worked a miracle of butchery.'

Wexford stooped down to re-tie the lace. A bright circle of gold, a little sunbeam refracted through a pane, had lighted on the wall beside his left leg. He stared at the trembling illumination. The gold flowers occurred on the paper in vertical lines about two inches apart, a thin black stripe dividing each line from the next, and the red leaves, pear-shaped, were printed in clusters of three between each flower. Flower, cluster, flower, followed each other immaculately and evenly to meet the bitumastic ridge. There were signs of faint blurring on the pattern, the result perhaps of washing the paper, but nothing had been obliterated. Three leaves, flower, three leaves . . .

'Mike,' he said in a strange voice, 'your sight's better than mine. Have a look at this.'

'I looked before and you stopped me. It's been washed. So what?'

'You were looking for signs of washing, maybe for a missing bit of the pattern. Look again.'

Impatiently Burden got to his knees. He concentrated on the puddle of light.

'Not a missing leaf,' said Wexford. 'In the lowest cluster there aren't three leaves but four.'

They squatted down side by side and examined the hall paper.

'You see,' Wexford said excitedly, 'in this one and this one, in all of them, there are three little pear-shaped leaves like the leaves in a fleur-de-lis. But in the one we're looking at there's a fourth leaf under the centre one.'

'And it's not quite the same colour. It's darker, it's browner.'

'It's blood,' said Wexford, and he added wonderingly, 'One little spot of blood.'

'Shall I . . . ?'

'No, don't touch it. The experts can come here, get their sample themselves. It's too precious for us to mess about with. Mike, d'you realize that's the one real piece of evidence we've got?'

'If it's blood, if it's hers.'

'I know it's hers. It has to be.'

They went outside where the sun blazed on the road, melting tar and creating, where concrete ended and fields began, a mirage like a veil of shimmering water. The car was oven-hot inside, its seats burning to the touch. Burden rolled down his window and drove in his shirt sleeves.

'Now to check the key,' said Wexford.

'Which one, sir? The one that didn't fit?'

'Yes. I think we'll find a door that it will open.' Sweating profusely, Wexford pulled down the eyeshade across the windscreen. 'But that's a simple job, a job for Martin.'

'I'm not with you,' said Burden, falling into line behind the bus that, with its load of Sundays estate passengers, made its way along the sunny road to Kingsmarkham. 'I haven't a clue what particular door you expect it to unlock.'

Wexford smiled. 'A lot of doors are beginning to unlock inside my head, Mike, but this one, this actual door, is in Myringham. It's the door to the house Dunsand lived in before he moved here.'

The afternoon wore on and the heat seemed to mount, reaching the eighties by four o'clock. Wexford shut himself up in his office, the windows open, the blinds down. He sat alone, waiting, thinking, and then, on the principle that it is better to shut away a problem whose answer continually eludes one, to exclude it and return to it later, he resumed work on that crime-prevention directive which had laid unattended since before the festival.

The reports began to come in. The blood was human and of Dawn Stonor's group. The key which Tate had given him in the hotel garden opened the door of Leonard Dunsand's former home in Myringham. But at Sundays, where questioning of housewives had continued all the afternoon, no one had been found to say that she had ever seen Nell Tate, much less observed her call at Dunsand's house.

The five-twelve bus stopped outside the Baptist church. Wexford watched the passengers get on it. A girl came out of the Luximart, carrying a brown paper bag. She wasn't wearing mauve, she wasn't in the least like Dawn, and she was going to her new house at Sundays, not to her death. Wexford phoned the Cheriton Forest Hotel. Yes, Mr Vedast was still there. Mr Vedast planned to leave that evening. The receptionist couldn't say any more, perhaps, if Wexford was the press, she had said too much already . . .

He turned the sheets of the crime-prevention directive face downwards. He returned to his problem as the day began to cool and the sun's rays slanted. At seven he went across the road to the Carousel café where he found Burden and his children eating steak and salad while Emmanuel Ellerman's hit song 'High Tide' brayed at them from wall speakers.

'Pity you've eaten,' said Wexford. 'I was going to take you out to dinner at the Cheriton Forest.' He ordered a sandwich. 'We shall have to be content to take our coffee with Zeno Vedast instead.'

'I don't suppose . . .' began John wistfully.

'I'm afraid you can't come, John. This is a serious visit, an official visit.'

'Pat and I were going to hang about in the High Street to see him pass though. He's going back to London tonight.'

'I don't think he'll be going just yet,' said Wexford.

CHAPTER TWENTY

The receptionist put a call through to the Elizabethan Suite. 'Mr Vedast says will you wait, please? Mr Vedast is engaged at present.' She was young, the right age to be among Vedast's adorers. 'If you'd care to go into the Shakespeare Lounge, it's over there on the . . .'

'We know the way,' said Wexford.

There was no one in the lounge but the dog. It got up when they came in, stared at them morosely, then collapsed again some two yards from where it had previously been lying.

'I'm in the dark,' said Burden, impatiently rejecting the magazines Wexford passed to him. 'I think you ought to tell me why we're here.'

'Why are we ever anywhere?' Wexford sighed. 'To ask, to deduce, to conclude and to catch. Only it's a little different this time.'

'Oh, riddles, philosophy. What I want to know is . . .'

'Wait.'

Godfrey Tate had come very quietly into the room, Godfrey Tate in his usual dapper black that made his torso look as thin as a teenager's and his limbs spidery.

'Zeno's got that guy Silk with him,' he said, without greeting, without preamble. 'He says to ask you what you want.'

Wexford said quietly, 'I want to tell him what I think of him.'

Tate was bemused with drink, not 'high' on alcohol, but low, dulled, cut off, almost somnambulistic. 'Do I tell him that?'

'Mr Tate, it's a matter of indifference to me what you tell him. Why is Silk here?'

'He'd heard Dunsand's been arrested. He came to tell Nell.'

'And now you're celebrating?'

Tate blinked at him. He turned, shuffled towards the door.

'See you,' said Wexford, looking at his watch, 'in ten minutes.'

But before the ten minutes were up – minutes in which Burden had picked up magazine after magazine, discarding them all, and Wexford had sat still, watching the hall – Martin Silk emerged from the lift. Long hair on the elderly makes its wearer look like a nineteenth-century statesman, but in Silk's case the resemblance ended at his neck. He wore a white tee-shirt with a bunch of grapes appliquéd on the chest. As he passed the reception desk he swaggered like a proud adolescent, thrusting his hips forward, but as he neared the lounge door he began to scuttle, an old man getting away from trouble.

'Mr Silk!'

Silk stopped and forced a broad smile, creasing his face into a thousand wrinkles, enclosing his eyes in cracked parchment skin.

'I hope we haven't driven you away,' said Wexford. 'You're welcome to stay as far as we're concerned.'

Sidling into the lounge, Silk perched himself on the arm of a chair. His knee joint cracked as he swung one leg.

'Merely a social call,' he said. 'I dropped by to tell Zeno there's quite a crowd waiting in Kingsmarkham to give him a send-off. Of course,' he added spuriously, 'I shall be seeing a lot of him now he's bought this lush pad.'

'But you've always seen a lot of him, haven't you, Mr Silk? One might say that you've been a sort of . . .' Wexford glanced meaningly at the shaggy grey hair, ' . . . a sort of *éminence grise* in his life. Or are you another slave?'

'I don't know what you mean.'

'But for you he'd still be Harold Goodbody and he never would have met Nell Dunsand.'

Silk stared at him. 'I acted for the best. We can't know what tragedies may hang on our small actions. I gave to youth a musical genius. If Dunsand freaked out, if certain people were – well, expendable . . .'

'Is that how you see it? Mr Silk, you interfere too much. You organize too much. Be warned, and don't interfere with Louis Mbowele. You might cause a war this time.'

'Really, I think you're twisted, sick. You're not together. Who is, at your age?' He sneered. 'The hung-up generation.'

'If I belong to it,' Wexford retorted, 'so do you. We're the same age. Only I know it, I accept it. You don't. I accept that all the sport is stale and all the wheels run down. And when I consider what some people call sport, I'm not all that sorry.'

At Wexford's words, particularly the reminder of his true age, a look of real pain crossed Silk's face. Mirrors show us what we want to see, but sometimes we look into living, human mirrors and then, briefly, the fantasizing has to stop. Wexford was fat, Silk skinny, the one in a crumpled old suit, the other in tee-shirt and jeans, but they were both sixty. The mirror comparison lay in their shared age, the shared weariness of muscle and bone, and painfully Silk saw it.

He said shrilly, 'What are you doing here?'

'Talking to you at the moment. Now we're going upstairs to talk to your genius.'

'But you've got Dunsand. Zeno wasn't even there. I was with Zeno and the Tates in Kensington. You've got Dunsand under lock and key!'

'What an old-fashioned expression!' Wexford mocked. 'Can't you find a more trendy way of putting it? Come on, Mike, we've wasted enough time.'

They walked up. Silk stood at the foot of the staircase watching them, hesitating, torn perhaps between a fear of his protégé coming to harm and an even greater fear of more cruel jibes levelled at him concerning his age.

Wexford said, 'He knows nothing about it. He knows less

even than Wexford.' He smiled obscurely, tapped on the door of the Elizabethan Suite.

They were packing. At last they were going home. His face an even duskier red than usual, Tate was on his knees, trying to fasten an overfull suitcase, while Vedast sat cross-legged on top of a lacquer cabinet watching him. Wordlessly, Nell led them through the labyrinth of piled luggage and mountains of frippery, magazines and records.

Dead flowers, smelling foetid, were heaped on the balcony. Fresh flowers had arrived that day, perhaps that afternoon, roses, lilies, carnations, and they were dying too. No one had bothered to put them in water.

Nell was as carefully dressed and made-up as usual, but her exertions in the heat had given her an air of dishevelment, for it was still hot, the evening air windless, the sun a smouldering crimson knot over the forest. She scowled at the policemen, met Vedast's cool gaze, and turned immediately to look at herself in one of the mirrors. Vedast gave a light laugh.

'Fasten that case, Goffo. Get a move on, dears. Why don't you go and order some coffee, Nello?' He swayed his body towards Wexford. 'That will give her a chance to repair her poor face,' he said as if she wasn't there.

Burden, who had followed the chief inspector's example and cleared a seat for himself, said gruffly, 'No coffee for us.'

'Just as you like.' Vedast flicked his fingers at Nell, who, still in front of the mirror, was apathetically fidgeting with her hair while watching the policemen in the glass. She sprang round as if those snapping fingers had actually touched her, fetched his orange juice and handed it to him with a pleading look. He removed a lump of ice and licked it. 'How glum you all look!' he said, surveying the four faces. 'You're frightening my little ones, Chief Inspector. Why don't we take it as read. I know what happened and so, presumably, do you – now. It *did* take you a long time. But you can't prove it. So why don't we just congratulate each other like clever cats and mice and you pop off home?'

Wexford quoted softly, ' "What need we fear who knows it when none can call our power to account?" '

The Tates looked at him uncomprehendingly, Nell edging closer to Vedast, who said, 'Macbeth. I sometimes think of changing over to the legitimate theatre. I've had no end of offers.' He swallowed what remained of his ice cube. 'But I don't want to start now, thank you so much. We're none of us feeling quite strong enough for drama.'

'You mean you've had enough of it? You've made your tragedy and now you're exhausted? The function of tragedy, as I'm sure you know, Mr Vedast, is to purge with pity and terror, and that's what I'm going to try to do to you – or some of you. So sit down, Mr Tate, and you too, Mrs Tate, and listen to me.'

Both Nell and her husband looked doubtfully at Vedast for instructions. He nodded lightly.

'Do what the man says, dears.'

Nell flounced on to the sofa, tipping off a heap of dirty clothes and what seemed to be a stack of fan letters. A full glass in his hand, a hand which trembled, Tate crept towards her.

She made a slight movement of rejection, turning her shoulder and at the same time spreading out her thick, stiffly embroidered skirts so that there was no room for her husband to sit beside her. He gave her a bitter look, a look of dark reproach, from under swollen veined eyelids. Clasping his drink as if it were a protective talisman, he perched himself on the sofa arm.

The singer watched them, amused that they had obeyed so easily. A law unto himself, he got down from the cabinet and lounged against the open french window. With the setting of the sun, a light breeze had begun to blow. It fanned his hair, lifting it into a golden aureole. Outside the blue of the sky was deepening to violet, feathered with flamingo red. The frosty orange glass glowed in his hand like a lamp. He stood as if he were about to sing, his chin lifted, his hips thrust forward, quite still, utterly relaxed.

'A tragedy,' said Wexford, 'in two parts.'

'It concerns,' he began, 'two people who by their looks and the power of their personalities were able to command obsessive love. You, Mr Vedast, and you, Mrs Tate. I'm not flattering you. Anyone may become the object of such love and, in my experience, those who do are usually shallow, narcissistic and self-centred.'

Nell said shrilly, 'Are you going to let him talk to me like that, Godfrey?'

Hunched up, nursing his glass, Tate gave her a black look. He said nothing. The breeze chilled him, making the dark hairs on his wrists stand erect.

'The need to love like this lies in the characters of the lovers who fasten generally on the first desirable person who comes in their way, fasten and, if they can, hold on. Unfortunately, the beloved objects trade on this and use it for their own ends, for cruelty and victimisation. Just in case Mrs Tate is under any misapprehension as to whom I mean when I speak of the man who loves her obsessively, in case she should be so obtuse as to suppose I mean Mr Vedast, I'll tell her now that I refer to her first husband, Leonard Dunsand. A foolish, clever, learned, dull and conventional little man who has loved her since she was eighteen when he married her.'

One of those people who will bear any insult provided it carries with it a hint of flattery, Nell apparently couldn't resist preening herself at this. She crossed her long and very shapely legs and gave a sidelong glance in Vedast's direction. Vedast stroked the string of beads he wore, running them through his fingers.

Wexford went on: 'Who is probably the only man sufficiently

capable of self-delusion to love her sincerely, the only man
who ever will.' He waited for some reaction from Nell's present
husband. Tate reacted characteristically, behaving as he always
did in crises or threatened crises. Without getting up, he
reached for the brandy bottle. 'If you are in a position to be
thankful for anything, Mr Tate, be thankful that you are more
sophisticated and have eyes to see. Pity you've clouded them
so much with that stuff.'

'I can look after myself,' said Tate in a low voice.

'I never saw a man less capable of doing so, unless it is
Mr Dunsand.'

'I'll look after Goffo.' Vedast turned idly, smiling, cooling
his hands on the glass, caressing it. 'Do tell us who's in love
with me. I'm dying to know.'

'Thousands, I imagine. The one in particular I speak of is
dead. She was dying for you too often and at last she really
died. You were her first lover. That's supposed to have some
profound effect on a woman and, whether it's true or not, it
had a profound effect on Dawn Stonor. I wonder how much
of that story Mr and Mrs Tate know?' While Vedast resumed
his scanning of the sky in which a few pale stars had appeared,
Wexford leant towards the Tates. 'They were at school together,
Dawn and a boy called Harold Goodbody, a boy who went
to tea with his girl friend's grandmother because he only had
baked beans at home; Harold Goodbody who wore his cousin's
cast-off shoes and whose father spent the housekeeping on dog
racing; Harold Goodbody who played April Fool tricks to
amuse his friends, who doubtless carried young Dawn's satchel
for her. A rustic idyll, wasn't it? Dawn Stonor and her first
love, Harold Goodbody.'

'I would prefer you not to call me that,' said Vedast, and
for the first time Wexford heard an edge of temper to his
voice.

'You'd prefer me to go away, but I shan't do that,'
Wexford flashed back. 'You said you were dying to hear and

you shall hear.' He leaned back, pleased at the unease his words had provoked in Nell, pleased by Tate's cringing. 'You left your friend,' he said to Vedast, 'and went to London. For you the idyll was over. Soon afterwards she went to London too, but by then you were beyond her reach. And yet she never forgot you. She told her friends and she pretended, perhaps to herself as well as to her friends, that you had always remained lovers and between you was some enduring bond.' Wexford glanced at Burden and inclined his head, giving the inspector honour for this idea which at first he had ridiculed. 'In fact,' he went on, 'nearly a decade passed by before you saw each other again. In that time you had become very famous, many exciting things had happened to you. Very little had happened to her. She was a waitress in a club and she remained a waitress.

'It was a pity you ever went into that club. If you hadn't, Dawn might at this moment be making wedding plans with her fiancé. Why did you go?'

Vedast shrugged. 'This bloke asked us. We hadn't anything better to do.'

'You could hardly have done worse.'

'I didn't kill her. I never touched her.'

Wexford turned towards the Tates, to Godfrey Tate whose bloodshot eyes were wide open and staring.

CHAPTER TWENTY-ONE

'I shall now go back,' said the chief inspector, 'to one of your exciting happenings, although I don't believe you'll regard it as a highspot when you come to write your memoirs. I refer to your meeting with Mrs Tate, and to describe that I must return to the other love story.'

A glance from Vedast was enough to make Nell get up and switch on the rose-shaded lamps. She moved stiffly, tripping over the red grip and cursing. Vedast gave her his empty glass and she refilled it. He took it without thanks like a duke receiving the drink he has ordered from a parlourmaid.

'Ice, Nello,' he said.

She spooned two cubes out of a pool of water in a bowl on the cabinet. Tate was crouched over his brandy, gazing into the golden liquid. The rosy light played on him, muting the harsh blackness of his hair. Nell gave Vedast his glass again, keeping her hands clasped round it so that his fingers would brush hers as he took it. They brushed them as a stranger's might without lingering. She seemed desperate to stay beside him, to remain with him on the cool, darkening balcony whose rail, reddened by the setting sun, was now a black filagree trellis behind the mound of dead blossoms.

'Go away, Nello. You fidget me.'

She hung her head, crept just inside the window and dropped on to an upright chair, her arms hanging limply by her sides.

'That's right, Mrs Tate, sit where I can see you. You're a very good-looking woman, but you've changed a good deal since you were a bride for the first time. For one thing, you've tinted your hair. I don't suppose you ever wear dark red these days, do you?

'Mr Dunsand liked your short dark hair. He liked you in simple, wifely dresses. I understand from what information was gathered today in Myringham that you were known as a quiet little thing, a good cook, fond of flowers, of homemaking, but inclined to be bored with the society you moved in. They were all so much older than you, those faculty wives, weren't they? You would have preferred the company of your husband's students. Those coffee mornings, those empty afternoons, were very dull for you. But they were nothing to the evenings when, after you had prepared the kind of meal Mr Dunsand liked, you had to sit for hours alone with him, the record player switched off, and plan together your annual holiday, plan your budget, decide what new equipment or furniture you could afford that year.

'To Mr Dunsand it was the very essence of contentment. I expect you played your part well. Women like you, born sycophants, usually do, and all the time they wait quietly for the means of escape. Your chance came when Zeno Vedast, your idol, gave a concert in Myringham. I don't suppose Mr Dunsand wanted you to go to that concert. The idea of his wife, the wife who depended on him utterly for her support, disporting herself among a bunch of teenagers at a pop concert, can hardly have appealed to him. No, he couldn't have liked to think of you raving among his own students, but you went. If you hadn't gone, Dawn Stonor would be alive today, making wedding plans with her fiancé.

'I don't think you threw yourself under Mr Vedast's car deliberately – you wouldn't have the courage – let's say it was an unconscious urge you couldn't control or resist.

'Mr Vedast had put you in a private room at the hospital. How you must have prayed for Mr Vedast himself to appear with the grapes and the chocolates! You didn't know him. You don't know him now. He sent his minion, and it was any port in a storm for you, Mrs Tate. But you're not unique, don't think it. Many a master in the past has married a likely wench off to his servant so that he can have the enjoying of her without any of the trouble.'

'You've no right to insult me!' Nell flared. She waited for her husband to defend her. When he said nothing, while Vedast smiled and sipped his orange juice, she said, 'Why shouldn't I have left my husband? Why shouldn't I have got married again? I'm not the only one. I was sick to death of living with Len.'

Vedast turned. He said smoothly, 'Like the judges say, this isn't a court of morals, Mr Wexford.'

'Oh, but it is. It must be because it can't be a court of justice.'

'In that case . . .' Nell got up. 'In that case, I'm going. Let's go, Zeno. He can't keep us here.'

'Do as you like, Nello.' Vedast gave her a sly sidelong glance. She couldn't do as she liked. She never had been able to. 'You go if you want,' he said in the voice, usual with him, that was both gentle and unkind. 'I'm staying. I'm fascinated. How about you, Goffo, are you going to take your wife away or stay and support your old mate?'

'Mr Tate stays,' said Burden sharply.

Wexford just glanced at him, raising his eyebrows. 'Let us have an intermission,' he said. 'An interval to relax in. If my voice were better, I'd offer to sing you a song, but in this company . . .' He hesitated, then said, 'You all know the song. It was written at the time of Mrs Tate's second marriage. It would be ingenuous of me to suppose it doesn't illustrate a true story, render someone's real suffering. That's why it was written. Poets,' he said, 'are said to make little songs out of their great sorrows. You . . .' His eyes went to the window, ' . . . amused yourself and feathered your luxurious nest by making a song out of someone else's.'

Vedast jerked round. He came into the room, his yellow eyes sharp and narrow.

'I'll sing it,' he said. 'There's nothing wrong with my voice.'

Wexford nodded. He could tell what Burden was thinking, that his son, that any fan at the festival, would have given a week's wages, a month's grant, a term's pocket money, to have been in their shoes. Vedast, who could command thousands for one concert, was going to sing in private for them. He felt a little sick.

In the pale rosy light, the soft kind light, Vedast looked very young, a teenager himself. He stood in a corner of the room, resting his bare elbows on a shelf from which rose-buds hung, young, fresh rose-buds dead before they opened from dehydration. He waited in the silence of the evening, the silence of the forest which surrounded them. The first word came loud like a note vibrating from a string, then the clear, light voice dropped a little, filling the room with sweet bitterness.

Nell watched the singer adoringly, tapping in time to the tune throughout the first verse, the first chorus. Wexford frowned at her and she tossed her head, flinging herself back petulantly against a cushion. His sickness was passing. He listened to the words as if he had never heard them before, as if he had never fully understood the depth of their meaning.

'Remember me and my life-without-life.
Come once more to be my wife,
Come today before I grieve,
Enter the web of let-me-believe.

So come by, come nigh,
   come try and tell why
   some sigh, some cry,
   some lie and some die . . .'

There was no applause. Vedast dropped his head. Then he flung it back, shaking his hair.

'Thank you,' said Wexford crisply. 'It's all in that song, isn't it? All Mr Dunsand's sorrow is there. He pleaded with

325

you, I imagine, not to break with him entirely, not to leave him utterly without life, to let him believe sometimes, very occasionally, that you were still his wife. And you repeated those conversations to Mr Vedast, giving him such a good idea for a song.'

Tate looked up, frowning, a trickle of brandy coursing down his chin. He wiped his mouth on his sleeve.

'Why did you agree to what Mr Dunsand asked?'

'I didn't want to hurt him too much,' Nell muttered.

A dull, humourless laugh escaped from Burden and it was echoed, surprisingly, by Tate. Wexford didn't laugh. 'Mrs Tate, is that you talking? *You?* When have you ever minded whom you hurt, you who are an expert treader on other people's dreams? If you won't tell me why, I shall have to guess.'

'It was to nark me,' Tate interrupted.

'But you didn't know until after the festival,' Wexford said quickly.

Bewildered, Tate said, 'That's true. She'd been seeing him two or three times a year, going to his house and bloody well sleeping with him. I blacked her eye for her.'

'So you told me. And you gave me a key. Only it wasn't the key to Mr Dunsand's house in The Pathway. It opens the front door of his former home in Myringham. Mrs Tate had never been to The Pathway house. She knew it only because Mr Dunsand described it to her over the phone as the middle house of the three. But he sent her a key, intending that she should keep up the custom of the Myringham days.'

Tate said slowly:

'What custom? What are you on about.'

'I believe you, Mr Tate, when you say you knew nothing of these visits of your wife's until after the festival when, frightened of what she had done but not frightened enough to confess everything, she told you she had been seeing her first husband. I believe you are entirely innocent of this crime, in no way an accessory. You had been kept in the dark as you

are, I daresay, about many things.' Tate shrugged awkwardly.
The level of golden liquor in the bottle was going steadily
down. He poured himself some more in silence. 'Nor do I
think you would have been a party to any of this had you
known about it,' said Wexford.

'Mr Vedast wasn't in the dark. He knew. Mrs Tate told him
she had promised these – shall I say loans? – loans of herself
to Mr Dunsand. And so I come back to why. Why did she
do it? You're not a very happy woman, are you, Mrs Tate?
Apparently you have everything you wanted, but only apparently. I think that very soon after your second marriage you
saw what you had got, luxury and excitement, yes, but at what
a price. Another not very inspiring husband – forgive me, Mr
Tate – though a complaisant one, a condescending master,
kind when you were obedient. So you agreed to Mr Dunsand's
requests for the sake of the contrast. Those few evenings, those
nights, you spent with him, showed you that what you had
was at least preferable to your former married life. After a
night in Myringham you could go back to London, to Europe,
to Bermuda, your loins girded, as it were, with the memory
of the alternative.'

'Is that true, Nello? I never knew that.'

'I'm glad to be able to tell you something you don't know,
Mr Vedast. But you knew of the part she played while she
was there, didn't you? I'm sure Mrs Tate told you all the
details, the props, the costume required, shall I say? I'm sure
she told you of the setting of the little play they enacted two
or three times a year, the activities, following always the same
pattern, in which the actors indulged, marriage *à la mode*
Dunsand. Indeed, I know she did. Had she not, you wouldn't
have been able to play your – your practical joke.'

Nell said, 'I want a drink, Godfrey.'

'Get it yourself.'

She did so, clattering the bottle neck against the glass,

spilling vermouth on to the pale embroidery on her white linen skirt. It made a red stain like blood.

Wexford said, 'I expect you thought all this very amusing, Mr Vedast, until there was a threat of the performance of this play interfering with your own plans. About a month ago Mrs Tate told you that she would be paying her first visit to Mr Dunsand's new home on the afternoon of Monday, June sixth. But that didn't suit you, for you and Mr and Mrs Tate would only just have returned from Manchester where you had a concert engagement.'

Tate shook his head. 'No, that's not right,' he said. 'He meant to stay over till the Monday. It was me said at the last moment it'd be too tiring for him.'

'Ah.' Wexford sighed. 'Even better – or worse. When Mrs Tate first confided in you, you intended that she and you and Mr Tate would all be away from the South on June sixth.' He looked at Nell, at the red stain on her dress which she had not attempted to remove, at the red colour that burned on her face. 'Why didn't you just change the date of your appointment with your first husband, Mrs Tate? Surely you could have put it off for a few days?'

For a moment she looked as if she were searching in her mind for an excuse. She put out a trembling hand to Vedast who ignored her, who smiled, his head on one side.

'Because that would have "hurt" Mr Dunsand?' Wexford went on relentlessly. 'Or did you do what you always do, obeyed Mr Vedast?'

In a small, thin voice, she said, 'I left it to Zeno.'

'You left it to Zeno. He was to get in touch with Mr Dunsand, was he? He, a world-famous singer, a pop idol, was to phone Mr Dunsand and tell him you couldn't make it but would, say, Wednesday do instead?'

She was near to tears. She held her hands crushed together so that the peeling nails dug into the flesh. 'You know it wasn't like that. You know you're just tormenting me.'

'Not everyone is as zealous as you, Mrs Tate, about the feelings of others. Not everyone is as anxious as you to go through life without doing hurt. But it's true that I know what happened.' Wexford got up and walked over to Vedast who had taken up a Yoga position, a half-Lotus, on the floor by the open window. He stood over the singer, looking down, his own grey eyes meeting the amber ones.

'No, Mr Vedast,' he said. 'To a person of your temperament it was far more amusing to keep the date, changing not the day but the female protagonist.'

Tate broke the silence.

'What d'you mean? I don't follow you. Female whatsit, what does it mean?'

Wexford came over to him. He spoke gently. 'It means, Mr Tate, that your employer saw a way of getting Mrs Tate out of her appointment, and perhaps all further similar appointments, and at the same time of playing one of his favourite jokes.

'He decided to send a substitute for your wife to The Pathway. First, I suspect, he thought of sending a call girl. But why go to all that trouble when he could send Dawn Stonor whose acquaintance he had renewed some weeks before and whom he had telephoned on May twenty-third?'

CHAPTER TWENTY-TWO

Wexford sat down in the centre of the room. 'I don't know why you phoned Dawn that last night,' he went on, addressing himself directly to Vedast. 'I think your motive was akin to Mrs Tate's motive for visiting her former husband. Probably at the Townsman Club you contrasted Dawn's humble situation with your successful one, remembering how you came from similar beginnings, how you had had even chances of money, fame, glory – but you had achieved them and she had not.

'On May twenty-third Mr and Mrs Tate were away. You were bored. Perhaps you even felt insecure. Why not phone Dawn, do a little slumming, so that afterwards you might have the pleasure of appreciating what you are and what you might have been? I daresay that phone conversation had the desired effect on you. You were quickly tired of her eagerness and you rang off, having vaguely suggested you see each other "sometime" but not, in fact, ever intending to see her again.

'During that week, I believe, Mrs Tate told you of the visit she planned to make to Mr Dunsand's new house. On the phone you had already, I think, boasted to Dawn of the house you were yourself thinking of buying near Kingsmarkham. Why not play a joke, the biggest joke of your career?'

'My thought processes,' said Vedast, 'don't work quite like that. Stop hovering, Nello. Go and sit down somewhere.'

The only spot in the room where she wanted to be was at his side. She looked at the sofa where her husband sat hunched, at the two occupied chairs, at the empty chairs which were either near her husband or near the policemen. And like an insect with bright antennae, bright wings, she fluttered desperately, hovered, as Vedast had put it, finally alighting –

her heels were high, her shoes platformed – on another spot
of carpet as near to him as she had been when he had shooed
her away. The insect had come back to the flame.

Wexford had paused when the interruption came but, apart
from hesitating briefly, he took no notice of her.

'The first of June,' he said to Vedast, 'was the birthday of
the man Dawn was very probably going to marry, the man
she would have married if you had left her alone. She was at
home, waiting for him to come to lunch. You didn't know
that. Would you have cared if you had? You phoned her in
the morning and asked her to meet you for a drink.' Burden
stirred in his chair, his eyebrows lifting. 'She wasn't very elated
about it. Perhaps she realized that a man like you, a man so
rich as you are, who could afford without noticing it the most
expensive restaurant in London, only takes a girl for drinks in
a pub if he despises her, if he thinks she isn't worth any more.
But she dressed carefully for you just the same; changing out
of the clothes that were good enough for an ordinary fiancé.

'And later, when the excitement of that lunchtime date
had begun to recede, she asked herself – and her flatmate –
if she *was* despised, if that was the reason why you were only
prepared to have a hole-in-corner, *sub rosa* affair with her,
hiding her in a house no one knew you had bought instead
of taking her to an hotel.

'In that pub, between one o'clock and three, you asked
her, after some preliminary flattery and flirtation, no doubt,
to spend the night of the following Monday with you in your
new house. Of course, she agreed. She would be on holiday.
She could go and see her mother and then go on to The
Pathway. That she and Dunsand were *people* with feelings never
entered your head, did it? You were as careless of his as of
hers. That Mrs Tate was in the habit of preparing for him on
these occasions a special meal of his favourite food, of bringing
good wine and beautiful flowers – to fill the void? – didn't
trouble you at all. You told Dawn anything would do, just

some quick picnic food for you and her to share. Any old wine, the cheapest she could get.

'She must go there first, you told her, and you gave her the key Mr Dunsand had sent to Mrs Tate and which Mrs Tate had given you. No responsibility, Mrs Tate? You left it all to Zeno?' Wexford turned back to Vedast. 'You'd be along around half past six. As soon as she was in the house she was to go upstairs where she would find a red dress.

'Now this dress had been laid out on the bed by Mr Dunsand. During his married life this dress of Mrs Tate's had been his favourite. When she wore it, sat down to dinner with him, listened to his account of his day and gave him account of hers, he could fancy himself protected from the "harsh light of day" and back safe and happy with his wife.

'Dawn knew nothing of this. She was told nothing of this. You asked her to wear this dress because it belonged to a fashion current when you were still together, still lovers, and you told her it would recall to you that past time.'

Looking ill, the colour all gone from his face, leaving a swarthy pallor, Tate lurched to his feet. He edged round the sofa and said to Vedast, 'Is that true?'

'We didn't mean any harm.'

'No harm? Christ... You did that and *she* knew it. God, I feel like I've never known either of you, never seen you before...'

'Godfrey...' Nell put out a feeble hand. 'I didn't do anything. I only told him – well, you know.'

'Have another drink, Goffo,' Vedast drawled.

'I don't want any more.' Tate made this remark in a thick but wondering voice. He swung on Wexford. 'Go on, then. What happened? Tell me the rest. Him...' He pointed at Vedast as if reluctant to use his name. 'Him and her, they were with me that evening. Honest, they were. They can't have killed her.'

'Who kills, Mr Tate, the one who holds the knife, the one who says "stab!" or the one who sends the victim to the appointed place? Which of the three Fates is responsible for our destinies, she who spins the thread, she who cuts it or she who merely holds the scissors?' Wexford could tell from Tate's puzzled, vacant expression that all this was going over his head. 'Maybe Mr Dunsand could tell us. He's the philosopher.' Glancing at Burden, hoping there would be no actual exclamation of shock, he said. 'He killed her, of course. He's admitted it. He isn't the kind of man to prevaricate for long. Only chivalry made him tell a few lies to avoid any involvement of...' Scornful eyes came to rest on Nell, '... of his beloved former wife.'

Wexford went on carefully, 'As to what he did, I'll tell you. He came home, longing, of course, for the evening and the night ahead. He let himself in with his own key at twenty to seven. By that time Dawn must have been feeling uneasy. There were many things to make her uneasy, the modest size of the place, the austere furnishings, the superabundance of learned books. And the dress – a dress that was too small for her, unbecoming, too tight. Of course she felt uneasy. Of course, when she heard a key in the lock, she came out of the living room shyly, not speaking, just standing there.

'Instead of Vedast, she saw a little middle-aged stranger. Instead of his wife, Dunsand saw – what? What, Mrs Tate?'

'Dawn Stonor,' she said in a small, sullen voice.

'Oh, no. She didn't exist for him. He never even knew her name. He saw his wife, yet not his wife, a girl of his wife's age but bigger, coarser, with even more make-up, with brassier hair, yet wearing his wife's dress, his favourite dress.

'Perhaps he didn't believe in the reality of this sight. Even to a better-balanced man than Dunsand, what he saw looming in the little hall would have seemed a hallucination. To him it wasn't just a travesty of his wife but a kind of succubus sent by something which existed in his clever sick mind to torment him. He wanted to destroy what he saw and he simply did so, attacking the hallucinatory shape with the first weapon that came to hand, the wine bottle his visitant had left on the hall table.'

Vedast got up, lifted his head sharply as he had lifted it at the festival, shook back his lion's mane. 'How was I to know things would go that way?' He held out his glass. 'Get me some more of that stuff, will you, Goffo.'

Tate said, 'Not me. Get your own bloody drink.'

'Temper, temper.' The golden eyebrows went up, the teeth showed in what was perhaps a smile.

'Can't you do anything to him?' Tate said to Wexford. 'He killed her. He's the real killer.'

'I know it, Mr Tate, but no, I can't do anything to him. What should be done to him? He is as sick as Mr Dunsand, a megalomaniac who lives on fantasies.'

'Don't give me that balls. He ought to be shot. Hanging'd be too good for him.'

' "Heaven hath no rage like love to hatred turned" . . . You are not obliged to associate with them, Mr Tate. You need not, just because you also married her, copy her first husband and be chivalrous.'

'Too bloody right, I needn't.' Shock had brought Tate complete cold sobriety. On his knees, he flung armfuls of garments into the red grip, seized it and a smaller suitcase. 'I'm going. I'm quitting.' He got up, said to Vedast, 'You owe me a hundred quid. You can sent it care of my mum's. *She* knows the address.'

'You can't go,' said Vedast and at last he wasn't playing. His voice had lost its lightness. 'We've been together for eight years. What'll I do without you?'

'Cut your bloody throat, but cut hers first.' Tate held out his hand to Wexford. 'I used to call you lot pigs,' he said, 'and maybe I will again. But, thanks, you've done me a good turn. If you've done nothing else you've got me away from them. I might even stop drinking now.' Then he used the first cultivated, literate phrase Wexford had ever heard from his lips but, even as he said it, the chief inspector knew he had learnt it parrot fashion from the 'scene' with which he had been associated. 'They'd have destroyed me utterly.'

'I really think they would, Mr Tate.'

When he had gone, slamming the suite door, the slave who remained seized Vedast's arm and said, 'Good riddance. I just feel relief, don't you?'

Vedast made no reply. He picked up the phone sullenly, asked for a porter. Immediately Nell, taking her cue, bundled heaps of clothes into cases, bags, carriers. Wexford and Burden, ready to leave, helpless, impotent, watched her. The cases were all packed in five minutes. Vedast stood at the window, his expression inscrutable. He looked over the balcony rail once, perhaps at the departing Tate. The porter came in, took two cases in his hands, one under his arm. Nell flung a white coat round her shoulders.

'I take it we shan't be wanted any more?'

'You will be wanted at Mr Dunsand's trial. Before that, statements will have to be taken from you.'

'Me?' said Vedast. 'I can't appear in court. It will be ghastly bad publicity. Why did Goffo have to go like that? Goffo could have coped.'

'I'll cope,' said Nell fondly. 'Let's go now, shall we? It's nearly midnight. Let's get going.'

He pushed her away. 'I'm going,' he said. 'I'm going by myself. You can get a taxi to whatever station there is in this hole.'

'But we've got the car!'

Petulantly, like a little boy, he said, 'It's my car. *I'm* going in it. You'd better face it, Nello, you're no use to me without Godfrey. He looked after me and then – then you came along.' His face cleared a little. 'You were a nice bit of decoration,' he said.

The flesh of her face seemed to sag. Her lip curled up, her eyes widened, stretching the skin, wrinkling it. 'You can't mean it, Zeno. Zeno, don't leave me! I've worshipped you since I was twenty. I've never thought of any man but you.'

'No, dear, I know. You just married them.'

As the porter returned to fetch the remaining luggage, Vedast tried to unhook her hands from his shoulders. 'Nello, do as I say. Let go of me. I'm going to pay the bill and then I'm going.' He went up to Wexford, the bantering tone quelled by what he had to say and by the presence of the inquisitive porter. 'I suppose we can keep all this quiet?' One of the long, lean hands sketched a gesture towards a jeans pocket. 'I imagine . . .'

'Mr Vedast, we are leaving.'

'I'll come down with you.'

'Zeno!' Nell screamed. 'Zeno, I love you!'

The two policemen had moved a pace or two away from the singer, moved distastefully. Nell flung herself upon Vedast. Her coat fell from her shoulders. She clung to his neck, pushing her fingers through the golden hair, pressing her body against him.

'Where am I to go? What am I to do?'

Struggling, pushing her, he said, 'You can go to Godfrey's mum. Go where you like, only get off me. Get off! Christ, Dawn Stonor'd have been a better bet than you. Get off!'

They grappled together like wrestlers, Nell screaming and clinging. Vedast was strong and muscular but not quite strong enough. He kicked and punched, grabbing at her hair, tearing it. They toppled and rolled on the floor among the dead flowers, the empty bottles, knocking over and breaking into fragments the orange-juice glass.

'Let's go,' said Wexford laconically.

In the corridor bedroom doors had been cautiously opened and sleepy people stared out. On the stairs the policemen passed four or five of the hotel night staff running up, alarmed by the screams, the thumps on the floorboards. Lights began to come on as the somnolent hotel woke to life.

The night was as clear, as softly violet-blue as the night of the festival, but now the moon was waning. And there were no ballads to be heard here, no plangent note from a string plucked with controlled power. Wexford could still hear Vedast's voice, though, raised now in a high-pitched lunatic scream, a sound none of his fans would have recognized. Instead of that vibrant twang came the crash of flying furniture; instead of melody, Nell's hysterical sobbing, and instead of applause, the manager gravely and quite ineffectively begging his guests to stop.

'Perhaps they'll kill each other,' said Burden as they passed the furred golden car.

'Perhaps they will. Who cares?' Wexford sighed. 'Vedast won't like it in court. Will it have any effect on his career?'

Once again Burden was being appealed to as the expert on such matters. 'I doubt it,' he said, starting the car. 'These singers, they're always appearing in court on drug offences. Did you ever hear of their records selling less well afterwards?'

'Drugs are one thing. Provided you don't deal in them, drugs harm no one but yourself. But there's a big thing among young people at the moment for loving your neighbour, for not hurting – above all, for keeping in mind that people are people. I don't think they'll be too pleased when they know their idol forgot or, rather, neglected to care for that fact.'

'Poor old Dunsand. What of him?'

'His career will be ruined, but it won't be prison for him. Mental hospital for years? Is that much better? It was a succubus he killed. Unfortunately for him, we know succubi don't exist – they're flesh and blood.'

A single light showed in Burden's bungalow. In an armchair in the living room John lay asleep, his hair tousled, a half-empty glass of milk beside him. The indicator light on the record player still glowed red.

'God, I forgot the kids! I was so carried away I forgot them.' Burden stooped tenderly over his son, but the boy didn't stir. 'He waited up for me,' he said wonderingly.

Wexford smiled rather sadly. 'Poor John. Somehow I don't think he'll get the Sundays album for his birthday now.'

'He certainly won't.' Burden took a stride to the record player, his face flushing with anger when he saw what lay on the turntable. Savagely, he seized 'Let-me-believe' in both hands and seemed about to twist it, to bend it double, when Wexford laid a gentle, warning hand on his arm.

'No, Mike,' he said. 'Don't do that. Leave it to John and – and all of them. Let them be his judges.'

Shake Hands
For Ever

For my aunts, Jenny Waldorff,
Laura Winfield, Margot Richards and
Phyllis Ridgway, with my love

CHAPTER ONE

The woman standing under the departures board at Victoria station had a flat rectangular body and an iron-hard rectangular face. A hat of fawn-coloured corrugated felt rather like a walnut shell encased her head, her hands were gloved in fawn-coloured cotton, and at her feet was the durable but scarcely used brown leather suitcase she had taken on her honeymoon forty-five years before. Her eyes scanned the scurrying commuters while her mouth grew more and more set, the lips thinning to a hairline crack.

She was waiting for her son. He was one minute late and his unpunctuality had begun to afford her a glowing satisfaction. She was hardly aware of this pleasure and, had she been accused of it, would have denied it, just as she would have denied the delight all failure and backsliding in other people brought her. But it was present as an undefined sense of well-being that was to vanish almost as soon as it had been born and be succeeded on Robert's sudden hasty arrival by her usual ill-temper. He was so nearly on time as to make any remarks about his lateness absurd, so she contented herself with offering her leathery cheek to his lips and saying:

'There you are then.'

'Have you got your ticket?' said Robert Hathall.

She hadn't. She knew that money had been tight with him for the three years of his second marriage, but that was his fault. Paying her share would only encourage him.

'You'd better go and get them,' she said, 'unless you want us to miss the train,' and she held even more tightly to her zipped-up handbag.

He was a long time about it. She noted that the Eastbourne train, stopping at Toxborough, Myringham and Kingsmarkham,

RUTH RENDELL

was due to depart at six twelve, and it was five past now. No
fully formed uncompromising thought that it would be nice to
miss the train entered her mind, any more than she had
consciously told herself it would be nice to find her daughter-
in-law in tears, the house filthy and no meal cooked, but once
more the seeds of pleasurable resentment began germinating.
She had looked forward to this weekend with a deep contentment, certain it would go wrong. Nothing would suit her better
than that it should begin to go wrong by their arriving late
through no fault of hers, and that their lateness should result
in a quarrel between Robert and Angela. But all this smouldered silent and unanalyzed under her immediate awareness
that Robert was making a mess of things again.

Nevertheless, they caught the train. It was crowded and
they both had to stand. Mrs Hathall never complained. She
would have fainted before citing her age and her varicose veins
as reasons why this or that man should give up his seat to
her. Stoicism governed her. Instead, she planted her thick body
which, buttoned up in a stiff fawn coat, had the appearance
of a wardrobe, in such a way as to prevent the passenger in
the window seat from moving his legs or reading his newspaper. She had only one thing to say to Robert and that could
keep till there were fewer listeners, and she found it hard to
suppose he could have anything to say to her. Hadn't they,
after all, spent every weekday evening together for the past
two months? But people she had noticed with some puzzlement, were prone to chatter when they had nothing to say.
Even her own son was guilty of this. She listened grimly while
he went on about the beautiful scenery through which they
would soon pass, the amenities of Bury Cottage, and how much
Angela was looking forward to seeing her. Mrs Hathall permitted herself a kind of snort at this last. A two-syllabled grunt
made somewhere in her glottis that could be roughly inter-
preted as a laugh. Her lips didn't move. She was reflecting on
the one and only time she had met her daughter-in-law, in

344

that room in Earls Court, when Angela had committed the outrage of referring to Eileen as a greedy bitch. Much would have to be done, many amends be made, before that indiscretion could be forgotten. Mrs Hathall remembered how she had marched straight out of that room and down the stairs, resolving never – never under any circumstances – to see Angela again. It only proved how forbearing she was that she was going to Kingsmarkham now.

At Myringham the passenger by the window, his legs numb, staggered out of the train and Mrs Hathall got his seat. Robert, she could tell, was getting nervous. There was nothing surprising in that. He knew very well this Angela couldn't compete with Eileen as cook and housekeeper and he was wondering just how far below his first wife's standards his second would fall. His next words confirmed her conviction that this was troubling his mind.

'Angela's spent the week spring-cleaning the place to make it nice for you.'

Mrs Hathall was shocked that anyone could make such a statement aloud and in front of a carriage full of people. What she would have liked to say was, firstly, that he should keep his voice down and, secondly, that any decent women kept her house clean at all times. But she contented herself with a 'I'm sure she needn't put herself out for me' and added repressively that it was time he got her suitcase down.

'It's five minutes yet,' said Robert.

She replied by getting heavily to her feet and struggling with the case herself. Robert and another man intervened to help her, the case nearly fell on to the head of a girl with a baby in her arms, and by the time the train drew to a halt at Kingsmarkham, sending them all staggering and clutching each other, the carriage was in a small uproar.

Out on the platform, Mrs Hathall said, 'That could have been avoided if you'd done as you were asked. You always were obstinate.'

She couldn't understand why he didn't retaliate and fight back. He must be more strung-up than she had thought. To goad him further, she said, 'I suppose we're going to have a taxi?'

'Angela's meeting us in the car.'

Then there wasn't much time for her to say what she had to. She pushed her suitcase at him and took hold of his arm in a proprietory manner. It wasn't that she needed his support or his reassurance, but she felt it essential that this daughter-in-law – how galling and disreputable to have two daughters-in-law! – should, in her first glimpse of them, see them consolidated and arm-in-arm.

'Eileen came in this morning,' she said as they gave up their tickets.

He shrugged absently. 'I wonder you two don't live together.'

'That'd make things easy for you. You wouldn't have to keep a roof over her head.' Mrs Hathall tightened her grip on the arm which he had attempted to jerk away. 'She said to give you her love and say why don't you go round one evening while you're in London.'

'You must be joking,' said Robert Hathall, but he said it vaguely and without much rancour. He was scanning the car park.

Pursuing her theme, Mrs Hathall began 'It's a wicked shame . . .' and then stopped in mid-sentence. A marvellous realization was dawning on her. She knew that car of Robert's, would know it anywhere, he'd had it long enough thanks to the straits that women had brought him to. She too let her sharp eyes rove round the tarmac square, and then she said in a satisfied tone, 'Doesn't look as if she'd put herself out to meet us.'

Robert seemed discomfited. 'The train was a couple of minutes early.'

'It was three minutes late,' said his mother. She sighed happily. Eileen would have been there to meet them all right.

Eileen would have been on the platform with a kiss for her mother-in-law and a cheerful promise of the nice tea that awaited them. And her granddaughter too ... Mrs Hathall remarked as if to herself but loud enough to be heard, 'Poor little Rosemary.'

It was very unlike Robert, who was his mother's son, to take this sort of aggravation without comment, but again he made none. 'It doesn't matter,' he said. 'It's not that far.'

'I can walk,' said Mrs Hathall in the stoical tone of one who realizes that there will be worse trials to come and that the first and lightest must be bravely borne. 'I'm quite used to walking.'

Their journey took them up the station approach and Station Road, across Kingsmarkham High Street and along the Stowerton Road. It was a fine September evening, the air aglow with sunset light, the trees heavily foliaged, the gardens bright with the last and finest flowers of summer. But Mrs Hathall, who might have said like the lover in the ballad, 'What are the beauties of nature to me?', disregarded it all. Her wistfulness had given way to certainty. Robert's depression could mean only one thing. This wife of his, this thief, this breaker of a happy marriage, was going to let him down and he knew it.

They turned into Wool Lane, a narrow tree-shaded byway without a pavement. 'That's what I call a nice house,' said Mrs Hathall.

Robert glanced at the detached, between-the-wars villa. 'It's the only one down here apart from ours. A woman called Lake lives there. She's a widow.'

'Pity it's not yours,' said his mother with a wealth of implication. 'Is it much further?'

'Round the next bend. I can't think what's happened to Angela.' He looked at her uneasily. 'I'm sorry about this, Mother. I really am sorry.'

She was so amazed that he should depart from family

tradition as actually to apologize for anything, that she could make no answer to this and remained silent until the cottage came into view. A slight disappointment marred her satisfaction, for this was a house, a decent though old house of brown brick with a neat slate roof. 'Is this it?'

He nodded and opened the gate for her. Mrs Hathall observed that the garden was untended, the flower-beds full of weeds and the grass inches high. Under a neglected-looking tree lay a scattering of rotten plums. She said, 'Hmm,' a noncommittal noise characteristic of her and signifying that things were turning out the way she expected. He put the key in the front-door lock and the door swung open. 'Come along in, Mother.'

He was certainly upset now. There was no mistaking it. She knew that way he had of compressing his lips while a little muscle worked in his left cheek. And there was a harsh nervous note in his voice as he called out, 'Angela, we're here!'

Mrs Hathall followed him into the living room. She could hardly believe her eyes. Where were the dirty teacups, finger-marked gin glasses, scattered clothes, crumbs and dust? She planted herself rectangularly on the spotless carpet and turned slowly round, scrutinizing the ceiling for cobwebs, the windows for smears, the ashtrays for that forgotten cigarette end. A strange uncomfortable chill took hold of her. She felt like a champion who, confident of victory, certain of her own superiority, loses the first set to a tyro.

Robert came back and said, 'I can't think where Angela's got to. She's not in the garden. I'll just go into the garage and see if the car's there. Would you like to go on upstairs, Mother? Your bedroom's the big one at the back.'

Having ascertained that the dining-room table wasn't laid and that there was no sign of preparations for a meal in the immaculate kitchen where the rubber gloves and dusting gloves of household labour lay beside the sink, Mrs Hathall mounted the stairs. She ran one finger along the picture rail on the landing. Not a mark, the woodwork might have been newly painted. The bedroom which was to be hers was as exquisitely clean as the rest of the house, the bed turned down to show candy-striped sheets, one dressing-table drawer open and lined with tissue paper. She noted it all but never once, as one revelation followed another, did she allow this evidence of Angela's excellence to mitigate her hatred. It was a pity that her daughter-in-law should have armed herself with this weapon, a pity and that was all. No doubt her other faults, such as this one of not being here to greet her, would more than compensate for this small virtue.

Mrs Hathall went into the bathroom. Polished enamel, clean fluffy towels, guest soap . . . She set her mouth grimly. Money couldn't have been as tight as Robert made out. She told herself only that she resented his deception, not putting even into thought-words that she was confronting a second deprivation, that of not being able to throw their poverty and the reason for it in their faces. She washed her hands and came out on to the landing. The door to the main bedroom was slightly ajar. Mrs Hathall hesitated. But the temptation to take a look inside and perhaps find a tumbled bed, a mess of squalid cosmetics, was too great to resist. She entered the room carefully.

The bed wasn't tumbled but neatly made. On top of the covers lay a girl face-downwards, apparently deeply asleep. Her dark, rather shaggy, hair lay spread over her shoulders and her left arm was flung out. Mrs Hathall said, 'Hmm,' all her warm pleasure welling back unalloyed. Robert's wife was lying asleep, perhaps even drunk. She hadn't bothered to take off her canvas shoes before collapsing there and she was dressed exactly as she had been that day in Earls Court, probably as she always dressed, in shabby faded blue jeans and a red check shirt. Mrs Hathall thought of Eileen's pretty afternoon dresses and short permed hair, of Eileen who would only have slept in the daytime if she had been at death's door, and then she went over to the bed and stared down, frowning. 'Hmm,' she said again, but this time it was a 'Hmm' of admonition, designed to announce her presence and get an immediate shamed response.

There was none. The genuine anger of the person who feels herself unbearably slighted seized Mrs Hathall. She put her hand on her daughter-in-law's shoulder to shake it. But she didn't shake it. The flesh of that neck was icy cold, and as she lifted the veil of hair, she saw a pallid cheek, swollen and bluish.

Most women would have screamed. Mrs Hathall made no sound. Her body became a little more set and cupboard-like as she drew herself upright and placed her thick large hand to her palpitating heart. Many times in her long life she had seen death, her parents', her husband's, uncles', aunts', but she had never before seen what the purplish mark on that neck showed – death by violence. No thought of triumph came to her and no fear. She felt nothing but shock. Heavily, she plodded across the room and began to descend the stairs.

Robert was waiting at the foot of them. In so far as she was capable of love, she loved him, and in going up to him and placing her hand on his arm, she addressed him in a muted reluctant voice, the nearest she could get to tenderness. And she used the only words she knew for breaking this kind of bad news.

'There's been an accident. You'd best go up and see for yourself. It's – it's too late to do anything. Try and take it like a man.'

He stood quite still. He didn't speak.

'She's gone, Robert, your wife's dead.' She repeated the words because he didn't seem to take them in. 'Angela's dead, son.'

A vague uncomfortable feeling came over her that she ought to embrace him, speak some tender word, but she had long ago forgotten how. Besides, she was shaking now and her heart was pumping irregularly. He had neither paled nor flushed. Steadily he walked past her and mounted the stairs. She waited there, impotent, awe-stricken, rubbing her hands together and hunching her shoulders. Then he called out from above in a harsh but calm voice:

'Phone the police, Mother, and tell them what's happened.'

She was glad of something to do, and finding the phone on a low table under a bookshelf, she set her finger to the nine slot in the dial.

CHAPTER TWO

He was a tall man, carrying insufficient weight for his wide frame. And he had an unhealthy look, his belly sagging a little, his skin a mottled red. Though still black, his hair was thinning and dry, and his features were bold and harsh. He sat in an armchair, slumped as if he had been injured and then flung there. By contrast, his mother sat upright, her solid legs pressed close together, her hands palm-downwards on her lap, her hard eyes fixed on her son with more of sternness than sympathy.

Chief Inspector Wexford thought of those Spartan mothers who preferred seeing their sons brought home on their shields to knowing they were taken captive. He wouldn't have been surprised if she had told this man to pull himself together, but she hadn't yet uttered a word or made any sign to himself and Inspector Burden beyond giving them a curt nod when admitting them to the house. She looked, he thought, like an old-style prison wardress or mistress of a workhouse.

From upstairs the footfalls of other policemen could be heard, passing to and fro. The woman's body had been photographed where it lay, had been identified by the widower and removed to the mortuary. But the men still had much to do. The house was being examined for fingerprints, for the weapon, for some clue as to how this girl had met her death. And it was a big house for a cottage, with five good-sized rooms apart from the kitchen and the bathroom. They had been there since eight and now it was nearly midnight.

Wexford, who stood by the table on which lay the dead woman's driving licence, purse and the other contents of her handbag, was examining her passport. It identified her as a British subject, born in Melbourne, Australia, thirty-two years old, occupation housewife, hair dark brown, eyes grey, height five feet five inches, no distinguishing marks. Angela Margaret Hathall. The passport was three years old and had never been used to pass any port. The photograph in it bore about as much resemblance to the dead woman as such photographs usually bear to their subjects.

'Your wife lived alone here during the week, Mr Hathall?' he said, moving away from the table and sitting down.

Hathall nodded. He answered in a low voice not much above a whisper. 'I used to work in Toxborough. When I got a new job in London I couldn't travel up and down. That was in July. I've been living with my mother during the week, coming home for weekends.'

'You and your mother arrived here at seven-thirty, I think?'

'Twenty past,' said Mrs Hathall, speaking for the first time. She had a harsh metallic voice. Under the South London accent lay a hint of North Country origins.

'So you hadn't seen your wife since – when? Last Sunday? Monday?'

'Sunday night,' said Hathall. 'I went to my mother's by train on Sunday night. My – Angela drove me to the station. I – I phoned her every day. I phoned her today. At lunchtime. She was all right.' He made a breath-catching sound like a sob, and his body swayed forward. 'Who – who would have done this? Who would have wanted to kill – *Angela?*'

The words had a stagy ring, a false sound, as if they had been learned from some television play or cliché-ridden thriller. But Wexford knew that grief can sometimes only be expressed in platitudes. We are original in our happy moments. Sorrow has only one voice, one cry.

He answered the question in similarly hackneyed words. 'That's what we have to find out, Mr Hathall. You were at work all day?'

'Marcus Flower, Public Relations Consultants. Half Moon Street. I'm an accountant.' Hathall cleared his throat. 'You can check with them that I was there all day.'

Wexford didn't quite raise his eyebrows. He stroked his chin and looked at the man in silence. Burden's face gave nothing away, but he could tell the inspector was thinking the same thought as his own. And during this silence Hathall, who had uttered this last sentence almost with eagerness, gave a louder sob and buried his face in his hands.

Rigid as stone, Mrs Hathall said, 'Don't give way, son. Bear it like a man.'

But I must feel it like a man . . . As the bit from *Macbeth* came into Wexford's mind, he wondered fleetingly why he felt so little sympathy for Hathall, why he wasn't moved. Was he getting the way he'd always sworn he wouldn't get? Was he getting hard and indifferent at last? Or was there really something false in the man's behaviour that gave the lie to these sobs and this abandonment to grief? Probably he was just tired, reading meanings where there were none; probably the woman had picked up a stranger and that stranger had killed her. He waited till Hathall had taken his hands away and raised his face.

'Your car is missing?'

'It was gone from the garage when I got home.' There were no tears on the hard thin cheeks. Would a son of that flint-faced woman be capable of squeezing out tears?

'I'll want a description of your car and its number. Sergeant Martin will get the details from you in a minute.' Wexford got up. 'The doctor has given you a sedative, I believe. I suggest you take it and try to get some sleep. In the morning I should like to talk to you again, but there's very little more we can do tonight.'

Mrs Hathall shut the door on them in the manner of one snapping 'Not today, thanks' at a couple of hawkers. For a moment or two Wexford stood on the path, surveying the place. Light from the bedroom windows showed him a couple of lawns that hadn't been mown for months and a bare plum tree. The path was paved but the drive which ran between the house wall and the right-hand fence was a strip of concrete.

'Where's this garage he was talking about?'

'Must be round the back,' said Burden. 'There wasn't room to build a garage on the side.'

They followed the drive round the back of the cottage. It led them to an asbestos hut with a felt roof, a building which couldn't be seen from the lane.

'If she went for a drive,' said Wexford, 'and brought someone back with her, the chances are they got the car into this garage without a soul seeing them. They'd have gone into the house by the kitchen door. We'll be lucky if we find anyone who saw them.'

In silence they regarded the moonlit empty fields that mounted towards wooded hills. Here and there, in the distance, an occasional light twinkled. And as they walked back towards the road, they were aware of how isolated the house was, how secluded the lane. Its high banks, crowned by massive over-hanging trees, made it a black tunnel by night, a sylvan unfrequented corridor by day.

'The nearest house,' said Wexford, 'is that place up by the Stowerton Road, and the only other one is Wool Farm. That's a good half-mile down there.' He pointed through the tree tunnel and then he went off to his car. 'We can say good-bye to our weekend,' he said. 'See you first thing in the morning.'

The chief inspector's own home was to the north of Kingsmarkham on the other side of the Kingsbrook. His bedroom light was on and his wife still awake when he let himself in. Dora Wexford was too placid and too sensible to wait up for her husband, but she had been baby-sitting for her elder daughter and had only just got back. He found her sitting up in bed reading, a glass of hot milk beside her, and although he had only parted from her four hours before, he went up to her and kissed her warmly. The kiss was warmer than usual because, happy as his marriage was, contented with his lot as

355

he was, it sometimes took external disaster to bring home to
him his good fortune and how much he valued his wife.
Another man's wife was dead, had died foully . . . He pushed
aside squeamishness, his small-hours sensitivity and, starting to
undress, asked Dora what she knew of the occupants of Bury
Cottage.

'Where's Bury Cottage?'

'In Wool Lane. A man called Hathall lives there. His wife
was strangled this afternoon.'

Thirty years of marriage to a policeman hadn't blunted
Dora Wexford's sensibilities or coarsened her speech or made
her untender, but it was only natural that she could no longer
react to such a statement with the average woman's horror.

'Oh, dear,' she said, and conventionally, 'How dreadful! Is
it going to be straightforward?'

'Don't know yet.' Her soft calm voice steadied him as it
always did. 'Have you ever come across these people?'

'The only person I've ever come across in Wool Lane is
that Mrs Lake. She came to the Women's Institute a couple of
times, but I think she was too busy in other directions to bother
much with that. Very much a one for the men, you know.'

'You don't mean the Women's Institute blackballed her?'
said Wexford in mock-horror.

'Don't so so silly, darling. We're not narrow-minded. She's
a widow, after all. I can't think why she hasn't married again.'

'Maybe she's like George the Second.'

'Not a bit. She's very pretty. What *do* you mean?'

'He promised his wife on her death-bed that he wouldn't
marry again but only take mistresses.' While Dora giggled,
Wexford studied his figure in the glass, drawing in the muscles
of his belly. In the past year he had lost three stone in weight,
thanks to diet, exercise and the terror inspired in him by his
doctor, and for the first time in a decade he could regard his
own reflection with contentment if not with actual delight.
Now he could feel that it had been worth it. The agony of

going without everything he liked to eat and drink had been worth while. *Il faut souffrir pour être beau.* If only there was something one could go without, some strenuous game one could play, that would result in remedying hair loss ...

'Come to bed,' said Dora. 'If you don't stop preening yourself, I'll think you're going to take mistresses, and I'm not dead yet.'

Wexford grinned and got into bed. Quite early in his career he had taught himself not to dwell on work during the night, and work had seldom kept him awake or troubled his dreams. But as he switched off the bed lamp and cuddled up to Dora – so much easier and pleasanter now he was thin – he allowed himself a few minutes' reflection on the events of the evening. It could be a straightforward case, it very well could be. Angela Hathall had been young and probably nice to look at. She was childless, and though house-proud, must have found time hanging heavily on her hands during those lonely weekdays and lonely nights. What more likely than that she had picked up some man and brought him back to Bury Cottage? Wexford knew that a woman need not be desperate or a nymphomaniac or on the road to prostitution to do this. She need not even intend infidelity. For women's attitudes to sex, whatever the new thought may hold, are not the same as men's. And though it is broadly true that a man who will pick up an unknown woman is only 'after one thing' and broadly speaking she knows it, she will cling to the generous belief that he wants nothing but conversation and perhaps a kiss. Had this been Angela Hathall's belief? Had she picked up a man in her car, a man who wanted more than that and had strangled her because he couldn't get it? Had he killed her and left her on the bed and then made a getaway in her car?

It could be. Wexford decided he would work along these lines. Turning his thoughts to more pleasant topics, his grand-children, his recent holiday, he was soon asleep.

CHAPTER THREE

'Mr Hathall,' Wexford said, 'you no doubt have your own ideas as to how this sort of enquiry should be conducted. You will perhaps think my methods unorthodox, but they are my methods and I can assure you they get results. I can't conduct my investigation on circumstantial evidence alone. It's necessary for me to know as much as I can about the persons involved, so if you can answer my questions simply and realistically we shall get on a lot faster. I can assure you I shall ask them from the pure and direct motive of wanting to discover who killed your wife. If you take offence we shall be delayed. If you insist that certain matters concern only your private life and refuse to disclose them, a good deal of precious time may be lost. Do you understand that and will you be cooperative?'

This speech had been occasioned by Hathall's reaction to the first query that Wexford had put to him at nine on the Saturday morning. It had been a simple request for information as to whether Angela had been in the habit of giving lifts to strangers, but Hathall who seemed refreshed by his night of drugged sleep, had flared at it in a burst of ill-temper.

'What right have you got to impugn my wife's moral character?'

Wexford had said quietly, 'The great majority of people who give lifts to hitchhikers have no thought in their minds beyond that of being helpful,' and then, when Hathall continued to stare at him with bitter angry eyes, he had delivered his lecture.

The widower made an impatient gesture, shrugging and throwing out his hands. 'In a case like this I should have thought you'd go on fingerprints and – well, that sort of thing.

I mean, it's obvious some man got in here and . . . He must have left traces. I've read about how these things are conducted. It's a question of deduction from hairs and footmarks and – well, fingerprints.'

'I've already said I'm sure you have your own ideas as to how an enquiry should be conducted. My methods include those you have put forward. You saw for yourself how thoroughly this house was gone over last night, but we're not magicians, Mr Hathall. We can't find a fingerprint or a hair at midnight and tell you whose it is nine hours later.'

'When will you be able to?'

'That I can't say. Certainly by later today I should have some idea as to whether a stranger entered Bury Cottage yesterday afternoon.'

'A *stranger*? Of course it was a stranger. I could have told you that myself at eight o'clock last night. A pathological killer who got in here, broke in, I daresay, and – and afterwards stole my car. Have you found my car yet?'

Very smoothly and coldly, Wexford said, 'I don't know, Mr Hathall. I am not God, nor have I second sight. I haven't yet even had time to contact my officers. If you'll answer the one question I've put to you, I'll leave you for a while and go and talk to your mother.'

'My mother knows nothing whatever about it. My mother never set foot in his house till last night.'

'My question, Mr Hathall.'

'No, she wasn't in the habit of giving lifts,' Hathall shouted, his face crimson and distorted. 'She was too shy and nervous even to make friends down here. I was the only person she could trust, and no wonder after what she'd been through. The man who got in here knew that, he knew she was always alone. You want to work on that, get to work on that one. That's my private life, as you call it. I'd only been married three years and I worshipped my wife. But I left her alone all week because I couldn't face the journey up and down and this is what it's come to. She was scared stiff of being alone here. I said it wouldn't be for much longer and to stick it for my sake. Well, it wasn't for much longer, was it?'

He threw his arm over the back of the chair and buried his face in the crook of his elbow, his body shaking. Wexford watched him thoughtfully but said no more. He made his way towards the kitchen where he found Mrs Hathall at the sink, washing breakfast dishes. There was a pair of rubber gloves on the counter but they were dry and Mrs Hathall's bare hands were immersed in the suds. She was the sort of woman, he decided, who would be masochistic about housework, would probably use a brush rather than a vacuum cleaner and aver that washing machines didn't get your clothes clean. He saw that instead of an apron she wore a checked tea towel tied round her waist, and this struck him as strange. Obviously she wouldn't have brought an apron with her for a weekend visit, but surely anyone as house-proud as Angela would have possessed several? However, he made no comment on it, but said good morning and asked Mrs Hathall if she would mind answering a few questions while she worked.

'Hmm,' said Mrs Hathall. She rinsed her hands and turned round slowly to dry them on a towel which hung from a rack. 'It's no good asking me. I don't know what she got up to while he was away.'

'I understand your daughter-in-law was shy and lonely, kept herself to herself, as you might say.' The noise she made fascinated him. It was part choke, part grunt, with a hint of the death rattle. He assumed it was, in fact, a laugh. 'She didn't impress you in that way?'

'Erotic,' said Mrs Hathall.

'*I beg your pardon?*'

She looked at him with scorn. 'Nervy. More like hysterical.'

'Ah,' said Wexford. This particular malapropism was new to him and he savoured it. 'Why was that, I wonder? Why was she – er, neurotic?'

'I couldn't say. I only saw her once.'

But they had been married for three years . . . 'I'm not sure I understand, Mrs Hathall.'

She shifted her gaze from his face to the window, from the window to the sink, and then she picked up another cloth and began drying the dishes. Her solid board of a body, its back turned to him, was as expressive of discouragement and exclusion as a closed door. She dried every cup and glass and plate and piece of cutlery in silence, scoured the draining board, dried it, hung the cloth up with the concentration of one practising an intricate and hard-learned skill. But at last she was obliged to turn again and confront his seated patient figure.

'I've got the beds to make,' she said.

'Your daughter-in-law has been murdered, Mrs Hathall.'

'I ought to know that. I found her.'

'Yes. How was that exactly?'

'I've already said. I've told it all already.' She opened the broom cupboard, took a brush, a duster, superfluous tools unneeded in that speckless house. 'I've got work to do, if you haven't.'

'Mrs Hathall,' he said softly, 'do you realize that you will have to appear at the inquest? You're a most important witness. You will be very closely questioned and you will *not be able* to refuse to answer then. I can understand that you have never before come into contact with the law, but I must tell you that there are serious penalties attached to obstructing the police.'

She stared at him sullenly, only a little awed. 'I should never have come here,' she muttered. 'I said I'd never set foot here and I should have stuck to it.'

'Why did you come?'

'Because my son insisted. He wanted things patched up.' She plodded to within a yard of him and stopped. Wexford was reminded of an illustration in a storybook belonging to one of his grandsons, a picture of a cabinet with arms and legs and a surly face. 'I'll tell you one thing,' she said, 'if that Angela was nervy, it was shame that did it. She was ashamed of breaking up his marriage and making him a poor man. And so she should have been, she ruined three people's lives. I'll say that at your inquest. I don't mind telling anyone that.'

'I doubt,' said Wexford, 'if you will be asked. I'm asking you about last night.'

She jerked up her head. Petulantly, she said, 'I'm sure I've nothing to hide. I'm thinking of him, having everything dragged out in the open. She was supposed to meet us at the station last night.' A dry 'Hmm' snapped off the last word.

'But she was dead, Mrs Hathall.'

Ignoring him, she went on shortly and rapidly, 'We got here and he went to look for her. He called out to her. He looked everywhere downstairs and in the garden and in the garage.'

'And upstairs?'

'He didn't go upstairs. He told me to go upstairs and take my things off. I went in their bedroom and there she was. Satisfied? Ask him and see if he can tell you different.' The walking cupboard stumped out of the room and the stairs creaked as it mounted them.

Wexford went back into the room where Hathall was, not moving stealthily but not making much noise either. He had been in the kitchen for about half an hour, and perhaps Hathall believed he had already left the house, for he had made a very rapid recovery from his abandonment to grief, and was standing by the window peering closely at something on the front page of the morning paper. The expression on his lean ruddy face was one of extreme concentration, intense, even calculating, and his hands were quite steady. Wexford gave a slight cough. Hathall didn't jump. He turned round and the anguish which Wexford could have sworn was real again convulsed his face.

'I won't bother you again, now Mr Hathall. I've been

thinking about this and I believe it would be much better for you to talk to me in different surroundings. Under the circumstances, these aren't perhaps the best for the sort of talk we must have. Will you come down to the police station at about three, please, and ask for me?'

Hathall nodded. He seemed relieved. 'I'm sorry I lost my temper just now.'

'That's all right. It was natural. Before you come this afternoon, would you have a look through your wife's things and tell me if you think anything is missing?'

'Yes, I'll do that. Your men won't want to go over the place any more?'

'No, all that's over.'

As soon as Wexford reached his own office in Kingsmarkham police station, he looked through the morning papers and found the one Hathall had been scrutinizing, the *Daily Telegraph*. At the foot of the front page, in the stop press, was a paragraph about an inch deep which read: 'Mrs Angela Hathall, 32, was last night found dead at her home in Wool Lane, Kingsmarkham, Sussex. She had been strangled. Police are treating the case as murder.' It was this on which Hathall's eyes had been fixed with such intensity. Wexford pondered for a moment. If his wife had been found murdered, the last thing he would have wanted would be to read about it in the paper. He spoke this thought aloud as Burden came into the room, adding that it didn't do to project one's own feelings on to others, for we can't all be the same.

'Sometimes,' said Burden rather gloomily, 'I think that if everyone was like you and me the world would be a better place.'

'Arrogant devil, you are. Have we got anything from the fingerprint boys yet? Hathall's dead keen on prints. He's one of those people who labour under the misapprehension that we're like foxhounds. Show us a print or a footmark and we put our noses to the ground and follow spoor until we run down our quarry about two hours later.'

Burden snorted. He thrust a sheaf of papers under the chief inspector's nose. 'It's all here,' he said. 'I've had a look and there are points of interest, but the fox isn't going to turn up in two hours or anything like it. Whoever he is, he's far, far away, and you can tell John Peel that one.'

Grinning, Wexford said, 'No sign of that car, I suppose?'

'It'll probably turn up in Glasgow or somewhere in the middle of next week. Martin checked with that company of Hathall's, Marcus Flower. He had a word with his secretary. She's called Linda Kipling and she says Hathall was there all day yesterday. They both came in at about ten – my God, I should be so lucky! – and apart from an hour and a half off for lunch, Hathall was there till he left at five-thirty.'

'Just because I said he'd been reading about his wife's murder in the paper, I didn't mean I thought he'd done it, you know.' Wexford patted the seat of the chair next to his own and said, 'Sit down, Mike, and tell me what's in that – that ream you've brought me. Condense it. I'll have a look at it myself later.'

The inspector sat down and put on his newly acquired glasses. They were elegant glasses with narrow black frames and they gave Burden the look of a successful barrister. With his large collection of well-tailored suits, his expertly cut fair hair and a figure that needed no dieting to keep it trim, he had never had the air of a detective – a fact which had been to his advantage. His voice was prim and precise, a little more selfconscious than usual, because he wasn't yet accustomed to the glasses which he seemed to regard as changing his whole appearance and indeed his personality.

'The first thing to note, I'd say,' he began, 'is that there weren't nearly as many prints about the house as one would expect. It was exceptionally well-kept house, everything very clean and well polished. She must have cleaned it very thoroughly indeed because there were hardly any of Hathall's own prints. There was a clear whole handprint on the front door and prints on other doors and the banisters, but those were obviously made after he got home last night. Mrs Hathall senior's prints were on the kitchen counter, the banisters, in the back bedroom, on the bathroom taps and lavatory cistern, on the telephone and, oddly enough, on the picture rail on the landing.'

'Not oddly enough at all,' said Wexford. 'She's the sort of old battleaxe who'd feel along a picture rail to see if her daughter-in-law had dusted it. And if she hadn't, she'd probably write "slut" or something equally provocative in the dust.'

Burden adjusted his glasses, smudged them with his fingertip and rubbed impatiently at them with his short cuff. 'Angela's prints were on the back door, the door from the kitchen into the hall, her bedroom door and on various bottles and jars on her dressing table. But they weren't anywhere else. Apparently she wore gloves for doing her housework, and if she took off her gloves to go to the bathroom, she wiped everything afterwards.'

'Sounds bloody obsessional to me. But I suppose some women do go on like that.'

Burden, whose expression conveyed that he rather approved of women who went on like that, said, 'The only other prints in the house were those of one unknown man and one unknown woman. The man's were found only on books and on the inside of a bedroom cupboard door, not Angela's bedroom. There's one single print of this other woman. It too was a whole handprint, the right hand, very clear, showing a small L-shaped scar on the forefinger, and it was found on the edge of the bath.'

'Hmm,' said Wexford, and because the sound reminded him of Mrs Hathall, he changed it to 'Huh.' He paused thoughtfully. 'I don't suppose these prints are on record?'

'Don't know yet. Give them time.'

'No, I mustn't be like Hathall. Is there anything else?'

'Some coarse long dark hair, three of them, on the bathroom

floor. They're not Angela's. Hers were finer. Hers alone were in her hairbrush on the dressing table.'

'Man's or woman's?'

'Impossible to tell. You know how long some blokes wear their hair these days.' Burden touched his own sleek crop and took off his glasses. 'We shan't get anything from the post-mortem till tonight.'

'OK. We have to find that car and we have to find someone who saw her go out in it and, let's hope, someone who saw her and her pick-up come back in it – if that's the way it was. We have to find her friends. She must have had *some* friends.'

They went down in the lift and crossed the black and white checkerboard foyer. While Burden paused for a word with the station sergeant, Wexford went up to the swing doors that gave on to the steps and the courtyard. A woman was coming up those steps, walking confidently in the manner of one who had never known rejection. Wexford held the right-hand door open for her, and as she came face to face with him she stopped and looked him full in the eyes.

She wasn't young. Her age couldn't have been far short of fifty, but it was at once apparent that she was one of those rare creatures whom time cannot wither or stale or devitalize. Every fine line on her face seemed the mark of laughter and mischievous wit, but there were few of these around her large bright blue and surprisingly young eyes. She smiled at him, a smile to make a man's heart turn over, and said:

'Good morning. My name is Nancy Lake. I want to see a policeman, the top one, someone very important. Are you important?'

'I daresay I will do,' said Wexford.

She looked him over as no woman had looked him over for twenty years. The smile became musing, delicate eyebrows went up. 'I really think you might,' she said, and stepping inside, 'However, we must be serious. I've come to tell you I think I was the last person to see Angela Hathall alive.'

CHAPTER FOUR

When a pretty woman ages, a man's reaction is usually to reflect on how lovely she must once have been. This was not Nancy Lake's effect. There was something very much of the here and now about her. When with her you thought no more of her youth and her coming old age than you think of spring or Christmas when you are enjoying late summer. She was of the season in which they were, a harvest-time woman, who brought to mind grape festivals and ripened fruit and long warm nights. These thoughts came to Wexford much later. As he led her into his office, he was aware only of how extremely pleasing this diversion was in the midst of murder and recalcitrant witnesses and fingerprints and missing cars. Besides, it wasn't exactly a diversion. Happy is the man who can combine pleasure and business . . .

'What a nice room,' she said. Her voice was low and sweet and lively. 'I thought police stations were brown and murky with photographs on the walls of great brutes all wanted for robbing banks.' She glanced with warm approval at his carpet, his yellow chairs, his rosewood desk. 'This is lovely. And what a nice view over all those delicious little roofs. May I sit down?'

Wexford was already holding the chair for her. He was recalling what Dora had said about this woman being 'very much for the men' and added to this statement one of his own: that the men would be very much for her. She was dark. Her hair was abundant and of a rich chestnut brown, probably dyed. But her skin had kept a rose and amber glow, the extreme of a peach, and a delicate light seemed to shine from beneath its surface as is sometimes seen in the faces of young girls or children, but which is rarely retained into middle age.

The red lips seemed always on the edge of a smile. It was as if she knew some delightful secret which she would almost, but never wholly, divulge. Her dress was just what, in Wexford's opinion, a woman's dress should be, full in the skirt, tight in the waist, of mauve and blue printed cotton, its low neck showing an inch or two of the upper slopes of a full golden bosom. She saw that he was studying her and she seemed to enjoy his scrutiny, basking in it, understanding more thoroughly than he himself what it meant.

He shifted his gaze abruptly. 'You live in the house at the Kingsmarkham end of Wool Lane, I believe?'

'It's called Sunnybank. I always think that sounds like a mental hospital. But my late husband chose the name and I expect he had his reasons.'

Wexford made a determined and eventually successful attempt to look grave. 'Were you a friend of Mrs Hathall's?'

'Oh, *no.*' He thought she was capable of saying she had no women friends, which would have displeased him, but she didn't. 'I only went there for the miracles.'

'The *what*?'

'An in-joke. I'm sorry. I meant the yellow egg plums.'

'Ah, mira*belles.*' This was the second malapropism of his day, but he decided this particular instance was a deliberate mistake. 'You went there yesterday to pick plums?'

'I always do. Every year. I used to when old Mr Somerset lived there, and when the Hathalls came they said I could have them. I make them into jam.'

He had a sudden vision of Nancy Lake standing in a sunfilled kitchen, stirring a pot full of the golden fruit. He smelled the scent of it, saw her face as she dipped in a finger and brought it to those full red lips. The vision threatened to develop into a fantasy. He shook it off. 'When did you go there?'

The roughness in his voice made her eyebrows go up. 'I phoned Angela at nine in the morning and asked if I could go up there and pick them. I'd noticed they were falling. She seemed quite pleased – for her. She wasn't a very gracious person, you know.'

'I don't know. I hope you'll tell me.'

She moved her hands a little, deprecatingly, casually. 'She said to come about half past twelve. I picked the plums and she gave me a cup of coffee. I think she only asked me in to show me how nice the house looked.'

'Why? Didn't it always look nice?'

'Goodness, no. Not that I care, that was her business. I'm not much for housework myself, but Angela's house was usually a bit of pigsty. Anyway, it was a mess last March which was when I was last in it. She told me she'd cleaned it up to impress Robert's mother.'

Wexford nodded. He had to make an effort of will to continue questioning her in the impersonal way, for she exercised a spell, the magical combination of feminine niceness and strong sexuality. But the effort had to be made. 'Did she tell you she was expecting another caller, Mrs Lake?'

'No, she said she was going out in the car, but she didn't say where.' Nancy Lake leaned across the desk rather earnestly, bringing her face to within a foot of his. Her perfume was fruity and warm. 'She asked me in and gave me coffee, but as soon as I'd had one cup she seemed to want to get rid of me. That's what I meant by saying she only wanted to show me how nice the house looked.'

'What time did you leave?'

'Let me see. It would have been just before half past one. But I was only in the house ten minutes. The rest of the time I was picking the miracles.'

The temptation to remain close to that vital, mobile and somehow mischievous face was great, but it had to be resisted. Wexford swivelled his chair round with deliberate casualness, turning to Nancy Lake a stern and businesslike profile. 'You didn't see her leave Bury Cottage or return to it later?'

'No, I went to Myringham. I was in Myringham the whole afternoon and part of the evening.'

For the first time there was something guarded and secretive in her reply, but he made no comment. 'Tell me about Angela Hathall. What sort of person was she?'

'Brusque, tough, ungracious.' She shrugged, as if such failings in a woman were beyond her comprehension. 'Perhaps that's why she and Robert got on so well together.'

'Did they? They were a happy couple?'

'Oh, very. They had no eyes for anyone else, as the saying is.' Nancy Lake gave a light laugh. 'All in all to each other, you know. They had no friends, as far as I could tell.'

'I've been given the impression she was shy and nervous.'

'Have you now? I wouldn't say that. I got the idea she was on her own so much because she liked it that way. Of course, they'd been very badly off till he got this new job. She told me they only had fifteen pounds a week to live on after all his outgoings. He was paying alimony or whatever it's called to his first wife.' She paused and smiled. 'People make such messes of their lives, don't they?'

There was a hint of ruthfulness in her voice as if she had experience of such messes. He turned round again, for a thought had struck him. 'May I see your right hand, Mrs Lake?'

She gave it to him without question, not laying it on the table but placing it palm-downwards in his. It was almost a lover-like gesture and one that has become typical of the beginning of a relationship between a man and a woman, this covering of hand by hand, a first approach, a show of comfort and trust. Wexford felt its warmth, observed how smooth and tended it was, noted the soft sheen of the nails and the diamond ring which encircled the middle finger. Bemused, he let it rest there a fraction too long.

'If anyone had told me,' she said, her eyes dancing, 'that I should be holding hands with a policeman this morning, I shouldn't have believed them.'

Wexford said stiffly, 'I beg your pardon,' and turned her hand over. No L-shaped scar marred the smooth surface of the tip of her forefinger, and he let the hand drop.

'Is that how you check fingerprints? Goodness, I always thought it was a much more complicated process.'

'It is.' He didn't explain. 'Did Angela Hathall have a woman in to help with the cleaning?'

'Not as far as I know. They couldn't have afforded it.' She was doing her best to conceal her delight at his discomfiture, but he saw her lips twitch and delight won. 'Can I be of any further service to you, Mr Wexford? You wouldn't care to make casts of my footprints, for instance, or take a blood sample?'

'No, thank you. That won't be necessary. But I may want to talk to you again, Mrs Lake.'

'I do hope you will.' She got up gracefully and took a few steps towards the window. Wexford, who was obliged to rise when she did, found himself standing close beside her. She had manoeuvred this, he knew she had, but he could only feel flattered. How many years was it since a woman had flirted with him, had wanted to be with him and enjoyed the touch of his hand? Dora had done so, of course, his wife had done so . . . As he was drawing himself up, conscious of his new firm figure, he remembered his wife. He remembered that he was not only a policeman but a husband who must be mindful of his marriage vows. But Nancy Lake had laid her hand lightly on his arm, was drawing his attention to the sunshine outside, the cars in the High Street that had begun their long progress to the coast.

'Just the weather for a day by the sea, isn't it?' she said. The remark sounded wistful, like an invitation. 'What a shame you have to work on a Saturday.' What a shame work and convention and prudence prevented him from leading this woman to his car, driving her to some quiet hotel. Champagne and roses, he thought, and that hand once more reaching across a table to lie warmly in his . . . 'And the winter will soon be here,' she said.

Surely she couldn't have meant it, couldn't have intended that double meaning? That the winter would soon be there for both of them, the flesh falling, the blood growing cold . . . 'I mustn't keep you,' he said, his voice as icy as that coming winter.

She laughed, not at all offended, but she took her hand from his arm and walked towards the door. 'You might at least say it was good of me to come.'

'It was. Very public-spirited. Good morning, Mrs Lake.'

'Good morning, Mr Wexford. You must come to tea quite soon and I'll give you some miracle jam.'

He sent for someone to see her out. Instead of sitting down once more behind his desk, he returned to the window and looked down, and there she was, crossing the courtyard with the assurance of youth, as if the world belonged to her. It didn't occur to him that she would look back and up but she did, suddenly, as if his thoughts had communicated themselves to her and called that swift glance. She waved. Her arm went up straight and she waved her hand. They might have known each other all their lives, so warm and free and intimate was that gesture, having separated after a delightful assignation that was no less sweet because it was customary. He raised his own arm in something like a salute, and then, when she had disappeared among the crowd of Saturday shoppers, he too went down to find Burden and take him off for lunch.

The Carousel Café, opposite the police station, was always crowded at Saturday lunchtime, but at least the juke box was silent. The real noise would start when the kids came in at six. Burden was sitting at the corner table they kept permanently reserved, and when Wexford approached, the proprietor, a meek Italian, came up to him deferentially and with considerable respect.

'My special today for you, Chief Inspector. The liver and bacon I can recommend.'

'All right, Antonio, but none of your reconstituted potato, eh? And no monosodium glutamate.'

Antonio looked puzzled. 'This is not on my menu, Mr Wexford.'

'No, but it's there all right, the secret agent, the alimentary fifth column. I trust you've had no more speedy goings-on of late?'

'Thanks to you, sir, we have not.'

The reference was to an act of mischief performed a couple of weeks before by one of Antonio's youthful part-time employees. Bored by the sobriety of the clientele, this boy had introduced into the glass tank of orange juice with its floating plastic oranges, one hundred amphetamine tablets, and the result had been a merry near-riot, a hitherto decorous businessman actually dancing on a table top. Wexford, chancing to call in and, on account of his diet, sampling the orange juice himself, had located the source of this almost Saturnalian jollity and, simultaneously, the joker. Recalling all this now, he laughed heartily.

'What's so funny?' said Burden sourly. 'Or has that Mrs Lake been cheering you up?' When Wexford stopped laughing but didn't answer, he said, 'Martin's taken a room in the church hall, a sort of enquiry post and general information pool. The public are being notified in the hope that anyone who may have seen Angela on Friday afternoon will come in and tell us about it. And if she didn't go out, there's a possibility her visitor was seen.'

'She went out,' said Wexford. 'She told Mrs Lake she was going out in the car. I wonder who the lady with the L-shaped scar is, Mike. Not Mrs Lake, and Mrs Lake says Angela didn't have a cleaner, or, come to that, any friends.'

'And who's the man who fingers the inside of cupboard doors?'

The arrival of the liver and bacon and Burden's spaghetti Bolognese silenced them for a few minutes. Wexford drank his orange juice, wistfully thinking how much he would enjoy it if this tankful had been 'speeded' up and Burden were suddenly to become merry and uninhibited. But the inspector, eating fastidiously, wore the resigned look of one who has sacrificed his weekend to duty. Deep lines, stretching from nostrils to the corners of his mouth, intensified as he said:

'I was going to take my kids to the seaside.'

Wexford thought of Nancy Lake who would look well in a swimsuit, but he switched off the picture before it developed into a full-colour three-dimensional image. 'Mike, at this stage of a case we usually ask each other if we've noticed anything odd, any discrepancies or downright untruths. Have you noticed anything?'

'Can't say I have, except the lack of prints.'

'She'd spring-cleaned the place to impress the old woman, though I agree it was strange she seems to have wiped everything again before going off on her car jaunt. Mrs Lake had coffee with her at about one, but Mrs Lake's prints aren't anywhere. But there's something else that strikes me as even odder than that, the way Hathall behaved when he got into the house last night.'

Burden pushed away his empty plate, contemplated the menu, and rejecting the idea of a sweet, signalled to Antonio for coffee. 'Was it odd?' he said.

'Hathall and his wife had been married for three years. During that time the old woman had only met her daughter-in-law once, and there had evidently been considerable antagonism between them. This appears to have something to do with Angela's having broken up Hathall's first marriage. Be that as it may – and I mean to learn more about it – Angela and her mother-in-law seem to have been at loggerheads. Yet there was a kind of *rapprochement*, the old woman had been persuaded to come for the weekend and Angela was preparing to receive her to the extent of titivating the place far beyond her normal standard. Now Angela was supposed to be meeting them at the station, but she didn't turn up. Hathall says she was shy and nervous, Mrs Lake that she was brusque and ungracious. Bearing this in mind, what conclusions would you expect Hathall to have drawn when his wife wasn't at the station?'

'That she'd got cold feet. That she was too frightened to face her mother-in-law.'

'Exactly. But what happened when he got to Bury Cottage? He couldn't find Angela. He looked for her *downstairs* and in the garden. He never went upstairs at all. And yet by then he must have suspected Angela's nervousness and concluded surely that a nervous woman takes refuge not in the garden but in her own bedroom. But instead of looking upstairs for her, *he sent his mother*, the very person he must have believed Angela to be frightened of. This shy and nervous girl to whom he is alleged to be devoted was cowering – he must have thought – in her bedroom, but instead of going up to reassure her and then bring her to confront his mother with him there to support her, he goes off to the garage. That, Mike, is very odd indeed.'

Burden nodded. 'Drink your coffee,' he said. 'You said Hathall was coming in at three. Maybe he'll give you an answer.'

CHAPTER FIVE

Although Wexford pretended to study the list of missing articles
– a bracelet, a couple of rings and a gilt neck chain – Hathall
had brought him, he was really observing the man himself.
He had come into the office with head bowed, and now he
sat silent, his hands folded in his lap. But the combination of
ruddy skin and black hair gives a man an angry look. Hathall,
in spite of his grief, looked angry and resentful. His hard
craggy features had the appearance of being carved out of
roseate granite, his hands were large and red, and even his
eyes, though not bloodshot, held a red gleam. Wexford wouldn't
have judged him attractive to women, yet he had had two
wives. Was it perhaps that certain women, very feminine or
nervous or maladjusted women, saw him as a rock to which
they might cling, a stronghold where they might find shelter?
Possibly that colouring of his indicated passion and tenacity
and strength as well as ill-temper.

Wexford placed the list on his desk and, looking up, said,
'What do you think happened yesterday afternoon, Mr Hathall?'

'Are you asking *me* that?'

'Presumably you knew your wife better than anyone else
knew her. You'd know who would be likely to call on her or
be fetched home by her.'

Hathall frowned, and the frown darkened his whole face.
'I've already said, some man got into the house for the purpose
of robbery. He took those things on that list and when my
wife interrupted him, he – he killed her. What else could it
have been? It's obvious.'

'I don't think so. I believe that whoever came to your
house wiped the place clean of a considerable number of

376

fingerprints. A thief wouldn't have needed to do that. He'd have worn gloves. And although he might have struck your wife, he wouldn't have strangled her. Besides, I see here that you value the missing property at less than fifty pounds all told. True, people have been killed for less, but I doubt if any woman has ever been strangled for such a reason.'

When Wexford repeated the word 'strangled,' Hathall again bowed his head. 'What alternative is there?' he muttered.

'Tell me who came to your house. What friends or acquaintances called on your wife?'

'We had no friends,' said Hathall. 'When we came here we were more or less on the breadline. You need money to make friends in a place like this. We hadn't got the money to join clubs or give dinner parties or even have people in for drinks. Angela often didn't see a soul from Sunday night till Friday night. And the friends I'd had before I married her – well, my first wife saw to it I'd lost them.' He coughed impatiently and tossed his head in the way his mother had. 'Look, I think I'd better tell you a bit about what Angela and I had been through, and then perhaps you'll see that all this talk of friends calling is arrant nonsense.'

'Perhaps you had, Mr Hathall.'

'It'll be my life history.' Hathall gave a humourless bark of laughter. It was the bitter laugh of the paranoiac. 'I started off as an office boy with a firm of accountants, Craig and Butler, of Gray's Inn Road. Later on, when I was a clerk there, the senior partner wanted me to be articled and persuaded me to study for the Institute's exams. In the meantime I'd got married and I was buying a house in Croydon on a mortgage, so the extra money was handy.' He looked up with another aggrieved frown. 'I don't think there's ever been a time till now when I've had a reasonable amount of money to live on, and now I've got it it's no good to me.

'My first marriage wasn't happy. My mother may think it was but outsiders don't know. I got married seventeen years ago and two years later I knew I'd made a mistake. But we'd got a daughter by that time, so there wasn't anything I could do about it. I expect I'd have jogged along and made the best of it if I hadn't met Angela at an office party. When I fell in love with her and knew that – well, what I felt for her was returned, I asked my wife for a divorce. Eileen – that's my first wife's name – made hideous scenes. She brought my mother into it and she even brought Rosemary in – a kid of eleven. I can't describe what my life was like and I won't try to.'

'This was five years ago?'

'About five years ago, yes. Eventually I left home and went to live with Angela. She had a room in Earls Court and she was working at the library of the National Archaeolgists' League.' Hathall, who had said he couldn't describe what his life had been like, immediately proceeded to do so. 'Eileen set about a – a campaign of persecution. She made scenes at my office and at Angela's place of work. She even came to Earls Court. I begged her for a divorce. Angela had a good job and I was doing all right. I thought I could have afforded it, whatever demands Eileen made. In the end she agreed, but by that time Butler had sacked me on account of Eileen's scenes, sacked me out of hand. It was a piece of outrageous injustice. And, to crown it all, Angela had to leave the library. She was on the verge of a nervous breakdown.

'I got a part-time job as accountant with a firm of toy manufacturers, Kidd and Co., of Toxborough, and Angela and I got a room nearby. We were on our beam ends. Angela couldn't work. The divorce judge awarded Eileen my house and custody of my daughter and a very unfairly large slice out of my very inadequate income. Then we had what looked like a piece of luck at last. Angela has a cousin down here, a man called Mark Somerset, who let us have Bury Cottage. It had been his father's, but of course there wasn't any question of its being rent-free – he didn't take his generosity that far, in spite of being a blood relation. And I can't say he ever did anything else for us. He didn't even befriend Angela, though he must have known how lonely she was.

'Things went on like this for nearly three years. We were literally living on about fifteen pounds a week. I was still paying off the mortgage on a house I haven't set foot in for four years. My mother and my first wife had poisoned my daughter's mind against me. What's the use of a judge giving you reasonable access to a child if the child refuses to come near you? I remember you said you'd want to know about my private life. Well, that was it. Nothing but harassment and persecution. Angela was the one bright spot in it and now – and now she's dead.'

Wexford, who believed that, with certain exceptions, a man only suffers chronic and acute persecution if something masochistic in his psychological makeup seeks persecution, pursed his lips. 'This man Somerset, did he ever come to Bury Cottage?'

'Never. He showed us over the place when he first offered it to us, and after that, apart from a chance meeting in the street in Myringham, we never saw him again. It was as if he'd taken an unreasonable dislike to Angela.'

So many people had disliked or resented her. She sounded, Wexford thought, as inclined to paranoia as her husband. Generally speaking, nice people are not much disliked. And a kind of widespread conspiracy of hatred against them, which Hathall seemed to infer, is never feasible.

'You say this was an unreasonable dislike. Mr Hathall. Was your mother's dislike equally unreasonable?'

'My mother is devoted to Eileen. She's old-fashioned and rigid and she was prejudiced against Angela for what she calls her taking me away from Eileen. It's complete nonsense to say that a woman can steal another woman's husband if he doesn't want to be – well, stolen.'

'They only met once, I believe. Was that meeting not a success?'

'I persuaded my mother to come to Earls Court and meet Angela. I should have known better, but I thought that when she actually got to know her she might get over the feeling she was a kind of scarlet woman. My mother took exception to Angela's clothes – she was wearing those jeans and that red shirt – and when she said something uncomplimentary about Eileen my mother walked straight out of the house.'

Hathall's face had grown even redder at the memory. Wexford said, 'So they weren't on speaking terms for the whole of your second marriage?'

'My mother refused to visit us or have us come to her. She saw me, of course. I tell you frankly, I'd have liked to cut myself off from her entirely but I felt I had a duty towards her.'

Wexford always took such assertions of virtue with a grain of salt. He couldn't help wondering if old Mrs Hathall, who must have been nearly seventy, had some savings to leave.

'What brought about the idea of the reunion you planned for this weekend?'

'When I landed this job with Marcus Flower – at, incidentally, double the salary I'd been getting from Kidd's – I decided to spend my week nights at my mother's place. She lives in Balham, so it wasn't too far for me to go into Victoria. Angela and I were looking for a flat to buy in London, so it wouldn't have gone on for too long. But, as usual with me, disaster hit me. However, as I was saying, I'd spent every week night at my mother's since July and I'd had a chance to talk to her about Angela and how much I'd like them to be on good terms. It took eight weeks of persuasion, but she did at last agree to come here for a weekend. Angela was very nervous at the whole idea. Of course she was as anxious for my mother to like her as I was, but she was very apprehensive. She scrubbed the whole place from top to bottom so that my mother couldn't find any fault there. I shall never know now whether it would have worked out.'

'Now, Mr Hathall, when you got to the station last night and your wife wasn't there to meet you as had been arranged, what was your reaction?'

'I don't follow you,' said Hathall shortly.

'What did you feel? Alarmed? Annoyed? Or just disappointed?'

Hathall hesitated. 'I certainly wasn't annoyed,' he said. 'I suppose I thought it was an unfortunate start to the weekend. I assumed Angela had been too nervous to come after all.'

'I see. And when you reached the house, what did you do?'

'I don't know what all this is leading up to, but I suppose there's some purpose behind it.' Again Hathall gave the impatient toss of the head. 'I called out to Angela. When she didn't answer, I looked for her in the dining room and in the kitchen. She wasn't there, so I went out into the garden. Then I told my mother to go upstairs while I looked to see if the car was in the garage.'

'You thought perhaps that you on foot and your wife in the car might have missed each other?'

'I don't know what I thought. I just naturally looked everywhere for her.'

'But not upstairs, Mr Hathall?' said Wexford quietly.

'Not at first. I would have done.'

'Wasn't it likely that of all places in the house a nervous woman, afraid to meet her mother-in-law, would have been, was her own bedroom? But you didn't go there first, as might have been expected. You went to the garage and sent your mother upstairs.'

Hathall, who might have blustered, who might have told Wexford to state plainly what he was getting at, said instead in a rather stiff and awkward tone, 'We can't always account for our actions.'

'I disagree. I think we can if we look honestly into our motives.'

'Well, I suppose I thought if she hadn't answered my call, she couldn't be in the house. Yes, I did think that. I thought she must have set off in the car and we'd missed each other because she'd gone some other way round.'

But some other way round would have meant driving a mile down Wool Lane to its junction with the Pomfret to Myringham road, then following this road to Pomfret or Stowerton before doubling back to Kingsmarkham station, a journey of five miles at least instead of a half-mile trip. But Wexford said no more about it. Another factor in the man's behaviour had suddenly struck him, and he wanted to be alone to think about it, to work out whether it was significant or merely the result of a quirk in his character.

As Hathall rose to go, he said, 'May I ask you something now?'

'By all means.'

But Hathall seemed to hesitate, as if still to postpone some burning question or to conceal it under another of less moment. 'Have you had anything from the – well, the pathologist yet?'

'Not yet, Mr Hathall.'

The red rock face tightened. 'These fingerprints. Have you got something from them yet? Isn't there some clue there?'

'Very little, as far as we can tell.'

'It seems a slow process to me. But I know nothing about it. You'll keep me informed, will you?'

He had spoken hectoringly, like a company chairman addressing a junior executive. 'Once an arrest has been made,' said Wexford, 'you may be sure you won't be left in the dark.'

'That's all very well, but neither will any newspaper reader. I should like to know about this . . .' He bit off the sentence as if he had been tending towards an end it might have been unwise to approach. 'I should like to know about this pathologist's report.'

'I will call on you tomorrow, Mr Hathall,' said Wexford.

'In the meantime, try to keep calm and rest as much as you can.'

Hathall left the office, bowing his head as he went. Wexford couldn't escape the notion that he had bowed it to impress the young detective constable who had shown him out. Yet the man's grief seemed real. But grief, as Wexford knew, is much easier to simulate than happiness. It demands little more than a subdued voice, the occasional outburst of righteous anger, the reiteration of one's pain. A man like Hathall, who believed the world owed him a living and who suffered from a persecution complex, would have no difficulty in intensifying his normal attitude.

But why had he shown no sign of shock? Why, above all, had he never shown that stunned disbelief which is the first characteristic reaction of one whose wife or husband or child has met with a violent death? Wexford thought back over the three conversations he had had with Hathall, but he wasn't able to recall a single instance of disbelief in awful reality. And he recalled similar situations, bereaved husbands who had interrupted his questions with cries that it couldn't be true, widows who had exclaimed that it couldn't be happening to them, that it was a dream from which they must soon awaken. Disbelief temporarily crowds out grief. Sometimes whole days pass before the fact can be realized, let alone accepted. Hathall had realized and accepted at once. It seemed to Wexford, as he sat musing and awaiting the post-mortem results, that he had accepted even before he let himself in at his own front door.

'So she was strangled with a gilt necklace,' said Burden. 'It must have been a pretty tough one.'

Looking up from the report, Wexford said, 'It could be the one on Hathall's list. It says here a gilt ligature. Some shreds of gilding were found embedded in her skin. No tissue from her killer found under her fingernails, so there was presumably no struggle. Time of death, between one-thirty and three-thirty. Well, we know it wasn't one-thirty because that was when Mrs Lake left her. She seems to have been a healthy woman, she wasn't pregnant, and there was no sexual assault.' He gave Burden a condensed version of what Robert Hathall had told him. 'The whole thing's beginning to look peculiar now, isn't it?'

'You mean you've got it into your head that Hathall had some sort of guilty knowledge?'

'I know he didn't kill her. He couldn't have done. When she died he was at this Marcus Flower place with Linda Whatsit and God knows how many other people. And I don't see any motive there. He seems to have been fond of her, if no one else was. But why didn't he go upstairs last night, why isn't he stunned with shock, and why does he get so worked-up about fingerprints?'

'The killer must have hung around after the deed was done to wipe off prints, you know. He must have touched things in the bedroom and the other rooms, and then forgotten what he *had* touched, so that he had to do a big clean-up job to be on the safe side. Otherwise Angela's and Mrs Lake's prints would have been in the living room. Doesn't that argue a lack of premeditation?'

'Probably. And I think you're right. I don't for a moment believe Angela was so fanatical or so frightened of her mother-in-law that she polished the living room after Mrs Lake had gone as well as before she came.'

'It's a funny thing, that he went to all that trouble, yet still left prints on the inside of a door to a cupboard in a spare room, a cupboard that was apparently never used.'

'If he did, Mike,' said Wexford, 'if he did. I think we're going to find that those prints belong to a Mr Mark Somerset, the owner of Bury Cottage. We'll find out just where in Myringham he lives and then we'd better get over to see him.'

CHAPTER SIX

Myringham, where the University of the South is situated, lies about fifteen miles from Kingsmarkham. It boasts a museum, a motte and bailey castle and one of the best-preserved remains of a Roman villa in Britain. And although a new centre has grown up between the university buildings and the railway station, a place of tower blocks and shopping precincts and multi-storey car parks, all this red brick and concrete has been kept well away from the old town which stands, unspoiled, on the banks of the Kingsbrook.

Here there are narrow lanes and winding by-streets that call to the mind of the visitor the paintings of Jacob Vrel. The houses are very old, some – of brown brick and worm-eaten grey-brown timber – built before the Wars of the Roses, or even, it is said, before Agincourt. Not all of them have owner-occupiers or steady tenants, for some have fallen into such disrepair, such dismal decay, that their owners cannot afford to put them in order. Squatters have taken possession of them, secure in their ancient right from police interference, safe from eviction because their 'landlords' are prevented by law from demolishing their property and by lack of money from repairing it.

But these form only a small colony of the Old Town. Mark Somerset lived in the smarter part, in one of the old houses by the river. In the days when England was Catholic it had been a priest's house and in one of the walls of its garden was a narrow and beautiful stained-glass window, for this was also a wall of St. Luke's Church. The Myringham Catholics had a new church now in the new town, and the presbytery was a modern house. But here where the brown walls clustered about the church and the mill, the fifteenth century still lingered.

There was nothing fifteenth century about Mark Somerset.

An athletic-looking man in his fifties, he wore neat black jeans and a tee-shirt, and Wexford detected his age only by the lines about his bright blue eyes and the veining of his strong hands. The man's belly was flat, his chest well muscled, and he had the good fortune to keep his hair which, having once been golden, was now silver-gilt.

'Ah, the fuzz,' he said, his smile and pleasant tone robbing the greeting of rudeness. 'I thought you'd turn up.'

'Shouldn't we have turned up, Mr Somerset?'

'Don't know. That's for you to decide. Come in, but be as quiet as you can in the hall, will you? My wife only came out of hospital this morning and she's just managed to get off to sleep.'

'Nothing serious, I hope?' said Burden fatuously – and unnecessarily, in Wexford's view.

Somerset smiled. It was a smile of sad experience, of endurance, tinged very slightly with contempt. He spoke in a near-whisper. 'She's been an invalid for years. But you haven't come to talk about that. Shall we go in here?'

The room had a beamed ceiling and panelled walls. A pair of glass doors, a later but pleasing addition, were open to a small paved garden backed by the riverside trees, and the foliage of these trees looked like black lace against the amber flare of the setting sun. Beside these doors was a low table on which was a bottle of hock in an ice-bucket.

'I'm a sports coach at the university,' said Somerset. 'Saturday night's the only time I allow myself a drink. Will you have some wine?'

The two policemen accepted and Somerset fetched three glasses from a cabinet. The Liebfraumilch had the delicate quality peculiar to some kinds of hock, that of tasting like liquid flowers. It was ice-cold, scented, dry.

'This is very kind of you, Mr Somerset,' said Wexford. 'You're disarming me. I hardly like to ask you now if we may take your fingerprints.'

SHAKE HANDS FOR EVER

Somerset laughed. 'You can take my fingerprints with pleasure. I suppose you've found the prints of some unknown mystery man at Bury Cottage, have you? They're probably mine, thought I haven't been in the place for three years. They can't be my father's. I had the whole place redecorated after he died.' He spread out his strong work-broadened hands with a kind of bold innocence.

'I understand you didn't get on with your cousin?'

'Well, now,' said Somerset, 'rather than let you interrogate me and probably put to me a lot of time wasting questions, wouldn't it be better if I told you what I know about my cousin and gave you a sort of history of our relationship? Then you can ask me what you like afterwards.'

Wexford said, 'That's exactly what we want.'

'Good.' Somerset had the good teacher's succinct crisp manner. 'You wouldn't want me to have any squeamish-ness about not speaking ill of the dead, would you? Not that I have much ill to speak of Angela. I was sorry for her. I thought she was feeble, and I don't much care for feeble people. I first met her about five years ago. She'd come to this country from Australia and I'd never seen her before. But she was my cousin all right, the daughter of my father's dead brother, so you needn't get any ideas she might have been an impostor.'

'You have been reading too many detective stories, Mr Somerset.'

'Maybe.' Somerset grinned and went on, 'She looked me up because I and my father were the only relatives she had in this country, and she was lonely in London. Or so she said. I think she was on the look-out for any pickings there might be for her. She was a greedy girl, poor Angela. She hadn't met Robert at that time. When she did she stopped coming out here and I didn't hear from her again until they were about to get married and hadn't anywhere to live. I'd written to her to tell her of my father's death – to which, by the way, she didn't reply – and she wanted to know if I'd let her and Robert have Bury Cottage.

'Well, I'd been meaning to sell it, but I couldn't get the price I wanted, so I agreed and let it to Angela and Robert for five pounds a week.'

'A very low rent, Mr Somerset,' said Wexford, interrupting him. 'You could have got at least twice that.'

Somerset shrugged. Without asking them he refilled their glasses. 'Apparently, they were very badly off, and she was my cousin. I have some silly old-fashioned ideas about blood being thicker than water, Mr Wexford, and I can't shake them off. I didn't in the least mind letting them have the place furnished at what was little more than a nominal rent. What I did mind was when Angela sent me her electricity bill for me to pay.'

'You'd made no agreement about that, of course?'

'Of course not. I asked her to come over here and we'd talk about it. Well, she came and spun me the old sob story I'd heard from her before about their poverty, her nerves and her unhappy adolescence with her mother who wouldn't let her go to university. I suggested that if money was so tight with them she should get a job. She was a qualified librarian and she could easily have got a library job at Kingsmarkham or Stowerton. She pleaded her mental breakdown, but she seemed perfectly healthy to me. I think she was just lazy. Anyway, she flounced out of the house, telling me I was mean, and I didn't see either her or Robert again until about eighteen months ago. On that occasion they didn't see me. I was out with a friend in Pomfret and I saw Robert and Angela through the windows of a restaurant. It was a very expensive restaurant and they seemed to be doing themselves proud, so I came to the conclusion they were doing a good deal better financially.

'We actually *met* again only once more. That was last April. We ran into each other in Myringham in that monstrosity the planners are pleased to call a shopping precinct. They were loaded down with stuff they'd bought, but they seemed depressed in spite of the fact that Robert had got himself this new job. Perhaps they were only embarrassed at coming face to face with me. I never saw Angela again. She wrote to me about a month ago to say that they'd want to leave the cottage as soon as they'd got a place in London, and that that would probably be in the New Year.'

'Were they a happy couple?' Burden asked when Somerset had finished.

'Very, as far as I could tell.' Somerset got up to close the glass doors as the sunset light faded and a little wind rose. 'They had so much in common. Should I be very mean-spirited if I said that what they had in common were paranoia, greed and a general idea that the world owed them a living? I'm sorry she's dead, I'm sorry to hear of anyone dying like that, but I can't say I liked her. Men can be as gauche and tough as they please, but I like a little grace in a woman, don't you? I don't want to be fanciful, but I sometimes thought Robert and Angela got on so well because they were united in gracelessness against the world.'

'You've been very helpful, Mr Somerset,' said Wexford more as a matter of form than with sincerity. Somerset had told him much he didn't know, but had he told him anything that mattered? 'You won't take it amiss, I'm sure, if I ask you what you were doing yesterday afternoon.'

He could have sworn the man hesitated. It was as if he had already thought up how he must answer, but still had to brace himself to give that answer. 'I was here alone. I took the afternoon off to get things ready for my wife's coming home. I'm afraid I was quite alone, and I didn't see anyone, so I can't give you confirmation.'

'Very well,' said Wexford. 'That can't be helped. I don't suppose you have any idea as to what friends your cousin had?'

'None at all. According to her, she had no friends. Everyone she'd ever known but Robert had been cruel to her, she said,

389

so making friends was just to invite more cruelty.' Somerset drained his glass. 'Have some more wine?'

'No, thank you. We've taken enough of your Saturday-night ration as it is.'

Somerset gave them his pleasant frank smile. 'I'll see you to the door.'

As they came out into the hall, a querulous voice sounded from upstairs: 'Marky, Marky, where are you?'

Somerset winced, perhaps only at the ugly diminutive. But blood is thicker than water, and a man and his wife are one. He went to the foot of the stairs, called out that he was just coming, and opened the front door. Wexford and Burden said good night quickly for the voice from above had risen to a thin petulant wail.

In the morning Wexford returned as he had promised to Bury Cottage. He had news, some of which had only just reached him, for Robert Hathall, but he had no intention of telling the widower what he most wanted to know.

Mrs Hathall let him in and said her son was still asleep. She showed him into the living room and told him to wait there, but she offered him neither tea nor coffee. She was the kind of woman, he decided, who had probably seldom if ever in her life dispensed refreshment to anyone but members of her own family. They were a strange guarded lot, the Hathalls, whose isolationism apparently infected the people they married, for when he asked Mrs Hathall if Angela's predecessor had ever been to the cottage, she said:

'Eileen wouldn't have lowered herself. She keeps herself to herself.'

'And Rosemary, your granddaughter?'

'Rosemary came once, and once was enough. Anyway, she's too busy with her schoolwork to go out and about.'

'Will you give me Mrs Eileen Hathall's address, please?'

Mrs Hathall's face grew as red as her son's, as red as the

wrinkled skin on a turkey's neck. 'No, I won't! You've no business with Eileen. Find it out for yourself.' She banged the door on him and he was left, alone.

It was the first time he had ever been alone there, so he used the waiting time to survey the room. The furniture, which he had supposed to be Angela's and had therefore credited her with taste, was in fact Somerset's, the lifelong collection perhaps of Somerset's father. It was the prettiest kind of late-Victorian with some earlier pieces, spindle-legged chairs, an elegant small oval table. By the window was a red and white Venetian glass oil-lamp that had never been converted to electricity. A glass-fronted bookcase contained, for the most part, the kind of works an old man would have collected and loved: a complete set of Kipling bound in red leather, some H.G. Wells, Gosse's *Father and Son*, a little of Ruskin and a lot of Trollope. But on the top shelf, where previously perhaps had stood an ornament, were the Hathall's own books. There were half a dozen thrillers in paperback, two or three works of 'pop' archaeology, a couple of novels which had aroused controversy over their sexual content when they had been published, and two handsomely jacketed imposing tomes.

Wexford took down the first of these. It was a volume of colour prints of ancient Egyptian jewellery, contained scarcely any text apart from the captions beneath the pictures, and bore inside its front cover a plate which proclaimed it as the property of the library of the National Archaeologists' League. Stolen, of course, by Angela. But books, like umbrellas, pens and boxes of matches, belong in a category of objects the stealing of which is a very venial offence, and Wexford thought little of it. He replaced the book and took out the last one on the shelf. Its title was *Of Men and Angels, A Study of Ancient British Tongues,* and when he opened it he saw that it was a very learned work with chapters on the origins of Welsh, Erse, Scottish Gaelic and Cornish and their common Celtic source. Its price was nearly six pounds, and he wondered that anyone as poor as the Hathalls had claimed to have been should have spent so much on something which was surely as far above their heads as it was above his own.

He was still holding the book when Hathall came into the room. He saw the man's eyes go warily to it, then look sharply away.

'I didn't know you were a student of Celtic languages, Mr Hathall,' he said pleasantly.

'It was Angela's. I don't know where it came from, but she'd had it for ages.'

'Strange, since it was only published this year. But no matter. I thought you'd like to know that your car has been found. It had been abandoned in London, in a side street near Wood Green station. Are you familiar with the district?'

'I've never been there.' Hathall's gaze kept returning, with a kind of reluctant fascination or perhaps apprehensively, to the book Wexford still kept hold of. And for this very reason Wexford determined to keep hold of it and not to remove the finger which he had slipped at random between its pages as if to keep a place. 'When can I have it back?'

'In two or three days. When we've had a good look at it.'

'Examined it for those famous fingerprints you're always on about, I suppose?'

'Am I, Mr Hathall? I? Aren't you rather projecting on to me what you think I ought to feel?' Wexford looked blandly at him. No, he wouldn't gratify the man's curiosity, though it was hard to tell now what Hathall most longed for. A revelation of what the fingerprints had disclosed? Or for that book to be laid down casually as of no account? 'My present feeling is that you should stop worrying about investigations which only we can make. Your mind may be eased a little when I tell your wife hadn't been sexually assaulted.' He waited for some sign of relief, but only saw those eyes with their red glint dart once more to the book. And there was no response when he said as he prepared to leave. 'Your wife died very quickly, in perhaps no more than fifteen seconds. It's possible that she scarcely knew what was happening to her.'

Getting up, he eased his finger from the pages of the book and slipped the jacket flap in where it had been. 'You won't mind if I borrow this for a few days, will you?' he said, and Hathall shrugged but still said nothing at all.

CHAPTER SEVEN

The inquest took place on Tuesday morning, and a verdict was returned of murder by person or persons unknown. Afterwards, as Wexford was crossing the courtyard between the coroner's court and the police station, he saw Nancy Lake go up to Robert Hathall and his mother. She began to speak to Hathall, to condole with him perhaps or offer him a lift home to Wool Lane in her car. Hathall snapped something short and sharp at her, took his mother's arm and walked off rapidly, leaving Nancy standing there, one hand up to her lips. Wexford watched this little pantomime, which had taken place out of earshot, and was nearing the car-park exit when a car drew up alongside him and a sweet vibrant voice said:

'Are you very busy, Chief Inspector?'

'Why do you ask, Mrs Lake?'

'Not because I have any fascinating clues to give you.' She put her hand out of the window and beckoned to him. It was a mischievous and seductive gesture. He found it irresistible and he went up to her and bent down. 'The fact is,' she said, 'that I have a table for two booked at the Peacock in Pomfret and my escort has most churlishly stood me up. Would you think it very forward of me if I asked you to lunch with me instead?'

He was staggered. There was no doubt now that this rich, pretty and entirely charming woman was making advances to him – *him*! It was forward all right, it was almost unprecedented. She looked at him calmly, the corners of her mouth tilted, her eyes shining.

But it wouldn't do. Along whatever paths of fantasy his imagination might lead him, into whatever picture galleries of erotica, it wouldn't do. Once though, when he was young and

without ties or prestige or pressures, it could have been a
different story. And in those days he had taken such offers or
made them without much appreciation and with little awareness of their delight. Ah, to be a little bit younger and know
what one knows now . . .!

'But I also have a table booked for lunch,' he said, 'at the
Carousel café.'

'You won't cancel that and be my guest?'

'Mrs Lake, I am, as you said, very very busy. Would you
think *me* forward if I said you would distract me from my
business?'

She laughed, but it wasn't a laugh of merriment, and her
eyes had ceased to dance. 'It's something, I suppose, to be a
distraction,' she said. 'You make me wonder if I've ever been
anything but a – distraction. Good-bye.'

He went quickly away and up in the lift to his office,
wondering if he had been a fool, if such a chance would ever
come to him again. He attached no special significance to her
words, neither to ponder on them nor to try and interpret
them, for he couldn't think of her intellectually. In his mind,
her face went with him, so seductive, so hopeful, then so
downcast because he had refused her invitation. He tried to
thrust this image away and concentrate on what was before
him, the dry and technical report on the examination of
Robert Hathall's car, but it kept returning, and with it her
entrancing voice, reduced now to a cajoling whisper.

Not that there was much in the report to get excited about.
The car had been found parked in a street near Alexandra
Park, and the discovery had been made by a constable on the
beat. It was empty but for a couple of maps and a ballpoint
pen on the dashboard shelf, and inside and out it had been
wiped clean. The only prints were those of Robert Hathall,
found on the outside of the boot and bonnet lids, and the only
hairs two of Angela's on the driving seat.

He sent for Sergeant Martin, but got nothing encouraging

from him. No one claiming to be a friend of Angela's had come forward, and nobody, apparently, had seen her go out or return home on Friday afternoon. Burden was out, making enquiries – for the second or third time – among the workers at Wool Farm, so Wexford went alone to the Carousel Café for a solitary lunch.

It was early, not much past midday, and the café was still half-empty. He had been sitting at his corner table for perhaps five minutes and had ordered Antonio's speciality of the day, roast lamb, when he felt a light touch that was almost a caress on his shoulder. Wexford had had too many shocks in his life to jump. He turned round slowly and said with a cool note in his voice that he didn't feel, 'This is an unexpected pleasure.'

Nancy Lake sat down opposite him. She made the place look squalid. Her cream silk suit, her chestnut silk hair, her diamonds and her smile threw into sordid relief Antonio's Woolworth cutlery and the tomato-shaped plastic sauce container.

'The mountain,' she said, 'wouldn't come to Mahomet.'

He grinned. It was pointless to pretend he wasn't delighted to see her. 'Ah, you should have seen me a year ago,' he said. 'Then I *was* a mountain. What will you eat? The roast lamb will be bad, but better than the pie.'

'I don't want to eat anything. I'll just have coffee. Aren't you flattered that I didn't come for the food?'

He was. Eyeing the heaped plate which Antonio set before him, he said, 'It's not much of a compliment, though. Coffee only for the lady, please.' Were her attractions enhanced, he asked himself, by Antonio's obvious admiration of them? She was aware of it all, he could see that, and in her awareness, her experienced acceptance of her powers, lay one of the few signs of her age.

She was silent for a few moments while he ate, and he

noticed that her expression was one of rueful repose. But suddenly, as he was preparing to ask her why Robert Hathall had repulsed her so violently that morning, she looked up and said:

'I'm sad, Mr Wexford. Things aren't going well for me.'

He was very surprised. 'Do you want to tell me about it?' How strange that their intimacy had advanced so far that he could ask her that ...

'I don't know,' she said. 'No, I don't think so. One gets conditioned into habits of secrecy and discretion, even if one doesn't personally see much point in them.'

'That's true. Or can be true in certain circumstances.' The circumstances Dora had referred to?

Yet she was on the brink of telling him. Perhaps it was only the arrival of her coffee and Antonio's admiring flutterings that deterred her. She gave a little shrug, but instead of the small-talk he expected, she said something that astonished him. It was so surprising and so intensely spoken that he pushed away his plate and stared at her.

'Is it very wrong, d'you think, to want someone to die?'

'Not,' he said, puzzled, 'if that wish remains just a wish. Most of us wish that sometimes, and most of us, fortunately, let I dare not wait upon I would.'

'Like the poor cat in the adage?'

He was delighted that she had capped his quotation. 'Is this – er, enemy of yours connected with these habits of secrecy and discretion?'

She nodded. 'But I shouldn't have brought it up. It was silly of me. I'm very lucky really, only it gets hard sometimes, alternating between being a queen and a – distraction. I shall get my crown back, this year, next year, sometime. I shall never abdicate. Goodness, all this mystery! And you're much too clever not to have guessed what I'm on about, aren't you?' He didn't reply to that one. 'Let's change the subject,' she said.

So they changed the subject. Afterwards, when she had left him and he found himself standing, bemused, in the High Street, he could hardly have said what they had talked about, only that it had been pleasant, too pleasant, and had left him with most unpleasant feelings of guilt. But he would see her no more. If necessary, he would eat his lunch in the police canteen, he would avoid her, he would never again be alone with her, even in a restaurant. It was as if he had committed adultery, had confessed it, and been told to 'avoid the occasion.' But he had committed nothing, not even himself. He had only talked and listened.

Had what he had listened to helped him? Perhaps. All that circumlocution, those hints at an enemy, at secrecy and discretion, that had been a pointer. Hathall, he knew, would admit nothing, would have had his ego boosted by the coroner's sympathy. Yet, knowing all this, he nevertheless set off along the High Street towards Wool Lane. He had no idea that it was to be his last visit to Bury Cottage, and that, although he would see Hathall again, it was to be more than a year before they exchanged another word.

Wexford had forgotten all about the book of Celtic languages, hadn't, in fact, bothered to glance at it again, but it was with a request for its immediate return that Hathall greeted him.

'I'll have it sent over to you tomorrow,' he said.

Hathall looked relieved. 'There's also the matter of my car. I need my car.'

'You can have that tomorrow as well.'

The sour old woman was evidently in the kitchen, closeted behind a shut door. She had maintained the house in the immaculate condition in which her dead daughter-in-law had left it, but the touch of an alien and tasteless hand was already apparent. On old Mr Somerset's oval table stood a vase of plastic flowers. What impulse, festive or funeral, had prompted Mrs Hathall to buy them and place them there? *Plastic* flowers, thought Wexford, in the season of mellow fruitfulness when real flowers filled the gardens and the hedgerows and the florist's shops.

Hathall didn't ask him to sit down and he didn't sit down himself. He stood with one elbow resting on the mantelpiece, his fist pressed into his hard red cheek.

'So you didn't find anything incriminating in my car?'

'I didn't say that, Mr Hathall.'

'Well, did you?'

'As a matter of fact, no. Whoever killed your wife was very clever. I don't know that I've ever come across anyone in this sort of situation who covered his tracks so expertly.' Wexford piled it on, letting a note of grudging admiration creep into his voice. Hathall listened impassively. And if gratified was too strong a word to use to describe his expression, satisfied wasn't. The fist uncurled and relaxed, and he leaned back against the fireplace with something like arrogance. 'He seems to have worn gloves to drive your car,' Wexford said, 'and to have given it a wash as well, for good measure. Apparently, he wasn't seen to park the car, and no one was seen driving it on Friday. At the moment, we really have very few leads to go on.'

'Will – will you find any more?' He was eager to know, but as anxious to disguise his eagerness.

'It's early days yet, Mr Hathall. Who knows?' Perhaps it was cruel to play with the man. Does the end ever justify the means? And Wexford didn't know what end he was aiming for, or where next to grab in this game of hide-and-seek in a dark room. 'I can tell you that we found the fingerprints of a man, other than your own, in this house.'

'Are they on – what d'you call it? – record?'

'They proved to be those of Mr Mark Somerset.'

'Ah, well . . .' Suddenly Hathall looked more genial than Wexford had ever seen him. Perhaps only an inhibition as to touching prevented him from stepping forward to pat the chief inspector on the back. 'I'm sorry,' he said. 'I'm not myself at the moment. I should have asked you to sit down. So the only prints you found were those of Mr Somerset, were they? Dear Cousin Mark, our tight-fisted landlord.'

'I didn't say that, Mr Hathall.'

'Well, and mine and – and Angela's, of course.'

'Of course. But apart from those, we found a whole handprint of a woman in your bathroom. It's the print of her right hand, and in the tip of the forefinger is an L-shaped scar.'

Wexford had expected a reaction. But he believed Hathall to be so well under control that he had thought that reaction would show itself only as fresh indignation. He would expostulate perhaps, ask why the police hadn't followed this evidence up, or with a shrug of impatience suggest that this was the handprint of some friend of his wife's whose existence, in his grief, he had forgotten to mention. Never had he supposed, feeling his way in the dark as he was, that his words would have had a cataclysmic effect.

For Hathall froze where he stood. Life seemed driven out of him. It was as if he had suddenly been stricken with a pain so great that it had paralyzed him or forced him to hold himself still for the protection of his heart and his whole nervous system. And yet he said nothing, he made no sound. His self-control *was* magnificent. But his body, his physical self, was triumphing over his mental processes. It was as strong an example of matter over mind as Wexford had ever seen. The shock had come to Hathall at last. The stunning, with its attendant disbelief and terror and realization of what the future must now be, which should have bludgeoned him when he first saw his wife's body, was taking effect five days later. He was poleaxed by it.

Wexford was excited but he behaved very casually. 'Perhaps you can throw some light on whose this handprint may be?'

Hathall drew in his breath. He seemed to have a very real need of oxygen. Slowly he shook his head.

'No idea at all, Mr Hathall?'

The head-shaking went on. It was robot-like, automatic, as if running on some dreadful cerebral clockwork, and Wexford had the notion that Hathall would have to take his head in both hands and grasp it to stop that slow mechanical movement.

'A clear handprint on the side of your bath. An L-shaped scar on the right forefinger. We shall, of course, take it as a lead for our main line of enquiry.'

Hathall jerked up his chin. A spasm ran through his body. He forced a thin constricted voice through stiff lips. 'On the bath, you said?'

'On the bath. I'm right, aren't I, in thinking you can guess whose it may be?'

'I haven't,' Hathall said tremulously and weakly, 'the faintest idea.' His skin had taken on a mottled pallor, but now the blood returned to it and pulsed in the veins on his forehead. The worst of the shock was over. It had been replaced by – what? Not anger, not indignation. Sorrow, Wexford thought, surprised. He was overcome at this late stage by real sorrow . . .

Wexford felt no impulse to be merciful. He said relentlessly, 'I've noticed how anxious you've been right through my enquiries to know what we've deduced from fingerprints. In fact, I've never known a bereaved husband to take quite such a keen interest in forensics. Therefore, I can't help feeling you expected a certain print to be found. If that's so and we've found it, I must tell you that you'll be obstructing this enquiry if you keep what may be vital information to yourself.'

'Don't threaten me!' Though the words were sharp, the voice that spoke them was feeble and the huffiness in the tone pathetically assumed. 'Don't think you can persecute me.'

'I should rather advise *you* to think over what I've said,

and then, if you are wise, you'll make a frank disclosure to us of what I'm sure you know.'

But even as he spoke, looking into the man's miserable, shocked eyes, he knew that any such disclosure would be far from wise. For whatever alibi the man might have, whatever love for her and devotion to her he might profess, he had killed his wife. And as he left the room, making his own way out of the house, he imagined Robert Hathall collapsing into a chair, breathing shallowly, feeling his racing heart, gathering his resources for very survival.

The revelation that they had found a woman's handprint had done this to him. Therefore, he knew who that woman was. He had been anxious about fingerprints because all the time he had dreaded she might have left this evidence behind. But his reaction hadn't been that of a man who merely suspects something or fears the confirmation of a fact he has guessed at. It had been the reaction of someone who fears for his own liberty and peace, the liberty and peace too of another, and, above all, that he and that other might not now have that liberty and peace together.

CHAPTER EIGHT

His discovery had driven from Wexford's mind memories of that lunchtime interlude. But when he walked into his own house soon after four they returned to him, discoloured by guilt. And if he hadn't spent that hour in Nancy Lake's company, or if it had been less enjoyable, he might not now have given Dora such a hearty kiss or asked her what he did ask her.

'How would you like to go up to London for a couple of days?'

'You mean you have to go?'

Wexford nodded.

'And you can't bear to be parted from me?' Wexford felt himself blushing. Why did she have to be so perceptive? It was almost as if she read his thoughts. But if she had been less perceptive, would he have married her? 'I'd love to darling,' she said blandly. 'When?'

'If Howard and Denise will have us, as soon as you can pack a bag.' He grinned, knowing the quantity of clothes she would want to take with her for even two days with her fashionable niece. 'Like – ten minutes?'

'Give me an hour,' said Dora.

'OK. I'll phone Denise.'

Chief Superintendent Howard Fortune, the head of Kenbourne Vale CID, was the son of Wexford's dead sister. For years Wexford had been in awe of him, his awe mixed with envy of this nephew, so aptly named, into whose lap so many good things had fallen, apparently without effort on his part, a first-class honours degree, a house in Chelsea, marriage to a beautiful fashion model, rapid promotion until his rank far surpassed his uncle's. And these two had taken on in his eyes the hard gloss of jet-set people, entering, although he hardly knew them, into that category of rich relations who will despise us from a distance and snub us if we make overtures to them. With misgivings he had gone to stay with them to convalesce after an illness, and his misgivings had turned out to be groundless, the silly suspicions that are borne only of a grudge. For Howard and Denise had been kind and hospitable and un-assuming, and when he had helped Howard solve a Kenbourne Vale murder case – solved it himself, Howard said – he had felt he was vindicated and a friendship established.

Just how firm that friendship was to be had been shown by the Fortunes' enjoyment of family Christmases at Wexford's house, by the new *rapport* between uncle and nephew, and revealed itself again in the greeting the chief inspector and his wife got as their taxi brought them to the house in Teresa Street. It was just after seven and one of Denise's elaborate dinners was almost ready.

'But you've got so thin, Uncle Reg,' she said as she kissed him. 'Here was I, counting calories for you, and now it looks as if it was all labour in vain. You look quite handsome.'

'Thank you, my dear. I must confess my weight loss has removed one of my principal fears of London.'

'And what would that be?'

'That *was* that I'd get myself inside one of those automatic ticket things on the Underground – you know, the kind with the snapping jaws – and be unable to get out.'

Denise laughed and took them into the living room. Since that first visit, Wexford had got over his fear of knocking over Denise's flower arrangements and conquered his awe of her fragile china ornaments and the pastel satin upholstery he was sure he would ruin with coffee stains. The abundance of everything, the smooth-running splendours and the air of gracious living, no longer intimidated him. He could sit with ease on a chair in one of those little circles of chairs and a silk sofa that reminded him of photographs of royal palace interiors. He could laugh about the tropical central heating, or as now when it wasn't on, comment on its summer counter-part, the newly installed air conditioning.

'It reminds me,' he said, 'of that description of Scott's of the Lady Rowena's apartments. "The rich hangings shook to the night blast . . . the flame of the torches streamed sideways into the air like the unfurled pennon of a chieftain." Only, in our case, it's house plants that stream and not flames.'

They had an in-joke about their exchange of quotations, for at one time Wexford had used them to assert his intellectual equality, and Howard had replied, or so his uncle believed, to keep discreetly off the subject of their shared occupation.

'Literary chit-chat, Reg?' said Howard, smiling.

'To break the ice only – and you'll get real ice on your flower vases if you keep that going, Denise. No, I want to talk to you about why I've come up here, but that'll keep till after dinner.'

'And I thought you'd come up here to see me!' said Denise.

'So I have, my dear, but another young woman is inter-esting me a good deal more at present.'

'What's she got that I haven't got?'

Wexford took her hand and, pretending to scrutinize it, said, 'An L-shaped scar on her forefinger.'

When Wexford was in London he always hoped people would take him for a Londoner. To sustain this illusion, he took certain measures such as remaining in his seat until the tube train had actually come to a halt at his destination instead of leaping up nervously thirty seconds beforehand as is the habit of non-Londoners. And he refrained from enquiring of other passengers if the train he was in was actually going to the place announced by the confusing indicator. As a result, he had once found himself in Uxbridge instead of Harrow-on-the-Hill. But there is no easy way of getting from the western reaches of Chelsea to the West End by Tube, so Wexford boarded the number 14 bus, an old friend.

Instead of one person, Marcus Flower turned out to be two, Jason Marcus and Stephen Flower, the former looking like a long-haired and youthful Ronald Colman and the latter a short-haired and superannuated Mick Jagger. Wexford refused a cup of the black coffee they were drinking – apparently as a hangover remedy – and said he had really come to talk to Linda Kipling. Marcus and Flower went off into a double act of innuendo at this, declaring that Miss Kipling was far better worth seeing than they, that no one ever came there except to look at the girls, and then, falling simultaneously grave, said almost in unison how frightfully sorry they had been to hear of 'poor old Bob's loss' about which they had been 'absolutely cut up.'

Wexford was then conducted by Marcus through a series of offices that were strangely lush and stark at the same time, rooms where the furniture was made of steel and leather and set against extravagant velvet drapes and high-pile carpets. On the walls were abstract paintings of the splashed ketchup and copulating spiders *genre*, and on low tables magazine pornography so soft as to be gently blancmange-like in texture and kind. The secretaries, three of them, were all together in a blue velvet room, the one who had received him, a red-headed one, and Linda Kipling. Two others, said Linda, were in one case at the hairdresser's and in the other at a wedding. It was that sort of place.

She led him into an empty office where she sat down on the kind of black leather and metal bench you find in airport lounges. She had the look of a dummy in the window of a very expensive dress shop, realistic but not real, as if made of high-quality plastic. Contemplating her fingernails, which were green, she told him that Robert Hathall had phoned his wife every day at lunchtime since he had been with them, either calling her himself or asking her to put the call through for him. This she had thought 'terribly sweet,' though now, of course, it was 'terribly tragic.'

'You'd say he was very happily married, would you, Miss Kipling? Talked about his wife a lot, kept her photograph on his desk, that sort of thing?'

'He did have her photograph, but Liz said it was frightfully bourgeois, doing things like that, so he put it away. I wouldn't know if he was happy. He was never very *lively*, not like Jason and Steve and some of the other blokes.'

'What was he like last Friday?'

'The same as usual. *Just* the same. I've told that to a policeman already. I don't know what's the good of saying the same thing over and over again. He was just the same as usual. He got in a bit before ten and he was in here all the morning working out the details of a sort of scheme for private hospital treatment for those of the staff who wanted it. Insurance, you know.' Linda looked her contempt for those executives who couldn't afford to pay for their own private treatment. 'He phoned his wife a bit before one and then he went out to lunch in a pub with Jason. They weren't gone long. I know he was back here by half past two. He dictated three letters to me.' She seemed aggrieved at the memory, as if this had been an unfairly demanding task. 'And he went off at five-thirty to meet his mother and take her off to wherever she lives, somewhere in Sussex.'

'Did he ever get phone calls here from women or a woman?'

'His wife never phoned *him*.' His meaning sank in and she stared at him. She was one of those people who are so narrow and who have imaginations so limited that hints at anything unexpected in the field of sex or social conduct or the emotions throw them into fits of nervous giggles. She giggled now. 'A girl-friend, d'you mean? Nobody like that phoned him. No one ever phoned him.'

'Was he attracted by any of the girls here?'

She looked astonished and edged slightly away. 'The girls *here?*'

'Well, there are five girls here, Miss Kipling, and if the three of you I've seen are anything to go by, you're not exactly repulsive. Did Mr Hathall have a special friendship with any girl here?'

The green fingernails fluttered. 'Do you mean a relationship? D'you mean, was he *sleeping* with anyone?'

'If you like to put it that way. After all, he was a lonely man, temporarily separated from his wife. I suppose you were all here on Friday afternoon, none of you out having her hair done or at a wedding?'

'Of course we were all here! And as to Bob Hathall having a relationship with any of us, you might care to know that June and Liz are married, Clare's engaged to Jason and Suzanne is Lord Carthew's daughter.'

'Does that exempt her from sleeping with a man?'

'It exempts her from sleeping with someone of Bob Hathall's – er, kind. And that goes for all of us. We mayn't be "exactly repulsive," as you put it, but we haven't come down to that!'

Wexford said good morning to her and walked out, feeling rather sorry he had paid her even that one grudging compliment. In Piccadilly, he went into a call-box and dialled the number of Craig and Butler, Accountants, of Gray's Inn Road. Mr Butler, he was told, was at present engaged, but would be happy to see him at three o'clock that afternoon. How should he spend the intervening time? Although he had discovered Mrs Eileen Hathall's address, Croydon was too far distant to sandwich in a visit there between now and three. Why not find out a little more about Angela herself and get some background to this marriage that everyone said was happy but which had ended in murder? He leafed through the directory and found it: The National Archaeologists' League Library, 17 Trident Place, Knightsbridge SW7. Briskly, he walked up to the Tube station in Piccadilly Circus.

Trident Place wasn't easy to find. Although he had con-

sulted his *A to Z Guide* in the privacy of the call-box, he found
he had to look at it again in full view of sophisticated Londo-
ners. As he was telling himself he was an old fool to be so
self-conscious, he was rewarded by the sight of Sloane Street
from which, according to the guide, Trident Place debouched.

It was a wide street of four-storey mid-Victorian houses,
all smart and well kept. Number seven had a pair of heavy
glass doors, framed in mahogany, through which Wexford
went into a hall hung with monochrome photographs of
amphorae and with portraits of gloomy-looking unearthers of
the past, and thence through another door into the library
itself. The atmosphere was that of all such places, utterly quiet,
scholarly, redolent of books, ancient and modern. There were
very few people about. A member was busy with one of the
huge leather-bound catalogues, another was signing for the
books he had taken out. Two girls and a young man were
occupied in a quiet and studious way behind the polished oak
counter, and it was one of these girls who came out and took
Wexford upstairs, past more portraits, more photographs, past
the sepulchrally silent reading room, to the office of the chief
librarian, Miss Marie Marcovitch.

Miss Marcovitch was a little elderly woman, presumably
of Central European Jewish origin. She spoke fluent academic
English with a slight accent. As unlike Linda Kipling as one
woman can be unlike another, she asked him to sit down and
showed no surprise that he had come to question her about a
murder case, although she had not at first connected the girl
who used to work for her with the dead woman.

'She left here, of course, before her marriage,' said Wexford. 'How would you describe her, as tough and ungracious,
or nervous and shy?'

'Well, she was quiet. I could put it like this — but, no, the
poor girl is dead.' After her small hesitation, Miss Marcovitch
went on hastily, 'I really don't know what I can tell you about
her. She was quite ordinary.'

'I should like you to tell me everything you know.'

'A tall order, even though she *was* ordinary. She came to work here about five years ago. It's not the usual practice of the library to employ people without university degrees, but Angela was a qualified librarian and she had some knowledge of archaeology. She'd no practical experience, but neither, for that matter, have I.'

The bookish atmosphere had reminded Wexford of a book he still had in his possession. 'Was she interested in Celtic languages?'

Miss Marcovitch looked surprised. 'Not that I know of.'

'Never mind. Please go on.'

'I hardly know how to go on, Chief Inspector. Angela did her work quite satisfactorily, though she was absent rather a lot on vague medical grounds. She was bad about money . . .' Again Wexford noticed the hesitation. 'I mean, she couldn't manage on her salary and she used to complain that it was inadequate. I gathered she borrowed small sums from other members of the staff, but that was no business of mine.'

'I believe she worked here for some months before she met Mr Hathall?'

'I'm not at all sure when she did meet Mr Hathall. First of all she was friendly with a Mr Craig who used to be on our staff but who has since left. Indeed, all the members of our staff from that time have left except myself. I'm afraid I never met Mr Hathall.'

'But you did meet the first Mrs Hathall?'

The librarian pursed her lips and folded her small shrivelled hands in her lap. 'This seems very much like scandal-mongering,' she said primly.

'So much of my work is, Miss Marcovitch.'

'Well . . .' She gave a sudden unexpected smile, bright and almost naughty. 'In for a penny, in for a pound, eh? I did meet the first Mrs Hathall. I happened to be in the library itself when she came in. You'll have noticed that this is a very quiet place. Voices aren't raised and movements aren't swift, an atmosphere which suits members and staff alike. I must confess to having been very angry indeed when this woman burst into the library, rushed up to where Angela was behind the counter and began to rant and rave at her. It was impossible for members not to realize that she was reproaching Angela for what she called stealing her husband. I asked Mr Craig to get rid of the woman as quietly as he could, and then I took Angela upstairs with me. When she calmed down I told her that, although her private affairs were no business of mine, such a thing mustn't be allowed to occur again.'

'It didn't occur again?'

'No, but Angela's work began to suffer. She was the kind that goes to pieces easily under strain. I was sorry for her, but not otherwise sorry, when she said she'd have to give up her job on her doctor's advice.'

The librarian finished speaking, seemed to have said everything she had to say and was on her feet. But Wexford, instead of getting up, said in a dry voice, 'In for a pound, Miss Marcovitch?'

She coloured and gave a little embarrassed laugh. 'How perspicacious of you, Chief Inspector! Yes, there is one more thing. I suppose you noticed my hesitations. I've never told anyone about this, but – well, I will tell you.' She sat down again, and her manner became more pedantic. 'In view of the fact that the library members pay a large subscription – twenty-five pounds annually – and are by their nature careful of books, we charge no fines should they keep books beyond the allotted period of one month. Naturally, however, we don't publicize this, and many new members have been pleasantly surprised to find that, on returning books they have kept for perhaps two or three months, no charge is made.

'About three and a half years ago, a little while after Angela had left us, I happened to be helping out at the returns counter when a member handed to me three books that I saw were six weeks overdue. I should have made no comment on this had the member not produced one pound eighty, which he assured me was the proper fine for overdue books, ten pence per week per book. When I told him no fines were ever exacted in this library, he said he'd only been a member for a year and had only once before kept books longer than a month. On that occasion the "young lady" had asked him for one pound twenty, and he hadn't protested, thinking it to be reasonable.

'Of course I made enquiries among the staff who all appeared perfectly innocent, but the two girls told me that other members had recently also tried to get them to accept fines for overdue books, which they had refused and had given an explanation of our rules.'

'You think Angela Hathall was responsible?' Wexford asked.

'Who else could have been? But she had gone, no very great harm was done, and I didn't relish raising this matter at a meeting of the trustees which might have led to trouble and perhaps to a prosecution with members called as witnesses and so on. Besides, the girl had been under a strain and it was a very small fraud. I doubt if she made more than ten pounds out of it at the most.'

CHAPTER NINE

A very small fraud . . . Wexford hadn't expected to encounter fraud at all, and it was probably irrelevant. But the shadowy figure of Angela Hathall had now, like a shape looming out of fog, begun to take more definite outlines. A paranoid personality with a tendency to hypochondria; intelligent but unable to persevere at a steady job; her mental state easily overthrown by adversity; financially unstable and not above making extra money by fraudulent means. How, then, had she managed on the fifteen pounds a week which was all she and her husband had had to live on for a period of nearly three years?

He left the library and took the Tube to Chancery Lane. Craig and Butler, Accountants, had their offices on the third floor of an old building near the Royal Free Hospital. He noted the place, had a salad and orange juice lunch in a café, and at one minute to three was shown up into the office of the senior partner, William Butler. The room was as old-fashioned and nearly as quiet as the library, and Mr Butler as wizened as Miss Marcovitch. But he wore a jolly smile, the atmosphere was of business rather than scholarship, and the only portrait a highly coloured oil of an elderly man in evening dress.

'My former partner, Mr Craig,' said William Butler.

'It would be his son, I imagine, who introduced Robert and Angela Hathall?'

'His nephew. Paul Craig, the son, has been my partner since his father's retirement. It's Jonathan Craig who used to work at the archaeologists' place.'

'I believe the introduction took place at an office party here?'

The old man gave a sharp scratchy little chuckle. 'A party *here?* Where would we put the food and drink, not to mention the guests? They'd be reminded of their income tax and get gloomy and depressed. No, that party was at Mr Craig's own home in Hampstead on his retirement from the firm after forty-five years.'

'You met Angela Hathall there?'

'It was the only time I did meet her. Nice-looking creature, though with a bit of that Shetland pony look so many of them have nowadays. Wearing trousers too. Personally, I think a woman should put on a skirt to go to a party. Bob Hathall was very smitten with her from the first, you could see that.'

'That can't have pleased Mr Jonathan Craig.'

Again Mr Butler gave his fiddle-string squawk. 'He wasn't serious about *her.* Got married since, as a matter of fact. His wife's nothing to look at but loaded, my dear fellow, pots of it. This Angela wouldn't have gone down at all well with the family, they're not easygoing like me. Mind you, even I took a bit of a dim view when she went up to Paul and said what a lovely job he'd got, just the thing for knowing how to fiddle one's tax. Saying that to an accountant's like telling a doctor he's lucky to be able to get hold of heroin.' And Mr Butler chortled merrily. 'I met the first Mrs Hathall too, you know,' he said. 'She was a lively one. We had quite a scene, what with her banging about trying to get to Bob, and Bob locking himself up in his office. What a voice she's got when she's roused! Another time she sat on the stairs all day waiting for Bob to come out. He locked himself up again and never went out all night. God knows when she went home. The next day she turned up again and screamed at me to make him go back to her and their daughter. Fine set-out that was. I'll never forget it.'

'As a result,' said Wexford, 'you gave him the sack.'

'I never did! Is that what he says?'

Wexford nodded.

'God damn it! Bob Hathall always was a liar. I'll tell you what happened, and you can believe it or not, as you like. I had him in here after all that set-out and told him he'd better manage his private affairs a bit better. We had a bit of an argument and the upshot was he flew into a rage and said he was leaving. I tried to dissuade him. He'd come to us as an office boy and done all his training here. I told him that if he was getting a divorce he'd need all the money he could lay his hands on and there'd be a rise for him in the New Year. But he wouldn't listen, kept saying everyone was against him and this Angela. So he left and got himself some tin-pot part-time job, and serve him right.'

Recalling Angela's fraud and her remark to Paul Craig, and telling himself that birds of a feather flock together, Wexford asked Mr Butler if Robert Hathall had ever done anything which could be construed even mildly as on the shady side of the law. Mr Butler looked shocked.

'Certainly not. I've said he wasn't always strictly truthful, but otherwise he was honest.'

'Susceptible to women, would you say?'

William Butler gave another squawk and shook his head vehemently. 'He was fifteen when he first came here, and even in those days he was walking out with that first wife of his. They were engaged for God knows how many years. I tell you, Bob was so narrow and downright repressed, he didn't know there were other women on the face of the earth. We'd got a pretty typist in here, and for all the notice he took, she might have been a type*writer*. No, that was why he went overboard for that Angela, went daft about her like some silly romantic schoolboy. He woke up, the scales fell from his eyes. It's often the way. Those late developers are always the worst.'

'So perhaps, having awakened, he began looking around some more?'

'Perhaps he did, but I can't help you there. You thinking he might have done away with that Angela?'

415

'I shouldn't care to commit myself on that, Mr Butler,' said Wexford as he took his leave.

'No. Silly question, eh? I thought he was going to murder that other one, I can tell you. That's just where she had her sit-in, the step you're on now. I'll never forget it, never as long as I live.'

Howard Fortune was a tall thin man, skeletally thin in spite of his enormous appetite. He had the Wexford family's pale hair, the colour of faded brown paper, and the light grey-blue eyes, small and sharp. In spite of the difference in their figures, he had always resembled his uncle, and now that Wexford had lost so much weight, that resemblance was heightened. Sitting opposite each other in Howard's study, they might have been father and son, for likeness apart, Wexford was now able to talk to his nephew as familiarly as he talked to Burden, and Howard to respond without the delicacy and self-conscious tact of former days.

Their wives were out. Having spent the day shopping, they had adjourned to a theatre, and uncle and nephew had eaten their dinner alone. Now, while Howard drank brandy and he contented himself with a glass of white wine, Wexford enlarged on the theory he had put forward the night before.

'As far as I see it,' he said, 'the only way to account for Hathall's horror – and it was horror, Howard – when I told him about the handprint, is that he arranged the killing of Angela with the help of a woman accomplice.'

'With whom he was having a love affair?'

'Presumably. That would be the motive.'

'A thin motive these days, isn't it? Divorce is fairly easy and there were no children to consider.'

'You've missed the point.' Wexford spoke with a sharpness that would once have been impossible. 'Even with this new job of his, he couldn't have afforded two discarded wives. He's just the sort of man who'd think himself almost justified in killing if killing was going to rid him of further persecution.'

'So this girl-friend of his came to the cottage in the afternoon . . .'

'Or was fetched by Angela.'

'I can't see that part, Reg.'

'A neighbour, a woman called Lake, says Angela told her she was going out.' Wexford sipped his drink to cover the slight confusion even the mention of Nancy Lake's name caused in him. 'I have to bear that in mind.'

'Well, maybe. The girl killed Angela by strangling her with a gilt necklace which hasn't been found, then wiped the place clean of her own prints but left one on the side of the bath. Is that the idea?'

'That's the idea. Then she drove Robert Hathall's car to London, where she abandoned it in Wood Green. I may go there tomorrow, but I haven't much hope. The chances are she lives as far from Wood Green as possible.'

'And then you'll go to this toy factory place in – what's it called? – Toxborough? I can't understand why you're leaving it till last. He worked there, after all, from the time of his marriage till last July.'

'And that's the very reason why,' said Wexford. 'It's just possible he knew this woman *before* he met Angela, or met her when his marriage was three years old. But there's no doubt he was deeply in love with Angela – everyone admits that – so is it likely he'd have begun a new relationship during the earliest part of his marriage?'

'No, I see that. Does it have to be someone he'd met at work? Why not a friend he'd met socially or the wife of a friend?'

'Because he doesn't seem to have had any friends, and that's not so difficult to understand. In his first marriage, the way I picture it, he and his wife would have been friendly with other married couples. But you know how it goes, Howard.

In these cases, a married couple's friends are their neighbours or her woman friends and their husbands. Isn't it probable that at the time of the divorce all these people would have rallied round Eileen Hathall? In other words, they'd remain her friends and desert him.'

'This unknown woman could be someone he'd picked up in the street or got talking to by chance in a pub. Have you thought of that?'

'Of course. If it's so, my chances of finding her are thin.'

'Well, Wood Green for you tomorrow. I'm taking the day off myself. I have to speak at a dinner at Brighton in the evening and I thought of taking a leisurely drive down, but maybe I'll come up to darkest Ally Pally with you first.'

The phone ringing cut short Wexford's thanks at this offer. Howard picked up the receiver and his first words, spoken cordially but without much familiarity, told his uncle that the caller was someone he knew socially but not very well. Then the phone was passed to him and he heard Burden's voice.

'Good news first,' said the inspector, 'if you can call it good,' and he told Wexford that at last someone had come forward to say he had seen Hathall's car driven into the drive of Bury Cottage at five past three on the previous Friday afternoon. But he had seen only the driver whom he described as a dark-haired young woman wearing some sort of red checked shirt or blouse. That she had had a passenger he was sure, and almost sure it had been a woman, but he was able to fill in no more details. He had been cycling along Wool Lane in the direction of Wool Farm and had therefore been on the left-hand side of the road, the side which would naturally give him a view of the car's driver but not necessarily of the other occupant. The car had stopped since he had the right of way, and he had assumed, because its right-hand indicator was flashing, that it was about to turn into the cottage drive.

'Why didn't this cyclist guy come forward before?'

'He was on holiday down here, he and his bicycle,' said Burden, 'and he says he never saw a paper till today.'

'Some people,' Wexford growled, 'live like bloody chrysalises. If that's the good news, what's the bad?'

'It may not be bad, I wouldn't know. But the Chief Constable's been in here after you, and he wants to see you at three sharp tomorrow afternoon.'

'That puts paid to our Wood Green visit,' said Wexford thoughtfully to his nephew, and he told him what Burden had said. 'I'll have to go back and try and take in Croydon or Toxborough on my way. I shan't have time for both.'

'Look, Reg, why don't I drive you to Croydon and then to Kingsmarkham via Toxborough? I'd still have three or four hours before I need to be in Brighton.'

'Be a bit of a drag for you, won't it?'

'On the contrary. I don't mind telling you I'm very keen to take a look at this virago, the first Mrs Hathall. You come back with me and Dora can stay on. I know Denise wants her to be here on Friday for some party or other she's going to.'

And Dora, who came in ten minutes later, needed no encouragement to remain in London till the Sunday.

'But will you be all right on your own?'

'I'll be all right. I hope you will. Personally, I should think you'll perish with the cold in this bloody awful air-conditioning.'

'I have my subcutaneous fat, darling, to keep me warm.'

'Unlike you, Uncle Reg,' said Denise who, coming in, had heard the last sentence. 'All yours has melted away quite beautifully. I suppose it really *is* all diet? I was reading in a book the other day that men who have a succession of love affairs keep their figures because a man unconsciously draws in his stomach muscles every time he pays court to a new woman.'

'So now we know what to think,' said Dora.

But Wexford, who had at that moment drawn his in

consciously, wasn't brought to the blush which would have been his reaction the day before. He was wondering what he was to think of his summons by the Chief Constable, and making a disagreeable guess at the answer.

CHAPTER TEN

The house which Robert Hathall had bought at the time of his first marriage was one of those semi-detached villas which sprang up during the thirties in their thousands, in their tens of thousands. It had a bay window in the front living room, a gable over the front bedroom window, and a decorative wooden canopy, of the kind sometimes seen sheltering the platforms of provincial railway stations, over the front door. There were about four hundred others exactly like it in the street, a wide thoroughfare along which traffic streamed to the south.

'This house,' said Howard, 'was built for about six hundred pounds. Hathall would have paid around four thousand for it, I should think. When did he get married?'

'Seventeen years ago.'

'Four thousand would be right. And now it would fetch eighteen.'

'Only he can't sell it,' said Wexford. 'I daresay he could have done with eighteen thousand pounds.' They got out of the car and went up to the front door.

She had none of the outward signs of a virago. She was about forty, short, high-coloured, her stout stocky figure crammed into a tight green dress, and she was one of those women who have been roses and are now cabbages. Ghostly shades of the rose showed in the pretty fat-obscured features, the skin which was still good, and the gingery hair that had once been blonde. She took them into the room with the bay window. Its furnishings lacked the charm of those at Bury Cottage, but it was just as clean. There was something oppressive about its neatness and the absence of any single object not totally conventional. Wexford looked in vain for some article, a hand-embroidered cushion maybe, an original drawing or a growing plant, that might express the personalities of the woman and the girl who lived here. But there was nothing, not a book, not a magazine even, no paraphernalia of a hobby. It was like a Times Furnishing window display before the shop assistant has added those touches that will give it an air of home. Apart from a framed photograph, the only picture was that reproduction of a Spanish gypsy with a black hat on her curls and a rose between her teeth, which Wexford had seen on a hundred lounge-bar walls. And even this stereotyped picture had more life about it than the rest of the room, the gypsy's mouth seeming to curl a little more disdainfully as she surveyed the sterile surroundings in which she was doomed to spend her time.

Although it was mid-morning and Eileen Hathall had been forewarned of their coming, she offered them nothing to drink. Her mother-in-law's ways had either rubbed off on her or else her own lack of hospitality had been one of the traits which so endeared the old woman to her. But that Mrs Hathall senior had been deluded in other respects soon showed. Far from keeping 'herself to herself,' Eileen was ready to be bitterly expansive about her private life.

At first, however, she was subdued. Wexford began by asking her how she had spent the previous Friday, and she replied in a quiet reasonable voice that she had been at her father's in Balham, remaining there till the evening because her daughter had been on a day trip to France, sponsored by her school, from which she hadn't returned until nearly midnight. She gave Wexford her widowed father's address which Howard, who knew London well, remarked was in the next street to where Mrs Hathall senior lived. That did it. Eileen's colour rose and her eyes smouldered with the resentment which was now perhaps the mainspring of her life.

'We grew up together, Bob and me. We went to the same school and there wasn't a day went by we didn't see each other. After we got married we were never apart for a single night till that woman came and stole him from me.'

Wexford, who held to the belief that it is impossible for an outsider to break up a secure and happy marriage, made no comment. He had often wondered too at the attitude of mind that regards people as things and marriage partners as objects which can be stolen like television sets or pearl necklaces.

'When did you last see your former husband, Mrs Hathall?'

'I haven't seen him for three and a half years.'

'But I suppose, although you have custody, he has reasonable access to Rosemary?'

Her face had grown bitter, a canker eating the blown rose. 'He was allowed to see her every other Sunday. I used to send her round to his mum and he'd fetch her from there and take her out for the day.'

'But you didn't see him yourself on these occasions?'

She looked down, perhaps to hide her humiliation. 'He said he wouldn't come if I was going to be there.'

'You said "used," Mrs Hathall. D'you mean this meeting between father and daughter has ceased?'

'Well, she's nearly grown-up, isn't she? She's old enough to have a mind of her own. Me and Bob's mum, we've always got on well, she's been like another mother to me. Rosemary could see the way we thought about it – I mean, she was old enough to understand what I'd suffered from her dad, and it's only natural she was resentful.' The virago was appearing and the tone of voice which Mr Butler had said would always remain in his memory. 'She took against him. She thought it was wicked what he'd done.'

'So she stopped seeing him?'

'She didn't *want* to see him. She said she'd got better things to do with her Sundays, and her gran and me, we thought she was quite right. Only once she went to that cottage place and when she came back she was in an awful state, tears and sobbing and I don't know what. And I don't wonder. Can you imagine a father actually letting his little girl see him kiss another woman? That's what happened. When the time came for him to bring Rosemary back, she saw him put his arms round that woman and kiss her. And it wasn't one of your ordinary kisses. Like what you'd see on the TV, Rosemary said, but I won't go into details, though I was disgusted, I can tell you. The upshot of it was that Rosemary can't stand her dad, and I don't blame her. I just hope it won't do something to her mentality the way these psychological people say it does.'

The red flush on her skin was high now and her eyes flashed. And now, as her bosom rose and she tossed her head, she had something in common with the gypsy on the wall.

'*He* didn't like it. He begged her to see him, wrote her letters and God knows what. Sent her presents and wanted to take her away on holiday. Him as said he hadn't got a penny to bless himself with. Fought tooth and nail he did to try and stop me getting this house and a bit of his money to live on. Oh, he's got money enough when he likes to spend it, money to spend on anyone but me.'

Howard had been looking at that single framed photograph and now he asked if it was of Rosemary.

'Yes, that's my Rosemary.' Still breathless from her outpouring of invective, Eileen spoke in gasps. 'That was taken six months ago.'

The two policemen looked at the portrait of a rather heavy-faced girl who wore a small gold cross hanging against her blouse, whose lank dark hair fell to her shoulders, and who bore a marked resemblance to her paternal grandmother. Wexford, who felt unable to tell an outright lie and say the girl was pretty, asked what she was going to do when she left school. This was a good move, for it had a calming effect on Eileen whose bitterness gave way, though only briefly, to pride.

'Go on to college. All her teachers say she's got it in her and I wouldn't stand in her way. It's not as if she's got to go out and earn money. Bob'll have plenty to spare *now*. I've told her I don't care if she goes on training till she's twenty-five. I'm going to get Bob's mum to ask him to give Rosemary a car for her eighteenth birthday. After all, that's like being twenty-one nowadays, isn't it? My brother's been teaching her to drive and she'll take her test the minute she's seventeen. It's his duty to give her a car. Just because he's ruined my life, that's no reason why he should ruin hers, is it?'

Wexford put out his hand to her as they left. She gave him hers rather reluctantly, but her reluctance was perhaps only part and parcel of that ungraciousness which seemed to be a feature of all the Hathalls and all their connections. Staring down, he held it just long enough to make sure there was no scar on the relevant finger.

'Let us be thankful for our wives,' said Howard devoutly when they were back in the car and driving southwards. 'He didn't kill Angela to go back to that one, at any rate.'

'Did you notice she didn't once mention Angela's death? Not even to say she wasn't sorry she was dead? I've never come across a family so nourished on hatred.' Wexford thought suddenly of his own two daughters who loved him, and on whose education he had spent money freely and happily because they loved him and he loved them. 'It must be bloody awful to have to support someone you hate and buy presents for someone who's been taught to hate you,' he said.

'Indeed it must. And where did the money come from for those presents and that projected holiday, Reg? Not out of fifteen pounds a week.'

By a quarter to twelve they were in Toxborough. Wexford's appointment at Kidd's factory was for half past, so they had a quick lunch in a pub on the outskirts before finding the industrial site. The factory, a large white concrete box, was the source of those children's toys which he had often seen on television commercials and which were marketed under the name of Kidd's Kits for Kids. The manager, a Mr Aveney, told him they had three hundred workers on the payroll, most of them women with part-time jobs. Their white-collar staff was small, consisting of himself, the personnel manager, the part-time accountant, Hathall's successor, his own secretary, two typists and a switchboard girl.

'You want to know what female office staff we had here when Mr Hathall was with us. I gathered that from what you said on the phone and I've done my best to make you a list of names and addresses. But the way they change and change about is ridiculous, Chief Inspector. Girls are crazy to change their jobs every few months these days. There isn't anyone in the office now who was here when Mr Hathall was here, and he's only been gone ten weeks. Not girls, that is. The personnel manager's been with us for five years, but his office is down in the works and I don't think they ever met.'

'Can you remember if he was particularly friendly with any girl?'

'I can remember he wasn't,' said Mr Aveney. 'He was crazy about that wife of his, the one who got herself killed. I never heard a man go on about a woman the way he went on about her. She was Marilyn Monroe and the Shah-ess of Persia and the Virgin Mary all rolled in one as far as he was concerned.'

But Wexford was tired of hearing about Robert Hathall's uxoriousness. He glanced at the list, formidably long, and there were the names, the sort of names they all seemed to have these days, Junes and Janes and Susans and Lindas and Julies. They had all lived in and around Toxborough and not one of them had stayed at Kidd's more than six months. He had a horrible prevision of weeks of work while half a dozen men scoured the Home Counties for this Jane, this Julie, this Susan, and then he put the list in his briefcase.

'Your friend said he'd like to have a look round the works, so if you'd care to, we'll go down and find him.'

They found Howard in the custody of a Julie who was

leading him between benches where women in overalls and with turbans round their heads were peeling the casts from plastic dolls. The factory was airy and pleasant, apart from the smell of cellulose, and from a couple of speakers came the seductive voice of Engelbert Humperdinck imploring his listeners to release him and let him love again.

'A bit of a dead loss that,' said Wexford when they had said good-bye to Mr Aveney. 'I thought it would be. Still, you'll be in plenty of time for your dinner date. It's no more than half an hour from here to Kingsmarkham. And I shall be in time to get myself promptly hauled over the coals. Would you like me to direct you round the back doubles so that we can miss the traffic and I can show you one or two points of interest?'

Howard said he would, so his uncle instructed him how to find the Myringham Road. They went through the centre of the town and past that shopping precinct whose ugliness had so offended Mark Somerset and where he had met the Hathalls on their shopping spree.

'Follow the signs for Pomfret rather than Kingsmarkham, and then I'll direct you into Kingsmarkham via Wool Lane.'

Obediently, Howard followed the signs and within ten minutes they were in country lanes. Here was unspoiled country, the soft Sussex of undulating hills topped with tree rings, of acres of fir forest and little brown-roofed farms nestling in woody hollows. The harvest was in, and where the wheat had been cut the fields were a pale blond, shining like sheets of silver gilt in the sun.

'When I'm out here,' said Howard, 'I feel the truth of what Orwell said about every man knowing in his heart that the loveliest thing to do in the world is to spend a fine day in the country. And when I'm in London I agree with Charles Lamb.'

'D'you mean preferring to see a theatre queue than all the flocks of silly sheep on Epsom Downs?'

Howard laughed and nodded. 'I take it I'm to avoid that turn that says Sewingbury?'

'You want the right turn for Kingsmarkham, coming up in about a mile. It's a little side road and eventually it becomes Wool Lane. I think Angela must have come along here in the car with her passenger last Friday. But where did she come *from?*'

Howard took the turn. They passed Wool Farm and saw the sign Wool Lane, at which the road became a narrow tunnel. If they had met another car, its driver or Howard would have had to pull right up on to the bank to allow the other's passage, but they met no cars. Motorists avoided the narrow perilous lane and few strangers took it for a through road at all.

'Bury Cottage,' Wexford said.

Howard slowed slightly. As he did so, Robert Hathall came round from the side of the house with a pair of garden shears in his hands. He didn't look up, but began chopping the heads off Michaelmas daisies. Wexford wondered if his mother had nagged him into this unaccustomed task.

'That's him,' he said. 'Did you get a look?'

'Enough to identify him again,' said Howard, 'though I don't suppose I shall have to.'

They parted at the police station. The Chief Constable's Rover was already parked on the forecourt. He was early for his appointment but so was Wexford. There was no need to rush up breathless and penitent, so he took his time about it, walking in almost casually to where the carpet and the coals awaited him.

'I can guess what it's about, sir. Hathall's been complaining.'

'That you can guess,' said Charles Griswold, 'only makes it worse.' He frowned and drew himself up to his full height which was a good deal more than Wexford's own six feet. The Chief Constable bore an uncanny likeness to the late General de Gaulle, whose initials he shared, and he must have been aware of it. A chance of nature may account for a physical resemblance to a famous man. Only knowledge of that resemblance, the continual reminders of it from friends and enemies, can account for similarities of the one personality to the other. Griswold was in the habit of speaking of Mid-Sussex, his area, in much the same tones as the dead statesman had spoken of *La France*. 'He's sent me a very strongly worded letter of complaint. Says you've been trying to trap him, using unorthodox methods. Sprang something about a fingerprint on him and then walked out of the house without waiting for his answer. Have you got any grounds for thinking he killed his wife?'

'Not with his own hands, sir. He was in his London office at the time.'

'Then what the hell are you playing at? I am proud of Mid-Sussex. My life's work has been devoted to Mid-Sussex. I was proud of the rectitude of my officers in Mid-Sussex, confident that their conduct might not only be beyond reproach but seen to be beyond reproach.' Griswold sighed heavily. In a moment, Wexford thought, he would be saying, '*L'état, c'est moi*.' 'Why are you harassing this man? Persecuting is what he calls it.'

'Persecuting,' said Wexford, 'is what he always calls it.'

'And that means?'

'He's paranoid, sir.'

'Don't give me that headshrinkers' jargon, Reg. Have you got one single piece of concrete evidence against this chap?'

'No. Only my personal and very strong feeling that he killed his wife.'

'Feeling? Feeling? We hear a damn sight too much about feelings these days and at your age you ought to bloody know better. What d'you mean then, that he had an accomplice? Have you got a *feeling* who this accomplice might be? Have you got any evidence about *him*?'

What could he say but 'No, sir, I haven't'? He added more firmly, 'May I see his letter?'

'No, you mayn't,' Griswold snapped. 'I've told you what's in it. Be thankful I'm sparing you his uncomplimentary remarks about your manners and your tactics. He says you've stolen a book of his.'

'For Christ's sake . . . You don't believe that?'

'Well, no, Reg, I don't. But have it sent back to him and fast. And lay off him pronto, d'you get that?'

'Lay off him?' said Wexford aghast. 'I have to talk to him. There's no other line of investigation I can pursue.'

'I said lay off him. That's an order. I won't have any more of it. I will not have the reputation of Mid-Sussex sacrificed to your *feelings*.'

CHAPTER ELEVEN

It was this which marked the end of Wexford's official investigation into the death of Angela Hathall.

Later, when he looked back, he was aware that three twenty-one on the afternoon of Thursday, October second, was the moment when all hope of solving her murder in a straightforward aboveboard way died. But at the time he didn't know that. He felt only grievance and anger, and he resigned himself to the delays and irritations which must ensue if Hathall couldn't be directly pursued. He still thought ways were open to him of discovering the identity of the woman without arousing fresh annoyance in Hathall. He could delegate. Burden and Martin could make approaches of a more tactful nature. Men could be put on the trail of those girls on Aveney's list. In a roundabout way it could be done. Hathall had betrayed himself, Hathall was guilty – therefore, the crime could ultimately be brought home to Hathall.

But he was disheartened. On his way back to Kingsmarkham he had considered phoning Nancy Lake, taking advantage – to put it into plain words – of Dora's absence, but even an innocent dinner with her, envisaged now, lost the savour the prospect of it had had. He didn't get in touch with her. He didn't phone Howard. He spent the lonely weekend of a grass widower, fulminating to himself about Hathall's good luck and about his own folly in being careless in his handling of an irritable and prickly personality.

Of Men and Angels was sent back, accompanied by a printed card on which Wexford had written a polite note regretting having kept it so long. No response came from Hathall, who must, the chief inspector thought, have been rubbing his hands with glee.

On Monday morning he went back to Kidd's factory at Toxborough.

Mr Aveney seemed pleased to see him – those who cannot be incriminated usually take a virtuous pleasure in their involvement in police enquiries – but he couldn't offer much help. 'Other women Mr Hathall might have met here?' he asked.

'I was thinking about sales reps. After all, it's children's toys you make.'

'The sales reps all work from our London office. There's only one woman among them and he never met her. What about those girls' names I gave you? No luck?'

Wexford shook his head. 'Not so far.'

'You won't. There's nothing there. That only leaves the cleaners. We've got one cleaning woman who's been here since we started up, but she's sixty-two. Of course she has a couple of girls working with her, but they're always changing like the rest of our staff. I suppose I *could* give you another list of names. I never see them and Mr Hathall wouldn't have. They've finished before we come in. The only one I can recall offhand I remember because she was so honest. She stayed behind one morning to hand me a pound note she'd found under someone's desk.'

'Don't bother with the list, Mr Aveney,' said Wexford. 'There's obviously nothing there.'

'You've got Hathall-itis,' said Burden as the second week after Angela's death came to an end.

'Sounds like bad breath.'

'I've never known you so – well, I was going to say pig-headed. You haven't got a scrap of evidence that Hathall so much as took another woman out, let alone conspired with her to do murder.'

'That handprint,' said Wexford obstinately, 'and those long dark hairs and that woman seen with Angela in the car.'

'He *thought* it was a woman. How many times have you and I seen someone across the street and not been able to make up our minds whether it was a boy or a girl. You always say the Adam's apple is the one sure distinguishing mark. Does a cyclist glancing into a car notice if the passenger's got an Adam's apple? We've followed up all the girls on that list, bar the one that's in the United States and the one who was in hospital on the nineteenth. Most of them could hardly remember who Hathall is.'

'What's your idea then? How do you account for that print on the bath?'

'I'll tell you. It was a bloke killed Angela. She was lonely and she picked him up like you said at first. He strangled her – by accident maybe – while he was trying to get the necklace off her. Why should he leave prints? Why should he touch anything in the house – except Angela? If he did, there wouldn't have been many and he could have wiped them off. The woman who left the print, she's not even involved. She was a passerby, a motorist, who called and asked to use the phone . . .'

'And the loo?'

'Why not? These things happen. A similar thing happened in my own home yesterday. My daughter was in on her own and a young fellow who'd walked from Stowerton because he couldn't hitch a lift, came and asked for a drink of water. She let him in – I had something to say about that, as you can imagine – and she let him use the bathroom too. Luckily, he was OK and no harm was done. But why shouldn't something like that have happened at Bury Cottage? The woman hasn't come forward because she doesn't even know the name of the house she called at or the name of the woman who let her in. Her prints aren't on the phone or anywhere else because Angela was still cleaning the place when she called. Isn't that more reasonable than this conspiracy idea that hasn't the slightest foundation?'

Griswold liked the theory. And Wexford found himself in charge of an enquiry based on a postulation he couldn't for a moment believe in. He was obliged to give his support to a nationwide hue and cry aimed at locating an amnesiac female motorist and a thief who killed by chance for a valueless necklace. Neither were found, neither took more definite shape than the vague outlines Burden had invented for them, but Griswold and Burden and the newspapers talked about them as if they existed. And Robert Hathall, Wexford learned at second-hand, had made a series of helpful suggestions as to one fresh lead after another. The Chief Constable couldn't understand – so the grass roots had it – what had given rise to the idea that the man suffered from a persecution complex or was bad-tempered. Nothing could have been more cooperative than his attitude once Wexford was removed from direct contact with him.

Wexford thought he would soon grow sick of the whole thing. The weeks dragged on and there were no new developments. At first it is maddening to have one's certain knowledge discounted and derided. Then, as fresh interests and fresh work enter, it becomes merely annoying; lastly, a bore. Wexford would have been very happy to have regarded Robert Hathall as a bore. After all, no one solves every murder case. Dozens have always, and always will have, eluded solution. Right should, of course, be done and justice hold sway, but the human element makes this impossible. Some must get away and Hathall was evidently going to be one of them. He ought by now to have been relegated to the ranks of the bores, for he wasn't an interesting man but essentially an irritating humourless bore. Yet Wexford couldn't think of him as such. In himself, he might be tedious but what he had done was not. Wexford wanted to know why he had done it and how and with what help and by what means. And above all he felt a righteous indignation that a man might kill his wife and bring his mother to find her body and yet be regarded by the powers-that-be as *cooperative*.

He mustn't let this thing develop into an obsession. He

reminded himself that he was a reasonable, level-headed man, a policeman with a job to do, not an executioner impelled to the hunt by some political mission or holy cause. Perhaps it was those months of starving himself that had robbed him of his steadiness, his equanimity. But only a fool would gain a good figure at the price of an unbalanced mind. Reminding himself of this excellent maxim, he kept cool when Burden told him Hathall was about to give up his tenancy of Bury Cottage, and replied with sarcasm rather than explosively.

'I suppose I'm to be allowed to know where he's going?'

Burden had been considered by Griswold as having a nice line in tact and had therefore, throughout the autumn, been the link with Hathall. The Mid-Sussex envoy was what Wexford called him, adding that he imagined 'our man' in Wool Lane would be in possession of such top-level secrets.

'He's staying with his mother in Balham for the time being and he talks of getting a flat in Hampstead.'

'The vendor will cheat him,' said Wexford bitterly, 'the train service will be appalling. He'll be made to pay an extortionate rent for his garage and someone's going to put up a tower block that'll spoil his view of the Heath. All in all, he'll be very happy.'

'I don't know why you make him out such a masochist.'

'I make him out a murderer.'

'Hathall didn't murder his wife,' said Burden. 'He's just got an unfortunate manner that got in your hair.'

'An unfortunate manner! Why not be blunt about it and say he has fits? He's allergic to fingerprints. Mention you've found one on his bath and he has an epileptic seizure.'

'You'd hardly call that evidence, would you?' said Burden rather coldly, and he put on his glasses for no better reason, Wexford thought than to peer censoriously through them at his superior officer.

But the idea of Hathall's departing and beginning the new life he had planned for himself and done murder to achieve was a disturbing one. That it had been allowed to happen was almost entirely due to his own mishandling of the investigation. He had spoiled things by being tough with and rude to the kind of man who would never respond to such treatment. And now there was nothing more he could do because Hathall's person was sacrosanct and every clue to the unknown woman's identity locked up in his sacrosanct mind. Was there any point in learning Hathall's new address? If he wasn't permitted to talk to him in Kingsmarkham, what hope had he of breaching his London privacy? For a long time personal pride stopped him asking Burden for news of Hathall, and Burden offered none until one day in spring, when they were lunching together at the Carousel. The inspector dropped Hathall's new address casually into their conversation, prefacing his remark with a 'by the by,' as if he were speaking of some slight acquaintance of theirs, a man in whom neither could have more than a passing interest.

'So now he tells me,' said Wexford to the tomato-shaped sauce bottle.

'There doesn't seem to be any reason why you shouldn't know.'

'Got it okayed by the Home Secretary first, did you?'

Having the address didn't really help matters and its location meant very little to Wexford. He was prepared to drop the subject there and then, knowing as he did that discussing Hathall with Burden only made them both feel awkward. Strangely enough, it was Burden who pursued it. Perhaps he hadn't cared for that crack about the Home Secretary or, more likely, disliked the idea of the significance that might attach to his announcement if he left it islanded.

'I've always thought,' he said, 'though I haven't said so before, that there was one major drawback to your theory. If Hathall had had an accomplice with that scar on her finger, he'd have insisted she wear gloves. Because if she left only one print, he'd never be able to live with her or marry her or even seen her again. And you say he killed Angela in order to do that. So he can't have. It's simple when you think about it.'

Wexford didn't say anything. He betrayed no excitement. But that night when he got home he studied his map of London, made a phone call and spent some time poring over his latest bank statement.

The Fortunes had come to stay for the weekend. Uncle and nephew walked down Wool Lane and paused outside the cottage which hadn't yet been re-let. The 'miracle' tree was laden with white blossom, and behind the house young lambs were pastured on the hillside whose peak was crowned by a ring of trees.

'Hathall doesn't prefer the flocks of silly sheep either,' said Wexford, recalling a conversation they had had near this spot. 'He's taken himself as far from Epsom Downs as can be, yet he's a South Londoner. West Hampstead is where he's living. Dartmeet Avenue. D'you know it?'

'I know where it is. Between the Finchley Road and West End Lane. Why did he pick Hampstead?'

'Just because it's as far as possible from South London where his mother and his ex-wife and his daughter are.' Wexford pulled down a branch of plum blossom to his face and smelled its faint honey scent. 'Or that's what I *think*.' The branch sprang back, scattering petals on the grass. Musingly, he said, 'He appears to lead a celibate life. The only woman he's been seen with is his mother.'

Howard seemed intrigued. 'You mean you have a – a watcher?'

'He's not much of a spy,' Wexford admitted, 'but he was the best and safest I could find. As a matter of fact, he's the brother of an old customer of mine, a chap called Monkey Matthews. The brother's name is Ginge, so-called on account of his hair. He lives in Kilburn.'

437

Howard laughed, but sympathetically. 'What does this Ginge do? Tail him?'

'Not exactly. But he keeps an eye. I give him a remuneration. Out of my own pocket, naturally.'

'I didn't realize you were that serious.'

'I don't know when I was ever so serious about a thing like this in my whole career.'

They turned away. A little wind had sprung up and it was growing chilly. Howard gave a backward glance at the hedge tunnel which was already greening and thickening, and said quietly, 'What is it you hope for, Reg?'

His uncle didn't reply at once. They had passed the isolated villa where Nancy Lake's car stood on the garage drive, before he spoke. He had been deep in thought, so silent and preoccupied that Howard had perhaps thought he had forgotten the question or had no answer to it. But now as they came to the Stowerton Road, he said, 'For a long time I wondered why Hathall was so horrified – and that's an understatement – when I told him about the print. Because he didn't want the woman discovered, of course. But it wasn't just fear he showed. It was something more like a terrible sorrow he showed – when he'd recovered a bit, that is. And I came to the conclusion that his reaction was what it was because he'd had Angela killed expressly so that he could be with that woman. And now he knew he'd never dare see her again.

'And then he reflected. He wrote that letter of protest to Griswold to clear the field of me because he knew I knew. But it might still be possible for him to get away with it and have what he wanted, a life with that woman. Not as he'd planned it. Not a flit to London, then after a few weeks a friendship with a girl, the lonely widower seeking consolation with a new woman friend whom, as time went by, he could marry. Not that – now. Even though he'd pulled the wool over Griswold's eyes, he wouldn't dare try that one on. The handprint had been found and however much we might seem to be ignoring him, he couldn't hope to go in for a public courtship and then marriage with a woman whose hand would betray her. Betray her to anyone, Howard, not just to an expert.'

'So what can he do?'

'He has two alternatives,' said Wexford crisply. 'He and the woman may have agreed to part. Presumably, even if one is madly in love, liberty is preferable to the indulgence of love. Yes, they could have parted.'

' "Shake hands forever, cancel all our vows?" '

'The next bit is even more appropriate.

> "And if we meet at any time again,
> Be it not seen in either of our brows
> That we one jot of former love retain."

'Or,' Wexford went on, 'they could have decided – let's say grandiloquently that their passion decided for them, love was bigger than both of them – to have gone on meeting clandestinely. Not to live together, never to meet in public, but to carry on as if each of them had a jealous suspicious spouse.'

'What, go on like that indefinitely?'

'Maybe. Until it wears itself out or until they find some other solution. But I think that's what they're doing, Howard. If it isn't so, why has he picked Northwest London where no one knows him as a place to live? Why not south of the river where his mother is and his daughter? Or somewhere near his work. He's earning a good salary now. He could just as well have got himself a place in Central London. He's hidden himself away so that he can sneak out in the evenings to be with *her*.

'I'm going to try and find her,' Wexford said thoughtfully. 'It'll cost me some money and take up my spare time, but I mean to have a go.'

CHAPTER TWELVE

In describing Ginge Matthews as not much of a spy, Wexford had rather underrated him. The miserable resources at his disposal made him bitter. He was perpetually irritated by Ginge's unwillingness to use the phone. Ginge was proud of his literary style which was culled from the witness-box manner of thick-headed and very junior police constables whose periphrasis he had overheard from the dock. In Ginge's reports his quarry never went anywhere, but always proceeded; his home was his domicile and, rather than going home, he withdrew or retired there. But in honesty and in fairness to Ginge, Wexford had to admit that, although he had learned nothing of the elusive woman during these past months, he had learned a good deal about Hathall's manner of life.

According to Ginge, the house where he had his flat was a big three-storeyed place and – reading between the lines – of Edwardian vintage. Hathall had no garage but left his car parked in the street. From meanness or the impossibility of finding a garage to rent? Wexford didn't know and Ginge couldn't tell him. Hathall left for work at nine in the morning and either walked or caught a bus from West End Green to West Hampstead Tube station where he took the Bakerloo Line train to (presumably) Piccadilly. He reached home again soon after six, and on several occasions Ginge, lurking in a phone box opposite number 62 Dartmeet Avenue, had seen him go out again in his car. Ginge always knew when he was at home in the evenings because then a light showed in the second floor bay window. He had never seen him accompanied by anyone except his mother – from his description it could only be old Mrs Hathall – whom he had brought to his flat by car one Saturday afternoon. Mother and son had had words, a harsh low-voiced quarrel on the pavement before they even got to the front door.

Ginge had no car. He had no job either, but the small amount of money Wexford could afford to give him didn't make it worth his while to spend more than one evening and perhaps one Saturday or Sunday afternoon a week watching Robert Hathall. It could easily have happened that Hathall brought his girl home on one or two of the other six evenings. And yet Wexford clung to hope. One day, sometime . . . He dreamed at night of Hathall, not very often, possibly once a fortnight, and in these dreams he saw him with the dark-haired girl with the scarred finger, or else alone as he had been when he had stood by the fireplace in Bury Cottage, paralyzed with fear and realization and – yes, with grief.

'On the afternoon of Saturday, June 15th inst., at 3.5 p.m., the party was seen to proceed from his domicile at 62 Dartmeet Avenue to West End Lane where he made purchases at a supermarket . . .' Wexford cursed. They were nearly all like that. And what proof had he that Ginge had even been there 'on the afternoon of Saturday, June 15th inst.'? Naturally, Ginge would say he had been there when there was a quid in it for every tailing session. July came and August, and Hathall, if Ginge was to be trusted, led a simple regular life, going to work, coming home, shopping on Saturdays, sometimes taking an evening drive. If Ginge could be trusted . . .

That he could be, up to a point, was proved in September just before the anniversary of Angela's death. 'There is reason to believe,' wrote Ginge, 'that the party had disposed of his motor vehicle, it having disappeared from its customary parking places. On the evening of Thursday, September 10th inst., having arrived home from his place of business at 6.10 p.m., he proceeded at 6.50 from his domicile and boarded the number 28 bus at West End Green NW6.'

Was there anything in it? Wexford didn't think so. On his salary Hathall could easily afford to run a car, but he might have got rid of it only because of the increasing difficulty of on-street parking. Still, it was a good thing from his point of view. Hathall could now be followed.

Wexford never wrote to Ginge. It was too risky. The little red-headed spy might not be above blackmail, and if any letters should fall into the hands of Griswold. . . . He sent his wages in notes in a plain envelope, and when he had to talk to him, which, on account of the paucity of news, happened rarely, he could always get him between twelve and one at a Kilburn public house called the Countess of Castlemaine.

'Follow him?' said Ginge nervously. 'What, on that bleeding 28?'

'I don't see why not. He's never seen you, has he?'

'Maybe he has. How should I know? It's not easy following a bloke on a bleeding bus.' Ginge's conversational manner was markedly different from his literary style, particularly as to his use of adjectives. 'If he goes up top, say, and I go inside, or vicey-versy . . .'

'Why does there have to be any vicey-versy?' said Wexford. 'You sit in the seat behind him and stick close. Right?'

Ginge didn't seem to think it was right at all, but he agreed rather dubiously to try it. Whether or not he had tried it, Wexford wasn't told, for Ginge's next report made no reference to buses. Yet the more he studied it with its magistrates' court circumlocutions, the more interested he was by it. 'Being in the neighborhood of Dartmeet Avenue NW6, at 3 p.m. on the 26th inst., I took it upon myself to investigate the party's place of domicile. During a conversation with the landlord, during which I represented myself as an official of the local rating authority, I enquired as to the number of apartments and was informed that only single rooms were to let in the establishment . . .'

Rather enterprising of Ginge, was Wexford's first thought, though he had probably only assumed this role to impress his employer and hope he would forget all about the more dangerous exercise of tailing Hathall on a bus. But that wasn't important. What astonished the chief inspector was that Hathall was a tenant rather than an owner-occupier and, moreover, the tenant of a room rather than a flat. Strange, very strange. He could have afforded to buy a flat on a mortgage. Why hadn't he? Because he didn't intend to be permanently domiciled (as Ginge would put it) in London? Or because he had other uses for his income? Both maybe. But Wexford seized upon this as the most peculiar circumstance he had yet discovered in Hathall's present life. Even with rents in London as extortionate as they were, he could hardly be paying more than fifteen pounds a week at the most for a room, yet, after deductions, he must be drawing sixty. Wexford had no confidant but Howard, and it was to Howard, on the phone, that he talked about it.

'You're thinking he could be supporting someone else?'

'I am,' said Wexford.

'Say fifteen a week for himself and fifteen for her on accommodation . . .? And if she's not working he has to keep her as well.'

'Christ, you don't know how good it is for me to hear someone talk about her as a real person, as "she." You believe she exists, don't you?'

'It wasn't a ghost made that print, Reg. It wasn't ectoplasm. She exists.'

In Kingsmarkham they had given up. They had stopped searching. Griswold had told the newspapers some rubbish – in Wexford's phrase – about the case not being closed, but it *was* closed. His statement was only face-saving. Mark Somerset had let Bury Cottage to a couple of young Americans, teachers of political economy at the University of the South. The front garden was tidied up and they talked of having the back garden landscaped at their own expense. One day the plums hung heavily on the tree, the next it was stripped. Wexford never found out if Nancy Lake had had them and made them into 'miracle' jam, for he had never seen Nancy since the day he was told to lay off Hathall.

Nothing came from Ginge for a fortnight. At last Wexford phoned him at the Countess of Castlemaine to be told that on his watching evenings Hathall had remained at home. He would, however, watch again that night and on the Saturday afternoon. On Monday his report came. Hathall had done his usual shopping on Saturday, but on the previous evening had walked down to the bus stop at West End Green at seven o'clock. Ginge had followed him, but being intimidated ('made cautious' was his expression) by Hathall's suspicious backward glances, hadn't pursued him on to the 28 bus which his quarry had caught at ten past seven. Wexford hurled the sheet of paper into the wastepaper basket. That was all he needed, for Hathall to get wise to Ginge.

Another week went by. Wexford was on the point of throwing Ginge's next communication away unopened. He felt he couldn't face another account of Hathall's Saturday shopping activities. But he did open the letter. And there, of course, was the usual nonsense about the supermarket visit. There too, appended casually as if it were of no importance, a throwaway line to fill up, was a note that after his shopping Hathall had called at a travel agency.

'The place he went to is called Sudamerica Tours, Howard. Ginge didn't dare follow him in, lily-livered idiot that he is.'

Howard's voice sounded thin and dry. 'You're thinking what I'm thinking.'

'Of course. Some place where we've no extradition treaty. He's been reading about train robbers and that gave him the idea. Bloody newspapers do more harm than good.'

'But, my God, Reg, he must be dead scared if he's prepared to throw up his job and flit to Brazil or somewhere. What's he going to do there? How will he live?'

'As birds do, nephew. God knows. Look, Howard, could

you do something for me? Could you get on to Marcus Flower and try and find out if they're sending him abroad? I daren't.'

'Well, I dare,' said Howard. 'But if they were, wouldn't they be arranging the whole thing and paying for it?'

'They wouldn't pay and arrange for his girl, would they?'

'I'll do my best and call you back this evening.'

Was that why Hathall had been living so economically? In order to save up his accomplice's fare? He would have to have a job there waiting for him, Wexford thought, or else be very desperate to get to safety. In that case, the money for two air fares would have to be found. In the *Kingsmarkham Courier*, which had been placed on his desk that morning, he remembered seeing an advertisement for trips to Rio de Janeiro. He fished it out from under a pile of papers and looked at the back page. There it was, the return fare priced at just under two hundred and fifty pounds. Add a bit more for two single fares, and Hathall's saving could be accounted for ...

He was about to discard the newspaper when a name in the deaths column caught his eye. Somerset. 'On October 15th, at Church House, Old Myringham, Gwendolen Mary Somerset, beloved wife of Mark Somerset. Funeral St. Luke's Church October 22nd. No flowers, please, but donations to Stowerton Home for Incurables.' So the demanding and querulous wife had died at last. The *beloved* wife? Perhaps she had been, or perhaps this was the usual hypocrisy, so stale, hackneyed and automatic a formula as to be hardly hypocrisy any more. Wexford smiled drily and then forgot about it. He went home early – the town was quiet and crimeless – and waited for Howard's telephone call.

The phone rang at seven, but it was his younger daughter, Sheila. She and her mother chatted for about twenty minutes, and after that the phone didn't ring again. Wexford waited till about half past ten and then he dialled Howard's number.

'He's bloody well out,' he said crossly to his wife. 'I call that the limit.'

'Why shouldn't he go out in the evening? I'm sure he works hard enough.'

'Don't I work? I don't go gallivanting about in the evenings when I've promised to phone people.'

'No, and if you did perhaps your blood pressure wouldn't rage the way it's doing at this moment,' said Dora.

At eleven he tried to get Howard again, but again there was no reply and he went off to bed in a peevish frame of mind. It wasn't surprising that he had another of those obsessive Hathall dreams. He was at an airport. The great jet aircraft was ready to take off and the doors had been closed, but they opened again as he watched and there appeared at the head of the steps, like a royal couple waving graciously to the well-wishing crowd, Hathall and a woman. The woman raised her right hand in a gesture of farewell and he saw the L-shaped scar burning red, an angry cicatrice – L for love, for loss, for leave-taking. But before he could rush up the steps as he had begun to do, the stairs themselves melted away, the couple retreated, and the aircraft sailed up, up into the ice-blue winter sky.

Why is it that as you get older you tend to wake up at five and are unable to get off to sleep again? Something to do with the blood sugar level being low? Or the coming of dawn exerting an atavistic pull? Wexford knew further sleep would elude him, so he got up at half past six and made his own breakfast. He didn't like the idea of phoning Howard before eight, and by a quarter to he was so fidgety and restless that he took a cup of tea in to Dora and went off to work. By now, of course, Howard would have left for Kenbourne Vale. He began to feel bitterly injured, and those old feelings he used to have about Howard reasserted themselves. True, he had listened sympathetically to all his uncle's ramblings about this case, but what was he really thinking? That this was an elderly man's fantasy? Country bumpkin rubbish? It seemed likely that he had only played along to humour him and had deferred that call to Marcus Flower until he could spare the time from his more important metropolitan business. He probably hadn't made it yet. Still, it was no use getting paranoid in Hathall style. He must humble himself, phone Kenbourne Vale and ask again.

This he did at nine-thirty. Howard hadn't yet come in, and he found himself involved in a gossipy chat with Sergeant Clements, an old friend from days when they had worked together on the Kenbourne Vale cemetery murder. Wexford was too kind a man to cut the sergeant short after he had discovered that Howard was delayed at some top-level conference, and resigned himself to hearing all about Clements' adopted son, prospective adopted daughter, and new maisonette. A message would be left for the chief superintendent, Clements said at last, but he wasn't expected in till twelve.

The call finally came at ten past.

'I tried to get you at home before I left,' said Howard, 'but Dora said you'd gone. I haven't had a moment since, Reg.'

There was a note of barely suppressed excitement in his nephew's voice. Maybe he'd been promoted again, Wexford thought, and he said not very warmly, 'You did say you'd phone last night.'

'So I did. At seven. But your line was engaged. I couldn't after that. Denise and I went to the pictures.'

It was the tone of amusement – no, of glee – that did it. Forgetting all about rank, Wexford exploded. 'Charming,' he snapped. 'I hope the people in the row behind you chattered the whole way through and the people in front had it off on the seats and the people in the circle dropped orange peel on you. What about my chap? What about my South America thing?'

'Oh, that,' said Howard, and Wexford could have sworn he heard a yawn. 'He's leaving Marcus Flower, he's resigned. I couldn't get any more.'

'Thanks a lot. And that's all?'

Howard was laughing now. 'Oh, Reg,' he said, 'it's wicked to keep you in suspense, but you were so ripe for it. You're such an irascible old devil, I couldn't resist.' He controlled his laughter and suddenly his voice became solemn, measured. 'That is by no means all,' he said. 'I've seen him.'

'You *what?* D'you mean you've talked to Hathall?'

'No, I've *seen* him. Not alone. With a woman. I've seen him with a woman, Reg.'

'Oh, my God,' said Wexford softly. 'The Lord hath delivered him into mine hands.'

CHAPTER THIRTEEN

'I wouldn't be so sure of that,' said Howard. 'Not yet. But I'll tell you about it, shall I? Funny, isn't it, the way I said I didn't suppose I'd ever have to identify him? But I did identify him last night. Listen, and I'll tell you how it was.'

On the previous evening, Howard had attempted to call his uncle at seven but the line had been engaged. Since he had nothing but negative news for him, he decided to try again in the morning as he was pressed for time. He and Denise were to dine in the West End before going on to the nine o'clock showing of a film at the Curzon Cinema, and Howard had parked his car near the junction of Curzon Street and Half Moon Street. Having a few minutes to spare, he had been drawn by curiosity to have a look at the exterior of the offices he had phoned during the day, and he and Denise were approaching the Marcus Flower building when he saw a man and a woman coming towards it from the opposite direction. The man was Robert Hathall.

At the plate-glass window they paused and looked inside, surveying velvet drapery and wall-to-wall Wilton and marble staircase. Hathall seemed to be pointing out to his companion the glossy splendours of the place where he worked. The woman was of medium height, good-looking but not startlingly so, with very short blonde hair. Howard thought she was in her late twenties or early thirties.

'Could the hair have been a wig?' Wexford asked.

'No, but it could have been dyed. Naturally, I didn't see her hand. They were talking to each other in what I thought was an affectionate way and after a bit they walked off down towards Piccadilly. And, incidentally, I didn't enjoy the picture. Under the circumstances, I couldn't concentrate.'

'They haven't shaken hands forever, Howard. They haven't cancelled all their vows. It's as I thought, and now it can only be a matter of time before we find her.'

The following day was his day of rest, his day off. The ten-thirty train from Kingsmarkham got him to Victoria just before half past eleven and by noon he was in Kilburn. What quirk of romantic imagination had prompted the naming of this squalid Victorian public house after Charles the Second's principal mistress, Wexford couldn't fathom. It stood in a turning off the Edgware Road and it had the air of a gone-to-seed nineteenth-century gin palace. Ginge Matthews was sitting on a stool at the bar in earnest and apparently aggrieved conversation with the Irish barman. When he saw Wexford his eyes widened – or, rather, one eye widened. The other was half-closed and sunk in purple swelling.

'Take your drink over to the corner,' said Wexford. 'I'll join you in a minute. May I have a glass of dry wine, please?'

Ginge didn't look like his brother or talk like him and he certainly didn't smoke like him, but nevertheless they had something in common apart from their partiality for petty crime. Perhaps one of their parents had been possessed of a dynamic personality, or there might even have been something exceptionally vital in their genes. Whatever it was, it made Wexford say that the Matthews brothers were just like other people only more so. Both were inclined to do things to excess. Monkey smoked sixty king-sized cigarettes a day. Ginge didn't smoke at all but drank, when he could afford it, a concoction of pernod and Guinness.

Ginge hadn't spoken to Monkey for fifteen years and Monkey hadn't spoken to him. They had fallen out as the result of the bungling mess they had made of an attempt to break into a Kingsmarkham furrier's. Ginge had gone to prison and Monkey had not – most unfairly, as Ginge had reasonably thought – and when he came out, the younger brother had taken himself off to London where he had married a widow who owned her own house and a bit of money. Ginge had soon spent the money and she, perhaps in revenge, had presented him with five children. He didn't, therefore, enquire after his brother whom he blamed for many of his misfortunes, but remarked bitterly to Wexford when he joined him at a corner table:

'See my eye?'

'Of course I see it. What the hell have you done to yourself? Walked into your wife's fist?'

'Very funny. I'll tell you who done it. That bleeding Hathall. Last night when I was following him down to the 28 stop.'

'For Christ's sake!' said Wexford, aghast. 'You mean he's on to you?'

'Thanks for the sympathy.' Ginge's small round face flushed nearly as red as his hair. 'Course he was bound to spot me sooner or later on account of my bleeding hair. He hadn't got no cause to turn round and poke me in the bleeding eye, though, had he?'

'Is that what he did?'

'I'm telling you. Cut me, he did. The wife said I looked like Henry Cooper. It wasn't so bleeding funny, I can tell you.'

Wearily, Wexford said, 'Could you stop the bleeding?'

'It stopped in time, naturally, it did. But it isn't healed up yet and you can see the bleeding...'

'Oh, *God*. I mean stop saying "bleeding" every other word. It's putting me off my drink. Look, Ginge, I'm sorry about your eye, but there's no great harm done. Obviously, you'll have to be a damn sight more careful. For instance, you could try wearing a hat...'

'I'm not going back there again, Mr Wexford.'

'Never mind that now. Let me buy you another of those what-d'you-call-'ems. What *do* you call them?'

'You ask for a half of draught Guinness with a double pernod in.' Ginge added proudly and more cheerfully, 'I don't know what *they* call 'em but I call 'em Demon Kings.'

451

The stuff smelled dreadful. Wexford fetched himself another glass of white wine and Ginge said, 'You won't get very
fat on that.'

'That's the idea. Now tell me where this 28 bus goes.'

Ginge took a swig of his Demon King and said with
extreme rapidity, 'Golders Green, Child's Hill, Fortune Green,
West End Lane, West Hampshire Station, Quex Road, Kilburn High Road . . .'

'For God's sake! I don't know any of these places, they
don't mean a thing to me. Where does it end up?'

'Wandsworth Bridge.'

Disappointed at this disclosure yet pleased for once to be
at an advantage in the face of so much sophisticated knowledge, Wexford said, 'He's only going to see his mother in
Balham. That's near Balham.'

'Not where that bus goes isn't. Look, Mr Wexford,' said
Ginge with patient indulgence, 'you don't know London, you've
said so yourself. I've lived here fifteen years and I can tell you
nobody as wasn't out of his bleeding twist would go to Balham
that way. He'd go to West Hampstead Tube and change on
to the Northern at Waterloo or the Elephant. Stands to reason
he would.'

'Then he's dropping off somewhere along the route. Ginge,
will you do one more thing for me? Is there a pub near this
bus stop where you've seen him catch the 28?'

'Oppo-sight,' said Ginge warily.

'We'll give him a week. If he doesn't complain about you
during the next week – Oh, all right, I know you think you're
the one with grounds for complaint – but if he doesn't we'll
know he either thinks you're a potential mugger . . .'

'Thanks very much.'

'. . . and doesn't connect you with me,' Wexford went on,
ignoring the interruption, 'or else he's too scared at this stage
to draw attention to himself. But, beginning next Monday, I
want you to station yourself in that pub by six-thirty every

night for a week. Just note how often he catches that bus. Will you do that? I don't want you to follow him and you won't be running any risk.'

'That's what you lot always say,' said Ginge. 'You want to remember he's already done some poor bleeder in. Who's going to see after my bleeding wife and kids if he gets throttling me with his bleeding gold chains?'

'The same as look after them now,' said Wexford silkily. 'The Social Security.'

'What a nasty tongue you've got.' For once Ginge sounded exactly like his brother, and briefly he looked like him as a greedy gleam appeared in his good eye. 'What's in it for me if I do?'

'A pound a day,' said Wexford, 'and as many of those – er, bleeding Demon Kings as you can get down you.'

Wexford waited anxiously for another summons from the Chief Constable, but none came, and by the end of the week he knew that Hathall wasn't going to complain. That, as he had told Ginge, didn't necessarily mean any more than that Hathall thought the man who was following him intended to attack him and had taken the law into his own hands. What was certain, though, was that whatever came out of Ginge's pub observations, he couldn't use the little red-headed man again. And it wasn't going to be much use finding out how often Hathall caught that bus if he could set no one to catch it with him.

Things were very quiet in Kingsmarkham. Nobody would object if he were to take the fortnight's holiday that was owing to him. People who take their summer holidays in November are always popular with colleagues. It all depended on Ginge. If it turned out that Hathall caught that bus regularly, why shouldn't he take his holiday and try to follow that bus by car? It would be difficult in the London traffic, which always intimidated him, but not all that difficult out of the rush hours. And ten to one, a hundred to one, Hathall wouldn't spot him.

Nobody on a bus looks at people in cars. Nobody on a bus can *see* the driver of a pursuing car. If only he knew when Hathall was leaving Marcus Flower and when he meant to leave the country . . .

But all this was driven out of his head by an event he couldn't have anticipated. He had been certain the weapon would never be found, that it was at the bottom of the Thames or tossed on to some local authority rubbish dump. When a young teacher of political science phoned him to say that a necklace had been found by the men excavating the garden of Bury Cottage and that her landlord, Mr Somerset, had advised her to inform the police, his first thought was that now he could overcome Griswold's scruples, now he could confront Hathall. He had himself driven down Wool Lane – observing on the way the For Sale board outside Nancy Lake's house – and then he walked into the wasteland, the area of open-cast mining, which had been Hathall's back garden. A load of Westmorland stone made a mountain range in one corner and a mechanical digger stood by the garage. Would Griswold say he should have had this garden dug over? When you're searching for a weapon, you don't dig up a garden that looks just like a bit of field without an exposed, freshly dug bit of earth in the whole of it. There hadn't been even a miniscule break in the long rank grass last September twelve-month. They had raked over every inch of it. How then had Hathall or his accomplice managed to bury the necklace and restore earth and grass without its being detected?

The teacher, Mrs Snyder, told him.

'There was a kind of cavity under here. A septic pit, would you call it? I guess Mr Somerset said something about a pit.'

'A cesspit or septic tank,' said Wexford. 'The main drainage came through to this part of Kingsmarkham about twenty years ago, but before that there'd have been a cesspit.'

'For heaven's sake! Why didn't they have it taken out?' said Mrs Snyder with the wonderment of a native of a richer and more hygiene-conscious country. 'Well, this necklace was in it, whatever it's called. That thing . . .' She pointed to the digger, '. . . smashed it open. Or so the workmen said. I didn't look personally. I don't want to seem to criticize your country, Captain, but a thing like that! A cess tank!'

Extremely amused by his new title which made him feel like a naval officer, Wexford said he quite understood that primitive methods of sewage disposal weren't pleasant to contemplate, and where was the necklace?

'I washed it and put it in the kitchen closet. I washed it in antiseptic.'

That hardly mattered now. It wouldn't, after its long immersion, bear prints, if it had ever done so. But the appearance of the necklace surprised him. It wasn't, as had been believed, composed of links, but was a solid collar of grey metal from which almost all the gilding had disappeared, and it was in the shape of a snake twisted into a circle, the snake's head passing, when the necklace was fastened, through a slot above its tail. Now he could see the answer to something that had long puzzled him. This was no chain that might snap when strained but a perfect strangler's weapon. All Hathall's accomplice had had to do was stand behind her victim, grasp the snake's head and pull . . .

But how could it have got into the disused cesspit? The metal cover, for use when the pit was emptied, had been buried under a layer of earth and so overgrown with grass that Wexford's men hadn't even guessed it might be there. He phoned Mark Somerset.

'I think I can tell you how it got there,' said Somerset. 'When the main drainage came through, my father, for the sake of economy, only had what's called the "black water" linked on to it. The "grey water" – that is, the waste from the bath, the hand basin and the kitchen sink – went on passing into the cesspit. Bury Cottage is on a bit of a slope, so he knew it wouldn't flood but would just soak away.'

'D'you mean someone could have simply dropped the thing down the sink plughole?'

'I don't see why not. If "someone" ran the taps hard, it'd get washed down.'

'Thank you, Mr Somerset. That's very helpful. By the way, I'd like to – er, express my sympathy for you in the loss of your wife.'

Was it his imagination, or did Somerset sound for the first time ill-at-ease? 'Well, yes, thanks,' he muttered and he rang off abruptly.

When he had had the necklace examined by laboratory experts, he asked for an appointment with the Chief Constable. This was granted for the following Friday afternoon and by two o'clock on that day he was in Griswold's own house, a tarted-up, unfarm-like farmhouse in a village called Millerton between Myringham and Sewingbury. It was known as High-trees Farm but Wexford privately called it Millerton-*Les-Deux-Églises*.

'What makes you think this is the weapon?' were Griswold's opening words.

'I feel it's the only type of necklace which could have been used, sir. A chain would have snapped. The lab boys say the gilt which remains on it is similar to the specimens of gilding taken from Angela Hathall's neck. Of course they can't be sure.'

'But I suppose they've got a "feeling"? Have you got any reason to believe that necklace hadn't been there for twenty years?'

Wexford knew better than to mention his feelings again. 'No, but I might have if I could talk to Hathall.'

'He wasn't there when she was killed,' said Griswold, his mouth turning down and his eyes growing hard.

'His girl-friend was.'

'Where? When? I am supposed to be the Chief Constable of Mid-Sussex where this murder was committed. Why am I not told if the identity of some female accomplice has been discovered?'

'I haven't exactly . . .'

'Reg,' said Griswold in a voice that had begun to tremble with anger, 'have you got any more evidence of Robert Hathall's complicity in this than you had fourteen months ago? Have you got one concrete piece of evidence? I asked you that before and I'm asking you again. *Have you?*'

Wexford hesitated. He couldn't reveal that he had had Hathall followed, still less that Chief Superintendent Howard Fortune, his own nephew, had seen him with a woman. What evidence of homicide lay in Hathall's economy or the sale of his car? What guilt was evinced by the man's living in North-west London or his having been seen to catch a London bus? There was the South American thing, of course . . . Grimly, Wexford faced just what that amounted to. Nothing. As far as he could prove, Hathall had been offered no job in South America, hadn't even bought a brochure about South America, let alone an air ticket. He had merely been seen to go into a travel agency, and seen by a man with a criminal record.

'No, sir.'

'Then the situation is unchanged. Totally unchanged. Remember that.'

CHAPTER FOURTEEN

Ginge had done as he was told, and on Friday, 8 November, a report arrived from him stating that he had been at his observation post in the pub each evening and on two of those evenings, the Monday and the Wednesday, Hathall had appeared at West End Green just before seven and had caught the 28 bus. That, at any rate, was something. There should have been another report on the Monday. Instead, the unheard-of happened and Ginge phoned. He was phoning from a call-box and he had, he told Wexford, plenty of two and ten pence pieces, and he knew a gentleman like the chief inspector would reimburse him.

'Give me the number and I'll call you myself.' For God's sake, how much of this was he supposed to stand out of his own pocket? Let the ratepayers fork out. Ginge picked up the receiver before the bell had rung twice. 'It has to be good, Ginge, to get you to the phone.'

'I reckon it's bleeding good,' said Ginge cockily. 'I seen him with a bird, that's what.'

The same climactic exultation is never reached twice. Wexford had heard those words – or words having the same meaning – before, and this time he didn't go off into flights about the Lord delivering Hathall into his hands. Instead he asked when and where.

'You know all that about me stationing myself in that pub and watching the bleeding bus stop? Well, I thought to myself there was no harm doing it again Sunday.' Make sure he got seven days' worth of cash and Demon Kings, thought Wexford. 'So I was in there Sunday dinnertime – that is, yesterday like – when I seen him. About one it was and pissing down with rain. He'd got a mac on and his umbrella up. He didn't stop to catch no bus but went right on walking down West End Lane. Well, I never give a bleeding thought to following him. I seen him go by and that was all. But I'd got to thinking I'd better be off to my own dinner – on account of the wife likes it on the table one-thirty sharp – so down I goes to the station.'

'Which station?'

'Wes' Haamsted Stesh'n,' said Ginge with a very lifelike imitation of a West Indian bus conductor. He chortled at his own wit. 'When I get there I'm putting a five-pee bit in the machine, on account of its being only one stop to Kilburn, when I see the party standing by the bleeding barrier. He'd got his back to me, thank Gawd, so I nips over to the bookstall and has a look at the girlie mags of what they've got a very choice selection. Well, bearing in mind my duty to you, Mr Wexford, I see my train come in but I don't run down the bleeding steps to catch it. I wait. And up the steps comes about twenty people. I never dared turn around, not wanting my other eye poked, but when I think the coast's clear, I has a bit of a shufty and he'd gone.

'I nips back into West End Lane like a shot and the rain's coming down like stair rods. But up ahead, on his way home, is bleeding Hathall with this bird. Walking very close, they was, under his bleeding umbrella, and the bird's wearing one of them see-through plastic macs with the hood up. I couldn't see no more of her, barring she was wearing a long skirt all trailing in the bleeding wet. So I went off home then and got a bleeding mouthful from the wife for being late for my dinner.'

'Virtue is its own reward, Ginge.'

'I don't know about that,' said Ginge, 'but you'll be wanting to know what my wages and the Demon Kings came to, and the bill's fifteen pound sixty-three. Terrible, the cost of bleeding living, isn't it?'

It wouldn't be necessary, Wexford decided as he put the phone down, to think any longer of ways and means of following a man on a bus. For this man had taken this bus only as far as West Hampstead station, had walked instead this Sunday because he had an umbrella and umbrellas are always a problem on buses. It must be possible now to catch Hathall and his woman together and follow them to Dartmeet Avenue.

'I've got a fortnight's holiday owing to me,' he said to his wife.

'You've got about three months' holiday owing to you with what's mounted up over the years.'

'I'm going to take a bit of it now. Next week, say.'

'What in November? Then we'll have to go somewhere warm. They say Malta's very nice in November.'

'Chelsea's very nice in November too, and that's where we're going.'

The first thing to do on the first day of his 'holiday' was to familiarize himself with a so far unknown bit of London's geography. Friday, 22 November, was a fine sunny day, June in appearance if January in temperature. How better to get to West Hampstead than on the 28 bus? Howard had told him that its route passed across the King's Road on its way to Wandsworth Bridge, so it wasn't a long walk from Teresa Street to the nearest stop. The bus went up through Fulham into West Kensington, an area he remembered from the time he had helped Howard on that former case, and he noticed to his satisfaction certain familiar landmarks. But soon he was in unknown territory and very varied and vast territory it was. The immense size of London always surprised him. He had had no inkling when he had interrupted Ginge's recitation of the stops on this route of how long the list would have been. Naively, he had supposed that Ginge would have named no more than two or three further places before the terminus, whereas in fact there would have been a dozen. As the conductor sang out, 'Church Street,' 'Notting Hill Gate,' 'Pembridge Road,' he felt a growing relief that Hathall had merely caught the bus to West Hampstead station.

This station was reached at last after about threequarters of an hour. The bus went on over a bridge above railway lines and past two more stations on the opposite side, West End Lane and another West Hampstead on some suburban line. It had been climbing ever since it left Kilburn and it went on climbing up narrow winding West End Lane till it reached West End Green. Wexford got off. The air was fresh here, not only fresh in comparison to that of Chelsea, but nearly as diesel-free as in Kingsmarkham. Surreptitiously, he consulted his guide. Dartmeet Avenue lay about a quarter of a mile to the east, and he was a little puzzled by this. Surely Hathall could have walked to West Hampstead station in five minutes and walked by the back doubles. Why catch a bus? Still, Ginge had seen him do it. Maybe he merely disliked walking.

Wexford found Dartmeet Avenue with ease. It was a hilly street like most of the streets round here and lined with fine tall houses built mostly of red brick, but some had been modernized and faced with stucco, their sash windows replaced by sheets of plain plate glass. Tall trees, now almost leafless, towered above roofs and pointed gables, and there were mature unpollarded trees growing in the pavements. Number 62 had a front garden that was all shrubbery and weeds. Three black plastic dustbins with 62 painted on their sides in whitewash stood in the side entrance. Wexford noted the phonebox where Ginge had kept his vigils and decided which of the bay windows must be Hathall's. Could anything be gained by calling on the landlord? He concluded that nothing could. The man would be bound to tell Hathall someone had been enquiring about him, would describe that someone, and then the fat would be in the fire. He turned away and walked slowly back to West End Green, looking about him as he did so for such nooks, crannies and convenient trees as might afford him shelter if he dared tail Hathall himself. Night closed in early now, the evenings were long and dark, and in a car . . .

The 28 bus sailed down Fortune Green Road as he reached
the stop. It was a good frequent service. Wexford wondered,
as he settled himself behind the driver, if Robert Hathall had
ever sat on that very seat and looked out through this window
upon the three stations and the radiating railway lines. Such
ruminations verged on the obsessional, though, and that he
must avoid. But it was impossible to refrain from wondering
afresh why Hathall had caught the bus at all just to reach this
point. The woman, when she came to Hathall's home, came
by train. Perhaps Hathall didn't like the tube train, got sick
of travelling to work by Tube, so that when he went to her
home, he preferred the relaxation of a bus ride.

It took about ten minutes to get to Kilburn. Ginge, who
was as sure to be found in the Countess of Castlemaine at
noon as the sun is to rise at daybreak or the sound of thunder
to follow the sight of lightning, was hunched on his bar stool.
He was nursing a half of bitter but when he saw his patron
he pushed the tankard away from him, the way a man leaves
his spoon in his half-consumed soup when his steak arrives.
Wexford ordered a Demon King by name and without description of its ingredients. The barman understood.

'He's got you on your toes, this bleeder, hasn't he?' Ginge
moved to an alcove table. 'Always popping up to the Smoke,
you are. You don't want to let it get on top of you. Once let
a thing like that get a hold on you and you could end up in
a bleeding bin.'

'Don't be so daft,' said Wexford, whose own wife had said
much the same thing to him that morning, though in more
refined terms. 'It won't be for much longer, anyway. This
coming week ought to see an end of it. Now what I want you
to do . . .'

'It won't be for *no* longer, Mr Wexford.' Ginge spoke with
a kind of shrinking determination. 'You put me on this to spot
him with a bird and I've spotted him with a bird. The rest's
up to you.'

'Ginge,' Wexford began cajolingly, 'just to watch the station next week while I watch the house.'

'No,' said Ginge.

'You're a coward.'

'Cowardness,' said Ginge, exhibiting his usual difficulty in making his command of the spoken language match up to his mastery of the written, 'don't come into it.' He hesitated and said with what might have been modesty or shame, 'I've got a job.'

Wexford almost gasped. 'A *job*?' In former days this monosyllable had exclusively been employed by Ginge and his brother to denote a criminal exercise. 'You mean you've got paid work?'

'Not me. Not exactly.' Ginge contemplated his Demon King rather sadly and, lifting his glass, he sipped from it delicately and with a kind of nostalgia. *Sic transit gloria mundi* or it had been good while it lasted. 'The wife has. Bleeding barmaid. Evenings and Sunday dinnertimes.' He looked slightly embarrassed. 'Don't know what's got into her.'

'What I don't know is why it stops you working for me.'

'Anyone'd think,' said Ginge, 'you'd never had no bleeding family of your own. Someone's got to stay home and mind the kids, haven't they?'

Wexford managed to delay his outburst of mirth until he was out on the pavement. Laughter did him good, cleansing him of the feverish balked feeling Ginge's refusal to cooperate further had at first brought him. He could manage on his own now, he thought as once more he boarded the 28 bus, and manage for the future in his car. From his car he could watch West Hampshire station on Sunday. With luck, Hathall would meet the woman there as he had done on the previous Sunday, and once the woman was found, what would it matter that Hathall knew he had been followed? Who would reproach him for breaking the rules when his disobedience had resulted in that success?

But Hathall didn't meet the woman on Sunday, and as the week wore on Wexford wondered at the man's elusiveness. He stationed himself in Dartmeet Avenue every evening but he never saw Hathall and he only once saw evidence of occupancy of the room with the bay window. On the Monday, the Tuesday and the Wednesday he was there before six and he saw three people enter the house between six and seven. No sign of Hathall. For some reason, the traffic was particularly heavy on the Thursday evening. It was six-fifteen before he got to Dartmeet Avenue. Rain was falling steadily and the long hilly street was black and glittering with here and there on its surface the gilt glare of reflected lamplight. The place was deserted but for a cat which snaked from between the dusbins and vanished through a fissure in the garden wall. A light was on in a downstairs room and a feebler glow showed through the fanlight above the front door. Hathall's window was dark, but as Wexford put on the handbrake and switched off the ignition, the bay window suddenly became a brilliant yellow cube. Hathall was in, had arrived home perhaps a minute before Wexford's own arrival. For a few seconds the window blazed, then curtains were drawn across it by an invisible hand until all that could be seen were thin perpendicular lines of light like phosphorescent threads gleaming on the dim wet façade.

The excitement this sight had kindled in him cooled as an hour, two hours, went by and Hathall didn't appear. At half past nine a little elderly man emerged, routed out the cat from among the sodden weeds and carried it back into the house. As the front door closed on him, the light that rimmed Hathall's curtains went out. That alerted Wexford and he started to move the car to a less conspicuous position, but the front door remained closed, the window remained dark, and he realized that Hathall had retired early to bed.

Having brought Dora to London for a holiday, he remembered his duty to her and squired her about the West End shopping centres in the daytime. But Denise was so much more adept at doing this than he that on the Friday he deserted his wife and his nephew's wife for a less attractive woman who was no longer a wife at all.

The first thing he saw when he came to Eileen Hathall's house was her ex-husband's car parked on the garage drive, the car which Ginge said had long ago been sold. Had Ginge made a mistake about that? He drove on till he came to a call-box where he phoned Marcus Flower. Yes, Mr Hathall was in, said the voice of a Jane or a Julie or a Linda. If he would just hold the line . . . Instead of holding the line, he put the receiver back and within five minutes he was in Eileen Hathall's arid living room, sitting on a cushionless chair under the Spanish gypsy.

'He gave his car to Rosemary,' she said in answer to his question. 'She sees him sometimes at her gran's, and when she said she'd passed her test he gave her his car. He won't need it where he's going, will he?'

'Where is he going, Mrs Hathall?'

'Brazil.' She spat out the rough r and the sibilant as if the word were not the name of a country but of some loathsome reptile. Wexford felt a chill, a sudden anticipation that something bad was coming. It came. 'He's all fixed up,' she said, 'to go the day before Christmas Eve.'

In less than a month . . .

'Has he got a job there?' he said steadily.

'A very good position with a firm of international accountants.' There was something pathetic about the pride she took in saying it. The man hated her, had humiliated her, would probably never see her again, yet for all that, she was bitterly proud of what he had achieved. 'You wouldn't believe the money he's getting. He told Rosemary and she told me. They're paying me from London, deducting what I get before it goes to him. He'll still have thousands and thousands a year to live on. And they're paying his fare, fixing it all up, got a house there waiting for him. He hasn't had to do a thing.'

Should he tell her Hathall wouldn't be going alone, wouldn't live in that house alone? She had grown stouter in the past year, her thick body – all bulges where there should be none – stuffed into salmon-pink wool. And she was permanently flushed as if she ran an endless race. Perhaps she did. A race to keep up with her daughter, keep pace with rage and leave the quiet dullness of misery behind. While he was hesitating, she said. 'Why d'you want to know? You think he killed that woman, don't you?'

'Do *you?*' he said boldly.

If she had been struck across the face her skin couldn't have crimsoned more deeply. It looked like flogged skin about to split and bleed. 'I wish he had!' she said on a harsh gasp, and she put up her hand, not to cover her eyes as he had at first thought, but her trembling mouth.

He drove back to London, to a fruitless Friday night vigil, an empty Saturday, a Sunday that might – just might – bring him what he desired.

December first, and once more pouring with rain. But this was no bad thing. It would clear the streets and make the chance of Hathall's peering into a suspicious-looking car less likely. By half past twelve he had parked as nearly opposite the station as he dared, for it wasn't only the chance of being spotted by Hathall that worried him, but also the risk of obstructing this narrow bottleneck. Rain drummed hard on the car roof, streamed down the gutter between the curb and the yellow painted line. But this rain was so heavy that, as it washed over the windscreen, it didn't obscure his view but had only a distorting effect as if there were a fault in the glass. He could see the station entrance quite clearly and about a hundred yards of West End Lane where it humped over the railway lines. Trains rattled unseen beneath him, 159 and 28 buses climbed and descended the hill. There were few people

about and yet it seemed as if a whole population were travelling, proceeding from unknown homes to unknown destinations
through the wet pallid gloom of this winter Sunday. The hands
of the dashboard clock crawled slowly through and past the
third quarter after twelve.

By now he was so used to waiting, resigned to sitting on
watch like a man who stalked some wary cunning animal, that
he felt a jolt of shock which was almost disbelief when at ten
to one he saw Hathall's figure in the distance. The glass played
tricks with him. He was like someone in a hall of mirrors, first
a skeletal giant, then a fat dwarf, but a single sweep of the
windscreen wipers brought him suddenly into clear focus. His
umbrella up, he was walking swiftly towards the station –
fortunately, on the opposite side of the road. He passed the
car without turning his head, and outside the station he
stopped, snapped the umbrella shut and open, shut, open and
shut, to shake off the water drops. Then he disappeared into
the entrance.

Wexford was in a dilemma. Was he meeting someone or
travelling himself? In daylight, even in this rain, he dared not
leave the car. A red train scuttled under the road and came
to a stop. He held his breath. The first people to get off the
train began to come out on to the pavement. One man put a
newspaper over his head and ran, a little knot of women
fluttered, struggling with umbrellas that wouldn't open. Three
opened simultaneously, a red one, a blue one and an orange
pagoda, blossoming suddenly in the greyness like flowers.
When they had lifted and danced off, what their brilliant
circles had hidden was revealed – a couple with their backs
to the street, a couple who stood close together but not
touching each other while the man opened a black umbrella
and enclosed them under its canopy.

She wore blue jeans and over them a white raincoat, the hood
of which was up. Wexford hadn't been able to catch a glimpse

of her face. They had set off as if they meant to walk it, but a taxi came splashing down with its For Hire light glowing orange like a cigarette end. Hathall hailed it and it bore them off northwards. Please God, thought Wexford, let it take them home and not to some restaurant. He knew he hadn't hope of tailing a London taxi-driver, and the cab had vanished before he was out into West End Lane and off.

And the journey up the hill was maddeningly slow. He was bogged down behind a 159 bus – a bus that wasn't red but painted all over with an advertisement for Dinky Toys which reminded him of Kidd's at Toxborough – and nearly ten minutes had passed before he drew up in front of the house in Dartmeet Avenue. The taxi had gone, but Hathall's light was on. Of course he'd have to put the light on at midday on such a day as this. Wondering with interest rather than fear if Hathall would hit him too, he went up the path and examined the bells. There were no names by the bell-pushes, just floor numbers. He pressed the first-floor bell and waited. It was possible Hathall wouldn't come down, would just refuse to answer it. In that case, he'd find someone else to let him in and he'd hammer on Hathall's room door.

This turned out to be unnecessary. Above his head the window opened and, stepping back, he looked up into Hathall's face. For a moment neither of them spoke. The rain dashed between them and they stared at each other through it while a variety of emotions crossed Hathall's features – astonishment, anger, cautiousness, but not, Wexford thought, fear. And all were succeeded by what looked strangely like satisfaction. But before he could speculate as to what this might mean, Hathall said coldly:

'I'll come down and let you in.'

Within fifteen seconds he had done so. He closed the door quietly, saying nothing, and pointed to the stairs. Wexford had never seen him so calm and suave. He seemed entirely relaxed. He looked younger and he looked triumphant.

'I should like you to introduce me to the lady you brought here in a taxi.'

Hathall didn't demur. He didn't speak. As they went up the stairs Wexford thought, has he hidden her? Sent her to some bathroom or up on to the top floor? His room door was on the latch and he pushed it open, allowing the chief inspector to precede him. Wexford walked in. The first thing he saw was her raincoat, spread out to dry over a chair back.

At first he didn't see her. The room was very small, no more than twelve feet by ten, and furnished as such places always are. There was a wardrobe that looked as if it had been manufactured round about the time of the Battle of Mons, a narrow bed with an Indian cotton cover, some wooden-armed chairs that are euphemistically known as 'fireside,' and pictures that had doubtless been painted by some relative of the landlord's. The light came from a dust-coated plastic sphere suspended from the pockmarked ceiling.

A canvas screen, canvas-coloured and hideous, shut off one corner of the room. Behind it, presumably, was a sink, for when Hathall gave a cautionary cough, she pushed it aside and came out, drying her hands on a tea towel. It wasn't a pretty face, just a very young one, heavy-featured, tough and confident. Thick black hair fell to her shoulders and her eyebrows were heavy and black like a man's. She wore a tee-shirt with a cardigan over it. Wexford had seen that face somewhere before, and he was wondering where when Hathall said:

'This is the "lady" you wanted to meet.' His triumph had changed to frank amusement and he was almost laughing. 'May I present my daughter, Rosemary?'

CHAPTER FIFTEEN

It was a long time since Wexford had experienced such an anticlimax. Coping with awkward situations wasn't usually a problem with him, but the shock of what Hathall had just said – combined with his realization that his own disobedience was now known – stunned him into silence. The girl didn't speak either after she had said a curt hello, but retreated behind the screen where she could be heard filling a kettle.

Hathall, who had been so withdrawn and aloof when Wexford first arrived, seemed to be getting the maximum possible enjoyment from his adversary's dismay. 'What's this visit in aid of?' he asked. 'Just looking up old acquaintances?'

In for a penny, in for a pound, thought Wexford, echoing Miss Marcovitch. 'I understand you're going to Brazil,' he said. 'Alone?'

'Can one go alone? There'll be about three hundred other people in the aircraft.' Wexford smarted under that one and Hathall saw him smart. 'I hoped Rosemary might go with me, but her school is here. Perhaps she'll join me in a few years' time.'

That fetched the girl out. She picked up her raincoat, hung it on a hanger and said, 'I haven't even been to Europe yet. I'm not burying myself in Brazil.'

Hathall shrugged at this typical sample of his family's ungraciousness, and said as brusquely, 'Satisfied?'

'I have to be, don't I, Mr Hathall?'

Was it his daughter's presence that kept his anger in check. He was almost mild, only a trace of his usual resentful querulousness sounding in his voice when he said, 'Well, if you'll excuse us, Rosemary and I have to get ourselves some lunch which isn't the easiest thing in the world in this little hole. I'll see you out.'

He closed the door instead of leaving it on the latch. It was dark and quiet on the landing. Wexford waited for the explosion of rage but it didn't come, and he was conscious only of the man's eyes. They were the same height and their eyes met on a level. Briefly, Hathall's showed white and staring around hard black irises in which that curious red spark glittered. They were at the head of the steep flight of stairs, and as Wexford turned to descend them, he was aware of a movement behind him, of Hathall's splayed hand rising. He grasped the banister and swung down a couple of steps. Then he made himself walk down slowly and steadily. Hathall didn't move, but when Wexford reached the bottom and looked back, he saw the raised hand lifted higher and the fingers closed in a solemn and somehow portentous gesture of farewell.

'He was going to push me down those stairs,' Wexford said to Howard. 'And I wouldn't have had much redress. He could have said I'd forced my way into his room. God, what a mess I've made of things! He's bound to put in another of his complaints and I could lose my job.'

'Not without a pretty full enquiry, and I don't think Hathall would want to appear at any enquiry.' Howard threw the Sunday paper he had been reading on to the floor and turned his thin bony face, his ice-blue penetrating eyes towards his uncle. 'It wasn't his daughter all the time, Reg.'

'Wasn't it? I know you saw this woman with short fair hair, but can you be sure it was Hathall you saw her with?'

'I'm sure.'

'You saw him once,' Wexford persisted. 'You saw him twenty yards off for about ten seconds from a car *you were driving*. If you had to go into court and swear that the man you saw outside Marcus Flower was the same man you saw in the garden of Bury Cottage, would you swear? If a man's life depended on it, would you?'

'Capital punishment is no longer with us, Reg.'

'No, and neither you nor I – unlike many of our calling – would wish to see it back. But if it were with us, then would you?'

Howard hesitated. Wexford saw that hesitation and he felt tiredness creep through his body like a depression drug. Even a shred of doubt could dispel what little hope he now had left.

At last, 'No, I wouldn't,' Howard said flatly.

'I see.'

'Wait a minute, Reg. I'm not sure nowadays if I could even swear to a man's identity if my swearing to it might lead to his death. You're pressing me too hard. But I'm sure beyond a reasonable doubt, and I'll still say to you, yes, I saw Robert Hathall. I saw him outside the offices of Marcus Flower in Half Moon Street with a fair-haired woman.'

Wexford sighed. What difference did it make, after all? By his own blundering of that day he had put an end to all hope of following Hathall. Howard mistook his silence for doubt and said, 'If he isn't with her, where does he go all those evenings he's out? Where did he go on that bus?'

'Oh, I still believe he's with her. The daughter just goes there sometimes on Sundays. But what good does that do me? I can't follow him on a bus. He'll be looking for me now.'

'He'll think, you know, that seeing him with his daughter will put you off.'

'Maybe. Maybe he'll get reckless. So what? I can't conceal myself in a doorway and leap on a bus after him. Either the bus would go before I got on or he'd turn round and see me. Even if I got on without his seeing me . . .'

'Then someone else must do it,' said Howard firmly.

'Easy to say. My Chief Constable says no, and you won't cross swords with my Chief Constable by letting me have one of your blokes.'

'That's true, I won't.'

'Then we may as well give over talking about it. I'll go

back to Kingsmarkham and face the music – a bloody great symphony in Griswold sharp major – and Hathall can go to the sunny tropics.'

Howard got up and laid a hand on his shoulder. 'I will do it,' he said.

The awe had gone long ago, giving way to love and comradeship: But that 'I will do it,' spoken so lightly and pleasantly, brought back all the old humiliation and envy and awareness of the other's advantages. Wexford felt a hot dark flush suffuse his face. '*You?*' he said roughly, 'you yourself? You must be joking. You take rank over me, remember?'

'Don't be such a snob. What if I do? I'd like to do it. It'd be fun. I haven't done anything like that for years and years.'

'Would you really do that for me, Howard? What about your own work?'

'If I'm the god you make me out to be, don't you think I have some say in the hours I work? Of course I shan't be able to do it every night. There'll be the usual crises that come up from time to time and I'll have to stay late. But Kenbourne Vale won't degenerate into a sort of twentieth-century Bridewell just because I pop up to West Hampstead every so often.'

So on the following evening Chief Superintendent Howard Fortune left his office at a quarter to six and was at West End Green on the hour. He waited until half past seven. When his quarry didn't come, he made his way along Dartmeet Avenue and observed that there was no light on in the window his uncle had told him was Hathall's.

'I wonder if he's going to her straight from work?'

'Let's hope he's not going to make a habit of that. It'll be almost impossible to follow him in the rush hour. When does he give up this job of his?'

'God knows,' said Wexford, 'but he leaves for Brazil in precisely three weeks.'

One of those crises at which he had hinted prevented Howard from tailing Hathall on the following night, but he

was free on the Wednesday and, changing his tactics, he got
to Half Moon Street by five o'clock. An hour later, in Teresa
Street, he told his uncle what had happened.

'The first person to come out of Marcus Flower was a
seedy-looking guy with a toothbrush moustache. He had a girl
with him and they went off in a Jaguar.'

'That'd be Jason Marcus and his betrothed,' said Wexford.

'Then two more girls and then – Hathall. I *was* right, Reg.
It's the same man.'

'I shouldn't have doubted you.'

Howard shrugged. 'He got into the Tube and I lost him.
But he wasn't going home. I know that.'

'How can you know?'

'If he'd been going home he'd have walked to Green Park
station, gone one stop on the Piccadilly Lane to Piccadilly
Circus or on the Victoria Line to Oxford Circus and changed
on to the Bakerloo. He'd have walked south. But he walked
north, and at first I thought he was going to get a bus home.
But he went to Bond Street station. You'd never go to Bond
Street if you meant to go to North-west London. Bond Street's
only on the Central Line until the Fleet Line opens.'

'And the Central Line goes where?'

'Due east and due west. I followed him into the station
but – well, you've seen our rush hours, Reg. I was a good
dozen people behind him in the ticket queue. The thing was
I had to be so damn careful he didn't get a look at me. He
went down the escalator to the westbound platform – and I
lost him.' Howard said apologetically, 'There were about five
hundred people on the platform. I got stuck and I couldn't
move. But it's proved one thing. D'you see what I mean?'

'I think so. We have to find where the west-bound Central
Line route crosses the 28 bus route, and somewhere in that
area lives our unknown woman.'

'I can tell you where that is straight off. The westbound
Central Line route goes Bond Street, Marble Arch, Lancaster

Gate, Queensway, Notting Hill Gate, Holland Park, Shepherd's Bush, and so on. The southbound 28 route goes Golders Green, West Hampstead, Kilburn, Kilburn Park, Great Western Road, Pembridge Road, Notting Hill Gate, Church Street, on through Kensington and Fulham to here and ultimately to Wandsworth. So it has to be Notting Hill. She lives, along with half the roving population of London, somewhere in Notting Hill. Small progress, but better than nothing. Have you made any?'

Wexford, on tenterhooks for two days, had phoned Burden, expecting to hear that Griswold was out for his blood. But nothing was further from the truth. The Chief Constable had been 'buzzing around' Kingsmarkham, as Burden put it, tearing between there and Myringham where there was some consternation over a missing woman. But he had been in an excellent frame of mind, had asked where Wexford had gone for his holiday, and on being told London ('For the theatres and museums, you know, sir,' Burden had said) had asked facetiously why the chief inspector hadn't sent him a picture postcard of New Scotland Yard.

'Then Hathall hasn't complained,' said Howard thoughtfully.

'Doesn't look like it. If I were to be optimistic, I'd say he thinks it safer not to draw attention to himself.'

But it was December third . . . Twenty days to go. Dora had dragged her husband round the stores, doing the last of her Christmas shopping. He had carried her parcels, agreed that this was just the thing for Sheila and that was exactly what Sylvia's elder boy wanted, but all the time he was thinking, twenty days, twenty days . . . this year Christmas for him would be the season of Robert Hathall's getaway.

Howard seemed to read his thoughts. He was eating one of those enormous meals he consumed without putting on a pound. Taking a second helping of *charlotte russe*, he said, 'If only we could get him on something.'

'What d'you mean?'

'I don't know. Some little thing you could hold him on that would stop him leaving the country. Like shoplifting, say, or travelling on the Tube without a ticket.'

'He seems to be an honest man,' said Wexford bitterly, 'if you can call a murderer honest.'

His nephew scraped the dessert bowl. 'I suppose he *is* honest?'

'As far as I know, he is. Mr Butler would have told me if there's been a smell of dishonesty about him.'

'I daresay. Hathall was all right for money in those days. But he wasn't all right for money when he got married to Angela, was he? Yet, in spite of their having only fifteen pounds a week to live on, they started doing all right. You told me Somerset had seen them on a shopping spree and then dining at some expensive place. Where did that money come from, Reg?'

Pouring himself a glass of Chablis from the bottle by Howard's elbow, Wexford said, 'I've wondered about that. But I've never been able to come to any conclusion. It didn't seem relevant.'

'Everything's relevant in a murder case.'

'True.' Wexford was too grateful to his nephew to react huffily at this small admonition. 'I suppose I reckoned that if a man's always been honest he doesn't suddenly become dishonest in middle age.'

'That depends on the man. This man suddenly became an unfaithful husband in middle age. In fact, although he'd been monogamous since puberty, he seems to have turned into a positive womanizer in middle age. And he became a murderer. I don't suppose you're saying he killed anyone before, are you?' Howard pushed away his plate and started on the gruyère. 'There's one factor in all this I don't think you've taken into sufficient account. One personality.'

'Angela?'

476

'Angela. It was when he met her that he changed. Some would say she'd corrupted him. This is an outside chance – a very wayout idea altogether – but Angela had been up to a little fraud on her own, one you know about, possibly others you don't. Suppose she encouraged him into some sort of dishonesty.'

'Your saying that reminds me of something Mr Butler said. He said he overheard Angela tell his partner, Paul Craig, that he was in a good position to fiddle his Income Tax.'

'There you are then. They must have got that money from somewhere. It didn't grow on trees like the "miracle" plums.'

'There hasn't been a hint of anything,' said Wexford. 'It would have to be at Kidd's. Aveney didn't drop so much as a hint.'

'But you weren't asking him about money. You were asking him about women.' Howard got up from the table and pushed aside his chair. 'Let's go and join the ladies. If I were you I'd take a little trip to Toxborough tomorrow.'

CHAPTER SIXTEEN

The rectangular white box set on green lawns, the screen of saplings, leafless and pathetic in December, and inside, the warm cellulose smell and the turbaned women painting dolls to the theme music from *Doctor Zhivago*. Mr Aveney conducted Wexford through the workshops to the office of the personnel manager, talking the while in a shocked and rather indignant way.

'Cooking the books? We've never had anything like that here.'

'I'm not saying you have, Mr Aveney. I'm working in the dark,' said Wexford. 'Have you ever heard of the old payroll fiddle?'

'Well, yes, I *have*. It used to be done a lot in the forces. No one'd get away with it here.'

'Let's see, shall we?'

The personnel manager, a vague young man with fair bristly hair, was introduced as John Oldbury. His office was very untidy and he seemed somewhat distraught as if he had been caught in the middle of searching for something he knew he would never find. 'Messing about with the wages, d'you mean?' he said.

'Suppose you tell me how you work with the accountant to manage the payroll.'

Oldbury looked distractedly at Aveney, and Aveney nodded, giving an infinitesimal shrug. The personnel manager sat down heavily and pushed his fingers through his unruly hair. 'I'm not very good at explaining things,' he began. 'But I'll try. It's like this: when we get a new worker I sort of tell the accountant details about her and he works them out for her wages. No, I'll have to be more explicit. Say we take on a – well, we'll call her Joan Smith, Mrs Joan Smith.' Oldbury, thought

Wexford, was as unimaginative as he was inarticulate. 'I tell
the accountant her name and her address – say . . .'

Seeing his total defeat, Wexford said, 'Twenty-four Gordon
Road, Toxborough.'

'Oh, fine!' The personnel manager beamed his admiration.
'I tell him Mrs Joan Smith, of whatever-it-is Gordon Road,
Toxborough . . .'

'Tell him by what means? Phone? A chit?'

'Well, either. Of course I keep a record. I haven't,' said
Oldbury unnecessarily, 'got a very good memory. I tell him
her name and her address and when she's starting and her
hours and whatever, and he feeds all that into the computer
and Bob's your uncle. And after that I do it every week for
her overtime and – whatever.'

'And when she leaves you tell him that too?'

'Oh, sure.'

'They're always leaving. Chop and change, it's everlasting,'
said Aveney.

'They're all paid in weekly wage packets?'

'Not all,' said Oldbury. 'You see, some of our ladies don't
use their wages for – well, housekeeping. Their husbands are
the – what's the word?'

'Breadwinners?'

'Ah, fine. Breadwinners. The ladies – some of them – keep
their wages for holidays and sort of improving their homes
and just saving up, I suppose.'

'Yes, I see. But so what?'

'Well,' said Oldbury triumphantly, '*they* don't get wage
packets. Their wages are paid into a bank account – more
likely the Post Office or a Trustee Savings Bank.'

'And if they are, you tell that to the accountant and he
feeds it into his computer?'

'He does, yes.' Oldbury smiled delightedly at the realization he had made himself so clear. 'You're absolutely right.
Quick thinking, if I may say so.'

'Not at all,' said Wexford, slightly stupefied by the man's zany charm. 'So the accountant could simply invent a woman and feed a fictitious name and address into the computer? Her wages would go into a bank account which the accountant – or, rather, his female accomplice – could draw on when they chose?'

'That,' said Oldbury severely, 'would be fraud.'

'It would indeed. But, since you keep records, we can easily verify if such a fraud has ever been committed.'

'Of course we can.' The personnel manager beamed again and trotted over to a filing cabinet whose open drawers were stuffed with crumpled documents. 'Nothing easier. We keep records for a whole year after one of our ladies has left us.'

A whole year . . . And Hathall had left them eighteen months before. Aveney took him back through the factory where the workers were now being lulled (or stimulated) by the voice of Tom Jones. 'John Oldbury' he said defensively, 'has got a very good psychology degree and he's marvellous with people.'

'I'm sure. You've both been very good. I apologize for taking up so much of your time.'

The interview had neither proved nor disproved Howard's theory. But since there were no records, what could be done? If the enquiry wasn't a clandestine one, if he had men at his disposal, he could send them round the local Trustee Savings Banks. But it was, and he hadn't. Yet he could see so clearly now how such a thing could have been done; the idea coming in the first place from Angela; the female accomplice brought in to impersonate the women Hathall had invented, and to draw money from the accounts. And then – yes, Hathall growing too fond of his henchwoman so that Angela became jealous. If he was right, everything was explainable, the deliberately contrived solitude of the Hathalls, their cloistral life, the money that enabled them to dine out and Hathall to buy presents for his daughter. And they would all have been in it together – until Angela realized the woman was more than an accomplice to her husband, more than a useful collector of revenues . . . What had she done? Broken up the affair and threatened that if it started again, she'd shop them both? That would have meant the end of Hathall's career. That would put paid to his job at Marcus Flower or any future accountancy job. So they had murdered her. They had killed Angela to be together, and knowing Kidd's kept records for only one year, to be safe forever from the risk of discovery . . .

Wexford drove slowly down the drive between the flat green lawns, and at the gateway to the main industrial estate road met another car coming in. Its driver was a uniformed police officer and its other occupant Chief Inspector Jack 'Brock' Lovat, a small snub-nosed man who wore small gold-rimmed glasses. The car slowed and Lovat wound his window down.

'What are you doing here?' Wexford asked.

'My job,' said Lovat simply.

His nickname derived from the fact that he kept three badgers, rescued from the diggers before badger-digging became an offence, in his back garden. And Wexford knew of old that it was useless questioning the head of Myringham CID about anything but this hobby of his. On that subject he was fulsome and enthusiastic. On all others – though he did his work in exemplary fashion – he was almost mute. You got a 'yes' or a 'no' out of him unless you were prepared to talk about setts and plantigrade quadrupeds.

'Since there are no badgers here,' Wexford said sarcastically, 'except possibly clockwork ones, I'll just ask this. Is your visit connected in any way with a man called Robert Hathall?'

'No,' said Lovat. Smiling closely, he waved his hand and told the driver to move on.

But for its new industries, Toxborough would by now have dwindled to a semi-deserted village with an elderly population. Industry had brought life, commerce, roads, ugliness, a community centre, a sports ground and a council estate. This last was traversed by a broad thoroughfare called Maynnot Way, where the concrete stilts of street lamps replaced the trees, and which had been named after the only old house that remained in it, Maynnot Hall. Wexford, who hadn't been this way for ten years when the concrete and the brick had first begun to spread across Toxborough's green fields, knew that somewhere, not too far from here, was a Trustee Savings Bank. At the second junction he turned left into Queen Elizabeth Avenue, and there it was, sandwiched between a betting shop and a place that sold cash-and-carry carpets.

The manager was a stiff pompous man who reacted sharply to Wexford's questions.

'Let you look at our books? Not without a warrant.'

'All right. But tell me this. If payments stop being made into an account and it's left empty or nearly empty, do you write to the holder and ask him or her if they want it closed?'

'We gave up the practice. If someone's only got fifteen pence in an account he's not going to waste money on a stamp saying he wants the account closed. Nor is he going to spend five pence on a bus fare to collect it. Right?'

'Would you check for me if any accounts held by women have had no payments made into them or withdrawals made from them since – well, last April or May twelvemonth? And if there are any, would you communicate with the holders?'

'Not,' said the manager firmly, 'unless this is an official police matter. I haven't got the staff.'

Neither, thought Wexford as he left the bank, had he. No staff, no funds, no encouragement; and still nothing but his own 'feelings' with which to convince Griswold that this was worth pursuing. Kidd's had a payroll, Hathall could have helped himself to money from it by the means of accounts held by fictitious women. Come to that, Kingsmarkham police station had a petty cash box and he, Wexford, could have helped himself out of it. There was about as much ground for suspicion in the latter case as in the former, and that was how the Chief Constable would see it.

'Another dead end,' he said to his nephew that night. 'But I understand how it all happened now. The Hathalls and the other woman work their fraud for a couple of years. The share-out of the loot takes place at Bury Cottage. Then Hathall gets his new job and there's no longer any need for the payroll fiddle. The other woman should fade out of the picture, but she doesn't because Hathall has fallen for her and wants to go on seeing her. You can imagine Angela's fury. It was *her* idea, she planned it, and it's led to this. She tells Hathall to give her up or she'll blow the whole thing, but Hathall can't. He pretends he has and all seems well between him and Angela, to the extent of Angela asking her mother-in-law to stay and cleaning up the cottage to impress her. In the afternoon Angela fetches her rival, perhaps to wind up the whole thing finally. The other woman strangles her as arranged, but leaves that print on the bath.'

'Admirable,' said Howard. 'I'm sure you're right.'

'And much good it does me. I may as well go home tomorrow. You're coming to us for Christmas?'

Howard patted his shoulder as he had done on the day he promised his vigilance. 'Christmas is a fortnight off. I'll keep on watching every free evening I get.'

At any rate, there was no summons from Griswold awaiting him. And nothing much had happened in Kingsmarkham during his absence. The home of the chairman of the rural council had been broken into. Six colour sets had been stolen from the television rental company in the High Street. Burden's son had been accepted by Reading University, subject to satisfactory A Levels. And Nancy Lake's house had been sold for a cool twenty-five thousand pounds. Some said she was moving to London, others that she was going abroad. Sergeant Martin had decorated the police station foyer with paper chains and mobiles of flying angels which the Chief Constable had ordered removed forthwith as they detracted from the dignity of Mid-Sussex.

'Funny thing Hathall didn't complain, wasn't it?'

'Lucky for you he didn't.' At ease now in his new glasses, Burden looked more severe and puritanical than ever. With a rather exasperated indrawing of breath, he said, 'You must give that up, you know.'

'Must? Little man, little man, *must* is not a word to be addressed to chief inspectors. Time was when you used to call me "sir." '

'And it was you asked me to stop. Remember?'

Wexford laughed. 'Let's go over to the Carousel and have a spot of lunch, and I'll tell you all about what I *must* give up.'

Antonio was delighted to see him back and offered him the speciality of the day – *moussaka.*

'I thought that was Greek.'

'The Greeks,' said Antonio, flinging out his hands, 'got it from us.'

'A reversal of the usual process. How interesting. I may as well have it, Antonio. And steak pie, which you got from *us*, for Mr Burden. Have I got thinner, Mike?'

'You're wasting away.'

'I haven't had a decent meal for a fortnight, what with chasing after that damned Hathall.' Wexford told him about it while they ate. 'Now do you believe?'

'Oh, I don't know. It's mostly in your head, isn't it? My daughter was telling me something the other day she got from school. About Galileo, it was. They made him recant what he'd said about the earth moving round the sun but he wouldn't give it up, and on his deathbed his last words were, "It does move." '

'I've heard it. What are you trying to prove? He was right. The earth does go round the sun. And on *my* deathbed I'll say, "He did do it." ' Wexford sighed. It was useless, may as well change the subject . . . 'I saw old Brock last week. He was as close as ever. Did he find his missing girl?'

'He's digging up Myringham Old Town for her.'

'As missing as that, is she?'

Burden gave Wexford's *moussaka* a suspicious look and a suspicious sniff, and attacked his own steak pie. 'He's pretty sure she'd dead and he's arrested her husband.'

'What, for murder?'

'No, not without the body. The bloke's got a record and he's holding him on a shop-breaking charge.'

'Christ!' Wexford exploded. 'Some people have all the luck.'

His eyes met Burden's, and the inspector gave him the kind of look we level at our friends when we begin to doubt their mental equilibrium. And Wexford said no more, breaking the silence only to ask after young John Burden's successes and prospects. But when they rose to go and a beaming Antonio had been congratulated on the cooking, 'When I retire or die, Antonio,' Wexford said, 'will you name a dish after me?'

The Italian crossed himself. 'Not to speak of such things, but yes, sure I will. *Lasagne* Wexford?'

'*Lasagne Galileo.*' Wexford laughed at the other's puzzlement. 'It sounds more Latin,' he said.

The High Street shops had their windows filled with glitter, and the great cedar outside the Dragon pub had orange and green and scarlet and blue light bulbs in its branches. In the toyshop window a *papier mâché* and cotton wool Santa Claus nodded and smiled and gyrated at an audience of small children who pressed their noses to the glass.

'Twelve more shopping days to Christmas,' said Burden.

'Oh, shut up,' Wexford snapped.

CHAPTER SEVENTEEN

A grey mist hung over the river, curtaining its opposite bank, shrouding the willows in veils of vapour, making colourless the hills and the leafless woods so that they appeared like a landscape in an out-of-focus monochrome photograph. On this side, the houses of the Old Town slept in the freezing mist, all their windows closed against it, their garden trees utterly still. The only motion was that of water drops falling gently and very slowly from threadlike branches. It was bitterly cold. As Wexford walked down past St. Luke's and Church House, it seemed wonderful to him that up there beyond those layers of cloud, miles of icy mist, must be a bright though distant sun. A few more days to the shortest day, the longest night. A few more days to the solstice when the sun would have moved to its extremest limit from this part of the earth. Or as he should put it, he thought, recalling Burden's snippet of pop education from the day before, when the ground on which he stood would have moved to its extremest limit of the sun . . .

He saw the police cars and police vans in River Lane before he saw any of the men who had driven them there or any signs of their purpose. They were parked all along the lane, fronting the row of almost derelict house whose owners had abandoned them and left them to be inhabited intermittently by the desperate homeless. Here and there, where the glass or even the frame of an ancient window had collapsed and gone, the cavity was patched with plastic sheeting. Against other windows hung bedspreads, sacks, rags, torn and soaking brown paper. But there were no squatters here now. Winter and the damp rising from the river had driven them to find other quarters, and the old houses, immeasurably more beautiful even now than any modern terrace, waited in the sour cold for new occupants or new purchasers. They were old but they were also very nearly immortal. No one might destroy them. All that could become of them was a slow disintegration into extreme decay.

An alley led between broken brick walls to the gardens which lay behind them, gardens which had become repositories of rubbish, rat-infested, and which sloped down to the river bank. Wexford made his way down this alley to a point where the wall had caved in, leaving a gap. A young police sergeant, standing just inside and holding a spade in his hand, barred his way and said, 'Sorry, sir. No one's allowed in here.'

'Don't you know me, Hutton?'

The sergeant looked again and, taken aback, said, 'It's Mr Wexford, isn't it? I beg your pardon, sir.'

Wexford said that was quite all right, and where was Chief Inspector Lovat to be found?

'Down where they're digging, sir. On the right-hand side at the bottom.'

'They're digging for this woman's body?'

'Mrs Morag Grey. She and her husband squatted here for a bit the summer before last. Mr Lovat thinks the husband may have buried her in this garden.'

'They lived *here*?' Wexford looked up at the sagging gable, shored up with a balk of timber. The leprous split plaster has scaled off in places, showing the bundles of wattle the house had been built of four hundred years before. A gaping doorway revealed interior walls which, slimy and running with water, were like those of a cave that the sea invades daily.

'It wouldn't be so bad in summer,' said Hutton by way of apology, 'and they weren't here for more than a couple of months.'

A great tangle of bushes, mud-spattered, under which lay empty cans and sodden newspaper, cut off the end of the garden. Wexford pushed his way through them into a waste-land. Four men were digging, and digging more than the three spits deep which is the gardener's rule. Mountains of earth, scattered with chalk splinters, were piled against the river wall. Lovat was sitting on this wall, his coat collar turned up, a thin damp cigarette stuck to his lower lip, watching them inscrutably.

'What makes you think she's here?'

'Got to be somewhere.' Lovat showed no surprise at his arrival but spread another sheet of newspaper on the wall for him to sit down. 'Nasty day,' he said.

'You think the husband killed her?' Wexford knew it was useless asking questions. You had to make statements and wait for Lovat to agree with them or refute them. 'You've got him on a shop-breaking charge. But you've got no body, just a missing woman. Someone must have made you take that seriously, and not Grey himself.'

'Her mother,' said Lovat.

'I see. Everyone thought she'd gone to her mother, and her mother thought she was elsewhere, but she didn't answer mother's letters. Grey's got a record, maybe living with another woman. Told a lot of lies. Am I right?'

'Yes.'

Wexford thought he had done his duty. It was a pity he knew so little about badgers, was even less interested in them than he was in the Grey affair. The icy mist was seeping through his clothes to his spine, chilling his whole body. 'Brock,' he said, 'will you do me a favour?'

Most people when asked that question reply that it all depends on what the favour is. But Lovat had virtues to offset his taciturnity. He took another crumpled cigarette from a damp and crumpled packet. 'Yes,' he said simply.

'You know that guy Hathall I'm always on about? I think he worked a payroll fiddle while he was with Kidd's at Toxborough. That's why I was there when we met the other day. But I've no authority to act. I'm pretty sure it was like this . . .' Wexford told him what he was pretty sure it was like.

'Would you get someone along to those Trustee Savings Banks and see if you can smell out any false accounts? And quick, Brock, because I've only got ten days.'

Lovat didn't ask why he only had ten days. He wiped his spectacles which the fog had misted and readjusted them on his red snub nose. Without looking at Wexford or showing the least interest, he fixed his eyes on the men and said, 'One way and another I've had a lot to do with digging in my time.'

Wexford made no response. Just at the moment he couldn't summon up much enthusiasm for a League-Against-Cruel-Sports homily. Nor did he repeat his request, which would only have annoyed Lovat, but sat silent in the damp cold listening to the sounds the spades made when they struck chalk, and the soft slump of earth lifted and slung heavily aside. Cans, waterlogged cartons, were lumped on to the growing heaps, to be followed by unearthed rose bushes, their roots scorpion-like and matted with wet soil. Was there a body under there? At any moment a spade might reveal, not a clod of ancient mortar or another mass of brown root, but a white and rotting human hand.

The mist was thickening over the almost stagnant water. Lovat threw his cigarette end into an oil-scummed puddle. 'Will do,' he said.

It was a relief to get away from the river and its miasma – the miasma that had once been thought of as a breeder of disease – and up into the fashionable part of the Old Town where he had parked his car. He was wiping its misted windscreen when he saw Nancy Lake, and he would have wondered what she was doing there had she not, at that moment, turned into a little baker's shop, famous for its home-baked bread and cakes. More than a year had passed since he had last seen her, and he had almost forgotten the sensation he had felt then, the catching of breath, the faint tremor in the heart. He felt it now as he saw the glass door close on her, the shop's warm orange glow receive her.

Although he was shivering now, his breath like smoke on the cold haze, he waited there for her on the kerb. And when she came out she rewarded him with one of her rich sweet smiles. 'Mr Wexford! There are policemen everywhere down here, but I didn't expect to see you.'

'I'm a policeman too. May I give you a lift back to Kingsmarkham?'

'Thank you, I'm not going back just now.' She wore a chinchilla coat that sparkled with fine drops. The cold which pinched other faces had coloured hers and brightened her eyes. 'But I'll come and sit in your car with you for five minutes, shall I?'

Someone, he thought, ought to invent a way of heating a car while the engine was switched off. But she didn't seem to feel the cold. She leaned towards him with the eagerness and the vitality of a young woman. 'Shall we share a cream cake?'

He shook his head. 'Bad for my figure, I'm afraid.'

'But you've got a lovely figure!'

Knowing that he shouldn't, that this was inviting a renewal of flirtation, he looked into those shining eyes and said, 'You are always saying things to me that no woman has said for half a lifetime.'

She laughed. 'Not always. How can it be "always" when I never see you?' She began to eat a cake. It was the kind of cake no one should attempt to eat without a plate, a fork and a napkin. She managed it with her bare fingers remarkably well, her small red tongue retrieving flecks of cream from her lips. 'I've sold my house,' she said. 'I'm moving out the day before Christmas Eve.'

The day before Christmas Eve ... 'They say that you're going abroad.'

'Do they? They've been saying things about me round here for twenty years and most of it has been a distortion of the truth. Do they say that my dream has come true at last?' She finished her cake, licked her fingers delicately. 'Now I must go. Once – Oh, it seems years ago – I asked you to come and have tea with me.'

'So you did,' he said.

'Will you come? Say – next Friday?' When he nodded, she said, 'And we'll have the last of the miracle jam.'

'I wish you'd tell me why you call it that.'

'I will, I will . . .' He held the car door open for her and she took the hand he held out. 'I'll tell you the story of my life. All shall be made clear. Till Friday, then.'

'Till Friday.' It was absurd, this feeling of excitement. You're old, he told himself sternly. She wants to give you plum jam and tell you the story of her life, that's all you're fit for now. And he watched her walk away until her grey fur had melted into the river mist and was gone.

'I can't follow him on the Tube, Reg. I've tried three times, but each night the crowds get worse with the pre-Christmas rush.'

'I can imagine,' said Wexford, who felt he never wanted to hear the word 'Christmas' again. He was more aware of the season's festive pressures than he had ever been in the past. Was Christmas more christmassy this year than usual? Or was it simply that he saw every card that flopped on to his front door mat, every hint of the coming celebrations, as a threat of failure? There was a bitter irony in the fact that this year they were going to fill the house with more people than ever before, both his daughters, his son-in-law, his two grandsons, Howard and Denise, Burden and his children. And Dora had already begun to put up the decorations. He had to hunch in his chair, the phone on his knees, to avoid prickling his face on the great bunch of holly that hung above his desk. 'That seems to be that then, doesn't it?' he said. 'Give it up, finish. Something may come out of the payroll thing. It's my last hope.'

Howard's voice sounded indignant. 'I didn't mean I want to give it up. I only meant that I can't do it that way.'

491

'What other way is there?'

'Why shouldn't I try to tail him from the other end?'

'The other end?'

'Last night after I'd lost him on the Tube, I went up to Dartmeet Avenue. You see, I'd reckoned he may stay all night with her some nights, but he doesn't always stay there. If he did, there'd be no point in his having a place of his own. And he didn't stay last night, Reg. He came home on the last 28 bus. So I thought, why shouldn't I also get on that last bus?'

'I must be getting thick in my old age,' said Wexford, 'but I don't see how that helps.'

'This is how. He'll get on at the stop nearest to her place, won't he? And once I find it I can wait at it the next night from five-thirty onwards. If he comes by bus I can follow him, if he comes by Tube it'll be harder, but there's still a good chance.'

Kilburn Park, Great Western Road, Pembridge Road, Church Street . . . Wexford sighed. 'There are dozens of stops,' he said.

'Not in Notting Hill, there aren't. And it has to be Notting Hill, remember. The last 28 bus crosses Notting Hill Gate at ten to eleven. Tomorrow night I'll be waiting for it in Church Street. I've got six more weekday evenings, Reg, six more watching nights to Christmas.'

'You shall have the breast of the turkey,' said his uncle, 'and the fifty-pence piece from the pudding.'

As he put the phone down, the doorbell rang and he heard the thin reedy voices of young carol singers.

> 'God rest you merry gentlemen,
> Let nothing you dismay . . .'

CHAPTER EIGHTEEN

The Monday of the week before Christmas passed and the Tuesday came and there was nothing from Lovat. Very likely he was too busy with the Morag Grey case to make much effort. Her body hadn't been found, and her husband, remanded in custody for a week, was due to appear in court again solely on the shop-breaking charge. Wexford phoned Myringham police station on Tuesday afternoon. It was Mr. Lovat's day off, Sergeant Hutton told him, and he wouldn't be found at home as he was attending something called the convention of the Society of Friends of the British Badger.

No word came from Howard. It wasn't awe that stopped Wexford phoning him. You don't harass someone who is doing you the enormous favour of giving up all his free time to gratify your obsession, pursue your chimera. You leave him alone and wait. *Chimera:* Monster, bogy, thing of fanciful conception. That was how the dictionary defined it, Wexford discovered, looking the word up in the solitude of his office. Thing of fanciful conception . . . Hathall was flesh and blood all right, but the woman? Only Howard had ever seen her, and Howard wasn't prepared to swear that Hathall – the monster, the bogy – had been her companion. Let nothing you dismay, Wexford told himself. Someone had made that handprint, someone had left those coarse dark hairs on Angela's bedroom floor.

And even if his chances of ever laying hands on her were now remote, growing more remote with each day that passed, he would still want to know how it had been done, fill in those gaps that still remained. He'd want to know where Hathall had met her. In the street, in a pub, as Howard had once suggested? Or had she originally been a friend of Angela's from those early London days before Hathall had been introduced to his second wife at that Hampstead party? Surely she must have lived in the vicinity of Toxborough or Myringham if hers had been the job of making withdrawals from those accounts. Or had that task been shared between her and Angela? Hathall had worked only part-time at Kidd's. On his day off, Angela might have used the car to collect.

Then there was the book on Celtic languages, another strange 'exhibit' in the case he hadn't even begun to account for. Celtic languages had some, not remote, connection with archaeology, but Angela had shown no interest in them while working at the library of the National Archaeologists' League. If the book wasn't relevant, why had Hathall been so upset by the sight of it in his, Wexford's hands?

But whatever he might deduce from the repeated examination of these facts, from carefully listing apparently unconnected pieces of information and trying to establish a link, the really important thing, the securing of Hathall before he left the country, depended now on finding evidence of that fraud. Putting those puzzle pieces together and making a picture of his chimera could wait until it was too late and Hathall was gone. That, he thought bitterly, would make an occupation for the long evenings of the New Year. And when he had still heard nothing from Lovat by Wednesday morning, he drove to Myringham to catch him in his own office, getting there by ten o'clock. Mr Lovat, he was told, was in court and wasn't expected back before lunch.

Wexford pushed his way through the crowds in Myringham's shopping precinct, climbing concrete steps, ascending and descending escalators – the whole lot strung with twinkling fairy lights in the shape of yellow and red daisies – and made his way into the magistrates' court. The public gallery was almost empty. He slid into a seat, looked round for Lovat, and spotted him sitting at the front almost under the Bench.

A pale-faced gangling man of about thirty was in the dock – according to the solicitor appearing for him, one Richard

George Grey, of no fixed abode. Ah, the husband of Morag. No wonder Lovat looked so anxious. But it didn't take long for Wexford to gather that the shop-breaking charge against Grey was based on very fragile evidence. The police, obviously, wanted a committal which it didn't look as if they would get. Grey's solicitor, youthful, suave and polished, was doing his best for his client, an effort that made Lovat's mouth turn down. With rare *schadenfreude*, Wexford found himself hoping Grey would get off. Why should he be the lucky one, able to hold a man until he had got enough evidence against him to charge him with the murder of his wife?

'And so you will appreciate, Your Worships, that my client has suffered from a series of grave misfortunes. Although he is not obliged to divulge to you any previous convictions, he wishes to do so, aware, no doubt, of how trivial you will find his one sole conviction to be. And of what does this single conviction consist? That, Your Worships, of being placed on probation for being found on enclosed premises at the tender age of seventeen.'

Wexford shifted along to allow for the entry of two elderly women with shopping bags. Their expressions were avid and they seemed to make themselves at home. This entertainment, he thought, was free, matutinal, and the real nittygritty stuff of life, three advantages it had over the cinema. Savouring Lovat's discomfiture, he listened as the solicitor went on.

'Apart from this, what do his *criminal proclivities* amount to? Oh, it is true that when he found himself destitute and without a roof over his head, he was driven to take refuge in a derelict house for which its rightful owner had no use and which was classified as *unfit for human habitation*. But this, as Your Worships are aware, is no crime. It is not even, as the law has stood for six hundred years, trespass. It is true too that he was dismissed by his previous employer for – he frankly admits, though no charge was brought – appropriating from his employer the negligible sum of two pounds fifty. As a result, he was obliged to leave his flat or tied cottage in Maynnot Hall, Toxborough, and as an even more serious result was deserted by his wife on the ground that she refused to live with a man whose honesty was not beyond reproach. This lady, whose whereabouts are not known and whose desertion has caused my client intense distress, seems to have something in common with the Myringham police, in particular that of hitting a man when he is down . . .'

There was a good deal more in the same vein. Wexford would have found it less boring, he thought, if he had heard more of the concrete evidence and less of this airy-fairy-pleading. But the evidence must have been thin and the identification of Grey shaky, for the magistrates returned after three minutes to dismiss the case. Lovat got up in disgust and Wexford rose to follow him. His elderly neighbours moved their shopping bags under protest, there was a press of people outside the court – a cloud of witnesses appearing for a grievous bodily harm case – and by the time he got through, Lovat was off in his car and not in the direction of the police station.

Well, he was fifteen miles north of Kingsmarkham, fifteen miles nearer London. Why waste those miles? Why not go on northwards for a last word with Eileen Hathall? Things could hardly be worse than they were. There was room only for improvement. And how would he feel if she were to tell him Hathall's emigration had been postponed, that he was staying a week, a fortnight, longer in London?

As he passed through Toxborough, the road taking him along Maynnot Way, a memory twitched at the back of his mind. Richard and Morag Grey had lived here once, had been servants presumably at Maynnot Hall – but it wasn't that. Yet it had something to do with what the young solicitor had said. Concentratedly, he reviewed the case, what he had come to think of as Hathall country, a landscape with figures. So many places and so many figures . . . Of all the personalities he had encountered or heard spoken of, one had been hinted at by the solicitor in his dramatic address to the Bench. But no name had been mentioned except Grey's . . . Yes, his wife. The lost woman, that was it. 'Deserted by his wife on the grounds that she refused to live with a man whose honesty was not beyond reproach.' But what did it remind him of? Way back in Hathall country, a year ago perhaps, or months or weeks, someone somewhere had spoken to him of a woman with a peculiar regard for honesty. The trouble was that he hadn't the slightest recollection of who that someone had been.

No effort of memory was required to identify Eileen Hathall's lunch guest. Wexford hadn't seen old Mrs Hathall for fifteen months and he was somewhat aghast to find her there. The ex-wife wouldn't tell the ex-husband of his call, but the mother would very likely tell the son. Never mind. It no longer mattered. Hathall was leaving the country in five days' time. A man who is fleeing his native land forever has no time for petty revenges and needless precautions.

And it seemed that Mrs Hathall, who was sitting at the table drinking an after-lunch cup of tea, was under a lucky misapprehension as to the cause of his visit. This tiresome policeman had called at a house where she was before; he was calling at a house where she was again. On each previous occasion he had wanted her son, therefore – 'You won't find him here,' she said in that gruff voice with its North Country undercurrent. 'He's busy getting himself ready for going abroad.'

Eileen met his questioning glance. 'He came here last night and said good-bye,' she said. Her voice sounded calm, almost complacent. And looking from one woman to the other, Wexford realized what had happened to them. Hathall, while living in England, had been to each of them a source of chronic bitterness, breeding in the mother a perpetual need to nag and harass, in the ex-wife resentment and humiliation. Hathall gone, Hathall so far away that he might as well be dead, would leave them at peace. Eileen would take on the status almost of a widow, and the old woman would have a ready-made respectable reason – her granddaughter's English education – as to why her son and daughter-in-law were parted.

'He's going on Monday?' he said.

Old Mrs Hathall nodded with a certain smugness. 'Don't suppose we shall ever set eyes on him again.' She finished her tea, got up and began to clear the table. The minute you finished a meal you cleared the remains of it away. That was the rule. Wexford saw her lift the lid from the teapot and contemplate its contents with an air of irritation, as if she regretted the wicked waste of throwing away half a pint of tea. And she indicated to Eileen with a little dumb show that there was more if she wanted it. Eileen shook her head and Mrs Hathall bore the pot away. That Wexford might have drunk it, might at least have been given the chance to refuse it, didn't seem to cross their minds. Eileen waited till her mother-in-law had left the room.

'I'm well rid of him,' she said. 'He'd no call to come here, I'm sure. I'd done without him for five years and I can do without him for the rest of my life. As far as I'm concerned, it's good riddance.'

It was as he had supposed. She was now able to pretend to herself that she had sent him away, that now Angela was gone she could have accompanied him to Brazil herself had she so chosen. 'Mum and me,' she said, surveying the bare room, unadorned by a single bunch of holly or paper streamer, 'Mum and me'll have a quiet Christmas by ourselves. Rosemary's going to her French pen-friend tomorrow and she won't be back till her school term starts. We'll be nice and quiet on our own.'

He almost shivered. The affinity between these women frightened him. Had Eileen married Hathall because he could bring her the mother she wanted? Had Mrs Hathall chosen Eileen for him because this was the daughter she needed?

'Mum's thinking of coming to live here with me,' she said as the old woman came plodding back. 'When Rosemary goes off to college, that is. No point in keeping up two homes, is there?'

A warmer, a more affectionate, woman might have reacted by smiling her gratification or by linking an arm with this ideal daughter-in-law. Mrs Hathall's small cold eyes flickered their approval over the barren room, resting briefly on Eileen's puffy face and crimped hair, while her mouth, rigid and down-turned, showed something like disappointment that she had no fault to find. 'Come along then, Eileen,' she said. 'We've got them dishes to do.'

They left Wexford to find his own way out. As he came from under the canopy that reminded him of a provincial railway station, the car that had been Hathall's turned into the drive, Rosemary at the wheel. The face that was an intelligent version of her grandmother's registered recognition but no polite expression of greeting, no smile.

'I hear you're going off to France for Christmas?'

She switched off the engine but otherwise she didn't move.

'I remember your saying once before that you'd never been out of England.'

'That's right.'

'Not even on a day trip to France with your school, Miss Hathall?'

'Oh, that,' she said with icy calm. 'That was the day Angela got herself strangled.' She made a quick chilling gesture of running one finger across her throat. 'I told my mother I was going with school. I didn't. I went out with a boy instead. Satisfied?'

'Not quite. You can drive, you've been able to drive for eighteen months. You disliked Angela and seem fond of your father . . .'

She interrupted him harshly. 'Fond of *him?* I can't stand the sight of any of them. My mother's a vegetable and the old woman's a cow. You don't know – no one knows – what they put me through, pulling me this way and that between them.' The words were heated but her voice didn't rise. 'I'm going to get away this year and none of them'll ever see me again for dust. Those two can live here together and one day they'll just die and no one'll find them for months.' Her hand went up to push a lock of coarse dark hair from her face, and he saw her fingertip, rosy red and quite smooth. 'Satisfied?' she said again.

'I am now.'

'Me kill Angela?' She gave a throaty laugh. 'There's others I'd kill first, I can tell you. Did you really think I'd killed her?'

'Not really,' said Wexford, 'but I'm sure you could have if you'd wanted to.'

He was rather pleased with this parting shot and thought of a few more *esprits d'escalier* as he drove off. It had only once before been his lot to confound a Hathall. He might, of course, have asked her if she had ever known a woman with a scarred fingertip, but it went against the grain with him to ask a daughter to betray her father, even such a daughter and such a father. He wasn't a medieval inquisitor or the pillar of a Fascist state.

Back at the police station he phoned Lovat who, naturally, was out and not expected to reappear till the following day. Howard wouldn't phone. If he had watched last night he had watched in vain, for Hathall had been making his farewells at Croydon.

Dora was icing the Christmas cake, placing in the centre of the white frosted circle a painted plaster Santa Claus and surrounding it with plaster robins, ornaments which came out each year from their silver paper wrappings and which had first been brought when Wexford's elder daughter was a baby.

'There! Doesn't it look nice?'

'Lovely,' said Wexford gloomily.

Dora said with calculated callousness, 'I shall be glad when that man's gone to wherever he's going and you're your normal self again.' She covered the cake and rinsed her hands. 'By the way, d'you remember once asking me about a woman called Lake? The one you said reminded you of George the Second?'

'I didn't say that,' said Wexford uneasily.

'Something like that. Well, I thought you might be interested to know she's getting married. To a man called Somerset. His wife died a couple of months ago. I imagine something has been going on there for years, but they kept it very dark. Quite a mystery. He can't have made any deathbed promises about only taking mistresses, can he? Oh, darling, I do wish you'd show a bit of interest sometimes and not look so perpetually fed up!'

CHAPTER NINETEEN

Thursday was his day off. Not that he would take a day off as he meant to run Lovat to earth – a fine metaphor, he thought, to use in connection with a protector of wildlife – but there was no reason for early rising. He had gone to sleep thinking what an old fool he was to suppose Nancy Lake fancied him when she was going to marry Somerset, and when morning came he was deep in a Hathall dream. This time it was totally nonsensical with Hathall and his woman embarking on to a flying 28 bus, and the phone ringing by his bed jerked him out of it at eight o'clock.

'I thought I'd get you before I left for work,' said Howard's voice. 'I've found the bus stop, Reg.'

That was more alerting than the alarm bell of the phone. 'Tell,' he said.

'I saw him leave Marcus Flower at five-thirty, and when he went up to Bond Street station I knew he'd be going to her. I had to go back to my own manor for a couple of hours, but I got down to the New King's Road by half past ten. God, it was easy. The whole exercise worked out better than I dared hope.

'I was sitting on one of the front seats downstairs, the near-side by the window. He wasn't at the stop at the top of Church Street or the next one just after Notting Hill Gate station. I knew if he was going to get on it would have to be soon and then, lo and behold, there he was all on his own at a request stop halfway up Pembridge Road. He went upstairs. I stayed on the bus and saw him get off at West End Green, and then,' Howard ended triumphantly, 'I went on to Golders Green and came home in a cab.'

'Howard, you are my only ally.'

502

'Well, you know what Chesterton said about that. I'll be at that bus stop from five-thirty onwards tonight and then we'll see.'

Wexford put on his dressing gown and went downstairs to find what Chesterton had said. 'There are no words to express the abyss between isolation and having one ally. It may be conceded to the mathematicians that four is twice two. But two is not twice one; two is two thousand times one . . .' He felt considerably cheered. Maybe he had no force of men at his disposal but he had Howard, the resolute, the infinitely reliable, the invincible, and together they were two thousand. Two thousand and one with Lovat. He must bathe and dress and get over to Myringham right away.

The head of Myringham CID was in, and with him Sergeant Hutton.

'Not a bad day,' said Lovat, peering through his funny little spectacles at the uniformly white, dull, sun-free sky.

Wexford thought it best to say nothing about Richard Grey. 'Did you get to work on that payroll thing?'

Lovat nodded very slowly and profoundly, but it was the sergeant who was appointed spokesman. 'We found one or two accounts which looked suspicious, sir. Three, to be precise. One was in the Trustee Savings Bank at Toxborough, one at Passingham St. John and one here. All had had regular payments made into them by Kidd and Co., and in all cases the payments and withdrawals ceased in March or April last year. The one in Myringham was in the name of a woman whose address turned out to be a sort of boarding house-cum-hotel. The people there don't remember her and we haven't been able to trace her. The one at Passingham turned out to be valid, all above board. The woman there worked at Kidd's, left in the March and just didn't bother to take the last thirty pee out of her account.'

'And the Toxborough account?'

'That's the difficulty, sir. It's in the name of a Mrs Mary

Lewis and the address is a Toxborough address, but the house is shut up and the people evidently away. The neighbours say they're called Kingsbury not Lewis, but they've taken in lodgers over the years and one of them could have been a Lewis. We just have to wait till the Kingsburys come back.'

'Do these neighbours know when they're coming back?'

'No,' said Lovat.

Does anyone ever go away the week before Christmas and not stay away till after Christmas? Wexford thought it unlikely. His day off stretched before him emptily. A year ago he had resolved to be patient, but the time had come when he was counting the hours rather than the days to Hathall's departure. Four days. Ninety-six hours. And that, he thought, must be the only instance when a large number sounds pitifully smaller than a small number. Ninety-six hours. Five thousand, seven hundred and sixty minutes. Nothing. It would be gone in the twinkling of an eye . . .

And the frustrating thing was that he had to waste those hours, those thousands of minutes, for there was nothing left for him personally to do. He could only go home and help Dora hang up more paper chains, arrange more coy bunches of mistletoe, plant the Christmas tree in its tub, speculate with her as to whether the turkey was small enough to lie on an oven shelf or big enough instead to be suspended by strings from the oven roof. And on Friday when only seventy-two hours remained (four thousand three hundred and twenty minutes) he went with Burden up to the police station canteen for the special Christmas dinner. He even put on a paper hat and pulled a cracker with Policewoman Polly Davies.

Ahead of him was his tea date with Nancy Lake. He nearly phoned her to cancel it, but he didn't do this, telling himself there were still one or two questions she could answer for him and that this was as good a way as any of using up some of those four thousand-odd minutes. By four o'clock he was in Wool Lane, not thinking about her at all, thinking how, eight months before, he had walked there with Howard, full of hope and energy and determination.

'We've been lovers for nineteen years,' she said. 'I'd been married for five and I'd come to live here with my husband, and one day when I was walking in the lane I met Mark. He was in his father's garden, picking plums. We knew its proper name, but we called it a miracle tree because it was a miracle for us.'

'The jam,' said Wexford, 'is very good.'

'Have some more.' She smiled at him across the table. The room where they were sitting was as bare as Eileen Hathall's and there were no Christmas decorations. But it wasn't barren or sterile or cold. He could see signs everywhere of the removal of a picture, a mirror, an ornament, and looking at her, listening to her, he could imagine the beauty and the character of those furnishings that were packed now, ready to be taken to her new home. The dark blue velvet curtains still hung at the French window, and she had drawn them to shut out the early mid-winter dusk. They made for her a sombre night sky background, and she glowed against them, her face a little flushed, the old diamond on her finger and the new diamond beside it, sparking rainbow fire from the light of the lamp at her side. 'Do you know,' she said suddenly, 'what it's like to be in love and have nowhere to go to make love?'

'I know it — vicariously.'

'We managed as best we could. My husband found out and then Mark couldn't come to Wool Lane any more. We'd tried not seeing each other and sometimes we kept it up for months, but it never worked.'

'Why didn't you marry? Neither of you had children.'

She took his empty cup and refilled it. As she passed it to him, her fingers just brushed his and he felt himself grow hot with something that was almost anger. As if it wasn't bad enough, he thought, her being there and looking like that without all this sex talk as well. 'My husband died,' she said. 'We were going to marry. Then Mark's wife got ill and he couldn't leave her. It was impossible.'

He couldn't keep the sneering note out of his voice. 'So you remained faithful to each other and lived in hopes?'

'No, there were others – for me.' She looked at him steadily, and he found himself unable to return that look. 'Mark knew, and if he minded he never blamed me. How could he? I told you once, I felt like a distraction, something to – to divert him when he could be spared from his wife's bedside.'

'Was it she you meant when you asked me if it was wrong to wish for someone's death?'

'Of course. Who else? Did you think – did you think I was speaking of *Angela?*' Her gravity went and she was smiling again. 'Oh, my dear . . .! Shall I tell you something else? Two years ago when I was very bored and very lonely because Gwen Somerset was home from hospital and wouldn't let Mark out of her sight, I – I made advances to Robert Hathall. There's confession for you! And he wouldn't have me. He turned me down. I am not accustomed,' she said with mock pomposity, 'to being turned down.'

'I suppose not. Do you think I'm blind,' he said rather savagely, 'or a complete fool?'

'Just unapproachable. If you've finished, shall we go into the other room? It's more comfortable. I haven't yet stripped it of every vestige of me.'

His questions were answered, and there was no need now to ask where she had been when Angela died or where Somerset had been, or probe any of those mysteries about her and Somerset, which were mysteries no more. He might as well say good-bye and go, he thought, as he crossed the hall behind her and followed her into a warmer room of soft textures and deep rich colours, and where there seemed no hard surfaces, but only silk melting into velvet and velvet into

brocade. Before she could close the door, he held out his hand
to her, meaning to begin a little speech of thanks and farewell.
But she took his hand in both of hers.

'I shall be gone on Monday,' she said, looking up into his
face. 'The new people are moving in. We shan't meet again.
I would promise you that, if you like.'

Up till then he had doubted her intentions towards him.
There was no room for doubt now.

'Why should you think I want to be the last fling for a
woman who is going to her first love?'

'Isn't it a compliment?'

He said, 'I'm an old man, and an old man who is taken
in by compliments is pathetic.'

She flushed a little. 'I shall soon be an old woman. We
could be pathetic together.' A rueful laugh shook her voice.
'Don't go yet. We can – talk. We've never really talked yet.'

'We have done nothing but talk,' said Wexford, but he
didn't go. He let her lead him to the sofa and sit beside him
and talk to him about Somerset and Somerset's wife and the
nineteen years of secrecy and deception. Her hand rested in
his, and as he relaxed and listened to her, he remembered the
first time he had held it and what she had said when he had
kept hold of it a fraction too long. At last she got up. He also
rose and put that hand to his lips. 'I wish you happy,' he said.
'I hope you're going to be very happy.'

'I'm a little afraid, you know, of how it will be after so
long. Do you understand what I mean?'

'Of course.' He spoke gently, all savagery gone, and when
she asked him to have a drink with her he said, 'I'll drink *to*
you and to your happiness.'

She put her arms round his neck and kissed him. The kiss
was impulsive, light, over before he could respond to her or
resist her. She was gone from the room for some minutes,
more minutes than were needful to fetch drinks and glasses.
He heard the sound of her footsteps overhead, and he guessed

how she would be when she came back. So he had to decide
what he should do, whether to go or stay. Gather ye rosebuds,
roses, other men's flowers, while ye may? Or be an old man,
dreaming dreams and being mindful of one's marriage vows?

The whole of his recent life seemed to him a long series
of failures, of cowardice and caution. And yet the whole of
his recent life had also been bent towards doing what he
believed to be right and just. Perhaps, in the end, it came to
the same thing.

At last he went out into the hall. He called her name,
'Nancy!', using that name for the first and only time, and when
he moved to the foot of the stairs, he saw her at the head of
them. The light there was soft and kind, unnecessarily kind,
and she was as he had known she would be, as he had seen
her in his fantasies – only better than that, better than his
expectations.

He looked up at her in wondering appreciation, looked for
long silent minutes. But by then he had made up his mind.

Only the unwise dwell on what is past with regret for rejected
opportunity or nostalgia for chosen delight. He regretted nothing, for he had only done what any man of sense would have
done in his position. His decision had been reached during
those moments while she had been away from the room and
he had stuck to that decision, confident he was acting according to his own standards and what was right for him. But he
was astonished to find it was so late when he let himself into
his own house, nearly eight o'clock. And at the recalling of
his mind to time's passing, he was back to counting the
minutes, back to calculating that only about three and a half
thousand of them remained. Nancy's face faded, the warmth
of her vanished. He marched into the kitchen where Dora was
making yet another batch of mince pies and said rather
brusquely, 'Has Howard phoned?'

She looked up. He had forgotten – he was always forgetting

– how astute she was. 'He wouldn't phone at this time, would he? It's last thing at night or first thing in the morning with him.'

'Yes, I know. But I'm strung up about this thing.'

'Indeed you are. You forgot to kiss me.'

So he kissed her, and the immediate past was switched off. No regrets, he reminded himself, no nostalgia, no introspection. And he took a mince pie and bit into the hot crisp crust.

'You'll get fat and gross and revolting.'

'Perhaps,' said Wexford thoughtfully, 'that wouldn't be such a bad thing – in moderation, of course.'

CHAPTER TWENTY

Sheila Wexford, the chief inspector's actress daughter, arrived on Saturday morning. It was good to see her in the flesh, her father said, instead of two-dimensionally and monotonally in her television serial. She pranced about the house arranging the cards more artistically and singing that she was dreaming of a white Christmas. It seemed, however, that it was going to be a foggy one. The long-range weather forecast had said it would be, and now the weather signs themselves fulfilled this prediction as a white morning mist shrouded the sun at noon and by evening was dense and yellowish.

The shortest day of the year. The Winter Solstice. It was arctic in light as well as in temperature, the fog closing out daylight at three and heralding seventeen hours of darkness. Along the streets lighted Christmas trees showed only as an amber blur in windows. God rest you merry, gentlemen, let nothing you dismay . . . Seventeen hours of darkness, thirty-six hours to go.

Howard had promised to phone and did so at ten. Hathall had been indoors alone at 62 Dartmeet Avenue since three. Howard was in the call-box opposite the house, but now he was going home. His six watching nights to Christmas were over – today's had been a bonus vigil, undertaken because he couldn't bear to be beaten and he was going home.

'I'll watch him tomorrow, Reg, for the last time.'

'Is there any point?'

'I shall feel I've done the job as thoroughly as it can be done.'

Hathall had been alone most of the day. Did that mean he had sent the woman on ahead of him? Wexford went to bed early and lay awake thinking of Christmas, thinking of himself and Howard retired to a quiet corner and holding their last inquest over what had happened, what else they could have done, what might have happened if on October second a year ago Griswold hadn't issued his ban.

On Sunday morning the fog began to lift. The vague hope Wexford had entertained that fog might force Hathall to postpone his departure faded as the sun appeared strong and bright by midday. He listened to the radio news but no airports were closed and no flights cancelled. And as the evening began with a bright sunset and a clear frosty sky – as if winter was already dying with the passing of the solstice – he knew he must resign himself to Hathall's escape. It was all over.

But though he could teach himself to avoid introspection where Nancy Lake was concerned, he couldn't help dwelling with regret and bitterness over the long period during which he and Robert Hathall had been adversaries. Things might have been very different if only he had guessed at that payroll fraud – if fraud there was – before. He should have known too that an angry paranoiac with much at stake wouldn't react passively to his clumsy probing and what that probing implied. But it was all over now and he would never know who the woman was. Sadly he thought of other questions that must remain unanswered. What was the reason for the presence in Bury Cottage of the Celtic languages book? Why had Hathall, who in middle life had come to enjoy sexual variety, repulsed such a woman as Nancy Lake? Why had his accomplice, in most ways so thorough and careful, left her handprint on, of all places, the side of the bath? And why had Angela, anxious to please her mother-in-law, desperate for a reconciliation, worn on the day of her visit the very clothes which had helped turn her mother-in-law against her?

It didn't cross his mind that, at this late stage, Howard would have any further success. Hathall's habit was to stay at home on Sundays, entertaining his mother or his daughter. And even

though he had already said good-bye to them, there seemed
no reason to suppose he would change his ways to the extent
of going to Notting Hill and her, when they were leaving
together on the following day. So when he lifted the receiver
at eleven that Sunday night and heard the familiar voice, a
little tired now and a little irritable, he thought at first Howard
was phoning only to say at what time he and Denise would
arrive on Christmas Eve. And when he understood the true
reason for the call, that at last when it was too late, Howard
was on the brink of accomplishing his task, he felt the sick
despair of a man who doesn't want hope to come in and
threaten his resignation.

'You saw her?' he said dully. 'You actually saw her?'

'I know how you're feeling, Reg, but I have to tell you. I
couldn't keep it to myself. I saw him. I saw her. I saw them
together. And I lost them.'

'Oh, *God*. My God, it's more than I can take.'

'Don't kill the messenger, Reg,' Howard said gently. 'Don't
do a Cleopatra on me. I that do bring the news made not the
match.'

'I'm not angry with you. How could I be after all you've
done? I'm angry with – fate, I suppose. Tell me what happened.'

'I started watching the house in Dartmeet Avenue after
lunch. I didn't know whether Hathall was in or not until I
saw him come out and put a great sackful of rubbish into one
of those dustbins. He was having a clear-out, packing, I expect,
and throwing out what he didn't want. I sat there in the car,
and I nearly went home when I saw his light go on at half
past four.

'Maybe it would have been better if I had gone home. At
least I couldn't have raised your hopes. He came out of the
house at six, Reg, and walked down to West End Green. I
followed him in the car and parked in Mill Lane – that's the
street that runs westwards off Fortune Green Road. We both

waited for about five minutes. The 28 bus didn't come and he got into a taxi instead.'

'You followed it?' said Wexford, admiration for a moment overcoming his bitterness.

'It's easier to follow a taxi than a bus. Buses keep stopping.

Following a taxi in London on a Sunday night is a different matter from trying to do it by day in the rush hours. Anyway, the driver took more or less the same route as the bus. It dropped Hathall outside a pub in Pembridge Road.'

'Near that stop where you saw him get on the bus before?'

'Quite near, yes. I've been to that bus stop and the streets round about it every night this week, Reg. But he must have used the back street to get to her from Notting Hill Gate station. I never saw him once.'

'You went into this pub after him?'

'It's called the Rosy Cross and it was very crowded. He bought two drinks, gin for himself and pernod for her, although she hadn't come in yet. He managed to find two seats in a corner and he put his coat on one of them to keep it. Most of the time the crowd blocked my view of him, but I could see that glass of yellow pernod waiting on the table for her to come and drink it.

'Hathall was early or she was ten minutes late. I didn't know she'd come in till I saw a hand go round that yellow glass and the glass lifted up out of my sight. I moved then and pushed through the crowd to get a better look. It was the same woman I saw him with outside Marcus Flower, a pretty woman in her early thirties with dyed blonde cropped hair. No, don't ask. I didn't see her hand. I was too close for safety as it was. I think Hathall recognized me. God, he'd have to be blind not to by now, even with the care I've taken.

'They drank their drinks quite quickly and pushed their way out. She must live quite near there, but where she lives I can't tell you. It doesn't matter now, anyway. I saw them walking away when I came out and I was going to follow them on foot. A taxi came and they got into it. Hathall didn't even wait to tell the driver where he wanted to go. He just got in and must have given his instructions afterwards. He wasn't going to run the risk of being followed, and I couldn't follow them. The taxi went off up Pembridge Road and I lost them. I lost them and went home.

'The last of Robert Hathall, Reg. It was good while it lasted. I really thought – well, never mind. You were right all along the line and that, I'm afraid, must be your consolation.'

Wexford said good night to his nephew and that he would see him on Christmas Eve. An aircraft sounded overhead, coming out of Gatwick. He stood by his bedroom window and watched its white and red lights like meteors crossing the clear starlit sky. Just a few more hours and Hathall would be on such an aircraft. First thing in the morning? Or an afternoon flight? Or would he and she be going by night? He found he knew very little about extradition. It hadn't come in his way to know about it. And things had taken such strange turns lately that a country would probably bargain, would want concessions or some sort of exchange before releasing a foreign national. Besides, though you might get an extradition order if you had irrefutable evidence of murder, surely you wouldn't on a fraud charge. Deception, the charge would be, he thought, deception under Section 15 of the Theft Act of 1968. It suddenly seemed fantastic to contemplate putting all that political machinery in motion to fetch a man out of Brazil for helping himself to the funds of a plastic doll factory.

He thought of Crippen being apprehended in mid-Atlantic by a wireless message, of train robbers caught after long periods of freedom in the distant South, of films he had seen in which some criminal, at ease now and believing himself secure, felt the heavy hand of the law descend on his shoulder as he sat drinking wine in a sunny pavement café. It wasn't his world. He couldn't see himself, even in a minor capacity, taking part in exotic drama. Instead he saw Hathall flying

away to freedom, to the life he had planned and had done
murder to get, while in a week or two perhaps Brock Lovat
was obliged to admit defeat because he had found no fraud
or theft or deception but only a few vague hints of something
underhand which Hathall might have been called to account
for – if only Hathall had been there to answer.

The day had come.

Waking early, Wexford thought of Hathall waking early
too. He had seen Howard the night before, had suspected he
was still being followed, so wouldn't have dared spend the
night with the woman or have her spend the night with him.
Now he was washing at the sink in that nasty little room,
taking a suit from the Battle of Mons wardrobe, shaving before
packing his razor into the small hand-case he would take with
him in the aircraft. Wexford could see the red granite face,
more heavily flushed from its contact with the razor's edge,
the thinning black hair slicked back with a wet comb. Now
Hathall would be taking a last look at the ten by twelve cell
which had been his home for nine months, and thinking with
happy anticipation of the home that was to be his; now across
to the call-box, at mid-winter daybreak, to check his flight with
the airport and harangue the girl who spoke to him for not
being prompt enough or efficient or considerate enough; now,
lastly, a call to *her*, wherever she was, in the labyrinth of
Notting Hill. No, perhaps one more call. To the taxi rank or
car-hire place for the car that would take him and his luggage
away forever . . .

Stop it, he told himself severely. Leave it. No more of this.
This way madness – or at least an obsessional neurosis – lies.
Christmas is coming, go to work, forget him. He took Dora a
cup of tea and went to work.

In his office he went through the morning mail and stuck
a few Christmas cards around. There was one from Nancy
Lake, which he looked at thoughtfully for a moment or two

before putting it inside his desk. No less than five calendars had come, including one of the glossy nudes *genre*, the offering of a local garage. It brought to mind Ginge at West Hampstead station, the offices of Marcus Flower . . . Was he going crazy? What was happening to him when he let erotica bring to mind a murder hunt? Stop it. From his selection he chose a handsome and immensely dull calendar, twelve colour plates of Sussex scenes, and pinned it on to the wall next to the district map. The gift of a grateful garage he put into a new envelope, marked it *For Your Eyes Only* and had it sent down to Burden's office. That would set the prim inspector fulminating against current moral standards and divert his, Wexford's, mind from that bloody, unspeakable, triumphant, God-damned crook and fugitive, Robert Hathall.

Then he turned his attention to the matters that were at present concerning Kingsmarkham police. Five women in the town and two from outlying villages had complained of obscene telephone calls. The only extraordinary thing about that was that their caller had also been a woman. Wexford smiled a little to note the odd corners of life into which Women's Liberation was infiltrating. He smiled more grimly and with exasperation at Sergeant Martin's attempt to make an issue out of the activities of four small boys who had tied a length of string from a lamppost to a garden wall in an effort to trip up passersby. Why did they waste his time with this rubbish? Yet sometimes it is better to have one's time wasted than spent on hankering ever and ever after a vain thing . . .

His internal phone was bleeping. He lifted the receiver, expecting the voice of a self-righteous and indignant Burden.

'Chief Inspector Lovat to see you, sir. Shall I show him up?'

CHAPTER TWENTY-ONE

Lovat came in slowly, and with him his inevitable interpreter, his *fidus Achates*, Sergeant Hutton.

'Lovely day.'

'Be damned to the day,' said Wexford in a throaty voice because his heart and his blood pressure were behaving very strangely. 'Never mind the day. I wish it would bloody well snow, I wish . . .'

Hutton said quietly. 'If we might just sit down a while, sir? Mr Lovat has something to tell you which he thinks will interest you greatly. And since it was you put him on to it, it seemed only a matter of courtesy . . .'

'Sit down, do as you like, have a calendar, take one each. I know why you've come. But just tell me one thing. Can you get a man extradited for what you've found out? Because if you can't, you've had it. Hathall's going to Brazil today, and ten to one he's gone already.'

'Dear me,' said Lovat placidly.

Wexford nearly put his head in his hands. 'Well, can you?' he shouted.

'I'd better tell you what Mr Lovat *has* found, sir. We called at the home of Mr and Mrs Kingsbury again last night. They'd just returned. They'd been on a visit to their married daughter who was having a baby. No Mrs Mary Lewis has ever lodged with them and they have never had any connection with Kidd and Co. Moreover, on making further enquiries at the boarding house Mr Lovat told you about, he could discover no evidence at all of the existence of the other so-called account holder.'

'So you've had a warrant sworn for Hathall's arrest?'

'Mr Lovat would like to talk to Robert Hathall, sir,' said

517

Hutton cautiously. 'I'm sure you'll agree we need a little more to go on. Apart from the – er, courtesy of the matter, we called on you for Hathall's present address.'

'His present address,' Wexford snapped, 'is probably about five miles up in the air above Madeira or wherever that damned plane flies.'

'Unfortunate,' said Lovat, shaking his head.

'Maybe he hasn't left, sir. If we could phone him?'

'I daresay you could if he had a phone and if he hasn't left.' Wexford looked in some despair at the clock. It was ten-thirty. 'Frankly, I don't know what to do. The only thing I can suggest is that we all get out to Millerton-*les-deux* – er, Hightrees Farm, and lay all this before the Chief Constable.'

'Good idea,' said Lovat. 'Many a fine night I've spent watching the badger setts there.'

Wexford could have kicked him.

He never knew what prompted him to ask the question. There was no sixth sense about it. Perhaps it was just that he thought he should have the facts of this fraud as straight in his mind as they were in Hutton's. But he did ask it, and afterwards he thanked God he had asked it then on the country lane drive to Millerton.

'The addresses of the account holders, sir? One was in the name of Mrs. Dorothy Carter of Ascot House, Myringham – that's the boardinghouse place – and the other of Mrs. Mary Lewis at 19 Maynnot Way, Toxborough.'

'Did you say Maynnot Way?' Wexford asked in a voice that sounded far away and unlike his own.

'That's right. It runs from the industrial estate to . . .'

'I know where it runs to, Sergeant. I also know who lived at Maynnot Hall in the middle of Maynnot Way.' He felt a constriction in his throat. 'Brock,' he said, 'what were you doing at Kidd's that day I met you at the gates?'

Lovat looked at Hutton and Hutton said, 'Mr Lovat was

pursuing his enquiries in connection with the disappearance of Morag Grey, sir. Morag Grey worked as a cleaner at Kidd's for a short while when her husband was gardener at the hall. Naturally, we explored every way open to us.'

'You haven't explored Maynnot Way enough.' Wexford almost gasped at the enormity of his discovery. His chimera, he thought, his thing of fanciful conception. 'Your Morag Grey isn't buried in anyone's garden. She's Robert Hathall's woman, she's going off to Brazil with him. My God, I can see it all . . . !' If only he had Howard beside him to explain all this to instead of the phlegmatic Lovat and this openmouthed sergeant. 'Listen,' he said. 'This Grey woman was Hathall's accomplice in the fraud. He met her when they both worked at Kidd's, and she and his wife had the job of making withdrawals from those accounts. No doubt, she thought up the name and address of Mrs Mary Lewis because she knew Maynnot Way and knew the Kingsburys let rooms. Hathall fell for her and she murdered Hathall's wife. She isn't dead, Brock, she's been living in London as Hathall's mistress ever since . . . When did she disappear?'

'As far as we know, in August or September of last year, sir,' said the sergeant, and he brought the car to a halt on the gravel outside Hightrees Farm.

For the sake of the reputation of Mid-Sussex, it would be most unfortunate for Hathall to escape. This, to Wexford's amazement, was the opinion of Charles Griswold. And he saw a faint flush of unease colour the statesmanlike face as the Chief Constable was forced to admit the theory was tenable.

'This is a little more than 'feeling,' I think, Reg,' he said, and it was he personally who phoned London Airport.

Wexford and Lovat and Hutton had to wait a long time before he came back. And when he did it was to say that Robert Hathall and a woman travelling as Mrs Hathall were on the passenger list of a flight leaving for Rio de Janeiro at twelve forty-five. The airport police would be instructed to hold them both on a charge of deception under the Theft Act, and a warrant had better be sworn at once.

'She must be travelling on his passport.'

'Or on Angela's,' Wexford said. 'He's still got it. I remember looking at it, but it was left with him in Bury Cottage.'

'No need to be bitter, Reg. Better late than never.'

'It happens, sir,' said Wexford very politely but with an edge to his voice, 'to be twenty to twelve now. I just hope we're in time.'

'Oh, he won't get out now,' Griswold said on a breezy note. 'They'll stop him at the airport where you can take yourselves forthwith. Forthwith, Reg. And tomorrow morning you can come over for a Christmas drink and tell me all about it.'

They went back to Kingsmarkham to pick up Burden. The inspector was in the foyer, peering through his glasses at the envelope he brandished, and angrily enquiring of a puzzled station sergeant who had had the effrontery to send him pornography for his exclusive perusal.

'Hathall?' he said when Wexford explained. 'You don't mean it. You're joking.'

'Get in the car, Mike, and I'll tell you on the way. No, Sergeant Hutton will tell *us* on the way. What have you got there? Art studies? Now I see why you needed glasses.'

Burden gave a snort of rage and was about to launch into a long explanation of his innocence, but Wexford cut him short. He didn't need diversions now. He had been waiting for this day, this moment, for fifteen months, and he could have shouted his triumph at the crisp blue air, the springlike sun. They left in two cars. The first contained Lovat and his driver and Polly Davies, the second Wexford, Burden and Sergeant Hutton with their driver.

'I want to know everything you can tell me about Morag Grey.'

'She was – well, is – a Scot, sir. From the northwest of Scotland, Ullapool. But there's not much work up there and she came south and went into service. She met Grey seven or eight years ago and married him and they got that job at Maynnot Hall.'

'What, he did the garden and she cleaned the place?'

'That's right. I don't quite know why as she seems to have been a cut above that sort of thing. According to her mother and – more to the point – according to her employer at the hall, she'd had a reasonable sort of education and was quite bright. Her mother says Grey had dragged her down.'

'How old is she and what does she look like?'

'She'd be about thirty-two now, sir. Thin, dark-haired, nothing special. She did some of the housework at the hall and did outside cleaning jobs as well. One of those was at Kidd's, in last March twelvemonth, but she only stayed two or three weeks. Then Grey got the sack for taking a couple of quid from his employer's wife's handbag. They had to leave their flat and go and squat in Myringham Old Town. But soon after that Morag turned him out. Grey says she found out the reason for their getting the push and wouldn't go on living with a thief. A likely story, I'm sure you'll agree, sir. But he insisted on it, despite the fact that he went straight from her to another woman who had a room about a mile away on the other side of Myringham.'

'It doesn't,' said Wexford thoughtfully, 'seem a likely story under the circumstances.'

'He says he spent the money he pinched on a present for her, a gilt snake necklace . . .'

'Ah.'

'Which may be true but doesn't prove much.'

'I wouldn't say that, Sergeant. What happened to her when she was left on her own?'

'We know very little about that. Squatters don't really have neighbours, they're an itinerant population. She had a series of cleaning jobs up until August and then she went on Social Security. All we know is that Morag told a woman in that row of houses that she'd got a good job in the offing and would be moving away. What that job was and where she was going we never found out. No one saw her after the middle of September. Grey came back around Christmas and took away what possessions she'd left behind.'

'Didn't you say it was her mother who started the hue and cry?'

'Morag had been a regular correspondent, and when her mother got no answers to her letters she wrote to Grey. He found the letters when he went back at Christmas and at last he wrote back with some cock-and-bull story about thinking his wife had gone to Scotland. Mother had never trusted Richard Grey and she went to the police. She came down here and we had to get an interpreter in on account of – believe it or not – her speaking only Gaelic.'

Wexford, who at that moment felt, like the White Queen, that he could have believed six impossible things before breakfast, said, 'Does Morag also – er, have the Gaelic?'

'Yes, sir, she does. She's bilingual.'

With a sigh Wexford sank back against the upholstery. There were a few loose ends to be tied, a few small instances of the unaccountable to be accounted for, but otherwise . . . He closed his eyes. The car was going very slowly. Vaguely he wondered, but without looking, if they were running into heavy traffic as they approached London. It didn't matter. Hathall would have been stopped by now, detained in some little side room of the airport. Even if he hadn't been told why he wasn't allowed to fly, he would know. He would know it was all over. The car was almost stopping. Wexford opened his eyes and seized Burden's arm. He wound down the window.

'See,' he said, pointing to the ground that now slid past at a snail's pace. 'It does move. And that . . .' his arm went upwards, skywards, '. . . that doesn't.'

'What doesn't?' said Burden. 'There's nothing to see. Look for yourself. We're fog-bound.'

CHAPTER TWENTY-TWO

It was nearly four o'clock before they reached the airport. All aircraft were grounded, and Christmas holiday travelers filled the lounges while queues formed at enquiry desks. The fog was all-enveloping, fluffy like aerated snow, dense earthbound clouds of it, a white gas that set people coughing and covering their faces.

Hathall wasn't there.

The fog had begun to come down at Heathrow at eleven-thirty, but it had affected other parts of London earlier than that. Had he been among the hundreds who had phoned the airport from fog-bound outer suburbs to enquire if their flights would leave? There was no way of knowing. Wexford walked slowly and painstakingly through the lounges, from bar to restaurant, out on to the observation terraces, looking into every face, tired faces, indignant faces, bored faces. Hathall wasn't there.

'According to the weather forecast,' said Burden, 'the fog'll lift by evening.'

'And according to the long-range, it's going to be a white Christmas, a white fog Christmas. You and Polly stay here, Mike. Get on to the chief constable and fix it so that we have every exit watched, not just Heathrow.'

So Burden and Polly remained while Wexford and Lovat and Hutton began the long drive to Hampstead. It was very slow going. Streams of traffic, bound for the M1, blocked all the north-west roads as the fog, made tawny by the yellow overhead lights, cast a blinding pall over the city. The landmarks on the route, which by now were all too familiar, had lost their sharp outlines and become amorphous. The winding hills of Hampstead lay under a smoky shroud and the great trees of Hampstead loomed like black clouds before being swallowed up in paler vapour. They crawled into Dartmeet Avenue at ten minutes to seven and pulled up outside number 62. The house was in darkness, every window tight shut and dead black. The dustbins were dewed where the fog had condensed on them. Their lids were scattered, and a cat darted out from under one of them, a chicken bone in its mouth. As Wexford got out of the car, the fog caught at his throat. He thought of another foggy day in Myringham Old Town, of men digging in vain for a body that had never been there. He thought of how his whole pursuit of Hathall had been befogged by doubt and confusion and obstruction, and then he went up to the front door and rang the landlord's bell.

He had rung it twice more before a light showed through the pane of glass above the lintel. At last the door was opened by the same little elderly man Wexford had once before seen come out and fetch his cat. He was smoking a thin cigar and he showed neither surprise nor interest when the chief inspector said who he was and showed him his warrant card.

'Mr Hathall left last night,' he said.

'Last night?'

'That's right. To tell you the truth, I didn't expect him to go till this morning. He'd paid his rent up to tonight. But he got hold of me in a bit of hurry last night and said he'd decided to go, so it wasn't for me to argue, was it?'

The hall was icy cold, in spite of the oil heater which stood at the foot of the stairs, and the place reeked of burning oil and cigar smoke. Lovat rubbed his hands together, then held them out over the guttering blue and yellow flames.

'Mr Hathall came back here about eight last night in a taxi,' said the landlord. 'I was out in the front garden, calling my cat. He came up to me and said he wanted to vacate his room there and then.'

'How did he seem?' Wexford said urgently. 'Worried? Upset?'

'Nothing out of the way. He was never what you'd call a

pleasant chap. Always grumbling about something. We went up to his room for me to take the inventory. I always insist on that before I give them back their deposits. D'you want to go up now? There's nothing to see, but you can if you want.'

Wexford nodded and they mounted the stairs. The hall and the landing were lit by the kind of lights that go off automatically after two minutes, and they went off now before Hathall's door was reached. In the pitch dark the landlord cursed, fumbling for his keys and for the light switch. And Wexford, his nerves tautening again, let out a grunt of shock when something snaked along the banister rail and jumped for the landlord's shoulder. It was, of course, only the cat. The light went on, the key was found, and the door opened.

The room was stuffy and musty as well as cold. Wexford saw Hutton's lip curl as he glanced at the First World War wardrobe, the fireside chairs and the ugly paintings, as he thought no doubt of an inventory being taken of this Junk City rubbish. Thin blankets lay untidily folded on the bare mattress beside a bundle of nickel knives and forks secured with a rubber band, a whistling kettle with a string-bound handle and a plaster vase that still bore on its base the price ticket indicating that it had cost thirty-five pence.

The cat ran along the mantelpiece and leaped on to the screen. 'I knew there was something fishy about him, mind you,' said the landlord.

'How? What gave you that idea?'

He favoured Wexford with a rather contemptuous smile. 'I've seen you before, for one thing. I can spot a copper a mile off. And there was always folks watching him. I don't miss much, though I don't say much either. I spotted the little fellow with the ginger hair – made me laugh when he came here and said he was from the council – and the tall thin one that was always in a car.'

'Then you'll know,' Wexford said, swallowing his humiliation, 'why he was watched.'

'Not me. He never did nothing but come and go and have his mother to tea and grouse about the rent.'

'He never had a woman come here? A woman with short fair hair?'

'Not him. His mother and his daughter, that's all. That's who he told me they were, and I reckon it was true seeing they was the spitting image of him. Come on, puss, let's get back where it's warm.'

Turning wearily away, standing on the spot where Hathall had been on the point of flinging him down those stairs, Wexford said, 'You gave him back his deposit and he left. What time was that?'

'About nine.' The landing light went off again and again the landlord flicked the switch, muttering under his breath while the cat purred on his shoulder. 'He was going abroad somewhere, he said. There were a lot of labels on his cases but I didn't look close. I like to see what they're doing, you know, keep an eye till they're off the premises. He went over the road and made a phone call and then a taxi came and took him off.'

They went down into the smelly hall. The light went off and this time the landlord didn't switch it on. He closed the door on them quickly to keep out the fog.

'He could have gone last night,' said Wexford to Lovat. 'He could have crossed to Paris or Brussels or Amsterdam and flown from there.'

'But why should he?' Hutton objected. 'Why should he think we're on to him after all this time?'

Wexford didn't want to tell them, at this stage, about Howard's involvement or Howard's encounter with Hathall on the previous evening. But it had come sharply into his mind up in that cold deserted room. Hathall had seen Howard at about seven, had recognized this man who was tailing him, and soon after had given him the slip. The taxi he had got into had dropped the girl off and taken him back to Dartmeet Avenue where he had settled with his landlord, taken his luggage and gone. Gone where? Back to her first and then . . .? Wexford shrugged unhappily and went across the road to the call-box.

Burden's voice told him the airport was still fog-bound. The place was swarming with disappointed stranded would-be travellers, and swarming by now with anxious police. Hathall hadn't appeared. If he had phoned, along with hundreds of other callers, he hadn't given his name.

'But he knows we're on to him,' said Burden.

'What d'you mean?'

'D'you remember a chap called Aveney? Manager of Kidd's?'

'Of course I remember. What the hell is this?'

'He got a phone call from Hathall at his home at nine last night. Hathall wanted to know – asked in a roundabout way, mind you – if we'd been asking questions about him. And Aveney, the fool, said not about his wife, that was all over, but only looking into the books in case there was something fishy about the payroll.'

'How do we know all this?' Wexford asked dully.

'Aveney had second thoughts, wondered if he ought to have told him anything, though he knew our enquiries had come to nothing. Apparently, he tried to get hold of you this morning and when he couldn't he at last contacted Mr Griswold.'

That, then, was the phone call Hathall had made from the call-box in Dartmeet Avenue, this very call-box, after leaving the landlord and before getting into that taxi. That, coupled with his recognition of Howard, would have been enough to frighten the wits out of him. Wexford went back across the road and got into the car where Lovat was smoking one of his nasty little damp cigarettes.

'I think the fog's thinning, sir,' said Hutton.

'Maybe. What time is it?'

'Ten to eight. What do we do now? Get back to the airport or try and find Morag Grey's place?'

With patient sarcasm, Wexford said, 'I have been trying

to do that for nine months, Sergeant, the normal period of gestation, and I've brought forth nothing. Maybe you think you can do better in a couple of hours.'

'We could at least go back through Notting Hill, sir, instead of taking the quicker way by the North Circular.'

'Oh, do as you like,' Wexford snapped, and he flung himself into the corner as far as possible from Lovat and his cigarette which smelled as bad as the landlord's cigar. Badgers! Country coppers, he thought unfairly. Fools who couldn't make a simple charge like shopbreaking stick. What did Hutton think Notting Hill was? A village like Passingham St. John where everyone knew everyone else and would be all agog and raring to gossip because a neighbour had gone off to foreign parts?

They followed the 28 bus route. West End Lane, Quex Road, Kilburn High Road, Kilburn Park ... The fog was decreasing, moving now, lying here in dense patches, there shivering and thinning into streaks. And Christmas colours began to glitter through it, garish paper banners in windows, sharp little starry lights that winked on and off. Shirland Road, Great Western Road, Pembridge Villas, Pembridge Road ...

One of these, Wexford thought, sitting up, must be the bus stop where Howard had seen Hathall board the 28. Streets debouched everywhere, streets that led into other streets, into squares, into a vast multitudinously peopled hinterland. Let Hutton make what he could of ...

'Stop the car, will you?' he said quickly.

Pink light streamed across the roadway from the glazed doors of a public house. Wexford had seen its sign and remembered. The Rosy Cross. If they had been regular customers, if they had often met there, the licensee or a barman might recall them. Perhaps they had met there again last night before leaving or had gone back just to say good-bye. At least he would know. This way he might know for sure.

The interior was an inferno of light and noise and smoke.

The crowd was of a density and a conviviality usually only reached much later in the evening, but this was Christmas, the night before the Eve. Not only was every table occupied and every bar stool and place by the bar, but every square foot of floor space too where people stood packed, pressed against each other, their cigarettes sending spirals of smoke to mingle with the blue pall that hung between gently swaying paper chains and smarting screwed-up eyes. Wexford pushed his way to the bar. Two barmen and a girl were working it, serving drinks feverishly, wiping down the counter, slopping dirty glasses into a steaming sink.

'And the next?' called the older of the barmen, the licensee maybe. His face was red, his forehead gleaming with sweat and his grey hair plastered against it in wet curls. 'What's for you, sir?'

Wexford said, 'Police. I'm looking for a tall black-haired man, about forty-five, and a younger blonde woman.' His elbow was jostled and he felt a trickle of beer run down his wrist. 'They were in here last night. The name is . . .'

'They don't give their names. There were about five hundred people in here last night.

'I've reason to think they came in here regularly.'

The barman shrugged. 'I have to attend to my customers. Can you wait ten minutes?'

But Wexford thought he had waited long enough. Let it pass into other hands, he could do no more. Struggling through the press of people, he made again for the door, bemused by the colours and the lights and the smoke and the heady reek of liquor. There seemed to be coloured shapes everywhere, the circles of red and purple balloons, the shining translucent cones of liqueur bottles, the squares of stained window glass. His head swimming, he realized he hadn't eaten all day. Red and purple circles, orange and blue paper spheres, here a green glass square, there a bright yellow rectangle . . .

A bright yellow rectangle. His head cleared. He steadied

and stilled himself. Jammed between a man in a leather coat
and a girl in a fur coat, he looked through a tiny space that
wasn't cluttered by skirts and legs and chair legs and handbags,
looked through the blue acrid smoke at that yellow rectangle
which was liquid in a tall glass, and saw it raised by a hand
and carried out of his sight.

Pernod. Not a popular drink in England. Ginge had drunk
it mixed with Guinness as a Demon King. And one other, she
that he sought, his chimera, his thing of fanciful conception,
drank it diluted and yellowed by water. He moved slowly,
pushing his way towards that corner table where she was, but
he could get only within three yards of her. There were too
many people. But now there was a space clear enough at eye
level for him to see her, and he looked long and long, staring
greedily as a man in love stares at the woman whose coming
he has awaited for months on end.

She had a pretty face, tired and wan. Her eyes were smarting
from the smoke and her cropped blonde hair showed half an
inch of dark at the roots. She was alone, but the chair beside
her was covered by a folded coat, a man's coat, and stacked
against the wall behind her, piled at her feet and walling her
in, were half a dozen suitcases. She lifted her glass again and
sipped from it, not looking at him at all, but darting quick
nervous glances towards a heavy mahogany door marked
Telephone and Toilets. But Wexford lingered, looking his fill at
his chimera made flesh, until hats and hair and faces converged
and cut off his view.

He opened the mahogany door and slipped into a passage.
Two more doors faced him, and at the end of the passage was
a glass kiosk. Hathall was bent over the phone inside it, his
back to Wexford. Phoning the airport, Wexford thought, phoning to see if his flight's on now the fog is lifting. He stepped
into the men's lavatory, pulling the door to, waiting till he
heard Hathall's footsteps pass along the passage.

The mahogany door swung and clicked shut. Wexford let a minute go by and then he too went back into the bar. The cases were gone, the yellow glass empty. Thrusting people aside, ignoring expostulation, he gained the street door and flung it open. Hathall and the woman were on the pavement edge, surrounded by their cases, waiting to hail a taxi.

Wexford flashed a glance at the car, caught Hutton's eye and raised his hand sharply, beckoning. Three of the car's doors opened simultaneously and the three policemen it had contained were on their feet, bounced on to the wet stone as if on springs. And then Hathall understood. He swung round to face them, his arm enclosing the woman in a protective but useless hold. The colour went out of his face, and in the light of the misted yellow lamps the jutting jaw, the sharp nose and the high forehead were greenish with terror and the final failure of his hopes. Wexford went up to him.

The woman said, 'We should have left last night, Bob,' and when he heard her accent, made strong by fear, he knew. He knew for sure. But he couldn't find his voice and, standing silent, he left it to Lovat to approach her and begin the words of the caution and the charge.

'Morag Grey . . .'

She brought her knuckles to her trembling lips, and Wexford saw the small L-shaped scar on her forefinger as he had seen it in his dreams.

CHAPTER TWENTY-THREE

Christmas Eve.

They had all arrived and Wexford's house was full. Upstairs, the two little grandsons were in bed. In the kitchen
Dora was again examining that turkey, consulting Denise this
time as to the all-important question of whether to hang it up
or lay it on the oven shelf. In the living room Sheila and her
sister were dressing the tree while Burden's teenage children
subjected the record player, which had to be in good order
for the following day, to a rather inexpert servicing. Burden
had taken Wexford's son-in-law down to the Dragon for a
drink.

'The dining room for us then,' said Wexford to his nephew.
The table was already laid for Christmas dinner, already
decorated with a handsome centrepiece. And the fire was laid
too, as sacrosanct as the table, but Wexford put a match to
the sticks. 'I shall get into trouble about that,' he said, 'but I
don't care. I don't care about anything now I've found her,
now *you*,' he added generously, 'and I have found her.'

'It was little or nothing I did,' said Howard. 'I never even
found where she was living. Presumably, you know now?'

'In Pembridge Road itself,' said Wexford. 'He only had
that miserable room but he paid the rent of a whole flat for
her. No doubt, he loves her, though the last thing I want is
to be sentimental about him.' He took a new bottle of whisky
from the sideboard, poured a glass for Howard and then,
recklessly, one for himself. 'Shall I tell you about it?'

'Is there much left to tell? Mike Burden's already filled me
in on the identity of the women, this Morag Grey. I tried to
stop him. I knew you'd want to tell me yourself.'

'Mike Burden,' said his uncle as the fire began to crackle

and blaze, 'had today off. I haven't seen him since I left him at London Airport yesterday afternoon. He hasn't filled you in, he doesn't know, unless – is it in the evening papers? The special court, I mean?'

'It wasn't in the early editions.'

'Then there is much left to tell.' Wexford drew the curtains against the fog which had returned in the afternoon. 'What did Mike say?'

'That it happened more or less the way you guessed, the three of them in the payroll fraud. Wasn't it that way?'

'My theory,' Wexford said, 'left far too many loopholes.' He pulled his armchair closer to the fire. 'Good to relax, isn't it? Aren't you glad you haven't got to get your tailing gear on and go off up to West End Green?'

'I'll say it again, I did very little. But at least I don't deserve to be kept in suspense.'

'True, and I won't keep you in it. There was a payroll fraud all right. Hathall set up at least two fictitious accounts, and maybe more soon after he joined Kidd's. He was pulling in a minimum of an extra thirty pounds a week for two years. But Morag Grey wasn't in on it. She wouldn't have helped anyone swindle a company. She was an honest woman. She was so honest she didn't even keep a pound note she found on an office floor, and so upright she wouldn't stay married to a man who'd stolen two pounds fifty. She couldn't have been in on it, still less have planned and collected from the Mary Lewis account because Hathall didn't meet her till the March. She was only at Kidd's for a couple of weeks and that was three months before Hathall left.'

'But Hathall was in love with her, surely? You said so yourself. And what other motive . . .?'

'Hathall was in love with his wife. Oh, I know we decided he's acquired amorous tastes, but what real evidence did we have of that?' With a slight self-consciousness too well covered for Howard to detect, Wexford said, 'If he was so susceptible, why did he reject the advances of a certain very attractive neighbour of his? Why did he give everyone who knew him the impression of being an obsessively devoted husband?'

'You tell me,' Howard grinned. 'You'll be saying in a minute that Morag Grey didn't kill Angela Hathall.'

'That's right. She didn't. Angela Hathall killed Morag Grey.'

A wail rose from the record player in the next room. Small feet scuttled across the floor above and there was a violent crash from the kitchen. The noise drowned Howard's low exclamation.

'I was pretty surprised myself,' Wexford went on casually. 'I suppose I guessed when I found out yesterday about Morag Grey being so honest and only being at Kidd's for such a short while. Then when we arrested them and I heard her Australian accent I knew.'

Howard shook his head slowly in astonishment and wonder rather than disbelief. 'But the identification, Reg? How could he hope to get away with it?'

'He did get away with it for fifteen months. You see, the secretive isolated life they led in order to make the payroll scheme work was in their favour when they planned this murder. It wouldn't have done for Angela to get well known in case she was recognized as not being Mrs Lewis or Mrs Carter when she went to make withdrawals from those accounts. Hardly a soul knew her even by sight. Mrs Lake did, of course, and so did her cousin, Mark Somerset, but who on earth would have called on them to identify the body? The natural person was Angela's husband. And just in case there was any doubt, he took his mother with him, taking care she should see the body first. Angela had dressed Morag in her own clothes, those very clothes she was wearing on the only previous occasion her mother-in-law had seen her. That was a fine piece of psychology, Howard, thought up, I'm sure, by

Angela who planned all the intricacies of this business. It was old Mrs Hathall who phoned us, old Mrs Hathall who put doubt out of court by telling us her daughter-in-law had been found dead in Bury Cottage.

'Angela started cleaning the place weeks ahead to clean off *her own fingerprints*. No wonder she had rubber gloves and dusting gloves. It wouldn't have been too difficult a task, seeing she was alone all week without Hathall there to leave his own prints about. And if we queried such extreme cleanliness, what better reason for it than that she was getting the cottage perfect for old Mrs Hathall's visit?'

'Then the handprint and the L-shaped scar were hers?'

'Of course.' Wexford drank his whisky slowly, making it last. 'The prints we thought were hers were Morag's. The hair in the brush we thought was hers were Morag's. She must have brushed the dead girl's hair – nasty, that. The coarser dark hairs were Angela's. She didn't have to clean the car in the garage or at Wood Green. She could have cleaned it any time she chose in the previous week.'

'But why did she leave that one print?'

'I think I can guess at that. On the morning of the day Morag died, Angela was up early getting on with her cleaning. She was cleaning the bathroom, had perhaps taken off her rubber gloves and was about to put on the others to polish the floor, when the phone rang. Mrs Lake rang to ask if she could come over and pick the miracle plums. And Angela, naturally nervous, steadied herself with her bare hand on the side of the bath when she got up to answer the phone.

'Morag Grey spoke, and doubtless read, Gaelic. Hathall must have known that. So Angela found out her address – they would have been keeping a close eye on her – and wrote to her, or more probably called on her, to ask if she would give her some assistance into the research she was doing into Celtic languages. Morag, a domestic servant, can only have been flattered. And she was poor too, she needed money. This,

RUTH RENDELL

I think, was the good job she spoke of to her neighbour, and she gave up her cleaning work at this time, going on to the Social Security until Angela was ready for her to start.'

'But didn't she know Angela?'

'Why should she? Angela would have given her a false name, and I see no reason why she should have known Hathall's address. On the nineteenth of September Angela drove over to Myringham Old Town, collected her and drove her to Bury Cottage for a discussion on their future work. She took Morag upstairs to wash or go to the loo or comb her hair. And there she strangled her, Howard, with her own gilt snake necklace.

'After that it was simple. Dress Morag in the red shirt and the jeans, imprint a few mobile objects with her fingerprints brush her hair. Gloves on, take the car down that tunnel of a lane, away to London. Stay a night or two in a hotel till she could find a room, wait for time to go by till Hathall could join her.'

'But why, Reg? Why kill her?'

'She was an honest woman and she found out what Hathall was up to. She was no fool, Howard, but rather one of those people who have potential but lack drive. Both her former employer and her mother said she was a cut above the kind of work she was doing. Her feckless husband dragged her down. Who knows? Maybe she would have had the ability to advise a *genuine* etymologist on demotic Gaelic, and maybe she thought this was her chance, now she was rid of Grey, to better herself. Angela Hathall, when you come to think of it, is a very good psychologist.'

'I see all that,' said Howard, 'but how did Morag find out about the payroll fraud?'

'That,' Wexford said frankly, 'I don't know – yet. I'd guess Hathall stayed late one evening while she was working there, and I'd guess she overheard a phone conversation he had with Angela on that occasion. Perhaps Angela had suggested a false address to him and he called her to check up he'd got it right

536

before he fed it into the computer. Don't forget Angela was the mainspring behind all this. You couldn't have been more right when you said she'd influenced and corrupted him. Hathall is just the sort of man to think of a cleaner as no more than a piece of furniture. But even if he'd spoken guardedly, that name, Mrs Mary Lewis, and that address, 19 Maynnot Way, would have alerted Morag. It was just down the road from where she and her husband lived and she knew no Mary Lewis lived there. And if, after that call, Hathall immediately began to feed the computer...'

'She blackmailed him?'

'I doubt it. She was an honest woman. But she'd have queried it, on the spot perhaps. Maybe she merely told him she'd overheard what he'd said and there was no Mary Lewis there, and if he'd seemed flustered − my God, you should see him when he's flustered! − she could have asked more and more questions until she had some hazy idea of what was actually going on.'

'They killed her for *that*?'

Wexford nodded. 'To you and me it seems a wretched motive. But to them? They would ever after have been in a panic of fear, for if Hathall's swindle were uncovered he'd lose his job, lose his new job at Marcus Flower, never get another job in the one field he was trained for. You have to remember what a paranoid pair they were. They expected to be persecuted and hounded, they suspected even the innocent and harmless of having a down on them.'

'You weren't innocent and harmless, Reg,' said Howard quietly.

'No, and perhaps I'm the only person who has ever truly persecuted Robert Hathall.' Wexford raised his almost empty glass. 'Happy Christmas,' he said. 'I shan't let Hathall's loss of liberty cloud the season for me. If anyone deserves to lose it, he does. Shall we join the others? I think I heard Mike come in with my son-in-law.'

The tree had been dressed. Sheila was jiving with John Burden to the thumping cacophony that issued from the record player. Having restored a sleepy little boy to his bed for the third time, Sylvia was wrapping the last of the presents, one of Kidd's Kits for Kids, a paint-box, a geographical globe, a picture book, a toy car. Wexford put an arm round his wife and an arm round Pat Burden and kissed them under the mistletoe. Laughing, he put his hand out to the globe and spun it. Three times it circled on its axis before Burden saw the point, and then he said:

'It does move. You were right. He did do it.'

'Well, you were right too,' said Wexford. 'He didn't murder his wife.' Seeing Burden's look of incredulity, he added, 'And now I suppose I shall have to tell the story all over again.'

A Sleeping Life

For Elaine and Leslie Gray,
with affection and gratitude

Those have most power to hurt us, that we love;
We lay our sleeping lives within their arms.
O, thou hast raised up mischief to his height,
And found one to outname thy other faults.

BEAUMONT AND FLETCHER: *The Maid's Tragedy*

CHAPTER ONE

Home early for once. Maybe he'd start getting home early regularly now August had begun, the silly season. Criminals as well as the law-abiding take their holidays in August. As he turned the car into his own road, Wexford remembered his grandsons would be there. Good. It would be light for another three hours, and he'd take Robin and Ben down to the river. Robin was always on about the river because his mother had read *The Wind in the Willows* to him, and his great desire was to see a water rat swimming.

Sylvia's car was parked outside the house. Odd, thought Wexford. He'd understood Dora was having the boys for the afternoon as well as the evening and that they'd be staying the night. As he edged his own car past his daughter's into the drive, she came running out of the house with a screaming Ben in her arms and six-year-old Robin looking truculent at her heels. Robin rushed up to his grandfather.

'You promised we could see the water rat!'

'So you can as far as I'm concerned and if there's one about. I thought you were staying the night.'

Sylvia's face was crimson, with rage or perhaps just from haste. It was very hot.

'Well, they're not. Thanks to my dear husband, nobody's going anywhere even though it does happen to be our wedding anniversary. Will you shut up, Ben! He's bringing a client home for dinner instead, if you please, and I of course as usual have to be the one to do the cooking and fetch the kids.'

'Leave them here,' said Wexford. 'Why not?'

'Yes, leave us here,' Robin shouted. '*Go on.*'

'Oh, no, that's out of the question. Why do you have to

encourage them, Dad? I'm taking them home and Neil can have the pleasure of putting them to bed for once.'

She thrust both children into the car and drove off. The windows of the car were all open, and the yells of the two little boys, for Robin had begun to back his brother up, vied with the roar of the ill-treated engine. Wexford shrugged and went indoors. Some sort of scene had evidently been taking place, but he knew his wife better than to suppose she would be much disturbed by it. True to his expectations, she was sitting placidly in the living room watching the tail end of a children's programme on television. A great many books had been pulled out of the shelves, and on a tower block of them sat a teddy bear.

'What's got into Sylvia?'

'Women's Lib,' said Dora Wexford. 'If Neil wants to bring a client home he ought to cook the meal. He ought to come home in the afternoon and clean the house and lay the table. She's taken the children home for the sole purpose of getting him to put them to bed. And she's taking care to stir them up on the way to make sure he has a hard time of it.'

'God. I always thought she was quite a sensible girl.'

'She's got a bee in her bonnet about it. It's been going on for months. You are the people, we are the others. You are the masters, we are the chattels.'

'Why haven't you told me about any of this?'

Dora switched off the television. 'You've been busy. You wouldn't have wanted to listen to all this nonsense when you got home. I've been getting it every day.'

Wexford raised his eyebrows. 'It's nonsense?'

'Well, not entirely, of course. Men still do have a better time of it in this world than women, it's still a man's world. I can understand she doesn't like being stuck at home with the boys, wasting her life, as she puts it, while Neil gets more and more successful in his career.' Dora smiled. 'And she says she got more A Levels than he did. I can understand she gets bored when people come and the men talk to Neil about architecture and the women talk to her about polishing the bedroom furniture. Oh, I can *understand* it.'

Her husband looked hard at her. 'You feel that way too?'

'Never you mind,' said Dora, laughing now. 'Let's forget our rather tiresome child. You're so early we might go out somewhere after we've eaten. Would you like to?'

'Love to.' He hesitated, said quickly, 'It's not threatening their marriage, is it? I've always thought of them as being so happy together.'

'We have to hope it'll pass. Anything we do or say would only make things worse, wouldn't it?'

'Of course. Now where shall we go? Cinema? Or how about the open-air theatre at Sewingbury?'

Before she could give him an answer, the phone rang.

'Sylvia,' she said. 'She's realized Ben left his teddy. You get it, darling. Oh, and Reg . . .? Would you say we'll drop it in on our way? I can't stand another session of the wounded wives tonight.'

Wexford lifted the receiver. It wasn't his daughter. Dora knew it wasn't even before he spoke. She knew that look. All he said was 'Yes' and 'Sure, I will', but she knew. He hung up and said, 'They don't all go on holiday in August. A body in a field not half a mile from here.'

'Is it . . .?'

'Not one of the people,' her husband said drily. 'One of the others.' He tightened the tie he had loosened, rolled down his shirtsleeves. 'I'll have to go straightaway. What'll you do? Stir up the telly so I have a hard time of it putting it to rights? You must regret marrying me.'

'No, but I'm working on it.'

Wexford laughed, kissed her and drove back the way he had come.

Kingsmarkham is a sizeable town somewhere in the middle of Sussex, much built-up now on the Stowerton and Sewingbury sides, though open and unspoilt country still remains at its northern end. There the High Street becomes the Pomfret Road, and there the pinewoods of Cheriton Forest clothe the hills.

Forest Road is the last street in the area to bear the postal address Kingsmarkham. It debouches directly from the Pomfret Road, but to reach it most of its few residents take the short cut from the end of the High Street by footpath across a field. Wexford parked his car at the point in Forest Road where this footpath entered it as an alley near the boundary fence of a pair of houses called Carlyle Villas. He swung into the alley and followed the footpath along a high privet hedge that bounded allotments. About a hundred yards ahead of him he could see a group of men gathered at the edge of a little copse.

Inspector Michael Burden was among them and so was Dr Crocker, the police doctor, and a couple of photographers. As Wexford approached, Burden came up to him and said something in a low voice. Wexford nodded. Without looking at the body, he went up to Detective Loring who stood a little apart with a younger man who looked pale and shaken.

'Mr Parker?'

'That's right.'

'I understand you found the body?'

Parker nodded. 'Well, my son did.'

He couldn't have been more than twenty-five himself.

'A *child?*' said Wexford.

'He doesn't realize. I hope not. He's only six.'

They sat down on a wooden seat the council had put there for pensioners to rest on. 'Tell me what happened.'

'I'd taken him round to my sister's, give the wife a bit of a break while she was putting the other two to bed. I live in one of the bungalows in Forest Road, Bella Vista, the one with the green roof. We were coming back, along the path here, and Nicky was playing with a ball. It went in the long grass under the hedge and he went to look for it. He said,

"Dad, there's a lady down there." I sort of knew, I don't know how. I went and looked and I – well, I know I shouldn't have, but I sort of pulled her coat over her chest. Nicky, you see, he's only six, there was – well, blood, a mess.'

'I do see,' said Wexford. 'You didn't move anything else?'

Parker shook his head. 'I told Nicky the lady was ill and we'd go home and phone the doctor. I said she'd be all right. I don't think he realized. I hope not. I got him home and phoned your people. Honestly, I wouldn't have touched her if I'd been on my own.'

'This was an exception, Mr Parker.' Wexford smiled at him. 'I'd have done the same in your place.'

'He won't have to . . .? I mean, there'll be an inquest, won't there? I mean, I'll have to go, I know that, but . . .'

'No, no. Good God, no. Get off home now and we'll see you again later. Thanks for your help.'

Parker got up off the seat, glanced at the photographers, the huddle round the body, then turned round. 'It's not for me to . . . Well, I mean, I do know who she is. Perhaps you don't . . .'

'No, we don't yet. Who is she?'

'Well, a Miss Comfrey. She didn't actually live here, her dad lives here.' Parker pointed back down the path. 'Carlyle Villas, the one with the blue paint. She must have been stopping there. Her dad's in hospital. He's an old man, he broke his hip, and she must have come down to see him.'

'Thanks, Mr Parker.'

Wexford crossed the sandy path, and Burden stepped aside for him to look down at the body. It was that of a middle-aged woman, biggish and gaunt. The face was coated with heavy make-up, clotted scarlet on the mouth, streaky blue on the crêpe eyelids, a ghastly ochreish layer on the planes of cheek and forehead. The grey eyes were wide and staring, and in them Wexford thought he saw – it must be his imagination – a sardonic gleam, a glare, even in death, of scorn.

A fringe of dark hair just showed under a tightly tied blue headscarf. The body was clothed in a blue and pink printed dress of some synthetic material, and the matching jacket had been drawn across the bodice. One of the high-heeled shoes had come off and hung suspended on a tangle of brambles. Across the hips lay a large scarlet handbag. There were no rings on the hands, no watch on either wrist, but a heavy necklace of red glass beads round the neck, and the nails, though short, were painted the same scarlet.

He knelt down and opened the handbag, covering his fingers with his handkerchief. Inside was a key ring with three keys on it, a box of matches, a packet of king-sized cigarettes from which four had been smoked, a lipstick, an old-fashioned powder compact, a wallet, in the bottom of the bag some loose change. No purse. No letters or documents. The wallet, which was an expensive new one of black leather, contained forty-two pounds. She hadn't been killed for the money she had on her.

There was nothing to give him a clue to her address, her occupation or even her identity. No credit card, no bank card, no cheque book.

He closed the bag and parted her jacket. The bodice of the dress was black with clotted blood, but plainly discernible in the dark matted mass were two cuts, the outward evidence of stab wounds.

CHAPTER TWO

Wexford moved away, and the doctor came back and knelt where he had knelt. He said to Loring:

'No sign of the weapon, I daresay?'

'No, sir, but we haven't made much of a search yet.'

'Well, get searching, you and Gates and Marwood. A knife of some sort.' The chances of it being there, he thought pessimistically, were slight. 'And when you haven't found it,' he said, 'you can do a house-to-house down Forest Road. Get all you can about her and her movements, but leave Parker and Carlyle Villas to me and Mr Burden.'

Back to Dr Crocker.

'How long has she been dead, Len?'

'Now, for God's sake, don't expect too much precision at this stage. Rigor's fully established, but the weather's been very hot, so its onset will have been more rapid. I'd say at least eighteen hours. Could be more.'

'OK.' Wexford jerked his head at Burden. 'There's nothing more here for us, Mike. Carlyle Villas and Parker next, I think.'

Michael Burden was properly of too high a rank to accompany a chief inspector on calls of inquiry. He did so because that was the way they worked, the way it worked. They had always done so, and always would, in spite of disapproving mutterings from the Chief Constable.

Two tall men. Nearly twenty years separated them, and once they had been so dissimilar in appearance as to provide that juxtaposition of incongruities which is the stuff of humour. But Wexford had lost his abundant fat and become almost a gaunt man, while Burden had always been lean. He was the better-looking of the two by far, with classical features that would have been handsome had they been less pinched by sour experience. Wexford was an ugly man, but his was the face that arrested the eye, compelled even the eyes of women, because it had in it so much lively intelligence and zest for life, so much vigour, and in spite of his seniority, so much more of the essence of youth.

Side by side, they walked along the footpath and down the alley into Forest Road, not speaking, for there was nothing yet to say. The woman was dead, but death by murder is in a way not an end but a beginning. The lives of the naturally dead may be buried with them. Hers would now gradually be exposed, event after event, obscure though she had been, until it took on the character of a celebrity's biography.

From the alley, they turned to the right and stood outside the pair of houses, cottages really, in front of which Wexford had parked his car. The houses shared a single gable, and in its apex was a plaster plaque bearing their name and the date of their construction: Carlyle Villas, 1902. Wexford knocked at the blue front door with little hope of getting an answer. There was none, and no one came when they rang the bell on the neighbouring front door, a far more trendy and ambitious affair of wrought iron and reeded glass.

Frustrated at this most promising port of call, they crossed the street. Forest Road was a cul-de-sac, ending in a stone wall, behind which meadows swelled and the forest sprawled. It contained about a dozen houses, apart from Carlyle Villas, a clutch of tiny cottages at the wall end, two or three newer bungalows, a squat grey stone lodge that had once stood at the gates of a long-vanished mansion. One of the bungalows, built at the period when Hollywood's influence penetrated even this corner of Sussex, had windows of curved glass and a roof of green pantiles. Bella Vista.

The child Nicky was still up, sitting with his mother in a living room that had the same sort of untidy look as the one Wexford had left an hour before. But if Parker hadn't introduced this girl as his wife, Wexford would have taken her for no more than an adolescent. She had the smooth brow and bunchy cheeks of a child, the silken hair, the innocent eyes. She must have been married at sixteen, though she looked no more than that now.

Parker said with ferocious winks, 'This gentleman's a doctor, come to tell us the poor lady's all right.'

Nicky buried his face in his mother's shoulder.

'Quite all right,' Wexford lied. 'She'll be fine.' They say the dead are well . . .

'You get along to Nanna's room then, Nicky, and she'll let you watch her TV.'

The tension lightened on his departure. 'Thanks,' said Parker. 'I only hope it isn't going to have a bad effect on him, poor kid.'

'Don't worry. He's too young to see newspapers, but you'll have to exercise a bit of censorship when it comes to the TV. Now, Mr Parker, I think you said Miss – er – Comfrey's father was in hospital. D'you know which hospital?'

'Stowerton. The infirmary. He had an accident last – when would it have been, Stell?'

'About May,' said Stella Parker. 'Miss Comfrey came down to see him, came in a taxi from the station, and when he saw her he rushed out of the house and fell over on the path and broke his hip. Just like that it happened. Her and the taxi-man, they took him to the hospital in the same taxi and he's been there ever since. I never saw it. Mrs Crown told me. Miss Comfrey's been down once to see him since. She never did come much, did she, Brian?'

'Not more than once or twice a year,' said Parker.

'I knew she was coming yesterday. Mrs Crown told me. I saw her in the Post Office and she said Rhoda'd phoned to say she was coming on account of old Mr Comfrey'd had a stroke. But I never saw her, didn't really know her to speak to.'

Burden said, 'Who is Mrs Crown?'

'Miss Comfrey's auntie. She lives in the next house to old Mr Comfrey. She's the one you want to see.'

'No doubt, but there's no one in.'

'I tell you what,' said Stella Parker who seemed to have twice her husband's grasp and intelligence, 'I don't want to put myself forward, but I do read detective books, and if it's sort of background stuff you want, you couldn't do better than talk to Brian's gran. She's lived here all her life, she was born in one of those cottages.'

'Your grandmother lives with you?'

'Helped us buy this place with her savings,' said Parker, 'and moved in with us. It works OK, doesn't it, Stell? She's a wonder, my gran.'

Wexford smiled and got up. 'I may want to talk to her but not tonight. You'll be notified about the inquest, Mr Parker. It shouldn't be too much of an ordeal. Now, d'you know when Mrs Crown will be home?'

'When the pubs turn out,' said Parker.

'I think the infirmary next, Mike,' said Wexford. 'From the vague sort of time Crocker gave us, it's beginning to look to me as if Rhoda Comfrey was killed on her way back from visiting her father in hospital. She'd have used that footpath as a short cut from the bus stop.'

'Visiting time at Stowerton's seven till eight in the evenings,' said Burden. 'We may be able to fix the time of death more accurately this way than by any post-mortem findings.'

'The pub-orientated aunt should help us there. If this old boy's *compos mentis*, we'll get his daughter's London address from him.'

'We'll also have to break the news,' said Burden.

Departing visitors were queueing at the bus stop outside Stowerton Royal Infirmary. Had Rhoda Comfrey queued there on the previous night? It was ten past eight.

A man in the porter's lodge told them that James Albert

Comfrey was a patient in Lytton Ward. They went along a corridor and up two flights of stairs. A pair of glass double doors, the entrance to Lytton Ward, were closed. As Wexford pushed them open, a young nurse of Malaysian or Thai origin popped up in their path and announced in a chirrup that they couldn't come in now.

'Police,' said Burden. 'We'd like to see the sister in charge.'

'If you please, my dear,' said Wexford, and the girl gave him a broad smile before hurrying off. 'Do you have to be so bloody rude, Mike?'

She came back with Sister Lynch, a tall dark-haired Irish-woman in her late twenties.

'What can I do for you gentlemen?' She listened, clicked her tongue as Wexford gave her the bare details. 'There's a terrible thing. A woman's not safe to walk abroad. And Miss Comfrey in here only last night to see her father.'

'We'll have to see him, Sister.'

'Not tonight you won't, Chief Inspector. I'm sure I'm sorry, but I couldn't allow it, not with the old gentlemen all settling down for the night. They'd none of them get a wink of sleep, and it's going off duty I am myself in ten minutes. I'll tell him myself tomorrow, though whether it'll sink in at all I doubt.'

'He's senile?'

'There's a word, Chief Inspector, that I'm never knowing the meaning of. Eighty-five he is, and he's had a major stroke. Mostly he sleeps. If that's to be senile, senile he is. You'll be wasting your valuable time seeing him. I'll break it to him as best I can. Now would there be anything else?'

'Miss Comfrey's home address, please.'

'Certainly.' Sister Lynch beckoned to a dark-skinned girl who had appeared, pushing a trolley of drugs. 'Would you get Miss Comfrey's home address from records, Nurse Mahmud?'

'Did you talk to Miss Comfrey last night, Sister?'

'No more than to say hallo and that the old gentleman was just the same. And I said good-bye to her too. She was talking to Mrs Wells and they left together. Mrs Wells's husband is in the next bed to Mr Comfrey. Here's the address you were wanting. Thank you, nurse. Number one, Carlyle Villas, Forest Road, Kingsmarkham.' Sister Lynch studied the card which had been handed to her. 'No phone I see.'

'I'm afraid you've got Mr Comfrey's address there,' said Wexford. 'It's his daughter's we want.'

'But that is his daughter's, his and his daughter's.'

Wexford shook his head. 'No. She lived in London.'

'It's the only one we have,' said Sister Lynch, a slight edge to her voice. 'As far as we know, Miss Comfrey lived in Kingsmarkham with her father.'

'Then I'm afraid you were misled. Suppose you had had to get in touch with her – for instance, if her father had taken a turn for the worse – how would you have done so?'

'Notified her by letter. Or sent a messenger.' Sister Lynch had begun to look huffy. He was questioning her efficiency. 'That wouldn't have been necessary. Miss Comfrey phoned in almost every day. Last Thursday, now, she phoned on the very day her father had his stroke.'

'And yet you say she hadn't a phone? Sister, I need that address. I shall have to see Mr Comfrey.'

Her eyes went to her watch and noted the time. She said very sharply, 'Aren't I telling you, the poor old gentleman's no more than a vegetable at all? As for giving you an address, you'd as likely get an answer out of my little dog.'

'Very well. In the absence of Miss Comfrey's address, I'll have Mrs Wells's please.' This was provided, and Wexford said. 'We'll come back tomorrow.'

'You must suit yourselves. And now I'll take my leave of you.'

Wexford murmured as they left, 'There is nothing you could take from me that I would more willingly part withal,' and then to Burden, who was smugly looking as if his early rudeness had been justified and he hoped his superior realized it, 'We'll get it from the aunt. Odd, though, isn't it, her not giving her home address to the hospital?'

'Oh, I don't know. Underhand, but not odd. These old people can be a terrible drag. And it's always the women who are expected to look after them. I mean, old Comfrey'll be let out some time and he won't be able to live on his own any more. A single woman and a daughter is a gift to all those busybody doctors and social workers. They'd seize on her. Wouldn't even consider expecting it of a son. If she gave them her real address they'd pounce on that as a convalescent home for the old boy.'

'You're the last person I thought I'd ever hear handing out Women's Lib propaganda,' said Wexford. 'Wonders will never cease. But doesn't it strike you that your theory only increases her chances of getting stuck with her father? They think she's on the spot, they think she lives with him already.'

'There'll be an explanation. It isn't important, is it?'

'It's a departure from the norm, and that makes it important to me. I think Mrs Wells next, Mike, and then back to Forest Road to wait for the aunt.

Mrs Wells was seventy years old, slow of speech and rather confused. She had seen and spoken to Rhoda Comfrey twice before on her previous visits to the hospital, once in May and once in July. On the evening before they had got on the bus together outside the hospital at eight-fifteen. What had they talked about? Mrs Wells thought it had mostly been about her husband's hip operation. Miss Comfrey hadn't said much, had seemed a bit nervous and uneasy. Worried about her father, Mrs Wells thought. No, she didn't know her London address, believed in fact that she lived in Forest Road where she had said she was returning. Mrs Wells had left the bus at the Kingsbrook Bridge, but her companion had remained on it, having a ticket to the next fare stage.

They returned to the police station. The weapon hadn't been found, and the house-to-house inquiry made by Loring, Marwood and Gates had produced negative results. No one in the cottages or the bungalows had heard or seen anything untoward on the previous evening. The inhabitants of the single detached house were away on holiday, and nobody had been working on the allotments. Rhoda Comfrey had been slightly known to everyone the three men had questioned, but only one had seen her on the previous day, and that had been when she left her father's house at six-twenty to catch the bus for Stowerton. Her London address was unknown to any of the residents of Forest Road.

'I want you to get back there,' Wexford said to Loring, 'and wait for Mrs Crown. I'm going home for an hour to get a bite to eat. When she comes in, call me on my home number.'

CHAPTER THREE

Dora had been sewing, but the work had been laid aside, and he found her reading a novel. She got up immediately and brought him a bowl of soup, chicken salad, some fruit. He seldom talked about work at home, unless things got very tough. Home was a haven – Oh, what know they of harbours that sail not on the sea? – and he had fallen in love with and married the kind of woman who would give him one. But did she mind? Did she see herself as the one who waited and served while he lived? He had never thought much about it. Thinking of it now reawakened the anxiety that had laid dormant for the past three hours, pushed out of mind by greater urgencies.

'Hear any more from Sylvia?' he said.

'Neil came round for the teddy bear. Ben wouldn't go to sleep without it.' She touched his arm, then rested her hand on his wrist. 'You mustn't worry about her. She's grown-up. She has to cope with her own problems.'

'Your son's your son,' said her husband, 'till he gets him a wife, but your daughter's your daughter the whole of your life.'

'There goes the phone.' She sighed, but not rebelliously. 'I have measured out my life in telephone bills.'

'Don't wait up for me,' said Wexford.

It was dark now, ten minutes to eleven, the wide sky covered all over with stars. And the moonlight was strong enough to cast bold shadows of tree and gate and pillar box along the length of Forest Road. A single street lamp shone up by the stone wall, and lights were on all over 2, Carlyle Villas, though the other houses were in darkness. He rang the bell on the reeded glass and wrought-iron front door.

'Mrs Crown?'

He had expected a negative answer because this woman was much younger than he had thought she would be. Only a few years older than he. But she said yes, she was, and asked him what he wanted. She smelt of gin and had about her the reckless air – no apparent fear of him or cautiousness or suspicion – that drink brings, though this might have been habitual with her. He told her who he was and she let him in. There, in a cluttered bizarre living room, he broke the news to her, speaking gently and considerately but all the time sensing that gentleness and consideration weren't needed here.

'Well, fancy,' she said. 'What a thing to happen! Rhoda, of all people. That's given me a bit of a shock, that has. A drink is called for. Want one?' Wexford shook his head. She helped herself from a gin bottle that stood on a limed oak sideboard whose surface was covered with drips and smears and ring marks. 'I won't make show of grief. We weren't close. Where did you say it happened? Down the footpath? You won't see me down there in a hurry, I can tell you.'

She was like the room they were in, small and over-dressed in bright colours and none too clean. The stretch nylon covers on her chairs were of a slightly duller yellow than the tight dress she wore, and unlike it, they were badly marked with cigarette burns. But all were disfigured with the same sort of liquor splashes and food stains. Mrs Crown's hair was of the same colour and texture as the dried grasses that stood everywhere in green and yellow vases, pale and thin and brittle but defiantly gold. She lit a cigarette and left it hanging in her mouth which was painted, as her niece's had been, to match her fingernails.

'I haven't yet been able to inform your brother,' Wexford said. 'It would appear he's not up to it.'

'Brother-in-*law*, if you don't mind,' said Mrs Crown. 'He's not my brother, the old devil.'

'Ah, yes,' said Wexford. 'Now, Mrs Crown, it's getting late

and I don't want to keep you up, but I'd like to know what you can tell me of Miss Comfrey's movements yesterday.'

She stared at him, blowing smoke through her sharp nose. 'What's that got to do with some maniac stabbing her? Killed her for her money, didn't he? She was always loaded, was Rhoda.' Horrifyingly, she added, with a Wife of Bath look, remembering the old dance, 'Wouldn't be for sex, not so likely.'

Wexford didn't take her up on that one. He said repressively, 'You saw her yesterday?'

'She phoned me on Friday to say she'd be coming. Thought I might get bothered if I saw lights on next door, not expecting anyone to be there, if you see what I mean. God knows why she put herself out. I was amazed. Picked up the phone and she says, "Hallo, Lilian. I wonder if you know who this is?" Of course I knew. I'd know that deep voice of hers anywhere and that put-on accent. She never got that from her mum and dad. But you don't want to know all that. She came in a taxi yesterday about one. All dressed-up she was, but miserable as sin. She was always down in the mouth when she came here, made no secret she hated the place, far cry from the way she sounded on the phone, all cocky, if you know what I mean. Sure you won't have a drink? I think I'll have a drop more.'

A good deal more than a drop of neat gin in her glass, Lilian Crown perched on the sofa arm and swung her legs. The calves were shapeless with varicose veins, but she still kept the high instep, the dancing foot, of one who has led a riotous youth. 'She never came in here till a quarter past six. "Feel like coming with me, Lilian?" she said, knowing damn well I wouldn't. I told her I'd got a date with my gentleman friend, which was the honest truth, but I could tell she didn't like it, always was jealous. "When'll you be back?" she said. "I'll come in and tell you how he is." "All right," I said, doing my best to be pleasant, though I never had any time for him or her after my poor sister went. "I'll be in by ten," I said, but she never came and no lights came on. Gone straight back to London, I thought, knowing her, never dreaming a thing like that had happened.'

Wexford nodded. 'I'll very likely want to speak to you again, Mrs Crown. In the meantime, would you give me Miss Comfrey's London address?'

'I haven't got it.'

'You mean you don't *know* it?'

'That's what I mean. Look, I live next door to the old devil, sure I do, but that's convenience, that is. I came here for my sister's sake and after she went I just stopped on. But that doesn't mean we were close. As a matter of fact, him and me, we weren't on speaking terms. As for Rhoda – well, I won't speak ill of the dead. She was my sister's girl, when all's said and done, but we never did get on. She left home must be twenty years ago, and if I've set eyes on her a dozen times since, that's it. She'd no call to give me her address or her phone number, and I'm sure I wouldn't have asked for it. Look, if I'd got it I'd give it you, wouldn't I? I'd have no call not to.'

'At least, I suppose, you know what she did for a living?'

'In business, she was,' said Lilian Crown. 'Got her own business.' Bitterness pinched her face. 'Money stuck to Rhoda, always did. And she hung on to it. None of it came my way or *his*. He's a proper old devil but he's her dad, isn't he?'

A woman who had said she wouldn't speak ill of the dead . . . Wexford went home, building up in his mind a picture of what Rhoda Comfrey had been. A middle-aged, well-off, successful woman, probably self-employed; a woman who had disliked the town of her origins because it held for her painful associations; who liked her privacy and had kept, in so far as she could, her address to herself; a clever, cynical, hard-bitten woman, indifferent to this country world's opinion, and owing to her unpleasant old father no more than a bare duty. Still, it was too early for this sort of speculation. In the morning they would have a warrant to search Mr Comfrey's house, the address, the nature of her business, would be discovered; and Rhoda Comfrey's life unfold. Already Wexford had a feeling – one of those illogical intuitive feelings the Chief Constable so much disliked – that the motive for her murder lay in that London life.

Kingsmarkham Police station had been built about fifteen years before, and the conservative townsfolk had been shocked by the appearance of this stark white box with its flat roof and wide picture windows. But a decade and a half had tripled the size of the saplings around it so that now its severity was half-screened by birches and laburnums. Wexford had his office on the second floor; buttercup-yellow walls with maps on them and a decorous calendar of Sussex views, a new blue carpet, his own desk of dark red rosewood that belonged to him personally and not to the Mid-Sussex Constabulary. The big window afforded him a fine view of the High Street, of higgledy-piggledy rooftops, of green meadows beyond. This morning, Wednesday, August tenth, it was wide open and the air-conditioning switched off. Another lovely day, exactly what the clear sky and stars and bright moon of the previous night had promised.

Since he had looked in first thing in the morning and left again for Stowerton Royal Infirmary, the clothes Rhoda Comfrey had been wearing had been sent up and left on the desk. Wexford threw down beside them the early editions of the evening papers he had just picked up. Middle-aged spinsters, even when stabbed to death, were apparently not news, and neither paper had allotted to this murder more than a couple of paragraphs on an inside page. He sat down by the window to cool down, for the front aspect of the police station was still in shade.

James Albert Comfrey. They had drawn cretonne curtains

printed with flowers round the old man's bed. His hands moved like crabs, gnarled and crooked, across the sheet. Sometimes they plucked at a tuft of wool on the red blanket, then they parted and crawled back, only to begin again on their journey. His mouth was open, he breathed stertorously. In the strong, tough yet enfeebled face, Wexford had seen the lineaments of the daughter, the big nose, long upper lip and cliff-like chin.

'Like I said,' said Sister Lynch, 'it never meant a thing to him when I passed on the news. There's little that registers at all.'

'Mr Comfrey,' said Wexford, approaching the bed.

'Sure, and you may as well save your breath.'

'I'd like to have a look in that locker.'

'I can't have that,' said Sister Lynch.

'I have a warrant to search his house.' Wexford was beginning to lose his patience. 'D'you think I couldn't get one to search a cupboard?'

'What's my position going to be if there's a come-back?'

'You mean *he's* going to complain to the hospital board?' Without wasting any more time, Wexford had opened the lower part of the locker. It contained nothing but a pair of slippers and a rolled-up dressing-gown. Irish ire making itself apparent behind him in sharp exhalations, he shook out the dressing-gown and felt in its pockets. Nothing. He rolled it up again. An infringement of privacy? he thought. The gown was made of red towelling with 'Stowerton Infirmary' worked in white cotton on its hem. Perhaps James Comfrey no longer possessed anything of his own.

He did. In the drawer above the cupboard was a set of dentures in a plastic box and a pair of glasses. Impossible to imagine this man owning an address book. There was nothing of that sort in the drawer, nothing else at all but a scrap of folded tissue.

So he had come away, baulked and wondering. But the

house itself would yield that address, and if it didn't those newspaper accounts, meagre as they were, would rouse the London friends and acquaintances, employers of employees, who must by now have missed her.

He turned his attention to the clothes. It was going to be a day of groping through other people's possessions – such closets to search, such alcoves to importune! Rhoda Comfrey's dress and jacket, shoes and underwear, were unremarkable, the medium-priced garments of a woman who had retained a taste for bright colours and fussy trimmings into middle age. The shoes were a little distorted by feet that had spread. No perfume clung to the fabric of dress and slip. He was examining labels which told him only that the shoes came from one of a chain of shops whose name had been a household word for a quarter of a century, that the clothes might have been bought in any Oxford Street or Knightsbridge emporium, when there came a knock at the door.

The head of Dr Crocker appeared. 'What seems to be the trouble?' said the doctor very breezily.

They were lifelong friends, having known each other since their schooldays when Leonard Crocker had been in the first form and Reginald Wexford in the sixth. And it had sometimes been Wexford's job – how he had loathed it! – to shepherd home to the street next his own in Pomfret the mischievous recalcitrant infant. Now they were both getting on in years, but the mischievousness remained. Wexford was in no mood for it this morning.

'What d'you think?' he growled. 'Guess.'

Crocker walked over to the desk and picked up one of the shoes. 'The old man's my patient, you know.'

'No, I don't know. And I hope to God you haven't come here just to be mysterious about it. I've had some of that nonsense from you before. "The secrets of the confessional" and "a doctor's like a priest" and all that rubbish.'

Crocker ignored this. 'Old Comfrey used to come to my

surgery regularly every Tuesday night. Nothing wrong with him bar old age till he broke his hip. These old people, they like to come in for a chat. I just thought you might be interested.'

'I am, of course, if it's interesting.'

'Well, it's the daughter that's dead and he was always on about his daughter. How she'd left him all on his own since her mother died and neglected him and didn't come to see him from one year's end to the next. He was really quite articulate about it. Now, how did he describe her?'

'A thwart disnatured torment?'

The doctor raised his eyebrows. 'That's good, but it doesn't sound old Comfrey's style. I've heard it somewhere before.'

'Mm,' said Wexford. 'No doubt you have. But let's not go into the comminations of Lear on his thankless child. You will, of course, know the thankless child's address.'

'London.'

'Oh, really! If anyone else says that to me I'll put them on a charge for obstruction. You mean even *you* don't know where in London? For God's sake, Len, this old boy's eighty-five. Suppose you'd been called out to him and found him at death's door? How would you have got in touch with his next of kin?'

'He wasn't at death's door. People don't have deathbeds like that any more, Reg. They get ill, they linger, they go into hospital. The majority of people die in hospital these days. During the whole long painful process we'd have got her address.'

'Well, you didn't,' Wexford snapped. 'The hospital haven't got it now. How about that? I have to have that address.'

'It'll be at old Comfrey's place,' said Crocker easily.

'I just hope so. I'm going over there now to find it if it's findable.'

The doctor jumped down from his perch on the edge of the desk. With one of those flashbacks to his youth, to his schooldays, he said on an eager note, 'Can I come too?'

'I suppose so. But I don't want you cavorting about and getting in everyone's way.'

'Thanks very much,' said Crocker in mock dudgeon. 'Who do you think the popularity polls show to be the most respected members of the community? General practitioners.'

'I knew it wasn't cops,' said Wexford.

CHAPTER FOUR

The house smelt as he had thought it would, of the old person's animal-vegetable-mineral smell, sweat, cabbage and camphor.

'What did moths live on before man wore woollen clothes?'

'Sheep, I suppose,' said the doctor.

'But do sheep have moths?'

'God knows. This place is a real tip, isn't it?'

They were turning out drawers in the two downstairs rooms. Broken pens and pencils, dried-out ink bottles, sticking plaster, little glass jars full of pins, dead matches, nails, nuts and bolts, screws of thread; an assortment of keys, a pair of dirty socks full of holes, pennies and threepenny bits from the old currency, pieces of string, a broken watch, some marbles and some dried peas; a five-amp electric plug, milk bottle tops, the lid of a paint tin encrusted with blue from the front door, cigarette cards, picture hangers and an ancient shaving brush.

'Nice little breeding ground for anthrax,' said Crocker, and he pocketed a dozen or so boxes and bottles of pills that were ranged on top of the chest. 'I may as well dispose of this lot while I'm here. They won't chuck them out, no matter how often you tell them. Though why they should be so saving when they get them for free in the first place, I never will know.'

The footfalls of Burden, Loring and Gates could be heard overhead. Wexford knelt down, opened the bottom drawer. Underneath a lot of scattered mothballs, more socks redolent of cheesy mustiness, and a half-empty packet of birdseed, he found an oval picture frame lying face-downwards. He turned it over and looked at a photograph of a young woman with short dark hair, strong jaw, long upper lip, biggish nose.

'I suppose that's her,' he said to the doctor.

'Wouldn't know. I never saw her till she was dead and she didn't look much like that then. It's the spitting image of the old man, though, isn't it? It's her all right.'

Wexford said thoughtfully and a little sadly, remembering the over-made-up, raddled face, 'It does look like her. It's just that it was taken a long time ago.' And yet she hadn't looked sad. The dead face, if it were possible to say such a thing, had looked almost pleased with itself. 'We'll try upstairs,' he said.

There was no bathroom in the house, and the only lavatory was outside in the garden. The stairs were not carpeted but covered with linoleum. Burden came out of the front bedroom which was James Comfrey's.

'Proper old glory hole in there. D'you know, there's not a book in the house, and not a letter or a postcard either.'

'The spare room,' said Crocker.

It was a bleak little place, the walls papered in a print of faded pink and mauve sweet pea, the bare floorboards stained dark brown, the thin curtains whitish now but showing faintly the remains of a pink pattern. On the white cotton counterpane that covered the single bed lay a freshly pressed skirt in a navy-checked synthetic material, a blue nylon blouse and a pair of tights still in their plastic wrapping. Apart from a wall cupboard and a very small chest of drawers, there was no other furniture. On the chest was a small suitcase. Wexford looked inside it and found a pair of cream silk pyjamas of better quality than any of Rhoda Comfrey's daytime wear, sandals of the kind that consist only of a rubber sole and rubber thong, and a sponge bag. That was all. The cupboard was empty as were the drawers of the chest.

The closets had been searched and the alcoves importuned in vain.

Wexford said hotly to Crocker and Burden, 'This is unbelievable. She doesn't give her address to her aunt or the hospital where her father is or to her father's doctor or his neighbours. It's not written down anywhere in his house, he hasn't got it with him in the hospital. No doubt, it was in his head where it's now either locked in or knocked out. What the hell was she playing at?'

'Possum,' said the doctor.

Wexford gave a snort. 'I'm going across the road,' he said. 'Mind you leave the place as you found it. That means untidying anything you've tidied up.' He grinned snidely at Crocker. It made a change for him to order the doctor about, for the boot was usually on the other foot. 'And get Mrs Crown formally to identify the body, will you, Mike? I wish you joy of her.'

Nicky Parker opened the door of Bella Vista, his mother close behind him in the hall. Again the reassuring game was played for the child's benefit and Wexford passed off as a doctor. Well, why not? Weren't doctors the most respected members of the community? A baby was crying somewhere, and Stella Parker looked harassed.

'Would it be convenient,' he said politely, 'for me to have a chat with your – er – grandmother-in-law?'

She said she was sure it would, and Wexford was led through to a room at the back of the house. Sitting in an armchair, on her lap a colander containing peas that she was shelling, sat one of the oldest people he had ever seen in his life.

'Nana, this is the police inspector.'

'How do you do, Mrs –?'

'Nana's called Parker too, the same as us.'

She was surrounded by preparations for the family's lunch. On the floor, on one side of her chair, stood a saucepanful of potatoes in water, the bowl of peelings in water beside it. Four cooking apples awaited her attention. Pastry was made, kneaded, and set on a plate. This, apparently, was one of the ways in which she, at her extreme age, contributed to the household management. Wexford remembered how Parker had called his grandmother a wonder, and he began to see why.

For a moment she took no notice of him, exercising perhaps the privilege of matriarchal eld. Stella Parker left them and shut the door. The old woman split open the last of her pods, an enormous one, and said as if they were old acquaintances:

'When I was a girl they used to say, if you find nine peas in a pod put it over your door and the next man to come in will be your own true love.' She scattered the nine peas into the full colander, wiped her greened fingers on her apron.

'Did you ever do it?' said Wexford.

'What d'you say? Speak up.'

'Did you ever do it?'

'Not me. Didn't need to. I'd been engaged to Mr Parker since we was both fifteen. Sit down, young man. You're too tall to be on your legs.'

Wexford was amused and absurdly flattered. 'Mrs Parker ...' he began on a bellow, but she interrupted him with what was very likely a favourite question.

'How old d'you think I am?'

There are only two periods in a woman's life when she hopes to be taken for older than she is, under sixteen and over ninety. In each case the error praises a certain achievement. But still he was wary.

She didn't wait for an answer. 'Ninety-two,' she said, 'and I still do the veg and make my own bed and do my room. And I looked after Brian and Nicky when Stell was in the hospital having Katrina. I was only eighty-nine then, though. Eleven children I've had and reared them all. Six of them gone now.' She levelled at him a girl's blue eyes in nests of wrinkles. 'It's not good to see your children go before you, young man.' Her face was white bone in a sheath of crumpled parchment. 'Brian's dad was my youngest, and he's been gone two years come November. Only fifty, he was. Still, Brian and Stell have been wonderful to me. They're a wonder, they are, the pair of them.' Her mind, drifting through the past, the ramifications of her family, returned to him, this stranger who must have come for something. 'What were you wanting? Police, Stell said.' She sat back, put the colander on the floor, and folded her hands. 'Rhoda Comfrey, is it?'

'Your grandson told you?'

''Course he did. Before he ever told you.' She was proud that she enjoyed the confidence of the young, and she smiled. But the smile was brief. Archaically, she said, 'She was wickedly murdered.'

'Yes, Mrs Parker. I believe you knew her well?'

'As well as my own children. She used to come and see me every time she come down here. Rather see me than her dad, she would.'

At last, he thought. 'Then you'll be able to tell me her address?'

'Speak up, will you?'

'Her address in London?'

'Don't know it. What'd I want to know that for? I've not written a letter in ten years and I've only been to London twice in my life.'

He had wasted his time coming here, and he couldn't afford to waste time.

'I can tell you all about her, though,' said Mrs Parker. 'Everything you'll want to know. And about the family. Nobody can tell you like I can. You've come to the right place for that.'

'Mrs Parker, I don't think . . .' That I care? That it matters? What he wanted at this stage was an address, not a biography, especially not one told with meanderings and digressions. But how to cut short without offence a woman of ninety-two whose deafness made interruption virtually impossible? He would have to listen and hope it wouldn't go on too long. Besides, she had already begun . . .

'They come here when Rhoda was a little mite. An only

child she was, and used to play with my two youngest. A poor feeble thing was Agnes Comfrey, didn't know how to stand up for herself, and Mr Comfrey was a real terror. I don't say he hit her or Rhoda, but he ruled them with a rod of iron just the same.' She rapped out sharply. 'You come across that Mrs Crown yet?'

'Yes,' said Wexford, 'But . . .' Oh, not the aunt, he thought, not the by-path. She hadn't heard him.

'You will. A crying scandal to the whole neighbourhood, she is. Used to come here visiting her sister when her first husband was alive. Before the war, that was, and she was a real fly-by-night even then, though she never took to drink till he was killed at Dunkirk. She had this baby about three months after – I daresay it was his all right, give her the benefit of the doubt – but it was one of them mongols, poor little love. John, they called him. Her and him come to live here with the Comfreys. Aggie used to come over to me in a terrible state of worry about what Lilian got up to and tried to keep dark, and Jim Comfrey threatening to throw her out.

'Well, the upshot of it was she met this Crown in the nick of time and they took the house next door when they was married on account of it had been empty all through the war. And d'you know what she done then?'

Wexford shook his head and stared at the pyramid of peas which were having a mesmeric effect on him.

'I'll tell you. She had little John put in a home. Have you ever heard the like, for a mother to do such a thing like that? Sweet affectionate little love he was too, the way them mongols are, and loved Rhoda, and she taking him out with her, not a bit ashamed.

'She'd have been how old then, Mrs Parker?' Wexford said for something to say. It was a mistake because he didn't really care, and he had to bawl it twice more before she heard.

'Twelve, she was, when he was born, and sixteen when Lilian had him put away. She was at the County High School, and Mr Comfrey wanted to take her away when she was fourteen like you could in them days. The headmistress herself, Miss Fowler that was, come to the house personally herself to beg him let Rhoda stay on, her being so bright. Well, he gave way for a bit, but he wasn't having her go on to no college, made her leave at sixteen, wanted her money, he said, the old skinflint.'

It was very hot, and the words began to roll over Wexford only half-heard. Just the very usual unhappy tale of the mean-spirited working-class parent who values cash in hand more than the career in the future. 'Got shop work – wanted to better herself, did Rhoda – always shut up in that back bedroom reading – taught herself French – went to typing classes –' How the hell was he going to get that address? Trace her through those clothes, those antique shoes? Not a hope. The sharp old voice cackled on. 'Nothing to look at – never had a boy – that Lilian always at her – "When you going to get yourself a boy-friend, Rhoda?" – got to be a secretary – poor thing, she used to get herself up like Lilian, flashy clothes and high heels and paint all over her face.' He'd have to get help from the Press: *Do You Know This Woman?* On the strength of that photograph? 'Aggie got cancer – never went to the doctor till it was too late – had an operation, but it wasn't no use – she passed on and poor Rhoda was left with the old man –'

Well, he wasn't going to allow publication of photos of her dead face, never had done that and never would. If only Mrs Parker would come to an end, if only she hadn't about twenty years still to go! 'And would have stayed, I daresay – been a slave to him – stayed for ever but for getting all that money – tied to him hand and foot –'

'What did you say?'

'I'm the one that's deaf, young man,' said Mrs Parker.

'I know, I'm sorry. But what was that about coming into money?'

'You want to listen when you're spoken to, not go off in day-dreams. She didn't come into money, she won it. On the pools, it was one of them office what-d'you-call-its.'

'Syndicates?'

'I daresay. Old Jim Comfrey, he thought he was in clover. 'My ship's come in,' he says to my eldest son. But he was wrong there. Rhoda upped and walked out on him, and so much for the house he was going to have and the car and all.'

'How much was it?'

'How much was what? What she won? Thousands and thousands. She never said and I wouldn't ask. She come round to my place one afternoon – I was living up the road then – and she'd got a big case all packed. Just thirty, she was, and twenty years ago nearly to the day. She had the same birthday as me, you see, August the fifth, and forty-two years between us. 'I'm leaving, Auntie Vi,' she says, 'going to London to seek my fortune,' and she gives me the address of some hotel and says would I have all her books packed up and sent on to her? Fat chance of that. Jim Comfrey burned the lot of them down the garden. I can see her now like it was yesterday, in them high heels she couldn't walk in properly and a dress all frills, and beads all over her and fingernails like she'd dipped them in red paint and . . .'

'You didn't see her yesterday, did you?' Wexford yelled rapidly. 'I mean, the day before yesterday?'

'No. Didn't know she was here. She'd have come, though, if it wasn't for some wicked . . .'

'What was she going to do in London, Mrs Parker?'

'Be a reporter on a paper. That's what she wanted. She was secretary to the editor of the *Gazette* and she used to write bits for them too. I told you all that only you wasn't listening.'

Puzzled, he said, 'But Mrs Crown said she was in business.'

'All I can say is, if you believe her you'll believe anything. Rhoda got to be a reporter and did well for herself, had a nice home, she used to tell me, and what with the money she'd won and her wages . . .'

He bellowed, 'What newspaper, d'you know? Whereabouts was this home of hers?'

Mrs Parker drew herself up, assuming a duchessy dignity. She said rather frigidly, 'Lord knows, I hope you'll never get to be deaf, young man. But maybe you'll never understand unless you do. Half the things folks say to you go over your head, and you can't keep stopping them to ask them what? Can you? They think you're going mental. Rhoda used to say she'd written a bit here and a bit there, and gone to this place or that, and bought things for her home and whatnot, and how nice it was and what nice friends she'd got. I liked to hear her talk, I liked her being friendly with an old woman, but I know better than to think I'm like to follow half the things she *said*.'

Defeated, flattened, bludgeoned and nearly stunned, Wexford got up. 'I must go, Mrs Parker.'

'I won't quarrel with that,' she said tartly and, showing no sign of fatigue, 'You've fair worn me out, roaring at me like a blooming bull.' She handed him the colander and the potatoes. 'You can make yourself useful and give these to Stell. And tell her to bring me in a pie dish.'

CHAPTER FIVE

Had she perhaps been a freelance journalist?

At the press conference Wexford gave that afternoon he asked this question of Harry Wild, of the *Kingsmarkham Courier*, and of the only reporter any national newspaper had bothered to send. Neither of them had heard of her in this connection, though Harry vaguely remembered a plain-featured dark girl called Comfrey, who twenty years before, had been secretary to the editor of the now defunct *Gazette*.

'And now,' Wexford said to Burden, 'we'll adjourn to the Olive for a well-earned drink. See if you can find Crocker. He's about somewhere, dying to get the low-down on the medical report.'

The doctor was found, and they made their way to the Olive and Dove where they sat outside at a table in the little garden. It had been the sort of summer that seldom occurs in England, the sort foreigners believe never occurs, though the Englishman of middle age can look back and truthfully assert that there have been three or four such in his lifetime. Weeks, months, of undimmed sunshine had pushed geraniums up to five feet and produced fuchsias of a size and profusion only generally seen inside a heated greenhouse. None of the three men wore a jacket, but the doctor alone sported a tee-shirt, a short-sleeved adolescent garment in which he made his rounds and entranced his female patients.

Wexford drank white wine, very dry and as cold as the Olive was able to produce it which, tonight, was around blood heat. The occasional beer was for when Crocker, a stern medical mentor, wasn't around. It was a while now since the chief inspector had suffered a mild thrombosis, but any excesses, as the doctor never tired of telling him, could easily lead to another.

He began by congratulating his friend on the accuracy of his on-the-spot estimate of the time of death. The eminent pathologist who had conducted the post-mortem had put it at between seven and nine-thirty.

'Eight-thirty's the most probable,' he said, 'on her way home from the bus stop.' He sipped his warm wine. 'She was a strong healthy woman – until someone put a knife in her. One stab wound pierced a lung and the other the left ventricle. No signs of disease, no abnormalities. Except one. I think in these days you could call it an abnormality.'

'What do you mean?' said Crocker.

'She was a virgin.'

Burden, that strait-laced puritan, jerked up his head. 'Good heavens, she was an unmarried woman, wasn't she? Things have come to a pretty pass, I must say, if a perfectly proper condition for a single woman is called abnormal.'

'I suppose you must say it, Mike,' said Wexford with a sigh, 'but I wish you wouldn't. I agree that a hundred years ago, fifty years ago, even twenty, such a thing wouldn't be unusual in a woman of fifty, but it is now.'

'Unusual in a woman of *fifteen*, if you ask me,' said the doctor.

'Look at it this way. She was only thirty when she left home, and that was just at the beginning of the stirrings of the permissive society. She had some money. Presumably, she lived alone without any kind of chaperonage. All right, she was never very attractive or charming, but she wasn't repulsive, she wasn't deformed. Isn't it very strange indeed that in those first ten years at least she never had one love affair, not even one adventure for the sake of the experience?'

'Frigid,' said Crocker. 'Everyone's supposed to be rolling about from bed to bed these days, but you'd be surprised how many people just aren't interested in sex. Women especially. Some of them put up a good showing, they really try, but they'd much rather be watching the TV.'

'So old Acton was right, was he? "A modest woman",'
Wexford quoted, ' "seldom desires any sexual gratification for
herself. She submits to her husband but only to please him
and, but for the desire for maternity, would far rather be
relieved from his attentions." '

Burden drained his glass and made a face like someone
who had taken unpalatable medicine. He had been a policeman for longer than Rhoda Comfrey had been free of paternal
ties, had seen human nature in every possible seamy or sordid
aspect, yet his experience had scarcely at all altered his attitude
towards sexual matters. He was still one of those people whose
feelings about sex are grossly ambivalent. For him it was both
dirty and holy. He had never read that quaint Victorian
manual, Dr Acton's *Functions and Disorders of the Reproductive
Organs*, male-orientated, prudish, repressive and biologically
very wide of the mark, but it was for such as he that it had
been written. Now, while Wexford and the doctor – who for
some reason beyond his comprehension seemed to know the
work well – were quoting from it with scathing laughter and
casting up of eyes, he said brusquely, interrupting them:

'In my opinion, this has absolutely nothing to do with
Rhoda Comfrey's murder.'

'Very likely not, Mike. It seems a small point when we
don't even know where she lived or how she lived or who her
friends were. But I hope all that will be solved tomorrow.'

'What's so special about tomorrow?'

'I think we shall see that this rather dull little backwoods
killing will have moved from the inside pages to be frontpage
news. I've been very frank with the newspapers – mostly via
Harry Wild who'll scoop a packet in lineage – and I think
I've given them the sort of thing they like. I've also given them
that photograph, for what it's worth. I'll be very much surprised if tomorrow morning we don't see headlines such
as "Murdered Woman Led Double Life" and "What Was
Stabbed Woman's Secret?" '

'You mean,' said Burden, 'that some neighbour of hers or employer or the man who delivers her milk will see it and let us know?'

Wexford nodded. 'Something like that. I've given the Press a number for anyone with information to ring. You see, that neighbour or employer may have read about her death today without its occurring to them that we're still in ignorance of her address.'

The doctor went off to get fresh drinks. 'All the nuts will be on the blower,' said Burden. 'All the men whose wives ran away in 1956, all the paranoiacs and sensation-mongers.'

'That can't be helped. We have to sort out the sheep from the goats. God knows, we've done it before often enough.'

The newspapers, as he put it, did him proud. They went, as always, too far with headlines more bizarre than those he had predicted. If the photograph, touched up out of recognition, struck no chords, he was sure the text must. Rhoda Comfrey's past was there, the circumstances of her Kingsmarkham life, the history of her association with the old *Gazette*, the details of her father's illness. Mrs Parker and Mrs Crown had apparently not been so useless after all.

By nine the phone began to ring.

For Wexford, his personal phone had been ringing throughout the night, but those calls had been from newspapermen wanting more details and all ready to assure him that Rhoda Comfrey hadn't worked for *them*. In Fleet Street she was unknown. Reaching the station early, he set Loring to trying all the London local papers, while he himself waited for something to come from the special line. Every call that had the slightest hint of genuineness about it was to be relayed to him.

Burden, of course, had been right. All the nuts were on the blower. There was the spiritualist whose sister had died fifteen years before and who was certain Rhoda Comfrey must have been that sister reincarnated; the son whose mother had abandoned him when he was twelve; the husband, newly released from a mental hospital, whose wife that he declared missing came and took the receiver from him with embarrassed apologies; the seer who offered to divine the dead woman's address from the aura of her clothes. None of these calls even reached Wexford's sanctum, though he was told of them. Personally he took the call from George Rowlands, former editor of the *Gazette*, who had nothing to tell him but that Rhoda had been a good secretary with the makings of a feature-writer. Every well-meant and apparently sane call he took, but the day passed without anything to justify his optimism. Friday came, and with it the inquest.

It was quickly adjourned, and nothing much came out of it but a reproof for Brian Parker from an unsympathetic coroner. This was a court, not a child guidance clinic, said the coroner, managing to imply that the paucity of evidence was somehow due to Parker's having rearranged Rhoda Comfrey's clothes.

The phone calls still came sporadically on the Saturday, but not one caller claimed to know Rhoda Comfrey by name or said he or she had lived next door to her or worked with her. No bank manager phoned to say she had an account at his bank, no landlord to say that she paid him rent.

'This,' said Wexford, 'is ridiculous. Am I supposed to believe she lived in a tent in Hyde Park?'

'Of course it has to be that she was living under an assumed name.' Burden stood at the window and watched the bus from Stowerton pause at the stop, let off a woman passenger not unlike Rhoda Comfrey, then move off towards Forest Road. 'I thought the papers were doing their usual hysterical stuff when they printed all that about her secret life.' He looked at Wexford, raising his eyebrows. 'I thought you were too.'

'My usual hysterical stuff. Thanks very much.'

'I meant melodramatic,' said Burden, as if that mitigated the censure. 'But they weren't. You weren't. Why would she behave like that?'

'For the usual melodramatic reason. Because she didn't want the people who knew Rhoda Comfrey to know what Rhoda Comfrey was up to. Espionage, drug-running, protection rackets, a call-girl ring. It's bound to be something like that.'

'Look, I didn't mean you always exaggerate. I've said I was wrong, haven't I? As a matter of fact, the call-girl idea did come into my mind. Only she was a bit old for that and nothing much to look at and – well . . .'

'Well, what? She was the only virgin prostitute in London, was she? It's a new line, Mike, it's an idea. It's a refreshing change in these dissolute times. I can think of all sorts of fascinating possibilities in that one, only I wouldn't like to burn your chaste ears. Shall we try to be realistic?'

'I always do,' said Burden gloomily. He sat down and rested his elbows on Wexford's desk. 'She's been dead since Monday night, and it's Sunday now and we don't even know where she lived. It seems hopeless.'

'That's not being realistic, that's defeatist. She can't be traced through her name or her description, therefore she must be traced by other means. In a negative sort of way, all this has shown us something. It's shown us that her murder is connected with that other life of hers. A secret life is almost always a life founded on something illicit or illegal. In the course of it she did something which gave someone a reason to kill her.'

'You mean we can't dismiss the secret life and concentrate on the circumstantial and concrete evidence we have?'

'Like what? No weapon, no witnesses, no smell of a motive?' Wexford hesitated and said more slowly, 'She seldom came back here, but she had been coming once or twice a year. The local people knew her by sight, knew who she was.

Therefore, I don't think this is a case of someone returning home after a long absence and being recognized – to put it melodramatically, Mike – by an old enemy. Nor was her real life here or her work or her interests or her involvements. Those, whatever they were, she left behind in London.'

'You don't think the circumstances point to local knowledge?'

'I don't. I say her killer knew she was coming here and followed her, though not, possibly, with premeditation to kill. He or she came from London, having known her in that other life of hers. So never mind the locals. We have to come to grips with the London life, and I've got an idea how to do it. Through that wallet she had in her handbag.'

'I'm listening,' said Burden with a sigh.

'I've got it here.' Wexford produced the wallet from a drawer in his desk. 'See the name printed in gold on the inside? Silk and Whitebeam.'

'Sorry, it doesn't mean a thing to me.'

'They're a very exclusive leather shop in Jermyn Street. That wallet's new. I think there's a chance they might remember who they sold it to, and I'm sending Loring up first thing in the morning to ask them. Rhoda Comfrey had a birthday last week. If she didn't buy it herself, I'm wondering what are the chances of someone else having bought it for her as a gift.'

'For a *woman*?'

'Why not? If she was in need of a wallet. Women carry banknotes as much as we do. The days of giving women a bottle of perfume or a brooch are passing, Mike. They are very nearly the people now. *Sic transit gloria mundi.*'

'*Sic transit gloria* Sunday, if you ask me,' said Burden.

Wexford laughed. His subordinate and friend could still surprise him.

CHAPTER SIX

As soon as he had let himself into his house, Dora came out from the kitchen, beckoned him into it and shut the door.

'Sylvia's here.'

There is nothing particularly odd or unusual about a married daughter visiting her mother on a Sunday afternoon, and Wexford said, 'Why shouldn't she be? What d'you mean?'

'She's left Neil. She just walked out after lunch and came here.'

'Are you saying she's seriously *left Neil*? Just like that? She's walked out on her husband and come home to mother? I can't believe it.'

'Darling, it's true. Apparently, they've been having a continuous quarrel ever since Wednesday night. He promised to take her to Paris for a week in September – his sister was going to have the children – and now he says he can't go, he's got to go to Sweden on business. Well, in the resulting row Sylvia said she couldn't stand it any longer, being at home all day with the children and never having a break, and he'd have to get an *au pair* so that she could go out and train for something. So he said – though I think she's exaggerating there – that he wasn't going to pay a girl wages to do what it was his wife's job to do. She'd only train for something and then not be able to get a job because of the unemployment. Anyway, all this developed into a great analysis of their marriage and the role men have made women play and how she was sacrificing her whole life. You can imagine. So this morning she told him that if she was only a nurse and a housekeeper she'd go and be a nurse and housekeeper with her parents – and here she is.'

'Where is she now?'

'In the living room, and Robin and Ben are in the garden. I don't know how much they realize. Darling, don't be harsh with her.'

'When have I ever been harsh with my children? I haven't been harsh enough. I've always let them do exactly as they liked. I should have put my foot down and not let her get married when she was only eighteen.'

She was standing up with her back to him. She turned round and said, 'Hallo, Dad.'

'This is a bad business, Sylvia.'

Wexford loved both his daughters dearly, but Sheila, the younger, was his favourite. Sheila had the career, the tough life, had been through the hardening process, and had remained soft and sweet. Also she looked like him, although he was an ugly man and everyone called her beautiful. Sylvia's hard classical features were those of his late mother-in-law, and hers the Britannia bust and majestic bearing. She had led the protected and sheltered existence in the town where she had been born. But while Sheila would have run to him and called him Pop and thrown her arms round him, this girl stood staring at him with tragic calm, one marmoreal arm extended along the mantelpiece.

'I don't suppose you want me here, Dad,' she said. 'I'd nowhere else to go. I won't bother you for long. I'll get a job and find somewhere for me and the boys to live.'

'Don't speak to me like that, Sylvia. Please don't. This is your home. What have I ever said to make you speak to me like that?'

She didn't move. Two great tears appeared in her eyes and coursed slowly down her cheeks. Her father went up to her and took her in his arms, wondering as he did so when it was that he had last held her like this. Years ago, long before she was married. At last she responded, and the hug he got was vice-like, almost breath-crushing. He let her sob and gulp into his shoulder, holding her close and murmuring to this fugitive goddess, all magnificent five feet ten of her, much the same words that he had used twenty years before when she had fallen and cut her knee.

More negative results awaited him on Monday evening. The phone calls were still coming in, growing madder as time went by. No newspaper in the country knew of Rhoda Comfrey either as an employee or in a freelance capacity, no Press agency, no magazine, and she was not on record as a member of the National Union of Journalists.

Detective Constable Loring had left for London by an early train, bound for the leather shop in Jermyn Street. Wexford wished now that he had gone himself, for he was made irritable by this enforced inactivity and by thoughts of what he had left behind him at home. Tenderness he felt for Sylvia, but little sympathy. Robin and Ben had been told their father was going away on business and that this was why they were there, but although Ben accepted this, Robin perhaps knew better. He was old enough to have been affected by the preceding quarrels and to have understood much of what had been said. Without him and Ben, their mother would have been able to lead a free, worthwhile and profitable life. The little boy went about with a bewildered look. That damned water rat might have provided a diversion, but the beast was as elusive as ever.

And Neil had not come. Wexford had been sure his son-in-law would turn up, even if only for more recriminations and mud-slinging. He had neither come nor phoned. And Sylvia, who had said she didn't want him to come, that she never wanted to see him again, first moped over his absence, then harangued her parents for allowing her to marry him in the first place. Wexford had had a bad night because Dora had hardly slept, and in the small hours he had heard Sylvia pacing her bedroom or roving the house.

Loring came back at twelve, which was the earliest he could possibly have made it, and Wexford found himself perversely wishing he had been late so that he could have snapped at him. That was no way to go on. Pleasantly he said:

'Did you get any joy?'

'In a sort of way, sir. They recognized the wallet at once. It was the last of a line they had left. The customer bought it on Thursday, August fourth.'

'You call that a sort of way? I call it a bloody marvellous break.'

Loring looked pleased, though it was doubtful whether this was praise or even directed at him. 'Not Rhoda Comfrey, sir,' he said hastily. 'A man. Chap called Grenville West. He's a regular customer of Silk and Whitebeam. He's bought a lot of stuff from them in the past.'

'Did you get his address?'

'Twenty-two, Elm Green, London, West 15,' said Loring.

No expert on the metropolis, Wexford nevertheless knew a good deal of the geography of the London Borough of Kenbourne. And now, in his mind's eye, he saw Elm Green that lay half a mile from the great cemetery. Half an acre or so of turf with elm trees on it, a white-painted fence bordering two sides of it, and facing the green, a row of late-Georgian houses, some with their ground floors converted into shops. A pretty place, islanded in sprawling, squalid Kenbourne which, like the curate's egg and all London boroughs, was good in parts.

It was a piece of luck for him that this first possible London acquaintance – friend, surely – of Rhoda Comfrey had been located here. He would get help, meet with no obstruction, for his old nephew, his dead sister's son, was head of Kenbourne Vale CID. That Chief Superintendent Howard Fortune was at present away on holiday in the Canary Islands was a pity but no real hindrance. Several members of Howard's team were known to him. They were old friends.

By two Stevens, his driver, was heading the car towards London. Wexford relaxed, feeling his confidence returning,

Sylvia and her troubles pushed to the back of his mind, and he felt stimulated by the prospect before him when Stevens set him down outside Kenbourne Vale Police Station.

'Inspector Baker in?'

It was amusing, really. If anyone had told him, those few years before, that the day would come when he would actually be asking for Baker, wanting to see him, he would have laughed with resentful scorn. For Baker had been the reverse of pleasant to him when, convalescing after his thrombosis with Howard and Denise, he had helped solve the cemetery murder. But Howard, Wexford thought secretly, would have refused that word 'helped', would have said his uncle had done all that solving on his own. And that had marked the beginning of Baker's respect and friendship. After that, there had been no more barbs about rustic policemen and interference and ignorance of London thugs.

His request was answered in the affirmative, and two minutes later he was being shown down one of those bottle-green painted corridors to the inspector's office with its view of a brewery. Baker got up and came to him delightedly, hand outstretched.

'This is a pleasant surprise, Reg!'

It was getting on for two years since Wexford had seen him. In that time, he thought, there had been more remarkable changes, and not just in the man's manner towards himself. He looked years younger, he looked happy. Only the harsh corncrake voice with its faint cockney intonation remained the same.

'It's good to see you, Michael.' Baker shared Burden's Christian name. How that had once riled him! 'How are you? You're looking fine. What's the news.'

'Well, you'll know Mr Fortune's away in Tenerife. Things are fairly quiet here, thank God. Your old friend Sergeant Clements is somewhere about, he'll be glad to see you. Sit down and I'll have some tea sent up.' There was a framed photograph of a fair-haired, gentle-looking woman on the desk.

Baker saw Wexford looking at it. 'My wife,' he said, self-conscious, proud, a little embarrassed. 'I don't know if Mr Fortune mentioned I'd got married –' a tiny hesitation '– again?'

Yes, Howard had, of course, but he had forgotten. The new ease of manner, the happiness, were explained. Michael Baker had once been married to a girl who had become pregnant by another man and who had left him for that other man. Finding that out from Howard had marked the beginnings of his toleration of Baker's rudeness and his thinly veiled insults.

'Congratulations. I'm delighted.'

'Yes, well . . .' Awkwardness brought out shades of Baker's old acerbity. 'You didn't come here to talk about my domestic bliss. You came about this Rose – no, Rhoda – Comfrey. Am I right?'

Wexford said on a surge of hope, 'You know her? You've got some . . .?'

'Wouldn't I have been in touch if I had? No, but I read the papers. I don't suppose you've got much else on your mind at the moment, have you?'

Sylvia, Sylvia . . . 'No, not much.' The tea came, and he told Baker about the wallet and Grenville West.

'I do know *him*. Well, not to say "know". He's what you might call our contribution to the arts. They put bits about him in the local paper from time to time. Come on, Reg, I always think of you as so damned intellectual. Don't tell me you've never heard of Grenville West?'

'Well, I haven't. What does he do?'

'I daresay he's not that famous. He writes books, historical novels. I can't say I've ever set eyes on him, but I've read one of his books – bit above my head – and I can tell you a bit about him from what I've seen in the paper. In his late thirties, dark-haired chap, smokes a pipe – they put his photo on his book jackets. You know those old houses facing the Green? He lives in a flat in one of them over a wine bar.'

Having courteously refused Baker's offer of assistance, sent his regards to Sergeant Clements, and promised to return later, he set off up Kenbourne High Street. The heat that was pleasant, acceptable in the country, made of this London suburb a furnace that seemed to be burning smelly refuse. A greyish haze obscured the sun. He wondered why the Green looked different, barer somehow, and bigger. Then he noticed the stumps where the trees had been. So Dutch Elm disease denuded London as well as the country...

He crossed the grass where black children and one white child were playing ball, where two Indian women in saris, their hair in long braids, walked slowly and gracefully as if they carried invisible pots on their heads. The wine bar had been discreetly designed not to mar the long elegant façade, as had the other shops in this row, and the sign over its bow window announced in dull gold letters: Vivian's Vineyard. The occasional slender tree grew out of the pavement, and some of the houses had window boxes with geraniums and petunias in them. Across the house next door to the bar rambled the vines of an *ipomaea*, the Morning Glory, its trumpet flowers open and glowing a brilliant blue. This might have been some corner of Chelsea or Hampstead. If you kept your eyes steady, if you didn't look south to the gasworks or east to St Biddulph's Hospital, if you didn't smell the smoky, diesel-y stench, it might even have been Kingsmarkham.

He rang repeatedly at the door beside the shop window, but no one came. Grenville West was out. What now? It was nearly five and, according to the notice on the shop door, the Vineyard opened at five. He sat down on one of the benches on the Green to wait until it did.

Presently a pale-skinned negroid girl came out, peered up and down the street and went back in again, turning the sign to 'Open'. Wexford followed her and found himself in a dim cavern, light coming only from some bulbs behind the bar itself and from heavily shaded Chianti-bottle lamps on the tables. The window was curtained in brown and silver and the curtains were fast drawn. On a high stool, under the most powerful of the lamps, the pale Negress had seated herself to leaf through a magazine.

He asked her for a glass of white wine, and then if the owner or manager or proprietor was about.

'You want Vic?'

'I expect I do if he's the boss.'

'I'll fetch him.'

She came back with a man who looked in his early forties. 'Victor Vivian. What can I do for you?'

Wexford showed him his warrant card and explained. Vivian seemed rather cheered by the unexpected excitement, while the girl opened enormous eyes and stared.

'Take a pew,' said Vivian not ineptly, for the place had the gloom of a chapel devoted to some esoteric cult. But there was nothing priestly about its proprietor. He wore jeans and a garment somewhere between a tee-shirt and a windcheater with a picture on it of peasant girls treading out the grape harvest. 'Gren's away. Went off on holiday to France, you know — let's see now — last Sunday week. He always goes to France for a month at this time of the year.'

'You own the house?'

'Not to say "own", you know. I mean, Notbourne Properties own it. I've got the under-lease.'

He was going to be an 'I mean-er' and 'you know-er'. Wexford could feel it coming. Still, such people usually talked a lot and were seldom discreet. 'You know him well?'

'We're old mates, Gren and me, you know. He's been here fourteen years and a damn good tenant. I mean, he does all his repairs himself and it's handy, you know, having someone always on the premises when the bar's closed. Most evenings he'll drop in here for a drink, you know, and then as often as not I'll have a quick one with him, up in his place, I mean, after we've knocked off for the night, and then, you know . . .'

Wexford cut this useless flow short. 'It's not Mr West I'm primarily interested in. I'm trying to trace the address of someone who may have been a friend of his. You've read of the murder of Miss Rhoda Comfrey?'

Vivian gave a schoolboy whistle. 'The old girl who was stabbed? You mean she was a friend of Gren's? Oh, I doubt that, I mean, I doubt that very much. I mean, she was fifty, wasn't she? Gren's not forty, I mean, I doubt if he's more than thirty-eight or thirty-nine. Younger than me, you know.'

'I wasn't suggesting the relationship was a sexual one, Mr Vivian. They could just have been friends.'

This possibility was apparently beyond Vivian's comprehension, and he ignored it. 'Gren's got a girl-friend. Nice little thing, you know, worships the ground he treads on.' A sly wink was levelled at Wexford. 'He's a wily bird, though, is old Gren. Keeps her at arm's length a bit. Afraid she might get him to the altar, you know, or that's my guess, I mean. Polly something-or-other, she's called, blonde – I mean, she can't be more than twenty-four or five. Came to do his typing, you know, and now she hangs on like the proverbial limpet. Have another drink? On the house, I mean.'

'No, thank you, I won't.' Wexford produced the photograph and the wallet. 'You've never seen this woman? She'd changed a lot, she didn't look much like that any more, I'm afraid.'

Vivian shook his head and his beard waggled. He had a variety of intense facial contortions, all stereotyped and suggesting the kind a ham actor acquired to express astonishment, sagacity, knowingness and suspicion. 'I've never seen her here or with Gren, you know,' he said, switching on the one that indicated disappointed bewilderment. 'Funny, though, I mean, there's something familiar about the face. Something, you know, I can't put a finger on it. Maybe it'll come back.' As Wexford's hopes leapt, Vivian crushed them. 'This picture wasn't in the papers, was it? I mean, could that be where I've seen her before?'

'It could.'

Two people came into the bar, bringing with them a momentary blaze of sunshine before the door closed again. Vivian waved in their direction, then, turning back, gave a low whistle. 'I say! That isn't old Gren's wallet, is it?'

Vague memories of Latin lessons came back to Wexford, of forms in which to put questions expecting the answer no. All Vivian's questions seemed to expect the answer no, perhaps so that he could whistle and put on his astounded face when he got a yes.

'Well, is it?'

'Now wait a minute. I mean, this one's new, isn't it? You caught me out for a minute, you know. Gren's got one like it, only a bit knocked around, I mean. Just like that, only a bit battered. Not new, I mean.'

And he had taken it with him to France, Wexford thought. He was making slow progress, but he kept trying. 'This woman was almost certainly living under an assumed name, Mr Vivian. never mind the name or the face. Did Mr West ever mention to you any woman friend he had who was older than himself?'

'There was his agent, his – what-d'you-call-it?' – literary agent. I can't remember her name. Mrs Something, you know. Got a husband living, I'm sure of that. I mean, it wouldn't be her, would it?'

'I'm afraid not. Can you tell me Mr West's address in France?'

'He's touring about, you know. Somewhere in the south, that's all I can tell you. Getting back to this woman, I'm racking my brains, but I can't come up with anyone. I mean, people chat to you about this and that, especially in my job, I mean, and a lot of it goes in one ear and out the other. Old Gren goes about a lot, great walker, likes his beer, likes to have a walk about Soho at night. For the pubs, I mean, nothing nasty, I don't mean that. He's got his drinking pals, you know, and he may have talked of some woman, but I wouldn't have the faintest idea about her name or where she lives, would I? I mean, I'm sorry I can't be of more help. But you know how it is, I mean, you don't think anyone's going to ask, I mean, it doesn't cross your mind, does it?'

As Wexford rose to go, he was unable to resist the temptation.

'I know what you mean,' he said.

CHAPTER SEVEN

'You're not having much luck,' said Baker over a fresh pot of
tea. 'I'll tell you what I'll do. I'll have someone go through
the Kenbourne street directory for you. If he did know her,
she might have been living only a stone's throw away.'

'Not as Rhoda Comfrey. But it's very good of you, Michael.'

Stevens was waiting for him, but they hadn't got far along
Kenbourne High Street when Wexford noticed a large newish
public library on the opposite side. It would close, he guessed,
at six, and it was a quarter to now. He told Stevens to drop
him and park the car as best he could in this jungle of buses
and container lorries and double yellow lines, and then he got
out and jay-walked in most unpoliceman-like fashion across
the road.

On the forecourt stood a bronze of a mid-nineteenth-cen-
tury gentleman in a frock-coat. 'Edward Edwards' said a
plaque at its feet, that and no more, as if the name ought to
be as familiar as Victoria R or William Ewart Gladstone. It
wasn't familiar to Wexford and he had no time to waste
wondering about it.

He went on into the library and its large fiction section,
and there he was, rubbing shoulders with Rebecca and Morris.
Three of Grenville West's novels were in, *Killed With Kindness*,
The Venetian Courtesan, *Fair Wind to Alicante*, and each was
marked on the spine with an H for Historical. The first title
appealed to him most and he took the book from the shelf
and looked at the publisher's blurb on the front inside flap of
the jacket.

'Once again,' he read, 'Mr West astonishes us with his
virtuosity in taking the plot and characters of an Elizabethan

drama and clothing them in his fine rich prose. This time it is Mistress Nan Frankford, from Thomas Heywood's *A Woman Killed with Kindness*, who holds the stage. At first a loving and faithful wife, she is seduced by her husband's trusted friend, and it is her remorse and Frankford's curious generosity which contribute to the originality of this compelling book. Mr West sticks closely to Heywood's plot, but he shows us what Heywood had no need to attempt for his contemporary audience, a vivid picture of domestic life in late sixteenth-century England with its passions, its cruelties, its conventions and its customs. A different world is unfolded before us, and we are soon aware that we are being guided through its halls, its knot gardens and its unspoilt pastoral countryside by a master of his subject.'

Hmm, thought Wexford, not for him. If *Killed With kindness* was from Heywood's play of almost identical title, *The Venetian Courtesan* was very likely based on Webster's *The White Devil* and *Fair Wind to Alicante* – on what? Wexford had a quick look at the blurb inside the jacket of that one and saw that its original was *The Changeling* of Middleton and Rowley.

A clever idea, he thought, for those who liked that sort of thing. It didn't look as if the author went in for too much intellectual stuff, but concentrated on the blood, thunder and passion which, from the point of view of his sales, was wise of him. There was a lot of Elizabethan and Jacobean plays, hundreds probably, so the possibilities of West going on till he was seventy or so seemed limitless.

Killed With Kindness had been published three years before. He turned to the back of the jacket. There Grenville West was portrayed in tweeds with a pipe in his mouth. He wore glasses and had a thick fringe of dark hair. The face wasn't very interesting but the photographer's lighting effects were masterful.

Under the picture was a biography:

'Grenville West was born in London. He has a degree in

history. His varied career has led him from teaching through freelance journalism, with short spells as a courier, barman and antique dealer, to becoming a highly successful writer of historical romance. In the twelve years since his first book, *Her Grace of Amalfi*, was published, he has delighted his readers with nine more novels of which several have been translated into French, German and Italian. His novels also appear in the United States and are regularly issued in paper-back.

'*Apes in Hell* was made into a successful television play, and *Arden's Wife* has been serialized for radio.

'Mr West is a francophile who spends most of his holidays in France, has a French car and enjoys French cooking. He is 35 years old, lives in London and is unmarried.'

On the face of it, Wexford thought, the man would appear to have little in common with Rhoda Comfrey. But then he didn't really know much about Rhoda Comfrey, did he? Maybe she too had been a francophile. Mrs Parker had told him, that when a young woman, she had taught herself French. And there was firm evidence that she had wanted to write and had tried her hand at journalism. It was possible that West had met her at a meeting of one of those literary societies, formed by amateurs who aspire to have their work published, and who had invited him to address them. Then why keep the relationship dark? In saying that there was nothing unpleasant in West's secretiveness, Vivian had only succeeded in suggesting that there was.

The library was about to close. Wexford went out and made a face at Edward Edwards who looked superciliously back at him. Stevens was waiting for him on the pavement, and together they walked back to the car which had necessarily been parked a quarter of a mile away.

He had made a mental note of the name of West's publishers, Carlyon Brent, of London, New York and Sydney. Would they tell him anything if he called them? He had a feeling they would be cagily discreet.

'I don't see what you're hoping to get, anyway,' said Burden in the morning. 'He's not going to have told his publishers who he gives birthday presents to, is he?'

'I'm thinking about this girl, this Polly something or other,' Wexford said. 'If she does his typing in his flat, which it seems as if she does, it's likely she also answers his phone. A sort of secretary, in fact. Therefore, someone at his publishers may be in the habit of speaking to her. Or, at any rate, it's possible West will have told them her name.'

Their offices were located in Russell Square. He dialled the number and was put through to someone he was told was Mr West's editor.

'Oliver Hampton speaking.' A dry cool public-school voice.

He listened while Wexford went somewhat awkwardly into his explanation. The awkwardness was occasioned not by Hampton's interruptions – he didn't interrupt – but by a strong extra-aural perception, carried along fifty miles of wires, that the man at the other end was incredulous, amazed and even offended.

At last Hampton said, 'I couldn't possibly give you any information of that nature about one of my authors.' The information 'of that nature' had merely been an address at which West could be written to or spoken to, or, failing that, the name of his typist. 'Frankly, I don't know who you are. I only know who you say you are.'

'In that case, Mr Hampton, I will give you a number for you to phone my Chief Constable and check.'

'I'm sorry, but I'm extremely busy. In point of fact, I have no idea where Mr West is at this moment except that he is somewhere in the South of France. What I will do is give you the number of his agent if that would help.'

Wexford said it might and noted the number down. Mrs Brenda Nunn, of Field and Bray, Literary Agents. This would be the woman Vivian had said was middle-aged and with a husband living. She was more talkative than Hampton and less suspicious, and she satisfied herself on his *bona fides* by calling him back at Kingsmarkham Police Station.

'Well, now we've done all that,' she said, 'I'm afraid I really can't be much help to you. I don't have an address for Mr West in France and I'd never heard of Rhoda Comfrey till I read about her in the papers. I do know the name of this girl who works for him. I've spoken to her on the phone. It's – well, it's Polly Flinders.'

'It's *what?*'

'I know. Now you can see why it stuck in my mind. Actually, it's Pauline Flinders – heaven knows what her parents were thinking about – but Grenville – er, Mr West – refers to her as Polly. I've no idea where she lives.'

Next Wexford phoned Baker. The search of the electoral register had brought to light no Comfrey in the parliamentary constituency of Kenbourne Vale. Would Baker do the same for him in respect of a Miss Pauline Flinders? Baker would, with pleasure. The name seemed to afford him no amusement or even interest. However, he was anxious to help, and in addition would send a man to Kenbourne Green to inquire in all the local shops and of Grenville West's neighbours.

'It's all so vague,' said Dr Crocker who came to join them for lunch at the Carousel Café. 'Even if the Comfrey woman was going under another name in London, this girl would have recognized her from the description in the papers. The photograph, unlike as it is, would have meant something to her. She'd have been in touch, she'd have read all your appeals.'

'So therefore doesn't it look as if she didn't because she has something to hide?'

'It looks to me,' said Burden, 'as if she just didn't know her.'

Waiting to hear from Baker, Wexford tried to make some sort of reasonable pattern of it. Rhoda Comfrey, who, for some unknown motive, called herself something else in London, had been a fan and admirer of Grenville West, had become his friend. Perhaps she performed certain services for him in connection with his work. She might – and Wexford was rather pleased with this notion – run a photocopying agency. That would fit in with what Mrs Crown had told him. Suppose she had made copies of manuscripts for West free of charge, and he, in gratitude, had given her a rather special birthday present? After all, according to old Mrs Parker, she had become fifty years old on 5 August. In some countries, Wexford knew, the fiftieth birthday was looked on as a landmark of great significance, an anniversary worthy of particular note. He had bought the wallet on the fourth, given it to her on the fifth, left for his holiday on the seventh, and she had come down to Kingsmarkham on the eighth. None of this got him nearer finding the identity of her murderer, but that was a long way off yet, he thought gloomily.

Into the midst of these reflections the phone rang.

'We've found her,' said the voice of Baker. 'Or we've found where she lives. She was in the register. West Kenbourne, All Souls Grove, number fifteen, flat one. Patel, Malina N. and Flinders, Pauline J. No number in the phone book for either of them, so I sent Dinehart round, and a woman upstairs said your Flinders usually comes in around half-four. D'you want us to see her for you? It's easily done.'

'No, thanks, Michael, I'll come up.'

Happiness hadn't eroded all the encrusting sourness from Baker's nature. He was still quick to sense a snub where no snub was intended, still looking always for an effusively expressed appreciation. 'Suit yourself,' he said gruffly. 'D'you know how to find All Souls Grove?' Implicit in his tone was the suggestion that this country bumpkin might be able to find a haystack or even a needle in one, but not a street delineated in every London guide. 'Turn right out of Kenbourne Lane Tube station into Magdalen Hill, right again into Balliol Street, and it's the second on the left after Oriel Mews.'

Forebearing to point out that with his rank he did rate a

car and a driver, Wexford said only, 'I'm most grateful, Michael, you're very good,' but he was too late.

'All in a day's work,' said Baker and put the phone down hard.

Wexford had sometimes wondered why it is that a plain woman so often chooses to live with, or share a flat with, or be companioned by, a beautiful woman. Perhaps choice does not enter into it; perhaps the pressure comes from the other side, from the beautiful one whose looks are set off by the contrast, while the ill-favoured one is too shy, too humble and too accustomed to her place to resist.

In this case, the contrast was very marked. Beauty had opened the front door to him, beauty in a peacock-green sari with little gold ornaments, and on hands of a fineness and delicacy seldom seen in Western women, the width across the broadest part less than three inches, rings of gold and ivory. An exquisite small face, the skin a smoky gold, peeped at him from a cloud of silky black hair.

'Miss Patel?'

She nodded, and nodded again rather sagely when he showed her his warrant card.

'I'd like to see Miss Flinders, please.'

The flat, on the ground floor, was the usual furnished place. Big rooms divided with improvised matchwood walls, old reject furniture, girls' clutter everywhere – clothes and magazines, pinned-up posters, strings of beads hanging from a door handle, half-burned coloured candles in saucers. The other girl, the one he had come to see, turned slowly from having been hunched over a typewriter. An ashtray beside her was piled with stubs. He found himself thinking:

> Little Polly Flinders
> Sat among the cinders,
> Warming her pretty little toes . . .

As it happened, her feet were bare under the long cotton skirt, and they were good feet, shapely and long. Perhaps, altogether, she wouldn't have been so bad if he hadn't seen Malina Patel first. She wouldn't have been bad at all but for that awful stoop, assumed no doubt in an attempt to reduce her height, though it was less than his Sylvia's, and but for the two prominent incisors in her upper jaw. Odd, he thought, in someone of her years, child of the age of orthodontics.

She came up to him, unsmiling and wary, and Malina Patel went softly away, having not spoken a word. He plunged straight into the middle of things.

'No doubt you've read the papers, Miss Flinders, and seen about the murder of a Miss Rhoda Comfrey. This photograph was in the papers. Imagine it, if you can, aged by about twenty years and its owner using another name.'

She looked at the photograph and he watched her. He could make nothing of her expression, it seemed quite blank.

'Do you think you have ever seen her? In, let us say, the company of Mr Grenville West?'

A flush coloured her face unbecomingly. Victor Vivian had described her as a blonde, and that word is very evocative, implying beauty and a glamorous femininity, a kind of Marilyn Monroe-ishness. Pauline Flinders was not at all like that. Her fairness was just an absence of colour, the eyes a watery pale grey, the hair almost white. Her blush was vivid and patchy under that pale skin, and he supposed it was his mention of the man's name that had caused it. Not guilty knowledge, though, but love.

'I've never seen her,' she said, and then, 'Why do you think Grenville knew her?'

He wasn't going to answer that yet. She kept looking towards the door as if she were afraid the other girl would come back. Because her flat-mate had teased her about her feelings for the novelist?

'You're Mr West's secretary, I believe?'

'I had an advertisement in the local paper saying I'd do typing for people. He phoned me. That was about two years ago. I did a manuscript for him and he liked it and I started sort of working for him part-time.' She had a graceless way of speaking, in a low dull monotone.

'So you answered his phone, no doubt, and met his friends. Was there anyone among his friends who might possibly have been this woman?'

'Oh, no, no one.' She sounded certain beyond a doubt, and she added fatuously, with a lover's obsessiveness, 'Grenville's in France. I had a card from him.' Why wasn't it on the mantelpiece? As she slipped the postcard out from under a pile of papers beside her typewriter, Wexford thought he knew the answer to that one too. She didn't want to be teased about it.

A coloured picture of Annecy, and 'Annecy' was clearly discernible on the otherwise smudged postmark. 'Greeting from France, little Polly Flinders, the sunshine, the food, the air and the *bel aujourd'hui.* I shan't want to come back. But I shall – So, see you. G. W.' Typical of one of those literary blokes, he thought, but not, surely, the communication of a lover. Why had she shown it to him with its mention of her whimsical nickname? Because it was all she had?

He brought out the wallet and laid it down beside the postcard. What he wanted was for her to shriek, turn pale, cry out, 'Where did you get that?' – demolish the structure of ignorance he fancied she might carefully have built up. She did nothing but stare at it with that same guarded expression.

'Have you ever seen this before, Miss Flinders?'

She looked at it inside and out. 'It looks like Grenville's wallet,' she said, 'the one he lost.'

'Lost?' said Wexford.

She seemed to gain self-confidence and her voice some

animation. 'He was coming back from the West End on a bus, and when he came in he said he'd left the wallet on the bus. That must have been Thursday or Friday week. Where did you find it?'

'In Miss Rhoda Comfrey's handbag.' He spoke slowly and heavily. So that was the answer. No connection, no relationship between author and admiring fan, no fiftieth birthday present. She had found it on a bus and kept it. 'Did Mr West report his loss?'

When she was silent she tried to cover her protruding teeth, as people with this defect do, by pushing her lower lip out over them. Now the teeth appeared again. They caused her to lisp a little. 'He asked me to but I didn't. I didn't exactly forget. But someone told me the police don't really like you reporting things you've lost or found. A policeman my mother knows told her it makes too much paperwork.'

He believed her. Who knew better than he that the police are not angels in uniform, sacrificing themselves to the public good? Leaving her to return to her typewriter, he went out into the big gloomy hall of the house. The flat door opened again behind him and Malina Patel appeared with a flash bright as a kingfisher. Her accent, as English and as prettily correct as his Sheila's surprised him nearly as much as what she said.

'Polly was here with me all the evening on the eighth. She was helping me to make a dress, she was cutting it out' Her smile was mischievous and her teeth perfect. 'You're a detective, aren't you?'

'That's right.'

'What a freaky thing to be. I've never seen one before except on the TV.' She spoke as if he were some rare animal, an eland perhaps. 'Do people give you a lot of money? Like "Fifty thousand dollars to find my daughter, she's all the world to me" that kind of thing?'

'I'm afraid not, Miss Patel.'

He could have sworn she was mocking her friend's dull

naivety. The lovely face became guileless, the eyes opened hugely.

'When you first came to the door,' she said, 'I thought you might be a bailiff. We had one of those before when we hadn't paid the rates.'

CHAPTER EIGHT

A red-hot evening in Kenbourne Vale, a dusty dying sun. The reek of cumin came to him from Kemal's Kebab House, beer and sweat from the Waterlily pub. All the eating and drinking places had their doors wide open, propped back. Children of all ages, all colours, pure races and mixed races, sat on flights of steps or rode two-and three-wheelers on hard pavements and up and down narrow stuffy alleys. An old woman, drunk or just old and sick, squatted in the entrance to a betting shop. There was nothing green and organic to be seen unless you counted the lettuces, stuffed tight into boxes outside a greengrocer's, and they looked as much like plastic as their wrappings.

One thing to be thankful for was that now he need not come back to Kenbourne Vale ever again if he didn't want to. The trail had gone cold, about the only thing that had this evening. Sitting in the car on the road back to Kingsmarkham, he thought about it. At first Malina Patel's behaviour had puzzled him. Why had she come out voluntarily to provide herself or Polly Flinders with an unasked-for alibi? Because she was a tease and a humorist, he now reflected, and in her beauty dwelt with wit. Everything she had said to him had been calculated to amuse – and how she herself had smiled at the time! – all that about telly detectives and bailiffs. Very funny and charming from such a pretty girl. But no wonder Polly kept the postcard hidden and feared her overhearing their conversation. He could imagine the Indian girl's comments.

But if she hadn't been listening at the door how the hell had she known what he had come for? Easy. The woman upstairs had told her. One of Baker's men – that none too

reliable Dinehart probably – had been round earlier in the
day and let slip not only that the Kingsmarkham police wanted
to talk to Polly but why they had wanted to talk to her. Malina
would have read the papers, noted the date of Rhoda Comfrey's death. He remembered how closely and somehow complacently she had looked at his warrant card. Rather a naughty
girl she was, playing detective stories and trying to throw cats
among pigeons to perplex him and tease her flat-mate.

Ah, well, it was over now. Rhoda Comfrey had found that
wallet on a bus or in the street, and he was back where he
started.

Just before nine he walked into his own house. Dora was
out, as he had known she would be, baby-sitting for Burden's
sister-in-law, Sylvia nowhere to be seen or heard. In the middle
of the staircase sat Robin in pyjamas.

'It's too hot to go to sleep. You aren't tired, are you,
Grandad?'

'Not really,' said Wexford who was.

'Granny said you would be but I know you, don't I? I said
to Granny that you'd want some fresh air.'

'River air? Put some clothes on, then, and tell Mummy
where you're going.'

Twilight had come to the water meadows. 'Dusk is a very
good time for water rats,' said Robin. 'Dusk.' He seemed to
like the word and repeated it over and over as they walked
along the river bank. Above the sluggish flow of the Kingsbrook gnats danced in lazy clouds. But the heat was not
oppressive, the air was sweet and a refreshment to a London-
jaded spirit.

However, 'I'm afraid we've had it for tonight,' Wexford
said as the darkness began to deepen.

Robin took his hand. 'Yes, we'd better go back because
my daddy's coming. I thought he was in Sweden but he's not.
I expect we'll go home tomorrow. Not tonight because Ben's
asleep.'

Wexford didn't know what answer to make. And when they came into the hall he heard from behind the closed door of the living room the angry but lowered voices of his daughter and son-in-law. Robin made no move towards that door. He looked at it, looked away, and rubbed his fists across his tired eyes.

'I'll see you into bed,' said his grandfather and lifted him more than usually tenderly in his arms.

In the morning they phoned him from Stowerton Royal Infirmary. They thought the police would wish to know that Mr James Comfrey had 'passed away' during the night, and since his daughter was dead, whom should they get in touch with?

'Mrs Lilian Crown,' he said, and then he thought he might as well go and see her himself. There was little else to do.

She was out. In Kingsmarkham the pubs open at ten on market day. To Bella Vista then. Today its name, its veridian roof and its sun-trap windows were justified. Light and heat beat down with equal force from a sky of the same hard dark blue as the late Mr Comfrey's front door.

'He's gone then,' the old woman said. News travels fast in these quiet backwoods places. During the hour that had passed since Wexford had been told the news, Mrs Crown also had been told and had informed at least some of her neighbours. 'It's a terrible thing to die, young man, and have no one shed a tear for you.'

She was stringing beans today, slicing them into long thin strips as few young housewives can be bothered to do. 'I daresay it'd have been a relief to poor Rhoda. Whatever'd she have done, I used to ask myself, if they'd turned him out of there and she'd had to look after him? Nursed her mother devotedly, she did, used to have to take time off work and all, but there was love there of course, and not a word of appreciation from old Jim.' The vital, youthful eyes fixed piercingly on him. 'Who'll get the money?'

'The money, Mrs Parker?'

'Rhoda's money. It'd have gone to him, being next of kin. I know that. Who'll get it now? That's what I'd like to know.'

This aspect hadn't occurred to him. 'Maybe there isn't any money. Few working people these days have much in the way of savings.'

'Speak up, will you?'

Wexford repeated what he had said, and Mrs Parker gave a scornful cackle.

''Course there's money. She got that lot from her pools win, didn't she? Wouldn't have blued that, not Rhoda, she wasn't one of your spendthrifts. I reckon you lot have been sitting about twiddling your thumbs or you'd have got to the bottom of it by now. A house there'll be somewhere, filled up with good furniture, and a nice little sum in shares too. D'you want to know what I think? It'll all go to Lilian Crown.'

Rather unwillingly he considered what she had said. But would it go to Mrs Crown? Possibly, but for that intervening heir, James Comfrey. If she had had anything to leave and if she had died intestate, James Comfrey had for nine days been in possession of his daughter's property. But a sister-in-law wouldn't automatically inherit from him, though her son, the mongol, if he were still alive ... A nephew by marriage? He knew little of the law relating to inheritance, and it hardly seemed relevant now.

'Mrs Parker,' he said, pitching his voice loud, 'you're quite right when you say we haven't got very far. But we do know Miss Comfrey was living under an assumed name, a false name. Do you follow me?' She nodded impatiently. 'Now when people do that, they often choose a name that's familiar to them, a mother's maiden name, for instance, or the name of some relative or childhood friend.'

'Whyever would she do that?'

'Perhaps only because her own name had very unpleasant associations for her. Do you know what her mother's maiden name was?'

Mrs Parker had it ready. 'Crawford. Agnes and Lilian Crawford, they was. Change the name and not the letter, change for worse and not for better. Poor Agnes changed for worse all right, and the same applies to that Lilian, though it wasn't a C for her the first time. Crown left her and he's got another wife somewhere, I daresay, for all she says he's dead.

'So she might have been calling herself Crawford?' He was speaking his thoughts aloud. 'Or Parker, since she was so fond of you. Or Rowlands after the editor of the old *Gazette*.' This spoken reverie had scarcely been audible to Mrs Parker, and he bawled out his last suggestion. 'Or Crown?'

'Not Crown. She hadn't no time for that Lilian. And no wonder, always mocking her and telling her to get herself a man.' The old face contorted and Mrs Parker put up her fists as the aged do, recalling that far distant childhood when such a gesture was natural. 'Why'd she call herself anything but her rightful name? She was a good woman was Rhoda, never did anything wrong nor underhand in her whole life.'

Could you truthfully say that of anyone? Not, certainly, of Rhoda Comfrey who had stolen something she must have known would be precious to its owner, and whose life could be described as a masterpiece of underhandedness.

'I'll go out this way, Mrs Parker,' he said, opening the french window to the garden because he didn't want to encounter Nicky.

'Mind you shut it behind you. They can talk about heat all they like, but my hands and feet are always cold like yours'll be, young man, when you get to my age.'

There was no sign of Mrs Crown. He hadn't checked her movements on the night in question, but was it within the bounds of possibility that she had killed her niece? The motive was very tenuous, unless she knew of the existence of a will. Certainly there might be a will, deposited with a firm of solicitors who were unaware of the testator's death, but Rhoda Comfrey would never have left anything to the aunt she so disliked. Besides, that little stick of a woman wouldn't have had the physical strength ...

His car, its windows closed and its doors locked for safety's sake, was oven-hot inside, the steering wheel almost too hot to hold. Driving back, he was glad he was a thin man now so that at least the trickling sweat didn't make him look like a pork carcase in the preliminary stages of roasting.

Before the sun came round, he closed the windows in his office and pulled down the blinds. Somewhere or other he had read that that was what they did in hot countries rather than let the air in. Up to a point it worked. Apart from a short break for lunch in the canteen, he sat up there for the rest of the day, thinking, thinking. He couldn't remember any previous case that had come his way in which, after nine days, he had had no possible suspect, could see no glimmer of a motive, or knew less about the victim's private life. Hours of thinking got him no further than to conclude that the killing had been, wildly incongruous though it seemed, a crime of passion, that it had been unpremeditated, and that Mrs Parker had allowed affection to sway her assessment of Rhoda Comfrey's character.

'Where's your mother?' said Wexford, finding his daughter alone.

'Upstairs, reading bedtime stories.'

'Sylvia,' he said, 'I've been busy, I'm still very busy, but I hope there'll never be a time when I've got too much on my hands to think about my children. Is there anything I can do to help? When I'm not being a policeman that's what I'm here for.'

She hung her head. Large and statuesque, she had a face designed, it seemed, to register the noble virtues, courage and fortitude. She was patience on a monument, smiling at grief. Yet she had never known grief, and in her life hardly any courage or fortitude had ever been called for.

'Wouldn't you like to talk about it?' he said.

The strong shoulders lifted. 'We can't change the facts. I'm a woman and that's to be a second-rate citizen.'

'You didn't used to feel like this.'

'Oh, Dad, what's the use of talking like that? People change. We don't hold the same opinions all our lives. If I say I read a lot of books and went to some meetings, you'll only say what Neil says, that I shouldn't have read them and I shouldn't have gone.'

'Maybe I shall and maybe I'd be right if what you've read has turned you from a happy woman into an unhappy one and is breaking up your marriage. Are you less of a second-rate citizen here with your parents than at home with your husband?'

'I shall be if I get a job, if I start training for something now.'

Her father forbore to tell her that he hardly cared for the idea of her attending some college or course while her mother was left to care for Robin and Ben. Instead he asked her if she didn't think that to be a woman had certain advantages. 'If you get a flat tyre,' he said, 'the chances are in five minutes some chap'll stop and change the wheel for you for no more reason than that you've got a good figure and a nice smile. But if it was me I could stand there flagging them down for twenty-four hours without a hope in hell of even getting the loan of a jack.'

'Because I'm pretty!' she said fiercely, and he almost laughed, the adjective was so inept. Her eyes flashed, she looked like a Medea. 'D'you know what that means? Whistles, yes, but no respect. Stupid compliments but never a sensible remark as from one human being to another.'

'Come now, you're exaggerating.'

'I am not, Dad. Look, I'll give you an example. A couple of weeks ago Neil backed the car into the gatepost and I took it to the garage to get a new rear bumper and light. When the mechanics had done whistling at me, d'you know what the manager said? "You ladies," he said, "I bet he had a thing or two to say when he saw what you'd done." *He took it for granted* I'd done it because I'm a woman. And when I corrected him he couldn't talk seriously about it. Just flirtatiousness and silly cracks and I was to explain this and that to Neil. "His motor", he said, and to tell *him* this, that and the other. I know as much about cars as Neil, it's as much my car as his.' She stopped and flushed. 'No, it isn't, though!' she burst out. 'It isn't! And it isn't as much my house as his. My children aren't even as much mine as his, he's their legal guardian. My God, my life isn't as much mine as his!'

'I think we'd better have a drink,' said her father, 'and you calm down a bit and tell me just what your grievances against Neil are. Who knows? I may be able to be your intermediary.'

Thus he found himself, a couple of hours later, closeted with his son-in-law in the house which he had, in former times, delighted to visit because it was noisy and warm and filled, it had seemed to him, with love. Now it was dusty, chilly and silent. Neil said he had had his dinner but, from the evidence, Wexford thought it had taken a liquid and spirituous form.

'Of course I want her back, Reg, and my kids. I love her, you know that. But I can't meet her conditions. I won't. I'm to have some wretched *au pair* here which'll mean the boys moving in together, pay her a salary I can ill afford, just so that Syl can go off and train for some profession that's already overcrowded. She's a damn good wife and mother, or she was. I don't see any reason to employ someone to do the things she does so well while she trains for something she may not do well at all. Have a drink?'

'No, thanks.'

'Well, I will, and you needn't tell me I've had too much already. I know it. The point is, why can't she go on doing her job while I do mine? I don't say hers is less important than mine. I don't say she's inferior and when she says others say so I think that's all in her head. But I'm not paying her a wage for doing what other women have done since time immemorial for love. Right? I'm not going to jeopardize my career by cancelling trips abroad, or exhaust myself cleaning the place and bathing the kids when I get home after a long day. I'll dry the dishes, OK, I'll see she gets any labour-saving equipment she wants, but I'd like to know just who needs the liberation if I'm to work all day and all night while she footles around at some college for God knows how many years. I wish I was a woman, I can tell you, no money worries, no real responsibility, no slogging off to an office day in and day out for forty years.'

'You don't wish that, you know.'

'I almost have done this week.' Neil threw out a despairing hand at the chaos surrounding him. 'I don't know how to do housework. I can't cook, but I can earn a decent living. Why the hell can't she do the one and I do the other like we used to? I could wring those damned Women's Libbers' necks. I love her, Reg. There's never been anyone else for either of us. We row, of course we do, that's healthy in a marriage, but we love each other and we've got two super kids. Doesn't it seem crazy that a sort of political thing, an impersonal thing, could split up two people like us?'

'It's not impersonal to her,' said Wexford sadly. 'Couldn't you compromise, Neil? Couldn't you get a woman in just for a year till Ben goes to school?'

'Couldn't she wait just for a year till Ben goes to school? OK, so marriage is supposed to be give and take. It seems to me I do all the giving and she does all the taking.'

'And she says it's the other way about. I'll go now, Neil.' Wexford laid his hand on his son-in-law's arm. 'Don't drink too much. It's not the answer.'

'Isn't it? Sorry, Reg, but I've every intention tonight of getting smashed out of my mind.'

Wexford said nothing to his daughter when he got home, and she asked him no questions. She was sitting by the still open french window, cuddling close to her Ben who had awakened and cried, and reading with mutinous concentration a book called *Woman and the Sexist Plot*.

CHAPTER NINE

Ben passed a fractious night and awoke at seven with a sore throat. Sylvia and her mother were discussing whether to send for Dr Crocker or take Ben to the surgery when Wexford had to leave for work. The last thing he expected was that he himself would be spending the morning in a doctor's surgery, for he saw the day ahead as a repetition of the day before, to be passed in fretful inertia behind drawn blinds.

He was a little late getting in. Burden was waiting for him, impatiently pacing the office.

'We've had some luck. A doctor's just phoned in. He's got a practice in London and he says Rhoda Comfrey was on his list, she was one of his patients.'

'My God. At last. Why didn't he call us sooner?'

'Like so many of them, he was away on holiday. In the South of France, oddly enough. Didn't know a thing about it till he got back last night and saw one of last week's newspapers.'

'I suppose you said we'd want to see him?'

Burden nodded. 'He expects to have seen the last of his surgery patients by eleven and he'll wait in for us. I said I thought we could be there soon after that.' He referred to the notes he had taken. 'He's a Dr Christopher Lomond and he's in practice at a place called Midsomer Road, Parish Oak, London, W19.'

'Never heard of it,' said Wexford. 'But come to that, I've only just about heard of Stroud Green and Nunhead and Earlsfield. All those lost villages swallowed up in ... What are you grinning at?'

'I know where it is. I looked it up. It may be W19 but it's still part of your favourite beauty spot, the London Borough of Kenbourne.'

'Back again,' said Wexford. 'I might have known it. And what's more, Stevens has gone down with the flu – flu in August! – so unless you feel like playing dodgem cars, it's train for us.'

Though unlikely to be anyone's favourite beauty spot, the district in which they found themselves was undoubtedly the best part of Kenbourne. It lay some couple of miles to the north of Elm Green and Kenbourne High Street and the library, and it was one of those 'nice' suburbs which sprang up to cover open country between the two world wars. The tube station was called Parish Oak, and from there they were directed to catch a bus which took them up a long hilly avenue, flanked by substantial houses whose front gardens had been docked for road-widening. Directly from it, at the top, debouched Midsomer Road, a street of comfortable-looking semi-detached houses, not unlike Wexford's own, where cars were tucked away into garages, doorsteps held neat little plastic containers for milk bottles, and dogs were confined behind wrought-iron gates.

Dr Lomond's surgery was in a flat-roofed annexe attached to the side of number sixty-one. They were shown in immediately by a receptionist, and the doctor was waiting for them, a short youngish man with a cheerful pink face.

'I didn't recognize Miss Comfrey from that newspaper photograph,' he said, 'but I thought I remembered the name and when I looked at the photo again I saw a sort of resemblance. So I checked with my records. Rhoda Agnes Comfrey, 6 Princevale Road, Parish Oak.'

'So she hadn't often come to you, Doctor?' said Wexford.

'Only came to me once. That was last September. It's often the way, you know. They don't bother to register with a doctor till they think they've got something wrong with them. She had herself put on my list and she came straight in.'

Burden said tentatively, 'Would you object to telling us what was wrong with her?'

The doctor laughed breezily. 'I don't think so. The poor woman's dead, after all. She thought she'd got appendicitis because she'd got pains on the right side of the abdomen. I examined her, but she didn't react to the tests and she hadn't any other symptoms, so I thought it was more likely to be indigestion and I told her to keep off alcohol and fried foods. If it persisted she was to come back and I'd give her a letter to the hospital. But she was very much against the idea of hospital and I wasn't surprised when she didn't come back. Look, I've got a sort of dossier thing here on her. I have one for all my patients.'

He read from a card: ' "Rhoda Agnes Comfrey. Age forty-nine. No history of disease, apart from usual childhood ailments. No surgery. Smoker —" I told her to give that up, by the way. "Social drinker" ' That can mean anything. "Formerly registered with Dr Castle of Glebe Road, Kingsmarkham, Sussex." '

'And he died last year,' said Wexford. 'You've been a great help, Doctor. Can I trouble you to tell a stranger in these parts where Princevale Road might be?'

'Half way down that hill you came up from the station. It turns off on the same side as this just above the block of shops.'

Wexford and Burden walked slowly back to the avenue which they now noted was called Montfort Hill.

'Funny, isn't it?' said Wexford. 'We know everyone else must have known her under an assumed name, but not her doctor, I wonder why not.'

'Too risky?'

'What's the risk? In English law one can call oneself what one likes. What you call yourself *is* your name. People think you have to change your name by deed poll but you don't. I could call myself Waterford tomorrow and you could call yourself Fardel without infringing a hairsbreadth of the law.'

Looking puzzled, Burden said, 'I suppose so. Look, I see the Waterford thing, but why Fardel?'

'You grunt and sweat under a weary life, don't you? Never mind, forget it. We won't go to Princevale Road immediately. First I want to introduce you to some friends of mine.'

Baker seemed to have forgotten his cause for offence and greeted Wexford cordially.

'Michael Baker, meet Mike Burden, and this, Mike, is Sergeant Clements.'

Once, though not for more than a few hours, Wexford had suspected the rubicund baby-faced sergeant of murder to be certain of the undisputed guardianship of his adopted son. It always made him feel a little guilty to remember that, even though that suspicion had never been spoken aloud. But the memory – how could he have entertained such ideas about this pillar of integrity? – had made him careful, in every subsequent conversation, to show kindness to Clements and not fail to ask after young James and the small sister chosen for him. However, the sergeant was too conscious of his subordinate rank to raise domestic matters now, and Wexford was glad of it for other reasons. He, in turn, would have been asked for an account of his grandsons, at present a sore and embarrassing subject.

'Princevale Road?' said Baker. 'Very pleasant district. Unless I'm much mistaken, number six is one of a block of what they call town houses, modern sort of places with a lot of glass and weatherboarding.'

'Excuse me, sir,' Clements said eagerly, 'but unless *I'm* much mistaken we were called to break-in down there a few months back. I'll nip downstairs and do a bit of checking.'

Baker seemed pleased to have guests and something to relieve the tedium of August in Kenbourne Vale. 'How about a spot of lunch at the Grand Duke, Reg? And then we could all get along there, if you've no objection.'

Anxious to do nothing which might upset the prickly Baker, who was a man of whom it might be said that one should not touch his ears, Wexford said that he and Burden would be most gratified, adding to Baker's evident satisfaction, that he didn't know how they would get on without his help.

The sergeant came back, puffed up with news.

'The occupant is a Mrs Farriner,' he said. 'She's away on holiday. It wasn't her place that was broken into, it was next door but one, but apparently she's got a lot of valuable stuff and she came in here before she went away last Saturday week to ask us to keep an eye on the house for her.'

'Should put it on safe deposit,' Baker began to grumble. 'What's the use of getting us to . . .'

Wexford interrupted him. He couldn't help himself. 'How old is she, Sergeant? What does she look like?'

'I've not seen her myself, sir. Middle-aged, I believe, and a widow or maybe divorced. Dinehart knows her.'

'Then get Dinehart to look at that photo, will you?'

'You don't mean you think Mrs Farriner could be that Comfrey woman, sir?'

'Why not?' said Wexford.

But Dinehart was unable to say one way or another. Certainly Mrs Farriner was a big tall woman with dark hair who lived alone. As to her looking like that girl in the picture – well, people change a lot in twenty years. He wouldn't like to commit himself.

Wexford was tense with excitement. Why hadn't he thought of that before? All the time he was frustrated or crossed by people being away on holiday, and yet he had never considered that Rhoda Comfrey might not have been missed by friends and neighbours because they *expected* her to be absent from her home. They supposed a Mrs Farriner to be at some resort, going under the name by which they knew her, so why connect her with a Miss Comfrey who had been found murdered in a Sussex town?

In the Grand Duke, an old-fashioned pub that had surely once been a country inn, they served themselves from the cold table. Wexford felt too keyed-up to eat much. Dealing diplomatically with people like Baker might be a social obligation, but it involved wasting a great deal of time. The others seemed to be taking what he saw as a major break-through far more placidly than he could. Even Burden showed a marked lack of enthusiasm.

'Doesn't it strike you as odd,' he said, 'that a woman like this Mrs Farriner, well-off enough to live where she lives and have all that valuable stuff, should keep a wallet she presumably found on a bus?'

'There's nowt so strange as folk,' said Wexford.

'Maybe, but it was you told me that any departure from the norm is important. I can imagine the Rhoda Comfrey *we* know doing it, but not this Mrs Farriner from what we know of her. Therefore it seems unlikely to me that they're one and the same.'

'Well, we're not going to find out by sitting here feeding our faces,' said Wexford crossly.

To his astonishment, Baker agreed with him. 'You're quite right. Drink up, then, and we'll get going.'

Ascending Montfort Hill on the bus, Wexford hadn't noticed the little row of five or six shops on the left-hand side. This time, in the car, his attention was only drawn to them by the fact of Burden giving them such an intense scrutiny. But he said nothing. At the moment he felt rather riled with Burden. The name of the street which turned off immediately beyond these shops was lettered in black on a white board, Princevale Road, W19, and Burden eyed this with similar interest, craning his neck to look back when they had passed it.

At the very end of the street – or perhaps, from the numbering, the very beginning – stood a row of six terraced houses. They looked less than ten years old and differed completely in style from the detached mock-Tudor, each with a generous front garden, that characterized Princevale Road. Wexford supposed that they had been built on ground left vacant after the demolition of some isolated old house. They were a sign of the times, of scarcity of land and builders' greed. But they were handsome enough for all that, three floors high, boarded in red cedar between the wide plateglass windows. Each had its own garage, integrated and occupying part of the ground floor, each having a different coloured front door, orange, olive, blue, chocolate, yellow and lime. Number six, at this end of the block, had the typical invitation-to-burglars look a house takes on when its affluent and prideful owner is away. All the windows were shut, all the curtains drawn back with perfect symmetry. An empty milk bottle rack stood on the doorstep, and there were no bottles, full or empty, beside it. Stuck through the letterbox and protruding from it were a fistful of letters and circulars in brown envelopes. So much for police surveillance, Wexford thought to himself.

It was rather unwillingly that he now relinquished a share of the investigating to Baker and Clements, though he knew Baker's efficiency. The hard-faced inspector and his sergeant went off to ring at the door of number one. With Burden beside him, Wexford approached the house next door to the empty one.

Mrs Cohen at number five was a handsome Jewess in her early forties. Her house was stuffed with ornaments, the wallpaper flocked crimson on gold, gold on cream. There were photographs about of nearly grown-up children, a buxom daughter in a bridesmaid's dress, a son at his bar mitzvah.

'Mrs Farriner's a very charming nice person. What I call a brave woman, self-supporting, you know. Yes, she's divorced. Some no-good husband in the background, I believe, though she's never told me the details and I wouldn't ask. She's got a lovely little boutique down at Montfort Circus. I've had some really exquisite things from her and she's let me have them at cost. That's what I call neighbourly. Oh, no, it couldn't be' – looking at the photograph '– not *murdered*. Not a false name, that's not Rose's nature. Rose Farriner, that's her name. I mean, it's laughable what you're saying. Of course I know where she is. First she went off to see her mother who's in a very nice nursing home somewhere in the country, and then she was going on to the Lake District. No, I haven't had a card from her, I wouldn't expect it.'

The next house was the one which had been burgled, and Mrs Elliott, when they had explained who they were, promptly assumed that there had been another break-in. She was at least sixty, a jumpy nervous woman who had never been in Rose Farriner's house or entertained her in her own. But she knew of the existence of the dress shop, knew that Mrs Farriner was away and had remarked that she sometimes went away for weekends, in her view a dangerous proceeding with so many thieves about. The photograph was shown to her and she became intensely frightened. No, she couldn't say if Mrs Farriner had looked like that when young. It was evident that the idea of even hazarding an identification terrified her, and it seemed as if by so doing she feared to put her own life in jeopardy.

'Rhoda,' said Wexford to Burden, 'means a rose. It's Greek for rose. She tells people she's going to visit her mother in a nursing home. What are the chances she's shifted the facts, and mother is father and the nursing home's a hospital?'

Baker and Clements met them outside the gate of number three. They too had been told of mother and the nursing home, of the dress shop, and they too had met only with doubt and bewilderment over the photograph. Together the four of them approached the last, the chocolate coloured, front door.

Mrs Delano was very young, a fragile pallid blonde with a pale blond baby, at present asleep in its pram in the porch.

'Rose Farriner's somewhere around forty or fifty,' she said as if one of those ages was much the same as the other and all the same to her. She looked closely at the photograph, turned even paler. 'I saw the papers, it never crossed my mind. It could be her. I can't imagine now why I didn't see it before.'

In the display window on the left side of the shop door was the trendy gear for the very young: denim jeans and waistcoats, tee-shirts, long striped socks. The other window interested Wexford more, for the clothes on show in it belonged in much the same category as those worn by Rhoda Comfrey when she met her death. Red, white and navy were the predominating colours. The dresses and coats were aimed at a comfortably-off middle-aged market. They were 'smart' – a word he knew would never be used by his daughters or by anyone under forty-five. And among them, trailing from an open sleeve to a scent bottle, suspended from a vase to the neck of a crimson sweater, were strings of glass beads.

A woman of about thirty came up to attend to them. She said her name was Mrs Moss and she was in charge while Rose Farriner was away. Her manner astonished, suspicious cautious – all to be expected in the circumstances. Again the photograph was studied and again doubt was expressed. She had worked for Mrs Farriner for only six months and knew her only in her business capacity.

'Do you know what part of the country Mrs Farriner originally came from?' Burden asked her.

'Mrs Farriner's never discussed private things with me.'

'Would you say she's a secretive person?'

Mrs Moss tossed her head. 'I really don't know. We aren't always gossiping to each other, if that's what you mean. She doesn't know any more about me than I know about her.'

Wexford said suddenly, 'Has she ever had appendicitis?'

'Has she *what*?'

'Has she had her appendix out? It's the kind of thing one often does know about people.'

Mrs Moss looked as if she were about to retort that she really couldn't say, but something in Wexford's serious and ponderous gaze seemed to inhibit her. 'I oughtn't to tell you things like that. It's a breach of confidence.'

'You're aware as to whom we think Mrs Farriner really is or was. I think you're being obstructive.'

'But she can't be that woman! She's in the Lake District. She'll be back in the shop on Monday.'

'Will she? Have you had a card from her? A phone call?'

'Of course I haven't. Why should I? I know she's coming home on Saturday.'

'I'll be as frank with you,' Wexford said, 'as I hope you'll be with me. If Mrs Rose Farriner has had her appendix removed she cannot be Miss Rhoda Comfrey. There was no scar from an appendicectomy on Miss Comfrey's body. On the other hand, if she has not, the chances of her having been Miss Comfrey are very strong. We have to know.'

'All right,' said Mrs Moss, 'I'll tell you. It must have been about six months ago, about February or March. Mrs Farriner took a few days off work. It was food poisoning, but when she came back she did say she'd thought at first it was a grumbling appendix because – well, because she'd had trouble like that before.'

CHAPTER TEN

The heat danced in waving mirages on the white roadway. Traffic kept up a ceaseless swirl round Montfort Circus, and there was headache-provoking noise, a blinding glare from sunlight flashing off chrome and glass. Wexford and Baker took refuge in the car which Clements had imperiously parked on a double yellow band.

'We'll have to get into that house, Michael.'

Baker said thoughtfully, 'Of course we do have a key . . .' His eye caught Wexford's. He looked away. 'No, that's out of the question. It'll have to be done on a warrant. Leave it to me, Reg, I'll see what can be done.'

Burden and Clements stood out on the pavement, deep in conversation. Well aware of Burden's prudishness and also of Clement's deep-rooted disapproval of pretty well all persons under twenty-five – which augured ill for James and Angela in the future – Wexford had nevertheless supposed that they would have little in common. He had been wrong. They were discussing, like old duennas, the indecent appearance of the young housewife who had opened the door of number two Princevale Road dressed only in a bikini. Wexford gave the inspector a discourteous and peremptory tap on the shoulder.

'Come on, John Knox. I want to catch the four-thirty-five back to Sussex, home and beauty.'

Burden looked injured, and when they had said good-bye and were crossing the Circus to Parish Oak station, remarked that Clements was a very nice chap.

'Very true,' sneered Wexford with Miss Austen, 'and this is a very nice day and we are taking a very nice walk.'

Having no notion of what he meant but suspecting he was being got at, Burden ignored this and said they would never get a warrant on that evidence.

'What d'you mean, on that evidence? To my mind, its conclusive. You didn't expect one of those women to come out with the whole story, did you? "Oh, yes, Rose told me in confidence her real name's Comfrey." Look at the facts. A woman of fifty goes to a doctor with what she thinks may be appendicitis. She gives the name of Comfrey and her address as 6 Princevale Road, Parish Oak. The only occupant of that house is a woman of around fifty called Rose Farriner. Six months later Rose Farriner is again talking of a possible appendicitis. Rhoda Comfrey is dead, Rose Farriner has disappeared. Rhoda Comfrey was comfortably-off, probably had her own business. According to Mrs Parker, she was interested in dress. Rose Farriner is well-off, has her own dress shop. Rose Farriner has a sick old mother living in a nursing home in the country. Rhoda Comfrey had a sick old father in a hospital in the country. Isn't that conclusive?'

Burden walked up and down the platform, looking gloomily at posters for pale blue movies. 'I don't know. I just think we'll have trouble getting a warrant.'

'There's something else bothering you, isn't there?'

'Yes there is. It's a way-out thing. Look, it's the sort of thing that usually troubles you, not me. It's the sort of thing I usually scoff at, to tell you the truth.'

'Well, what the hell is it? You might as well tell me.'

Burden banged the palm of his hand with his fist. His expression was that of a man who, sceptical, practical, down-to-earth, hesitates from a fear of being laughed at to confess that he has seen a ghost. 'It was when we were driving up Montford Hill and we passed those shops, and I thought it hadn't really been worth getting a bus up that first time, it not being so far from the station to the doctor's place. And then I sort of noticed the shops and the name of the street facing us and . . . Look, it's stupid, forget it. Frankly, the more I think about it the more I can see I was just reading something into nothing. Forget it.'

'*Forget it?* After all that build-up? Are you crazy?'

'I'm sorry, sir,' said Burden very stiffly, 'but I don't approve of police work being based on silly conjectures and the sort of rubbish women call intuition. As you say, we have some very firm and conclusive facts to go on. No doubt, I was being unduly pessimistic about that warrant. Of course we'll get one.'

An explosion of wrath rose in Wexford with a fresh eruption of sweat. 'You're a real pain in the arse,' he snapped, but the rattle of the incoming train drowned his words.

His temper was not improved by Friday morning's newspaper. 'Police Chief Flummoxed by Comfrey Case' said a headline running across four columns at the foot of page one. And there, amid the text, was a photograph of himself, the block for which they had presumably had on file since the days when he had been a fat man. Piggy features glowered above three chins. He glowered at himself in the bathroom mirror and, thanks to Robin running in and out and shouting that grandad had got his picture in the paper, cut himself shaving the chicken skin where the three chins used to be.

He drove to Forest Road and let himself into the late James Comfrey's house with Rhoda Comfrey's key. There were two other keys on the ring, and one of them, he was almost sure, would open Rose Farriner's front door. At the moment, though, he was keeping that to himself for comparison with the one in the possession of Kenbourne police only if the obtaining of the warrant were held up. For if they weren't identical – and, in the light of Rhoda Comfrey's extreme secrecy about her country life in town and her town life in the country, it was likely enough they wouldn't be – he might as well say good-bye to the chance of that warrant here and now. But he did wonder about the third key. To the shop door perhaps? He walked into the living room, insufferably musty now, that Crocker had called a real tip, and flung open the window.

From the drawers which had been re-filled with their

muddled and apparently useless assortment of string and pins and mothballs and coins he collected all the keys that lay amongst it. Fifteen, he counted. Three Yale keys, one Norlond, one stamped RST, one FGW Ltd., seven rusted or otherwise corroded implements for opening the locks of back doors or privy doors or garden gates, a car ignition key and a smaller one, the kind that is used for locking the boot of a car. On both of these last were stamped the Citröen double chevron. They had not been together in the same drawer and to neither of them was attached the usual leather tag.

A violent pounding on the front door made him jump. He went out and opened it and saw Lilian Crown standing there.

'Oh, it's you', she said. 'Thought it might be kids got in. Or squatters. Never know these days, do you?'

She wore red trousers and a tee-shirt which would have been better suited to Robin. Brash fearlessness is not a quality generally associated with old women, especially those of her social stratum. Timidity, awe of authority, a need for self-effacement so often get the upper hand after the climacteric – as Sylvia might have pointed out to him with woeful examples – but they had not triumphed over Mrs Crown. She had the boldness of youth, and this surely not induced by gin at ten in the morning.

'Come in, Mrs Crown,' he said, and he shut the door firmly behind her. She trotted about, sniffing.

'What a pong! Haven't been in here for ten years.' She wrote something in the dust on top of the chest of drawers and let out a girlish giggle.

His hands full of keys, he said, 'Does the name Farriner mean anything to you?'

'Can't say it does.' She tossed her dried grass hair and lit a cigarette. She had come to check that the house hadn't been invaded by vandals, come from only next-door, but she had brought her cigarettes with her and a box of matches. To have a companionable smoke with squatters? She was amazing.

'I suppose your niece had a car,' he said, and he held up the two small keys.

'Never brought it here if she did. And she would've. Never missed a chance of showing off.' Her habit of omitting pronouns from her otherwise not particularly economical speech irritated him. He said rather sharply, 'Then whom do these keys belong to?'

'No good asking me. If she'd got a car left up in London, what's she leave her keys about down here for? Oh, no, that car'd have been parked outside for all the world to see. Couldn't get herself a man, so she was always showing what she could get. Wonder who'll get her money? Won't be me. though, not so likely.'

She blew a blast of smoke into his face, and he retreated, coughing.

'I'd like to know more about that phone call Miss Comfrey made to you on the Friday evening.'

'Like what? said Mrs Crown, smoke issuing dragon-like from her nostrils.

'Exactly what you said to each other. You answered the phone and she said, "Hallo, Lilian. I wonder if you know who this is." Is that right?' Mrs Crown nodded. 'Then what?' Wexford said. 'What time was it?'

'About seven. I said hallo and she said what you've said. In a real put-on voice, all deep and la-di-da. "Of course I know," I said. "If you want to know about your dad," I said, "you'd best get on to the hospital," "Oh, I know all about that," she said. "I'm going away on holiday," she said, "but I'll come down for a couple of days first." '

'You're sure she said that about a holiday?' Wexford interrupted.

' 'Course I'm sure. There's nothing wrong with my memory. Tell you another thing. She called me darling. I was amazed. "I'll come down for a couple of days first, darling," she said. Mind you, there was someone else with her while she was phoning. I know what she was up to. She'd got some woman there with her and she wanted her to think she was talking to a man.'

'But she called you Lilian.

'That's not to say the woman was in there with her when she started talking, is it? No, if you want to know what I think, she'd got some friend in the place with her, and this friend came in after she'd started talking, so she put in that "darling" to make her think she'd got a boy-friend she was going to see. I'm positive, I knew Rhoda. She said it again, or sort of "My dear", she said. "Thought you might be worried if you saw lights on, my dear. I'll come in and see you after I've been to the infirmary." And then whoever it was must have gone out again, I heard a door slam. Her voice went very low after that and she just said in her usual way, "See you Monday then. Good-bye." '

'You didn't wish her Many Happy Returns of the day?'

If a spider had shoulders they would have looked like Lilian Crown's. She shrugged them up and down, up and down, like a marionette. 'Old Mother Parker told me afterwards it was her birthday. You can't expect me to remember a thing like that. I knew it was in August sometime. Sweet fifty and never been kissed!'

'That's all, Mrs Crown,' said Wexford distastefully and escorted her back to the front door. Sometimes he thought how nice it would be to be a judge so that one could boldly and publicly rebuke people. With his sleeve he rubbed out of the dust the arrowed heart – B loves L – she had drawn there, wondering as he did so if B were the 'gentleman friend' she went drinking with, and wondering too about incidence of adolescent souls lingering on in mangy old carcases.

He made the phone call from home.

'I can tell you that here and now,' said Baker. 'Dinehart happened to mention it. Rose Farriner runs a Citröen. Any help to you?'

'I think so, Michael. Any news of my Chief Constable's get-together with your Super?'

'You'll have to be patient a bit longer, Reg.'

Wexford promised he would be. The air was clearing. Rhoda Comfrey Farriner had made that call to her aunt from Princevale Road on the evening of her birthday when, not unnaturally, she had had a friend with her. A woman, as Lilian Crown had supposed? No, he thought, a man. Late in life, she had at last found herself a man whom she had been attempting to inspire with jealousy. He couldn't imagine why. But never mind. That man, whoever he was, had indeed been inspired, had heard enough to tell him where Rhoda Rose Comfrey Farriner was going on Monday. Wexford had no doubt that that listener had been her killer.

It had been a crime of passion. Adolescent souls linger on, as Mrs Crown had shown him, in ageing bodies. Not in everyone does the heyday in the blood grow tame. Had he not himself even recently, good husband though he tried to be, longed wistfully for the sensation of being again in love? Hankered for the feeling of it and murmured to himself the words of Stendhal – though it might be with the ugliest kitchen-maid in Paris, as long as he loved her and she returned his ardour . . .

The girl who sat in the foyer of Kingsmarkham Police Station was attracting considerable attention. Sergeant Camb had given her a cup of tea, and two young detective constables had asked her if she was quite comfortable and was she sure there was nothing they could do to help her? Loring had wondered if it would cost him his job were he to take her up to the canteen for a sandwich or the cheese on toast Chief Inspector Wexford called Fuzz Fondue. The girl looked nervous and upset. She had with her a newspaper at which she kept staring in an appalled way, but she would tell no one what she wanted, only that she must see Wexford.

Her colouring was exotic. There is an orchid, not pink or green or gold, but of a waxen and delicate beige, shaded with sepia, and this girl's face had the hue of such an orchid. Her features looked as if drawn in charcoal on oriental silk, and her hair was black silk, massy and very finely spun. For her country-women the sari had been designed, and she walked as if she were accustomed to wearing a sari, though for this visit she was in Western dress, a blue skirt and a white cotton shirt.

'Why is he such a long time?' she said to Loring, and Loring who was a romantic young man thought that it was in just such a tone that the Shunamite had said to the watchman: Have ye seen him whom my soul loveth?

'He's a busy man,' he said. 'but I'm sure he won't be long.' And for the first time he wished he were ugly old Wexford who could entertain such a visitor in seclusion.

And then, at half past twelve, Wexford walked in.

'Good morning, Miss Patel.'

'You remember me!'

Loring had the answer to that one ready. Who could forget her, once seen? Wexford said only that he did remember her, that he had a good memory for faces, and then poor Loring was sharply dismissed with the comment that if he had nothing to do the chief inspector could soon remedy that. He watched beauty and the beast disappear into the lift.

'What can I do for you, Miss Patel?'

She sat down in the chair he offered her. 'You're going to be very angry with me. I've done something awful. No, really, I'm afraid to tell you. I've been so frightened ever since I saw the paper. I got on the first train. You're all so nice to me, everyone was so nice, and I know it's going to change and it won't be nice at all when I tell you.'

Wexford eyed her reflectively. He remembered that he had put her down as a humorist and a tease, but now her wit had deserted her. She seemed genuinely upset. He decided

CHAPTER ELEVEN

He could hardly comfort her as he would have comforted his
Sylvia or his Sheila whom he would have taken in his arms.
So he picked up the phone and asked for someone to bring
up coffee and sandwiches for two, and remarked as much to
himself as to her that he wouldn't be able to get angry when
he had his mouth full.

Crying did nothing to spoil her face. She wiped her eyes,
sniffed and said, 'You *are* nice. And I've been such an idiot.
I must be absolutely out of my tree.'

'I doubt it. D'you feel like beginning or d'you want your
coffee first?'

'I'll get it over.'

Should he tell her he was no longer interested in Grenville
West, for it must have been he she had come about, or let it
go? Might as well hear what it was.

'I told you a deliberate lie,' she said.

He raised his eyebrows. 'You aren't the first to do that by
a long chalk. I could be in the *Guinness Book of Records* as the
man who's had more deliberate lies told him than anyone else
on earth.'

'But I told this one. I'm so ashamed.'

The coffee arrived and a plate of ham sandwiches. She
took one and held it but didn't begin to eat. 'It was about
Polly,' she said. 'Polly never goes out in the evenings alone,
but *never*. If she goes to Grenville's he always runs her home
or puts her in a taxi. She had a horrible thing happen about
a year back. She was walking along in the dark and a man
came up behind her and put his arms round her. She screamed
and kicked him and he ran off, but after that she was afraid
to be out alone in the dark. She says if people were allowed
to have guns in this country she'd have one.'

Wexford said gently, 'Your deliberate lie, Miss Patel? I think you're stalling.'

'I know I am. Oh, dear. Well, I told you Polly was at home with me that Monday evening, but she wasn't. She went out before I got home from work and she came back alone – oh, I don't know, after I was in bed. Anyway, the next day I asked her where she'd been because I knew Grenville was away, and she said she'd got fed up with Grenville and she'd been out with someone else. Well, I knew she'd been unhappy about him for a long time, Grenville, I mean. She wanted to go and live with him. Actually, she wanted to marry him, but he wouldn't even kiss her.' Malina Patel gave a little shudder. 'Ooh, I wouldn't have wanted him to kiss me! There's something really funny about him, something queer – I don't mean gay-queer, or I don't *think* so – but something sort of hard to . . .'

'On with your story, please, Miss Patel!'

'I'm sorry. So what I was going to say was that Polly had met this man who was married and that Monday they'd been to some motel and had a room there for the evening. And she said this man of hers was afraid of his wife finding out, she'd put a private detective on him, and if that detective came round, would I say she'd been at home with me?'

'*You thought I was a private detective?*'

'Yes! I told you I was mad. I told Polly I'd do what she said if a detective came, and a detective did come. It didn't seem so very awful, you see, because it's not a crime, sleeping with someone else's husband, is it? It's not very nice but it's not a crime. I mean, not against the law.'

Wexford did his best to suppress his laughter and succeeded fairly well. Those remarks of hers, then, which he had thought witty and made at his expense, had in fact come from a genuine innocence. If she wasn't so pretty and so sweet, he would have been inclined to call her – it seemed sacrilege – downright stupid.

She ate a sandwich and took a gulp of coffee.

'And I was glad Polly had got someone after being so miserable about Grenville. And I thought private detectives are awful people, snooping and prying and getting paid for doing dirty things like that. So I thought it didn't really matter telling a lie to that sort of person.'

This time Wexford had to let his laughter go. She looked at him dubiously over the top of her coffee cup.

'Have you ever known any private detectives, Miss Patel?'

'No but I've seen lots of them in films.'

'Which enabled you to identify me with such ease? Seriously, though . . .' He stopped smiling. 'Miss Flinders knew who I was. Didn't she tell you afterwards?'

It was the crucial question, and on her answer depended whether he accompanied her at once back to Kenbourne Vale or allowed her to go alone.

'Of course she did! But I was too stupid to see. She said you hadn't come about the man and the motel at all, but it was something to do with Grenville and that wallet he'd lost and she was going to tell me a whole lot more, but I wouldn't *listen*. I was going out, you see, I was late already, and I was sick of hearing her on and on about Grenville. And she tried again to tell me the next day, only I said not to go on about Grenville, please, I'd rather hear about her new man, and she hasn't mentioned him – Grenville, I mean – since.'

He seized on one point. 'You knew before that the wallet had been lost, then?'

'Oh, yes! She'd been full of it. Long before she told me about the motel and the man and the private detective. Poor Grenville had lost his wallet on a bus and he'd asked her to tell the police but she hadn't because she thought they wouldn't be able to do anything. That was *days* before she went to the motel.'

He believed her. His case for indentifying Rhoda Comfrey as Rose Farriner was strengthened. What further questions he asked Malina Patel would be for his amusement only.

'May I ask what made you come and tell me the awful truth?'

'Your picture in the paper. I saw it this morning and I recognized you.'

From *that* picture? Frivolous inquiries may lead to humiliation as well as amusement.

'Polly had already gone out. I wished I'd listened to her before. I suddenly realized it had all been to do with that murdered woman, and I realized who you were and everything. I felt awful. I didn't go to work. I phoned and said I'd got gastro-enteritis which was another lie, I'm afraid, and I left a note for Polly saying I was going to see my mother who was ill, and then I got the train and came here. I've told so many lies now I've almost forgotten who I've told what.'

Wexford said, 'When you've had more practice you'll learn how to avoid that. Make sure to tell the same lie.'

'You don't mean it!'

'No, Miss Patel, I don't. And don't tell lies to the police, will you? We usually find out. I expect we should have found this one out, only we're no longer very interested in that line of inquiry. Another cup of coffee?'

She shook her head. 'You've been awfully nice to me.'

'You don't go to prison till next time,' said Wexford. 'What they call a suspended sentence. Come on, I'll take you downstairs and we'll see if we can fix you up with a lift to the station. I have an idea Constable Loring has to go that way.'

Large innocent eyes of a doe or calf met his. 'I'm afraid I'm being an awful lot of trouble.'

'Not a bit of it,' Wexford said breezily. 'He'll bear it with the utmost fortitude, believe me.'

Once again he got home early with a free evening ahead. Such a thing rarely happened to him in the middle of a murder case. There was nothing to do but wait and wonder. Though not to select or discard from a list of suspects, for he had none, nor attempt to read hidden meanings and calculated falsehoods between the lines of witnesses' statements. He had no witnesses. All he had were four keys and a missing car; a wallet that beyond all doubt now had been lost on a bus; and a tale of a phone call overheard by a man who, against all reasonable probability, loved withered middle-aged gawky Rhoda Comfrey so intensely that he had killed her from jealousy.

Not a very promising collection of objects and negativities and conjectures.

The river was golden in the evening light, having on its shallow rippling surface a patina like that on beaten bronze. There were dragonflies in pale blue or speckled armour, and the willow trailed his hoar leaves in the grassy stream.

'Wouldn't it be nice,' said Robin, 'if the river went through your garden?'

'My garden would have to be half a mile longer,' said Wexford.

Water rats having failed to appear, the little boys had taken off sandals and socks and were paddling. It was fortunate that Wexford, rather against his will, had consented to remove his own shoes, roll up his trousers and join them. For Ben, playing boats with a log of willow wood, leant over too far and toppled in up to his neck. His grandfather had him out before he had time to utter a wail.

'Good thing it's so warm. You'll dry off on the way back.'

'Grandad carry.'

Robin looked anything but displeased. 'There'll be an awful row.'

'Not when you tell them how brave grandad jumped in and saved your brother's life.'

'Come on. It's only about six inches deep. He'll get in a row and so will you. You know what women are.'

But there was no row, or rather, no fresh row to succeed that already taking place. How it had begun Wexford didn't know, but as he and the boys came up to the french windows he heard his wife say with, for her, uncommon tartness, 'Personally, I think you've got far more than you deserved, Sylvia. A good husband, a lovely home and two fine healthy sons. D'you think you've ever done anything to merit more than that?'

Sylvia jumped up. Wexford thought she was going to shout some retort at her mother, but at that moment, seeing her mudstained child, she seized him in her arms and rushed away upstairs with him. Robin, staring in silence, at last followed her, his thumb in his mouth, a habit Wexford thought he had got out of years before.

'And you tell me not to be harsh with her!'

'It's not very pleasant,' said Dora, not looking at him, 'to have your own daughter tell you a woman without a career is a useless encumbrance when she gets past fifty. When her looks have gone. Her husband only stays with her out of duty and because someone's got to support her,'

He was aghast. She had turned away because her eyes had filled with tears. He wondered when he had last seen her cry. Not since her own father died, not for fifteen years.

The second woman to cry over him that day. Coffee and sandwiches were hardly the answer here, though a hug might have been. Instead he said laconically, 'I often think if I were a bachelor now at my age, and you were single – which, of course, you wouldn't be – I'd ask you to marry me.'

She managed a smile. 'Oh, Mr Wexford, this is so sudden. Will you give me time to think it over?'

'No,' he said. 'Sorry. We're going out to celebrate our engagement.' He touched her shoulder. 'Come on. Now. We'll go and have a nice dinner somewhere and then we'll go to the pictures. You needn't tell Sylvia. We'll just sneak out.'

'We can't!'

'We're going to.'

So they dined at the Olive and Dove, she in an old cotton dress and he in his water-rat-watching clothes. And then they saw a film in which no one got murdered or even got married, still less had children or grandchildren, but in which all the characters lived in Paris and drank heavily and made love all day long. It was half past eleven when they got back, and Wexford had the curious feeling, as Sylvia came out into the hall to meet them, that they were young lovers again and she the parent. As if she would say: Where had they been and what sort of a time was this to come home? Of course she didn't.

'The Chief Constable's been on the phone for you, Dad.'

'What time was that?' said Wexford.

'About eight and then again at ten.'

'I can't phone him now. It'll have to wait till the morning.'

Sharing the initials and, to some extent, the appearance of the late General de Gaulle, Charles Griswold lived in a converted farmhouse in the village of Millerton – Millerton *Les-Deux-Églises*, Wexford called it privately. Wexford was far from being his favourite officer. He regarded him as an eccentric and one who used methods of the kind Burden had denounced on Parish Oak station platform.

'I hoped to get hold of you last night,' he said coldly when Wexford presented himself at Hightrees Farm at nine-thirty on Saturday morning.

'I took my wife out, sir.'

Griswold did not exactly think that policemen shouldn't have wives. He had one himself, she was about the place now, though some said he had more or less mislaid her decades ago. But that females of any kind should so intrude as to have to be taken out displeased him exceedingly. He made no comment. His big forehead rucked up into a frown.

'I sent for you to tell you that this warrant has been sworn. The matter is in the hands of the Kenbourne police. Superintendent Rittifer foresees entering the house tomorrow morning, and it is entirely by his courtesy that you and another officer may accompany him.'

It's my case, Wexford thought resentfully. She was killed in my manor. Oh, Howard, why the hell do you have to be in Tenerife now? Aloud he said, not very politely:

'Why not today?'

'Because it's my belief the damned woman'll turn up today, the way she's supposed to.'

'She won't, sir. She's Rhoda Comfrey.'

'Rittifer thinks so too. I may as well tell you that if it rested on your notions alone the obtaining of this warrant wouldn't have my support. I know you. Half the time you're basing your inquiries on a lot of damn-fool intuitions and *feelings*.'

'Not this time, sir. One woman has positively identified Rhoda Comfrey as Rose Farriner from the photograph. She is the right age, she disappeared at the right time. She complained of appendicits symptoms only a few months after we know Rhoda Comfrey went to a doctor with such symptoms. She . . .'

'All right, Reg.' The Chief Constable delivered the kind of dismissive shot of which only he was capable. 'I won't say you know your own business best because I don't think you do.'

CHAPTER TWELVE

The courtesy of Superintendent Rittifer did not extend to his putting in an appearance at Princevale Road. No blame to him for that, Wexford thought. He wouldn't have done so either in the superintendent's position and on a fine Sunday afternoon. For it was two by the time they got there, he and Burden with Baker and Sergeant Clements.

Because it was a Sunday they had come up in Burden's car and the traffic hadn't been too bad. Now that the time had come he was beginning to have qualms, the seeds of which had been well sown by Burden and the Chief Constable. The very thing which had first put him on to Rose Farriner now troubled him. Why should she go to a doctor and give only to him the name of Rhoda Comfrey while everyone else knew her as Rose Farriner? And a local doctor too, one who lived no more than a quarter of a mile away, who might easily and innocently mention that other name to those not supposed to know it. Then there were the clothes in which Rhoda Comfrey's body had been dressed. He remembered thinking that his own wife wouldn't have worn them even in the days when they were poor. They had been of the same sort of colours as those sold in the Montfort Circus boutique, but had they been of anything like the same standard? Would Mrs Cohen have wanted to get them at cost and have described them as 'exquisite'? How shaky too had been that single identification, made by a very young woman who looked anaemic and neurotic, who might even be suffering from some kind of post-natal hysteria.

Could Burden have been right about the wallet? He got out of the car and looked up at the house. Even from their linings he could see that the curtains were of the kind that cost a hundred pounds for a set. The windows were double-glazed, the orange and white paintwork fresh. A bay tree stood in a tub by the front door. He had seen a bay tree like that in a garden centre priced at twenty-five pounds. Would a woman who could afford all that steal a wallet? Perhaps, if she were leading a double life, had two disparate personalities inside that strong gaunt body. Besides, the wallet had been stolen, and from a bus that passed through Kenbourne Vale . . .

Before Baker could insert the key Mrs Farriner had given Dinehart, Wexford tested out the two which had been on Rhoda Comfrey's ring. Neither fitted.

'That's a bit of a turn-up for the books,' said Burden.

'Not necessarily. I should have brought all the keys that were in that drawer.' Wexford could see Baker didn't like it, but he unlocked the door just the same and they went in.

Insufferably hot and stuffy inside. The temperature in the hall must have been over eighty and the air smelt strongly. Not of mothballs and dust and sweat, though, but of pine-scented cleansers and polish and those deodorizers which, instead of deodorizing, merely provide a smell of their own. Wexford opened the door to the garage. It was empty. Clean towels hung in the yellow and white shower room and there was an unused cake of yellow soap on the washbasin. The only other room on this floor was carpeted in black, and black and white geometrically patterned curtains hung at its french window. Otherwise, it contained nothing but two black arm-chairs, a glass coffee table and a television set.

They went upstairs, bypassing for the time being the first floor, and mounting to the top. Here were three bedrooms and a bathroom. One of these bedrooms was totally empty, a second, adjoining it, furnished with a single bed, a wardrobe and a dressing table. Everything was extremely clean and sterile-looking, the wastepaper baskets emptied, the flower vases empty and dry. Again, in this bathroom, there were fresh towels hanging. A medicine chest contained aspirins, nasal spray, sticking plaster, a small bottle of antiseptic. Wexford was beginning to wonder if Rhoda Comfrey had ever stamped anything with her personality, but the sight of the principal bedroom changed his mind.

It was large and luxurious. Looking about him, he recalled that spare room in Carlyle Villas. Since then she had come a long way. The bed was oval, its cover made of some sort of beige-coloured furry material, with furry beige pillows piled at its head. A chocolate-coloured carpet, deep-piled, one wall all mirror, one all glass overlooking the street, one filled with built-in cupboards and dressing table counter, the fourth entirely hung with brown glass beads, strings of them from ceiling to floor. On the glass counter stood bottles of French perfume, a pomander and a crystal tray containing silver brushes.

They looked at the clothes in the cupboards. Dresses and coats and evening gowns hung there in profusion, and all were not only as different from those on Rhoda Comfrey's body as a diamond is different from a ring in a cracker, but of considerably higher quality than those in Mrs Farriner's shop.

On the middle floor the living room was L-shaped, the kitchen occupying the space between the arms of the L. A refrigerator was still running on a low mark to preserve two pounds of butter, some plastic-wrapped vegetables and a dozen eggs.

Cream-coloured carpet in the main room, coffee-coloured walls, abstract paintings, a dark red leather suite – real leather, not fake. Ornaments, excluded elsewhere, abounded here. There was a good deal of Chinese porcelain, a bowl that Wexford thought might be Sung, a painting of squat peasants and yellow birds and red and purple splashes that surely couldn't be a Chagall original – or could it?

'No wonder she wanted us to keep an eye on it,' said Baker, and Clements began on a little homily, needless in this company, on the imprudence of householders, the flimsiness of locks and the general fecklessness of people who had more money than they knew what to do with.

Wexford cut him short. 'That's what I'm interested in.' He pointed to a long teak writing desk in which were four drawers and on top of which stood a white telephone. He pictured Rhoda Comfrey phoning her aunt from there, her companion coming in from the kitchen perhaps with ice for drinks. Dr Lomond had warned her to keep off alcohol. There was plenty of it here in the sideboard, quite an exotic variety, Barcardi and Pernod and Campari as well as the usual whisky and gin. He opened the top drawer in the desk.

A cardboard folder marked 'Car' held an insurance policy covering the Citroën, a registration document and a manufacturer's handbook. No driving licence. In another, marked 'House', a second policy and a mass of services bill counterfoils. There was a third folder, marked 'Finance', but it held only a paying-in book from Barclays Bank, Montfort Circus, W19.

'And yet she didn't have a cheque-book or a credit card on her,' Wexford remarked more or less to himself.

Writing paper in the second drawer, with the address of the house on it in a rather ornate script. Under the box was a personal phone directory. Wexford turned to C for Comfrey, F for father, D for dad, H for hospital, S for Stowerton, and back to C for Crown. Nothing...

Burden said in a curiously high voice, 'There's some more stuff here.' He had pulled out the drawer in a low table that stood under the window. Wexford moved over to him. A car door banged outside in the street.

'You ought to look at this,' Burden said, and he held out a document. But before Wexford could take it there was a sound from below as of the front door being pushed open.

'Not expecting any more of your people, are you?' Wexford said to Baker.

Baker didn't answer him. He and the sergeant went to the head of the stairs. They moved like burglars surprised in the course of robbery, and 'burglars' was the first word spoken by the woman who came running up the stairs and stopped dead in front of them.

'Burglars! Don't tell me there's been a break-in!'

She looked round her at the open drawers, the disarranged ornaments. 'Mrs Cohen said the police were in the house. I couldn't believe it, not on the very day I come home.' A man had followed her. 'Oh, Bernard, look, my God! For heaven's sake, what's happened?'

In a hollow voice, Baker said, 'It's quite all right, madam, nothing has been taken, there's been no break-in. I'm afraid we owe you an apology.'

She was a tall well-built woman who looked about forty but might have been older. She was handsome, dark, heavily made-up, and she was dressed in expensively tailored denim jeans and waistcoat with a red silk shirt. The man with her seemed younger, a blond burly man with a rugged face.

'What are you doing with my birth certificate?' She said to Burden.

He handed it to her meekly along with a certificate of a divorce decree. Her face registered many things, mainly disbelief and nervous bewilderment. Wexford said:

'You are Mrs Rose Farriner?'

'Well, of course I am. Who did you think I was?'

He told her. He told her who he was and why they were there.

'Lot of bloody nonsense,' said the man called Bernard. 'If you want to make an issue of this, Rosie, you can count on my support. I never heard of such a thing.'

Mrs Farriner sat down. She looked at the photograph of Rhoda Comfrey, she looked at the newspaper Wexford gave her.

'I think I'd like a drink, Bernard. Whisky, please. I thought you were here because burglars had got in and now you say you thought *I* was this woman. What did you say your name was? Wexford? Well, Mr Wexford, I am forty-one years old, not fifty, my father has been dead for nine years and I've never been to Kingsmarkham in my life. Thanks, Bernard. That's better. It was a shock, you know. My God, I don't understand how you could make a mistake like that.' She passed the documents to Wexford who read them in silence.

Rosemary Julia Golbourne, born forty-one years before in Northampton. The other piece of paper, which was a certificate making a decree nisi absolute, showed that the marriage which had taken place between Rosemary Julia Golbourne and Godfrey Farriner at Christ Church, Lancaster Gate, in April 1959 had been dissolved fourteen years later at Kenbourne Country Court.

'Had you delayed another week,' said Mrs Farriner, 'I should have been able to show you my second marriage certificate.' The blond man rested his hand on her shoulder and glowered at Wexford.

'I can only apologize very profoundly, Mrs Farriner, and assure you we have done no damage and that everything will be restored as it was.'

'Yes, but look here, that's all very well,' said Bernard. 'You come into my future wife's home, break in more or less, go through her private papers, and all because . . .'

But Mrs Farriner had begun to laugh. 'Oh, it's so ridiculous! A secret life, a mystery woman. And that photograph! Would you like to see what I looked like when I was thirty? For God's sake, there's a picture in that drawer.' There was. A pretty girl with dark brown curls, a smiling wide-eyed face only a little softer and smoother than the same face now. 'Oh, I shouldn't laugh. That poor creature. But to mix me up with some old spinster who got herself mugged down a country lane!'

'I must say you take it very well, Rosie.'

Mrs Farriner looked at Wexford. She stopped laughing. He thought she was a nice woman, if insensitive. 'I shan't take it further, if that's what you're worrying about,' she said. 'I shan't complain to the Home Secretary. I mean, now I've got over the shock, it'll be something to dine out on, won't it? And now I'll go and make us all some coffee.'

Wexford wasn't over the shock. He refused Baker's offer of a lift to Victoria. Burden and he walked slowly along the pavement. Well-mannered as were the residents of Princevale Road, a good many of Mrs Farriner's neighbours had come out to watch their departure. What some of them were afterwards to call a 'police raid' had made their weekend, though they pretended as they watched that they were clipping their hedges or admonishing their children.

The sun shone strongly on Kenbourne Tudor, on subtly coloured paintwork and unsubtly coloured flowers, petunias striped and quartered like flags, green plush lawns where sprinklers fountained. Wexford felt hollow inside. He felt that hollow sickness that follows exclusively the making of some hideous howler or *faux pas*.

'There'll be an awful row,' said Burden unhelpfully, using the very words Robin had used two days before.

'I suppose so. I should have listened to you.'

'Well . . . I didn't say much. It was just that I had this feeling all the time, and you know how I distrust "feelings".'

Wexford was silent. They had come to the end of the street where it joined Montfort Hill. There he said, 'What was the feeling? I suppose you can tell me now.'

'You've asked me at exactly the right point, OK, I'll tell you. It struck me the first time we passed this spot.' Burden led the chief inspector a little way down Montfort Hill, away from the bus stop they had been making for. 'We'll suppose Rhoda Comfrey is on her way to Dr Lomond's, whose name she's got out of the phone book. She isn't exactly sure where Midsomer Road is, so she doesn't get the bus, she walks from Parish Oak station.

'For some reason which we don't know she doesn't want to give Dr Lomond her true address, so she has to give him a false one, and one that's within the area of his practice. So far she hasn't thought one up. But she passes these shops and looks up at that tobacconist, and what's the first thing she sees?'

Wexford looked up. 'A board advertising Wall's ice cream. My God, Mike, a hanging sign for Player's Number Six cigarettes. Was that what your feeling was about. Was that why you kept looking back that first time we came in the car? She sees the number six, and then that black and white street sign for Princevale Road?'

Burden nodded unhappily.

'I believe you're right, Mike. It's the way people do behave. It could happen almost unconsciously. Dr Lomond's receptionist asks her for her address when she comes to register and she comes out with number six, Princevale Road.' Wexford struck his forehead with the heel of his hand. 'I ought to have seen it! I've come across something like it before, and here in Kenbourne Vale, years ago. A girl called herself Loveday because she'd seen the name on a shop.' He turned on Burden. 'Mike, you should have told me about this, you should have told me last week.'

'Would you have believed me if I had?'

Hot-tempered though he might be, Wexford was a fair man. 'I might've – but I'd have wanted to get into that house just the same.'

Burden shrugged. 'We're back to square one, aren't we?'

CHAPTER THIRTEEN

There was no point in delaying. He went straight to Hightrees Farm. Griswold listened to him with an expression of lip-curling disgust. In the middle of Wexford's account he helped himself to a brandy and soda, but he offered nothing to his subordinate.

When it was ended he said, 'Do you ever read the newspapers?'

'Yes, sir. Of course.'

'Have you ever noticed how gradually over the past ten years or so the Press have been ramming it home to people that their basic freedoms are constantly under threat? And who comes in for most of the shit-throwing? The police. You've just given them a big helping of it on a plate, haven't you? All ready for throwing tomorrow morning.'

'I don't believe Mrs Farriner will tell the Press, sir.'

'She'll tell her friends, won't she? Some busybody dogooder will get hold of it.' The Chief Constable, who referred to Mid-Sussex as the General had been in the habit of referring to *la belle France*, with jealousy and with reverence, said, 'Understand, I will not have the hitherto unspotted record of the Mid-Sussex Constabulary smeared all over by the gutter Press. I will not have it endangered by one foolish man who acts on psychology and not on circumstantial evidence.'

Wexford smarted under that one. 'Foolish man' was hard to take. And he smarted more when Griswold went on, even though he now called him Reg which meant there would be no immediate retribution.

'This woman's been dead for two weeks, Reg, and as far as you've got, she might as well have dropped from Mars. She might as well have popped off in a space ship every time she left Kingsmarkham.' I'm beginning to think she did, Wexford thought, though he said nothing aloud. 'You know I don't care to call the Yard in unless I must. By the end of this coming week I'll have to if my own men can't do better than this. It seems to me . . .' and he gave Wexford a ponderous bull-like glare '. . . that all you can do is get your picture in the papers like some poove of a film actor.'

Sylvia sat in the dining room, the table covered with application forms for jobs and courses.

'You've picked the wrong time of year,' her father said, picking up a form that applied for entry to the University of London. 'Their term starts next month.'

'The idea is I get a job to fill in the year and start doing my degree next year. I have to get a grant, you see.'

'My dear, you don't stand a chance. They'll assess you on Neil's salary. At least, I suppose so. He's your husband.'

'Maybe he won't be by then. Oh, I'm so sick of you men ruling the world! It's not fair just taking it for granted my husband pays for me like he'd pay for a child.'

'Just as fair as taking it for granted the taxpayers will. I know you're not interested in my views or your mother's, but I'm going to give you mine just the same. The way the world still is, women have to prove they're as capable as men. Well, you prove it. Do an external degree or a degree by correspondence and in something that's likely to lead to a good job. It'll take you five years and by that time the boys'll be off your hands. Then when you're thirty-five you and Neil will be two professional people with full-times jobs and a servant you both pay for. Nobody'll treat you like a chattel or a furniture polisher then. You'll see.'

She pondered, looking sullen. Very slowly she began filling in the section of a form headed 'Qualifications'. The list of them, Wexford noted sadly, was sparse. She scrawled a line through *Mr/Mrs/Miss* and wrote *Ms*. Her head came up and the abundant hair flew out.

'I'm glad I've got boys. I'd feel sick with despair for them if they were girls. Didn't you want a son?'

'I suppose I did before Sheila was born. But after she was born I didn't give it another thought.'

'Didn't you think what we'd suffer? You're aware and sensitive, Dad. Didn't you think how we'd be exploited and humiliated by men and *used?*'

It was too much. There she sat, tall and powerful, blooming with health, the youthful hue sitting on her skin like morning dew, a large diamond cluster sparkling on her hand, her hair scented with St Laurent's *Rive Gauche*. Her sister, described by critics as one of England's most promising young actresses, had a big flat of her own in St John's Wood where, it had often seemed to her father, she sweetly exploited and used all the men who frequented it.

'I couldn't send you back, could I?' he snapped. 'I couldn't give God back your entrance ticket and ask for a male variety instead. I know exactly what Freud felt when he said there was one question that would always puzzle him. What is it that women want?'

'To be people,' she said.

He snorted and walked out. The Crockers and a couple of neighbours were coming in for drinks. The doctor hustled Wexford upstairs and produced his sphygmomanometer.

'You look rotten, Reg. What's the matter with you?'

'That's for you to say. How's my blood pressure?'

'Not bad. Is it Sylvia?'

He hated explaining why his daughter and the children were in the house. People categorize others into the limited compartments their imaginations permit. They assumed that either Sylvia or her husband had been unfaithful or that Neil had been cruel. He couldn't spell it all out, but just had to watch the speculating gleam in their eyes and take their pity.

'Partly,' he said, 'and it's this Comfrey case. I dream about her, Len. I rack my brains, such as they are, about her. And

I've made a crazy mistake. Griswold half-crucified me this afternoon, called me a foolish man.'

'We all have to fail, Reg,' said Crocker like a liberal headmaster.

'There was a sort of sardonic gleam in her eyes when we found her. I don't know if you noticed. I feel as if she's laughing at me from beyond the grave. Hysterical, eh? That's what Mike says I am.'

But Mike didn't say it again. He knew when to tread warily with the chief inspector, though Wexford had become a little less glum when there was nothing in the papers on Monday or Tuesday about the Farriner fiasco.

'And that business wasn't all vanity and vexation of spirit,' he said. 'We've learnt one thing from it. The disappearance of Rhoda Comfrey, alias whatever, may not have been re-marked by her neighbours because they expect her to be away on holiday. So we have to wait and hope a while longer that someone from outside will still come to us.'

'Why should they at this stage?'

'Exactly because it is at this stage. How long do the majority of people go on holiday for?'

'A fortnight,' said Burden promptly.

Wexford nodded. 'So those friends and neighbours who knew her under an assumed name would have expected her back last Saturday. Now they wouldn't have been much con-cerned if she wasn't back by Saturday, but by Monday when she doesn't answer her phone, when she doesn't turn up for whatever work she does? By today?'

'You've got a point there.'

'God knows, every newspaper reader in the country must be aware we still don't know her London identity. The Press has rammed it home hard enough. Wouldn't it be nice, Mike, if at this very moment some public-spirited citizen were to be walking into a nick somewhere in north or west London to say she's worried because her boss or the woman next door hasn't come back from Majorca?'

Burden always took Wexford's figurative little flights of fancy literally. 'She couldn't have been going there, wouldn't have had a passport.'

'As Rhoda Comfrey she might have. Besides, there are all sorts of little tricks you can get up to with passports. You're not going to tell me a woman who's fooled us like this for two weeks couldn't have got herself a dozen false passports if she'd wanted them.'

'Anyway, she didn't go to Majorca. She came here and got herself stabbed.' Burden went to the window and said wonderingly, 'There's a cloud up there.'

'No bigger than a man's hand, I daresay.'

'Bigger than that,' said Burden, not recognizing this quotation from the Book of Kings. 'In fact, there are quite a lot of them.' And he made a remark seldom uttered by Englishmen in a tone of hope, still less of astonishment. 'It's going to rain.'

The room went very dark and they had to switch the light on. Then a golden tree of forked lightning sprang out of the forest, splitting the purple sky. A great rolling clap of thunder sent them retreating from where they had been watching the beginnings of this storm, and Burden closed the windows.

At last the rain came, but sluggishly at first in the way rain always does come when it has held off for weeks, slow intermittent plops of it. Wexford remembered how Sylvia, when she was a tiny child, had believed until corrected that the rain was contained up there in a bag which someone punctured and then finally sliced open. He sat down at his desk and again phoned the Missing Persons Bureau, but no one had been reported missing who could remotely be identified as Rhoda Comfrey.

It was still only the middle of the afternoon. Plenty of time for the public-spirited citizen's anxiety and tension to mount until . . . Today was the day, surely, when that would happen if it was going to happen. The bag was sliced open and rain crashed in a cataract against the glass, bringing with it a sudden drop in the temperature. Wexford actually shivered; for the first time in weeks he felt cold, and he put on his jacket. He found himself seeing the storm as an omen, this break in the weather signifying another break. Nonsense, of course, the superstition of a foolish man. He had thought he had had breaks before, hadn't he? Two of them, and both had come to nothing.

By six there had come in no phone calls relevant to Rhoda Comfrey, but still he waited, although it was not necessary for him to be there. He waited until seven, until half past, by which time all the exciting pyrotechnics of the storm were over and the rain fell dully and steadily. At a quarter to eight, losing faith in his omen, in the importance of this day above other days – it had been one of the dreariest he had spent for a long time – he drove home through the grey rain.

CHAPTER FOURTEEN

It was like a winter's evening. Except at night, the french windows had not been closed since the end of July and now it was August twenty third. Tonight they were not only closed, but the long velvet curtains were drawn across them.

'I thought of lighting a coal fire,' said Dora who had switched on one bar of the electric heater.

'You've got quite enough to do without that.' Child-minding, Wexford thought, cooking meals for five instead of two. 'Where's Sylvia gone?' he snapped.

'To see Neil, I think. She said something earlier about presenting him with a final ultimatum.'

Wexford made an impatient gesture. He began to walk about the room, then sat down again because pacing can only provoke irritation in one's companion. Dora said:

'What is it, darling? I hate to see you like this.'

He shrugged. 'I ought to rise above it. There's a story told about St Ignatius of Loyola. Someone asked him what he would do if the Pope decided to dissolve the Society of Jesus on the morrow, and he said, "Ten minutes at my orisons and it would be all the same to me." I wish I could be like that.'

She smiled. 'I won't ask you if you want to talk about it.'

'Wouldn't do any good. I've talked about it to the point of exhaustion – the Comfrey case, that is. As for Sylvia, is there anything we haven't said? I suppose there'll be a divorce and she'll live here with the boys. I told her this was her home and of course I meant it. I read somewhere the other day that one in three marriages now come to grief, and hers is going to be one of them. That's all. It just doesn't make me feel very happy.'

The phone rang, and with a sigh Dora got up to answer it.

'I'll get it,' Wexford said, almost pouncing on the receiver. The voice of Dora's sister calling from Wales as she mostly did on a mid-week evening. He said, yes, there had been a storm and, yes, it was still raining, and then he handed the phone to Dora, deflated. Two weeks before, just a bit earlier than this, he had received the call that told him of the discovery of Rhoda Comfrey's body. He had been confident then, full of hope, it had seemed simple.

Through layers of irrelevant facts, information about people he would never see again and whom he need not have troubled to question, through a mind-clogging jumble of trivia, a gaunt harsh face looked up at him out of his memory, the eyes still holding that indefinable expression. She had been fifty and ugly and shapeless and ill-dressed, but someone had killed her from passion and in revenge. Some man who loved her had believed her to be coming here to meet another man. It was inconceivable but it must be so. Stabbing in those circumstances is always a crime of passion, the culmination of a jealousy or a rage or an anguish that suddenly explodes. No one kills in that way because he expects to inherit by his victim's death, or thereby to achieve some other practical advantage . . .

'They had the storm in Pembroke this morning,' said Dora, coming back.

'Fantastic,' said her husband, and then quickly, 'Sorry, I shouldn't snipe at you. Is there anything on the television?'

She consulted the paper. 'I think I know your tastes by now. If I suggested any of this lot I might get that vase chucked at me. Why don't you read something?'

'What is there?'

'Library books. Sylvia's and mine. They're all down there by your chair.'

He humped the stack of them on to his lap. It was easy to sort out which were Sylvia's. Apart from *Woman and the Sexist Plot*, there was Simone de Beauvoir's *The Second Sex* and Mary Wollstonecraft's *A Vindication of the Rights of Woman*.

Dora's were a detective story, a biography of Marie Antoinette and Grenville West's *Apes in Hell*. His reaction was to repudiate this last, for it reminded him too forcibly of his first mistake. Women's Lib as seen through the eyes of Shelley's mother-in-law would almost have been preferable. But that sort of behaviour was what Burden called hysterical.

'What's this like?'

'Not bad,' said Dora. 'I'm sure it's very well researched. As far as I'm concerned, the title's way-out, quite meaningless.'

'It probably refers to an idea the Elizabethans had about unmarried women. According to them, they were destined to lead apes in hell.'

'How very odd. You'd better read it. It's based on some play called *The Maid's Tragedy*.'

But Wexford, having looked at the portrait of its author, pipe in mouth, on the back of the jacket, turned to Marie Antoinette. For the next hour he tried to concentrate on the childhood and youth of the doomed Queen of France, but it was too real for him, too factual. These events had taken place, they were history. What he needed tonight was total escape. A detective story, however bizarre, however removed from the actualities of detection, was the last thing to give it to him. By the time Dora had brought in the tray with the coffee things, he had again picked up *Apes in Hell*.

Grenville West's biography was no longer of interest to him, but he was one of those people who, before reading a novel, like to acquaint themselves with that short summary of the plot publishers generally display on the front flap of the jacket and sometimes in the preliminary pages. After all, if this précis presents too awful an augury one need read no further. But in this instance the jacket flap had been obscured by the library's own covering of the book, so he turned the first few pages.

Apparently, it was West's third novel, having been preceded by *Her Grace of Amalfi* and *Arden's Wife*. The plot summary informed him that the author's source had been Beaumont and Fletcher's *The Maid's Tragedy*, a Jacobean drama set in classical Rhodes. West, however, had shifted the setting to the England of his favourite half-timbering and knot gardens, and with an author's omnipotent conjuring trick – his publisher's panegyric, this – had transformed kings and princes into a seventeenth-century aristocracy. Not a bad idea, Wexford thought, and one which Beaumont and Fletcher might themselves have latched on to if writing about one's contemporaries and fellow nationals had been more in favour at the time.

Might as well see what it was like. He turned the page, and his fingers rested on the open pages, his breath held. Then he gave a gasp.

'What on earth is it?' said Dora.

He made her no answer. He was looking at two lines of type in italics on an otherwise blank sheet. The dedication.

For Rhoda Comfrey, without whom this book could never have been written.

CHAPTER FIFTEEN

'Our first red herring,' Burden said.

'Only it wasn't a red herring. If this isn't proof West knew her I don't know what would be. He's known her for years, Mike. This book was published ten years ago.'

It was a cool clean day. The rain had washed roofs and pavements and had left behind it a thin mist, and the thermometer on Wexford's wall recorded a sane and satisfactory sixty-five degrees. Burden was back to a normal-weight suit. He stood by the window, closed against the mist, examining *Apes in Hell* with a severe and censorious expression.

'What a load of rubbish,' was his verdict. He had read the plot summary. 'Ten years ago, yes,' he said. 'That Hampton guy, his publisher, why didn't he tell you West had dedicated a book to this woman?'

'Maybe he'd forgotten or he'd never known. I don't know anything about publishing, Mike. They call Hampton West's editor, but for all I know an editor may never see a writer's dedication. In any case, I refuse to believe that a perfectly respectable and no doubt disinterested man like Hampton was involved in a plot to conceal from me West's friendship with Rhoda Comfrey. And the same goes for his literary agent and for Vivian and Polly Flinders. They simply didn't know about the dedication.'

'It's a funny thing about the wallet, isn't it?' said Burden after a pause. 'He must have given it to her. The alternative is inconceivable.'

'The alternative being that he lost it and it was found by chance and deliberately kept by a friend of his? That's impossible, but there's a possibility between those two alternatives, that he left it behind in her house or flat or wherever she lived and she, knowing he was to be away for a month, just kept it for him.'

'And *used* it? I don't think much of that idea. Besides, those two girls told you he lost it, and that he asked this Polly to report the loss to the police.'

'Are they both lying then?' said Wexford. 'Why should they lie?'

Burden didn't answer him. 'You'll have him fetched back now, of course.'

'I shall try. I've already had a word with the French police. Commissaire Laquin in Marseilles. We worked together on a case once, if you remember. He's a nice chap.'

'I'd like to have heard that conversation.'

Wexford said rather coldly, 'He speaks excellent English. If West's in the South of France he'll find him. It shouldn't be too difficult even if he's moving from one hotel to another. He must be producing his passport wherever he goes.'

Burden rubbed his chin, gave Wexford the sidelong look that presages a daring or even outrageous suggestion. 'Pity we can't get into West's flat.'

'Are you insane? D'you want to see me back on the beat or in the sort of employment Malina Patel marked out for me? Christ, Mike, I can just see us rifling through West's papers and have him come walking in in the middle of it.'

'OK, OK. You're getting this Laquin to send West home? Suppose he won't come? He may think it a bit thin, fetching him back from his holiday merely because he knew someone who got herself murdered.'

'Laquin will ask him to accompany him to a police station and then he'll phone me so that I can speak to West. That'll be a start. If West can give me Rhoda Comfrey's London address he may not need to come home. We'll see. We can't take any steps to enforce his return, Mike. As far as we know, he's committed no offence and it's quite possible he hasn't seen an English newspaper since he left this country. It's more than likely, if he's that much of a francophile.'

Given to *non sequiturs* this morning, Burden said, 'Why couldn't this book have been written without her?'

'It only means she helped him in some way. Did some research for him, I daresay, which may mean she worked in a library. One thing, this dedication seems to show West had no intention of concealing their friendship.'

'Let's hope not. So you're going to glue yourself to this phone for the next few days, are you?'

'No,' Wexford retorted. 'You are. I've got other things to do.'

The first should have been to question those girls, but that would have to wait until they were both home in the evening. The second perhaps to visit Silk and Whitebeam in Jermyn Street and discover in detail the circumstances of the purchase of that wallet. And yet wouldn't all be made plain when West was found? Wexford had a feeling – what anathema that would have been to the Chief Constable – that West was not going to be easily found.

He sent Loring back to the leather shop and Bryant to inquiring of every library in London as to whether any female member of their staff had not returned to work after a holiday as she should have done. Then he took himself to Forest Road.

Young Mrs Parker with a baby on her hip and old Mrs Parker with a potato peeler in her hand looked at *Apes in Hell* not so much as if it were an historical novel as any hysterical novelty. Babies and beans might be all in the day's work to them. Books were not.

'A friend of Miss Comfrey's?' said Stella Parker at last. It seemed beyond her comprehension that anyone she knew or had known could also be acquainted with the famous. Grenville West was famous in her eyes simply because he had his name in print and had written things which got into print. She repeated what she had said, this time without the interrogative note, accepting the incredible just as she accepted nuclear fission or the fact that potatoes now cost fifteen pence a pound. 'A friend of Miss Comfrey's. Well!'

Her grandmother-in-law was less easily surprised. 'Rhoda was a go-getter. I shouldn't wonder if she'd known the Prime Minister.'

'But do you know for a fact that she was a friend of Grenville West's?'

'Speak up.'

'He wants to know,' said Stella Parker, 'if you know if she knew him, Nanna.'

'Me? How should I know. The only West I ever come across was that Lilian.'

Wexford bent over her. 'Mrs Crown?'

'That's right. Her first husband's name was West. She was Mrs West when she first come here to live with Agnes. And poor little John, he was called West too, of course he was. I thought I told you that, young man, when we was talking about names that time.'

'I didn't ask you,' said Wexford.

West is a common name. So he thought as he waited in the car for Lilian Crown to come home from the pub. But if Grenville West should turn out to be some connection by marriage of Rhoda Comfrey's how much more feasible would any acquaintance between them be. If, for instance, they called each other cousin as many people do with no true blood tie to justify it. Their meeting, their casual affection, would then be explained. And might she not have called herself West, preferring this common though euphonious name over the rarer Comfrey?

Lilian Crown arrived home on the arm of an elderly man whom she did not attempt to introduce to Wexford. They were neither of them drunk, that is to say unsteady on their feet or slurred in their speech, but each reeked of liquor, Lilian Crown of spirits and the old man of strong ale. There was even a dampish look about them, due no doubt to the humid weather, but suggesting rather that they had been dipped into vats of their favourite tipple.

Mrs Crown evidently wanted her friend to accompany her and Wexford into the house, but he refused with awed prot-estations and frenetic wobblings of his head. Her thin shoulders went up and she made a monkey face at him.

'OK, be like that.' She didn't say good-bye to him but marched into the house, leaving Wexford to follow her. He found her already seated on the food-stained sofa, tearing open a fresh packet of cigarettes.

'What is it this time?'

He knew he was being over-sensitive with this woman, who was herself totally insensitive. But it was difficult for him, even at his age and after his experiences, to imagine a woman whose only child was a cripple and an idiot not to have had her whole life blighted by her misfortune. And although he sensed that she might answer any question he asked her about her son with indifference, he still hoped to avoid asking her. Perhaps it was for himself and not for her that he felt this way, perhaps he was, even now, vulnerable to man's or woman's, inhumanity.

'You were Mrs West, I believe,' he said, 'before you married for the second time?'

'That's right. Ron – Mr West, that is – got himself killed at Dunkirk.' She put it in such a way as to imply that her first husband had deliberately placed himself as the target for a German machine-gun or aircraft. 'What's that got to do with Rhoda?'

'I'll explain that in a moment, if you don't mind. Mr West had relatives, I suppose?'

'Of course he did. His mum didn't find him under a gooseberry bush. Two brothers and a sister he had.'

'Mrs Crown, I have good reason to be interested in anyone connected with your late niece who bears the name of West. Did these people have children? Do you know where they are

663

now?' Would she, when she hadn't known the address of her own niece? But very likely they had no reason to be secretive.

'Ethel, the sister, she never spoke a word to me after I married Ron. Gave herself a lot of mighty fine airs, for all her dad was only a farm labourer. Married a Mr Murdoch, poor devil, and I reckon they'd both be over eighty now if they're not dead. The brothers was Len and Sidney, but Sidney got killed in the war like Ron. Len was all right, I got on OK with Len.' Mrs Crown said this wonderingly, as if she had surprised herself by admitting that she got on with anyone connected to her by blood or by marriage. 'Him and his wife, they still send me Christmas cards.'

'Have they any children?'

Mrs Crown lit another cigarette from the stub of the last, and Wexford got a blast of smoke in his face. 'Not to say *children*. They'll be in their late thirties by now. Leslie and Charley, they're called.' The favour in which she held the parents did not apparently extend to their sons. 'I got an invite to Leslie's wedding, but he treated me like dirt, acted like he didn't know who I was. Don't know if Charley's married, wouldn't be bothered to ask. He's a teacher, fancies himself a cut above his people, I can tell you.'

'So as far as you know there isn't a *Grenville* West among them?'

Like Mrs Parker, Lilian Crown had evidently set him down as stupid. They were both the sort of people who assume authority, any sort of authority, to be omniscient, to know all sorts of private and obscure details of their own families and concerns as well as they know them themselves. This authority did not, and therefore this authority must be stupid. Mrs Crown cast up her eyes.

'Of course there is. They're all called Grenville, aren't they? It's like a family name, though what right a farm labourer thinks he's got giving his boys a fancy handle like that I never will know.'

'Mrs Crown,' said Wexford, his head swimming, 'what do you mean, they're all called Grenville?'

She reeled it off rapidly, a list of names. 'Ronald Grenville West, Leonard Grenville West, Sidney Grenville West, Leslie Grenville West, Charles Grenville West.'

'And these people,' he said, half-stunned by it, 'your niece Rhoda knew them?'

'May have come across Leslie and Charley when they was little kids, I daresay. She'd have been a lot older.'

He had written the names down. He looked at what he had written. Addresses now, and Mrs Crown was able, remarkably, to provide them or some of them. The parents lived at Myfleet, a village not far from Kingsmarkham, the son Leslie over the county boundary in Kent. She didn't know the whereabouts of Charley, but his school was in South London, so his father said, which meant he must live down there somewhere, didn't it?

And now he had to ask it, as tactfully as he could. For if every male of the West family . . .

'And that is all?' he said almost timorously. 'There's no one else called Grenville West?'

'Don't think so. Not that I recall.' She fixed him with a hard stare. 'Except my boy, of course, but that wouldn't count, him not being normal. Been in a home for the backward like since he was so high. He's called John Grenville West, for what it's worth.'

CHAPTER SIXTEEN

No word came from Commissaire Laquin that day. But Loring's inquiries were more fruitful, clearing up at last the matter of the wallet.

'Those girls weren't lying,' Wexford said to Burden. 'He did lose a wallet on a bus, but it was his *old* one he lost. That's what he told the assistant at Silk and Whitebeam when he went on Thursday, 4 August, to replace it with a new one.'

'And yet it was the new one we found in the possession of Rhoda Comfrey.'

'Mike, I'm inclined to believe that the old one did turn up and he gave her the new one, maybe on the Saturday when it was too late to tell Polly Flinders. She told him she had reached the age of fifty the day before, and he said OK, have this for a present.'

'You think he was a sort of cousin of hers?'

'I do, though I don't quite see yet how it can help us. All these people on the list have been checked out. Two of them, in any case, are dead. One is in an institution at Myringham, the Abbotts Palmer Hospital. One is seventy-two years old. One had emigrated with his wife to Australia. The last of them, Charles Grenville West, is a teacher, has been married for five years and lives in Carshalton. The father, also John Grenville West, talks of cousins and second cousins who may bear the name, but he's doddery and vague. He can't tell us the whereabouts of any of them. I shall try this Charles.'

Almost the first thing Wexford noticed when he was shown into Charles Grenville West's living room was a shelf of books with familiar titles: *Arden's Wife, Apes in Hell, Her Grace of Amalfi, Fair Wind to Alicante, Killed with Kindness.* They had pride of place in the bookcase and were well cared for. The whole room was well cared for, and the neat little house itself, and smiling, unsuspicious, cooperative Mr and Mrs West.

On the phone he had told Charles West only that he would like to talk to him about the death of a family connection of his, and West had said he had never met Rhoda Comfrey – well, he might have seen her when he was a baby – but Wexford would be welcome to call just the same. And now Wexford, having accepted a glass of beer, having replied to kind inquiries about the long journey he had made, looked again at the books, pointed to them and said:

'Your namesake would appear to be a favourite author of yours.'

West took down *Fair Wind to Alicante*. 'It was the name that first got me reading them,' he said, 'and then I liked them for themselves. I kept wondering if we were related.' He turned to the back of the jacket and the author's photograph. 'I thought I could see a family resemblance, but I expect that was imagination or wishful thinking, because the photo's not very clear, is it? And then there were things in the books, I mean in the ones with an English setting . . .'

'What sort of things?' Wexford spoke rather sharply. His tone wasn't one to give offence, but rather to show Charles West that these questions were relevant to the murder.

'Well, for instance, in *Killed with Kindness* he describes a manor house that's obviously based on Clythorpe Manor near Myringham. The maze is described and the long gallery. I've been in the house, I know it well. My grandmother was in service there before she married.' Charles West smiled. 'My people were all very humble farm workers and the women were all in service, but they'd lived in that part of Sussex for generations, and it did make me wonder if Grenville West was one of us, some sort of cousin, because he seemed to know the countryside so well. I asked my father but he said the family was so huge and with so many ramifications.'

'I wonder you didn't write to Grenville West and ask *him*,' said Wexford.

'Oh, I did. I wrote to him care of his publishers and I got a very nice letter back. Would you like to see it? I've got it somewhere.' He went to the door and called out, 'Darling, d'you think you could find that letter from Grenville West? But he's not a relation,' he said to Wexford. 'You'll see what he says in the letter.'

Mrs West brought it in. The paper was headed with the Elm Green address. 'Dear Mr West,' Wexford read. 'Thank you for your letter. It gives me great pleasure that you have enjoyed my novels, and I hope you will be equally pleased with *Sir Bounteous,* which is to be published next month and which is based on Middleton's *A Mad World, My Masters.*

'This novel also has an English setting or, more precisely, a Sussex setting. I am very attached to your native county and I am sorry to have to tell you that it is not mine, nor can I trace any connection between your ancestry and mine. I was born in London. My father's family came originally from Lancashire and my mother's from the West Country. Grenville was my mother's maiden name.

'So, much as I should have liked to discover some cousins – as an only child of two only children, I have scarcely any living relatives – I must disappoint myself and perhaps you too.

'With best wishes,
'Yours sincerely,
'Grenville West.'

With the exception, of course, of the signature, it was typewritten. Wexford handed it back with a shrug. Whatever the information, or lack of it, had done for the author and for Charles West, it had certainly disappointed him. But there was something odd about it, something he couldn't quite put his finger on. The style was a little pretentious with a whisper of arrogance, and in the calculated leading from paragraph to paragraph, the almost too elegant elision of the professional writer. That wasn't odd, though, that wasn't odd at all . . . He was growing tired of all these hints, these 'feelings', these pluckings at his mind and at the *fingerspitzengefühl* he seemed to have lost. No other case had ever been so full of whispers that led nowhere. He despised himself for not hearing and understanding them, but whatever Griswold might say, he knew they were sound and true.

'A very nice letter,' he said dully. Except, he would have liked to add, that most of it is a carefully spun fabric of lies.

There was one more Grenville West to see, the one who dragged out his life in the Abbotts Palmer Hospital. Wexford tried to picture what that man would be like now, and his mind sickened. Besides, he knew he had only contemplated going there to keep himself away from the police station, away from hearing that Laquin had nothing for him, that Griswold had called in the Yard over his head, for it was getting to the end of the week now, it was Thursday.

That was no attitude for a responsible police officer to take. He went in. The weather was hot and muggy again, and he felt he had gone back a week in time, for there, waiting for him again, was Malina Patel.

An exquisite little hand was placed on his sleeve, limpid eyes looked earnestly up at him. She seemed tinier and more fragile than ever. 'I've brought Polly with me.'

Wexford remembered their previous encounters. The first time he had seen her as a provocative tease, the second as an enchanting fool. But now an uneasiness began to overcome his susceptibility. She gave the impression of trying hard to be good, of acting always on impulse, of a dotty and delightful innocence. But was innocent dottiness compatible with such careful dressing, calculated to stun? Could that sweet guilelessness be natural? He cursed those susceptibilities of his, for they made his voice soft and gallant when he said:

'Have you now? Then where is she?'

'In the loo. She said she felt sick and one of the policemen showed her where the loo was.'

'All right. Someone will show you both up to my office when she's feeling better.'

Burden was there before him. 'It would seem, according to your pal, that the whole of France is now being scoured for our missing author. He hasn't been in Annecy, whatever your little nursery rhyme friend may say.'

'She's on her way up now, perhaps to elucidate.'

The two girls came in. Pauline Flinders' face was greenish from nausea, her lower lip trembling under the ugly prominent teeth. She wore faded frayed jeans and a shirt which looked as if they had been picked out of a crumpled heap on a bedroom floor. Malina too wore jeans, of toffee-brown silk, stitched in white, and a white clinging sweater and gold medallions on a long gold chain.

'I made her come,' said Malina. 'She was in an awful state. I thought she'd been really ill.' And she sat down, having given Burden a shy sidelong smile.

'What is it, Miss Flinders?' Wexford said gently.

'Tell him, Polly. You promised you would. It's silly to come all this way for nothing.'

Polly Flinders lifted her head. She said rapidly, in a monotone, 'I haven't had a card from Grenville. That was last year's. The postmark was smudged and I thought you wouldn't know, and you didn't know.'

The explosion of wrath she perhaps expected didn't come. Wexford merely nodded. 'You also thought I wouldn't know he knew Rhoda Comfrey. But he had known her for years, hadn't he?'

Breathlessly, Polly said, 'She helped him with his books. She was there in his flat a lot. But I don't know where she lived. I never asked, I didn't want to know. About the postcard, I . . .'

'Never mind the postcard. Were you and Miss Comfrey in Mr West's flat on the evening of August fifth?' A nod answered him and a choking sound like a sob. 'And you both overheard her make a phone call from there, saying where she would be on the Monday?'

'Yes, but . . .'

'Tell him the truth, Polly. Tell him everything and it'll be all right.'

'Very well, Miss Patel, I'll do the prompting.' He hadn't taken his eyes from the other girl, and now he said to her, 'Have you any idea of Mr West's present whereabouts? No? I think you told me the lie about the postcard because you were afraid for Mr West, believing him to have had something to do with Miss Comfrey's death.'

She gave him an eager pathetic nod, her hands clenched.

'I don't think we'll talk any more now,' he said. 'I'll come and see you tomorrow evening. That will give you plenty of time to get into a calmer frame of mind.' Malina looked disappointed, less so when he went on, 'I shall want you to give me the name of the man with whom you spent that Monday evening. Will you think about that?'

Again she said yes, a sorrowful and despairing monosyllable, and then Burden took them both away, returning to say, 'Rhoda Comfrey was blackmailing West. I wonder why we didn't think of that before.'

'Because it isn't a very bright idea. I can see how someone might succeed in blackmailing *her*. She had a secret life she genuinely wanted kept secret. But West?'

'West,' said Burden repressively, 'is almost certainly homosexual. Why else reject Polly? Why else mooch about Soho at night? Why hobnob with all those blokes in bars? And why, most of all, have a long-standing friendship with an older woman on a completely platonic basis? That's the sort of thing these queers do. They like to know women, but it's got to be *safe* women, married ones or women much older than they are.'

Wexford wondered why he hadn't thought of that. Once again he had come up against Burden's solid common sense. And hadn't his own 'feelings' also been hinting at it when he read the letter to Charles West?

He jeered mildly just the same. 'So this long-standing friend suddenly takes it into her head to blackmail him, does she? After ten years? Threatens to expose his gay goings-on, I suppose.' He had never liked the word 'queer'. 'Why should he care? It's nothing these days. He probably advertises his – his inversion in *Gay News*.'

'Does he? Then why doesn't your Indian lady friend know about it? Why doesn't his agent or Vivian or Polly? It mightn't do him any good with his readership if ordinary decent people were to find what he gets up to in London at night. It wouldn't with me, I can tell you.'

'Since when have you been one of his readers?'

Burden looked a little shamefaced as he always did when confessing to any even mild intellectual lapse. 'Since yesterday morning,' he admitted. 'Got to do something while I'm being a phone operator, haven't I? I sent Loring out to get me two of them in paperback. I thought they'd be above my head, but they weren't. Quite enjoyable, lively sort of stuff, really, and the last thing you'd feel is that their author's homosexual.'

'But you say he is.'

'And he wants to keep it dark. He's queer but he's still thinking of settling down with Polly – they do that when they get middle-aged – and Rhoda mightn't have liked the idea of only being able to see him with a wife around. So she threatens to spill the beans unless he gives Polly up. And there's your motive.'

'It doesn't account for how he happens to have the same name as a whole tribe of her aunt's relatives.'

'Look,' said Burden, 'your Charles West wrote to him, thinking he might be a cousin. Why shouldn't Rhoda have done the same thing years ago, say after she'd read his first book? Charles West didn't pursue it, but she may have done. That could be the reason for their becoming friends in the first place, and then the friendship was strengthened by Rhoda doing research for him for that book that's dedicated to her. The name is relevant only in that it brought them together.'

'I just hope,' said Wexford, 'that tomorrow will bring West and us together.'

Robin came up and opened the car door for him.

'Thanks very much,' said Wexford. 'You're the new hall porter, are you? I suppose you want a tip.' He handed over the ices he had bought on the way home. 'One for your brother, mind.'

'I'll never be able to do it again,' said Robin.

'Why's that? School starting? You'll still get in before I do.'

'We're going home, Grandad. Daddy's coming for us at seven.'

To the child Wexford couldn't express what he felt. There was only one thing he could say, and in spite of his longing to be alone once more with Dora in peace and quiet and orderliness, it was true. 'I shall miss you.'

'Yes,' said Robin complacently. Happy children set a high valuation on themselves. They expect to be loved and missed. 'And we never saw the water rat.'

'There'll be other times. You're not going to the North Pole.'

The little boy laughed inordinately at that one. Wexford sent him off to find Ben and hand the ice over, and then he let himself into the house. Sylvia was upstairs packing. He put his arm round her shoulder, turned her face towards him.

'Well, my dear, so you and Neil have settled your differences?'

'I don't know about that. Not exactly. Only he's said he'll give me all the support I need in taking a degree if I start next year. And he's – he's bought a dishwasher!' She gave a little half-ashamed laugh. 'But that's not why I'm going back.'

'I think I know why.'

She pulled away from him, turning her head. For all her height and her majestic carriage, there was something shy and gauche about her. 'I can't live without him, Dad,' she said. 'I've missed him dreadfully.'

'That's the only good reason for going back, isn't it?'

'The other thing – well, you can say women are equal to men but you can't give them men's position in the world. Because that's in men's minds and it'll take hundreds of years to change it.' She came out with a word that was unfamiliar to her wellread father. 'One would just have to practise aeonism,' she said.

What had she been reading now? Before he could ask her, the boys came in.

'We could have a last try for the water rat, Grandad.'

'Oh, Robin! Grandad's tired and Daddy's coming for us in an hour.'

'An hour,' said Robin with a six-year-old's view of time, 'is ever so long.'

So they went off together, the three of them, over the hill and across the meadow to the Kingsbrook. It was damp and misty and still, the willows bluish amorphous shadows, every blade of grass glistening with water drops. The river had risen and was flowing fast, the only thing in nature that moved.

'Grandad carry,' said Ben somewhat earlier in the expedition than usual.

But as Wexford bent down to lift him up, something apart from the river moved. A little way to the right of them, in the opposite bank, a pair of bright eyes showed themselves at the mouth of a hole.

'Ssh,' Wexford whispered. 'Keep absolutely still.'

The water rat emerged slowly. It was not at all rat-like but handsome and almost rotund with spiky fur the colour of sealskin and a round alert face. It approached the water with slow stealth but entered it swiftly and began to swim, spreading and stretching its body, towards the bank on the side where they stood. And when it reached the bank it paused and looked straight at them seemingly without fear, before scurrying off into the thick green rushes.

Robin waited until it had disappeared. Then he danced up and down with delight. 'We saw the water rat! We saw the water rat!'

'Ben wants to see Daddy! Ben want to go home! Poor Ben's feet are cold!'

'Aren't you pleased we saw the water rat, Grandad?'

'Very pleased,' said Wexford, wishing that his own quest might come to so simple and satisfying an end.

CHAPTER SEVENTEEN

Grenville West's elusiveness could no longer be put down to chance. He was on the run and no doubt had been for nearly three weeks now. Everything pointed to his being the killer of Rhoda Comfrey, and by Friday morning Wexford saw that the case had grown too big for him, beyond the reach of his net. Far from hoping to dissuade the Chief Constable from carrying out his threat, he saw the inevitability of calling in Scotland Yard and also the resources of Interpol. But his call to the Chief Constable left him feeling a little flat, and the harsh voice of Michael Baker, phoning from Kenbourne Vale, made him realize only that now he must begin confessing failure.

Baker asked him how he was, referred to their 'red faces' over the Farriner business, then said:

'I don't suppose you're still interested in that chap Grenville West, are you?'

To Wexford it had seemed as if the whole world must be hunting for him, and yet here was Baker speaking as if the man were still a red herring, incongruously trailed across some enormously more significant scent.

'Am I still interested! Why?'

'Ah,' said Baker. 'Better come up to the Smoke then. It'd take too long to go into details on the phone, but the gist is that West's car's been found in an hotel garage not far from here, and West left the hotel last Monday fortnight without paying his bill.'

Wexford didn't need to ask any more now. He remembered to express effusive gratitude, and within not much more than an hour he was sitting opposite Baker at Kenbourne Vale

Police Station, Stevens having recovered from his flu or perhaps only his antipathy to London traffic.

'I'll give you a broad outline,' said Baker, 'and then we'll go over to the Trieste Hotel and see the manager. We got a call from him this morning and I sent Clements up there. West checked in on the evening of Sunday, August seventh, and parked his car, a red Citroën, in one of the hotel's lock-up garages. When he didn't appear to pay his bill on Wednesday morning, a chambermaid told Hetherington – that's the manager – that his bed hadn't been slept in for two nights.'

'Didn't he do anything about it?' Wexford put in.

'Not then. He says he knew who West was, had his address and had no reason to distrust him. Besides, he'd left a suitcase with clothes in it in his room and his car in the garage. But when it got to the end of the week he phoned West's home, and getting no reply sent someone round to Elm Green. You can go on from there, Sergeant, you talked to the man.'

Clements, who had come in while Baker was speaking, greeted Wexford with a funny little half-bow. 'Well, sir, this Hetherington, who's a real smoothie but not, I reckon, up to anything he shouldn't be, found out from the girl in that wine bar place where West was, and he wasn't too pleased. But he calculated West would write to him from France.'

'Which didn't happen?'

'No, sir. Hetherington didn't hear a word and he got to feeling pretty sore about it. Then, he says, it struck him the girl had said a motoring holiday, which seemed fishy since West's car was still at the Trieste. Also West had gone off with his room key and hadn't left an ignition key with the hotel. Hetherington began to feel a bit worried, said he suspected foul play, though he didn't get on to us. Instead he went through West's case and found an address book. He got the phone numbers of West's publishers and his agent and Miss Flinders and he phoned them all. None of them could help him, they all said West was in France, so this morning, at long last, he phoned us.'

They were driven up to North Kenbourne, round Montfort Circus and down a long street of lofty houses. Wexford noted that Undine Road was within easy walking distance of Parish Oak tube station, and not far therefore from Princevale Road and Dr Lomond's surgery. Formerly the Trieste Hotel had been a gigantic family house, but its balconies and turrets and jutting gables had been masked with new brickwork or weather-boarding, and its windows enlarged and glazed with plain glass. Mr Hetherington also seemed to have been smoothed out, his sleek fair hair, pink china skin and creaseless suit. He presented as spruce an appearance compared with the four policemen as his hotel did with its neighbours. His careful grooming reminded Wexford of Burden's fastidiousness, though the inspector never quite had the look of having been sprayed all over with satin-finish lacquer.

He took them into his office, a luxurious place that opened off a white-carpeted, redwood panelled hallway in which very large houseplants stood about on Corinthian columns.

Neither Baker nor Clements were the sort of men to go in for specious courtesies or obsequious apology. In his rough way, Baker said, 'You'll have to tell the whole story again, sir. We're taking a serious view.'

'My pleasure.' Hetherington flashed a smile that bore witness to his daily use of dental floss, and held it steadily as if for unseen cameras. 'I'm feeling considerable concern about Mr West myself. I feel convinced something dreadful has happened. Do please sit down.' He eyed Wexford's raincoat uncertainly, ushered him away from the white upholstered chair in which he had been about to sit, and into a duncol-oured one. He said, 'You'll be more comfortable there, I think,' as to a caller of low social status directed to the servants' entrance. 'Now where shall I begin?'

'At the beginning,' said Wexford with perfect gravity. 'Go on to the end and then stop.'

This time he got an even more uncertain look. 'The beginning,' said Hetherington, 'would be on the Saturday, Saturday the sixth. Mr West telephoned and asked if he could have a room for three nights, the Sunday, Monday and Tuesday. Naturally, that would usually be an impossible request in August, but it so happened that a very charming lady from Minneapolis who stays with us regularly every year had cancelled on account of...' He caught Wexford's eye, stern censor of snobbish digression. 'Yes, well, as I say, it happened to be possible and I told Mr West he could have Mrs Gruber's room. He arrived at seven on the Sunday and signed the register. I have it here.'

Wexford and Baker looked at it. It was signed 'Grenville West' and the Elm Green address was given. Certain that the manager was incapable of obeying his injunction, Wexford said:

'He had been here before, I think?'

'Oh, yes, once before.'

'Mr Hetherington, weren't you surprised that a man who lived within what is almost walking distance of the hotel should want to stay here?'

'Surprised?' said Hetherington. 'Certainly not. Why should I be? What business was it of mine? I shouldn't be *surprised* if a gentleman who lived next door wanted to stay in the hotel.'

He took the register away from them. While his back was turned Clements murmured with kindly indulgence, 'It happens a lot, sir. Men have tiffs with their wives or forget their keys.'

Maybe, Wexford thought, but in those cases they don't book their night's refuge some fifteen hours in advance. Even if the others didn't find it odd, he did. He asked Hetherington if West had brought much luggage.

'A suitcase. He may have had a handbag as well.' Although Hetherington was strictly correct in employing this word, the rather quaint usage made Wexford want to repeat, in Lady Bracknell's outraged echo, '*A handbag?*' But he only raised his eyebrows, and Hetherington said, 'He asked if he could garage his car – he didn't want to leave it on the hardtop parking – so I let him have number five which happened to be vacant. He put the car away himself.' There was a small hesitation. 'As a matter of fact, it was a little odd now I come to think of it. I offered to get the car garaged for him and asked for his key, but he insisted on doing it himself.'

'When did you last see him?' Baker asked.

'I never saw him again. He ordered breakfast in his room on the Monday morning. No one seemed to have seen him go out. I expected him to vacate his room by noon on Wednesday but he didn't appear to pay his bill.' Hetherington paused, then went on to tell the story broadly as Wexford had heard it from Clements. When he had finished Wexford asked him what had become of West's room key.

'Heaven knows. We do stress that our guests hand in their keys at reception when they go out, we make them too heavy to be comfortably carried in a pocket, but it's of no avail. They will take them out with them. We lose hundreds. I have his suitcase here. No doubt you will wish to examine the contents.'

For some moments Wexford had been regarding a suitcase which, standing under Hetherington's desk, he had guessed to be the luggage West had left behind him. It was of brown leather, not new but of good quality and stamped inside the lid with the name and crest of Silk and Whitebeam, Jermyn Street. Baker opened it. Inside were a pair of brown whipcord slacks, a yellow roll-neck shirt, a stone-coloured lightweight pullover, a pair of white underpants, brown socks and leather sandals.

'Those were the clothes he arrived in,' said Hetherington, his concern for West temporarily displaced by distaste for anyone who would wear trousers with a shiny seat and a pullover with a frayed cuff.

'How about this address book?' said Baker.

'Here.'

The entries of names, addresses and phone numbers were sparse. Field and Bray, Literary Agents; Mrs Brenda Nunn's personal address and phone number; several numbers and extensions for West's publishers; Vivian's Vineyard; Polly Flinders; Kenbourne Town Hall; a number for emergency calls to the North Thames Gas Board; London Electricity; the London Library and Kenbourne Public Library, High Road Branch; some French names and numbers and places – and Crown, Lilian, with the Kingsmarkham telephone number of Rhoda Comfrey's aunt.

Wexford said, 'Where's the car now?'

'Still in number five garage. I couldn't move it, could I? I hadn't the means.'

I wonder if I have, thought Wexford. They trooped out to the row of garages. The red Citroën looked as if it had been well maintained and it was immaculately polished. The licence plates showed that it was three years old. The doors were locked and so was the boot.

'We'll get that open,' Baker said. 'Should have a key to fit, or we'll get one. It won't take long.'

Wexford felt through the jangling mass in his pocket. Two keys marked with a double chevron. 'Try these,' he said.

The keys fitted.

There was nothing inside the car but a neat stack of maps of Western Europe on the dashboard shelf. The contents of the boot were more rewarding. Two more brown leather suitcases, larger than the one West had left in his room, and labelled 'Grenville West, Hotel Casimir, Rue Victor Hugo, Paris'. Both were locked, but the opening of suitcases is child's play.

'To hell with warrants,' Wexford said out of range of Hetherington's hearing. 'Can we have these taken back to the nick?'

'Surely,' said Baker, and to Hetherington in the grating tones of admonition that made him unpopular with the public and colleagues alike, 'You've wasted our time and the tax-payers' money by delaying like this. Frankly, you haven't a hope in hell of getting that bill paid.'

Loring drove the car back with Baker beside him, while Wexford went with Clements. A lunchtime traffic jam held the police car up, Clements taking this opportunity during a lull in events to expound on lack of public cooperation, laxity that amounted to obstruction, and Hetherington's hair which he averred had been bleached. At last Wexford managed to get him off this – anyone whose conversation consists in continual denunciation is wearying to listen to – and on to James and Angela. By the time they got to the police station both cases had been opened and were displayed in the centre of the floor of Baker's drab and gloomy sanctum.

The cases were full of clothes, some of which had evidently been bought new for West's holiday. In a leather bag was a battery-operated electric shaver, a tube of suntan cream and an aerosol of insect repellant, but no toothbrush, toothpaste, soap, sponge or flannel, cologne or after-shave.

'If he's a homosexual,' said Wexford, 'these are rather odd omissions. I should have expected a fastidious interest in his personal appearance. Doesn't he even clean his teeth?'

'Maybe he's got false ones.'

'Which he scrubs at night with the hotel nailbrush and the hotel soap?'

Baker had brought to light a large brown envelope, sealed. 'Ah, the documents.' But there was something else inside apart from papers. Carefully, Baker slit the envelope open and pulled out a key to which was attached a heavy wood and metal tag, the metal part engraved with the name of the Trieste Hotel and the number of the room West had occupied for one night.

'How about this?' said Baker. 'He isn't in France, he never left the country.'

What he handed to Wexford was a British passport, issued according to its cover to Mr J.G. West.

CHAPTER EIGHTEEN

Wexford opened the passport at page one.

The name of the bearer was given as Mr John Grenville West and his national status as that of a citizen of the United Kingdom and Colonies. Page two gave West's profession as a novelist, his place of birth as Myringham, Sussex, his date of birth 9 September 1940, his country of residence as the United Kingdom, his height as five feet nine, and the colour of his eyes as grey. In the space allotted to the bearer's usual signature, he had signed it 'Grenville West'.

The photograph facing this description was a typical passport photograph and showed an apparent lunatic or psychopath with a lock of dark hair grimly falling to meet a pair of black-framed glasses. At the time it was taken West had sported a moustache.

Page four told Wexford that the passport had been issued five years before in London, and on half a dozen of the subsequent pages were stamps showing entries to and exists from France, Belgium, Holland, Germany, Italy, Turkey and the United States, and there was also a visa for the United States. West, he noted, had left the country at least twelve times in those five years.

'He meant to go this time,' said Baker. 'Why didn't he go? And where is he?'

Wexford didn't answer him. He said to Loring:

'I want you to go now, as fast as you can make it, to the Registry of Births and look this chap West up. You get the volume for the year 1940, then the section with September in, then all the Wests. Have you got that? There'll be a lot of them but it's unlikely there'll be more than one John Grenville West born on 9 September. I want his mother's name and his father's.'

Loring went. Baker was going through the remaining contents of the envelope. 'A cheque-book,' he said, 'a Eurocard and an American Express card, travellers' cheques signed by West, roughly a thousand francs. . . . He meant to come back for this lot all right, Reg.'

'Of course he did. There's a camera here under some of these clothes, nice little Pentax.' Suddenly Wexford wished Burden were with him. He had reached one of those points in a case when, to clear his mind and dispel some of this frustration, he needed Burden and only Burden. For rough argument with no punches pulled, for a free exchange of insults with no offence taken if such words as 'hysterical' or 'prudish' were hurled in the heat of the moment. Baker was a very inadequate substitute. Wexford wondered how he would react to some high-flown quotation, let alone to being called a pain in the arse. But needs must when the devil drives. Choosing his words carefully, toning down his personality, he outlined to Baker Burden's theory.

'Hardly germane to this inquiry,' said Baker, and Wexford's mind went back years to when he and the inspector had first met and when he had used those very words. 'All this motive business. Never mind motive. Never mind whether West was this Comfrey woman's second cousin or, for that matter, her grandmother's brother-in-law.' A bigtoothed laugh at this witticism. 'It's all irrelevant. If I may say so, Reg –' Like all who take offence easily, Baker never minded giving offence to others or even noticed he was giving it '– if I may say so, you prefer the trees to the wood. Ought to have been one of these novelist chappies yourself. Plain facts aren't your cup of tea at all.'

Wexford took the insult – for it is highly insulting to be told that one would be better at some profession other than that which one has practised for forty years – without a word. He chuckled to himself at Baker's mixed metaphors, sylvan and refective. Was refective the word? Did it mean what he thought it did, pertaining to mealtimes? There was another word he had meant to look up. It was there, but not quite there, on the tip of his tongue, the edge of his memory. He needed a big dictionary, not that potty little *Concise Oxford* which, in any case, Sheila had appropriated long ago . . .

'Plain facts, Reg,' Baker was saying. 'The principal plain fact is that West scarpered on the day your Comfrey got killed. I call that evidence of guilt. He meant to come back to the Trieste and slip off to France but something happened to scare him off.'

'Like what?'

'Like being seen by someone where he shouldn't have been. That's like what. That's obvious. Look at that passport. West wasn't born in London, he was born somewhere down in your neck of the woods. There'll be those around who'll know him, recognize him.' Baker spoke as if the whole of Sussex were a small rural spot, his last sentence having a *Wind in the Willows* flavour about it as if West had been the Mole and subject to the scrutiny of many bright eyes peering from the boles of trees. 'That's where these second cousins and grandmother's whatsits come in. One of them saw him, so off into hiding he went.'

'Under the protection, presumably, of another of them?'

'Could be,' said Baker seriously. 'But we might just as well stop speculating and go get us a spot of lunch. You can't do any more. I can't do any more. You can't find him. I can't find him. We leave him and his gear to the Yard, and that's that. Now how about a snack at the Hospital Arms?'

'Would you mind if we went to Vivian's Vineyard instead, Michael?'

With some casting up of eyes and pursing of lips, Baker agreed. His expression was that of a man who allows a friend with an addiction one last drink or cigarette. So on the way to Elm Green Wexford was obliged to argue it out with himself. It seemed apparent that West had booked into the

Trieste to establish an alibi, but it was a poor sort of alibi since he had signed the register in his own name. Baker would have said that all criminals are fools. Wexford knew this was often not so, and especially not so in the case of the author of books praised by critics for their historical accuracy, their breadth of vision and their fidelity to their models. He had not meant to kill her, this was no premeditated crime. On the face of it, the booking into the Trieste looked like an attempt at establishing an alibi, but it was not. For some other purpose West had stayed there. For some other reason he had gone to Kingsmarkham. How had his car keys come into Rhoda Comfrey's possession? And who was he? Who was he? Baker called that irrelevant, yet Wexford knew now the whole case and its final solution hung upon it, upon West's true identity and his lineage.

It was true that he couldn't see the wood for the trees, but not that he preferred the latter. Here the trees would only coalesce into a wood when he could have each one before him individually and then, at last, fuse them. He walked in a whispering forest, little voices speaking to him on all sides, hinting and pleading – 'Don't you see now? Can't you put together what he has said and she has said and what I am saying?'

Wexford shook himself. He wasn't in a whispering wood but crossing Elm Green where the trees had all been cut down, and Baker was regarding him as if he had read in a medical journal that staring fixedly at nothing, as Wexford had been doing, may symptomize a condition akin to epilepsy.

'You OK, Reg?'

'Fine,' said Wexford with a sigh, and they went into the brown murk of Vivian's Vineyard. The girl with the pale brown face sat on a high stool behind the bar, swinging long brown legs, chatting desultorily to three young men in what was probably blue denim, though in here it too looked brown. The whole scene might have been a sepia photograph.

Baker had given their order when Victor Vivian appeared from the back with a wine bottle in each hand.

'Hallo, hallo, hallo!' He came over to their table and sat down in the vacant chair. Today the tee-shirt he wore was printed all over with a map of the vineyards of France, the area where his heart was being covered by Burgundy and the Auvergne.

'What's happened to old Gren, then? I didn't know a thing about it, you know, till Rita here gave me the low-down. I mean, told me there was this hotel chap after him in a real tizz, you know.'

Baker wouldn't have replied to this but Wexford did. 'Mr West didn't go to France,' he said. 'He's still in this country. Have you any idea where he might go?'

Vivian whistled. He whistled like the captain of the team in the *Boy's Own Paper*. 'I say! Correct me if I'm wrong, you know, but I'm getting your drift. I mean, it's serious, isn't it? I mean, I wasn't born yesterday.'

From a physical point of view this was apparent, though less so from Vivian's mental capacity. Not for the first time Wexford wondered how a man of West's education and intelligence could have borne to spend more than two minutes in this company unless he had been obliged to. What had West seen in him? What had he seen, for that matter, in Polly Flinders, dowdy and desperate, or in the unprepossessing, graceless Rhoda Comfrey?

'You reckon old Gren's on the run?'

The girl put two salads, a basket of rolls and two glasses of wine in front of them. Wexford said, 'You told me Mr West came here fourteen years ago. Where did he come from?'

'Couldn't tell you that, you know. I mean, I didn't come here myself till a matter of five years back. Gren was here. *In situ*, I mean.'

'You never talked about the past? About his early life?'

Vivian shook his head, his beard waggling. 'I'm not one

to push myself in where I'm not wanted, you know. Gren never talked about any family. I mean, he may have said he'd lost his parents, I think he did say that, you know, I think so.'

'He never told you where he'd been born?'

Baker was looking impatient. If it is possible to eat ham and tomatoes with an exasperated air, he was doing so. And he maintained a total disapproving silence.

Vivian said vaguely, 'People don't, you know. I mean, I reckon Rita here was born in Jamaica, but I don't know, you know. I don't go about telling people where I was born. Gren may have been born in France, you know, France wouldn't surprise me.' He banged his chest. 'Old Gren brought me this tee-shirt back from his last hols, you know. Always a thoughtful sort of chap. I mean, I don't like to think of him in trouble, I don't at all.'

'Did you see him leave for this holiday of his? I mean . . .' How easy it was to pick up the habit! 'When he left here on Sunday, the seventh?'

'Sure I did. He popped in the bar. About half-six it was, you know. "I'm just off, Vic," he says. He wouldn't have a drink, you know, on account of having a long drive ahead of him. I mean, his car was parked out here in the street, you know, and I went out and saw him off. "Back on September fourth," he says, and I remember I thought to myself, his birthday's round about then, I thought, eighth or the ninth, you know, and I thought I'd look that up and check and have a bottle of champers for him.'

'Can you also remember what he was wearing?'

'Gren's not a snappy dresser, you know. I mean, he went in for those roll-neck jobs, seemed to like them, never a collar and tie if he could get away with it. His old yellow one, that's what he was wearing, you know, and a sweater and kind of dark-coloured trousers. Never one for the gear like me, you know. I'd have sworn he went to France, I mean I'd have taken my oath on it. This is beyond me, frankly, you know.

I'm lost. When I think he called out to me, "I'll be in Paris by midnight, Vic," in that funny high voice of his, and he never went there at all – well, I go cold all over, you know. I mean, I don't know what to think.'

Baker could stand no more. Abruptly he said, 'We'll have the bill, please.'

'Sure, yes, right away. Rita! When he turns up – well, if there's anything I can do, you know, any sort of help I can give, you can take that as read, you know. I mean, this has knocked me sideways.'

It was evident that Baker thought the representatives of the Mid-Sussex Constabulary would return to their rural burrow almost at once. He had even looked up the time of a suitable train from Victoria and offered a car to take them there. Wexford hardened himself to hints – there were so many other hints he would have softened to if he had known how – and marched boldly back into the police station where Loring sat patiently waiting for him.

'Well?'

'Well, sir, I've found him.' Loring referred to his notes. 'The birth was registered at Myringham. In the county,' he said earnestly, 'of Sussex. 9 September 1940. John Grenville West. His father's name is given as Ronald Grenville West and his mother's name as Lilian West, born Crawford.'

CHAPTER NINETEEN

Little John. Sweet affectionate little love, the way them mongols are ... Mrs Parker's voice was among the whisperers. He could hear it clearly in the receiver of his mind, and hear too Lilian Crown's, brash and tough and uncaring. Been in a home for the backward like since he was so high ...

'I looked up the parents too, sir, just to be on the safe side. Ronald West's parents were John Grenville West and Mary Ann West, and Ronald's birth was also registered in Myringham in 1914. The mother, Lilian West, was the daughter of William and Agnes Crawford, and her birth was registered in Canterbury in 1917. Ronald and Lilian West were married in Myringham in 1937.'

'You're sure there's no other John Grenville West born on that date and registered at Myringham?'

How could there be? Such a coincidence would evince the supernatural.

'Quite sure, sir,' said Loring.

'I know who this man is. He's mentally retarded. He's been in an institution for the greater part of his life.' Wexford was uncertain whom he was addressing. Not Baker or Loring or the baffled Clements. Perhaps only himself. 'It can't be!' he said.

'It is, sir,' said Loring, not following, anxious only that his thoroughness should not be questioned.

Wexford turned from him and buried his face in his hands. Burden would have called this hysterical or maybe just melodramatic. For Wexford, at this moment, it was the only possible way of being alone. Fantastic pictures came to him of a normal child being classified as abnormal so that his mother, in order to make a desired marriage, might be rid of

691

him. Of that child somehow acquiring an education, of being adopted but retaining his true name. Then why should Lilian Crown have concealed it?

He jumped up. 'Michael, may I use your phone?'

'Sure you can, Reg.'

Baker had ceased to hint, had stopped his impatient fidgeting. Wexford knew what he was thinking. It was as if there had been placed before him, though invisible to others, a manual of advice to ambitious policemen. Always humour the whims of your chief's uncle, even though in your considered opinion the old boy is off his rocker. The uses of nepotism must always be borne in mind when looking to promotion.

Burden's voice, from down there in the green country, sounded sane and practical and encouraging.

'Mike, could you get over to the Abbotts Palmer Hospital? Go there, don't phone. I could do that myself. They have, or had, an inmate called John Grenville West. See him if you can.'

'Will do,' said Burden. 'Is he seeable? What I'm trying to say is, is he some sort of complete wreck or is he capable of communicating?'

'If he's who he seems to be, he's more than capable of communicating, in which case he won't be there. But I'm not sending you on a wild goose chase. You have to find out when he entered the institution, when he left and how. Everything you can about him, OK? And if you find he's not there but was cured, if that's possible, and went out into the world, confront the man's mother with it, will you? You may have to get tough with her. Get tough. Find out if she knew he was Grenville West, the author, and why the hell she didn't tell us.'

'Am I going to find out who his mother is?'

'Mrs Lilian Crown, 2 Carlyle Villas, Forest Road.'

'Right,' said Burden.

'I'll be here. I'd come back myself, only I want to wait in Kenbourne till Polly Flinders gets home this evening.'

Baker accepted this last so philosophically as to send down for coffee. Wexford took pity on him.

'Thanks, Michael, but I'm going to take myself off for a walk.' He said to Loring, 'You can get over to All Soul Grove and find out when the Flinders girl is expected home. If Miss Patel is taking another of her days off, I daresay you won't find the work too arduous.'

He went out into the hazy sunshine. Sluggishly people walked, idled on street corners. It seemed strange to him, as it always does to us when we are in a state of turbulence, that the rest of humanity was unaffected. He that is giddy thinks the world turns round. Giddiness exactly described his present condition, but it was a giddiness of the mind, and he walked steadily and slowly along Kenbourne High Road. At the cemetery gate he turned into the great necropolis. Along the aisles, between the serried tombs, he walked, and sat down at last on a toppled gravestone. On a warm summer's day there is no solitude to be found on a green or in a park, but one may always be sure of being alone in the corner of a cemetery. The dead themselves seem to decree silence, while the atmosphere of the place and its very nature are repellent to most people.

Very carefully and methodically he assembled the facts, letting the whispers wait. West had been cagey about his past, had made few friends, and those he had were somehow unsuitable and of an intellect unequal to his own. He gave his publishers and his readers his birthplace as London, though his passport and the registration of his birth showed he had been born in Sussex. His knowledge of the Sussex countryside and its great houses also showed a familiarity with that county. No one seemed to know anything of his life up to fourteen years before, and when he had first come to Elm Green and two years before his book was published. Not to his neighbour and intimate friend did he ever speak of his origins, and to one other bearer of the name Grenville West he had denied any connection with the family.

Why?

Because he had something to keep hidden, while Rhoda Comfrey was similarly secretive because she had her blackmailing activities to keep hidden. Put the two together and what do you get? A threat on the part of the blackmailer to disclose something. Not perhaps that West was homosexual – Wexford could not really be persuaded that these days this was of much significance – but that he had never been to a university (as his biography claimed he had), never been a teacher or a courier or a freelance journalist, been indeed nothing till the age of twenty-four when he had somehow emerged from a home for the mentally handicapped.

As his first cousin, Rhoda Comfrey would have known it; from her it could never have been kept as it had been kept from others. Had she used it as a final weapon – Burden's theory here being quite tenable – when she saw herself losing her cousin to Polly Flinders? West had overheard that phone call made by her to his own mother, even though she had called Lilian Crown 'darling' to put him off the scent. Had he assumed that she meant to see his mother and wrest from her the details of his early childhood, the opinions of doctors, all Mrs Crown's knowledge of the child's incarceration in that place and his subsequent release?

Here, then, was a motive for the murder. West had booked into the Trieste Hotel because it was simpler to allow Polly Flinders and Victor Vivian to believe him already in France. But that he had booked in his own name and for three nights showed surely that he had never intended to kill his cousin. Rather he had meant to use those three days for argument with Rhoda and to attempt to dissuade her from her intention.

But how had he done it? Not the murder, that might be clear enough, that unpremeditated killing in a fit of angry despair. How had he contrived in the first place such an escape and then undergone such a metamorphosis? Allowing for the fact that he might originally have been unjustly placed in the Abbotts Palmer or its predecessor, how had he surmounted his terrible difficulties? Throughout his childhood and early youth he must have been there, and if not in fact retarded, retardation would surely have been assumed for some years so that education would have been withheld and his intellect dulled and impeded by the society of his fellow inmates. Yet at the age of twenty-five or-six he had written and published a novel which revealed a learned knowledge of the Elizabethan drama, of history and of the English usage of the period.

If, that is, he were he.

It couldn't be, as Wexford had said to Loring, and yet it must be. For though John Grenville West might not be the author's real name, though he might be a suitable pseudonym by chance have alighted on it – inventing it, so to speak, himself – other aspects were beyond the possibility of coincidence. True, the chance use of this name (instead, for example, of his real one which might be absurd or dysphonious) could have brought him and Rhoda together, the cousinship at first having been assumed on her part as Charles West had also assumed it. But he could not by chance have also chosen her cousin's birthday and parentage. It must be that John Grenville West, the novelist, the francophile, the traveller, was also John Grenville West, the retarded child his mother had put away when he was six years old. From this dismal state, from this position in the world . . .

He stopped. The words he had used touched a bell and rang it. Again he was up in the spare bedroom with his daughter, and Sylvia was talking about men and women and time, saying something about men's position in the world. And after that she had said this position could only be attained by practising something or other. Deism? No, of course not. Aeolism? Didn't that mean being long-winded? Anyway, it wasn't that, she hadn't said that. What had she said?

He tried placing one letter of the alphabet after another to follow the diphthong and the O, and settled at last with absolute conviction for 'aeonism'. Which must have something to do with aeons. So she had only meant that, in order for sexual equality to be perfected, those who desired it would have to transcend the natural course of time.

He felt disappointed and let down, because, with a curious shiver in that heat, he had felt he had found the key. The word had not been entirely new to him. He fancied he had heard it before, long before Sylvia spoke it, and it had not meant transcending time at all.

Well, he wasn't getting very far cogitating like this. He might as well go back. It was after five, and by now Burden might have got results. He left the cemetery as they were about to close the gates and got a suspicious look from the keeper who had been unaware of his presence inside. But outside the library he thought of that elusive word again. He had a large vocabulary because in his youth he had always made a point of looking up words whose meaning he didn't know. It was a good rule and not one reserved to the young.

This was the place for which Grenville West had a ticket and where Wexford himself had first found his books. Now he spared them a glance on his way to the reference room. Four were in, including *Apes in Hell*, beneath whose covers Rhoda Comfrey's name lurked with such seeming innocence.

The library had only one English dictionary, the *Shorter Oxford* in two bulky volumes. Wexford took the first one of these down, sat at the table and opened it. 'Aeolism' was not given, and he found that 'aeolistic' meant what he thought it did and that it was an invention of Swift's. 'Aeon' was there – 'an age, or the whole duration of the world, or of the universe; an immeasurable period of time; eternity'. 'Aeonian' too and 'aeonial', but no 'aeonism'.

Could Sylvia have made it up, or was it perhaps the etymologically doubtful brain-child of one of her favourite

Women's Lib writers? That wouldn't account for his certainty that he had himself previously come across it. He replaced the heavy tome and crossed the street to the Police Station.

Baker was on the phone when he walked in, chatting with such tenderness and such absorption that Wexford guessed he could only be talking to his wife. But the conversation, though it appeared only to have been about whether he would prefer fried to boiled potatoes for his dinner and whether he would be home by six or could make it by ten to, put him in great good humour. No, no calls had come in for Wexford. Loring had not returned, and he, Baker, thought it would be a good idea for the two of them to adjourn at once to the Grand Duke. Provided, of course, that this didn't delay him from getting home by ten to six.

'I'd better stay here, Michael,' Wexford said rather awkwardly, 'if that's all right with you.'

'Be my guest, Reg. Here's your young chap now.'

Loring was shown in by Sergeant Clements. 'She came in at half past four, sir. I told her to expect you some time after six-thirty.'

He had no idea what he would say to her, though he might have if only Burden would phone. The word still haunted him. 'Would you mind if I made a call?' he said to Baker.

Humouring him had now become Baker's line. 'I said to be my guest, Reg. Do what you like.' His wife and the fried potatoes enticed him irresistibly. 'I'll be off then.' With stoical resignation, he added, 'I daresay we'll be seeing a good deal of each other in the next few days.'

Wexford dialled Sylvia's number. It was Robin who answered.

'Daddy's taken Mummy up to London to see Auntie Sheila in a play.'

The Merchant of Venice at the National. She was playing Jessica, and her father had seen her in the part a month before. Another of those whispers hissed at him from the text – 'But

love is blind, and lovers cannot see the pretty follies that
themselves commit.' To the boy he said:

'Who's with you, then? Grandma?'

'We've got a sitter,' said Robin. 'For Ben,' he added.

'See you,' said Wexford just as laconically, and put the
receiver back. Clements was still there, looking, he thought,
rather odiously sentimental. 'Sergeant,' he said, 'would you by
any chance have a dictionary in this place?'

'Plenty of them, sir. Urdu, Bengali, Hindi, you name it,
we've got it. Have to have on account of all these immigrants.
Of course we do employ interpreters, and a nice packet they
make out of it, but even they don't know all the words. And
just as well, if you ask me. We've got French too and German
and Italian for our Common Market customers, and common
is the word. Oh, yes, we've got more Dick, Tom and Marias,
as my old father used to call them, than they've got down the
library.'

Wexford controlled an impulse to throw the phone at him.
'Would you have an *English* dictionary?'

He was almost sure Clements would say this wasn't necessary as they all spoke English, whatever the *hoi polloi* might
do. But to his surprise he was told that they did and Clements
would fetch it for him, his pleasure.

He hadn't been gone half a minute when the switchboard,
with many time-wasting inquiries, at last put through a call
from Burden. He sounded as if the afternoon had afforded
him work that had been more distressing than arduous.

'Sorry I've been so long. I'm not so tough as I think I am.
But, God, the sights you see in these places. What it boils
down to is that John Grenville West left the Abbotts Palmer
when he was twenty . . .'

'*What?*'

'Don't get excited,' Burden said wearily. 'Only because
they hadn't the facilities for looking after him properly. He
isn't a mongol at all, whatever your Mrs Parker said. He was

born with serious brain damage and one leg shorter than the other. Reading between the lines, from what they said and didn't say, I gather this was the result of his mother's attempt to procure an abortion.'

Wexford said nothing. The horror was all in Burden's voice already.

'Don't let anyone ever tell me,' said the inspector savagely, 'that it was wrong to legalize abortion.'

Wexford knew better than to say at this moment that it was Burden who had always told himself, and others, that. 'Where is he now?'

'In a place near Eastbourne. I went there. He's been nothing more than a vegetable for eighteen years. I suppose the Crown woman was too ashamed to tell you. I've just come from her. She said it was ever so sad, wasn't it, and offered me a gin.'

CHAPTER TWENTY

The dictionaries Clements brought him, staggering under their weight, turned out to be the *Shorter Oxford* in its old vast single volume and *Webster's International* in two volumes.

'There's a mighty lot of words in those, sir. I doubt if anyone's taken a look at them since we had that nasty black magic business in the cemetery a couple of years back and I couldn't for the life of me remember how to spell mediaeval.'

It was the associative process which had led Rhoda Comfrey to give Dr Lomond her address as 6 Princevale Road, and that same process that had brought Sylvia's obscure expression back to Wexford's mind. Now it began to operate again as he was looking through the *Addenda and Corrigenda* to the *Shorter Oxford.*

'Mediaeval?' he said. 'You mean you weren't sure whether there was a diphthong or not?' The sergeant's puzzled frown made him say hastily, 'You weren't sure whether it was spelt i, a, e or i, e, was that it?'

'Exactly, sir.' Clements' need to put the world right – or to castigate the world – extended even to criticizing lexicographers. 'I don't know why we can't have simplified spelling, get rid of all these unnecessary letters. They only confuse schoolkids, I know they did me. I well remember when I was about twelve . . .'

Wexford wasn't listening to him. Clements went on talking, being the kind of person who would never have interrupted anyone when he was speaking, but didn't think twice about assaulting a man's ears while he was reading.

'. . . And day after day I got kept in after school for mixing up "there" and "their", if you know what I mean, and my father said . . .'

Diphthongs, thought Wexford. Of course. That ae was just

an anglicization of Greek eeta, wasn't it, or from the Latin which had a lot of ae's in it? And often these days the diphthong was changed to a single e, as in modern spelling of mediaeval. So his word, Sylvia's word, might appear among the E's and not the A's at all. He heaved the thick wedge of pages back to the E section. 'Eolienne' – 'a fine dress farbric' . . . 'Eosin' – 'a red dye-stuff' . . .

Maybe Sylvia's word had never had a diphthong, maybe it didn't come from Greek or Latin at all, but from a name or a place. That wasn't going to help him, though, if it wasn't in the dictionaries. Wild ideas came to him of getting hold of Sylvia ·here and now, of calling a taxi and having it take him down over the river to the National Theatre, finding her before the curtain went up in three-quarters of an hour's time . . . But there was still another dictionary.

'Harassment, now,' the sergeant was saying. 'There's a word I've never been able to spell, though I always say over to myself, "possesses possesses five s's".'

Webster's International. He didn't want it to be international, only sufficiently comprehensive. The E section. 'Eocene', 'Eolienne' – and there it was.

'Found what you're looking for, sir?' said Clements.

Wexford leant back with a sigh and let the heavy volume fall shut. 'I've found, Sergeant, what I've been looking for for three weeks.'

Rather warily, Malina Patel admitted them to the flat. Was it for Loring's benefit that she had dressed up in harem trousers and a jacket of some glossy white stuff, heavily embroidered? Her black hair was looped up in complicated coils and fastened with gold pins.

'Polly's in an awful state,' she said confidingly. 'I can't do anything with her. When I told her you were coming I thought she was going to faint, and then she cried so terribly. I didn't know what to do.'

Perhaps, Wexford thought, you could have been a friend

to her and comforted her, not spent surely a full hour making yourself look like something out of a seraglio. There was no time now, though, to dwell on forms of hypocrisy, on those who will seek to present themselves as pillars of virtue and archetypes of beauty even at times of grave crisis.

Making use of those fine eyes – could she even cry at will? – she said sweetly, 'But I don't suppose you want to talk to me, do you? I think Polly will be up to seeing you. She's in there. I said to her that everything would be all right if she just told the truth, and then you wouldn't frighten her. Please don't frighten her, will you?'

Already the magic was working on Loring who looked quite limp. It had ceased to work on Wexford.

'I'd rather frighten you, Miss Patel,' he said. Her eyelashes fluttered at him. 'And you're wrong if you think I don't want to talk to you. Let us go in here.'

He opened a door at random. On the other side of it was a squalid and filthy kitchen, smelling of strong spices and of decay, as if someone had been currying meat and vegetables that were already rotten. The sink was stacked up to the level of the taps with unwashed dishes. She took up her stand in front of the sink, too small to hide it, a self-righteous but not entirely easy smile on her lips.

'You're very free with your advice,' he said. 'Do you find in your experience that people take it?'

'I was only trying to help,' she said, slipping into her little girl role. 'It was good advice, wasn't it?'

'You didn't take my good advice.'

'I don't know what you mean.'

'Not to lie to the police. The scope of the truth, Miss Patel, is very adequately covered by the words of the oath one takes in the witness box. I swear to tell the truth, the whole truth and nothing but the truth. After I had warned you, you obeyed – as far as I know – the first injunction and the third but not the second. You left out a vital piece of truth.'

She seized on only one point. 'I'm not going into any witness box!'

'Oh, yes you will. One thing you may be sure of is that you will. Yesterday morning you received a phone call, didn't you? From the manager of the Trieste Hotel.'

She said sullenly, 'Polly did.'

'And when Miss Flinders realized that Mr West's car had been found, you told her that the police would be bound to find out. Did you advise her to tell us? Did you remember my advice to you? No. You suggested that the best thing would be to bring her to us with the old story that your conscience had been troubling you.'

She shifted her position, and the movement sent the dirty plates subsiding over the edge of the bowl.

'When did you first know the facts, Miss Patel?'

A flood of self-justification came from her. Her voice lost its soft prettiness and took on a near-cockney inflexion. She was shrill.

'What, that Polly hadn't been in a motel with a married man? Not till last night. I didn't, I tell you, I didn't till last night. She was in an awful state and she'd been crying all day, and she said I can't tell him that man's address because there isn't a man. And that made me laugh because Polly's never had a real boy-friend all the time I've known her, and I said, "You made it up?" And she said she had. And I said, "I bet Grenville never kissed you either, did he?" So she cried some more and . . .' The faces of the two men told her she had gone too far. She seemed to remember the personality she wished to present and to grab at it in the nick of time. 'I knew you'd find out because the police always did, you said. I warned her you'd come, and then what was she going to say?'

'I meant,' Wexford tried, 'when did you know where Miss Flinders had truly been that night?'

Anxiety gone – he wasn't really cross, men would never really be cross with her – she smiled the amazed smile of someone on whom a great revelatory light has shone. 'What a weird thing! I never thought about that.'

No, she had never thought about that. About her own attractions and her winning charm she had thought, about establishing her own ascendancy and placing her friend in a foolish light, about what she called her conscience she had thought, but never about the aim of all these inquiries. What a curiously inept and deceiving term Freud had coined, Wexford reflected, when he named the conscience the superego!

'It never occurred to you then that a girl who never went out alone after dark must have had some very good reason for being out alone all that evening and half the night? You didn't think of that aspect? You had forgotten perhaps that that was the evening of Rhoda Comfrey's murder?'

She shook her head guilelessly. 'No, I didn't think about it. It couldn't have had anything to do with me or Polly.'

Wexford looked at her steadily. She looked back at him, her fingers beginning to pick at the gold embroideries on the tunic whose whiteness set off her orchid skin. At last the seriousness of his gaze affected her, forcing her to use whatever powers of reasoning she had. The whole pretty sweet silly façade broke, and she let out a shattering scream.

'Christ,' said Loring.

She began to scream hysterically, throwing back her head. The heroine, Wexford thought unsympathetically, going mad in white satin. 'Oh, slap her face or something,' he said and walked out into the hall.

Apart from the screeches, and now the choking sounds and sobs from the kitchen, the flat was quite silent. It struck him that Pauline Flinders must be in the grip of some over-powering emotion, or stunned into a fugue, not to have reacted to those screams and come out to inquire. He looked forward with dread and with distaste to the task ahead of him.

All the other doors were closed. He tapped on the one that led to the living room where he had interviewed her before. She didn't speak, but opened the door and looked at him with great sorrow and hopelessness. Everything she wore and everything about her seemed to drag her down, the flopping hair, the stooping shoulders, the loose overblouse and the long skirt, compelling the eye of the beholder also to droop and fall.

Today there was no script on the table, no paper in the typewriter. No book or magazine lay open. She had been sitting there waiting – for how many hours? – paralysed, capable of no action.

'Sit down, Miss Flinders,' he said. It was horrible to have to torture her, but if he was to get what he wanted he had no choice. 'Don't try to find excuses for not telling me the name of the man you spent the evening of August eighth with. I know there was no man.'

She tensed at that and darted him a look of terror, and he knew why. But he let it pass. Out of pity for her, his mind was working quickly, examining this which was so fresh to him, so recently realized, trying to get enough grasp on it to decide whether the whole truth need come out. But even at this stage, with half the facts still to be understood, he knew he couldn't comfort her with that one.

She hunched in a chair, the pale hair curtaining her face. 'You were afraid to go out alone at night,' he said, 'and for good reason. You were once attacked in the dark by a man, weren't you, and very badly frightened?'

The hair shivered, her bent body nodded.

'You wished it were legal in this country for people to carry guns for protection. It's illegal too to carry knives but knives are easier to come by. How long is it, Miss Flinders, since you have been carrying a knife in your handbag?'

She murmured, 'Nearly a year.'

'A flick knife, I suppose. The kind with a concealed blade that appears when you press a projection on the hilt. Where is that knife now?'

'I threw it into the canal at Kenbourne Lock.'

Never before had he so much wished he could leave someone in her position alone. He opened the door and called to Loring to come in. The girl bunched her lips over her teeth, straightened her shoulders, her face very white.

'Let us at least try to be comfortable,' said Wexford, and he motioned her to sit beside him on the sofa while Loring took the chair she had vacated. 'I'm going to tell you a story.' He chose his words carefully. 'I'm going to tell you how this case appears.'

'There was a woman of thirty called Rhoda Comfrey who came from Kingsmarkham in Sussex to London where she lived for some time on the income from a football pools win, a sum which I think must have been in the region of ten thousand pounds.

'When the money began to run out she supplemented it with an income derived from blackmail, and she called herself West, Mrs West, because the name Comfrey and her single status were distasteful to her. After some time she met a young man, a foreigner, who had no right to be in this country but who, like Joseph Conrad before him, wanted to live here and write his books in English. Rhoda Comfrey offered him an identity and a history, a mother and father, a family and a birth certificate. He was to take the name of someone who would never need national insurance or a passport because he had been and always would be in an institution for the mentally handicapped – her cousin, John Grenville West. This the young man did.

'The secret bound them together in a long uneasy friendship. He dedicated his third novel to her, for it was certain that without her that book would never have been written. He would not have been here to write it. Was he Russian perhaps? Or some other kind of Slav? Whatever he was, seeking asylum, she gave him the identity of a real person who would never need to use his reality and who was himself in an asylum of a different kind.

'And what did she get from him? A young and personable man to be her escort and her companion. He was homosexual, of course, she knew that. All the better. She was not a highly sexed woman. It was not love and satisfaction she wanted, but a man to show off to observers.

'How disconcerting for her, therefore, when he took on a young girl to type his manuscripts for him, and that young girl fell in love with him . . .'

Polly Flinders made a sound of pain, a single soft 'Ah!', perhaps irrepressible. Wexford paused, then went on.

'He wasn't in love with her. But he was growing older, he was nearly middle-aged. What sort of dignified future has a homosexual who follows the kind of life-style he had been following into his forties? He decided to marry, to settle down – at least superficially – to add another line to that biography of his on the back of his books.

'Perhaps he hadn't considered what this would mean to the woman who had created him and received his confidences. It was not she, twelve years his senior, he intended marrying, but a girl half her age. To stop him, she threatened to expose his true nationality, his illegalities and his homosexual conduct. He had no choice but to kill her.'

Wexford looked at Polly Flinders who was looking hard at him.

'But it wasn't quite like that, was it?' he said.

CHAPTER TWENTY-ONE

While he was speaking a change had gradually come over her. She was suffering still but she was no longer tortured with fear. She had settled into a kind of resigned repose until, at his last sentence, apprehensiveness came back. But she said nothing, only nodding her head and then shaking it, as if she wished to please him, to agree with him, but was doubtful whether he wanted a yes or a no.

'Of course he had a choice,' Wexford went on. 'He could have married and left her to go ahead. His readers would have felt nothing but sympathy with a man who wanted asylum in this country, even though he had used illegal means to get it. And there was not the slightest chance of his being deported after so long. As for his homosexuality, who but the most old-fashioned would care? Besides, the fact of his marriage would have put paid to any such aspersions. And where and how would Rhoda Comfrey have published it? In some semi-underground magazine most of his readers would never see? In a gossip column where it would have to be written with many circumlocutions to avoid libel? Even if he didn't feel that *any* publicity is good publicity, he still had a choice. He could have agreed to her demands. Marriage for him was only an expedient, not a matter of passion.'

The girl showed no sign that these words had hurt her. She listened calmly, and now her hands lay folded in her lap. It was as if she were hearing what she wanted to hear but had hardly dared hope she would. Her pallor, though, was more than usually marked. Wexford was reminded of how he had once read in some legend or fairy story of a girl so fair and with skin so transparent, that when she drank the course the red wine followed could be seen as it ran down her throat.

But Polly Flinders was in no legend or fairy story – or even nursery rhyme – and her dry bunched lips looked parched for wine or love.

'It was for this reason,' he said, 'that someone else was alarmed – the girl he could so easily be prevented from marrying. She loved him and wanted to marry him, but she knew that this older woman had far more influence over him than she did.

'August fifth was Rhoda Comfrey's birthday. Grenville West showed her – and showed the girl too – how little malice or resentment he felt towards her by giving her an expensive wallet for a birthday present. Indicating, surely, that he meant to let her rule him? That evening they were all together, the three of them, in Grenville West's flat, and Rhoda Comfrey asked if she might make a phone call. Now when a guest does that, a polite host leaves the room so that the person making the call may be private. You and Mr West left the room, didn't you, Miss Flinders? But perhaps the door was left open.

'She was only telephoning her aunt to say she was going to visit her father in Stowerton Infirmary on the following Monday, but to impress you and Mr West she made it appear as if she were talking to a man. You were uninterested in that aspect of it, but you were intrigued to find out where she would be on the Monday. In the country where you could locate her as you never could on her own in London.'

He paused, deciding to say nothing about the Trieste Hotel and West's disappearance, guessing that she would be thankful for his name to be omitted.

'On the evening of Monday, August eighth, you went to Stowerton, having found out when visiting time was. You saw Miss Comfrey get on to a bus with another woman, and you got on to it too, without letting her see you. You left the bus at the stop where she left it and followed her across the footpath – intending what? Not to kill her then. I think you wished only to be alone with her to ask why and to try to dissuade her from interfering between you and Mr West.

'But she laughed at you, or was patronizing, or something of that sort. She said something hurtful and cruel, and driven beyond endurance, you stabbed her. Am I right, Miss Flinders?'

Loring sat up stiffly, bracing himself, waiting perhaps for more screams. Polly Flinders only nodded. She looked calm and thoughtful as if she had been asked for verbal confirmation of some action, and not even a reprehensible action, she had performed years before. Then she sighed.

'Yes, that's right. I killed her. I stabbed her and wiped the knife on the grass and got on another bus and then a train and came home. I threw the knife into Kenbourne Lock on the way back. I did it just like you said.' She hesitated, added steadily, 'And why you said.'

Wexford got up. It was all very civilized and easy and casual. He could tell what Loring was thinking. There had been provocation, no real intent, no premeditation. The girl realized all this and that she would get off with three or four years, so better confess it now and put an end to the anxiety that had nearly broken her. Get it over and have peace, with no involvement for Grenville West.

'Pauline Flinders,' he said, 'you are charged with the murder on August eighth of Rhoda Agnes Comfrey. You are not obliged to say anything in answer to the charge, but anything you do say may be taken down and used in evidence.'

'I don't want to say anything,' she said. 'Do I have to go with you now?'

'It seems,' said Burden when Wexford phoned him, 'a bit of a sell.'

'You want more melodrama? You want hysterics?'

'Not exactly that. Oh, I don't know. There seems to have been so many oddities in this case, and what it boils down to is that it was this girl all along. She killed the woman just because she was coming between her and West.' Wexford said nothing. 'I suppose she *did* kill her? She's not confessing in an attempt to protect West?'

'Oh, she killed her all right. No doubt about that. In her statement she's given us the most precise circumstantial account of times, the geography of the Forest Road area, what Rhoda Comfrey was wearing and even the fact that the London train, the nine-twenty-four Kingsmarkham to Victoria, was ten minutes late that night. Tomorrow Rittifer will have Kenbourne Lock dragged and we'll find that knife.'

'And West himself had nothing to do with it?'

'He had everything to do with it. Without him there'd have been no problem. He was the motive. I'm tired now, Mike, and I've got another call to make. I'll tell you the rest after the special court tomorrow.'

His other call was to Michael Baker. A woman with a soft voice and a slight North Country accent answered. 'It's for you, darling,' she called out, and Baker called back, 'Coming, darling.' His voice roughened, crackling down the phone when he heard who it was, and implicit in his tone was the question, 'Do you know what time it is?' though he didn't actually say this. But when Wexford had told him the bare facts he became immediately cocky and rather took the line that he had predicted such an outcome all along.

'I knew you were wasting your time with all those names and dates and birth certificates, Reg. I told you so.' Wexford had never heard anyone utter those words in seriousness before, and had he felt less tired and sick he would have laughed. 'Well, all's well that ends well, eh?'

'I daresay. Good night, Michael.'

Maybe it was because he forgot to add something on the lines of his eternal gratitude for all the assistance rendered him by Kenbourne police that Baker dropped the receiver without another word. Or, rather, without more than a fatuous cry of

'Just coming, sweetheart,' which he hardly supposed could be addressed to him.

Dora was in bed, sitting up reading the Marie Antoinette book. He sat down beside her and kicked off his shoes.

'So it's all over, is it?' she said.

'I've behaved very badly,' he muttered. 'I've strung that wretched girl along and told her lies and accepted lies from her just to get a confession. I've got a horrible job. She still thinks she's got away with it.'

'Darling,' Dora said gently, 'you do realize I haven't the least idea what you're talking about?'

'Yes, in a way I'm talking to myself. Maybe being married is talking to oneself with one's other self listening.'

'That's one of the nicest things you've ever said to me.'

He went into the bathroom and looked at his ugly face in the glass, at the bags under his tired eyes and the wrinkles and the white stubble on his chin that made him look like an old man.

'I am alone the villain of the earth,' he said to the face in the glass, 'and feel I am so most.'

In court on Saturday morning, Pauline Flinders was charged with the murder of Rhoda Comfrey, committed for trial and remanded in custody.

After it was over Wexford avoided the Chief Constable – it was supposed to be his day off, wasn't it? – and gave Burden the slip and pretended not to see Dr Crocker, and got into his own car and drove to Myringham. What he had to do, would spend most of the day doing, could only be done in Myringham.

He drove over the Kingsbrook Bridge and through the old town to the centre. There he parked on the top floor of the multi-storey car park, for Myringham was given over to shoppers' cars on Saturdays, and went down in the lift to enter the building on the opposite side of the street.

In marble this time, Edward Edwards, a book in his hand, looked vaguely at him. Wexford paused to read what was engraved on the plinth and then went in, the glass doors opening of their own accord to admit him.

CHAPTER TWENTY-TWO

For years before it became a hotel – for centuries even – the Olive and Dove had been a coaching inn where the traveller might not get a bedroom or, come to that, a bed to himself, but might be reasonably sure of securing a private parlour. Many of these parlours, oak-panelled, low-ceilinged cubby-holes, still remained, opening out of passages that led away from the bar and the lounge bar, though they were private no longer but available to any first-comer. In the smallest of them where there was only one table, two chairs and a settle, Burden sat at eight o'clock on Sunday evening, waiting for the chief inspector to come and keep the appointment he had made himself. He waited impatiently, making his half-pint of bitter last, because to leave the room now for another drink would be to invite invasion. Coats thrown over tables imply no reservation in the Olive at weekends. Besides, he had no coat. It was too warm.

Then at ten past, when the bitter was down to its last inch, Wexford walked in with a tankard in each hand.

'You're lucky I found you at all, hidden away like this,' he said. 'This is for plotters or lovers.'

'I thought you'd like a bit of privacy.'

'Maybe you're right. I am Sir Oracle, and when I ope my lips let no dog bark.'

Burden raised his tankard and said, 'Cheers! This dog's going to bark. I want to know where West is, why he stayed in that hotel, who he is, come to that, and why I had to spend Friday afternoon inspecting mental hospitals. That's for a start. I want to know why, on your admission, you told that girl two entirely false stories and where you spent yesterday.'

'They weren't entirely false,' said Wexford mildly. 'They had elements of the truth. I knew by then that she had killed

714

Rhoda Comfrey because there was no one else who could have done so. But I also knew that if I presented her with the absolute truth at that point, she would have been unable to answer me and not only should I not have got a confession, but she would very likely have become incoherent and perhaps have collapsed. What was true was that she was in love with Grenville West, that she wanted to marry him, that she overheard a phone conversation and that she stabbed Rhoda Comfrey to death on the evening of August eighth. All the rest, the motive, the lead up to the murder and the characters of the protagonists to a great degree – all that was false. But it was a version acceptable to her and one which she might not have dreamed could be fabricated. The sad thing for her is that the truth must inevitably be revealed and has, in fact, already been revealed in the report I wrote yesterday for Griswold.

'I spent yesterday in the new public library in Myringham, in the reference section, reading Havelock Ellis, a biography of the Chevalier d'Eon, and bits of the life histories of Isabelle Eberhardt, James Miranda Barry and Martha Jane Burke – if those names mean anything to you.'

'There's no need to be patronizing,' said Burden. 'They don't.'

Wexford wasn't feeling very light-hearted, but he couldn't, even in these circumstances, resist teasing Burden who was already looking irritable and aggrieved.

'Oh, and Edward Edwards,' he said. 'Know who Edward Edwards was? The Father of Public Libraries, it said underneath his statue. Apparently, he was instrumental in getting some bill through Parliament in 1850 and . . .'

'For God's sake,' Burden exploded, 'can't you get on to West? What's this Edwards got to do with West?'

'Not much. He stands outside libraries and West's books are inside.'

'Then where is West? Or are you saying he's going to turn

up now he's read in the paper that one of his girl-friends has murdered the other one?'

'He won't turn up.'

'Why won't he?' Burden said slowly. 'Look, d'you mean there were two people involved in murdering Rhoda Comfrey? West as well as the girl?'

'No. West is dead. He never went back to the Trieste Hotel because he was dead.'

'I need another drink,' said Burden. In the doorway he turned round and said scathingly, 'I suppose Polly Flinders bumped him off too?'

'Yes,' said Wexford. 'Of course.'

The Olive was getting crowded and Burden was more than five minutes fetching their beer. 'My God,' he said, 'who d'you think's out there? Griswold. He didn't see me. At least, I don't think so.'

'Then you'd better make that one last. I'm not running the risk of bumping into him.'

Burden sat down again, his eye on the doorway which held no door. He leant across the table, his elbows on it. 'She can't have. What became of the body?'

Wexford didn't answer him directly. 'Does the word eonism mean anything to you?'

'No more than all those names you flung at me just now. Wait a minute, though. An aeon means a long time, an age. An aeonist is – let's see – is someone who studies changes over long periods of time.'

'No. I thought something like that too. It has nothing to do with aeons, there's no a in it. Havelock Ellis coined the word in a book published in 1928 called *Studies in the Psychology of Sex, Eonism and other Studies*. He took the name from that of the Chevalier d'Eon, Charles Eon de Beaumont, who died in this country in the early part of the nineteenth century...' Wexford paused and said, '... Having masqueraded for thirty-three years as a woman.

'Rhoda Comfrey masqueraded for twenty years as a man. When I agreed that Pauline Flinders had murdered Grenville West, I meant that she had murdered him in the body of Rhoda Comfrey. Rhoda Comfrey and Grenville West were one and the same.'

'That's not possible,' said Burden. 'People would have known or at least suspected.' Intently staring at Wexford's face, he was oblivious of the long bulky shadow that had been cast across the table and his own face.

Wexford turned round, said, 'Good evening, sir,' and smiled pleasantly. It was Burden who, realizing, got to his feet.

'Sit down, Mike, sit down,' said the Chief Constable, casting upon Wexford a look that implied he would have liked the opportunity to tell him to sit down also. 'May I join you? Or is the chief inspector here indulging his well-known habit of telling a tale with the minimum of celerity and the maximum of suspense? I should hate to interrupt before the climax was reached.'

In a stifled voice, Burden said, 'The climax was reached just as you came in, sir. Can I get you a drink?'

'Thank you, but I have one.' Griswold produced, from where he had been holding it, for some reason, against his trouser leg, a very small glass of dry sherry. 'And now I too would like to hear this wonderful exposition, though I have the advantage over you, Mike, of having read a condensed version. I heard your last words. Perhaps you'll repeat them.'

'I said she couldn't have got away with it. Anyone she knew well would have known.'

'Well, Reg?' Griswold sat down on the settle next to Burden. 'I hope my presence won't embarrass you. Will you go on?'

'Certainly I will, sir.' Wexford considered saying he wasn't easily embarrassed but thought better of it. 'I think the answer to that question is that she took care, as we have seen, only to know *well* not very sensitive or intelligent people. But even so, Malina Patel had noticed there was something odd about Grenville West, and she said she wouldn't have liked him to kiss her. Even Victor Vivian spoke of a "funny high voice" while, incidentally, Mrs Crown said that Rhoda's voice was deep. I think it probable that such people as Oliver Hampton and Mrs Nunn did know, or rather, if they didn't know she was a woman, they suspected Grenville West of being of ambivalent sex, of being physically a hermaphrodite, or maybe an effeminate homosexual. But would they have told me? When I questioned them I suspected West of nothing more than being acquainted with Rhoda Comfrey. They are discreet people, who were connected with West in a professional capacity. As for those men Rhoda consorted with in bars, they wouldn't have been a bunch of conservative suburbanites. They'd have accepted her as just another oddity in a world of freaks.

'Before you came in, sir, I mentioned three names. Isabelle Eberhardt, James Miranda Barry and Martha Jane Burke. What they had in common was that they were all eonists. Isabelle Eberhardt became a nomad in the North African desert where she was in the habit of sporadically passing herself off as male. James Barry went to medical school as a boy in the days before girls were eligible to do so, and served for a lifetime as an army doctor in the British colonies. After her death she was found to be a woman, and a woman who had had a child. The last named is better known as Calamity Jane who lived with men as a man, chewed tobacco, was proficient in the use of arms, and was only discovered to be a woman while she was taking part in a military campaign against the Sioux.

'The Chevalier d'Eon was a physically normal man who successfully posed as a female for thirty years. For half that period he lived with a woman friend called Marie Cole who never doubted for a moment that he also was a woman. She nursed him through his last illness and didn't learn he was a man until after his death. I will quote to you Marie Cole's reaction to the discovery from the words of the Notary Public, Doctors' Commons, 1810: "She did not recover from the shock for many hours."

'So you can see that Rhoda Comfrey had precedent for what she did, and that the lives of these predecessors of hers show that cross-dressing succeeds in its aim. Many people are totally deceived by it, others speculate or doubt, but the subject's true sex is often not detected until he or she become ill or wounded, or until, as in Rhoda's case, death supervenes.'

The Chief Constable shook his head, as one who wonders rather than denies. 'What put you on to it, Reg?'

'My daughters. One saying a woman would have to be an eonist to get a man's rights, and the other dressing as a man on the stage. Oh, and Grenville West's letter to Charles West – that had the feel of having been written by a woman. And Rhoda's fingernails painted but clipped short. And Rhoda having a toothbrush in her luggage at Kingsmarkham and West not having one in his holiday cases. All feelings, I'm afraid, sir.'

'That's all very well,' said Burden, 'but what about the age question? Rhoda Comfrey was fifty and West was thirty-eight.'

'She had a very good reason for fixing her age as twelve years less than her true one. I'll go into that in a minute. But also you must remember that she saw herself as having lost her youth and those best years. This was a way of regaining them. Now think what are the signs of youth in men and women. A woman's subcutaneous fat begins to decline at fifty or thereabouts, but a man never has very much of it. So even a young man may have a hard face, lined especially under the eyes without looking older than he is. A woman's youthful looks largely depend on her having no lines. Here, as else-where, we apply a different standard for the sexes. You're what, Mike? In your early forties? Put a wig and make-up on you and you'll look an old hag, but cut off the hair of a woman of your age, dress her in a man's suit, and she could pass for thirty. My daughter Sheila's twenty-four, but when she puts on doublet and hose for Jessica in *The Merchant of Venice* she looks sixteen.'

Remarkably, it was the Chief Constable who supported him. 'Quite true. Think of Crippen's mistress, Ethel Le Neve. She was a mature woman, but when she tried to escape across the Atlantic disguised in men's clothes she was taken for a youth. And by the way, Reg, you might have added Maria Marten, the Red Barn victim, to your list. She left her father's house disguised as a farm labourer, though I believe transvestism was against the law at the time.'

'In seventeenth-century France,' said Wexford, 'men, at any rate, were executed for it.'

'Hmm. You have been doing your homework. Get on with the story, will you?'

Wexford proceeded: 'Nature had not been kind to Rhoda as a woman. She had a plain face and a large nose and she was large-framed and flat-chested. She was what people call "mannish", though incidentally no one did in this case. As a young girl she tried wearing ultra-feminine clothes to make herself more attractive. She copied her aunt because she saw that her aunt got results. She, however, did not, and she must have come to see her femaleness as a grave disadvantage. Because she was female she had been denied an education and was expected to be a drudge. All her miseries came from being a woman, and she had none of a woman's advantages over a man. My daughter Sylvia complains that men are attentive to her because of her physical attractions but accord her no respect as a person. Rhoda had no physical attractions so, because she was a woman, she received neither attention nor respect. No doubt she would have stayed at home and become an embittered old maid, but for a piece of luck. She won a large sum of money in an office football pools syndicate. Where she first lived in London and whether as a man or a woman, I don't know and I don't think it's relevant. She began to write. Did she at this time cease to wear those unsuitable clothes and take to trousers and sweaters and jackets instead? Who knows? Perhaps, dressed like that, she was once or twice mistaken for a man, and that gave her the idea. Or what is more likely, she took to men's clothes because, as Havelock Ellis says, cross-dressing fulfilled a deep demand of her nature.

'It must have been then that she assumed a man's name, and perhaps this was when she submitted her first manuscript to a publisher. It was then or never, wasn't it? If she was going to have a career and come into the public eye there must be no ambivalence of sex.

'By posing – or passing – as a man she had everything to gain: the respect of her fellows, a personal feeling of the rightness of it for her, the freedom to go where she chose and do what she liked, to walk about after dark in safety, to hobnob with men in bars on an equal footing. And she had very little to lose. Only the chance of forming close intimate friendships, for this she would not dare to do – except with unobservant fools like Vivian.'

'Well,' said Burden, 'I've just about recovered from the shock, unlike Marie Cole who took some hours. But there's something else strikes me she had to lose.'

He looked with some awkwardness in the direction of the Chief Constable, and Griswold, without waiting for him to say it, barked, 'Her sexuality, eh? How about that?'

'Len Crocker said at the start of this case that some people are very low-sexed. And if I may again quote Havelock Ellis, eonists often have an almost asexual disposition. "In people", he says, "with this psychic anomaly, physical sexual urge seems often subnormal." Rhoda Comfrey, who had had no sexual experience, must have decided it was well worth sacrificing the possibility – the remote possibility – of ever forming a satisfactory sexual relationship for what she had to gain. I am sure she did sacrifice it and became a man whom other men and women just thought rather odd.

'And she took pains to be as masculine as she could be. She dressed plainly, she used no colognes or toilet waters, she carried an electric shaver, though we must suppose it was never used. Because she couldn't grow an Adam's apple she wore high necklines to cover her neck, and because she couldn't achieve on her forehead an M-line, she always wore a lock of hair falling over her brow.'

'What d'you mean?' said Burden. 'An M-line?'

'Look in the mirror,' said Wexford.

The three men got up and confronted themselves in the ornamented glass on the wall above their table. 'See,' said Wexford, putting his own hands up to his scanty hairline, and the other two perceived how their hair receded in two triangles at the temples. 'All men,' he said, 'have to some degree, but no woman does. Her hairline is oval in shape. But for Rhoda Comfrey these were small matters and easily dealt with. It was only when she paid a rare visit to Kingsmarkham to see her father that she was obliged to go back to being a woman. Oh, and on one other occasion. No wonder people said she was happy in London and miserable in the country. For her, dressing as a woman was very much what it would be like for a normal man to be forced into drag.

'But she played it in character, or in her old character, dressing fussily, wearing heavy make-up, painting her finger-nails which, however, she couldn't grow long for the purpose. For these visits she kept women's underclothes and an old pair of stiletto-heeled shoes. When you come to think of it, she might buy a woman's dress without trying it on, but hardly a pair of shoes.'

'But you said,' put in Griswold, 'that there were other occasions when she went back to being a woman.'

'I said there was one, sir. She might deceive her friends and her acquaintances. They weren't going to subject her to a physical examination. She had been a patient of old Dr Castle in Kingsmarkham, though I imagine she was a strong healthy woman who seldom needed medical attention. Last year, however, he died, but when she suspected she had appendicitis, she had to go to a doctor. Even the most cursory examination would have revealed she was no man, so to Dr Lomond she went reluctantly as a woman, giving her true name and an address she thought up on the way. Hence the Farriner confusion.

'That was a year ago, by which time she had already met Polly Flinders – and Polly Flinders had fallen in love with her.'

CHAPTER TWENTY-THREE

'Everything points to Rhoda Comfrey's having been aware of the girl's feelings,' Wexford went on, 'and to some extent to her having encouraged them. She let her act as her secretary instead of just an occasional typist, took her into the wine bar for drinks, drove her home if she was kept late at Elm Green, sent her whimsical postcards. What she did not do, and probably felt she was behaving ethically in not doing – although I daresay she didn't want to either – was show her the least demonstrative affection.'

'It was cruel and unjustifiable all the same,' said Burden.

'I think it was natural,' Wexford said hesitantly. 'I think it was very *human*. After all, look at it from Rhoda's point of view. As a girl of twenty-five she hadn't been remotely attractive to men. Mustn't it have enormously gratified her to know that at fifty she had someone of twenty-five in love with her? A poor obtuse innocent creature perhaps, but still a young human being in love with her. A poor ill-favoured thing, but mine own. Who else had ever really loved her? Her mother, long ago. Mrs Parker? This was a love of a different kind, and the kind everyone wants once in a lifetime.'

Griswold had started to look impatient. 'All right, Reg, all right. Get back to the nitty-gritty, can't you? You're a policeman, not a shrink.'

'Well, for the nitty-gritty, sir, we have to come to a month or so ago. Rhoda was planning to go on holiday, but her father had had a stroke. She meant to go, no doubt about that, but perhaps she ought to see the old man first and find out how the land lay.'

'What d'you mean by that?'

'I mean that if he was very seriously incapacitated she

would know that her greatest fear, that her father might have to be parked on her one day, would be groundless and she could go off to France with a light heart. But she had to go down there and find out, even though this would mean putting off her holiday for a day or two. Never mind. That was no great inconvenience. She phoned her aunt to tell her she would be coming and when she did so Polly Flinders was in the flat, but not all the time in the room.

'Now, if no one else did, Polly knew that Grenville West had once or twice before disappeared mysteriously at week-ends. I think we can assume that Rhoda rather enjoyed keeping her in the dark about that, and guessed she was giving her cause for jealousy. On that Friday evening Polly had very likely been troublesome – she may, for instance, have wanted West to take her away on holiday with him – and Rhoda vented her annoyance by calling Lilian Crown "darling". Polly overheard, as she was meant to overhear, and believed that West was involved with another woman living in the country. No doubt she asked questions, but was told it was no business of hers, so she determined to go to Stowerton on the Monday and find out for herself what was going on.'

Burden interrupted him. 'Why didn't Rhoda or West or whatever we're going to call him or her – it gets a bit complicated – go to Kingsmarkham that day? Then there wouldn't have been any need to postpone the holiday. Where does the Trieste Hotel come in?'

'Think about it,' said Wexford. 'Walk out of Elm Green in make-up and high-heeled shoes and a dress?'

'I should have thought a public lavatory . . .' Burden stopped himself proceeding further with this gaffe, but not in time to prevent Griswold's hoot of laughter.

'How does he manage to go in the Gents' and come out of the Ladies', Mike?'

Wexford didn't feel like laughing. He had never been amused by drag or the idea of it, and now the humorous aspects of this particular case of cross-dressing seemed to him quenched by its consequences. 'She used hotels for the change-over,' he said rather coldly, 'and usually hotels in some distant part of London. But this time she had left it too late to pick and choose, especially with the tourist season as its height. On that Saturday she must have tried to book in at a number of hotels without success. The only one which could take her was the Trieste which she had used once before – on the occasion of the visit to Dr Lomond. You can see, Mike, how she walked out of the Trieste on that day, crossed Montfort Circus, went up Montfort Hill, and chose an address from a street name and an advertisement.

'So back to the Trieste she went, with her car packed up for the French holiday and allowing Vivian to believe she was leaving directly for France. The car was left in a garage at the hotel with her passport and French currency locked up in the boot. On her person she retained the car keys and her new wallet, and these went into her handbag when on the following day she left the hotel as Rhoda Comfrey.'

'That must have been as bad as walking out of Elm Green. Suppose she'd been seen?'

'By whom? An hotel servant? She says she's calling on her friend, Mr West. It would have been easy enough to mingle with the other guests or conceal herself in a cloakroom, say, if Hetherington had appeared. As a respectable middle-aged lady, she'd hardly have been suspected of being there for what you'd call an immoral purpose.'

'Hotels don't take much notice of that these days,' said the Chief Constable easily. Forgetting perhaps that it was he who had told Wexford to get back to the nitty-gritty, he said, 'This passport, though. I'm still not clear about it. I see she had to have a man's name and a man's identity, but why that one? She could have changed her name by deed poll or kept Comfrey and used one of those Christian names that will do for either sex. Leslie, for instance, or Cecil.'

'Deed poll means a certain amount of publicity, sir. But I don't think that was entirely the reason. She needed a passport. Of course she could have used some ambiguous Christian name for that. And with her birth certificate and her change of name document she could have submitted to the Passport Office a photograph that gave no particular indication of whether she was male or female . . .'

'Exactly,' said Griswold. 'A British passport isn't required to state the holder's home address or marital status or,' he added with some triumph, 'the holder's sex.'

'No, sir, not in so many words. If the holder is accompanied by a child, that child must be declared as male or female, but not the holder. Yet on the cover and on page one the holder's *style* is shown. It wouldn't have helped her much, would it, to have a man's Christian name and a man's photograph but be described as *Miss* Cecil Comfrey?'

'You're a shrewd man, Reg,' said the Chief Constable.

Wexford said laconically, 'Thanks,' and remembered that it wasn't long since that same voice had called him a foolish one. 'Instead she chose to acquire and submit the birth certificate of a man who would never need a passport because he would never, in any conceivable circumstances, be able to leave this country. She chose to assume the identity of her mentally defective and crippled first cousin. And to him, I discovered yesterday, she left everything of which she died possessed and her royalties as long as they continue.'

'They won't do poor John West much good,' said Burden. 'What happened when Polly encountered Rhoda on the Monday evening?'

Not much caring what reaction he would get, Wexford said, 'At the beginning of *Apes in Hell*, two lines are quoted from Beaumont and Fletcher's play:

Those have most power to hurt us, that we love;
We lay our sleeping lives within their arms.

'Rhoda wrote that book long before she met Polly. I wonder if she ever thought what they really meant or ever thought about them again. Possibly she did. Possibly she understood that Polly had laid her sleeping life within her arms, and that though she might have to repudiate the girl, she must never let her know the true state of affairs. For eonists, Ellis tells us, are often "educated, sensitive, refined and reserved".

'On that Monday evening Polly came to the gates of Stowerton Infirmary prepared to see something which would make her upset and unhappy. She expected to see West either with another woman or on his way to see another woman. At first she didn't see West at all. She joined the bus queue, watching a much bedizened middle-aged woman who was in conversation with an old woman. When did she realize? I don't know. It may be that at first she took Rhoda for some relative of West's, even perhaps a sister. But one of the things we can never disguise is the way we walk. Rhoda never attempted to disguise her voice. Polly got on the bus and went upstairs, feeling that the unbelievable was happening. But she followed Rhoda and they met on that footpath.

'What she saw when they confronted each other must have been enough to cause a temporary loss of reason. Remember she had come, prepared to be distressed, but nothing had prepared her for this. Marie Cole's shock would have been nothing to hers. She saw, in fact, a travesty in the true meaning of the word, and she stabbed to death an abomination.'

Griswold looked embarrassed. 'Pity she couldn't have seen it for what it was, a lucky escape for her.'

'I think she saw it as the end of the world,' Wexford said sombrely. 'It was only later on that she came to feel anything would be preferable to having it known she'd been in love with a man who was no man at all. And that's why she agreed to my story.'

'Cheer up, Reg,' said the Chief Constable. 'We're used to

your breaking the rules. You always do.' He laughed, adding, 'The end justifies the means,' as if this aphorism were invariably accepted by all as pithy truth instead of having for centuries occasioned controversy. 'Let's all have another drink before they shut up shop.'

'Not for me, sir,' said Wexford. 'Good night.' And he walked out into the dark and went home, leaving his superior planning reprisals and his subordinate affectionately incensed.